PENGUIN BOOKS

The Sword of Honour Trilogy

Evelyn Waugh was born in Hampstead in 1903, second son of Arthur Waugh, publisher and literary critic, and brother of Alec Waugh, the popular novelist. He was educated at Lancing and Hertford College, Oxford, where he read Modern History. In 1927 he published his first work, a life of Dante Gabriel Rossetti, and in 1928 his first novel, *Decline and Fall*, which was soon followed by *Vile Bodies* (1930), *Black Mischief* (1932), *A Handful of Dust* (1934), and *Scoop* (1938). During these years he travelled extensively in most parts of Europe, the Near East, Africa, and tropical America. In 1939 he was commissioned in the Royal Marines and later transferred to the Royal Horse Guards, serving in the Middle East and in Yugoslavia. In 1942 he published *Put Out More Flags* and then, in 1945, *Brideshead Revisited*. *When the Going Was Good* and *The Loved One* were followed by *Helena* (1950), his historical novel. *Men at Arms*, which came out in 1952, is the first volume of *The Sword of Honour Trilogy*, and won the James Tait Black Memorial Prize; the other volumes, *Officers and Gentlemen* and *Unconditional Surrender*, were published in 1955 and 1961. Evelyn Waugh was received into the Roman Catholic Church in 1930 and his earlier biography of the Elizabethan Jesuit martyr, *Edmund Campion*, was awarded the Hawthornden Prize in 1936. In 1959 he published the official *Life of Ronald Knox*. For many years he lived with his wife and six children in the West Country. He died in 1966.

EVELYN WAUGH

The Sword of Honour Trilogy

MEN AT ARMS

OFFICERS AND GENTLEMEN

UNCONDITIONAL SURRENDER

PENGUIN BOOKS

Penguin Books Ltd, Harmondsworth, Middlesex, England
Penguin Books, 40 West 23rd Street, New York, New York 10010, U.S.A.
Penguin Books Australia Ltd, Ringwood, Victoria, Australia
Penguin Books Canada Ltd, 2801 John Street, Markham, Ontario, Canada L3R 1B4
Penguin Books (N.Z.) Ltd, 182–190 Wairau Road, Auckland 10, New Zealand

Men at Arms first published by Chapman & Hall 1952
Published in Penguin Books 1964
Copyright © the Estate of Evelyn Waugh, 1952
Officers and Gentlemen first published by Chapman & Hall 1955
Published in Penguin Books 1964
Copyright © the Estate of Evelyn Waugh, 1955
Unconditional Surrender first published by Chapman & Hall 1961
Published in Penguin Books 1964
Copyright © the Estate of Evelyn Waugh, 1961
Published in one volume as *The Sword of Honour Trilogy* 1984
Copyright © the Estate of Evelyn Waugh, 1984
All rights reserved

Made and printed in Great Britain by
Richard Clay (The Chaucer Press) Ltd, Bungay, Suffolk
Filmset in Monophoto Baskerville by
Northumberland Press Ltd, Gateshead

MEN
AT
ARMS

TO CHRISTOPHER SYKES
Companion in arms

CONTENTS

Prologue SWORD OF HONOUR   9

Book One APTHORPE GLORIOSUS   35

Book Two APTHORPE FURIBUNDUS   107

Book Three APTHORPE IMMOLATUS   155

PROLOGUE

Sword of Honour

I

When Guy Crouchback's grandparents, Gervase and Hermione, came to
Italy on their honeymoon, French troops manned the defences of Rome, the
Sovereign Pontiff drove out in an open carriage and Cardinals took their
exercise side-saddle on the Pincian Hill.

Gervase and Hermione were welcomed in a score of frescoed palaces.
Pope Pius received them in private audience and gave his special blessing
to the union of two English families which had suffered for their Faith and
yet retained a round share of material greatness. The chapel at Broome had
never lacked a priest through all the penal years and the lands of Broome
stretched undiminished and unencumbered from the Quantocks to the
Blackdown Hills. Forbears of both their names had died on the scaffold. The
City, lapped now by the tide of illustrious converts, still remembered with
honour its old companions in arms.

Gervase Crouchback stroked his side-whiskers and found a respectful
audience for his views on the Irish question and the Catholic missions in
India. Hermione set up her easel among the ruins and while she painted
Gervase read aloud from the poems of Tennyson and Patmore. She was
pretty and spoke three languages; he was all that the Romans expected of
an Englishman. Everywhere the fortunate pair were praised and petted but
all was not entirely well with them. No sign or hint betrayed their distress
but when the last wheels rolled away and they mounted to their final
privacy, there was a sad gap between them, made by modesty and tender-
ness and innocence, which neither spoke of except in prayer.

Later they joined a yacht at Naples and steamed slowly up the coast,
putting in at unfrequented harbours. And there, one night in their state
room, all at last came right between them and their love was joyfully
completed.

Before they fell asleep they felt the engines stop and heard the rattle of
the anchor-chain, and when Gervase came on deck at dawn, he found that
the ship lay in the shelter of a high peninsula. He called Hermione to join
him and so standing together hand-in-hand, at the moist taffrail, they had

their first view of Santa Dulcina delle Rocce and took the place and all its people into their exulting hearts.

The waterfront was thronged as though the inhabitants had been shaken from bed by an earthquake; their voices came clearly across the water, admiring the strange vessel. Houses rose steeply from the quay; two buildings stood out from the ochre and white walls and rusty pantiles, the church domed, with a voluted façade, and a castle of some kind comprising two great bastions and what seemed a ruined watch-tower. Behind the town for a short distance the hillside was terraced and planted, then above broke wildly into boulders and briar. There was a card game which Gervase and Hermione had played together in the schoolroom in which the winner of a trick called, 'I claim.'

'I claim,' cried Hermione, taking possession of all she saw by right of her happiness.

Later in the morning the English party landed. Two sailors went first to prevent any annoyance from the natives. There followed four couples of ladies and gentlemen; then the servants carrying hampers and shawls and sketching materials. The ladies wore yachting caps and held their skirts clear of the cobbles; some carried lorgnettes. The gentlemen protected them with fringed sunshades. It was a procession such as Santa Dulcina delle Rocce had never seen before. They sauntered through the arcades, plunged briefly into the cool twilight of the church and climbed the steps which led from the piazza to the fortifications.

Little remained. The great paved platform was broken everywhere with pine and broom. The watch-tower was full of rubble. Two cottages had been built in the hillside from the finely cut masonry of the old castle and two families of peasants ran out to greet them with bunches of mimosa. The picnic luncheon was spread in the shade.

'Disappointing when you get up here,' said the owner of the yacht apologetically. 'Always the way with these places. Best seen from a distance.'

'I think it's quite perfect,' said Hermione, 'and we're going to live here. Please don't say a word against our castle.'

Gervase laughed indulgently with the others but later, when his father died and he seemed to be rich, the project came to life. Gervase made inquiries. The castle belonged to an elderly lawyer in Genoa who was happy to sell. Presently a plain square house rose above the ramparts and English stocks added their sweetness to the myrtle and the pine. Gervase called his new house the Villa Hermione, but the name never caught the local fancy. It was cut in large square letters on the gate-posts but honeysuckle spread and smothered it. The people of Santa Dulcina spoke always of the 'Castello Crouchback' until eventually that title found its way to the head of the writing-paper and Hermione, proud bride, was left without commemoration.

Whatever its name, however, the Castello kept the character of its origin. For fifty years, until the shadows closed on the Crouchback family, it was a place of joy and love. Guy's father and Guy himself came there for their honeymoons. It was constantly lent to newly married cousins and friends. It was the place of Guy's happiest holidays with his brothers and sister. The town changed a little but neither railway nor high road touched that happy peninsula. A few more foreigners built their villas there. The inn enlarged itself, installed sanitation of a sort and a café-restaurant, took the name of 'Hotel Eden' and abruptly changed it during the Abyssinian crisis to 'Albergo del Sol'. The garage proprietor became secretary of the local Fascists. But as Guy descended to the piazza on his last morning, he saw little that would have been unfamiliar to Gervase and Hermione. Already, an hour before midday, the heat was fierce but he walked as blithely as they on that first morning of secret jubilation. For him, as for them, frustrated love had found its first satisfaction. He was packed and dressed for a long journey, already on his way back to his own country to serve his King.

Just seven days earlier he had opened his morning newspaper on the headlines announcing the Russian-German alliance. News that shook the politicians and young poets of a dozen capital cities brought deep peace to one English heart. Eight years of shame and loneliness were ended. For eight years Guy, already set apart from his fellows by his own deep wound, that unstaunched, internal draining away of life and love, had been deprived of the loyalties which should have sustained him. He lived too close to Fascism in Italy to share the opposing enthusiasms of his countrymen. He saw it neither as a calamity nor as a rebirth; as a rough improvisation merely. He disliked the men who were edging themselves into power around him, but English denunciations sounded fatuous and dishonest and for the past three years he had given up his English newspapers. The German Nazis he knew to be mad and bad. Their participation dishonoured the cause of Spain, but the troubles of Bohemia, the year before, left him quite indifferent. When Prague fell, he knew that war was inevitable. He expected his country to go to war in a panic, for the wrong reasons or for no reason at all, with the wrong allies, in pitiful weakness. But now, splendidly, everything had become clear. The enemy at last was plain in view, huge and hateful, all disguise cast off. It was the Modern Age in arms. Whatever the outcome there was a place for him in that battle.

Everything was now in order at the Castello. His formal farewells were made. The day before he had visited the Arciprete, the Podestà, the Reverend Mother at the Convent, Mrs Garry at the Villa Datura, the Wilmots at the Castelletto Musgrave, Gräfin von Gluck at the Casa Gluck. Now there was a last piece of private business to transact. Thirty-five years old, slight and trim, plainly foreign but not so plainly English, young now, in heart and step, he came to bid good-bye to a life-long friend who lay, as was proper for a man dead eight hundred years, in the parish church.

St Dulcina, titular patroness of the town, was reputedly a victim of Diocletian. Her effigy in wax lay languorously in a glass case under the high altar. Her bones, brought from the Greek islands by a medieval raiding party, lay in their rich casket in the sacristy safe. Once a year they were carried shoulder high through the streets amid showers of fireworks, but except on her feast day she was not much regarded in the town to which she had given her name. Her place as benefactor had been usurped by another figure whose tomb was always littered with screws of paper bearing petitions, whose fingers and toes were tied in bows of coloured wool as *aides-mémoire*. He was older than the church, older than anything in it except the bones of St Dulcina and a pre-Christian thunderbolt which lay concealed in the back of the altar (whose existence the Arciprete always denied). His name, just legible still, was Roger of Waybrooke, Knight, an Englishman; his arms five falcons. His sword and one gauntlet still lay beside him. Guy's uncle, Peregrine, a student of such things, had learned some of his story. Waybroke, now Waybrook, was quite near London. Roger's manor had long ago been lost and over-built. He left it for the Second Crusade, sailed from Genoa and was shipwrecked on this coast. There he enlisted under the local Count, who promised to take him to the Holy Land but led him first against a neighbour, on the walls of whose castle he fell at the moment of victory. The Count gave him honourable burial and there he had lain through the centuries, while the church crumbled and was rebuilt above him, far from Jerusalem, far from Waybroke, a man with a great journey still all before him and a great vow unfulfilled; but the people of Santa Dulcina delle Rocce, to whom the supernatural order in all its ramifications was ever present and ever more lively than the humdrum world about them, adopted Sir Roger and despite all clerical remonstrance canonized him, brought him their troubles and touched his sword for luck, so that its edge was always bright. All his life, but especially in recent years, Guy had felt an especial kinship with 'il Santo Inglese'. Now, on his last day, he made straight for the tomb and ran his finger, as the fishermen did, along the knight's sword. 'Sir Roger, pray for me,' he said, 'and for our endangered kingdom.'

The confessional was occupied that morning, for it was the day when Suora Tomasina brought the schoolchildren to their duties. They sat on a bench along the wall, whispering and pinching one another, while the sister flapped over them like a hen leading them in turn to the grille and thence to the high altar to recite their penance.

On an impulse, not because his conscience troubled him but because it was a habit learned in childhood to go to confession before a journey, Guy made a sign to the sister and interrupted the succession of peasant urchins.

'*Beneditemi, padre, perche ho peccato* ...' Guy found it easy to confess in Italian. He spoke the language well but without nuances. There was no risk of going deeper than the denunciation of his few infractions of law, of his habitual weaknesses. Into that wasteland where his soul languished he need not, could not, enter. He had no words to describe it. There were no words in any language. There was nothing to describe, merely a void. His was not an 'interesting case', he thought. No cosmic struggle raged in his sad soul. It was as though eight years back he had suffered a tiny stroke of paralysis; all his spiritual faculties were just perceptibly impaired. He was 'handi-capped' as Mrs Garry of the Villa Datura would have put it. There was nothing to say about it.

The priest gave him absolution and the traditional words of dismissal: '*Sia lodato Gesù Cristo*,' and he answered '*Oggi, sempre*.'* He rose from his knees, said three 'Aves' before the waxen figure of St Dulcina and passed through the leather curtain into the blazing sunlight of the piazza.

Children, grandchildren, great-grandchildren of the peasants who first greeted Gervase and Hermione still inhabited the cottages behind the Castello and farmed the surrounding terraces. They grew and made the wine; they sold the olives; they kept an almost etiolated cow in an under-ground stable from which sometimes she escaped and trampled the vege-table beds and plunged over the low walls until she was, with immense drama, recaptured. They paid for their tenancy in produce and service. Two sisters, Josefina and Bianca, did the work of the house. They had laid Guy's last luncheon under the orange trees. He ate his spaghetti and drank his *vino scelto*, the brownish, heady wine of the place. Then with a fuss Josefina brought him a large ornamental cake which had been made in celebration of his departure. His slight appetite was already satisfied. He watched with alarm as Josefina carved. He tasted it, praised it, crumbled it. Josefina and Bianca stood implacable before him until he had finished the last morsel.

The taxi was waiting. There was no carriage drive to the Castello. The gates stood in the lane at the bottom of a flight of steps. When Guy rose to leave, all his little household, twenty strong, assembled to see him go. They would remain come what might. All kissed his hand. Most wept. The children threw flowers into the car. Josefina put into his lap the remains of the cake wrapped in newspaper. They waved until he was out of sight, then returned to their siestas. Guy moved the cake to the back seat and wiped his hands with his handkerchief. He was glad that the ordeal was over and waited resignedly for the Fascist secretary to start a conversation.

He was not loved, Guy knew, either by his household or in the town. He was accepted and respected but he was not *simpatico*. Gräfin von Gluck, who spoke no word of Italian and lived in undisguised concubinage with her

* 'Jesus Christ be praised.' 'Today, always.'

butler, was *simpatica*. Mrs Garry was *simpatica*, who distributed Protestant tracts, interfered with the fishermen's methods of killing octopuses and filled her house with stray cats.

Guy's uncle, Peregrine, a bore of international repute whose dreaded presence could empty the room in any centre of civilization – Uncle Peregrine was considered *molto simpatico*. The Wilmots were gross vulgarians; they used Santa Dulcina purely as a pleasure resort, subscribed to no local funds, gave rowdy parties and wore indecent clothes, talked of 'wops' and often left after the summer with their bills to the tradesmen unpaid; but they had four boisterous and ill-favoured daughters whom the Santa-Dulcinesi had watched grow up. Better than this, they had lost a son bathing from the rocks. The Santa-Dulcinesi participated in these joys and sorrows. They observed with relish their hasty and unobtrusive departures at the end of the holidays. They were *simpatici*. Even Musgrave who had the Castelletto before the Wilmots and bequeathed it his name, Musgrave who, it was said, could not go to England or America because of warrants for his arrest, 'Musgrave the Monster', as the Crouchbacks used to call him – *he* was *simpatico*. Guy alone, whom they had known from infancy, who spoke their language and conformed to their religion, who was open-handed in all his dealing and scrupulously respectful of all their ways, whose grandfather built their school, whose mother had given a set of vestments embroidered by the Royal School of Needlework for the annual procession of St Dulcina's bones – Guy alone was a stranger among them.

The black-shirt said: 'You are leaving for a long time?'

'For the duration of the war.'

'There will be no war. No one wants it. Who would gain?'

As they drove they passed on every windowless wall the lowering, stencilled face of Mussolini and the legend '*The Leader is always right*'. The Fascist secretary took his hands off the wheel and lit a cigarette, accelerating as he did so. '*The Leader is always right*' ... '*The Leader is always right*' flashed past and was lost in the dust. 'War is foolishness,' said the imperfect disciple. 'You will see. Everything will be brought to an arrangement.'

Guy did not dispute the matter. He was not interested in what the taxi-driver thought or said. Mrs Garry would have thrown herself into argument. Once, driving with this same man, she had stopped the cab and walked home, three hot miles, to show her detestation of his political philosophy. But Guy had no wish to persuade or convince or to share his opinions with anyone. Even in his religion he felt no brotherhood. Often he wished that he lived in penal times when Broome had been a solitary outpost of the Faith, surrounded by aliens. Sometimes he imagined himself serving the last mass for the last Pope in a catacomb at the end of the world. He never went to communion on Sundays, slipping into the church, instead, very early on weekdays when few others were about. The people of Santa Dulcina preferred Musgrave the Monster. In the first years after his divorce Guy had prosecuted a few sad little love affairs but he had always hidden them from the village. Lately he had fallen into a habit of dry and negative chastity which even the priests felt to be unedifying. On the lowest, as on the highest plane, there was no sympathy between him and his fellow men. He could not listen to what the taxi-driver was saying.

'History is a living force,' said the taxi-driver, quoting from an article he had lately read. 'No one can put a stop to it and say: "After this date there shall be no changes." With nations as with men, some grow old. Some have too much, others too little. Then there must be an arrangement. But if it comes to war, everyone will have too little. *They* know that. *They* will not have a war.'

Guy heard the voice without vexation. Only one small question troubled him now: what to do with the cake. He could not leave it in the car; Bianca and Josefina would hear of it. It would be a great nuisance in the train. He tried to remember whether the Vice-Consul, with whom he had to decide certain details of closing the Castello, had any children to whom the cake might be given. He rather thought he had.

Apart from this one sugary encumbrance, Guy floated free; as untouchable in his new-found contentment as in his old despair. *Sia lodato Gesù Cristo. Oggi, sempre.* Today especially; today of all days.

2

The Crouchback family, until quite lately rich and numerous, was now much reduced. Guy was the youngest of them and it seemed likely he would be the last. His mother was dead, his father over seventy. There had been four children. Angela, the eldest; then Gervase, who went straight from Downside into the Irish Guards and was picked off by a sniper his first day in France, instantly, fresh and clean and unwearied, as he followed the duckboard across the mud, carrying his blackthorn stick, on his way to report to company headquarters. Ivo was only a year older than Guy but they were never friends. Ivo was always odd. He grew much odder and finally, when he was twenty-six, disappeared from home. For months there was no news of him. Then he was found barricaded alone in a lodging in Cricklewood where he was starving himself to death. He was carried out emaciated and delirious and died a few days later stark mad. That was in 1931. Ivo's death sometimes seemed to Guy a horrible caricature of his own life, which at just that time was plunged in disaster.

Before Ivo's oddness gave real cause for anxiety Guy had married, not a Catholic but a bright, fashionable girl, quite unlike anyone that his friends or family would have expected. He took his younger son's share of the diminished family fortune, and settled in Kenya, living, it seemed to him afterwards, in unruffled good-humour beside a mountain lake where the air was always brilliant and keen and the flamingos rose at dawn first white, then pink, then a whirl of shadow passing across the glowing sky. He farmed assiduously and nearly made it pay. Then unaccountably his wife said that her health required a year in England. She wrote regularly and affectionately until one day, still affectionately, she informed him that she had fallen deeply in love with an acquaintance of theirs named Tommy Blackhouse; that Guy was not to be cross about it; that she wanted a divorce. '*And, please,*' her letter ended, '*there's to be no chivalrous nonsense of your going to Brighton and playing "the guilty party". That would mean six months separation from Tommy and I won't trust him out of my sight for six minutes, the beast.*'

So Guy left Kenya and shortly afterwards his father, widowed and despairing of an heir, left Broome. The property was reduced by then to the house and park and home farm. In recent years it had achieved a certain celebrity. It was almost unique in contemporary England, having been held in uninterrupted male succession since the reign of Henry I. Mr Crouchback did not sell it. He let it, instead, to a convent and himself retired to Matchet, a near-by watering-place. And the sanctuary lamp still burned at Broome as of old.

No one was more conscious of the decline of the House of Crouchback than Guy's brother-in-law, Arthur Box-Bender, who had married Angela in 1914 when Broome seemed set unalterably in the firmament, a celestial body emanating tradition and unobtrusive authority. Box-Bender was not a man of family and he respected Angela's pedigree. He even at one time considered the addition of Crouchback to his own name, in place of either Box or Bender, both of which seemed easily dispensable, but Mr Crouchback's chilling indifference and Angela's ridicule quickly discouraged him. He was not a Catholic and he thought it Guy's plain duty to marry again, preferably someone with money, and carry on his line. He was not a sensitive man and he could not approve Guy's hiding himself away. He ought to take over the home farm at Broome. He ought to go into politics. People like Guy, he freely stated, owed something to their country; but when at the end of August 1939 Guy presented himself in London with the object of paying that debt, Arthur Box-Bender was not sympathetic.

'My dear Guy,' he said, 'be your age.'

Box-Bender was fifty-six and a Member of Parliament. Many years ago he had served quite creditably in a rifle regiment; he had a son serving with them now. For him soldiering was something that belonged to extreme youth, like butterscotch and catapults. Guy at thirty-five, shortly to be thirty-six, still looked on himself as a young man. Time had stood still for him during the last eight years. It had advanced swiftly for Box-Bender.

'Can you seriously imagine yourself sprinting about at the head of a platoon?'

'Well, yes,' said Guy. 'That's exactly what I did imagine.'

Guy usually stayed with Box-Bender in Lowndes Square when he was in London. He had come straight to him now from Victoria but found his sister Angela away in the country and the house already half dismantled. Box-Bender's study was the last room to be left untouched. They were sitting there now before going out to dinner.

'I'm afraid you won't get much encouragement. All that sort of thing happened in 1914 – retired colonels dyeing their hair and enlisting in the ranks. I remember it. I was there. All very gallant of course but it won't happen this time. The whole thing is planned. The Government know just how many men they can handle; they know where they can get them; they'll take them in their own time. At the moment we haven't got the accommodation or the equipment for any big increase. There may be casualties, of course, but personally I don't see it as a soldier's war at all. Where are we going to fight? No one in his senses would try to break either the Maginot or the Siegfried Lines. As I see it, both sides will sit tight until they begin to feel the economic pinch. The Germans are short of almost every industrial essential. As soon as they realize that Mr Hitler's bluff has been called, we shan't hear much more of Mr Hitler. That's an internal matter for the Germans to settle for themselves. We can't treat with the present gang of course, but as soon as they produce a respectable government we shall be able to iron out all our differences.'

'That's rather how my Italian taxi-driver talked yesterday.'

'Of course. Always go to a taxi-driver when you want a sane, independent opinion. I talked to one today. He said: "When we are at war then it'll be time to start talking about war. Just at present we aren't at war." Very sound that.'

'But I notice you are taking every precaution.'

Box-Bender's three daughters had been dispatched to stay with a commercial associate in Connecticut. The house in Lowndes Square was being emptied and shut. Some of the furniture had gone to the country; the rest would go into store. Box-Bender had taken part of a large brand-new luxury flat, going cheap at the moment. He and two colleagues from the House of Commons would share these quarters. The cleverest of his dodges had been to get his house in the constituency accepted as a repository for 'National Art Treasures'. There would be no trouble there with billeting officers, civil or military. A few minutes earlier Box-Bender had explained these provisions with some pride. Now he merely turned to the wireless and said: 'D'you mind awfully if I just switch this thing on for a moment to hear what they're saying? There may be something new.'

But there was not. Nor was there any message of peace. The evacuation of centres of population was proceeding like clockwork; happy groups of mothers and children were arriving punctually at their distributing centres and being welcomed into their new homes. Box-Bender switched it off.

'Nothing new since this afternoon. Funny how one keeps twiddling the thing these days. I never had much use for it before. By the way, Guy, that's a thing that might suit you, if you really want to make yourself useful. They're very keen to collect foreign language speakers at the B.B.C. for monitoring and propaganda and that sort of rot. Not very exciting of course but someone has to do it and I think your Italian would come in very handy.'

There was no great affection between the two brothers-in-law. It never occurred to Guy to speculate about Box-Bender's view of him. It never occurred to him that Box-Bender had any particular view. As a matter of fact, which he freely admitted to Angela, Box-Bender had for some years been expecting Guy to go mad. He was not an imaginative man, nor easily impressionable, but he had been much mixed up in the quest for Ivo and his ghastly discovery. That thing had made an impression. Guy and Ivo were remarkably alike. Box-Bender remembered Ivo's look in the days when his extreme oddness still tottered this side of lunacy; it had not been a wild look at all; something rather smug and purposeful; something 'dedicated'; something in fact very much like the look in Guy's eyes now as he presented himself so inopportunely in Lowndes Square talking calmly about the Irish Guards. It could bode no good. Best get him quickly into something like the B.B.C., out of harm's way.

They dined that night at Bellamy's. Guy's family had always belonged to this club. Gervase's name was on the 1914–18 Roll of Honour in the front hall. Poor crazy Ivo had often sat in the bay window alarming passers-by with his fixed stare. Guy had joined in early manhood, seldom used it in recent years, but kept his name on the list notwithstanding. It was an historic place. Once fuddled gamblers, attended by linkmen, had felt their way down these steps to their coaches. Now Guy and Box-Bender felt their way up in utter blindness. The first glass doors were painted out. Within them in the little vestibule was a perceptible eerie phosphorescence. Beyond the second pair of doors was bright light, noise, and a thick and stagnant fog of cigar-smoke and whisky. In these first days of the black-out the problem of ventilation was unsolved.

The club had only that day re-opened after its annual cleaning. In normal times it would have been quite empty at this season. Now it was thronged. There were many familiar faces but no friends. As Guy passed a member who greeted him, another turned and asked: 'Who was that? Someone new, isn't it?'

'No, he's belonged for ages. You'll never guess who he is. Virginia Troy's first husband.'

'Really? I thought she was married to Tommy Blackhouse.'

'This chap was before Tommy. Can't remember his name. I think he lives in Kenya. Tommy took her from him, then Gussie had her for a bit, then Bert Troy picked her up when she was going spare.'

'She's a grand girl. Wouldn't mind having a go myself one of these days.'

For in this club there were no depressing conventions against the bandying of ladies' names.

Box-Bender and Guy drank, dined and drank with a group which fluctuated and changed throughout the evening. The conversation was briskly topical and through it Guy began to make acquaintance with this changed city. They spoke of domestic arrangements. Everyone seemed to be feverishly occupied in disencumbering himself of responsibilities. Box-Bender's arrangements were the microcosm of a national movement. Everywhere houses were being closed, furniture stored, children transported, servants dismissed, lawns ploughed, dower-houses and shooting lodges crammed to capacity; mothers-in-law and nannies were everywhere gaining control.

They spoke of incidents and crimes in the black-out. So-and-so had lost all her teeth in a taxi. So-and-so had been sandbagged in Hay Hill and robbed of his poker-winnings. So-and-so had been knocked down by a Red Cross ambulance and left for dead.

They spoke of various forms of service. Most were in uniform. Everywhere little groups of close friends were arranging to spend the war together. There was a territorial searchlight battery manned entirely by fashionable aesthetes who were called 'the monstrous regiment of gentlemen'. Stockbrokers and wine salesmen were settling into the offices of London District Headquarters. Regular soldiers were kept at twelve hours' notice for active service. Yachtsmen were in R.N.V.R. uniform growing beards. There seemed no opportunity for Guy in any of this.

'My brother-in-law here is looking for a job,' said Box-Bender.

'You've left it rather late, you know. Everyone's pretty well fixed. Of course things will start popping once the balloon goes up. I should wait till then.'

They sat on late, for no one relished the plunge into darkness. No one attempted to drive a car. Taxis were rare. They made up parties to walk homeward together. At length Guy and Box-Bender joined a group walking to Belgravia. They stumbled down the steps together and set out into the baffling midnight void. Time might have gone back two thousand years to the time when London was a stockaded cluster of huts down the river, and the streets through which they walked, empty sedge and swamp.

In the following fortnight Guy came to spend most of the day in Bellamy's. He moved to an hotel and immediately after breakfast daily walked to St James's Street as a man might go to his office. He wrote letters there, a thick batch of them every day, written shamefacedly with growing facility in a corner of the morning-room.

'Dear General Cutter, Please forgive me for troubling you at this busy time. I hope you remember as I do the happy day when the Bradshawes brought you to my house at Santa Dulcina and we went out together in the boat and so ignominiously failed to spear pulpi ...'

'Dear Colonel Glover, I am writing to you because I know you served with my brother Gervase and were a friend of his ...'

'Dear Sam, Though we have not met since Downside I have followed your career with distant admiration and vicarious pride ...'

'Dear Molly, I am sure I ought not to know, but I *do* know that Alex is Someone Very Important and Secret at the Admiralty. I know that you have him completely under your thumb. So do you think you could possibly be an angel ...'

He had become a facile professional beggar.

Usually there was an answer; a typewritten note or a telephone call from a secretary or aide-de-camp; an appointment or an invitation. Always there was the same polite discouragement. 'We organized skeleton staffs at the time of Munich. I expect we shall expand as soon as we know just what our commitments are' – from the civilians – 'Our last directive was to go slow on personnel. I'll put you in our list and see you are notified as soon as anything turns up.'

'We don't want cannon-fodder this time' – from the Services – 'we learned our lesson in 1914 when we threw away the pick of the nation. That's what we've suffered from ever since.'

'But I'm not the pick of the nation,' said Guy. 'I'm natural fodder. I've no dependants. I've no special skill in anything. What's more I'm getting old. I'm ready for immediate consumption. You should take the 35s now and give the young men time to get sons.'

'I'm afraid that's not the official view. I'll put you on our list and see you're notified as soon as anything turns up.'

In the following days Guy's name was put on many lists and his few qualifications summarized and filed in many confidential registers where they lay unexamined through all the long years ahead.

England declared war but it made no change in Guy's routine of appeals and interviews. No bombs fell. There was no rain of poison or fire. Bones were still broken after dark. That was all. At Bellamy's he found himself one of a large depressed class of men older than himself who had served without glory in the First World War. Most of them had gone straight from school to the trenches and spent the rest of their lives forgetting the mud and lice and noise. They were under orders to await orders and spoke sadly of the various drab posts that awaited them at railway stations and docks and dumps. The balloon had gone up, leaving them on the ground.

Russia invaded Poland. Guy found no sympathy among these old soldiers for his own hot indignation.

'My dear fellow, we've quite enough on our hands as it is. We can't go to war with the whole world.'

'Then why go to war at all? If all we want is prosperity, the hardest bargain Hitler made would be preferable to victory. If we are concerned with justice the Russians are as guilty as the Germans.'

'Justice?' said the old soldiers. 'Justice?'

'Besides,' said Box-Bender when Guy spoke to him of the matter which seemed in no one's mind but his, 'the country would never stand for it. The socialists have been crying blue murder against the Nazis for five years but they are all pacifists at heart. So far as they have any feeling of patriotism it's for Russia. You'd have a general strike and the whole country in collapse if you set up to be just.'

'Then what are we fighting for?'

'Oh we had to do that, you know. The socialists always thought we were pro-Hitler, God knows why. It was quite a job in keeping neutral over Spain. You missed all that excitement living abroad. It was quite ticklish, I assure you. If we sat tight now there'd be chaos. What we have to do now is to limit and localize the war, not extend it.'

The conclusion of all these discussions was darkness, the baffling night that lay beyond the club doors. When the closing hour came the old soldiers and young soldiers and the politicians made up their same little companies to grope their way home together. There was always someone going Guy's way towards his hotel, always a friendly arm. But his heart was lonely.

Guy heard of mysterious departments known only by their initials or as 'So-and-so's cloak and dagger boys'. Bankers, gamblers, men with jobs in oil companies seemed to find a way there; not Guy. He met an acquaintance, a journalist, who had once come to Kenya. This man, Lord Kilbannock, had lately written a racing column; now he was in Air Force uniform.

'How did you manage it?' Guy asked.

'Well, it's rather shaming really. There's an air marshal whose wife plays bridge with my wife. He's always been mad keen to get in here. I've just put him up. He's the most awful shit.'

'Will he get in?'

'No, no, I've seen to that. Three blackballs guaranteed already. But he can't get me out of the Air Force.'

'What do you do?'

'That's rather shaming too. I'm what's called a "conducting officer". I take American journalists round fighter stations. But I shall find something else soon. The great thing is to get into uniform; then you can start moving yourself round. It's a very exclusive war at present. Once you're *in*, there's every opportunity. I've got my eye on India or Egypt. Somewhere where there's no black-out. Fellow in the flats where I live got coshed on the head the other night, right on the steps. All a bit too dangerous for me. I don't want a medal. I want to be known as one of the soft-faced men who did well out of the war. Come and have a drink.'

So the evenings passed. Every morning Guy awoke in his hotel bedroom, early and anxious. After a month of it he decided to leave London and visit his family.

He went first to his sister, Angela, to the house in Gloucestershire which Box-Bender bought when he was adopted as Member for the constituency.

'We're living in the most frightful squalor,' she said on the telephone. 'We can't meet people at Kemble any more. No petrol. You'll have to change and take the local train. Or else the bus from Stroud if it's still running. I rather think it isn't.'

But at Kemble, when he emerged from the corridor in which he had stood for three hours, he found his nephew Tony on the platform to greet him. He was in flannels. Only his close-cropped hair marked him as a soldier.

'Hullo, Uncle Guy. I hope I'm a pleasant surprise. I've come to save you from the local train. They've given us embarkation leave and a special issue of petrol coupons. Jump in.'

'Shouldn't you be in uniform?'

'Should be. But no one does. It makes me feel quite human getting out of it for a few hours.'

'I think I shall want to stay in mine once I get it.'

Tony Box-Bender laughed innocently. 'I should love to see you. Somehow I can't imagine you as one of the licentious soldiery. Why did you leave Italy? I should have thought Santa Dulcina was just the place to spend the war. How did you leave everyone?'

'Momentarily in tears.'

'I bet they miss you.'

'Not really. They cry easily.'

They bowled along between low Cotswold walls. Presently they came into sight of the Berkeley Vale far below them with the Severn shining brown and gold in the evening sun.

'You're glad to be going to France?'

'Of course. It's hell in barracks being chased round all day. It's pretty good hell at home at the moment – art treasures everywhere and Mum doing the cooking.'

Box-Bender's house was a small, gabled manor in a sophisticated village where half the cottages were equipped with baths and chintz. Drawing-room and dining-room were blocked to the ceiling with wooden crates.

'Such a disappointment, darling,' said Angela. 'I thought we'd been so clever. I imagined us having the Wallace Collection and luxuriating in Sèvres and Boulle and Bouchers. Such a cultured war, I imagined. Instead we've got Hittite tables from the British Museum, and we mayn't even peep at them, not that we want to, heaven knows. You're going to be hideously uncomfortable, darling. I've put you in the library. All the top floor is shut so that if we're bombed we shan't panic and jump out of the windows. That's Arthur's idea. He's really been too resourceful. He and I are in the cottage. I know we shall break our necks one night going to bed across the garden. Arthur's so strict about the electric torch. It's all very idiotic. No one can possibly see into the garden.'

It seemed to Guy that his sister had grown more talkative than she had been.

'Ought we to have asked people in for your last night, Tony? I'm afraid it's very dull, but who is there? Besides there really isn't elbow room for ourselves now we eat in Arthur's business-room.'

'No, Mum, it's much nicer being alone.'

'I so hoped you'd say that. We like it of course, but I do think they might give you two nights.'

'Have to be in at reveille on Monday. If you'd stayed in London . . .'

'But you'd sooner be *at home* your last night?'

'Wherever you are, Mum.'

'Isn't he a dear boy, Guy?'

The library was now the sole living-room. The bed already made up for Guy on a sofa at one end consorted ill with the terrestrial and celestial globes at its head and foot.

'You and Tony will both have to wash in the loo under the stairs. He's sleeping in the flower-room, poor pet. Now I must go and see to dinner.'

'There's really not the smallest reason for all this,' said Tony. 'Mum and Dad seem to enjoy turning everything topsy-turvy. I suppose it comes from having been so very correct before. And of course Dad has always been jolly close about money. He hated paying out when he felt he had to. Now he thinks he's got a splendid excuse for economizing.'

Arthur Box-Bender came in carrying a tray. 'Well, you see how we're roughing it,' he said. 'In a year or two, if the war goes on, everyone will have to live like this. We're starting early. It's the greatest fun.'

'You're only here for week-ends,' said Tony. 'I hear you're very snug in Arlington Street.'

'I believe you would sooner have spent your leave in London.'

'Not really,' said Tony.

'There wouldn't have been room for your mother in the flat. No wives. That was part of the concordat we made when we decided to share. Sherry, Guy? I wonder what you'll think of this. It's South African. Everyone will be drinking it soon.'

'This zeal to lead the fashion is something new, Arthur.'

'You don't like it?'

'Not very much.'

'The sooner we get used to it the better. There is no more coming from Spain.'

'It all tastes the same to me,' said Tony.

'Well, the party is in your honour.'

A gardener's wife and a girl from the village were now the only servants. Angela did all the lighter and cleaner work of the kitchen. Presently she called them in to dinner in the little study which Arthur Box-Bender liked to call his 'business-room'. He had a spacious office in the City; his election agent had permanent quarters in the market town; his private secretary had files, a typewriter and two telephones in South-West London; no business was ever done in the room where they now dined, but Box-Bender had first heard the expression used by Mr Crouchback of the place where he patiently transacted all the paper work of the estate at Broome. It had an authentic rural flavour, Box-Bender rightly thought.

In the years of peace Box-Bender often entertained neat little parties of eight or ten to dinner. Guy had memories of many candle-lit evenings, of a rather rigid adequacy of food and wine, of Box-Bender sitting square in his place and leading the conversation in humdrum topical subjects. Tonight with Angela and Tony frequently on their feet moving the plates, he seemed less at his ease. His interests were still topical and humdrum but Guy and Tony had each his own preoccupation.

'Shocking thing about the Abercrombies,' he said. 'Did you hear? They packed up and went to Jamaica bag and baggage.'

'Why shouldn't they?' said Tony. 'They couldn't be any use here. Just extra mouths to feed.'

'It looks as though I am going to be an extra mouth,' said Guy. 'It's a matter of sentiment, I suppose. One wants to be with one's own people in war time.'

'Can't see it,' said Tony.

'There's plenty of useful work for the civilian,' said Box-Bender.

'All the Prentices' evacuees have gone back to Birmingham in a huff,' said Angela. 'They always were unnaturally lucky. We've got the Hittite horrors for life, I know.'

'It's an awful business for the men not knowing where their wives and families are,' said Tony. 'Our wretched Welfare Officer spends his whole day trying to trace them. Six men in my platoon have gone on leave not knowing if they've got a home to go to.'

'Old Mrs Sparrow fell out of the apple-loft and broke both legs. They wouldn't take her in at the hospital because all the beds are kept for air-raid casualties.'

'We have to keep a duty officer on day and night doing P.A.D. It's a ghastly bore. They ring up every hour to report "All clear".'

'Caroline Maiden was stopped in Stroud by a policeman and asked why she wasn't carrying a gas-mask.'

'Chemical Warfare is the end. I'm jolly grateful I had a classical education. We had to send an officer from the battalion on a C.W. course. They had me down for it. Then by the mercy of God a frightfully wet fellow turned up in C Company who'd just got a science scholarship, so I stood the adjutant a couple of drinks and got him sent instead. All the wettest fellows are in C.W.'

Tony was from another world; their problems were not his. Guy belonged to neither world.

'I heard someone say that this was a very exclusive war.'

'Well, surely, Uncle Guy, the more who can keep out of it the better. You civilians don't know when you're well off.'

'Perhaps we don't want to be particularly well off at the moment, Tony.'

'I know exactly what I want. An M.C. and a nice neat wound. Then I can spend the rest of the war being cosseted by beautiful nurses.'

'*Please*, Tony.'

'Sorry, Mum. Don't look so desperately serious. I shall begin to wish I'd spent my leave in London.'

'I thought I was keeping such a stiff upper lip. Only please, darling, don't talk like that about being wounded.'

'Well, it's the best one can hope for, isn't it?'

'Look here,' said Box-Bender, 'aren't we all getting a bit morbid? Take Uncle Guy away while your mother and I clear the table.'

Guy and Tony went into the library. The french windows were open on the paved garden. 'Damn, we must draw the curtains before we put on the light.'

'Let's go out for a minute,' said Guy.

It was just light enough to see the way. The air was scented by invisible magnolia flowers, high in the old tree which covered half the house.

'Never felt less morbid in my life,' said Tony, but as he and Guy strolled out into the gathering darkness, he broke the silence by saying suddenly, 'Tell me about going mad. Are lots of Mum's family cuckoo?'

'No.'

'There was Uncle Ivo, wasn't there?'

'He suffered from an excess of melancholy.'

'Not hereditary?'

'No, no. Why? Do you feel your reason tottering?'

'Not yet. But it's something I read, about an officer in the last war who seemed quite normal till he got into action and then went barking mad and his sergeant had to shoot him.'

' "Barking" is scarcely the word for your uncle's trouble. He was in every sense a most retiring man.'

'How about the others?'

'Look at me. Look at your grandfather – and your great-uncle Peregrine; he's appallingly sane.'

'He's spending his time collecting binoculars and sending them to the War Office. Is that sane?'

'Perfectly.'

'I'm glad you told me.'

Presently Angela called: 'Come in, you two. It's quite dark. What are you talking about?'

'Tony thinks he's going mad.'

'Mrs Groat is. She left the larder un-blacked-out.'

They sat in the library with their backs to Guy's bed. Quite soon Tony rose to say good night.

'Mass is at eight,' said Angela. 'We ought to start at twenty to. I'm picking up some evacuees in Uley.'

'Oh I say, isn't there something later? I was looking forward to a long lie.'

'I thought we might all go to communion tomorrow. Do come, Tony.'

'All right, Mum, of course I will. Only make it twenty-five to in that case. I shall have to go to scrape after weeks of wickedness.'

Box-Bender looked self-conscious, as he still did, always, when religious practices were spoken of. He did not get used to it – this ease with the Awful.

'I shall be with you in spirit,' he said.

Then he left too, and stumbled across the garden to the cottage. Angela and Guy were left alone.

'He's a charming boy, Angela.'

'Yes, so military, isn't he? All in a matter of months. He doesn't mind a bit going to France.'

'I should think not indeed.'

'Oh, Guy, you're too young to remember. I grew up with the first war. I'm one of the girls you read about who danced with the men who were being killed. I remember the telegram coming about Gervase. You were just a schoolboy going short of sweets. I remember the first lot who went out. There wasn't one of them left at the end. What chance has a boy of Tony's age starting now at the very beginning? I worked in a hospital, you remember. That's why I couldn't bear it when Tony talked of a nice neat wound and being cosseted.'

'He oughtn't to have said that.'

'There weren't any nice little wounds. They were all perfectly beastly and this time there'll be all kinds of ghastly new chemicals too, I suppose. You heard how he spoke about Chemical Warfare – a hobby for "wet" officers. He doesn't know what it will be like. There isn't even the hope of his being taken prisoner this time. Under the Kaiser the Germans were still a civilized people. These brutes will do anything.'

'Angela, there's nothing I can say except that you know very well you wouldn't have Tony a bit different. You wouldn't want him to be one of those wretched boys I hear about who have run away to Ireland or America.'

'That's quite inconceivable, of course.'

'Well, then?'

'I know. I know. Time for bed. I'm afraid we've filled your room with smoke. You can open the window when the light's out. Thank goodness Arthur has gone ahead. I can use my torch across the garden without being accused of attracting Zeppelins.'

That night, lying long awake, obliged to choose between air and light, choosing air, not reading, Guy thought; Why Tony? What crazy economy was it that squandered Tony and saved himself? In China when called to the army it was honourable to hire a poor young man and send him in one's place. Tony was rich in love and promise. He himself destitute, possessed of nothing save a few dry grains of faith. Why could he not go to France in Tony's place, to the neat little wound or the barbarous prison?

But next morning as he knelt at the altar-rail beside Angela and Tony he seemed to hear his answer in the words of the canon: *Domine non sum dignus.*

3

Guy had planned to stay two nights and go on Monday to visit his father at Matchet. Instead he left before luncheon on Sunday so as to leave Angela uninterrupted in her last hours with Tony. It was a journey he had often made before. Box-Bender used to send him into Bristol by car. His father used to send for him to the mainline station. Now all the world seemed on the move and he was obliged to travel tediously with several changes of bus and train. It was late afternoon when he arrived at Matchet station and found his father with his old golden retriever waiting on the platform.

'I don't know where the hotel porter is,' said Mr Crouchback. 'He should be here. I told him he would be needed. But everyone's very busy. Leave your bag here. I expect we'll meet him on the way.'

Father and son and dog walked out together into the sunset down the steep little streets of the town.

Despite the forty years that divided them there was a marked likeness between Mr Crouchback and Guy. Mr Crouchback was rather the taller and he wore an expression of steadfast benevolence quite lacking in Guy. '*Racé* rather than *distingué*' was how Miss Vavasour, a fellow resident at the Marine Hotel, defined Mr Crouchback's evident charm. There was nothing of the old dandy about him, nothing crusted, nothing crotchety. He was not at all what is called 'a character'. He was an innocent, affable old man who had somehow preserved his good humour – much more than that, a mysterious and tranquil joy – throughout a life which to all outward observation had been overloaded with misfortune. He had like many another been born in full sunlight and lived to see night fall. England was full of such Jobs who had been disappointed in their prospects. Mr Crouchback had lost his home. Partly in his father's hands, partly in his own, without extravagance or speculation, his inheritance had melted away. He had rather early lost his beloved wife and been left to a long widowhood. He had an ancient name which was now little regarded and threatened with extinction. Only God and Guy knew the massive and singular quality of Mr Crouchback's family pride. He kept it to himself. That passion, which is often so thorny a growth, bore nothing save roses for Mr Crouchback. He was quite without class consciousness because he saw the whole intricate social structure of his country divided neatly into two unequal and unmistakable parts. On one side stood the Crouchbacks and certain inconspicuous, anciently allied families; on the other side stood the rest of mankind, Box-Bender, the butcher, the Duke of Omnium (whose onetime wealth derived from monastic spoils), Lloyd George, Neville Chamberlain – all of a piece together. Mr Crouchback acknowledged no monarch since James II. It was not an entirely sane conspectus but it engendered in his gentle breast two rare qualities, tolerance and humility. For nothing much, he assumed, could reasonably be expected from the commonalty; it was remarkable how well some of them did behave on occasions; while, for himself, any virtue he had came from afar without his deserving, and every small fault was grossly culpable in a man of his high tradition.

He had a further natural advantage over Guy; he was fortified by a memory which kept only the good things and rejected the ill. Despite his sorrows, he had had a fair share of joys, and these were ever fresh and accessible in Mr Crouchback's mind. He never mourned the loss of Broome. He still inhabited it as he had known it in bright boyhood and in early, requited love.

In his actual leaving home there had been no complaining. He attended every day of the sale seated in the marquee on the auctioneer's platform, munching pheasant sandwiches, drinking port from a flask and watching the bidding with tireless interest, all unlike the ruined squire of Victorian iconography.

'... Who'd have thought those old vases worth £18? ... Where did that table come from? Never saw it before in my life ... Awful shabby the carpets

look when you get them out . . . What on earth can Mrs Chadwick want with
a stuffed bear? . . .'

The Marine Hotel, Matchet, was kept by old servants from Broome. They
made him very welcome. There he brought a few photographs, the bedroom
furniture to which he was accustomed, complete and rather severe – the
brass bedstead, the oak presses and boot-rack, the circular shaving glass, the
mahogany prie-dieu. His sitting-room was furnished from the smoking-room
at Broome with a careful selection of old favourites from the library. And
there he had lived ever since, greatly respected by Miss Vavasour and the
other permanent residents. The original manager sold out and went to
Canada; his successor took on Mr Crouchback with the other effects. Once
a year he revisited Broome, when a requiem was sung for his ancestors. He
never lamented his changed state or mentioned it to newcomers. He went
to mass every day, walking punctually down the High Street before the
shops were open; walking punctually back as the shutters were coming down,
with a word of greeting for everyone he passed. All his pride of family was
a schoolboy hobby compared with his religious faith. When Virginia left
Guy childless, it did not occur to Mr Crouchback, as it had never ceased
occurring to Box-Bender, that the continuance of his line was worth a tiff
with the Church; that Guy should marry by civil law and beget an heir and
settle things up later with the ecclesiastical authorities as other people
seemed somehow to do. Family pride could not be served in dishonour.
There were in fact two medieval excommunications and a seventeenth-
century apostasy clearly set out in the family annals, but those were among
the things that Mr Crouchback's memory extruded.

Tonight the town seemed fuller than usual. Guy knew Matchet well. He
had picnicked there as a child and visited his father whenever he came to
England. The Marine Hotel lay outside the town, on the cliff beside the
coast-guard station. Their way led down the harbour, along the waterfront,
then up again by a red rock track. Lundy Island could be seen in the setting
sun, beyond the brown waters. The channel was full of shipping held by the
Contraband Control.

'I should have liked to say good-bye to Tony,' said Mr Crouchback. 'I
didn't know he was off so soon. There's something I looked out for him the
other day and wanted to give him. I know he'd have liked to have it –
Gervase's medal of Our Lady of Lourdes. He bought it in France on a
holiday the year the war broke out and he always wore it. They sent it back
after he was killed with his watch and things. Tony ought to have it.'

'I don't think there'd be time to get it to him now.'

'I'd like to have given it to him myself. It's not the same thing sending
it in a letter. Harder to explain.'

'It didn't protect Gervase much, did it?'

'Oh, yes,' said Mr Crouchback, 'much more than you might think. He told me when he came to say good-bye before going out. The army is full of temptations for a boy. Once in London, when he was in training, he got rather drunk with some of his regiment and in the end he found himself left alone with a girl they'd picked up somewhere. She began to fool about and pulled off his tie and then she found the medal and all of a sudden they both sobered down and she began talking about the convent where she'd been at school and so they parted friends and no harm done. I call that being protected. I've worn a medal all my life. Do you?'

'I have from time to time. I haven't one at the moment.'

'You should, you know, with bombs and things about. If you get hit and taken to hospital, they know you're a Catholic and send for a priest. A nurse once told me that. Would *you* care to have Gervase's medal, if Tony can't?'

'Very much. Besides I hope to get into the army too.'

'So you said in your letter. But they've turned you down?'

'There doesn't seem to be much competition for me.'

'What a shame. But I can't imagine you a soldier. You never liked motor-cars, did you? It's all motor-cars now, you know. The yeomanry haven't had any horses since the year before last, a man was telling me, and they haven't any motor-cars either. Seems a silly business. But you don't care for horses either, do you?'

'Not lately,' said Guy, remembering the eight horses he and Virginia had kept in Kenya, the rides round the lake at dawn; remembering, too, the Ford van which he had driven to market twice a month over the dirt track.

'Trains de luxe are more in your line, eh?'

'There wasn't anything very luxurious about today's trains,' said Guy.

'No,' said his father. 'I've no business to chaff you. It's very nice of you to come all this way to see me, my boy. I don't think you'll be dull. There are all kinds of new people in the inn – most amusing. I've made a whole new circle of friends in the last fortnight. Charming people. You'll be surprised.'

'More Miss Vavasours?'

'No, no, different people. All sorts of quite young people. A charming Mrs Tickeridge and her daughter. Her husband is a major in the Halberdiers. He's come down for Sunday. You'll like them awfully.'

The Marine Hotel was full and overflowing, as all hotels seemed to be all over the country. Formerly when he came to visit his father, Guy had been conscious of a stir of interest among guests and staff. Now he found it difficult to get any attention.

'No, we're quite full up,' said the manageress. 'Mr Crouchback did ask for a room for you but we were expecting you tomorrow. There's nothing at all tonight.'

'Perhaps you could fix him up in my sitting-room.'

'We'll do what we can, if you don't mind waiting a bit.'

The porter who should have been at the station was helping hand round drinks in the lounge.

'I'll go just as soon as I can, sir,' he said. 'If you don't mind waiting until after dinner.'

Guy did mind. He wanted a change of shirt after his journey, but the man was gone with his tray of glasses before Guy could answer.

'Isn't it a gay scene?' said Mr Crouchback. 'Those are the Tickeridges over there. Do come and meet them.'

Guy saw a mousy woman and a man in uniform with enormous handle-bar moustaches. 'I expect they've sent their little girl up to bed. She's a remarkable child. Only six, no nannie, and does everything for herself.'

The mousy woman smiled with unexpected charm at Mr Crouchback's approach. The man with the moustaches began moving furniture about to make room.

'Cheeroh,' he said. 'Pardon my glove.' (He was holding a chair above his head with both hands.) 'We were about to do a little light shopping. What's yours, sir?'

Somehow he cleared a small space and filled it with chairs. Somehow he caught the porter. Mr Crouchback introduced Guy.

'So you're joining the lotus-eaters too? I've just settled madam and the offspring here for the duration. Charming spot. I wish I could spend a few weeks here instead of in barracks.'

'No,' said Guy, 'I'm only here for one night.'

'Pity. The madam wants company. Too many old pussycats around.'

In addition to his huge moustaches Major Tickeridge had tufts of wiry ginger whisker high on his cheekbones, almost in his eyes.

The porter brought them their drinks. Guy tried to engage him on the subject of his bag but he was off in a twinkling with 'I'll be with you in one minute, sir.'

'Baggage problems?' said the major. 'They're all in rather a flap here. What's the trouble?'

Guy told him at some length.

'That's easy. I've got the invaluable but usually invisible Halberdier Gold standing easy somewhere in the rear echelon. Let him go.'

'No, I say, please. . . .'

'Halberdier Gold has not done a hand's turn since we got here except call me too damned early this morning. He needs exercise. Besides he's a married man and the housemaids won't let him alone. It'll do Halberdier Gold good to get away from them for a bit.'

Guy warmed towards this kind and hairy man.

'Here's how,' said the major.

'Here's how,' said the mousy wife.

'Here's how,' said Mr Crouchback with complete serenity.

But Guy could only manage an embarrassed grunt.

'First today,' said the major, downing his pink gin. 'Vi, order another round while I winkle out the Halberdier.'

With a series of collisions and apologies Major Tickeridge made his way across the hall.

'It's awfully kind of your husband.'

'He can't bear a man standing idle,' said Mrs Tickeridge. 'It's his Halberdier training.'

Later when they separated for dinner Mr Crouchback said: 'Delightful people, didn't I tell you? You'll see Jenifer tomorrow. A beautifully behaved child.'

In the dining-room the old residents had their tables round the wall. The newcomers were in the centre, and, it seemed to Guy, got more attention. Mr Crouchback by a long-standing arrangement brought his own wine and kept it in the hotel cellars. A bottle of Burgundy and a bottle of port were already on the table. The five courses were rather better than might have been expected.

'It's really remarkable how the Cuthberts cope with the influx. It's all happened so suddenly. Of course one has to wait a bit between courses but they manage to turn out a very decent dinner, don't they? There's only one change I mind. They've asked me not to bring Felix in to meals. Of course he did take up an awful lot of room.'

With the pudding the waiter put a plate of dog's dinner on the table. Mr Crouchback studied it carefully, turning it over with his fork.

'Yes, that looks delicious,' he said. 'Thank you so very much,' and to Guy, 'D'you mind if I take it up to Felix now? He's used to it at this time. Help yourself to the port. I'll be back directly.'

He carried the plate through the dining-room up to his sitting-room, now Guy's bedroom, and soon returned.

'We'll take him out later,' said Mr Crouchback. 'At about ten. I see the Tickeridges have finished dinner. The last two nights they've joined me in a glass of port. They seem a little shy tonight. You don't mind if I ask them over, do you?'

They came.

'A beautiful wine, sir.'

'Oh, it's just something the people in London send down to me.'

'I wish you could come to our mess one day. We've got some very fine port we bring out for guest nights. You, too,' he added, addressing Guy.

'My son, in spite of his advanced years, is making frantic efforts to join the army himself.'

'I say, not really? I call that jolly sporting.'

'I'm not seeing much sport,' said Guy, and wryly described the disappointments and rebuffs of the last fortnight.

Major Tickeridge was slightly puzzled by the ironic note of the recitation.

'I say,' he said. 'Are you serious about this?'

'I try not to be,' said Guy. 'But I'm afraid I am.'

'Because if you *are* serious, why don't you join *us*?'

'I've pretty well given up,' said Guy. 'In fact I've as good as signed on in the Foreign Office.'

Major Tickeridge showed deep concern.

'I say, that is a pretty desperate thing to do. You know, if you're really serious, I think the thing can be managed. The old corps never quite does things in the ordinary army style. I mean none of that Hore-Belisha stuff of starting in the ranks. We're forming a brigade of our own, half regulars, half temporaries, half National Service men, half long-service. It's all on bumf at present but we're starting cadre training any day now. It's going to be something rather special. We all know one another in the corps, you know, so if you'd like me to put in a word with the Captain-Commandant, just say so. I heard him saying the other day he could do with a few older chaps among the temporary officers.'

By ten o'clock that night, when Guy and his father let Felix go bounding into the blackness, Major Tickeridge had made notes of Guy's particulars and promised immediate action.

'It's remarkable,' said Guy. 'I spent weeks badgering generals and Cabinet Ministers and getting nowhere. Then I come here and in an hour everything is fixed up for me by a strange major.'

'That's often the way. I told you Tickeridge was a capital fellow,' said Mr Crouchback, 'and the Halberdiers are a magnificent regiment. I've seen them on parade. They're every bit as good as the Foot Guards.'

At eleven lights went out downstairs in the Marine Hotel and the servants disappeared. Guy and his father went up to bed. Mr Crouchback's sitting-room smelled of tobacco and dog.

'Doesn't look much of a bed, I'm afraid.'

'Last night at Angela's I slept in the library.'

'Well, I hope you'll be all right.'

Guy undressed and lay down on the sofa by the open window. The sea beat below and the sea-air filled the room. Since that morning his affairs had greatly changed.

Presently his father's door opened: 'I say, are you asleep?'

'Not quite.'

'There's this thing you said you'd like. Gervase's medal. I might forget it in the morning.'

'Thanks most awfully. I'll always wear it from now on.'

'I'll put it here on the table. Good night.'

Guy stretched out in the darkness and felt the light disc of metal. It was strung on a piece of cord. He tied it round his neck and heard his father moving about in his room. The door opened again. 'I say, I'm afraid I get up rather early and I'll have to come through. I'll be as quiet as I can.'

'I'll come to mass with you.'

'Will you? Do. Good night again.'

Soon he heard his father lightly snoring. His last thought before falling asleep was the uneasy question: 'Why couldn't I say "Here's how" to Major Tickeridge? My father did. Gervase would have. Why couldn't I?'

BOOK ONE

Apthorpe Gloriosus

I

'Here's how,' said Guy.

'Cheers,' said Apthorpe.

'Look here, you two, you'd better have those drinks on me,' said Major Tickeridge, 'junior officers aren't supposed to drink in the ante-room before lunch.'

'Oh Lord. I am sorry, sir.'

'My dear chap, you couldn't possibly know. I ought to have warned you. It's a rule we have for the youngsters. It's all rot applying it to you chaps, of course, but there it is. If you want a drink tell the corporal-of-servants to send it to the billiards-room. No one will mind that.'

'Thanks for telling us, sir,' said Apthorpe.

'I expect you work up quite a thirst pounding the square. The C.O. and I had a look at you this morning. You're coming along.'

'Yes, I think we are.'

'I heard from my madam today. All's well on the Matchet front. Pity it's too far for week-end leave. I expect they'll give you a week at the end of the course.'

It was early November. Winter had set in early and cold that year. A huge fire blazed in the ante-room. Junior officers, unless invited, did not sit by it; but its warmth reached the humble panelled corners.

The officers of the Royal Corps of Halberdiers, from the very fact of their being poor men, lived in great comfort. In fashionable regiments the mess was deserted after working hours by all except the orderly-officer. The Halberdiers had made this house their home for two hundred years. As Major Tickeridge often said: 'Any damn fool can make himself comfortable.' In their month in the regiment neither Guy nor Apthorpe had once been out to a meal.

They were the eldest of the batch of twenty probationary officers now under instructions in barracks. Another similar group was said to be at the Depot. Presently they would be brought together. Some hundreds of National Service recruits were in training on the coast. Eventually in the spring they would all be interjoined with the regular battalions and the Brigade would form. This was a phrase in constant use: 'When the brigade forms . . .' It was the immediate end of all their present activity, awaited like a birth; the start of a new unknown life.

Guy's companions were mostly young clerks from London offices. Two or three had come straight from public schools. One, Frank de Souza, was just down from Cambridge. They had been chosen, Guy learned, from more than two thousand applicants. He wondered, sometimes, what system of selection had produced so nondescript a squad. Later he realized that they typified the peculiar pride of the Corps, which did not expect distinguished raw materials but confided instead in its age-old methods of transformation. The discipline of the square, the traditions of the mess, would work their magic and the *esprit de corps* would fall like blessed unction from above.

Apthorpe alone looked like a soldier. He was burly, tanned, moustached, primed with a rich vocabulary of military terms and abbreviations. Until recently he had served in Africa in some unspecified capacity. His boots had covered miles of bush trail.

Boots were a subject of peculiar interest to Apthorpe.

He and Guy first met on the day they joined. Guy got into the carriage at Charing Cross and found Apthorpe seated in the corner opposite to him. He recognized the badges of the Halberdiers and the regimental horn buttons. His first thought was that he had probably committed some heinous breach of etiquette by travelling with a senior officer.

Apthorpe had no newspaper or book. He stared fixedly at his own feet for mile after mile. Presently by a process of furtive inspection Guy realized that the insignia of rank on Apthorpe's shoulders were not crowns but single stars like his own. Still neither spoke, until after twenty minutes Apthorpe took out a pipe and began carefully filling it from a large rolled pouch. Then he said: 'This is my new pair of porpoises. I expect you wear them too.'

Guy looked from Apthorpe's boots to his own. They seemed very much alike. Was 'porpoise' Halberdier slang for 'boot'?

'I don't know. I just told the man I always go to, to make me a couple of pairs of thick black boots.'

'He may have given you cow.'

'Perhaps he did.'

'A great mistake, old man, if you don't mind my saying so.'

He puffed his pipe for another five minutes, then spoke again: 'Of course, it's really the skin of the white whale, you know.'

'I didn't know. Why do they call it "porpoise"?'

'Trade secret, old man.'

More than once after their meeting Apthorpe reverted to the topic. Whenever Guy gave evidence of sophistication in other matters, Apthorpe would say: 'Funny you don't wear porpoises. I should have thought you were just the sort of chap who would.'

But the Halberdier servant who looked after them in barracks – one between four probationary officers – found great difficulty in polishing Apthorpe's porpoises and the only criticism ever made of his turn-out on parade was that his boots were dull.

Because of their age Guy and Apthorpe became companions in most things and were called 'Uncle' by the younger officers.

'Well,' said Apthorpe, 'we'd better get a move on.'

The luncheon break allowed no time for dawdling. On paper there was an hour and a half but the squad drilled in suits of privates' dungarees (battle-dress had not yet been issued) and they had to change before appearing in the mess. Today Colour Sergeant Cook had kept them five minutes after the dinner call in expiation of Trimmer's being late on parade that morning.

Trimmer was the only member of the batch whom Guy definitely disliked. He was not one of the youngest. His large, long-lashed, close-set eyes had a knowing look. Trimmer concealed under his cap a lock of golden hair which fell over his forehead when he was bare-headed. He spoke with a slightly refined Cockney accent and when the wireless in the billiards-room played jazz, Trimmer trucked about with raised hands in little shuffling dance steps. Nothing was known of his civilian antecedents; theatrical, possibly, Guy supposed. He was no fool but his talents were not soldierly. The corporate self-esteem of the Halberdiers did not impress Trimmer, nor did the solemn comforts of the mess attract him. The moment work ended Trimmer was off, sometimes alone, sometimes with a poor reflection of himself, his only friend, named Sarum-Smith. As surely as Apthorpe was marked for early promotion, Trimmer was marked for ignominy. That morning he had appeared at the precise time stated in orders. Everyone else had been waiting five minutes and Colour Sergeant Cork called out the marker just as Trimmer appeared. So it was twelve thirty-five when they were dismissed.

Then they had doubled to their quarters, thrown their rifles and equipment on their beds, and changed into service-dress. Complete with canes and gloves (which had to be buttoned before emerging. A junior officer seen buttoning his gloves on the steps would be sent back to dress) they had marched in pairs to the Officers' House. This was the daily routine. Every ten yards they saluted or were saluted. (Salutes in the Halberdiers' Barracks were acknowledged as smartly as they were given. The senior of the pair was taught to count: 'Up. One, two, three. Down.') In the hall they removed their caps and Sam-Brownes.

Theoretically there was no distinction of rank in the mess 'Except, Gentle-men, the natural deference which youth owes to age', as they were told in the address of welcome on their first evening; Guy and Apthorpe were older than most of the regular captains and were, in fact, treated in many ways as seniors. Together they now went into the mess at a few minutes after one.

Guy helped himself to steak-and-kidney pie at the sideboard and carried his plate to the nearest place at the table. A mess orderly appeared immediately at his elbow with salad and roast potatoes. The wine butler put a silver goblet of beer before him. No one spoke much. 'Shop' was banned and there was little else in their minds. Over their heads two centuries of commanding officers stared dully at one another from their gilt frames.

Guy had joined the Corps in a mood of acute shyness born of conflicting apprehension and exultation. He knew little of military life save stories he had heard from time to time of the humiliations to which new officers were liable; of 'subalterns' courts martial' and gross ceremonies of initiation. He remembered a friend telling him that in his regiment no one noticed him for a month and that the first words spoken to him were: 'Well, Mr Bloody, and what may your name be?' In another regiment a junior officer said 'Good morning' to a senior and was answered: 'Good morning, good morning, good morning, good morning, good morning, good morning, good morning. Let that last you for a week.' There had been nothing at all like that in the hospitable welcome he and his fellows received from the Halberdiers. It seemed to Guy that in the last weeks he had been experiencing something he had missed in boyhood, a happy adolescence.

Captain Bosanquet, the adjutant, coming cheerfully into the mess after his third pink gin, stopped opposite Guy and Apthorpe and said: 'It must have been pretty bloody cold on the square this morning.'

'It was rather, sir.'

'Well, pass the word to your chaps to wear great-coats this afternoon.'

'Very good, sir.'

'Thank you, sir.'

'Oh, you two poops,' said Frank de Souza, the Cambridge man opposite. 'That means we'll have to let out all our equipment again.'

So there was no time for coffee or a cigarette. At half past one Guy and Apthorpe put on their belts, buttoned their gloves, looked in the glass to see that their caps were straight, tucked their canes under their arms and strode off in step to their quarters.

'Up. One, two, three. Down.' They acknowledged a fatigue party called to attention as they passed.

At their steps they broke into a run. Guy changed, and began hastily adjusting his webbing equipment. Blanco got under his fingernails. (This was the time of day which, all his life since school, Guy had spent in an easy chair.) It was permissible to double in drill suits. Guy arrived on the edge of the barrack square with half a minute in hand.

Trimmer looked terrible. Instead of buttoning his great-coat across the chest and clipping it tight at the throat, he had left it open. Moreover he had made a mess of his equipment. He had let one side-strap down at the back, the other in front with monstrous effect.

'Mr Trimmer, fall out, sir. Go to your quarters and come back here properly dressed in five minutes. *As you were.* One pace *back* from the rear rank, Mr Trimmer. *As you were.* On the command "Fall out" you take one pace back with the left foot. About turn, quick march. *As you were.* Swing the right arm level with the belt as the left foot goes forward. Now get it right. Fall out. And let me not see any laughter, Mr Sarum-Smith. There's not an officer in this squad so smart as he can laugh at another. Any officer I see laughing at another officer on parade will find himself up before the adjutant. All right. Stand easy. While we wait for Mr Trimmer, we'll just run through a little Corps history. The Royal Corps of Halberdiers was first raised by the Earl of Essex, for service in the Low Countries in the reign of Queen Elizabeth. It then bore the name of the Earl of Essex's Honourable Company of Free Halberdiers. What other sobriquets has it earned, Mr Crouchback?'

' "The Copper Heels", and the "Applejacks", Sergeant.'

'Right. Why the "Applejacks", Mr Sarum-Smith?'

'Because after the Battle of Malplaquet a detachment of the Corps under Halberdier Sergeant Major Breen were bivouacked in an orchard when they were surprised by a party of French marauders whom they drove away by pelting them with apples, Sergeant.'

'Very good, Mr Sarum-Smith. Mr Leonard, what part did the Corps play in the First Ashanti War . . .'

Presently Trimmer returned.

'Very well. Now we can get on. This afternoon we are going to the kitchens where Halberdier Sergeant Major Groggin will show you how to tell meat. Every officer must know how to tell meat. Many frauds are attempted on the military by civilian contractors and the health of his men depends on the alertness of the officer. All right? Then, Mr Sarum-Smith, will you take command. At the command, "Move", step smartly out of the ranks, about turn, face your men. Move. This is your squad now. I'm not here. I want them without arms, marched in a soldierly fashion to the kitchen yard. If you don't know where that is, follow your nose, sir. First run through the detail for piling arms, just for refreshment, and then give the executive order.'

The detail for piling arms was the most elaborate part of their education to date. Sarum-Smith faltered. Guy was called out and faltered also. De Souza ran on confidently, but incorrectly. At last Apthorpe, the safe stand-by, was called on. With an expression of strain he got it right – '. . . the odd numbers of the front rank will seize the rifles of the even numbers with the left hand crossing the muzzles, magazines turned outward, at the same time

raising the piling swivels with the forefinger and thumb of both hands ...'
and the squad marched off. For the rest of the afternoon period they
inspected the kitchens in great heat and the meat store in great cold. They
saw vast, purple and yellow, carcasses of beef and were taught to distinguish
cat from rabbit by the number of ribs.

At four they were dismissed. There was tea in the mess for those who
thought it worth another change of uniform. Most lay on their beds until
it was time for Physical Training.

Sarum-Smith came to Guy's room.

'I say, Uncle, have you had any pay yet?'

'Not a penny.'

'Can't we do anything about it?'

'I did mention it to the Second-in-Command. He says it always takes some
time to get through. It's just a matter of waiting.'

'That's all right for those who can afford it. Some firms are making up
their fellows' salaries so they don't lose by joining the army. Mine doesn't.
You're quite happily placed, aren't you, Uncle?'

'Well, I'm not quite broke yet.'

'Wish I wasn't. It's jolly awkward for me. Did you realize when we joined
they'd make us pay for our food?'

'Well, we don't really. We pay for what we have to supplement rations.
It's very good value.'

'That's all very well, but I'd have thought the least they could do would
be to feed us in war-time. It was a shock when I found my first mess bill.
How do they expect us to live? I'm absolutely stony.'

'I see,' said Guy without enthusiasm or surprise, for this was not the first
conversation of the kind he suffered in the last few weeks and Sarum-Smith
was not a man whom he particularly liked. 'I suppose you want a loan.'

'I say, Uncle, you're a thought-reader. I would be glad of a fiver if you
can spare it. Just till the Army pays up.'

'Don't tell everyone else.'

'No, of course not. A lot of us are in a bit of a fix, I can tell you. I tried
Uncle Apthorpe first. He advised me to come to you.'

'Thoughtful of him.'

'Of course if it's putting *you* in a fix. ...'

'No, that's all right. But I don't want to become banker for the whole
Corps.'

'You shall have it back the moment I get my pay ...'

Guy was owed fifty-five pounds.

Soon it was time to change into flannels and go to the gym. This was the
one part of the day Guy hated. The squad of probationary officers assembled
under the arc lights. Two Halberdier corporals were kicking a football about.

40

One of them kicked it so that it smacked against the wall over their heads.

'That's damned cheek,' said a young man named Leonard.

The ball came again, rather closer.

'I believe the fellow's doing it deliberately,' said Sarum-Smith.

Suddenly there was a loud authoritative shout from Apthorpe. 'You two men, there. Can't you see there's a squad of officers here? Take that ball and get out.'

The corporals looked sulky, picked up their ball and strolled out with a plausible suggestion of nonchalance. Outside the door they laughed loudly. The gym seemed to Guy to institute a sort of extra-territorial area, the embassy of an alien and hostile people, that had no part in the well-ordered life of the barracks.

The Physical Training instructor was a sleek young man with pomaded hair, a big behind and unnaturally glittering eyes. He performed his great feats of strength and agility with a feline and, to Guy, most offensive air of sang-froid.

'The purpose of P.T. is to loosen up,' he said, 'and counteract the stiffening effects of the old-fashioned drill. Some of you are older than others. Don't strain. Don't do more than you feel you can. I want to see you *enjoy* yourselves. We'll start with a game.'

These games had a deeply depressing effect even on the youngest. Guy stood in line, took a football when it came to him from between the legs of the man in front, and passed it on. They were supposed to compete, one rank against the other.

'Come on,' said the instructor, 'you're letting them get away with it. I'm backing you. Don't let me down.'

After the game came exercises.

'Make it smooth and graceful, gentlemen, as though you were waltzing with your best girl. That's the way, Mr Trimmer. That's very rhythmic. In the old days a soldier's training consisted of standing stiff at attention for long periods and stamping the feet. Modern science has shown that stamping the feet can seriously jar the spinal column. That's why nowadays every day's work ends with half an hour's limbering up.'

This man would never fight, Guy thought. He would stay in his glaring shed, rippling his muscles, walking on his hands, bouncing about the boards like an india-rubber ball, though the heavens were falling.

'At Aldershot today the advance courses are all done to music.'

There would have been no place for this man, Guy reflected, in the Earl of Essex's Honourable Company of Free Halberdiers. He was no Copper Heel, no true Applejack.

After Physical Training another change of clothes and a lecture on Military Law from Captain Bosanquet. Lecturer and audience were equally comatose. Captain Bosanquet demanded no more than silence.

'... The great thing to remember is to stick in all the amendments of King's Regulations as soon as they're issued. Keep your King's Regulations up to date and you can't go far wrong.'

At six-thirty they were roused, dismissed and the day's work was at last over. This evening Captain Bosanquet called Guy and Apthorpe back.

'I say,' he said, 'I looked in at your P.T. this evening. Do you think it does you any particular good?'

'I can't say I do, sir,' said Guy.

'No, it's rather rot for people like yourselves. If you like, you can cut it out. Keep clear of the ante-room. Just stay in your quarters and, if anyone asks, say you are mugging up Military Law.'

'Thanks awfully, sir.'

'You'll probably find yourself commanding companies one day. Military Law will be more use to you then than P.T.'

'I think I'll stay on in the gym, if I may,' said Apthorpe. 'I find that after the square I need limbering up a bit.'

'Just as you like.'

'I've always been used to plenty of exercise,' said Apthorpe to Guy, as they returned to their quarters. 'There's a lot of sense in what Sergeant Pringle said about jarring the spinal column. I think I may have jarred mine a bit. I've been feeling a bit off colour lately. It may be that. I don't want anyone to think I'm not as fit as the rest of the crowd. The truth is I've lived hard, old man, and it tells.'

'Talking about being different from the rest of the crowd, did you by any chance pass Sarum-Smith on to me?'

'That's right. I don't believe in borrowing or lending. Seen too much of it.'

There were two baths on every staircase. Coal fires had now been lighted in the bedrooms. Toiling old Halberdiers, recalled to the colours and put on barrack duties, kept them stoked. This was the best hour of the day. Guy heard the feet of the young officers scampering down and out to local cinemas, hotels and dance-halls. He soaked in hot water and later lay dozing in the wicker Oxford chair before his fire. No Mediterranean siesta had ever given such ease.

Presently Apthorpe came to summon him to the Officers' House. Patrol dress was optional for probationary officers. Only he and Guy had bought it and this tended to set them apart and make them more acceptable to the regulars, not because they could afford twelve guineas which the others could not, but because they had chosen to make a private investment in the traditions of the Corps.

When the two 'Uncles' in their blues arrived in the ante-room, Major Tickeridge and Captain Bosanquet were alone before the fire.

'Come and join us,' said Major Tickeridge. He clapped his hands. 'Music and dancing-girls. Four pink gins.'

Guy loved Major Tickeridge and Captain Bosanquet. He loved Apthorpe. He loved the oil-painting over the fireplace of the unbroken square of Halberdiers in the desert. He loved the whole Corps deeply and tenderly.

Dinner was formal that night. The mess-president struck the table with an ivory hammer and the chaplain said Grace. The young officers, accustomed to swifter and sparser meals, found all this rather oppressive. 'I call it a bit thick,' Sarum-Smith had remarked, 'the way they even make a drill-movement out of eating.'

The table was lit with huge many-branched candlesticks which commemorated the military history of the last century in silver palm trees and bowed silver savages. There were about twenty officers in mess that night. Many of the young were out in the town; the older were in neighbouring villas with their wives. No one drank wine except on guest nights. Guy had made the mistake of ordering claret his first evening and had been rebuked with a jocular: 'Hullo, blood? Is it someone's birthday?'

'There's an Ensa show tonight. Shall we go?'

'Why not?'

'I rather thought of sticking some amendments into the King's Regulations.'

'I'm told the orderly-room clerk will do it for a pound.'

'Looks better to do it oneself,' said Apthorpe. 'Still I think I'll come for once. The Captain-Commandant may be there. I haven't spoken to him since the first day.'

'What d'you want to say to him?'

'Oh, nothing particular. Anything that crops up, you know.'

After a pause Guy said: 'You heard what the adjutant said about our probably getting companies.'

'Doesn't that verge rather on shop, old man?'

Presently the hammer sounded again, the chaplain said Grace and the table was cleared. The removal of the cloth was a feat of dexterity which never failed to delight Guy. The corporal-of-servants stood at the foot of the table. The mess orderlies lifted the candlesticks. Then with a single flick of his wrists the corporal drew the whole length of linen into an avalanche at his feet.

Port and snuff went round. The party broke up.

The Halberdiers had their own Garrison Theatre within the barrack walls. It was nearly full when Guy and Apthorpe arrived. The first two rows were kept for officers. In the centre sat the full colonel, who by an idiosyncrasy of the Corps was called the Captain-Commandant, with his wife and daughter. Guy and Apthorpe looked for places, saw only two empty seats in the centre. They hesitated, Guy seeking to withdraw, Apthorpe rather timidly advancing.

'Come along,' said the Captain-Commandant. 'Ashamed to be seen sitting with us? Meet madam and the brat.'

43

They took their places with the distinguished party.

'Do you go home for the week-end?' asked the brat.

'No. You see my home's in Italy.'

'Not really. Are you artistic or something? How thrilling.'

'My home used to be in Bechuanaland,' said Apthorpe.

'I say,' said the Captain-Commandant. 'You must have some interesting yarns. Well, I suppose I'd better get this thing started.'

He gave a nod; the footlights went up; he rose and climbed the steps to the stage.

'We're all greatly looking forward to this show,' he said. 'These charming ladies and accomplished gentlemen have come a long way on a cold night to entertain us. Let's see we give them a real Halberdier welcome.'

Then he returned to his place amid loud applause.

'It's really the chaplain's job,' he said to Guy. 'But I give the little fellow a rest now and then.'

A piano began playing behind the curtain. The curtain rose. Before the stage was fully revealed, the Captain-Commandant sank into deep but not silent sleep. Under the Corps crest in the proscenium there was disclosed a little concert party comprising three elderly women, over-made-up, a cadaverous old man, under-made-up, and a neuter beast of indeterminable age at the piano. All wore the costume of pierrots and pierrettes. There was a storm of loyal applause. A jaunty chorus opened the show. One by one the heads in the first two rows sank into their collars. Guy slept too.

He was awakened an hour later by a volume of song striking him from a few feet away. It came from the cadaverous man whose frail northern body seemed momentarily possessed by the ghost of some enormous tenor from the south. He woke the Captain-Commandant, too.

'I say, that's not "God Save The King", is it?'

'No, sir. "There'll always be an England".'

The Captain-Commandant collected his wits and listened.

'Quite right,' he said. 'Never can tell a tune till I've heard the words. The old fellow's got a voice, hasn't he?'

It was the last item. Soon everyone was at attention. The tenor did more. He stood at attention while company and audience joined in the National Anthem.

'On these occasions we always have the performers in for a drink. You might round up some of the young chaps to do the honours, will you? I expect you've more experience in entertaining the theatrical world than we have. And, I say, if you're here for Sunday and have nothing better to do, come and lunch.'

'Very glad to, sir,' said Apthorpe, whose inclusion in the invitation was by no means clear.

'You'll be here, too? Yes, of course, do come. Delighted.'

The Captain-Commandant did not go with them to the Officers' House. Two regulars and three or four of Guy's batch formed the reception committee. The ladies had shed all theatrical airs with their make-up and their fancy dress. They might have come in from a day's household shopping.

Guy found himself next to the tenor, who had shed his wig, revealing a few grey wisps of hair which made him appear somewhat younger, but still very old. His cheeks and nose were blotchy and bright-veined, his eyes watery in a nest of wrinkles. It was many weeks since Guy had looked into a sick man's face. He might have taken the tenor for an alcoholic, but he chose only coffee to drink.

'Find I don't sleep if I drink whisky nowadays,' he said apologetically. 'You're all wonderfully hospitable. Especially the Corps. I've always had a very warm corner for the Copper Heads.'

'Copper Heels.'

'Yes, of course. I meant Copper Heels. We were next to you in the line once in the last show. We got on very well with your chaps. I was in the Artists. Not with a commission, mind you. I wasn't the age for that, even then. Joined up in the ranks and saw it all through.'

'I only just scraped in.'

'Oh, you're young. I wonder if I might have another cup of this excellent coffee. Takes it out of one, singing.'

'You've got a fine voice.'

'D'you think it went down all right? One never knows.'

'Oh, yes, a great success.'

'Of course we aren't a No. 1 Company.'

'You were all a great success.'

They stood silent. A burst of laughter rose from the group round the ladies. Everything was going easily there.

'More coffee?'

'No more, thank you.'

Silence.

'The news looks better,' said the tenor at last.

'Does it?'

'Oh, *much* better.'

'We don't get much time to read the papers.'

'No, I suppose you don't. I envy you. There's nothing in them but lies,' he added sadly. 'You can't believe a word they say. But it's all good. Very good indeed. It helps to keep one's spirits up,' he said from the depths of his gloom. 'Something cheerful every morning. That's what we need in these times.'

Quite soon the party bowled away into the night.

'That looked a very interesting man you were talking to,' said Apthorpe. 'Yes.'

45

'A real artist. I should think he's been in opera.'

'I daresay.'

'Grand Opera.'

Ten minutes later Guy was in bed. In youth he had been taught to make a nightly examination of conscience and an act of contrition. Since he joined the army this pious exercise had become confused with the lessons of the day. He had failed dismally in the detail of the pile-arms ... – '... the even numbers of the centre rank will incline their muzzles to the front and place their rifles under their right arms, guards uppermost, at the same time seizing the piling swivel. ...' – He was not now certain which had the more ribs, a cat or a rabbit. He wished it had been he, not Apthorpe, who had called the impudent corporals to order in the gym. He had snubbed that decent, melancholy old man about the 'Copper Heads'. Was that the real 'Halberdier welcome' expected of him? There was much to repent and repair.

2

On Saturday at twelve there was a large exodus from barracks. Guy as usual remained. More than his longer and more bitter memories, his modest bank balance, his blue patrols, his boredom in the gym or any of the small symptoms of age which distinguished him from his youthful fellows, there was this recurring need for repose and solitude. Apthorpe went off to play golf with one of the regulars. It was holiday enough for Guy to change at his leisure, wear the same clothes all the afternoon, to smoke a cigar after luncheon, walk down the High Street to collect his weekly papers – the *Spectator*, the *New Statesman*, the *Tablet* – from the local newsagent, to read them drowsily over his own fire in his own room. He was thus employed when, long after nightfall, Apthorpe returned from golf. He wore flannel trousers and a tweed coat much patched and bound with leather. There was a fatuous and glassy squint in his eyes. Apthorpe was tight.

'Hallo. Have you had dinner?'

'No. I don't intend to. It's a sound rule of health not to have dinner.'

'Never, Apthorpe?'

'Now, old man, I never said that. Of course not *never*. Sometimes. Gives the juices a rest. You have to be your own doctor in the bush. First rule of health, keep your feet dry; second, rest the juices. D'you know what the third is?'

'No.'

'Nor do I. Just stick to two rules and you'll be all right. You know you don't look well to me, Crouchback. I've been worrying about you. You know Sanders?'

'Yes.'

'I've been playing golf with him.'

'Good game?'

'Terrible. High wind, poor visibility. Played nine holes and knocked off. Sanders has a brother in Kasanga. I suppose you think that's near Makarikari.'

'Isn't it?'

'Just about twelve hundred miles, that's how near it is. You know, old man, for a chap who's knocked about as much as you have, you don't know much, do you? Twelve hundred bloody miles of bush and you call that near.' Apthorpe sat down and stared at Guy sadly. 'Not that it really matters,' he said. 'Why worry? Why go to Makarikari? Why not stay in Kasanga?'

'Why not indeed?'

'Because Kasanga's a perfectly awful hole, that's why. Still if you like the place, stay there by all means. Only don't ask me to join you, that's all, old man. Of course you'd have Sanders' brother. If he's anything like Sanders he plays pretty rotten golf, but I've no doubt you'd be jolly glad of his company in Kasanga. It's a perfectly awful hole. Don't know what you see in the place.'

'Why don't you go to bed?'

'Lonely,' said Apthorpe. 'That's why. It's always the same, wherever you are, Makarikari, Kasanga, anywhere. You have a good time drinking with the chaps in the club, you feel fine, and then at the end of it all you go back alone to bed. I need a woman.'

'Well, you won't find one in barracks.'

'For company, you understand. I can do without the other thing. Not, mind you, that I haven't done myself well in my time. And I will do again I hope. But I can take it or leave it. I'm above sex. You have to be, in the bush, or it gets a grip on you. But I can't do without company.'

'I can.'

'You mean you want me to go? All right, old man, I'm not as thick-skinned as you might think. I know when I'm not wanted. I'm sorry I inflicted myself on you for so long, very sorry.'

'We'll meet again tomorrow.'

But Apthorpe did not move. He sat goggling sadly. It was like watching the ball at roulette running slower and slower, trickling over the numbers. What would turn up next: Women? Africa? Health? Golf? It clicked into boots.

'I was wearing rubber soles today,' he said. 'I regret it now. Spoiled my drive. No grip.'

'Don't you think you'd better get to bed?'

It was half an hour before Apthorpe rose from the chair. When he did so, he sat heavily on the floor and continued the conversation, without apparently noticing his change of position. At last he said with a new lucidity: 'Look here, old man, I've enjoyed this talk tremendously. I hope we can go on with it some other night but at the moment I'm rather sleepy so if you don't mind I think I'll turn in.'

He then rolled over and lay silent. Guy went to bed to the sound of Apthorpe's breathing, turned off the light and slept also. He woke in the dark to hear groaning and stumbling. He turned on the light. Apthorpe was on his feet blinking.

'Good morning, Crouchback,' he said with dignity. 'I was just looking for the latrines. Must have taken a wrong turning. Good night.'

And he staggered from the room leaving the door ajar.

Next morning when Guy was called, the batman said: 'Mr Apthorpe's sick. He asked for you to go in and see him when you're dressed.'

Guy found him in bed with a japanned tin medicine chest on his knees.

'I'm a bit off colour, today,' he said. 'Not quite the thing at all. I shan't be getting up.'

'Anything I can do?'

'No, no, it's just a touch of Bechuana tummy. I get it from time to time. I know just how to take it.' He was stirring a whitish mixture with a glass rod. 'The hell of it is I promised to lunch with the Captain-Commandant. I must make a signal putting him off.'

'Why not just send him a note?'

'That's what I mean, old man. You always call it "making a signal" in the service, you know.'

'Do you remember calling on *me* last night?'

'Yes, of course. What an extraordinary question, old man. I'm not a talkative bloke as you well know, but I do enjoy a regular chinwag now and then in the right company. But I don't feel so good today. It was bloody cold and wet on the links and I'm liable to this damned Bechuana tummy if I get a chill. I wondered if you could let me have some paper and an envelope. I'd better let the Captain-Commandant know in good time.' He drank his mixture. 'Be a good chap and put this down for me somewhere where I can reach it.'

Guy lifted the medicine chest, which on inspection seemed to contain only bottles labelled 'Poison', put it on a table, and brought Apthorpe paper.

'D'you suppose I ought to begin: "Sir, I have the honour"?'

'No.'

'Just "Dear Colonel Green"?'

'Or "Dear Mrs Green".'

'That's the ticket. That's exactly the right note. Good for you, old man. "Dear Mrs Green" of course.'

One of the characteristics of the Halberdiers was a tradition of firm churchmanship. Papistry and Dissent were almost unknown among the regulars. Long-service recruits were prepared for Confirmation by the chaplain as part of their elementary training. The parish church of the town was the garrison chapel. For Sunday Mattins the whole back of the nave was reserved for the Halberdiers who marched there from the barracks behind their band. After church the ladies of the garrison – wives, widows and daughters in whom the town abounded, whose lawns were mown by Halberdiers and whose joints of beef were illicitly purchased from the Halberdier stores – assembled with hymn books in their hands at the Officers' House for an hour's refreshment and gossip. Nowhere in England could there be found a survival of a Late-Victorian Sunday so complete and so unselfconscious, as at the Halberdier barracks.

As the only Catholic officer Guy was in charge of the Catholic details. There were a dozen of them, all National Service men. He inspected them on the square and marched them to mass at the tin church in a side street. The priest was a recent graduate from Maynooth who had little enthusiasm for the Allied cause or for the English army, which he regarded merely as a provocation to immorality in the town. His sermon that morning was not positively offensive; there was nothing in it to make the basis of a complaint; but when he spoke of 'this terrible time of doubt, danger and suffering in which we live,' Guy stiffened. It was a time of glory and dedication.

After mass, as the men were waiting to fall in for their return march, the priest accosted Guy at the gate. 'Won't you just slip in to the presbytery, Captain, and pass the time of day? I've a bottle of whisky a good soul gave me, that needs opening.'

'I won't, thank you, Father Whelan. I've got to take the men back to barracks.'

'Well now and what a wonderful thing the army is to be sure, that a lot of grown lads can't walk half a mile by themselves.'

'Those are the orders, I'm afraid.'

'Now that little matter of the list of names, Captain. His Lordship wants a list of all the names of the Catholic serving men for his records as I think I mentioned to you last Sunday.'

'Very good of you to take so much interest in us. I think you get a capitation grant from the War Office, don't you, Father Whelan, when there's no Catholic chaplain?'

'Well, I do now, Captain, and isn't it me right at law?'

'I'm not a captain. You'd better write to the adjutant.'

'And how would I be telling one officer from another and me not a military man at all?'

'Just write "the Adjutant, the Royal Corps of Halberdiers". That'll get to him all right.'

'Well, if you won't help, you won't, I suppose. God bless you, Captain,' he said curtly and turned to a woman who had been standing unnoticed at his elbow. 'Well, my dear woman, and what's troubling you now?'

On the march home they passed the parish church, a lofty elaborate tower rising from a squat earlier building of flint and grey stone, with low dog-toothed arches. It stood in a well-kept graveyard behind ancient yews. Within from the hammer-beams hung the spider's-web Colours of the Corps. Guy knew them well. He often stopped there on Saturday afternoons with his weekly papers. From such a doorway as that Roger de Waybroke had stepped out on his unaccomplished journey, leaving his madam padlocked.

Less constrained than the Lady of Waybroke, the womenfolk of the Halberdiers were all over the ante-room when Guy returned. He knew most of them now and for half an hour he helped order sherry, move ashtrays and light cigarettes. One of his own batch, the athletic young man named Leonard, had brought his wife that morning. She was plainly pregnant. Guy knew Leonard little for he lodged in the town and spent his evenings there, but he recognized him as peculiarly fitted for the Halberdiers. Apthorpe looked like any experienced soldier but Leonard seemed made of the very stuff that constituted the Corps. In peace he had worked in an insurance office and had travelled every winter Saturday afternoon, carrying his 'change' in an old leather bag, to outlying football grounds to play scrum-half for his club.

In his first speech of welcome the Captain-Commandant had hinted that there might be permanent commissions for some of them after the war. Guy could imagine Leonard in twelve years' time as hairy and kindly and idiomatic as Major Tickeridge. But that was before he met his madam.

The Leonards sat with Sarum-Smith talking of money.

'I'm here because I've got to be,' Sarum-Smith was saying. 'I went to town last week-end and it cost me over a fiver. I shouldn't have thought twice of it when I was in business. Every penny counts in the army.'

'Is it true, Mr Crouchback, that they're moving you all after Christmas?'

'I gather so.'

'Isn't it a shame? No sooner settled in one place than you're off somewhere else. I don't see the sense of it.'

'One thing I won't do,' said Sarum-Smith, 'and that's buy a map-case. Or King's Regulations.'

'They say we've got to pay for our battle-dress when it comes. I call that a bit thick,' said Leonard.

'It's no catch being an officer. They're always making you buy something you don't want. The War Office is so busy sucking up to the other ranks it hasn't time for the poor bloody officers. There was three bob on my mess bill yesterday marked "entertainment". I asked what that was for and they told me it was my share of the drinks for the Ensa party. I didn't even go to the show, let alone stand any drinks.'

'Well, you wouldn't want them to come to the Corps and not have any hospitality, would you?' asked Leonard.

'I could survive it,' said Sarum-Smith. 'And I bet half those drinks went down the throats of the regular officers.'

'Steady on,' said Leonard. 'Here's one of them.'

Captain Sanders approached. 'I say, Mrs Leonard,' he said. 'You know that the Captain-Commandant's expecting you both to luncheon today?'

'We got our orders,' said Mrs Leonard sourly.

'Grand, I'm trying to find another man. Apthorpe's chucked. You're booked for it already, aren't you, Crouchback? How about you, Sarum-Smith?'

'Spare me,' said Sarum-Smith.

'You'll enjoy it. They're grand people.'

'Oh, very well then.'

'I haven't seen Uncle Apthorpe this morning. How's he looking?'

'Terrible.'

'He had rather a load on last night. He got into a pretty hearty school at the golf club.'

'He has Bechuana tummy this morning.'

'Well, that's a new name for it.'

'I wonder what he'd call *my* tummy,' said Mrs Leonard.

Sarum-Smith laughed loudly. Captain Sanders wandered away. Leonard said: 'Keep it clean, Daisy, for heaven's sake. I'm glad you're coming to lunch, Uncle. We'll have to sit on Daisy. She's in a wicked mood today.'

'Well, all I can say, I wish *Jim* had something wrong with himself. Here he is playing soldiers all the week. I never see him. They might at least give him his Sunday free. Any decent job you get that.'

'The Captain-Commandant seemed awfully nice.'

'I daresay he is, if you know him. So is my Aunt Margie. But I don't expect the Captain-Commandant to spend his day off with her.'

'You mustn't mind Daisy,' said Leonard. 'It's just she looks forward to Sundays and she isn't one for going out and meeting people particularly at the moment.'

'If you ask me the Halberdiers think far too much of themselves,' said Mrs Leonard. 'It's different in the R.A.F. My brother's a wing commander on the catering side and he says it's just like any ordinary job only easier. Halberdiers can't ever forget to be Halberdiers even on Sunday. Look at them all now.'

Sarum-Smith looked at his brother officers and at their ladies, whose laps were full of prayer-books and gloves, their hands full of cigarettes and sherry; their voices high and happy.

'I suppose we shall find *these* drinks on the mess bill too. How much d'you suppose the Captain-Commandant charges for lunch?'

'I say, steady on,' said Leonard.

'I wish Jim had joined the R.A.F.,' said Mrs Leonard. 'I'm sure it could have been managed. You know where you are with them. You just settle down at an R.A.F. station as though it was business with regular hours and a nice crowd. Of course I shouldn't let Jim fly, but there's plenty of jobs like my brother's got.'

'Ground staff is all right in war-time,' said Sarum-Smith. 'It won't sound so good afterwards. One's got to think of peace. It'll do one more good in business to have been in the Halberdiers than the R.A.F. ground staff.'

At five minutes to one Mrs Green and Miss Green, wife and daughter of the Captain-Commandant, rose from their places and collected the guests.

'We mustn't be late,' said Mrs Green. 'Ben Ritchie-Hook is coming. He's a terror if he's kept waiting for his food.'

'I find him rather a terror always,' said Miss Green.

'You oughtn't to say that about their future brigadier.'

'Is it the man you were telling me about?' asked Mrs Leonard, whose way of showing her disapproval of the expedition was to speak only to her husband, 'the man who cuts off people's heads?'

'Yes. He sounds a regular fizzer.'

'We're all very fond of him really,' said Mrs Green.

'I've heard of him,' said Sarum-Smith as though to be known to him had some sinister connotation like being 'known' to the police.

Guy too had heard of him often. He was the great Halberdier *enfant terrible* of the First World War; the youngest company commander in the history of the Corps; the slowest to be promoted; often wounded, often decorated, recommended for the Victoria Cross, twice court martialled for disobedience to orders in the field, twice acquitted in recognition of the brilliant success of his independent actions; a legendary wielder of the entrenching tool; where lesser men collected helmets Ritchie-Hook once came back from a raid across no-man's-land with the dripping head of a German sentry in either hand. The years of peace had been years of unremitting conflict for him. Wherever there was blood and gunpowder from County Cork to the Matto Grosso, there was Ritchie-Hook. Latterly he had wandered about the Holy Land tossing hand-grenades into the front parlours of dissident Arabs. These were some of the things Guy had heard in the mess.

The Captain-Commandant inhabited a square, solid house at an extremity of the barrack area. As they approached it, Mrs Green said: 'Do any of you smoke a pipe?'

'No.'

'No.'

'No.'

'That's a pity. Ben prefers men who smoke pipes. Cigarettes?'

'Yes.'

'Yes.'

'Yes.'

'That's a pity, too. He likes you not to smoke at all if you don't smoke pipes. My husband always smokes a pipe when Ben's about. Of course he's senior but that doesn't count with Ben. My husband is rather afraid of him.'

'He's in a blue funk,' said Miss Green. 'It's pitiful to see.'

Leonard laughed heartily.

'I don't see it's funny,' said Mrs Leonard. '*I* shall smoke if I want to.'

But no one else in the party shared Mrs Leonard's mood of defiance. The three probationary Halberdiers stood back for the ladies to pass and followed them through the garden-gate with adolescent misgivings and there before them unmistakably, separated from them only by the plate glass of the drawing-room window, stood Lieutenant-Colonel, shortly to be gazetted Brigadier Ritchie-Hook glaring out at them balefully with a single, terrible eye. It was black as the brows above it, this eye, black as the patch which hung on the other side of the lean skew nose. It was set in a steel-rimmed monocle. Colonel Ritchie-Hook bared his teeth at the ladies, glanced at his huge wrist-watch with studied pantomime and said something inaudible but plainly derisive.

'Oh dear,' said Mrs Green. 'We must be late.'

They entered the drawing-room; Colonel Green, hitherto a figure of awe, smirked at them from behind a little silver tray of cocktails. Colonel Ritchie-Hook, not so much usurping the position of host as playing the watch dog, the sentinel perhaps at one of those highly secret headquarters which Guy had visited in his search for employment, strode to meet them. Mrs Green attempted some conventional introductions but was interrupted.

'Names again, please. Must get them clear. Leonard, Sarum-Smith, Crouchback? — I can only count three. Where's Crouchback? Oh, I see. And which owns the madam?'

He flashed his huge eye-teeth at Mrs Leonard.

'*I* own *this* one,' she said.

It was braver and better than Guy would have expected, and it went down well. Leonard alone seemed put out.

'Splendid,' said Ritchie-Hook. 'Jolly good.'

'That's the way to treat him,' said Mrs Green.

Colonel Green goggled in admiration.

'Gin for the lady,' cried Colonel Ritchie-Hook. He stretched out a maimed right hand, two surviving fingers and half a thumb in a black glove, clutched a glass and presented it to Mrs Leonard. But the light mood passed and he immediately refused to take one for himself.

'Very nice if you don't have to keep awake after lunch.'

'Well, I don't,' said Mrs Leonard. 'Sunday's my day of rest – usually.'

'There are no Sundays in the firing-line,' said Colonel Ritchie-Hook. 'The week-end habit could lose us the war.'

'You're spreading alarm and despondency, Ben.'

'I'm sorry, Geoff. The Colonel here was always the brainy one,' he added, as though to explain his meek acceptance of criticism. 'He was brigade major when I only had a platoon. That's why he's sitting in this fine mansion while I'm going under canvas. Any camping experience?' he asked suddenly of Guy.

'Yes, sir, a little. I lived in Kenya at one time and did several trips in the bush.'

'Good for you. Gin for the old settler.' The black claw struck, grappled and released a second cocktail into Guy's hand. 'Did you get much shooting?'

'I bagged an old lion once who wandered into the farm.'

'Which are you? Crouchback? I knew one of my young officers came from Africa. I thought it was some other name. You'll find your African experience worth a hundred pounds a minute. There's one wretched fellow on my list spent half his life in Italy. I didn't care for the sound of that much.'

⋅ Miss Green winked at Guy and he kept silent.

'I've had fun in Africa too,' said Ritchie-Hook. 'After one of my periodical disagreements with the powers that be, I got seconded to the African Rifles. Good fellows if you keep at them with a stick but devilish scared of rhinos. One camp we had was by a lake and an old rhino used to come down for a drink every evening across the parade ground. Devilish cheek; I wanted to shoot him but the C.O. talked a lot of rot about having to get a game licence. He was a stuffy fellow, the sort of chap,' he said as though defining a universally recognized and detestable type, 'the sort of chap who owns a dozen shirts. So the next day I fixed up a flare-path right across rhino's drinking place, with a line of fuses, and touched it off right under his nose. I never saw a rhino move faster, smack through the camp lines. Caught a black fellow bang through the middle. You never heard such a yelling. They couldn't stop me shooting him then, not when he had a sergeant stuck on his nose.'

'Sounds like Bechuana tummy,' said Mrs Leonard.

'Eh? What's that?' said Colonel Ritchie-Hook, not so pleased now at her cheeky ways.

'Where was this, Ben?' Mrs Green interposed.

'Somaliland. Ogaden border.'

'I didn't know there was any rhino in Somaliland,' said Colonel Green.

'There's one less now.'

'How about the sergeant?'

'Oh, he was on parade again in a week.'

'You mustn't take all Colonel Ritchie-Hook says quite literally,' said Mrs Green.

They went into luncheon. Two Halberdiers waited at table. Mrs Green carved. Ritchie-Hook grasped his fork in his gloved fingers, impaled his meat, cut it rapidly into squares, laid down his knife, changed hands with the fork and ate fast and silently, plunging the pieces into horse-radish sauce and throwing them back to his molars. Then he began to talk again. Had he followed any less chivalrous calling, had he worn any other uniform than a Halberdier's, it might have seemed that Colonel Ritchie-Hook, piqued by her interruption, was seeking to discomfort Mrs Leonard, so hard did he fix her with his single, ferocious eye, so directly aimed seemed all his subsequent words at the hopes and susceptibilities of a bride.

'You'll be glad to hear that I've got the War House to play. They've recognized our Special Role. I drafted the minute myself. It went right up the line and came down again approved. We're HOO.'

'What does that mean, please?' asked Mrs Leonard.

'Hazardous Offensive Operations. We've been given our own heavy machine-guns and heavy mortars; no divisional organization; we come direct under the Chiefs of Staff. There was some opposition from an idiot gunner in Military Training but I soon scotched him. We've got a whizz of an area in the Highlands.'

'Scotland? Is that where we've got to settle?'

'That is where we shall form.'

'But is that where we shall be in the summer? I've got my arrangements to make.'

'Summer arrangements will depend on our friend the Boche. By summer I hope to report the brigade as efficient and then immediate action. No good hanging about. There's a limit to the amount of training men can take. After a point they get stale and go back. You must use them when they're on their toes ... Use them,' he repeated dreamily, 'spend them. It's like slowly collecting a pile of chips and then plonking them all down on the roulette board. It's the most fascinating thing in life, training men and staking them against the odds. You get a perfect force. Everyone knows everyone else. Everyone knows his commander so well they can guess his intention before they're told. They can work without orders, like sheep-dogs. Then you throw them into action and in a week, perhaps in a few hours, the whole thing is expended. Even if you win your battle, you're never the same again. There are reinforcements and promotions. You have to "start all over again from your beginnings, and never breathe a word about your loss". Isn't that how the poem goes? So you see, Mrs Leonard, it's no good asking where or when we shall settle. Do you all play footer?'

'No, sir.'

'No, sir.'

'Yes,' from Leonard.

'Soccer?'

'No, sir. Rosslyn Park.'

'Pity. The men don't understand rugger, except Welshmen and we don't get many of those. It's a great thing to play with them. The men go for you and you go for them and there's no hard feeling when bones get broken. In my company at one time we had more casualties from soccer than from the enemy and I can assure you we gave more than we took. Permanent injuries some of them. There was a plucky little fellow played right half for C Company lamed for life in the rest camp. You ought to follow footer even if you don't play. I remember once a sergeant of mine got his leg blown off. There was nothing to be done for the poor beggar. It had taken half his body with it. He was a goner all right but quite sensible and there was the padre one side of him trying to make him pray and me the other side and all he'd think about was football. Luckily I knew the latest League results and those I didn't know, I made up. I told him his home team was doing fine and he died smiling. If ever I see a padre getting above himself, I pull his leg about that. Of course it's different with Catholics. Their priests hold on to them to the last. It's a horrible sight to see them whispering at a dying man. They kill hundreds just with fright.'

'Mr Crouchback is a Catholic,' said Mrs Green.

'Oh, sorry. Am I talking out of turn as usual? Never had any tact. Of course it's because you live in Africa,' said Colonel Ritchie-Hook, turning to Guy. 'You get a very decent type of missionary out there. I've seen 'em myself. They don't stand any nonsense from the natives. None of the "me velly Clistian boy got soul all same as white boss". But mind you, Crouchback, you've only seen the best. If you lived in Italy like this other young officer of mine, you'd see them as they are at home. Or in Ireland; the priests there were quite openly on the side of the gunmen.'

'Eat your pudding, Ben,' said Mrs Green.

Colonel Ritchie-Hook turned his eye down to his apple-pie and for the rest of luncheon spoke mainly against air-raid precautions, an uncontroversial subject.

In the drawing-room with the coffee Colonel Ritchie-Hook showed the softer side of his character. There was a calendar on the chimney-piece, rather shabby now in November and coming to the end of its usefulness. Its design was fanciful, gnomes, toadstools, hare-bells, pink bare babies and dragonflies.

'I say,' he said. 'That's a lovely thing. My word it *is* lovely. Isn't it lovely?'

'Yes, sir.'

'Well, we mustn't stand here getting sentimental. I've a long ride ahead of me on my motor-bike. I need a stretch. Who's coming with me?'

'Not Jim,' said Mrs Leonard, 'I'm taking him home.'

'All right. Coming you two?'

'Yes, sir.'

The town where the Halberdiers lived was ill suited to walking for pleasure. It was a decent old place at the heart revealing concentric layers of later ugliness. Pleasant country had to be sought three miles out or more, but Colonel Ritchie-Hook's aesthetic appetites had been sated by the calendar.

'There's a round I always go when I'm here,' he said. 'It takes fifty minutes.'

He set off at a fast irregular lope, with which it was impossible to keep in step. He led them to the railway beside which, separated from it by a fence of black, corrugated iron, ran a cinder path.

'Now we're out of earshot of the Captain-Commandant,' he began, but a passing train put him out of earshot of his two companions. When he could next be heard he was saying '... altogether too much flannel in the Corps. Necessary in peace time. No use for it in war. You want more than automatic obedience. You want Grip. When I commanded a company and a man came up to me on a charge I used to ask him whether he'd take my punishment or go to the C.O. He always chose mine. Then I'd bend him over and give him six of the best with a cane. Court-martial offence, of course, but there was never a complaint and I had less crime than any Company in the Corps. That's what I call "Grip".' He strode on. Neither companion found any suitable reply. At length he added: 'I shouldn't try that out yourselves though – not at first.'

The walk continued mostly in silence. When Ritchie-Hook spoke it was mostly to recount practical jokes or *gaffes raisonnées*. For this remarkable warrior the image of war was not hunting or shooting; it was the wet sponge on the door, the hedgehog in the bed; or, rather, he saw war itself as a prodigious booby trap.

After twenty-five minutes Colonel Ritchie-Hook looked at his watch.

'We ought to be crossing now. I'm getting slow.'

Soon they came to an iron foot-bridge. On the farther side of the line was a similar cinder track, bounded by corrugated iron. They turned along it towards home.

'We'll have to spurt a bit if we're going to keep the scheduled time.'

They went at a great pace. At the barrack gates he looked at his watch. 'Forty-nine minutes,' he said. 'Good going. Well, glad to have got to know you. We'll be seeing plenty of each other in the future. I left my motor-bike at the guard-room.' He opened his respirator haversack and showed them a tight wad of pyjamas and hair brushes. 'That's all the luggage I carry. Best use for this damn silly thing. Good-bye.'

Guy and Sarum-Smith saluted as he drove off.

'Regular old fire-eater, isn't he?' said Sarum-Smith. 'Seems to have made up his mind to get us all killed.'

That evening Guy looked in on Apthorpe to see if he was coming to dinner.

'No, old man. Going slow today. I think I can shake this thing off but I've got to go slow. How was lunch?'

'Our future brigadier was there.'

'I'm sorry I missed that, very sorry. But it wouldn't have been much of a first impression. I shouldn't want him to see me under the weather. How did things go?'

'Not so badly. Largely because he thought I was you.'

'I don't quite get you, old man.'

'He'd heard one of us lived in Italy and the other in Africa. He thinks I'm the African one.'

'I say, old man, I don't much like that.'

'He began it. Then it had gone too far to put him right.'

'But he *must* be put right. I think you ought to write and tell him.'

'Don't be an ass.'

'But it's not a joking matter at all. It seems to me you've pulled rather a fast one, taking advantage of another chap's illness to impersonate him. It's just the sort of thing that might make a lot of difference. Did you take my name, too?'

'No, of course not.'

'Well, if you won't write, I will.'

'I shouldn't. He'd think you were mad.'

'Well, I shall have to consider what is best. The whole thing's extremely delicate. I can't think how you let it happen.'

Apthorpe did not write to Colonel Ritchie-Hook but he nursed his resentment and was never again quite off his guard in Guy's company.

3

Shortly before Christmas the course of elementary training came to an end and Guy and his batch were sent on a week's leave. Before they left and largely in their honour, there was a guest night. They were urged to bring guests to what, for the time being at any rate, was to be their last night in the barracks. Each felt on his mettle to provide someone creditable to himself. Apthorpe, in particular, was proud of his choice.

'Great bit of luck,' he said, 'I've got hold of "Chatty" Corner. I didn't know he was in England till I saw it in the paper.'

'Who's Chatty Corner?'

'I should have thought you would have heard of him. Perhaps it's different in the posh ranches of Kenya. If you asked that question in *Real* Africa – anywhere between Chad and Moçambique – people would think you were chaffing. He is a great character, Chatty. Queer sort of devil to look at. You wouldn't think he knew how to use a knife and fork. Actually he's a Bishop's son, Eton and Oxford and all that, and he plays the violin like a pro. He's mentioned in all the books.'

'Books on music, Apthorpe?'

'Books on gorillas, of course. And who are you bringing, old man, if one may ask?'

'I haven't found anyone yet.'

'Funny. I should have thought a chap like you would have known quite a number of people.'

He was still huffy over the affair of mistaken identity.

Guy proposed himself for Christmas to the Box-Benders. In her reply Angela said that Tony was coming on Christmas leave. Guy was able at the last moment to intercept him in London and lure him down to the Halberdiers for the night. It was the first time either had seen the other in uniform.

'I wouldn't miss seeing you masquerading as a young officer for anything in the world, Uncle Guy,' he said on arrival.

'Everyone else here calls me "Uncle", too, you'll find.'

They were walking across the gravel to the quarters where the guests had been given rooms. A Halberdier passed them at the salute and Guy shrank to see his nephew's careless flick of acknowledgement.

'I say, Tony, that may be all right in your regiment. Here we return the salute as smartly as it's given.'

'Uncle Guy, do I have to remind you that I am your superior officer?'

But that evening he was proud of his nephew, conspicuous in green patrols and black leather, as he led him up to the Mess President in the ante-room.

'Back from France, eh? I'm going to exercise my presidential privilege and put you next to me. I'd very much like a first-hand account of what's going on out there. Can't make head or tail of the papers.'

The identity of Chatty Corner was apparent to all without introduction; a brown man with grizzled hair *en brosse* stood morosely at Apthorpe's side. It was easy to see how he had gained a footing among the gorillas; easy, too, to recognize English irony in his nickname. He swung his head from side to side, gazing about him from under shaggy brows as though seeking some high path by which he could swing himself aloft and lie cradled in solitude among the rafters. Not till the band struck up 'The Roast Beef of Old England' did Chatty seem at ease. Then he beamed, nodded and gibbered confidentially into Apthorpe's ear.

The band was in the minstrels' gallery. They passed under it to enter the mess and met its full force as they took their places at the table. The Mess President was in the centre opposite the Vice. Tony, next to him, began to sit down before Grace and was hastily restrained by his uncle. The band ceased, the hammer struck, the chaplain prayed. Band and general conversation burst out once more together.

Drawn out by the senior officers round him, Tony began to talk about his service in France, of field-craft, night patrols, and booby traps, of the extreme youth and enthusiasm of the handful of enemy prisoners whom he had seen, of the admirable style and precision of their raiding tactics. Guy looked down the table to Chatty Corner to see whether he was displaying any notable dexterity with his knife and fork and saw him drink with an odd little rotary swirling motion of head and wrist.

At length when the cloth was drawn for dessert, the brass departed and the strings came down from the minstrels' gallery and stationed themselves in the window embrasure. Now there was silence over all the diners while the musicians softly bowed and plucked. It all seemed a long way from Tony's excursions in no-man's-land; farther still, immeasurably far, from the frontier of Christendom where the great battle had been fought and lost; from those secret forests where the trains were, even then, while the Halberdiers and their guests sat bemused by wine and harmony, rolling east and west with their doomed loads.

They played two pieces, in the second of which a carillon was brightly struck. Then the Captain of the Musicke presented himself in traditional form to the Mess President. Room was made for him on a chair placed next to Tony's and a bumper of port brought by the corporal-of-servants. He was a shiny, red man no more to be recognized as a man of the arts, Guy thought, than Chatty himself.

The Mess President hammered the table. All rose to their feet.

'Mr Vice, our Colonel-in-Chief, the Grand-Duchess Elena of Russia.'

'The Grand-Duchess, God bless her.'

This ancient lady lived in a bed-sitting-room at Nice, but she was still as loyally honoured by the Halberdiers as when, a young beauty, she had graciously accepted the rank in 1902.

Smoke began to curl among the candles. The horn of snuff was brought round. This huge, heavy-mounted object was hung about with a variety of little silver tools – spoon, hammer, brush – which had to be employed ritualistically and in the right order on pain of a half-crown fine. Guy instructed his nephew in their proper use.

'Do you have all this sort of thing in your regiment?'

'Not quite all this. I'm awfully impressed.'

'So am I,' said Guy.

No one was quite sober when he left the dining-room; no one was quite drunk except Chatty Corner. This man of the wilds, despite his episcopal origin, succumbed to the advance of civilization, was led away and never seen again. Had he been competing for prestige, as Apthorpe thought he was, this would have been an hour of triumph for Guy. Instead the whole evening was one simple sublime delight.

In the ante-room there was an impromptu concert. Major Tickeridge gave an innocently obscene performance called 'The One-Armed Flautist', an old favourite in the Corps, new to Guy, a vast success with all. The silver goblets, which normally held beer, began to circulate brimming with champagne. Guy found himself talking religion with the chaplain.

'. . . Do you agree,' he asked earnestly, 'that the Supernatural Order is not something added to the Natural Order, like music or painting, to make everyday life more tolerable? It *is* everyday life. The supernatural is real; what we call "real" is a mere shadow, a passing fancy. Don't you agree, Padre?'

'Up to a point.'

'Let me put it another way . . .'

The chaplain's smile had become set during Major Tickeridge's performance; it was like an acrobat's, a professional device concealing fear and exhaustion.

Presently the adjutant started a game of football with a waste-paper basket. They changed from soccer to rugger. Leonard had the basket. He was tackled and brought down. All the young officers began to leap on the struggling bodies. Apthorpe leapt. Guy leapt. Others leapt on them. Guy was conscious of a wrench in the knee; then the wind was knocked out of him and he lay momentarily paralysed. Dusty, laughing, sweating, panting, they disentangled themselves and got to their feet. Guy felt a remote but serious pain in his knee.

'I say, Uncle, are you hurt?'

'No, no, it's nothing.'

Somewhere the order had been given to disperse. Tony gave Guy his arm across the gravel.

'I hope you weren't too bored, Tony?'

'I wouldn't have missed it for anything. D'you think you ought to see a doctor?'

'It'll be all right in the morning. It's just a twist.'

But in the morning, when he awoke from deep sleep, his knee was swollen large and he could not walk with it.

4

Tony was driving home. He took Guy with him as they had arranged, and for four days Guy lay up at Box-Bender's with his leg bandaged stiff. On Christmas Eve they bore him to midnight mass and then put him back on his bed in the library. There was anti-climax in Tony's return. All the stage properties remained, the crates of Hittite tablets, the improvised beds, but there was no drama. After the spacious life of his barracks Guy felt himself penned and straightened so that when after Boxing-Day his brother-in-law returned to London, Guy went with him and spent the last days of his leave in an hotel.

Those days of lameness, he realized much later, were his honeymoon, the full consummation of his love of the Royal Corps of Halberdiers. After them came domestic routine, much loyalty and affection, many good things shared, but intervening and overlaying them all the multitudinous, sad little discoveries of marriage, familiarity, annoyance, imperfections noted, discord. Meanwhile it was sweet to wake and to lie on in bed; the spirit of the Corps lay beside him: to ring the bell; it was in the service of his unseen bride.

London had not yet lost its store of riches. It was the same city he had avoided all his life, whose history he had held to be mean, whose aspect drab. Here it was, all round him, as he had never seen it before, a royal capital. Guy was changed. He hobbled out into it with new eyes and a new heart.

Bellamy's, where last he had slunk in corners to write his begging letters, offered him now an easy place in the shifting population of the bar. He drank hard and happily, saying mechanically 'Cheerioh' and 'Here's how', quite unconscious of the mild surprise these foreign salutations roused.

One evening he went alone to the theatre and heard behind him a young voice say: 'Oh my prophetic soul, my uncle.'

He turned and saw immediately behind him Frank de Souza. He was dressed in what the Halberdiers called 'plain clothes' and civilians, more exotically, 'mufti'. His clothes were not particularly plain – a brown suit, a green silk shirt, an orange tie. Beside him sat a girl. Guy knew Frank de Souza little. He was a dark, reserved, drily humorous, efficient young man. He remembered vaguely hearing that Frank had a girl in London whom he visited at week-ends.

'Pat, this is my Uncle Crouchback.'

The girl smiled, without humour or welcome.

'Must you be facetious?' she said.

'Enjoying it?' Guy asked. They were at what was known as an 'intimate revue'.

'Quite.'

Guy had thought it very bright and pretty. 'Have you been in London all the time?'

'I've got a flat in Earls Court,' said the girl. 'He lives with me.'

'That must be nice,' said Guy.

'Quite,' said the girl.

Further conversation was stopped by the return of their neighbours from the bar and the rise of the curtain. The second half of the programme seemed less bright and pretty to Guy. He was conscious all the time of this cold odd couple behind him. At the end he said: 'Won't you come and have some supper with me?'

'We're going to the Café from here,' said the girl.

'Is that far?'

'The Café Royal,' Frank explained. 'Come too.'

'But Jane and Constant said they might be meeting us there,' said the girl.

'They never do,' said Frank.

'Come and eat oysters with me,' said Guy. 'There's a place just next door.'

'I hate oysters,' said the girl.

'Perhaps we'd better not,' said Frank. 'Thanks all the same.'

'Well, we'll meet again soon.'

'At Philippi,' said Frank.

'Oh God,' said the girl. 'Come on.'

On his last evening, the last day of the old year, after dinner Guy was at Bellamy's, standing at the bar, when he heard: 'Hullo, Tommy, how are the staff-officer's piles?' and, turning, found at his side a major of the Coldstream.

It was Tommy Blackhouse, whom he had last seen from his solicitor's window in Lincoln's Inn when he and Tommy's soldier-servant had been summoned to make a formal recognition during the divorce proceedings. Tommy and Virginia had come through the square laughing, had paused at the door by arrangement showing their faces, Virginia's under a bright new hat, Tommy's under a bowler, and had immediately gone on, without looking up towards the windows from one of which, they knew, they were being watched. Guy had testified: 'That is my wife.' The guardsman had said: 'That is Captain Blackhouse and the lady with him is the one I found when I called him on the morning of the 14th.' Each had then signed a statement and the solicitor had stopped Guy from giving the guardsman a ten shilling note. 'Entirely irregular, Mr Crouchback. The offer of an emolument might jeopardize the action.'

Tommy Blackhouse had had to send in his papers and leave the Brigade of Guards, but, because his heart was in soldiering, he had transferred to a line regiment. Now, it seemed, he was back in the Coldstream. Before that time Guy and Tommy Blackhouse had known one another very slightly. Now they said:

'Hullo, Guy.'

'Hullo, Tommy.'

'So you're in the Halberdiers. They're very efficient, aren't they?'

'Much too efficient for me. They nearly broke my leg the other night. I see you're back in the Coldstream.'

'I don't know where I am. I'm a sort of shuttlecock between the War House and the Lieutenant-Colonel. I got back to the Brigade all right last year – adultery doesn't matter in war-time apparently – but like an ass I spent the last two or three years at the Staff College and somehow managed to pass. So I'm called "G.2. Training" and spend all my time trying to get back to regimental soldiering. I knew one of yours at the Staff College. Awfully good chap with a big moustache. Forget his name.'

'They've all got big moustaches.'

'You're in for a pretty interesting role it seems to me. I saw a file about it today.'

'We know nothing.'

'Well, it'll be a long war. There'll be fun for us all in the end.'

It was all quite effortless.

Half an hour later the group broke up. In the hall Tommy said: 'I say you *are* going lame. Let me give you a lift.'

They drove up Piccadilly in silence. Then Tommy said: 'Virginia's back in England.'

Guy had never considered what Tommy thought about Virginia. He did not know precisely in what circumstances they had parted.

'Has she been away?'

'Yes, for quite a time. In America. She's come back for the war.'

'Typical of her – when everyone else is running the other way.'

'She's in great form. I saw her this evening in Claridge's. She asked after you but I didn't know then where you were.'

'She asked after me?'

'Well, to tell you the truth she asked after all her old boy friends – but you especially. Go and see her if you've got time. We all ought to rally round.'

'Where is she?'

'At Claridge's, I imagine.'

'I don't suppose she wants to see me really.'

'I got the impression she wants to see the whole world. She was all over *me*.'

Here they reached Guy's hotel and parted. Guy in correct Halberdier fashion absurdly saluted this superior officer in the utter darkness.

Next morning, New Year's Day, Guy awoke, as always now, at the hour when the bugles were sounding reveille in barracks; his first thought was of Virginia. He was full of over-mastering curiosity, but after eight years, after all that he had felt and left unsaid, he could not pick up the telephone at his bedside and call her as, he had no doubt, she would have called him had she known where to find him. Instead he dressed and packed and settled his hotel bill with his head full of Virginia. He had until four that afternoon before setting out to his new destination.

He drove to Claridge's, asked at the desk, learned that Mrs Troy had not yet come down, and stationed himself in the hall where he could watch both lifts and staircase. From time to time people he knew passed, stopped, asked him to join them, but he kept his unwinking vigil. At length someone who might be she, came swiftly from the lift and crossed to the desk. The concierge pointed towards where Guy was sitting. The woman turned and immediately beamed with pleasure. He limped forward; she came to meet him with a skip and a jump.

'Guy, *pet*; what a treat! How lovely London is!' She hugged him; then examined him at arm's length. 'Yes,' she said. 'Very nice indeed. I was asking about you only yesterday,'

'So I heard. Tommy told me.'

'Oh, I asked absolutely everyone.'

'But it was funny hearing of it from him.'

'Yes, come to think of it, I suppose it was in a way. Why are your clothes a different colour from everyone else's?'

'They aren't.'

'Well from Tommy's and his over there and his and his?'

'They're in the Foot Guards.'

'Well, I think your colour's *much* more chic. And how it suits you. I do believe you're growing a little moustache, too. It does make you look so *young*.'

'You too.'

'Oh yes, me more than anyone. I thrive on the war. It's such heaven being away from Mr Troy.'

'He's not with you?'

'Darling, just between us two, I don't think I'm going to see much more of Mr Troy. He hasn't been behaving at all well lately.'

Guy knew nothing of this Hector Troy except his name. He knew that for eight years Virginia had floated on a tide of unruffled popularity. He willed her no evil but this prosperity of hers had stiffened the barrier between them. In destitution she would have found him at her side, but as she drifted into ever ampler felicity, Guy shrank the further into his own dry, empty place. Now in the changes of war, here she was, pretty and smart and pleased to see him.

'Are you lunching anywhere?'

'I was. I won't. Come on. I say, you're lame. Not wounded already?'

'No. Believe it or not, I've been playing football with a waste-paper basket.'

'Not true?'

'Literally.'

'Darling, how madly unlike you.'

'You know, you're the first person I've met who hasn't been surprised to find me in the army.'

'Why, wherever else would you be? Of course I've always known you were brave as a lion.'

They lunched together and afterwards went up to her room and talked continuously until it was time for Guy's train.

'You've still got the farm at Eldoret?'

'I sold it at once; didn't you know?'

'Perhaps I did hear at the time, but you know I had such a lot on my mind just then. First divorce, then marriage, then divorce again, before I had time to look round. Tommy didn't last any time at all, the beast. I might almost just as well have stayed put. I hope you got a big price?'

'Practically nothing. It was the year everyone went broke.'

'So it was. Don't I remember! That was another of the troubles with Tommy. The chief thing was that his regiment turned so stuffy. We had to leave London and stay in a ridiculous little town full of the dreariest people. He even talked of going to India. That was the end. I really did adore him, too. You never married again?'

'How could I?'

'Darling, don't pretend your heart was broken for life.'

'Apart from my heart, Catholics can't remarry, you know.'

'Oh, *that*. You still keep to all that?'

'More than ever.'

'Poor Guy, you did get in a mess, didn't you? Money gone, me gone, all in one go. I suppose in the old days they'd have said I'd ruined you.'

'They might.'

'Have you had lots of lovely girls since?'

'Not many, not very lovely.'

'Well, you must now. I'll take you in hand and find you something special.'

And.

'There's one thing I always did feel rather bad about. How did your father take it all? He was such a lamb.'

'He just says: "Poor Guy, picked a wrong 'un." '

'Oh, I don't like that at all. What a perfectly beastly way to speak.'

And.

'But it can't be possible just to have done *nothing* for eight years.'

It amounted to nothing. There was nothing worth the telling. When he first came to Santa Dulcina from Kenya, with the habit of farming still fixed in him, he had tried to learn viticulture, had pruned the straggling vines, attempted to introduce a system for selection among the pickers, a new French press. The wine of Santa Dulcina was delicious on the spot but turned sour after an hour's travel. Guy had tried to bottle it scientifically. But it all came to nothing.

He had tried to write a book. It went well enough for two chapters and then petered out.

He had put a little money and much work into a tourist agency which a friend of his tried to organize. The intention was to provide first-rate aesthetic guides in Italy and to take specially deserving visitors into little-known districts and to palaces normally kept shut. But the Abyssinian crisis had cut off the flow of visitors, deserving and undeserving alike.

'No, nothing,' he agreed.

'Poor Guy,' said Virginia. 'How wretched you make it sound. No work. No money. Plain girls. Anyway you've kept your wool. Tommy's almost bald. It was quite a shock to see him again. And your figure. Augustus is as fat as butter.'

'Augustus?'

'I don't think we ever knew him in your time. He came after Tommy. But I never married Augustus. He was getting fat even then.'

And so on for three hours.

When they parted Virginia said: 'But we must *keep* meeting. I'm here indefinitely. We mustn't ever lose touch again.'

It was dark when Guy reached the station. Under the faint blue lamp he found half a dozen of his batch of Halberdiers.

'Here comes our gouty uncle,' they said as he joined them. 'Tell us all about this new course. You're always in the know.'

But Guy knew no more than was typed on his move order. It was a destination quite unknown.

5

The Movement Order said: '*Destination, Kut-al-Imara House, Southsand-on-sea.*' It was issued on the morning of the guest night without explanation. Guy had consulted Major Tickeridge, who said: 'Never heard of the place. It must be something new the Corps has thought up,' and the adjutant, who said: 'Not our pigeon. You'll come under the Training Depot from now on until the brigade forms. It'll probably be a pretty fair shambles.'

'None of the regulars from here will be coming?'

'Not on your life, Uncle.'

But to Guy sitting there with them in the ante-room among all the trophies of the Corps, in the order and comfort of two centuries' uninterrupted inhabitation, it seemed impossible that anything conducted by the Halberdiers could fall short of excellence. And to him now, as the train rolled through the cold and misty darkness, there remained the same serene confidence. His knee was stiff and painful. He shifted his leg among the legs that crossed and crowded in the twilight. The little group of subalterns sat listless. High overhead their piled kitbags, equipment, and suitcases loomed darkly and were lost in the shadows. Faces were hidden. Only their laps were lit by shafts too dim for easy reading. From time to time one of them struck a match. From time to time they spoke of their leave. Mostly they were silent. In the fog and chill Guy was full of clear and comforting memories and he sat listening inwardly to the repeated voices of the afternoon as though he were playing a gramophone record over and over to himself. A ghost had been laid that day which had followed him for eight years, lurked in every strange passage barring his way, crossing him everywhere. Now he had met it face to face in the daylight and found it to be kind and unsubstantial; that airy spirit could never again block him, he thought.

For the last three quarters of an hour of the journey all were quite silent, all save Guy asleep. At length they reached Southsand, dragged out their gear and stood in sharper cold on the platform. The train moved off. For long after its feeble lamp had disappeared the sound of the engine came to them on the east wind. A porter said: 'You from the Halberdiers? You ought to have been on the six-eight.'

'This is the train on our orders.'

'Well, the rest of you came through an hour ago. The R T O just locked up. You might catch him in the yard. No, that's him driving away now. He said not to expect any more military tonight.'

'Hell.'

'Well, that's the army all over, isn't it?'

The porter moved off into the darkness.

'What are we going to do?'

'Better telephone.'

'Who to?'

Leonard pursued the porter.

'Is Kut-al-Imara House on the telephone?'

'Only the military line. That's locked up in the RTO's office.'

'Have you a telephone book?'

'You can try. Expect it's been cut off.'

In the dim office of the station-master they found the local directory.

'Here's Kut-al-Imara House Preparatory School. Let's try it.'

After a time a hoarse voice answered: 'Ullo, yes; what, who? Can't hear a thing. This line's supposed to be cut off. This is a military establishment.'

'There are eight officers here waiting for transport.'

'Are you the officers what's expected?'

'We thought so.'

'Well, 'old on, sir. I'll try and find someone.'

After many minutes a new voice said: 'Where are you?'

'Southsand station.'

'Why the devil didn't you get on the bus with the others?'

'We've only just arrived.'

'Well, you're late. The bus has gone back. We haven't any transport. You'll have to find your own way here.'

'Is it far?'

'Of course it's far. You'd better hurry or there won't be anything left to eat. There's bloody little now.'

. They managed to find one taxi, and then a second, and so drove huddled and laden to their new home. Nothing was visible. There was no impression of anything until twenty minutes later they stood beside their bags in a hall quite devoid of furniture. The floor-boards had recently been washed and were still damp and reeking of disinfectant. An aged Halberdier, much decorated for long years of good conduct, said: 'I'll get Captain McKinney.'

Captain McKinney, when he came, had his mouth full.

'Here you are,' he said, chewing. 'There seems to have been a balls-up about your move order. I daresay it's not your fault. Everything's rather a shambles. I'm acting camp-commandant. I didn't know I was coming here at all till nine o'clock this morning, so you can imagine how much I know about anything. Have you had dinner? Well, you'd better come and get something now.'

'Is there anywhere to wash?'

'In there. But there's no soap I'm afraid and the water's cold.'

They followed him unwashed through the door by which he had come to greet them, and found a dining-room, soon to become familiar in every horrid aspect but now affording merely a glare of nakedness. Two trestle tables were laid with enamel plates and mugs and the grey cutlery they had seen in the mess-rooms during one of their conducted tours of barracks. There were dishes of margarine, sliced bread, huge bluish potatoes and a kind of drab galantine which Guy seemed to remember, but without relish, from his school-days during the First World War. On a side table an urn stood in a pool of tea, dripping. Beetroot alone gave colour to the spread.

'What price Dotheboys Hall?' said Trimmer.

But it was not the room nor the rations that caught Guy's chief notice. It was a group of strange second lieutenants who occupied one of the tables and now looked up, staring and munching. Those evidently were the Depot Batch about whom they had so often heard.

Half a dozen familiar figures from the Barrack Batch sat at the other table.

'You'd better settle there for the time being,' said Captain McKinney. 'There's some of your chaps still adrift. Sorting out will have to wait till morning.' Then he raised his voice and addressed the room at large.

'I'm pushing off now to my billet,' he said. 'I hope you've got everything you want. If you haven't, you'll just have to do without. Your quarters are upstairs. They aren't allotted. Arrange all that between yourselves. Lights out downstairs at twelve. Reveille at seven. Parade tomorrow at eight-fifteen. You're free to come and go up to twelve. There are six orderlies about the place but they've been at work all day scrubbing out, so I'd be glad if you'd let them stand-easy for a bit. It won't kill you to hump your own gear for once. We haven't been able to start a bar yet. The nearest pub is on the front about half a mile down the road. It's called the Grand and it's in bounds to officers. The pub nearer is for Other Ranks only. Well, good night.'

'Do I remember a lecture on "Man-management" not long ago?' said Trimmer. ' "When you make camp or move into new billets, remember that the men under your command come first, second and third. You come nowhere. A Halberdier officer never eats until he has seen the last dinner served. A Halberdier officer never sleeps until he has seen the last man bedded down." Didn't it go something like that?' He took one of the forks and moodily bent it till it broke. 'I'm off to the Grand to see if there's anything edible there.'

He was the first to go. Soon after him the Depot Batch rose from their table. One or two of them hesitated, wondering whether they ought not to speak to the newcomers, but by now all heads at the Barrack Batch table were bent over their plates. The moment passed before it was recognized.

'Matey bastards, aren't they?' said Sarum-Smith.

The meal did not last long. Soon they were in the hall with the luggage.

'Let me take yours up, Uncle,' said Leonard and Guy gratefully surrendered his kitbag and limped upstairs behind him.

The doors round the stairhead were locked. A notice scrawled in chalk on the wall-paper pointed to '*Officers Quarters*' through a baize door. A step down, bare light bulbs, a strip of linoleum with open doors on either side. The first-comers had already established themselves but it could not be said that they had gained by their priority. The rooms were uniform. Each contained six service bedsteads and a pile of blankets and palliasses.

'Let's keep away from Trimmer and Sarum-Smith,' said Leonard. 'How about this, Uncle? Take your pick.'

Guy chose a corner bed and Leonard swung his kitbag on it.

'Shan't be a jiffy with the rest,' he said. 'Hold the fort.'

Other second lieutenants looked in. 'Any room, Uncle?'

'Room for three. I'm keeping a place for Apthorpe.'

'There's four of us. We'll try farther down.'

He heard their voices next door: 'To hell with unpacking. If we're going to get a drink before closing time we've got to hurry.'

Leonard returned laden.

'I thought I'd better keep a place for Apthorpe.'

'Rather. Can't have our uncles separated. This is going to be very cosy. I don't know how long I'll be here though. Daisy's coming down as soon as I find rooms. There's a rumour married men can sleep out.'

Three cheerful youths brought in their luggage and appropriated the remaining beds.

'Coming to the pub, Leonard?'

'How about you, Uncle?'

'Don't worry about me. I'll be all right.'

'Sure?'

'We might be able to get a taxi.'

'No, you run along.'

'Well, we'll be seeing you.'

Soon Guy was left quite alone in the new quarters. He began to unpack. There were no cupboards or presses. He hung his greatcoat on a hook in the wall and laid his hair-brushes, washing things and books on the window-sill. He got out his sheets and made the bed and stuffed his pillow-case with a rolled blanket. Everything else was left unpacked. Then, leaning on his stick, he made a tour of the empty house.

The sleeping quarters had plainly been the boys' dormitories. Each was named after a battle in the First War. His was *Paschendael*. He passed the doors of *Loos*, *Wipers* (so spelt) and *Anzac*. Then he found a small unnamed room, a master's perhaps, containing a single unappropriated bed and a chest of drawers. Here lay luxury. Guy's spirits rose. 'Any damn fool can make himself uncomfortable,' he thought. The old soldier 'made his recce', 'appreciated the situation', 'conformed his plan to the ground'. He began to drag his kit-bag down the linoleum. And then he remembered Leonard dragging it up there. He remembered how he had been given choice of beds. If he moved now he would be denying the welcome of his juniors, setting himself apart again, as he had already been too much set apart in barracks, from the full fellowship of his batch. He closed the door of the single room and dragged his bag back to Paschendael.

He continued his tour. The place had been thoroughly emptied, presumably during the summer holidays. On the first floor he found a row of baths in doorless cubicles; on the ground floor a changing-room with many pegs, wash basins, and a shower. He found a notice board which still bore a list of cricket colours. Certain locked rooms must have been the headmaster's private quarters. Here was plainly the masters' common-room – an empty set of oak bookshelves, cigarette burns all over the chimney-piece, a broken waste-paper basket. '*O.Rs*' was chalked on the door which led to the kitchen-quarters; beyond it the wireless was playing. In the hall a tabletop had been put on the mantelpiece. It was divided vertically with a chalk line. Over one half was written '*Standing Orders*', over the other '*Daily Orders*'. Standing Orders comprised printed notices about black-out and protection from gas, a typewritten alphabetical list of names, and *Routine: Reveille 0700. Breakfast 0730. Parade and Instruction 0830. Lunch 1300. Parade and Instruction 1415. Tea 1700. Dinner 1930. Unless otherwise ordered officers will be free from 1700.* There were no Daily Orders. A painting too large to move – acquired when, how and why? – hung in a gilt composition frame opposite the fire-place; it represented a wintry sea-scape empty save for a few distant dishing boats and an enormous illegible signature. He leant against a coil of antiquated iron pipes and was surprised to find them hot. They seemed to lack all power of radiation; a yard from them there was no sensible warmth. He could imagine a row of little boys struggling to sit on them, tight-trousered boys with adenoids and chilblains; or perhaps it was a privilege to sit there enjoyed only by prefects and the First Eleven. In its desolation he could see the whole school as it had been made familiar to him in many recent realistic novels; an enterprise neither progressive nor prosperous. The assistant masters changed often, he supposed, arriving with bluff, departing with bluster; half the boys were taken at surreptitiously reduced fees; none of them ever won a scholarship or passed into a reputable public school or returned for an Old Boys' Day or ever thought of his years there with anything but loathing and shame. The History lessons were patriotic in design, turned to ridicule by the young masters. There was no school song at Kut-al-Imara House. All this Guy thought he snuffed in the air of the forsaken building.

Well, he reflected, he had not joined the army for his own comfort. He had expected a grim initiation. Life in barracks had been a survival from long years of peace, something rare and protected, quite unconnected with his purpose. That was over and done with; this was war.

And yet on this dark evening, his spirit sank. The occupation of this husk of a house, perhaps, was a microcosm of that new world he had enlisted to defeat. Something quite worthless, a poor parody of civilization, had been driven out; he and his fellows had moved in, bringing the new world with them; the world that was taking firm shape everywhere all about him, bounded by barbed wire and reeking of carbolic.

His knee hurt more tonight than ever before. He stumped woefully to Paschendael, undressed, spread his clothes on the foot of his bed, and lay down leaving the single bulb shining in his eyes. Soon he fell asleep and soon after was awakened by the cheery return of his companions.

6

There was nothing obnoxious about the batch from the Training Depot. There were no grounds on which the Barrack batch could assume superiority. The disconcerting quality about them was their resemblance at every point. They had their Trimmer, a black sheep named Hemp. They had their Sarum-Smith, a malcontent named Colenso. They even had their 'uncles', a genial, stoutish schoolmaster named 'Tubby' Blake and a rubber planter from Malaya named Roderick. It was as though in their advance the Barrack batch had turned a corner and suddenly been brought up sharp by a looking-glass in which they found themselves reflected. There was no enmity between the two groups but there was little friendship. They continued as they had begun, eating at separate tables and inhabiting separate bedrooms. To Guy it seemed that there were just twice too many young officers at Kut-al-Imara House. They were diminished and caricatured by duplication, and the whole hierarchic structure of army life was affronted by this congregation of so many men of perfectly equal rank. The regular officers charged with their training lived in billets, appeared more or less punctually for duty, sauntered from class to class during working hours and punctually departed. Often at their approach a sergeant instructor would say: 'Come on now, look alive. Officer coming,' oblivious of the rank of his squad. The orderlies and non-commissioned instructors were under the command of a quartermaster-sergeant. The second lieutenants had no responsibility for, nor authority over them.

Living conditions grew slightly more tolerable. Rudimentary furniture appeared; a mess-committee was formed consisting of the camp-commandant, Guy and 'Tubby' Blake; the food was improved, the bar stocked. A motion to hire a wireless-set was hotly debated and narrowly lost through the combination of the elderly with the thrifty. The regimental Comforts Fund lent a dart board and a ping-pong table; but in spite of these amenities the house was generally deserted in the evening. Southsand offered a dance hall, a cinema and several hotels and there was more money about. Each officer was greeted on his return from leave with a note crediting him with back-pay and a number of quite unexpected allowances. All Guy's creditors save Sarum-Smith repaid their loans. Sarum-Smith said: 'With regard to that little matter of a fiver, uncle, if it's all the same to you, I'll let it run a bit longer.'

It seemed to Guy that there was now a slight nuance in the use of 'Uncle'. What had before been, at heart, an expression of respect, of 'the deference which youth owes to age', was now perceptibly derisive. The young officers were much at their ease in Southsand; they picked up girls of the town, they drank in congenial palm-lounges and snuggeries, they felt their leisure free from observation. In barracks Guy had been a link between them and their seniors. Here he was a lame old buffer who did not shine at the work or join in the fun. He had always stood in their esteem on the very verge of absurdity. Now his stiff knee and supporting stick carried him over.

He was excused from parades and Physical Training. He hobbled alone to instruction in the gym where they marched as a squad, and hobbled back alone behind them. They had been given battle-dress and now wore it for classes. At night they changed into service-dress if they wished. There was no order about it. 'Blues' were out. The work of the course was Small Arms, morning and afternoon. The lessons followed the Manual page by page, designed for the comprehension of the dullest possible recruit.

'Just imagine, gentlemen, that you're playing football. I daresay some of you wish you were. All right? You're outside right. There's a wind blowing straight down the field. All right? You're taking a corner kick. All right? Do you aim straight at the goal? Can't anyone tell me? Mr Trimmer, do you aim straight at the goal?'

'Oh, yes, Sergeant.'

'You do, do you? What does anyone else think?'

'No, Sergeant.'

'No, Sergeant.'

'No Sergeant.'

'Oh, you don't, don't you? Well, where do you aim?'

'I'd try and pass.'

'That's not the answer I want. Suppose you *want* to shoot a goal, do you aim straight at it?'

'Yes.'

'No.'

'No, Sergeant.'

'Well, where *do* you aim? Come along, doesn't anyone here play football? You aim *up* field, don't you?'

'Yes, Sergeant.'

'Why? Can't any of you think? You aim *up* field because it's *into the wind*, isn't it? ...'

Guy took his turn at the aiming-rest and laid off for wind. Later he lowered himself painfully to the gymnasium floor and pointed a rifle at Sarum-Smith's eye while Sarum-Smith squinnied at him through an 'aiming-disc' and declared all his shots wide.

It was generally known that Guy had once shot a lion. The non-commissioned officers took up the theme: 'Dreaming of big game, Mr Crouchback?' they asked when Guy's attention wandered, and they gave their fire order: 'Ahead a bushy-top tree. Right, four o'clock, ten degrees, corner of yellow field. In that corner a lion. At that lion, two rounds fire.'

Guy's position on the mess-committee was far from being a hollow dignity, indeed, it lacked dignity of any kind for it exposed him to rather sharp complaints: 'Uncle, why can't we have better pickles?' 'Uncle, why isn't whisky cheaper here than at the Grand Hotel?' 'Why do we take in *The Times*? No one reads it except you.' Throughout all the smooth revolutions of barracks life there had been accumulating tiny grits of envy which were now generating heat.

All that week Guy was increasingly lonely and dispirited. The news on the eighth day that Apthorpe was rejoining them cheered him throughout a tedious session of 'Judging Distance'.

'... Why do we judge distance? To estimate the range of the target correctly. All right? Correct range makes fire effective and avoids waste of ammunition. All right? At two hundred yards all parts of the body are distinctly seen. At three hundred yards the outline of the face is blurred. At four hundred yards no face. At six hundred yards the head is a dot and the body tapers. Any questions? ...'

As he limped back from the gym to the house he repeated to himself: 'Six hundred yards the head is a dot; four hundred yards, no face,' not to fix it in his mind, but as a meaningless jingle. Before he reached the house he was saying: 'Four hundred yards, the head is a face; six hundred yards, no dot.' It was the worst afternoon since he joined the army.

Then he found Apthorpe sitting in the hall.

'I'm delighted to see you back,' said Guy, with sincerity. 'Are you all right again?'

'No, no, far from it. But I've been passed fit for light duties.'

'Bechuana tummy again?'

'It's no joking matter, old man. I met with rather a nasty accident. In the bathroom when I hadn't a stitch on.'

'Do tell me.'

'I was going to, only you seem to find it so funny. I was staying with my aunt at Peterborough. There wasn't a great deal to do and I didn't want to get out of condition, so I decided to run through some of the P.T. tables. Somehow the very first morning I slipped and came the most awful cropper. I can tell you it hurt like the devil.'

'Whereabouts, Apthorpe?'

'In my knee. It was literally agony. I quite thought I'd broken it. I had quite a business finding an MO. My aunt wanted me to see her doctor but I insisted on going through service channels. When I did, he took it very seriously. Packed me off to hospital. As a matter of fact that was interesting. I don't think you've ever been in a military hospital, Crouchback?'

'Not yet.'

'It's well worth while. One should get to know all arms of the service. I had a sapper in the next bed to mine – with ulcers.'

'Apthorpe, there's one thing I must ask you –'

'I was there over Christmas. The VADs sang carols –'

'Apthorpe, are you lame?'

'Well, what d'you expect, old man? A thing like this doesn't clear up in a day even with the best treatment.'

'I'm lame too.'

'Very sorry to hear it. But I was telling you about Christmas in the ward. The SMO made punch –'

'Don't you realize what awful fools we're going to look, the two of us, I mean, both going lame?'

'No.'

'Like a pair of twins.'

'Frankly, old man, I think that's a bit far-fetched.'

But when he and Apthorpe appeared at the dining-room, each leaning on his stick, there was a general turning of heads, then laughter, then a round of clapping from both tables.

'I say, Crouchback, has this been pre-arranged?'

'No. It seems quite spontaneous.'

'Well, I consider it's in pretty poor taste.'

They filled their mugs at the urn and sat down.

'Not the first tea I've had in this room!' said Apthorpe.

'How is that?'

'We used to play Kut-al-Imara when I was at Staplehurst. I was never quite first-class at cricket but I played goal for the First Eleven my last two seasons.'

Guy had come to rejoice in facts about Apthorpe's private life. They were rather rare. The aunt at Peterborough was a new character; now there was Staplehurst.

'Was that your prep school?'

'Yes. It's that rather prominent building I expect you've noticed the other side of the town. I should have thought you'd have heard of it. It's very well known. My aunt was rather High Church,' he added with the air of thus somehow confirming the school's reputation.

'Your aunt at Peterborough?'

'No, no, of course not,' said Apthorpe crossly. 'My aunt at Tunbridge Wells. My aunt at Peterborough doesn't go in for that sort of thing at all.'

'Was it a good school?'

'Staplehurst? One of the best. Quite outstanding. At least it was in my day.'

'I meant Kut-al-Imara.'

'We thought them awful little ticks. They usually beat us, of course, but then they made a fetish of games. We just took them in our stride at Staplehurst.'

Leonard joined them.

'We've kept a bed for you in our room, Uncle,' he said.

'Jolly decent of you, but to tell you the truth I've got rather a lot of gear. I had a look round before you chaps dismissed and found an empty room, so I'm moving in there alone. I shall have to read a bit at night, I expect, to catch up with you. The sapper I met in hospital lent me some very interesting books, pretty confidential ones. The sort of thing you aren't allowed to take into the front line trenches in case it fell into the hands of the enemy.'

'Sounds like an ATM.'

'This *is* an ATM.'

'We've all been issued with those.'

'Well, it can't be at all the same thing. I got it from this sapper major. He had an internal ulcer so he passed it on to me.'

'Is this the thing?' asked Leonard, taking from the pocket of his battle-dress trousers a copy of the January Army Training Memorandum that was issued to all officers.

'I couldn't say offhand,' said Apthorpe. 'Anyway I don't think I ought to talk about it.'

So Apthorpe's gear, that vast accumulation of ant-proof boxes, water-proof bundles, strangely shaped, heavily initialled tin trunks and leather cases all bound about with straps and brass buckles, was shut away from all eyes but his.

Guy had seen them often enough in barracks, incuriously. He could have asked about them then, in the days of confidence before the Captain-Commandant's luncheon party, and learned their secrets. All he knew now, from an early chance reference, was that somewhere among these possessions lay something rare and mysterious which Apthorpe spoke of as his 'Bush Thunder-box'.

That night for the first time Guy went out into the town. He and Apthorpe hired a car for the evening and drove from hotel to hotel, finding Halberdiers everywhere, drinking and moving on in search of greater privacy.

'It seems to me you've let the young gentlemen become rather uppish in my absence,' said Apthorpe.

In particular they sought an hotel called the Royal Court where Apthorpe's aunts had stayed when they came to visit him at school.

'Not one of the showy places, but everything just right. Only a few people know of it.'

No one knew of it that evening. At length when all bars were shut Guy said: 'Couldn't we visit Staplehurst?'

'There wouldn't be anyone there, old man. Holidays. And anyway it's a bit late.'

'I mean, couldn't we just go and look at it?'

'Sound scheme. Driver, go to Staplehurst.'

'Staplehurst Grove or Staplehurst Drive?'

'Staplehurst House.'

'Well, I know the Grove and the Drive. I'll try there, shall I? Is it a Private?'

'I don't follow you, driver.'

'A private hotel?'

'It is a Private School.'

There was a moon and a high wind off-shore. They followed the Parade and mounted to the outskirts of the town.

'It all seems rather changed,' said Apthorpe. 'I don't remember any of this.'

'We're in the Grove now, sir. The Drive is round on the left.'

'It stood just about here,' said Apthorpe. 'Something must have happened to it.'

They got out into the moonlight and the bitter North wind. All round them lay little shuttered villas. Here, under their feet and beyond the neat hedges, lay the fields where muddy Apthorpe had kept goal. Somewhere among these gardens and garages bits of brickwork, perhaps, survived from the sanctuary where clean Apthorpe in lace cotta had lighted the tapers.

'Vandals,' said Apthorpe bitterly.

Then the two lame men climbed into the car and drove back to Kut-al-Imara in alcoholic gloom.

7

Next day Apthorpe had a touch of Bechuana tummy but he rose none the less. Guy was first down, driven from bed by thirst. It was a grey and bitter morning, heavy with coming snow. He found one of the regular officers in the hall engaged at the notice board with a large sheet headed in red chalk: 'READ THIS. IT CONCERNS YOU.'

'Great bit of luck,' he said. 'We've got Mudshore for today. Embus at eight-thirty. Draw haversack rations. You'd better pass the word to your chaps.'

Guy climbed the stairs and put his head into each dormitory in turn saying: 'We've got Mudshore for today. Bus leaves in twenty minutes.'

'Who's Mudshore?'

'I've no idea.'

Then he returned to the notice board and learned that Mudshore was a rifle-range some ten miles distant.

Thus began the saddest day of the new dispensation.

Mudshore range was a stretch of sea-marsh transected at regular intervals by banks and ending in a colourless natural escarpment. It was surrounded by wire and cautionary notices; there was a tin hut by the nearest bank, the firing point. When they arrived they found a soldier in his shirt-sleeves shaving at the door; another was crouching by a Soyer stove; a third appeared buttoning his tunic, unshaved.

The major in charge of the expedition went forward to investigate. They heard his tones, ferocious at first, grow gradually softer and end with: 'Very well, Sergeant. It's clearly not your fault. Carry on. I'll try and get through to Area.'

He returned to his party.

'There seems to have been some sort of misunderstanding. The last order the range-keeper got from Area was that firing was cancelled for today. They're expecting snow. I'll see what can be done. Meanwhile since we're here, it's a good opportunity to run through Range Discipline.'

For an hour, while the light broadened into a leaden glare, they learned and practised the elaborate code of precautions which, at this stage of the Second World War, surrounded the firing of live ammunition. Then the major returned to them from the hut where he had been engaged on the telephone. 'All right. They don't expect snow for an hour or two. We can carry on. Our walking wounded can make themselves useful in the butts.'

Guy and Apthorpe set off across the five hundred yards of sedge and took their places in the brick-lined trench below the targets. A corporal and two details from the Ordnance Corps joined. After much telephoning red flags were hoisted and eventually firing began. Guy looked at his watch before marking the first shot. It was now ten minutes to eleven. At half past twelve fourteen targets had been shot and the message came to stand easy. Two of the Depot Branch arrived to relieve Guy and Apthorpe.

'They're getting pretty fed up at the firing point,' one of them said. 'They say you're marking too slow. And I'd like to see my target. I'm certain my third was on it. It must have gone through the same hole as the second. I was dead on aim.'

'It's patched out, anyway.'

Guy stumped away and emerged from the side of the trench to be greeted with distant yells and arm waving. He hobbled on, disregarding, until he was within talking distance. Then he heard from the major: 'For Christ's sake, man, d'you want to be killed? Can't you see the red flag's up?'

Guy looked and saw that it was. No one was at the firing point. All were crowded in the lee of the hut eating sandwiches. He continued his walk among the hummocks.

'Get down, for Christ's sake. Now, look for the flag.'

He lay, looked and presently saw the flag lowered. 'All right, come on now.'

When he came up with the major he said: 'I'm sorry, sir. Those other people had just come up and we'd been told to stand easy.'

'Exactly. That's how fatal accidents happen. The flag and only the flag is the signal to go by. Pay attention, everyone. You've just seen a typical example of bad range discipline. Remember it.'

Apthorpe meanwhile had just started out and was making heavy going. When he arrived, Guy said: 'Did *you* see the bloody flag?'

'Of course. One always looks out for it. It's the first rule. Besides the corporal up there tipped me off. They often play that trick the first day on the range, running up the red flag when everyone knows it ought to be down. It's simply done to impress the need of range discipline.'

'Well, you might have passed the tip on to me.'

'Hardly the thing, old man. It would defeat the whole object of the exercise. There'd be no lessons learned if everyone tipped everyone else off, if you see what I mean.'

They ate their sandwiches. The cold was intense. 'Couldn't we carry on firing, sir? Everyone's ready.'

'I daresay, but we've got to think of the men. They expect their stand-easy.'

At last firing began again.

'We shan't get through on time,' said the major. 'Cut down to five rounds a man.'

But it was not the firing which took the time; it was the falling in of details, the drill on the firing point, the inspection of arms. Light was failing when it came to Guy's turn. He and Apthorpe joined the last detail, hobbling up independently. As he lay and sighted his rifle before loading, Guy made the disconcerting discovery that the target entirely disappeared when he covered it. He lowered his rifle and looked with two eyes. There was a discernible white square. He closed one eye; the square became dimmed, flickered. He raised the rifle and at once there was a total black at the end of his foresight.

He loaded and quickly fired his five observed shots. After the first, the disc rose and covered the bull.

'Nice work, Crouchback, keep it up.'

After the second, the flag signalled a miss. After the third, the flag again.

'Hullo, Crouchback, what's gone wrong?'

The fourth was a high outer. After the fifth, the flag.

Then a telephone message: 'Correction on target two. The first shot was wrongly marked a bull. A patch had blown off. The first shot on target two was a miss.'

Apthorpe, next to him, had done very nicely.

The major led Guy aside and said gravely: 'That was a very poor show, Crouchback. What on earth went wrong?'

'I don't know, sir. The visibility was rather poor.'

'It was the same for everyone. You'll have to work hard at elementary aiming. You put up a very poor show today.'

Then began the ritual of counting the ammunition and collecting shell cases. 'Pull through now. Boil out as soon as you're dismissed.'

Then the snow began. It was dark before they took their seats in the bus and began slowly nosing a way home.

'I reckon that lion was unlucky, Uncle,' said Trimmer. But no one in his numbed audience laughed.

Even Kut-al-Imara House seemed warm and welcoming. Guy pressed himself to the hot pipes in the hall while the rush on the stairs cleared. A mess waiter passed and Guy ordered a glass of rum. Slowly he began to feel the blood move and irrigate his hands and feet.

'Hullo, Crouchback, boiled out already?'

It was the major.

'Not yet, sir. I was just waiting till the crowd had finished.'

'Well, you've no business to wait. What were the orders? Boil out *immediately* you dismiss. Nothing was said about waiting till you'd had a couple of drinks.'

The major was cold too; he, also, had had a beastly day. Moreover he had nearly a mile to walk through the snow to his billet and when he got there, he remembered now, the cook would be out and he had promised to take his wife to dinner at one of the hotels.

'Not one of your better days, Crouchback. You may not be much of a marksman but might at least keep your rifle clean for someone who is,' he said; he went off into the snow and entirely forgot the matter before he had gone a hundred yards.

Trimmer was on the stairs during this conversation.

'Hullo, Uncle, did I hear you getting a rocket?'

'You did.'

'Quite a change for our blue-eyed boy.'

A spark was struck in Guy's darkened mind; a fuse took fire. 'Go to hell,' he said.

'Tut, tut, Uncle. Aren't we a little crusty this evening?'

Bang.

'You bloody, half-baked pipsqueak, pipe down,' he said. 'One more piece of impudence out of you and I'll hit you.'

The words were not well chosen; lame or sound, Guy was not built to inspire great physical fear, but sudden wrath is always alarming, recalling as it does the awful unpredictable dooms of childhood; moreover Guy was armed with a strong stick which he now involuntarily raised a little. A court martial might or might not have construed this gesture as a serious threat against the life of a brother officer. Trimmer did.

'Here, I say, steady on. No offence meant.'

Anger carries its own propulsive mechanism and soars far from the point of ignition. It carried Guy now into a red incandescent stratum where he was a stranger.

'God rot your revolting little soul, I told you to pipe down, didn't I?'

He gave the stick a definite, deliberate flourish and advanced a halting step. Trimmer fled. Two swift *chassés* and he was round the corner, muttering inaudibly about '... taking a joke without flying off the handle ...'

Quite slowly Guy's rage subsided and touched ground; self-satisfaction sank with it, rather more slowly but at last that too was on the common level.

Just such a drama, he reflected, must have been enacted term by term at Kut-al-Imara House, when worms turned and suddenly revealed themselves as pythons; when nasty, teasing little boys were put to flight. But the champions of the upper fourth needed no rum to embolden them.

Was it for this that the bugles sounded across the barrack square and the strings sang over the hushed dinner table of the Copper Heels? Was this the triumph for which Roger de Waybroke took the Cross; that he should exult in putting down Trimmer?

In shame and sorrow Guy stood last in the queue for boiling water, leaning on his fouled weapon.

8

The week that followed brought consolation.

Health returned to Guy's knee. It had grown stronger every day while he was acquiring a habitual limp; the pain, lately, had come from the elastic bandage. Now, haunted by Apthorpe in the role of *doppelgänger*, he abandoned stick and strapping and found he could move normally, and he fell in with his squad as proudly as on his second day in barracks.

At the same time the moustache which he had let grow for some weeks suddenly took shape, as suddenly as the child learns to swim; one morning it was a straggle of hair, the next a firm and formal growth. He took it to a barber in the town who trimmed it and brushed it and curled it with a hot iron. He rose from the chair transmogrified. As he left the shop he noticed an optician's over the street in whose window lay a single enormous china eyeball and a notice proclaiming: FREE TESTS. EYE-GLASSES OF ALL KINDS FITTED WHILE YOU WAIT. The solitary organ, the idiosyncratic choice of word 'eye-glasses' in preference to 'spectacles', the memory of the strange face which had just looked at him over the barber's basin, the memory of countless German Uhlans in countless American films, drew him across.

'I was thinking of a monocle,' he said quite accurately.

'Yes, sir. Merely the plain lens for smart appearance, or do you suffer from faulty vision?'

'It's for shooting. I can't see the target.'

'Dear, dear, *that* won't do, will it, sir?'

'Can you cure it?'

'We *must*, mustn't we, sir?'

Quarter of an hour later Guy emerged, having purchased for fifteen shillings a strong lens in a 'rolled-gold' double rim. He removed it from its false-leather purse, stopped before a window and stuck the glass in his right eye. It stayed there. Slowly he relaxed the muscles of his face; he stopped squinting. The monocle remained firmly in place. The man reflected to him had a cynical leer; he was every inch a junker. Guy returned to the optician.

'I think I'd better have two or three more of these, in case I break one.'

'I'm afraid that's the only one I have in stock of that particular strength.'

'Never mind. Give me the nearest you have.'

'Really, sir, the eye is a most delicate instrument. You shouldn't play ducks and drakes with it. *That* is the lens for which you have been tested. It is the only one I can recommend professionally.'

'Never mind.'

'Well, sir, I have made my protest. The man of science demurs. The man of business submits.'

The monocle combined with the moustaches, set him up with his young companions, none of whom could have transformed himself so quickly. It also improved his shooting.

A few days after he bought it, they went to Mudshore to fire the Bren. Through his eye-glass Guy saw, distinct from the patchy snow, a plain white blob and hit it every time, not with notable marksmanship but as accurately as anyone else in his detail.

He did not attempt to keep the monocle permanently in his eye but he used it rather often and regained much of his lost prestige by discomfiting the sergeant-instructor with it.

His prestige rose also with the renewed incidence of poverty. Palm lounges and dance halls cost dear and the first flood-tide of ready cash ebbed fast. Young officers began counting the days until the end of the month and speculating whether, now that their existence had once been recognized by the pay-office, they could depend on regular funds. One by one all Guy's former clients returned to him; one or two others diffidently joined; and all, save Sarum-Smith, he helped (Sarum-Smith got a cold stare through the monocle), and although you could not say that the Halberdiers sold 'the deference which youth owed to age' for three or four pounds down, it was a fact that his debtors were more polite to him and often remarked to one another in extenuation of their small acts of civility: 'Old Uncle Crouchback is an awfully generous good-natured fellow really.'

His life was further mitigated by his discovery of two agreeable retreats. The first was a small restaurant on the front called 'the Garibaldi' where Guy found Genoese cooking and a warm welcome. The proprietor was a part-time spy. This Giuseppe Pelecci, fat and philoprogenitive, welcomed Guy on his first visit as a possible source of variety in the rather monotonous and meagre lists of shipping which hitherto had been his sole contribution to his country's knowledge, but when he found Guy spoke Italian, patriotism gave place to simple home-sickness. He had been born not far from Santa Dulcina and knew the Castello Crouchback. The two became more than *patron* and patron, more than agent and dupe. For the first time in his life Guy felt himself *simpatico* and he took to dining at the Garibaldi most evenings.

The second was the Southsand and Mudshore Yacht Squadron.

Guy found this particularly congenial resort in a way which was itself a joy, for it added some hard facts to the incomplete history of Apthorpe's youth.

It would be a travesty to say that Guy suspected Apthorpe of lying. His claims to distinction – porpoise-skin boots, a High Church aunt in Tunbridge Wells, a friend who was on good terms with gorillas – were not what an impostor would invent in order to impress. Yet there was about Apthorpe a sort of fundamental implausibility. Unlike the typical figure of the J.D. lesson, Apthorpe tended to become faceless and tapering the closer he approached. Guy treasured every nugget of Apthorpe but under assay he found them liable to fade like faery gold. Only so far as Apthorpe was himself true, could his enchantment work its spell. Any firm passage between Apthorpe's seemingly dreamlike universe and the world of common experience was a thing to cherish, and just such a way Guy found on the Sunday following his fiasco on Mudshore range; the start of the week which ended triumphantly with his curled moustaches and his single eye-glass.

Guy went alone to mass. There were no Halberdiers to march there and the only other Catholic officer was Hemp, the Trimmer of the Depot. Hemp was not over scrupulous in his religious duties, from which (he claimed to have read somewhere) all servicemen were categorically dispensed.

The church was as old as most buildings in Southsand and sombrely embellished by the legacies of many widows. In the porch, as he left, Guy was accosted by the neat old man who had earlier carried the collection plate.

'I think I saw you here last week, didn't I? My name is Goodall, Ambrose Goodall. I didn't speak to you last Sunday as I didn't know if you were here for long. Now I hear you are at Kut-al-Imara for some time, so may I welcome you to St Augustine's?'

'My name is Crouchback.'

'A great name, if I may say so. One of the Crouchbacks of Broome perhaps?'

'My father left Broome some years ago.'

'Of course, yes, I know. Very sad. I make a study, in a modest way, of English Catholicism in penal times so of course Broome means a lot to me. I'm a convert myself. Still I daresay I've been a Catholic nearly as long as you have. I usually take a little turn along the front after mass. If you are walking back may I accompany you a short way?'

'I'm afraid I ordered a taxi.'

'Oh dear. I couldn't induce you to stop at the Yacht Club? It's on your way.'

'I don't think I can stop, but let me drop you there.'

'That's very kind. It *is* rather sharp this morning.'

As they drove away, Mr Goodall continued. 'I'd like to do anything I can for you while you are here. I'd like to talk about Broome. I went there last summer. The sisters keep it very well all things considered.

'I might be able to show you round Southsand. There are some very interesting old bits. I know it very well. I was a master at Staplehurst House once, you see, and I stayed on all my life.'

'You were at Staplehurst House?'

'Not for very long. You see when I became a Catholic I had to leave. It wouldn't have mattered at any other school but Staplehurst was so very High Church that of course they minded particularly.'

'I *long* to hear about Staplehurst.'

'Do you, Mr Crouchback? Do you? There's not very much to tell. It came to an end nearly ten years ago. There were said to be abuses of the Confessional. I never believed it myself. You must be descended from the Grylls, too, I think. I have always had a particular veneration for the Blessed John Gryll. And, of course, for the Blessed Gervase Crouchback. Sooner or later they'll be canonized, I'm quite sure of it.'

'Do you by any chance remember a boy at Staplehurst called Apthorpe?'

'Apthorpe? Oh dear, here we are at the Club. Are you sure I can't induce you to come in?'

'May I, after all? It's earlier than I thought.'

The Southsand and Mudshore Yacht Squadron occupied a solid villa on the front. A flag and burgee flew from a pole on the front lawn. Two brass cannon stood on the steps. Mr Goodall led Guy to a chair in the plate-glass windows and rang the bell.

'Some sherry, please, steward.'

'It must be more than twenty years since Apthorpe left.'

'That would be just the time I was there. The name seems familiar. I could look him up if you're really interested. I keep all the old Mags.'

'He's with us at Kut-al-Imara.'

'Then I will certainly look him up. He's not a Catholic?'

'No, but he has a High Church aunt.'

'Yes, I suppose so. Most of our boys did, but quite a number came into the church later. I try to keep touch with them but parish affairs take up so much time, particularly now that Canon Geoghan can't get about as he did. And then I have my work. I had rather a hard time of it at first but I get along. Private tutoring, lectures at convents. You may have seen some of my reviews in the *Tablet*. They generally send me anything connected with heraldry.'

'I'm sure Apthorpe would like to meet you again.'

'Do you think he would? After all this time? But I must look him up first. Why don't you bring him here to tea? My rooms aren't very suitable for entertaining, but I'd be very pleased to see him here. You also stem from Wrottman of Speke, do you not?'

'I've some cousins of that name.'

'But not of Speke, surely? The Wrottmans of Speke are extinct in the male line. Don't you mean Wrottman of Garesby?'

'Perhaps I do. They live in London.'

'Oh yes, Garesby was demolished under the usurper George. One of the saddest things in all that whole unhappy century. The very stones were sold to a building contractor and dragged away by oxen.'

But when a few days later the meeting was arranged Guy and Apthorpe kept the conversation on the affairs of Staplehurst.

'I was able to find two references to your football in the Mag. I copied them out. I'm afraid neither is very laudatory. First in November 1913. "*In the absence of Brinkman ma. Apthorpe acted as understudy in goal but repeatedly found the opposing forwards too strong for him.*" The score was 8–0. Then in February 1915: "*Owing to mumps we could only put up a scratch XI against St Olaf's. Apthorpe in goal was unfortunately quite outclassed.*" Then in the summer of '16 you are in the *Vale* column. It doesn't give the name of your public school.'

'No, sir. It was still rather uncertain at the time of going to press.'

'Was he ever in your form?'

'Were you, Apthorpe?'

'Not exactly. We came to you for Church History.'

'Yes. I taught that through the school. In fact I owe my conversion to it. Otherwise I only took the scholarship boys. You were never one of those, I think?'

'No,' said Apthorpe. 'There was a muddle about it. My aunt wanted me to go to Dartmouth. But somehow I made a hash of the Admiral's interview.'

'I always think it's too formidable an ordeal for a small boy. Plenty of good candidates fail purely on nerves.'

'Oh, it wasn't that exactly. We just couldn't seem to hit it off.'

'Where *did* you go after leaving?'

'I chopped and changed rather,' said Apthorpe.

They ate their tea in deep leather arm-chairs before a fire. Presently Mr Goodall said: 'I wonder if either of you would like to become temporary members of the club while you are here. It's a cosy little place. You don't have to have a yacht. That was the original idea but lots of our members can't run to one nowadays. I can't myself. But we keep up a general interest in yachting. There's usually a very pleasant crowd in here between six and eight and you can get dinner if you give the steward a day's notice.'

'I should like it very much,' said Guy.

'There's a lot to be said for it,' said Apthorpe.

'Then let me introduce you to our Commodore. I just saw him come in. Sir Lionel Gore, a retired Harley Street man. A very good fellow in his way.'

They were introduced. Sir Lionel spoke of the Royal Corps of Halberdiers and with his own hand filled in their entries in the Candidates Book, leaving a blank for the names of their yachts.

'You'll hear from the secretary in due course. In fact at the moment *I* am the secretary. If you'll wait a minute I'll make out your cards and post you on the board. We charge temporary members ten bob a month. I don't think that's unreasonable these days.'

So Guy and Apthorpe joined the Yacht Club, and Apthorpe said: 'Thanks, Commodore' when he was handed his ticket of membership.

It was dark and freezing hard when they left. Apthorpe had not yet recovered the full use of his leg and insisted on travelling by taxi.

As they drove back he said: 'I reckon we are on a good thing there, Crouchback. I suggest we keep it to ourselves. I've been thinking lately, it won't hurt to be a bit aloof with our young friends. Living cheek by jowl breeds familiarity. It may prove a bit awkward later when one's commanding a company and they're one's platoon commanders.'

'I shan't ever get a company. I've been doing badly all round lately.'

'Well, awkward for me, at any rate. Of course, old man, I don't mind being familiar with you because I know you'd never try to take advantage of it. Can't say the same for all the batch. Besides, you never know, you might get made second-in-command and that's a captain's appointment.'

Later, he said: 'Funny old Goodall taking such a fancy to you,' and later still, when they had reached Kut-al-Imara and were sitting in the hall with their gin and vermouth, he broke a long silence with: 'I never claimed to be anything much at football.'

'No. You said you didn't make a fetish of it.'

'Exactly. To tell you the truth I never made much mark at Staplehurst. It's strange, looking back on it now, but in those days I might just have passed for one of the crowd. Some men develop late.'

'Like Winston Churchill.'

'*Exactly.* We might go back to the Club after dinner.'

'D'you think tonight?'

'Well, I'm going and it's cheaper sharing a taxi.'

So that evening and most subsequent evenings Guy and Apthorpe went to the Yacht Club. Apthorpe was welcome as a fourth in the card-room and Guy read happily before the fire surrounded by charts, burgees, binnacles, model ships and other nautical decorations.

9

All that January was intensely cold. In the first week an exodus began from the dormitories of Kut-al-Imara, first of the married men who were given permission to sleep in lodgings; then, since many of the controlling staff were themselves unmarried yet comfortably quartered, the order was stretched to include all who could afford or contrive it. Guy moved to the Grand Hotel, which was conveniently placed between Kut-al-Imara and the Club. It was a large hotel built for summer visitors, almost empty now in war-time winter. He engaged good rooms very cheaply. Apthorpe was taken in by Sir Lionel Gore. By the end of the month less than half the original draft remained in quarters. They spoke of 'boarders and dayboys'. The local bus service did not fit the times of parade nor did it strictly conform to its timetable. Many 'dayboys' had lodgings far from the school and the bus route. The weather showed no sign of breaking. Even the march to and from the bus stop was now laborious on the icebound road. There were many cases of officers late on parade with plausible excuses. The gym was un-heated and long hours there became increasingly irksome. For all these reasons working hours were cut. They began at nine and ended at four. There was no bugler at Kut-al-Imara and Sarum-Smith one day facetiously rang the school bell five minutes before parade. Major McKinney thought this a helpful innovation and gave orders to continue it. The curriculum followed the textbooks, lesson by lesson, exercise by exercise, and the preparatory school way of life was completely re-created. They were to stay there until Easter – a whole term.

The first week of February filled no dykes that year. Everything was hard and numb. Sometimes about midday there was a bleak glitter of sun; more often the skies were near and drab, darker than the snowbound downland inshore, leaden and lightless on the seaward horizon. The laurels round Kut-al-Imara were sheathed in ice, the drive rutted in crisp snow.

On the morning of Ash Wednesday Guy rose early and went to mass.

With the ash still on his forehead he breakfasted and tramped up the hill to Kut-al-Imara, where he found the place full of boyish excitement.

'I say, Uncle, have you heard? The Brigadier's arrived.'

'He was here last night. I came into the hall and there he was, covered in red, glaring at the notice board.'

'I'd made a resolution to dine in every night till the end of the month, but I slipped out by the side door. So did everyone else.'

'Something tells me he's up to no good.'

The school bell rang. Apthorpe was now restored to general duties and fell in with the squad.

'The Brigadier has come.'

'So I hear.'

'High time, too, if you ask me. There are quite a number of things here need putting in order, starting with the staff.'

They marched to the gymnasium and broke up into the usual four classes.

All were being initiated in the same hard way into the mysteries of Fixed Lines.

'Stores,' said the colour sergeant instructor. 'Gun, spare barrel, dummies, magazines, carrier's wallet, tripod, aiming peg and night firing lamp. All right?'

'Right, Sergeant.'

'Right, eh? Any gentleman see anything not right? Where's the peg; where's the lamp? Not available. So this here piece of chalk will substitute for peg and lamp. All right?'

Every half-hour they stood easy for ten minutes. During the second of these periods of glacial rest there was a warning: 'Pipes out. Officers coming. Party, shun.'

'Carry on, Sergeants,' said a voice unfamiliar to most. 'Never hold up instruction. Don't look at me, gentlemen. All eyes on the guns.'

Ritchie-Hook was among them, clothed as a brigadier, attended by the officer commanding the course and his second-in-command. He went from class to class. Parts of what was said reached the corner where Guy's squad worked. Most of it sounded cross. At last he reached Guy's squad.

'First detail; prepare for action.'

Two young officers flung themselves on the floorboards and reported: 'Magazines and spare barrel correct.'

'Action.'

The Brigadier watched. Presently he said: 'Get up, you two. Stand easy, everyone. Now tell me what a fixed line is for.'

Apthorpe said: 'To deny an area to the enemy by means of interlocking beaten zones.'

'Sounds as though you'd stopped giving him sweets. I'd like to hear less about denying things to the enemy and more about biffing him. Remember that, gentlemen. All fire-plans are just biffing. Now, you, number one at the gun. You've just been laying an aim on that chalk mark on the floor, haven't you? D'you think you'd hit it?'

'Yes, sir.'

'Look again.'

Sarum-Smith lay down and carefully checked his aim.

'Yes, sir.'

'With the sights at 1800?'

'That's the range we were given, sir.'

'But God damn it, man, what's the use of aiming at a chalk mark ten yards away with the sights at 1800?'

'That's the fixed line, sir.'

'Fixed on what?'

'The chalk mark, sir.'

'Anyone care to help him?'

'There is no aiming peg or night firing lamp available, sir,' said Apthorpe.

'What the hell's that got to do with it?'

'That's why we're using a chalk mark, sir.'

'You young officers have been doing small arms for six weeks. Can none of you tell me what a fixed line is for?'

'For biffing, sir,' suggested Trimmer.

'For biffing what?'

'The aiming peg or night firing lamp if available, sir. Otherwise the chalk mark.'

'I see,' said the Brigadier, baffled. He strode out of the gym followed by the staff.

'Now you've been and let me down,' said the sergeant-instructor.

In a few minutes a message arrived that the Brigadier would see all officers in the mess at twelve o'clock.

'Rockets all round,' said Sarum-Smith. 'I shouldn't wonder if the staff aren't having rather a sticky morning, too.'

So it seemed from their glum looks as they sat facing their juniors assembled in the school dining-hall. Places were already laid for luncheon and there was a smell of brussels sprouts boiling not far away. They sat silent as in a monastery refectory. The Brigadier rose, *Cesare armato con un occhio grifano*, as though to say Grace. He said: 'Gentlemen, you may not smoke.'

It had not occurred to anyone to do so.

'But you need not sit at attention,' he added, for everyone was instinctively stiff and motionless. They tried to arrange themselves less formally but there was no ease in that audience. Trimmer rested an elbow on the table and rattled the cutlery.

'It is not yet time to eat,' said the Brigadier.

Guy remembered the anecdote about 'six of the best'. It would really not have surprised him greatly if the Brigadier had produced a cane and called Trimmer up for correction. No charge had been preferred, no specific rebuke (except to Trimmer) uttered but under that solitary ferocious eye all were held in universal guilt.

The spirits of countless scared schoolboys still haunted and dominated the hall. How often must the word have been passed under those rafters of painted and grained plaster, in this same stench of brussels sprouts: 'the Head's in a frightful wax.' 'Who is it this time?' 'Why me?'

The words of that day's liturgy echoed dreadfully in Guy's mind: *Memento, homo, quia pulvis es, et in pulverem reverteris*.

Then the Brigadier began his speech: 'Gentlemen, it seems to me that you could all do with a week's leave,' and his smile, more alarming than any scowl, convulsed the grey face. 'In fact some of you needn't bother to come back at all. They'll be notified later through what are laughingly called the "correct channels".'

It was a masterly opening. The Brigadier was no scold and he was barely one part bully. What he liked was to surprise people. In gratifying this simple taste he had often to resort to violence, sometimes to heavy injury, but there was no pleasure for him in these concomitants. Surprise was everything. He must have known, glaring at his audience, that morning, that he had scored a triumph. He continued:

'I can only say that I am sorry I have not been to visit you before. There is more work than you can possibly know in forming a new brigade. I have been looking after that side of your affairs. I heard reports that when you arrived the accommodation was not perfect but Halberdier officers must learn to look after themselves. I came here last night on a friendly visit expecting to find you all happily settled in. I arrived at seven o'clock. There was not one officer in camp. Of course there is no military rule that you must dine in on any particular night. I supposed you were all out on some celebration. I asked the civilian caterer and learned that yesterday was not an exceptional occasion. He did not know the name of a single member of the mess committee. This does not strike me as being what the blue-jobs call a "happy ship".

'I looked at your work this morning. It was pretty moderate – and in case any young officer doesn't know what that means, it means damned awful. I do not say that it is entirely your fault. No military offence that I know of has been committed. But an officer's worth does not consist in avoiding military offences.

'What's more, gentlemen, you aren't officers. There are advantages in your present equivocal position. Advantages for you and for me. You none of you hold His Majesty's Commission. You are on probation. I can send the lot of you packing tomorrow without giving any explanation.

'As you know, the normal channel to a commission nowadays in the rest of the army is through the ranks and then to an OCTU. Halberdiers have been specially privileged to collect and train our new officers by direct entry. It won't occur again. We were given this single opportunity to train one batch of young officers because the War Office have faith in the traditions of the Corps. They know we wouldn't take a dud. Your replacements, when you're "expended"' – a cyclopean flash – 'will have gone through the modern mill of the ranks and an OCTU. You are the last men to be accepted and trained in the old way. And I'd sooner report total failure than let in one man I can't trust.

'Don't think you've done something clever in getting a commission easily by the backstairs. You'll go down those stairs arse over tip with my foot behind you, if you don't pull yourselves together.

'The rule of attack is "Never reinforce failure". In plain English that means: if you see some silly asses getting into a mess, don't get mixed up with 'em. The best help you can give is to go straight on biffing the enemy where it hurts him most.

'This course has been a failure. I'm not going to reinforce it. We'll start again this time next week. I shall be in charge.'

The Brigadier did not stay for luncheon. He mounted his motor-cycle and drove away noisily among the icy ruts. Major McKinney and the directing staff packed into their cosy private cars. The probationary officers remained. Strangely enough the atmosphere was one of exhilaration, not at the prospect of leave (that created many problems), but because all, or nearly all, had been unhappy during the past weeks. They were all, or nearly all, brave, unromantic, conscientious young men who joined the army expecting to work rather harder than they had done in peace time. Regimental pride had taken them unawares and quite afflated them. At Kut the Bitter they had been betrayed; deserted among dance halls and slot machines.

'Rather strong worded, I thought,' said Apthorpe. 'He might have made it clearer that there were certain exceptions.'

'You don't think he meant you when he said some of us need not come back?'

'Hardly, old man,' Apthorpe said, and added: 'I think in the circumstances I shall dine in mess tonight.'

Guy went alone to the Garibaldi where he found it difficult to explain to Mr Pelecci, a deeply superstitious Catholic but in the manner of his townsmen not given to ascetic practices, that he did not want meat that evening. Ash Wednesday was for Mrs Pelecci. Mr Pelecci feasted for St Joseph and fasted for no one.

But that evening Guy felt full of meat, gorged like a lion on Ritchie-Hook's kill.

I O

Perhaps the Brigadier believed that besides clearing space for his own work, he was softening the force of his reprimand by sending the course on leave. The 'boarders' left cheerfully but the 'dayboys' were committed to various arrangements in the town. Many had overspent themselves in establishing their wives. For them there was the prospect of five days loafing in lodgings. Guy was not rich. He was spending rather more than usual. There was no great attraction in changing an hotel bedroom in Southsand for a more expensive one in London. He decided to remain.

On the second evening Mr Goodall was due to dine with him at the Garibaldi. Afterwards they went to the Yacht Club, and sat alone among the trophies in the shuttered morning-room. Both were elated by that evening's news, the boarding of the *Altmark*, but soon Mr Goodall was back on his favourite topic. He was very slightly flown with wine and looser than usual in his conversation.

He spoke of the extinction (in the male line), some fifty years back, of an historic Catholic family.

'... They were a connexion of yours through the Wrottmans of Garesby. It was a most curious case. The last heir took his wife from a family (which shall be nameless) which has an unfortunate record of instability in recent generations. They had two daughters and then the wretched girl eloped with a neighbour. It made a terrible ado at the time. It was before divorce was common. Anyway they *were* divorced and this woman married this man. If you'll forgive me I won't tell you his name. Then ten years later your kinsman met this woman alone, abroad. A kind of rapprochment occurred but she went back to her so-called husband and in due time bore a son. It was in fact your kinsman's. It was by law the so-called husband's, who recognized it as his. That boy is alive today and in the eyes of God the rightful heir to all his father's quarterings.'

Guy was less interested in the quarterings than in the morality.

'You mean to say that theologically the original husband committed no sin in resuming sexual relations with his former wife?'

'Certainly not. The wretched girl of course was guilty in every other way and is no doubt paying for it now. But the husband was entirely blameless. And so under another and quite uninteresting name a great family has been preserved. What is more the son married a Catholic so that *his* son is being brought up in the Church. Explain it how you will, I see the workings of Providence there.'

'Mr Goodall,' Guy could not resist asking, 'do you seriously believe that God's Providence concerns itself with the perpetuation of the English Catholic aristocracy?'

'But, of course. And with sparrows, too, we are taught. But I am afraid that genealogy is a hobby-horse I ride too hard when I get the chance. So much of my life is spent with people who aren't interested and might even think it snobbish or something – one evening a week for the Vincent de Paul Society, one evening at the boys' club; then I go to the Canon one evening to help him with his correspondence. And I have to keep some time for my sister who lives with me. She's not really interested in genealogy. Not that it matters. We are both unmarried and the last of our family, such as it was. Oh dear, I think your hospitality has made my tongue run away with me.'

'Not at all, dear Mr Goodall. Not at all. Some port?'

'No more, thank you.' Mr Goodall looked crestfallen. 'I must be on my way.'

'You're quite sure about that point you raised. About the husband committing no sin with his former wife?'

'Quite sure, of course. Think it out for yourself. What possible sin could he have committed?'

Guy did think long and late about that blameless and auspicious pseudo-adultery. The thought was still with him when he woke next day. He went to London by a morning train.

The name of Crouchback, so lustrous to Mr Goodall, cut no ice at Claridge's: Guy was politely informed that there was no room available for him. He asked for Mrs Troy and learned that she had left instructions not to be disturbed. He went crossly to Bellamy's and explained his predicament at the bar, which, at half past eleven, was beginning to fill.

Tommy Blackhouse said: 'Who did you ask?'

'Just the chap at the desk.'

'That's no good. When in difficulties always take the matter to a higher level. It never fails. I'm staying there myself at the moment. In fact I'm going round there now. Would you like me to fix it for you?'

Half an hour later the hotel telephoned to say that there was a room awaiting him. He returned and was welcomed at the desk. 'We are so grateful to Major Blackhouse for telling us where to find you. There was a cancellation just as you left the hotel and we had no address for you.' The receptionist took a key from his rack and led Guy to the lift. 'We are fortunate in being able to offer you a very nice little suite.'

'I was thinking of a bedroom only.'

'This has a very nice little sitting-room that goes with it. I'm sure you will find it more quiet.'

They reached the floor; doors were thrown open on rooms which in all points proclaimed costliness. Guy remembered why he had come and the laws of propriety which govern hotels; a sitting-room constituted a chaperon.

'Yes,' he said, 'I think these will do very nicely.'

When he was left alone, he asked on the telephone for Mrs Troy.

'Guy? *Guy*. Where are you?'

'Here in the hotel.'

'Darling, how *beastly* of you not to let me know.'

'But I am letting you know now. I've only this minute arrived.'

'I mean let me know in advance. Are you here for a lovely long time?'

'Two days.'

'How *beastly*.'

'When am I going to see you?'

'Well, it's rather difficult. You should have let me know. I've got to go out almost at once. Come now. Number 650.'

It was on his floor, not a dozen rooms away, round two corners. The doors all stood ajar.

'Come in, I'm just finishing my face.'

He passed through the sitting-room – also a chaperon? he wondered. The bedroom door was open; the bed unmade; clothes and towels and newspapers all over the place. Virginia sat at a dressing-table covered with powder and wads of cotton wool and crumpled paper napkins. She was staring intently in the glass doing something to her eye. Tommy Blackhouse came unconcernedly from the bathroom.

'Hullo, Guy,' he said. 'Didn't know you were in London.'

'Make a drink for us all,' Virginia told him. 'I'll be with you in a second.'

Guy and Tommy went into the sitting-room where Tommy began cutting up a lemon and shovelling ice into a cocktail-shaker.

'They fixed you up all right?'

'Yes. I'm most grateful to you.'

'No trouble at all. By the way, better not say anything to Virginia' – Guy noticed that he had shut the bedroom door behind him – 'about our having met at Bellamy's. I told her I came straight from a conference, but as you know I stopped on the way. She's never jealous of other women, but she does hate Bellamy's. Once, while we were married, she said: "Bellamy's. I'd like to burn the place down." Meant it, too, bless her. Here for long?'

'Two nights.'

'I go back to Aldershot tomorrow. I ran into a brigadier of yours the other day at the War Office; they're scared stiff of him there. Call him "the one-eyed monster". Is he a bit cracked?'

'No.'

'I didn't think so either. They all say he's stark crazy at the War Office.'

Soon from the disorderly slum of her bedroom Virginia emerged spruce as a Halberdier.

'I hope you haven't made them too strong, Tommy. You know how I hate strong cocktails. Guy, *your moustache*.'

'Don't you like it?'

'It's perfectly awful.'

'I must say,' said Tommy, 'it took me aback rather.'

'It's greatly admired by the Halberdiers. Is this any better?' He inserted the monocle.

'I think it is,' said Virginia. 'It was just plain common before. Now it's comic.'

'I thought that, taken together, they achieved a military effect.'

'There you're wrong,' said Tommy. 'You must accept my opinion on a point of that kind.'

'Not attractive to women?'

'No,' said Virginia. 'Not to nice women.'

'Damn.'

'We ought to be going,' said Tommy. 'Drink up.'

'Oh dear,' said Virginia. 'What a short meeting. Am I going to see you again? I shall be free of this burden tomorrow. Couldn't we do something in the evening?'

'Not before?'

'How can I, darling, with this lout around? Tomorrow evening.'

They were gone.

Guy returned to Bellamy's as though to the Southsand Yacht Club. He washed and gazed in the glass over the basin as steadfastly as Virginia had done in hers. The moustache was fair, inclined to ginger, much lighter than the hair of his head. It was strictly symmetrical, sweeping up from a neat central parting, curled from the lip, cut sharp and slightly oblique from the corners of his mouth, ending in firm points. He put up his monocle. How, he asked himself, would he regard another man so decorated? He had seen such moustaches before and such monocles on the faces of clandestine homosexuals, on touts with accents to hide, on Americans trying to look European, on business-men disguised as sportsmen. True, he had also seen them in the Halberdier mess, but on faces innocent of all guile, quite beyond suspicion. After all, he reflected, his whole uniform was a disguise, his whole new calling a masquerade.

Ian Kilbannock, an arch-imposter in his Air Force dress, came up behind him and said: 'I say, are you doing anything this evening? I'm trying to get some people in for cocktails. Do come.'

'I might. Why?'

'Sucking up to my air marshal. He likes to meet people.'

'Well, I'm not much of a catch.'

'He won't know that. He just likes meeting people. I'd be awfully grateful if you could bear it.'

'I've certainly nothing else to do.'

'Well, come then. Some of the other people won't be quite as awful as the marshal.'

Later, upstairs in the coffee-room, Guy watched Kilbannock going round the tables, collecting his party.

'What's the point of all this, Ian?'

'Well, I told you. I've put the marshal up for this club.'

'But they aren't letting him in?'

'I hope not.'

'But I thought it was all fixed.'

'It's not quite as easy as that, Guy. The marshal is rather fly in his way. He's not giving anything away except for value received. He insists on meeting some members and getting their support. If he only knew, his best chance of getting in is to meet no one. So it's all in a good cause really.'

That afternoon Guy had his moustache shaven. The barber expressed professional admiration for the growth and did his work with reluctance, like the gardeners who all over the country had that autumn ploughed up their finest turf and transformed herbaceous borders into vegetable plots. When it was done, Guy studied himself once more in the glass and recognized an old acquaintance he could never cut, to whom he could never hope to give the slip for long, the uncongenial fellow traveller who would accompany him through life. But his naked lip felt strangely exposed.

Later he went to Ian Kilbannock's party. Virginia was there with Tommy. Neither noticed the change until he called attention to it.

'I knew it wasn't real,' said Virginia.

The air marshal was the centre of the party, in the sense that everyone was introduced to him and almost immediately withdrew. He stood like the entrance to a bee-hive, a point of vacuity with a constant buzzing movement to and from it. He was a stout man, just too short to pass for a Metropolitan policeman, with a cheerful manner and shifty little eyes.

There was a polar-bear rug before the fire.

'That reminds me of a clever rhyme I once heard,' he said.

> 'Would you like to sin
> With Eleanor Glyn
> On a tiger skin?
> Or would you prefer
> With her
> To err
> On some other fur?'

All in his immediate ambience looked at the rug in sad embarrassment.

'Who's Eleanor Glyn?' asked Virginia.

'Oh, just a name, you know. Put in to make it rhyme, I expect. Neat, isn't it?'

When he came to go, Guy found himself at the door with Ian and the marshal.

'My car's here. Can I give you a lift?'

It was snowing again and dark as the grave.

'That's very good of you, sir. I was going to St James's Street.'

'Hop in.'

'I'll come too, sir, if I may,' said Ian, surprisingly for there were still guests lingering upstairs.

When they reached Bellamy's, Ian said: 'Won't you come in for a final one, sir?'

'A sound idea.'

The three of them went to the bar.

'By the way, Guy,' said Ian, 'Air Marshal Beech is thinking of joining us here. Parsons, got the Candidates Book with you?'

The book was brought and the marshal's virgin page presented to view. Ian Kilbannock's fountain-pen was gently put into Guy's hand. He signed.

'I'm sure you'll find it amusing here, sir,' said Ian.

'I've no doubt I shall,' said the air marshal. 'I often thought of joining in the piping days of peace, but I wasn't in London often enough for it to be worth while. Now I need a little place like this where I can slip away and relax.'

It was St Valentine's Day.

Februato Juno, dispossessed, has taken a shrewish revenge on that steadfast clergyman, bludgeoned and beheaded seventeen centuries back, and set him in the ignominious role of patron to killers and facetious lovers. Guy honoured him for the mischance and whenever possible went to mass on his feast-day. He walked from Claridge's to Farm Street, from Farm Street to Bellamy's and settled down to a bleak day of waiting.

The newspapers were still full of the *Altmark*, now dubbed 'the Hell Ship'. There were long accounts of the indignities and discomforts of the prisoners, officially designed to rouse indignation among a public quite indifferent to those trains of locked vans still rolling East and West from Poland and the Baltic, that were to roll on year after year bearing their innocent loads to ghastly unknown destinations. And Guy, oblivious also, thought all that winter's day of his coming meeting with his wife. In the late afternoon when all was black, he telephoned to her room.

'What are our plans for the evening?'

'Oh good, are there plans? I quite forgot. Tommy's just left and I was thinking of a lonely early night, dinner in bed with the cross-word. I'd *much* rather have plans. Shall I come along to you? Everything looks rather squalid here.' So she came to the six-guinea chaperon sitting-room and Guy ordered cocktails.

'Not as cosy as mine,' she said, looking round the rich little room.

Guy sat beside her on the sofa. He put his arm on the back, edged towards her, put his hand on her shoulder.

'What's going on?' she asked in unaffected surprise.

'I just wanted to kiss you.'

'What an odd way to go about it. You'll make me spill my drink. Here.' She put her glass carefully on the table at her side, took hold of him by the ears and gave him a full firm kiss on either cheek.

'Is that what you want?'

'Rather like a French general presenting medals.' He kissed her on the lips. 'That's what I want.'

'Guy, are you tight?'

'No.'

'You've been spending the day at that revolting Bellamy's. Admit.'

'Yes.'

'Then of course you're tight.'

'No. It's just that I want you. D'you mind?'

'Oh, nobody ever minds about being wanted. But it's rather unexpected.'

The telephone bell rang.

'Damn,' said Guy.

The telephone was on the writing-table. Guy rose from the sofa and lifted the receiver. Familiar tones greeted him.

'Hullo, old man, Apthorpe here. I thought I'd just give you a ring. Hullo, hullo. That is Crouchback, isn't it?'

'What d'you want?'

'Nothing special. I thought I could do with a change from Southsand so I ran up to town for the day. I got your address out of the Leave Book. Are you doing anything this evening?'

'Yes.'

'You mean, you have an engagement?'

'Yes.'

'I couldn't join you anywhere?'

'No.'

'Very well, Crouchback. I'm sorry I disturbed you.' Huffily: 'I can tell when I'm not wanted.'

'It's a rare gift.'

'I don't quite get you, old man.'

'Never mind. See you tomorrow.'

'Things seem a bit flat in town.'

'I should go and have a drink.'

'I daresay I shall. Forgive me if I ring off now.'

'Who was that?' asked Virginia. 'Why were you so beastly to him?'

'He's just a chap from my regiment. I didn't want him butting in.'

'Some horrible member at Bellamy's?'

'Not at all like that.'

'Mightn't he have been rather fun?'

'No.'

Virginia had now moved to an arm-chair.

'What were we talking about?' she asked.

'I was making love to you.'

'Yes. Let's think of something different for a change.'

'It *is* a change. For me, anyway.'

'Darling, I haven't had time to get my breath from Tommy. Two husbands in a day is rather much.'

Guy sat down and stared at her.

'Virginia, did you ever love me at all?'

'But of course, darling. Don't you remember? Don't look so gloomy. We had lovely times together, didn't we? Never a cross word. *Quite* different to Mr Troy.'

They talked of old times together. First of Kenya. The group of bungalows that constituted their home, timber-built, round stone chimneys and open English hearths, furnished with wedding presents and good old pieces of furniture from the lumber-rooms at Broome; the estate, so huge by European standards, so modest in East Africa, the ruddy earth roads, the Ford van and the horses; the white-gowned servants and their naked children always tumbling in the dust and sunshine round the kitchen quarters; the families always on the march to and from the native reserves, stopping to beg for medicine; the old lion Guy shot among the mealies. Evening bathes in the lake, dinner parties in pyjamas with their neighbours. Race Week in Nairobi, all the flagrant, forgotten scandals of the Muthaiga Club, fights, adulteries, arson, bankruptcies, card-sharping, insanity, suicides, even duels – the whole Restoration scene re-enacted by farmers, eight thousand feet above the steaming seaboard.

'Goodness it was fun,' said Virginia. 'I don't think anything has been quite such fun since. How things just do happen to one!'

In February 1940 coal still burned in the grates of six-guinea hotel sitting-rooms. Virginia and Guy sat in the fire-light and their talk turned to gentle matters, their earliest meeting, their courtship, Virginia's first visit to Broome, their wedding at the Oratory, their honeymoon at Santa Dulcina. Virginia sat on the floor with her head on the sofa, touching Guy's leg. Presently Guy slid down beside her. Her eyes were wide and amorous.

'Silly of me to say you are drunk,' she said.

It was all going as Guy had planned, and, as though hearing his unspoken boast, she added: 'It's no good planning anything,' and she said again: 'Things just happen to one.'

What happened then was a strident summons from the telephone.

'Let it ring,' she said.

It rang six times. Then Guy said: 'Damn. I must answer it.'

Once again he heard the voice of Apthorpe.

'I'm doing what you advised, old man; I've had a drink. Rather more than one as it happens.'

'Good. *Continuez, mon cher.* But for Christ's sake don't bother me.'

'I've met some very interesting chaps. I thought perhaps you'd like to join us.'

'No.'

'Still engaged?'

'Very much so.'

'Pity. I'm sure you'd like these chaps. They're in Ack-Ack.'

'Well, have a good time with them. Count me out.'

'Shall I ring up later to see if you can give your chaps the slip?'

'No.'

'We might all join forces.'

'No.'

'Well, you're missing a very interesting palaver.'

'Good night.'

'Good night, old man.'

'I'm sorry about that,' said Guy, turning from the telephone.

'While you're there you might order some more to drink,' said Virginia. She rose to her feet and arranged herself suitably for the waiter's arrival. 'Better put on the lights,' she said.

They sat opposite one another on either side of the fire, estranged and restless. The cocktails were a long time in coming. Virginia said: 'How about some dinner?'

'Now?'

'It's half past eight.'

'Here?'

'If you like.'

He sent for the menu and they ordered. There was half an hour in which waiters came and went, wheeling a table carrying an ice bucket, a hot-plate, eventually food. The sitting-room suddenly seemed more public than the restaurant below. All the fire-side intimacy was dissipated. Virginia said: 'What are we going to do afterwards?'

'I can think of something.'

'Can you indeed?'

Her eyes were sharp and humorous, all the glowing expectation and acceptance of an hour ago quite extinguished. Finally the waiter removed all his apparatus; the chairs on which they had sat at dinner were back against the wall; the room looked just as it had when it was first thrown open to him, costly and uninhabited. Even the fire, newly banked up with coal and smoking darkly, had the air of being newly lit. Virginia leaned on the chimney-piece with a cigarette training a line of smoke between her fingers. Guy came to stand by her and she moved very slightly away.

'Can't a girl have time to digest?' she said.

Virginia had a weak head for wine. She had drunk rather freely at dinner and there was a hint of tipsiness in her manner, which, he knew from of old, might at any minute turn to truculence. In a minute it did.

'As long as you like,' said Guy.

'I should just think so. You take too much for granted.'

'That's an absolutely awful expression,' said Guy. 'Only tarts use it.'

'Isn't that rather what you think I am?'

'Isn't it rather what you are?'

They were both aghast at what had happened and stared at one another, wordless. Then Guy said: 'Virginia, you know I didn't mean that. I'm sorry. I must have gone out of my mind. Please forgive me. Please forget it.'

'Go and sit down,' said Virginia. 'Now tell me just what you did mean.'

'I didn't mean anything at all.'

'You had a free evening and you thought I was a nice easy pick-up. That's what you meant, isn't it?'

'No. As a matter of fact I've been thinking about you ever since we met after Christmas. That's why I came here. Please believe me, Virginia.'

'And anyway what do you know about picking up tarts? If I remember our honeymoon correctly, you weren't so experienced. Not a particularly expert performance as I remember it.'

The moral balance swung sharply up and tipped. Now Virginia had gone too far, put herself in the wrong. There was another silence until she said: 'I was wrong in thinking the army had changed you for the better. Whatever your faults in the old days you weren't a cad. You're worse than Augustus now.'

'You forget I don't know Augustus.'

'Well, take it from me he was a monumental cad.'

A tiny light gleamed in their darkness, a pin-point in each easy tear which swelled in her eyes and fell.

'Admit I'm not as bad as Augustus.'

'Very little to choose. But he was fatter. I'll admit that.'

'Virginia, for God's sake don't let's quarrel. It's my last chance of seeing you for I don't know how long.'

'There you go again. The warrior back from the wars. "I take my fun where I find it."'

'You know I didn't mean that.'

'Perhaps you didn't.'

Guy was beside her again with his hands on her. 'Don't let's be beastly.'

She looked at him, not loving yet, but without any anger; sharp and humorous again.

'Go back and sit down,' she said, giving him one friendly kiss. 'I haven't finished with you yet. Perhaps I do look like an easy pick-up. Lots of people seem to think so, anyway. I suppose I shouldn't complain. But I can't understand you, Guy, not at all. You were never one for casual affairs. I can't somehow believe you are now.'

'I'm not. This isn't.'

'You used to be so strict and pious. I rather liked it in you. What's happened to all that?'

'It's still there. More than ever. I told you so when we first met again.'

'Well, what would your priests say about your goings-on tonight; picking up a notorious divorcee in an hotel?'

'They wouldn't mind. You're my wife.'

'Oh, rot.'

'Well, you asked what the priests would say. They'd say: "Go ahead." '

The light that had shone and waxed in their blackness suddenly snapped out as though at the order of an air-raid warden.

'But this is horrible,' said Virginia.

Guy was taken by surprise this time.

'What's horrible?' he said.

'It's absolutely disgusting. It's worse than anything Augustus or Mr Troy could ever dream of. Can't you see, you pig, you?'

'No,' said Guy in deep, innocent sincerity. 'No, I don't see.'

'I'd far rather be taken for a tart. I'd rather have been offered five pounds to do something ridiculous in high heels or drive you round the room in toy harness or any of the things they write about in books.' Tears of rage and humiliation were flowing unresisted. 'I thought you'd taken a fancy to me again and wanted a bit of fun for the sake of old times. I thought you'd chosen me specially, and by God you had. Because I was the only woman in the whole world your priests would let you go to bed with. That was my attraction. You wet, smug, obscene, pompous, sexless, lunatic pig.'

Even in this discomfiture Guy was reminded of his brawl with Trimmer.

She turned to leave him. Guy sat frozen. On the silence left by her strident voice there broke a sound more strident still. While her hand was on the door-knob, she instinctively paused at the summons. For the third time that evening the telephone bell sang out between them.

'I say, Crouchback, old man, I'm in something of a quandary. I've just put a man under close arrest.'

'That's a rash thing to do.'

'He's a civilian.'

'Then you can't.'

'That, Crouchback, is what the prisoner maintains. I hope you aren't going to take his part.'

'Virginia, don't go.'

'What's that? I don't get you, old man. Apthorpe here. Did you say it was "No go"?'

Virginia went. Apthorpe continued.

'Did you speak or was it just someone on the line? Look here, this is a serious matter. I don't happen to have my King's Regulations with me. That's why I'm asking for your help. Ought I to go out and try and collect an NCO and some men for prisoner's escort in the street? Not so easy in the black-out, old man. Or can I just hand the fellow over to the civilian police? ... I say, Crouchback, are you listening? I don't think you quite appreciate that this is an official communication. I am calling on you as an officer of His Majesty's Forces . . .'

Guy hung up the receiver and from the telephone in his bedroom gave instructions that he was taking no more calls that night, unless by any chance he was rung up from Number 650 in the hotel.

He went to bed and lay restless, half awake, for half the night. But the telephone did not disturb him again.

Next day when he met Apthorpe at the train he said: 'You got out of your trouble last night?'

'Trouble, old man?'

'You telephoned to me, do you remember?'

'Did I? Oh, yes, about some point of military law. I thought you might be able to help.'

'Did you solve the problem?'

'It blew over, old man. It just blew over.'

Presently he said: 'Not wishing to be personal, may I ask what's happened to your moustache?'

'It's gone.'

'Exactly. Just what I mean.'

'I had it shaved off.'

'Did you? What a pity. It suited you, Crouchback. Suited you very well.'

BOOK TWO

Apthorpe Furibundus

I

Orders were to report back at Kut-al-Imara by 1800 hours on 15 February.

Guy travelled through the familiar drab landscape. The frost was over and the countryside sodden and dripping. He drove through the darkling streets of Southsand where blinds were going down in the lightless windows. This was no homecoming. He was a stray cat, slinking back mauled from the rooftops, to a dark corner among the dustbins where he could lick his wounds.

Southsand was a place of solace. Hotel and Yacht Club would shelter him, he thought. Giuseppe Pelecci would feed him and flatter him; Mr Goodall raise him. Mist from the sea and the melting snow would hide him. The spell of Apthorpe would bind him, and gently bear him away to the far gardens of fantasy.

In his melancholy Guy had taken no account of the Ritchie-Hook Seven Day Plan.

Later in his military experience, when Guy had caught sight of that vast uniformed and bemedalled bureaucracy by whose power alone a man might stick his bayonet into another, and had felt something of its measureless obstructive strength, Guy came to appreciate the scope and speed of the Brigadier's achievement. Now he innocently supposed that someone of the Brigadier's eminence merely said what he wanted, gave his orders and the thing was done; but even so he marvelled, for in seven days Kut-al-Imara had been transformed, body and soul.

Gone were Major McKinney and the former directing staff and the civilian caterers. Gone, too, was Trimmer. A notice on the board, headed *Strength, Decrease of*, stated that his temporary commission had been terminated. With him went Helm and a third delinquent, a young man from the Depot whose name was unfamiliar to Guy for the sufficient reason that he had been absent without leave for the whole of the course at Southsand. In their stead were a group of regular officers, Major Tickeridge among them, many of whom Guy recognized from the barracks. They sat at the back of the mess behind the Brigadier when at six o'clock on the first evening he rose to introduce them.

He held his audience for a moment with his single eye. Then he said: 'Gentlemen, these are the officers who will command you in battle.'

At those words Guy's shame left him and pride flowed back. He ceased for the time being to be the lonely and ineffective man – the man he so often thought he saw in himself, past his first youth, cuckold, wastrel, prig – who had washed and shaved and dressed at Claridge's, lunched at Bellamy's and caught the afternoon train; he was one with his regiment, with all their historic feats of arms behind him, with great opportunities to come. He felt from head to foot a physical tingling and bristling as though charged with galvanic current.

The rest of his speech was an explanation of the new organization and régime. The brigade had already taken embryonic form. The temporary officers were divided into three battalion groups of a dozen each under the regular major and captain who would eventually become respectively their commanding officer and adjutant. All would live in. Permission to sleep out would be given to married men for Saturday and Sunday nights only. All would dine in mess at least four nights a week.

'That is all, gentlemen. We will meet again at dinner.'

When they left the mess, they found that the table top over the fireplace in the hall had been covered in their brief absence with type-written sheets. Gradually spelling his way through the official abbreviations Guy learned that he was in the Second Battalion under Major Tickeridge and the Captain Sanders with whom Apthorpe had once so notably played golf. With him were Apthorpe, Sarum-Smith, de Souza, Leonard and seven others all from the barracks. Sleeping quarters had been reallocated. They lived by battalions, six to a room. He was back in Paschendael; as was Apthorpe.

Then and later he learned of other changes. The closed rooms of the house were now thrown open. One was labelled '*Bde. HQ*' and held a brigade major and two clerks. The headmaster's study housed three Battalion Orderly Rooms. There were also a regular quartermaster, with an office and a clerk, three regimental sergeant majors, Halberdier cooks, new, younger Halberdier servants, three lorries, a Humber Snipe, three motor-bicycles, drivers, a bugler. The day's routine was a continuous succession of parades, exercises and lectures from eight in the morning till six. 'Discussions' would be held after dinner on Mondays and Fridays. 'Night Operations', also, were two a week.

'I don't know how Daisy will take this,' said Leonard.

She took it, Guy learned later, very badly, and returned heavy and cross to her parents.

Guy welcomed the new arrangements. After the expenses of London he had been uneasy about his hotel bill at the Grand. But most of the young officers were worried. Apthorpe, who had mentioned in the train that he was suffering from 'a touch of tummy', looked more worried than anyone.

'It's the question of my gear,' he said.

'Why not leave it at your digs?'

'At the Commodore's? Pretty awkward, old man, in the case of a sudden move. I think I'd better have a palaver with the Q.M. about it.'

And later: 'D'you know, the Q.M. wasn't a bit helpful. Said he was busy. Seemed to think I was talking about superfluous clothing. He even suggested I might have to scrap half of it when we move under canvas. He's just one of those box-wallahs. No experience of campaigning. I told him so and he said he'd served in the ranks in Hong Kong. Hong Kong – I ask you! About the cushiest spot in the whole empire. I told him that too.'

'Why is it all so important to you, Apthorpe?'

'My dear fellow, it's taken me years to collect.'

'Yes, but what's in it?'

'That, old man, is not an easy question to answer in one word.'

Everyone dined in the mess that first evening. There were three tables now, one for each battalion. The Brigadier, who from now on sat wherever his fancy took him, said Grace, banging the table with the handle of his fork and saying simply and loudly: 'Thank God.'

He was in high good humour and gave evidence of it first by providing a collapsible spoon for the brigade major which spilt soup over his chest, and secondly by announcing after dinner: 'When the tables have been cleared there will be a game of Housey-housey, here. For the benefit of the young officers I should explain that it is what civilians, I believe, call Bingo. As you are no doubt aware, it is the only game which may be played for money by His Majesty's Forces. Ten per cent of each bank goes to the Regimental Comforts Fund and Old Comrades' Association. The price of each card will be three pence.'

'Housey-housey?'

'Bingo?'

The junior officers looked at one another in wild surmise. 'Tubby' Blake alone, the veteran of the Depot Batch, claimed he had played the game on board ship crossing the Atlantic to Canada.

'It's quite simple. You just cross out the numbers as they're called.'

'What numbers?'

'The ones they call.'

Mystified, Guy returned to the mess. The brigade major sat at the corner of a table with a tin cash box and a heap of cards printed with squares and numbers. Each bought a card as he came in. The Brigadier, smiling ferociously, stood at the brigade major's side with a pillow-case in his hands. When they were all seated the Brigadier said: 'One object of this exercise is to see how many of you carry pencils.'

About half did. Sarum-Smith, surprisingly, had three or four, including a metal one with different coloured leads.

Someone asked: 'Will a fountain-pen do, sir?'

'Every officer should always carry a pencil.'

It was back to prep school again, but a better school than McKinney's.

At last after much borrowing and searching of pockets the game began suddenly with the command: 'Eyes down for a house.'

Guy stared blankly at the Brigadier, who now plunged his hand in the pillow-case and produced a little square card.

'Clickety-click,' said the Brigadier disconcertingly. Then: 'Sixty-six.' Then in rapid succession, in a loud sing-song tone: 'Marine's breakfast number 10 add two twelve all the fives fifty-five never been kissed sweet sixteen key of the door twenty-one add six twenty-seven legs eleven Kelly's eye number one and we'll . . .'

He paused. The regular officers and 'Tubby' Blake gave tongue: 'Shake the bag.'

Slowly the terms of this noisy sport became clearer to Guy and he began making crosses on his card until there was a cry of 'House' from Captain Sanders, who then read his numbers aloud.

'House correct,' said the brigade major, and Sanders collected about nine shillings, and the other players crowded round the brigade major to buy new cards.

They played for two hours. The Brigadier's eye teeth flashed like a questing tiger's. As the players began to grasp what was going on, an element of enjoyment just perceptible warmed them here and there. The Brigadier became more jolly. 'Who wants one number?'

'Sir.'

'Sir.'

'Sir.'

'What do you want?'

'Eight.'

'Fifteen.'

'Seventy-one.'

'Well it's . . . .' Pause. The Brigadier made a pantomime of being unable to read it; fixed the card with his monocle. 'Did someone say they *wanted* seventy-one. Well it is seventy . . .' pause 'seven. All the sevens and we'll . . .'

'Shake the bag.'

At half past ten the Brigadier said: 'Well, gentlemen, Bedfordshire for you. I've got work. You haven't got a training programme yet.'

He led his staff away into the room marked '*Bde. HQ*'. It was two o'clock when Guy heard them disperse.

The Training Programme followed no textbook. Tactics as interpreted by Brigadier Ritchie-Hook consisted of the art of biffing. Defence was studied cursorily and only as the period of reorganization between two bloody assaults. The Withdrawal was never mentioned. The Attack and the Element of Surprise were all. Long raw misty days were passed in the surrounding country with maps and binoculars. Sometimes they stood on the beach and biffed imaginary defenders into the hills; sometimes they biffed imaginary invaders from the hills into the sea. They invested downland hamlets and savagely biffed imaginary hostile inhabitants. Sometimes they merely collided with imaginary rivals for the use of the main road and biffed them out of the way.

Guy found that he had an aptitude for this sort of warfare. He read his map easily and had a good eye for country. When townsmen like Sarum-Smith gazed blankly about them Guy could always recognize 'dead ground' and 'covered lines of approach'. Sometimes they worked singly, sometimes in 'syndicates'; Guy's answers usually turned out to be the 'staff solution'. At night when they were dropped about the downs, with compass bearings to guide them to a meeting-place, Guy was usually home one of the first. There were great advantages in a rural upbringing. In the 'discussions', too, he did well. These were debates on the various more recondite aspects of biffing. The subjects were announced beforehand with the implication that the matter should be given thought and research. When the evening came most were drowsy and Apthorpe's fine show of technical vocabulary fell flat. Guy spoke up clearly and concisely. He realized that he was once more attracting favourable notice.

The thaw gave place to clear, cold weather. They returned to Mudshore range but with the Brigadier in charge. This was a period before the invention of 'Battle Schools'. The firing of a live round, as Guy well knew, was attended with all the solemnity of a salute at a funeral, always and everywhere, except when Brigadier Ritchie-Hook was about. The sound of flying bullets exhilarated him to heights of levity.

He went to the butts to organize snap-shooting. Markers raised figure-targets at unpredictable points drawing bursts of Bren fire. The Brigadier soon tired of this, put his hat on his stick and ran up and down the trench, raising, lowering, waving it, promising down the telephone a sovereign to the man who hit it. All missed. Enraged he popped his head over the parapet shouting: 'Come on, you young blighters, shoot me.' He did this for some time, running, laughing, ducking, jumping, until he was exhausted though unwounded.

It was a period when ammunition was short. Five rounds a man was the normal training allowance. Brigadier Ritchie-Hook had all the Brens firing at once, continuously, their barrels overheated, changed, plunged sizzling into buckets of water, while he led his young officers on all fours in front of the targets a few inches below the rain of bullets.

2

The newspapers, hastily scanned, were full of Finnish triumphs. Ghostly ski-troops, Guy read, swept through the sunless Arctic forests harassing the mechanized divisions of the Soviet who had advanced with massed bands and portraits of Stalin expecting a welcome, whose prisoners were ill-equipped, underfed, quite ignorant of whom they were fighting and why. English forces, delayed only by a few diplomatic complications, were on their way to help. Russian might had proved to be an illusion. Mannerheim held the place in English hearts won in 1914 by King Albert of the Belgians. Then quite suddenly it appeared that the Finns were beaten.

No one at Kut-al-Imara House seemed much put out by the disaster. For Guy the news quickened the sickening suspicion he had tried to ignore, had succeeded in ignoring more often than not in his service in the Halberdiers; that he was engaged in a war in which courage and a just cause were quite irrelevant to the issue.

That day Apthorpe said: 'After all, it's only what one expected.'

'Did you, Apthorpe? You never told me.'

'Stuck out a mile, old man, to anyone who troubled to weigh the pros and cons. It was simply the case of Poland over again. But there was no point in talking about it. It would only have spread alarm and despondency among the weaker brethren. Personally I can see quite a few advantages in the situation.'

'What, for instance?'

'Simplifies the whole strategy, if you know what I mean.'

'Am I to take this as part of your campaign to prevent alarm and despondency?'

'Take it how you like, old man. I've other things to worry about.'

And Guy at once knew that there must have been a new development in the tense personal drama which all that Lent was being played against the background of the Brigadier's training methods; which, indeed, drew all its poignancy from them and itself formed their culminating illustration.

This adventure had begun on the first Sunday of the new régime.

The schoolrooms were almost deserted that afternoon; everyone was either upstairs asleep or else in the town. Guy was reading his weekly papers in the hall when he saw through the plate-glass window a taxi drive up and

Apthorpe emerge carrying, with the help of the driver, a large square object, which they placed in the porch. Guy went out to offer his help.

'That's all right, thank you,' said Apthorpe rather stiffly. 'I'm just shifting some of my gear.'

'Where d'you want to put it?'

'I don't quite know yet. I shall manage quite well, thank you.'

Guy returned to the hall and stood in the window gazing idly out. It was getting too dark to read comfortably and the man had not yet appeared to put up the black-out screens. Presently he saw Apthorpe emerge from the front door into the twilight and begin furtively burrowing about in the shrubbery. He watched fascinated until some ten minutes later he saw him return. The front porch opened directly into the hall. Apthorpe entered backwards dragging his piece of gear.

'Are you sure I can't help?'

'Quite sure, thank you.'

There was a large cupboard under the stairs. Into this Apthorpe with difficulty shoved his burden. He removed his gloves and coat and cap and came with an air of unconcern to the fire saying: 'The Commodore sent you his compliments. Says he misses us at the Club.'

'Have you been there?'

'Not exactly. I just dropped in on the old man to fetch something.'

'That piece of gear?'

'Well, yes, as a matter of fact.'

'Is it something very private, Apthorpe?'

'Something of no general interest, old man. None at all.'

At that moment the duty servant came in to fix the black-out. Apthorpe said: 'Smethers.'

'Sir.'

'Your name is Smethers, isn't it?'

'No, sir. Crock.'

'Well, never mind. What I wanted to ask you was about the offices, the back-parts of the house.'

'Sir?'

'I need some sort of little shed or store-house, a gardener's hut would do, a wash-house, dairy, anything of that kind. Is there such a place?'

'Was you wanting it just for the moment, sir?'

'No, no, no. For as long as we're here.'

'Couldn't say, I'm sure, sir. That's for the Q.M.'

'Yes. I was only wondering,' and when the man had gone: 'Stupid fellow that. I always thought he was called Smethers.'

Guy turned back to his weekly papers. Apthorpe sat opposite him gazing at his boots. Once he got up, walked to the cupboard, peered in, shut it and returned to his chair.

'I can *keep* it there, I suppose, but I can't possibly *use* it there, can I?'

'Can't you?'

'Well, how *can* I?'

There was a pause during which Guy read an article about the inviolability of the Mikkeli Marshes. (These were the brave days before the fall of Finland.) Then Apthorpe said:

'I thought I could find a place for it in the shrubbery but it's all much more open than I realized.'

Guy said nothing and turned a page of the *Tablet*. It was clear that Apthorpe was longing to divulge his secret and would shortly do so.

'It is no good going to the Q.M. *He* wouldn't understand. It's not exactly an easy thing to explain to anyone.'

Then, after another pause, he said: 'Well, if you *must* know, it's my thunder-box.'

This was far above Guy's hopes; his mind had been running on food, medicine, fire-arms; at the very best he had hoped for something exotic in footwear.

'May I see it?' he asked reverently.

'I don't see why not,' said Apthorpe. 'As a matter of fact I think it will interest you; it's pretty neat, a type they don't make any more. Too expensive, I suppose.'

He went to the cupboard and dragged out the treasure, a brass-bound, oak cube.

'It's a beautiful piece of work really.'

He opened it, showing a mechanism of heavy cast-brass and patterned earthenware of solid Edwardian workmanship. On the inside of the lid was a plaque bearing the embossed title of *Connelly's Chemical Closet*.

'What do you think of it?' said Apthorpe.

Guy was not sure of the proper terms in which to praise such an exhibit.

'It's clearly been very well looked after,' said Guy.

It seemed Guy had said the right thing.

'I got it from a High Court Judge, the year they put drains into the Government buildings at Karonga. Gave him five pounds for it. I doubt if you could find one for twenty today. There's not the craftsmanship any more.'

'You must be very proud of it.'

'I am.'

'But I don't quite see why you need it here.'

'Don't you, old man? Don't you?' A curiously solemn and fatuous expression replaced the innocent light of ownership that had until now beamed from Apthorpe. 'Have you ever heard of a rather unpleasant complaint called "clap", Crouchback?'

Guy was dumbfounded.

'I say, what a beastly thing. I am sorry. I had no idea. I suppose you picked it up the other night in London when you were tight. But are you having it properly seen to? Oughtn't you to go sick?'

'No, no, no, no. *I* haven't got it.'

'Then who has?'

'Sarum-Smith for one.'

'How do you know?'

'I don't *know*. I simply chose Sarum-Smith as an example. He's just the sort of young idiot who would. Any of them might. And I don't intend to take any risks.'

He shut his box and pushed it away under the stairs. The effort seemed to rile him.

'What's more, old man,' he said, 'I don't much like the way you spoke to me just now, accusing me of having clap. It's a pretty serious thing, you know.'

'I'm sorry. It was rather a natural mistake in the circumstances.'

'Not natural to me, old man, and I don't quite know what you mean by "circumstances". I *never* get tight. I should have thought you would have noticed that. Merry, perhaps, on occasions, but never *tight*. It's a thing I keep clear of. I've seen far too much of it.'

Apthorpe was up at first light next day exploring the outbuildings and before breakfast had discovered an empty shed where the school perhaps had kept bats and pads. There with the help of Halberdier Crock he installed his chemical closet and thither for several tranquil days he resorted for his comfort. It was two days after the fall of Finland that his troubles began.

Back from biffing about the downs and, after a late luncheon inclined for half an hour's rest, Guy was disturbed by Apthorpe. He wore a face of doom.

'Crouchback, a word with you.'

'Well.'

'In private if you don't mind.'

'I do mind. What is it?'

Apthorpe looked round the ante-room. Everyone seemed occupied.

'You've been using my thunder-box.'

'No, I haven't.'

'Someone has.'

'Well, it isn't me.'

'No one else knows of it.'

'How about Halberdier Crock?'

'He wouldn't dare.'

'Nor would I, my dear fellow.'

'Is that your last word?'

'Yes.'

'Very well. But in future I shall keep a look-out.'

'Yes, I should.'

'It's a serious matter, you know. It almost amounts to pilfering. The chemical is far from cheap.'

'How much a go?'

'It isn't the money. It's the principle.'

'And the risk of infection?'

'Exactly.'

For two days Apthorpe posted himself in the bushes near his shed and spent every available minute on watch. On the third day he drew Guy aside and said: 'Crouchback, I owe you an apology. It isn't you who has been using my thunder-box.'

'I knew that.'

'Yes, but you must admit the circumstances were very suspicious. Anyway I've found out who it is, and it's most disturbing.'

'Not Sarum-Smith?'

'No. Much more disturbing that that. *It's the Brigadier*.'

'Do you think *he*'s got clap?'

'No. Most unlikely. Far too much a man of the world. But the question arises, what action ought I to take?'

'None.'

'It's a matter of principle. As my superior officer he has no more right to use my thunder-box than to wear my boots.'

'Well, I'd lend him my boots if he wanted them.'

'Perhaps; but then, if you'll forgive my saying so, you're not very particular about your boots, are you, old man? Anyway you think it my duty to submit without protest.'

'I think you'll make a tremendous ass of yourself if you don't.'

'I shall have to think about it. Do you think I ought to consult the B.M.?'

'No.'

'You may be right.'

Next day Apthorpe reported: 'Things are looking worse.'

It showed how much the thunder-box had occupied Guy's thoughts that he at once knew what Apthorpe meant.

'More intruders?'

'No, not that. But this morning as I was coming out I met the Brigadier going in. He gave me a very odd look – you may have noticed he has rather a disagreeable stare on occasions. His look seemed to suggest that *I* had no business there.'

'He's a man of action,' said Guy. 'You won't have to wait long to know what he thinks about it.'

All day Apthorpe was distracted. He answered haphazard when asked an opinion on tactics. His solutions of the problems set them were wild. It was a particularly cold day. At every pause in the routine he kept vigil by the hut. He missed tea and did not return until ten minutes before the evening lecture. He was red-nosed and blue-cheeked.

'You'll make yourself ill, if this goes on,' said Guy.

'It can't go on. The worst has happened already.'

'What?'

'Come and see. I wouldn't have believed it, if I hadn't seen it with my own eyes.'

They went out into the gloom.

'Just five minutes ago. I'd been on watch since tea and was getting infernally cold, so I started walking about. And the Brigadier came right past me. I saluted. He said nothing. Then he did this thing right under my very eyes. Then he came past me again and I saluted and he positively grinned. I tell you, Crouchback, it was *devilish*.'

They had reached the hut. Guy could just see something large and white hanging on the door. Apthorpe turned his torch on it and Guy saw a neatly inscribed notice: *Out of Bounds to all ranks below Brigadier.*

'He must have had it specially made by one of the clerks,' said Apthorpe awfully.

'It's put you in rather a fix, hasn't it?' said Guy.

'I shall send in my papers.'

'I don't believe you can in war-time.'

'I can ask for a transfer to another regiment.'

'I should miss you, Apthorpe, more than you can possibly believe. Anyway there's a lecture in two minutes. Let's go in.'

The Brigadier himself lectured. Booby traps, it appeared, were proving an important feature of patrol-work on the Western front. The Brigadier spoke of trip-wires, detonators, anti-personnel mines. He described in detail an explosive goat which he had once contrived and driven into a Bedouin encampment. Seldom had he been more exuberant.

This was one of the evenings when there was no discussion or night exercise and it was generally accepted that those who wished might dine out.

'Let's go to the Garibaldi,' said Apthorpe. 'I won't sit at the same table with that man. You must dine with me as my guest.'

There, in the steam of *minestrone*, Apthorpe's face became a healthier colour and strengthened by Barolo his despair gave place to defiance. Pelecci leant very near while Apthorpe rehearsed his wrongs. The conversation was abstruse. 'Thunder-box', an invention of this capable officer's, unjustly misappropriated by a superior, was clearly a new weapon of value.

'I don't think,' said Apthorpe, 'it would be any good appealing to the Army Council, do you?'

'No.'

'You could not expect them to meet a case like this with purely open minds. I don't suggest positive prejudice but, after all, it's in their interest to support authority if they possibly can. If they found a loophole ...'

'You think there are loopholes in your case?'

'Quite frankly, old man, I do. In a court of honour, of course, the thing would be different, but in its purely legal aspect one has to admit that the Brigadier is within his rights in putting any part of the brigade premises out of bounds. It is also true that I installed my thunder-box without permission. That's just the sort of point the Army Council would jump on.'

'Of course,' said Guy, 'it's arguable that since the thunder-box has not risen to the rank of brigadier, it is itself at the moment out of bounds.'

'You've got it, Crouchback. You've hit the nail right on the head.' He goggled across the table with frank admiration. 'There's such a thing, you know, as being too near to a problem. Here I've been turning this thing over and over in my mind till I felt quite ill with worry. I knew I needed an outside opinion; anybody's, just someone who wasn't personally implicated. I've no doubt I'd have come to the same solution myself sooner or later, but I might have worried half the night. I owe you a real debt of gratitude, old man.'

More food arrived and more wine. Giuseppe Pelecci was out of his depth. 'Thunder-box', it now appeared, was the code-name of some politician of importance but no military rank, held concealed in the district. He would pass the information on for what it was worth; keener brains than his should make what they could of it. He had no ambition to rise in his profession. He was doing nicely out of the restaurant. He had worked up the good-will of the place himself. Politics bored him and battles frightened him. It was only in order to escape military service that he had come here in the first place.

'And afterwards a special *zabaglione*, gentlemen?'

'Yes,' said Apthorpe. 'Yes, rather. Let's have all you've got.' And to Guy: 'You must understand that this is *my* dinner.'

So Guy had understood from the first; this reminder, Guy thought, was perhaps a clumsy expression of gratitude. It was in fact a sly appeal for further services.

'I think we've cleared up the whole legal aspect very neatly,' Apthorpe continued. 'But there's now the question of action. How are we going to get the thunder-box out?'

'The way you got it in, I suppose.'

'Not so easy, old man. There's wheels within wheels. Halberdier Crock and I carried it there. How can we carry it away without going out of bounds? One can't order a man to perform an unlawful action. You must remember that. Besides I shouldn't really care to *ask* him. He was distinctly uncooperative about the whole undertaking.'

'Couldn't you lasso it from the door?'

'Pretty ticklish, old man. Besides, my lariat is with the rest of my gear at the Commodore's.'

'Couldn't you draw it out with a magnet?'

'I say, are you trying to be funny, Crouchback?'

'It was just a suggestion.'

'*Not* a very practical one, if you don't mind my saying so. No. Someone must go in and get it.'

'Out of bounds?'

'Someone who doesn't know, or at least who the Brigadier doesn't know knows, that the hut is out of bounds. If he was caught he could always plead that he didn't see the notice in the dark.'

'You mean me?'

'Well, you're more or less the obvious person, aren't you, old man?'

'All right,' said Guy, 'I don't mind.'

'Good for you,' said Apthorpe, greatly relieved.

They finished their dinner. Apthorpe grumbled about the bill but he paid it. They returned to Kut-al-Imara. There was no one about. Apthorpe kept *cave* and Guy, without much difficulty, dragged the object into the open.

'Where to now?'

'That's the question. Where do you think will be the best place?'

'The latrines.'

'Really, old man, this is scarcely the time or place for humour.'

'I was only thinking of Chesterton's observation. "Where is the best place to hide a leaf? In a tree." '

'I don't get you, old man. It would be jolly awkward up a tree, from *every* point of view.'

'Well, let's not take it far. It's bloody heavy.'

'There's a potting shed I found when I was making my recce.'

They took it there, fifty yards away. It was less commodious than the hut, but Apthorpe said it would do. As they were returning from their adventure he paused in the path and said with unusual warmth: 'I shan't forget this evening's work, Crouchback. Thank you very much.'

'And thank you for the dinner.'

'That wop did pile it on, didn't he?'

After a few more steps Apthorpe said: 'Look here, old man, if you'd care to use the thunder-box, too, it's all right with me.'

It was a moment of heightened emotion; an historic moment, had Guy recognized it, when in their complicated relationship Apthorpe came nearest to love and trust. It passed, as such moments do between Englishmen.

'It's very good of you but I'm quite content as I am.'

'Sure?'

'Yes.'

'That's all right then,' said Apthorpe, greatly relieved.

Thus Guy stood high in Apthorpe's favour and became with him joint custodian of the thunder-box.

3

In full retrospect all the last weeks of March resolved themselves into the saga of the chemical closet. Apthorpe soon forgot his original motive for installing it.

He was no longer driven by fear of infection. His right of property was at stake. Waiting to fall in, on the morning after the first translation, Apthorpe drew Guy aside. Their new comradeship was on a different plane from frank geniality; they were fellow conspirators now. 'It's still there.'

'Good.'

'Untouched.'

'Fine.'

'I think, old man, that in the circumstances we had better not be seen talking together too much.'

Later, as they went into the mess for luncheon Guy had the odd impression that someone in the crowd was attempting to hold his hand. He looked about him and saw Apthorpe near, with averted face, talking with great emphasis to Captain Sanders. Then he realized that a note was being passed to him.

Apthorpe made for a place at table as far as possible from his. Guy opened the screw of paper and read: '*The notice has been taken down from the hut. Unconditional surrender?*'

Not until tea-time did Apthorpe consider it safe to speak.

'I don't think we've any more to worry about. The Brig. has given us best.'

'It doesn't sound like him.'

'Oh, he's unscrupulous enough for anything. I know that. But he has his dignity to consider.'

Guy did not wish to upset Apthorpe's new, gleeful mood, but he doubted whether these adversaries had an identical sense of dignity. Next day it was apparent that they had not.

Apthorpe arrived for parade (under the new régime there was half an hour's drill and physical training every morning) with a face of horror. He fell in next to Guy. Again there was an odd inter-fumbling of fingers and Guy found himself holding a message. He read it at the first stand-easy while

Apthorpe turned ostentatiously away. '*Must speak to you alone first opportunity. Gravest developments.*'

An opportunity came half-way through the morning.

'The man's mad. A dangerous, certifiable maniac. I don't know what I ought to do about it.'

'What's he done now?'

'He came within an inch of killing me, that's all. If I hadn't been wearing my steel helmet I shouldn't be here to tell you. He caught me with a bloody great flower-pot, full of earth and a dead geranium, square on the top of my head. That's what he did this morning.'

'He threw it at you?'

'It was on top of the potting-shed door.'

'Why were you wearing your tin-hat?'

'Instinct, old man. Self-preservation.'

'But you said last night you thought the whole thing was over. Apthorpe, do you always wear your tin-hat on the thunder-box?'

'All this is irrelevant. The point is that this man simply isn't responsible. It's a very serious matter for someone in his position – and ours. A time may come when he holds our lives in his hands. What ought I to do?'

'Move the box again.'

'And not report the matter?'

'Well, there's your dignity to consider.'

'You mean there are people who might think it funny?'

'Awfully funny.'

'Damn,' said Apthorpe. 'I hadn't considered that side of the question.'

'I wish you'd tell me the truth about the tin-hat.'

'Well, if you must know, I *have* been wearing it lately. I suppose it really boils down to home-sickness, old man. The helmet has rather the feel of a solar topee, if you see what I mean. It makes the thunder-box more homely.'

'You don't start out wearing it?'

'No, under my arm.'

'And when do you put it on, before or after lowering the costume? I must know.'

'On the threshold, as it happens. Very luckily for me this morning. But, you know, really, old man, I don't quite get you. Why all the interest?'

'I must visualize the scene, Apthorpe. When we are old men, memories of things like this will be our chief comfort.'

'Crouchback, there are times when you talk almost as though you found it funny.'

'Please don't think that, Apthorpe. I beg you, think anything but that.'

Already after so brief a reconciliation Apthorpe was getting suspicious. He would have liked to be huffy but did not dare. He was pitted against a ruthless and resourceful enemy and must hold fast to Guy or go down.

'Well, what is our next move?' he asked.

That night they crept out to the potting-shed and Apthorpe in silence showed with his torch the broken shards, the scattered mould and the dead geranium of that morning's great fright. In silence he and Guy lifted the box and bore it as they had planned, back to its original home in the games-hut.

Next day, the Brigadier appeared at first parade.

'ATM 24, as no doubt you all know, recommends the use of games for training in observation and field-craft. This morning, gentlemen, you will play such a game. Somewhere about these grounds has been concealed an antiquated field latrine, no doubt left here as valueless by the former occupants of the camp. It looks like a plain square box. Work singly. The first officer to find it will report to me. Fall out.'

'His effrontery staggers me,' said Apthorpe. 'Crouchback, guard the shed. I will draw off the hunt.'

New strength had come to Apthorpe. He was master of the moment. He strode off purposefully towards the area of coal bunkers and petrol dump and, sure enough, the Brigadier was soon seen to follow behind him. Guy made deviously for the games-hut and sauntered near it. Twice other seekers approached and Guy said: 'I've just looked in there. Nothing to see.'

Presently the bugle recalled them. The Brigadier received the 'nil report', mounted his motor-cycle and drove away scowling ominously but without a word; he did not reappear at all that day.

'A bad loser, old man,' said Apthorpe.

But next day the *Out of Bounds* notice was back on the shed.

As Guy foresaw, those mad March days and nights of hide-and-seek drained into a deep well of refreshment in his mind, but in retrospect the detail of alternate ruse and counter-ruse faded and grew legendary. He never again smelled wet laurel, or trod among pine needles, without reliving those encumbered night prowls with Apthorpe, those mornings of triumph or disappointment. But the precise succession of episodes, indeed their very number, faded and were lost among later, less child-like memories.

The climax came in Holy Week at the very end of the course. The Brigadier had been in London for three days on the business of their next move. The thunder-box stood in a corner of the playing field, unhoused but well hidden between an elm tree and a huge roller. There for the three days Apthorpe enjoyed undisputed rights of property.

The Brigadier returned in alarmingly high spirits. He had bought some trick glasses at the toy-shop which, when raised, spilled their contents down the drinker's chin, and these he secretly distributed round the table before dinner. After dinner there was a long session of Housey-housey. When he had called the last house he said: 'Gentlemen, everyone except the B.M. and I goes on leave tomorrow. We meet under canvas in the lowlands of Scotland where you will have ample space to put into practice the lessons you have learned here. Details of the move will be posted as soon as the B.M. has sweated them out. You will particularly notice that officers' baggage and equipment is defined by a scale laid down at the War House. Those limits will be strictly observed. I think that's all, isn't it, B.M.? Oh, no, one other thing. You are all improperly dressed. You've been promoted as from this morning. Get those second pips up before leaving camp.'

That night there was singing in the dormitories:

> 'This time tomorrow I shall be
> Far from this Academee.'

Leonard improvised

> 'No more TEWTS and no more drill,
> No night ops to cause a chill.'

'I say,' said Guy to Apthorpe. 'That scale of equipment won't allow for your gear.'

'I know, old man. It's very worrying.'

'And the thunder-box.'

'I shall find a place for it. Somewhere quite safe, a crypt, a vault, somewhere like that where I shall know it's waiting for me until the end of the war.'

> 'No more swamps through which to creep,
> No more lectures to make me sleep.'

The cheerful voices reached the room marked '*Bde. HQ*' where the Brigadier was at work with his brigade major.

'That reminds me,' he said, 'I've some unfinished business to attend to outside.'

Next morning as soon as the sun touched the unshaded window of Paschendael, Apthorpe was up, jabbing his shoulder straps with a pair of nail scissors. Then he tricked himself out as a lieutenant. He nothing common did or mean on their morning of departure. His last act before leaving the dormitory was a friendly one; he offered to lend Guy a pair of stars from a neat leather stud-box which he now revealed to be full of such adornments and of crowns also. Then before Guy had finished shaving, Apthorpe, correctly dressed and bearing his steel helmet under his arm, set out for his corner of the playing field.

The spot was not a furlong away. In less than five minutes an explosion rattled the windows of the schoolhouse. Various jolly end-of-term voices rose from the dormitories: 'Air raid'; 'Take cover'; 'Gas'.

Guy buckled his belt and hurried out to what he knew must be the scene of the disaster. Wisps of smoke were visible. He crossed the playing field. At first there was no sign of Apthorpe. Then he came upon him, standing, leaning against the elm, wearing his steel helmet, fumbling with his trouser buttons and gazing with dazed horror on the wreckage which lay all round the roller.

'I say, are you hurt?'

'Who is that? Crouchback? I don't know. I simply don't know, old man.'

Of the thunder-box there remained only a heap of smoking wood, brass valves, pinkish chemical powder scattered many yards, and great jags of patterned china.

'What happened?'

'I don't know, old man. I just sat down. There was a frightful bang and the next thing I knew I was on all fours on the grass, right over there.'

'Are you hurt?' Guy asked again.

'Shock,' said Apthorpe. 'I don't feel at all the thing.'

Guy looked more closely at the wreckage. It was plain enough from his memories of the last lecture what had happened.

Apthorpe removed his steel helmet, recovered his cap, straightened his uniform, put up a hand to assure himself that his new stars were still in place. He looked once more on all that remained of his thunder-box; the *mot juste*, thought Guy.

He seemed too dazed for grief.

Guy was at a loss for words of condolence.

'Better come back to breakfast.'

They turned silently towards the house.

Apthorpe walked unsteadily across the wet, patchy field with his eyes fixed before him.

On the steps he paused once and looked back.

There was more of high tragedy than of bitterness in the epitaph he spoke. '*Biffed.*'

4

Guy had considered going to Downside for Holy Week but decided instead on Matchet. The Marine Hotel was still crowded but there was now no sense of bustle. Management and servants had settled down to the simple policy of doing less than they had done before, for rather more money. A notice board hung in the hall. Except that they began: '*Guests are respectfully reminded*

...', '*Guests are respectfully requested* ...', '*Guests are regretfully informed* ...', the announcements were curiously like military orders and each proclaimed some small curtailment of amenity.

'Seems to me this place is going off rather,' said Tickeridge, who now wore the badges of lieutenant-colonel.

'I'm sure they're doing their best,' said Mr Crouchback.

'I notice they've put up the prices too.'

'I believe they're finding everything rather difficult.'

All his life Mr Crouchback abstained from wine and tobacco during Lent, but his table still bore its decanter of port and the Tickeridges joined them every evening.

As they stood at the windy front door that Maundy Thursday night, while Felix gambolled off into the darkness, Mr Crouchback said:

'I'm so glad you're in Tickeridge's battalion. He's such a pleasant fellow. His wife and little girl miss him dreadfully. ...

'He tells me you're probably being given a company.'

'Hardly that. I think I may get made second-in-command.'

'He said you'd get your own company. He thinks the world of you. I'm so glad. You're wearing that medal?'

'Yes, indeed.'

'I really am delighted you're doing so well. Not that I'm at all surprised. By the way I shall be taking my turn at the Altar of Repose. I don't suppose you care to come too?'

'What time?'

'Well, they seem to find it hardest to get people for the early morning watches. It's all the same for me so I said I'd be there from five to seven.'

'That's a bit long for me. I might look in for half an hour.'

'Do. They've got it looking very pretty this year.'

Dawn was breaking that Good Friday when Guy arrived at the little church, but inside it was as still as night. The air was heavy with the smell of flowers and candles. His father was alone, kneeling stiff and upright at a prie-dieu before the improvised altar, gazing straight before him into the golden lights of the altar. He turned to smile at Guy and then resumed his prayer.

Guy knelt not far from him and prayed too.

Presently a sacristan came in and drew the black curtains from the east windows; brilliant sunlight blinded their eyes, momentarily, to candles and chalice.

At that moment in London – for in this most secret headquarters it was thought more secret to work at unconventional hours – Guy was being talked about.

'There's some more stuff come in about the Southsand affair, sir.'

'Is that the Welsh professor who's taken against the RAF?'

'No, sir. You remember the short-wave message from L18 we intercepted. It's here. *Two Halberdier officers state that important politician Box visited Southsand in secret and conferred with high military commander.*'

'I've never thought there was much in that. We've no suspect called Box as far as I know and there's no high military commander anywhere near Southsand. Might be a code name, of course.'

'Well, sir, we got to work on it as you told us and we've learned that there's a Member of Parliament named Box-Bender who has a brother-in-law named Crouchback in the Halberdiers. Now Box-Bender was born plain Box. His father added to the name in 1897.'

'Well, that seems to dispose of it, eh? No reason why this fellow shouldn't visit his own brother-in-law.'

'In secret, sir?'

'Have we anything on this Box? Nothing very suspicious about a hyphenated name, I hope?'

'We've nothing very significant, sir,' said the junior officer whose name was Grace-Groundling-Marchpole, each junction of which represented a provident marriage in the age of landed property. 'He went to Salzburg twice, ostensibly for some kind of musical festival. But Crouchback's quite another fish. Until September of last year he lived in Italy and is known to have been on good terms with the Fascist authorities. Don't you think I'd better open a file for him?'

'Yes, perhaps it would be as well.'

'For both, sir?'

'Yes. Pop 'em all in.'

They, too, took down the black-out screens and admitted the dawn.

Thus two new items were added to the Most Secret index, which later was micro-filmed and multiplied and dispersed into a dozen indexes in all the Counter-Espionage Headquarters of the Free World and became a permanent part of the Most Secret archives of the Second World War.

5

The great promised event, 'When the brigade forms', had glowed in Guy's mind, as in the minds of nearly all his companions, for more than five months; a numinous idea. None knew what to expect.

Once Guy saw a film of the Rising of 45. Prince Charles and his intimates stood on a mound of heather, making a sad little group, dressed as though for the Caledonian Ball, looking, indeed, precisely as though they were a party of despairing revellers mustered in the outer suburbs to meet a friend with a motor-car who had not turned up.

An awful moment came when the sun touched the horizon behind them. The Prince bowed his head, sheathed his claymore and said in rich Milwaukee accents: 'I guess it's all off, Mackingtosh.' (Mackingtosh from the first had counselled immediate withdrawal.)

At that moment, suddenly, a faint skirl of pipes rose and swelled to an unendurable volume, while from all the converging glens files of kilted extras came winding into view. ''Tis Invercauld comes younder.' 'Aye and Lochiel', 'And stout Montrose', 'The Laird of Cockpen', 'The bonnets of bonnie Dundee', 'The Campbells are coming. Hurrah, Hurrah ...' until across the crimson panorama the little bands swept together into one mighty army. Unconquerable they seemed to anyone ignorant of history, as they marched into the setting sun; straight, as anyone knowledgeable in Highland geography could have told them, into the chilly waters of Loch Moidart.

Guy had come to expect something almost like that; something at any rate totally different from what did happen.

They reassembled from Easter leave at Penkirk, a lowland valley some twenty miles from Edinburgh, covered in farm land and small homesteads. At its head stood a solid little mid-Victorian Castle. It was there they met and there they messed and slept for the first two days. Their numbers were swollen by many unfamiliar regulars of all ranks, a Medical Officer, an Undenominational Chaplain and a cantankerous, much beribboned veteran who commanded the Pioneers. Still there were only officers. The drafts of men had been postponed until there was accommodation for them.

The Pioneers, it was supposed, had prepared a camp, but on the appointed day nothing was visible above ground. They had been there all the winter cosily established in the Castle stables. Some of them had grown fond of the place, particularly the reservists who made friends in the neighbourhood, sheltered at their hearths during working hours and paid for their hospitality with tools and provisions from the company stores. These veterans were designed to be the stiffening of a force otherwise composed of anti-fascist 'cellists and dealers in abstract painting from the Danubian Basin.

'If they'd given me one section of *fascists*,' said their commander, 'I'd have had the place finished in a week.'

But he did not repine. He had billeted himself in very fair comfort at the Station Hotel three miles distant. He was versed in all the arcana of the Pay Office and drew a multitude of peculiar special allowances. If he liked the new commander he was quite ready to prolong his task until the end of the summer.

Five minutes with Brigadier Ritchie-Hook decided him to make an end and be gone. The veterans were caught and put to bully the anti-fascists. Construction began in earnest but not earnestly enough for Ritchie-Hook. A second Ruskin, on the first morning at Penkirk, he ordered his young officers to dig and carry. Unfortunately he had had them all inoculated the evening before with every virus in the medical store. Noting a lack of enthusiasm he tried to stir up competition between Halberdiers and Pioneers. The musicians responded with temperamental fire; the art-dealers less zealously, but seriously and well; the Halberdiers not at all, for they could barely move.

They dug drains and carried tent-boards (the most awkward burden ever devised by man for man); they unloaded lorryloads of Soyer stoves and zinc water pipes; they ached and staggered and in a few cases fainted. Not until the work was nearly done, did the poisons lose their strength.

For the first two nights they spread their blankets and messed higgledy-piggledy in the Castle. It was Major McKinney's Kut-al-Imara all over again. Then on the third day officers' lines were complete in each battalion area, with a mess tent, a water tap and a field kitchen. They moved out and in. The adjutant procured a case of spirits. The quartermaster improvised a dinner. Colonel Tickeridge stood round after round of drinks and later gave his obscene performance of 'The One-Armed Flautist'. The Second Battalion had found a home and established its identity.

Guy groped his way among the ropes and tent pegs that first evening under canvas, fuddled with gin, fatigue, and germs, to the tent he was sharing with Apthorpe.

Apthorpe, the old campaigner, had defied orders (as, it soon appeared, had done all the regulars) and brought with him a substantial part of his 'gear'. He had left the mess before Guy. He lay now, on a high collapsible bed, in a nest of white muslin illuminated from inside by a patent, incandescent oil lamp, like a great baby in a bassinette, smoking his pipe and reading his Manual of Military Law. A table, a chair, a bath, a wash-hand-stand all collapsible; chests and trunks, very solid, surrounded his roost; also a curious structure like a gallows from which hung his uniforms. Guy gazed, fascinated by this smoky, luminous cocoon.

'I trust I've left you enough room,' said Apthorpe.

'Yes, rather.'

Guy had only a rubber mattress, a storm lantern and a three-legged canvas wash-basin.

'You may think it odd that I prefer to sleep under a net.'

'I expect it's wise to take every precaution.'

'No, no, no. This isn't a *precaution*. It's just that I sleep better.'

Guy undressed, throwing his clothes on his suitcase, and lay down on the floor, between blankets, on his strip of rubber. It was intensely cold. He felt in his bag for a pair of woollen socks and a balaclava helmet knitted for him by one of the ladies at the Marine Hotel, Matchet. He added his great-coat to his mattress.

'Chilly?' asked Apthorpe.

'Yes.'

'It's not really a cold night,' said Apthorpe. 'Far from it. Of course we're some way north of Southsand.'

'Yes.'

'If you'd care to have a rub down with liniment, I can lend you some.'

'Thanks awfully. I shall be all right.'

'You ought to, you know. It makes a lot of difference.'

Guy did not answer.

'Of course this is only a temporary arrangement,' said Apthorpe, 'until the lists are out. Company commanders have tents to themselves. I'd double in with Leonard if I were you. He's about the best of the subalterns. His wife had a baby last week. I should have thought it the kind of thing that would rather spoil one's leave, but he seems quite cheerful about it.'

'Yes. He told me.'

'What you want to avoid in a room-mate is someone who's always trying to borrow one's gear.'

'Yes.'

'Well, I'm turning in now. If you have to get up in the night you'll take care where you walk, won't you? I've got some pretty valuable stuff lying around I haven't found a place for yet.'

He laid his pipe on his table and extinguished his light. Soon, invisible in his netting, embraced in cloud, soothed and wooed and gently overborne like Hera in the arms of Zeus, he was asleep.

Guy turned down his lantern and lay long awake, cold and aching but not discontented.

He was thinking of this strange faculty of the army of putting itself into order. Shake up a colony of ants and for some minutes all seems chaos. The creatures scramble aimlessly, frantically about; then instinct reasserts itself. They find their proper places and proper functions. As ants, so soldiers.

In the years to come he was to see the process at work again and again, sometimes in grim circumstances, sometimes in pleasant domesticity. Men unnaturally removed from wives and family began at once to build substitute homes, to paint and furnish, to make flower-beds and edge them with white-washed pebbles, to stitch cushion-covers on lonely gun-sites.

He thought, too, about Apthorpe.

Apthorpe had been in his proper element during the building operations. When his turn had come to be inoculated that first evening he had insisted on waiting until last and had then given the Medical Officer such an impressive account of the diseases from which he had, from time to time, suffered, of the various inoculations he had undergone and their precise effects, of the warnings he had been given by eminent specialists about the dangers of future inoculations, of idiosyncratic allergies and the like, that the Medical Officer readily agreed to perform a purely ceremonial injection of quite non-injurious matter.

He was thus in full vigour of mind and was usually to be found in consultation with the Pioneer officer giving sage advice about the siting of camp kitchens in relation to the prevailing wind, or pointing out defects in the guy-ropes.

He had taken advantage of the two days mucking-in with the brigade staff to make himself well known to them all. He had discovered an old friendship with a cousin of the brigade major's. He had done very well indeed.

And yet, Guy thought, and yet there was something rum about him; not 'off colour'; far from it; gloriously over-Technicolored like Bonnie Prince Charlie in the film. It was not anything that could be defined. Just a look in the eye; not even that; an aura. But it was distinctly rum.

So fitfully sleeping and thinking he passed the hours until reveille.

6

On the fourth afternoon the last tent went up. Across and down the valley, from the Castle to the main road, lay the battalion lines, the kitchens, stores, mess-tents, latrines. Much was missing, much had been scamped, but it was ready for occupation. On the morrow the men were due to arrive. That evening the officers assembled in the Castle, which for now was the Brigade Headquarters, and the Brigadier addressed them:

'Gentlemen,' he began, 'tomorrow you meet the men you will lead in battle.'

It was the old, potent spell, big magic. Those two phrases, 'the officers who will command you ...', 'the men you will lead ...', set the junior officers precisely in their place, in the heart of the battle. For Guy they set swinging all the chimes of his boyhood's reading ...

'... "I've chosen your squadron for the task, Truslove." "Thank you, sir. What are our chances of getting through?" "It can be done, Truslove, or I shouldn't be sending you. If anyone can do it, you can. And I can tell you this, my boy, I'd give all my seniority and all these bits of ribbon on my chest to be with you. But my duty lies here with the Regiment. Good luck to you, my boy. You'll need it" ...'

The words came back to him from a summer Sunday evening at his preparatory school, in the headmaster's drawing-room, the three top forms sitting about on the floor, some in a dream of home, others – Guy among them – spell-bound.

That was during the First World War but the story came from an earlier chapter of military history. Pathans were Captain Truslove's business. Troy, Agincourt and Zululand were more real to Guy in those days than the world of mud and wire and gas where Gervase fell. Pathans for Truslove; paynims for Sir Robert de Waybroke; for Gervase, Bernard Partridge's flamboyant, guilty Emperor, top-booted, eagle-crowned. For Guy at the age of twelve there were few enemies. They, in their hordes, came later.

The Brigadier continued. It was the first of April, a day which might have provoked him to fun, but he was serious and for once Guy listened with only half his mind. This crowd of officers, many quite strange to him, seemed no longer his proper habitat. In less than forty-eight hours he had made his new, more hallowed home with the Second Battalion and his thoughts were with the men who were coming next day.

The assembly was dismissed and from that moment the Brigadier, who until then had been the dominant personality in their lives, became for the time remote. He lived in his castle with his staff. He came and went, to London, to Edinburgh, to the Training Depot, and no one knew why or when. He became the source of annoying, impersonal orders. 'Brigade says we have to dig slit trenches' ... 'Brigade says only a third of the battalion can be absent from camp at any given time' ...

'More bumf from Brigade' ... That was Ritchie-Hook with his wounds and his escapades; a stupendous warrior shrunk to a mean abstraction – 'Brigade'.

Each battalion went to its lines. There were four oil-stoves in the mess-tent now but the evening chill entered the Second Battalion as they sat on the benches to hear Colonel Tickeridge's list of appointments.

He read slowly: first the headquarters; himself, the second-in-command, the adjutant, all regulars; intelligence-gas-welfare-transport-assistant-adjutant and 'general dogsbody', Sarum-Smith; Headquarter Company; commander, Apthorpe; second-in-command, one of the very young regulars.

This caused a stir of interest. There had been rumours among the temporary officers that one or two of them might be promoted; no one except Apthorpe supposed he might get his own company at this early stage; not even Apthorpe imagined he would be put in command of a regular, however juvenile.

It was a shock, too, to the regulars, who looked at one another askance. A Company had a regular commander and second-in-command, three temporary officers as platoon commanders. B Company followed the same plan. In C Company Leonard was second-in-command. There were now left Guy, two other temporary officers and one of the cockiest young regulars, named Hayter.

'D Company,' said Colonel Tickeridge. 'Commander Major Erskine, who apparently can't be spared at the moment. He ought to be with us in the next few days. Meanwhile the second-in-command, Hayter, will be in command single-handed. Platoon commanders, de Souza, Crouchback and Jervis.'

It was a bitter moment. At no previous stage in his life had Guy expected success. His 'handkerchief' at Downside took him by surprise. When a group of his College suggested he should stand as secretary of the J.C.R. he had at once assumed that his leg was being inoffensively pulled. So it had been throughout his life. The very few, very small distinctions that had come to him had all come as a surprise. But in the Halberdiers he had had a sense of well-doing. There had been repeated hints. He had not expected or desired much but he had looked forward rather confidently to promotion of some kind and he had come to want it simply as a sign that he had, in fact, done well in training and that the occasional words of approbation had not been merely 'the deference due to age'. Well, now he knew. He was not as bad as Trimmer, not quite as bad as Sarum-Smith, whose appointment was contemptible; he had just scraped through without honours. He should have realized, he saw now, that Leonard was obviously the better man. Moreover he was the poorer man and newly a father; Leonard needed the extra pay that would come eventually with his captaincy. Guy felt no resentment; he was a good loser – at any rate an experienced one. He merely felt a deep sinking of spirit such as he had felt in Claridge's with Virginia, such as he had felt times beyond number through all his life. Sir Roger, maybe, had felt thus when he drew his dedicated sword in a local brawl, not foreseeing that one day he would acquire the odd title of 'il Santo Inglese'.

Colonel Tickeridge continued: 'Of course all these appointments are just a try-out. We may have a reshuffle later. But they're the best we can think of at the moment.'

The meeting broke up. The orderly behind the bar busily served pink gins.

'Congratulations, Apthorpe,' said Guy.

'Thanks, old man. I confess I never expected the Headquarter Company. It's twice the size of any other, you know.'

'I'm sure you'll manage it very well.'

'Yes. I may have to sit on my 2IC a bit.'

'On your what, Apthorpe? Is that a new sort of thunder-box?'

'No, no, no. Second-in-command, of course. You really ought to get the correct terms, you know. It's the kind of thing they notice higher up. By the way I think it's bad luck you didn't do better. I heard a buzz that one of our batch was going to be a 2IC. I quite thought that meant you.'

'Leonard's very efficient.'

'Yes. *They* know best, of course. Still I'm sorry it wasn't you. If it's a bore to move your gear immediately, you can use my tent for tonight.'

'Thanks. I will.'

'But get it clear first thing tomorrow, won't you, old man.'

It was so cold in the mess-tent that they dined in great-coats. In accordance with regimental custom, Apthorpe and Leonard stood drinks to all.

Several of the temporary officers said; 'Bad luck, Uncle.' Guy's reverse seemed to have made him more *simpatico*.

Hayter said: 'You're Crouchback, aren't you? Have a drink. Time I got to know my little flock. You won't find me a hard chap to work with, when you're used to my ways. What did you do in the piping days of peace?'

'Nothing.'

'Oh.'

'What's Major Erskine like?'

'Brainy. He's spent a lot of his service in rather special jobs. But you'll get on all right with him if you do what you're told. He won't expect anything much of you new chaps at first.'

'What time do the men arrive tomorrow?'

'The Brig. was shooting rather a line about that. It's only the old sweats who come tomorrow. The National Service chaps won't be here for some days.'

They drank pink gin together and eyed one another without confidence.

'Which are de Souza and Jervis? I ought to have a word with them, too, I suppose.'

That evening when Guy went in for the last time to Apthorpe's tent, he found his host awake and illuminated.

'Crouchback,' he said, 'there's something I have to say to you. I never want to hear another word about that happening at Southsand. Never. Do you understand? Otherwise I shall have to take action.'

'What sort of action, Apthorpe?'

'*Drastic* action.'

Rum. Very rum indeed.

7

Nearly three weeks later there appeared *Army Training Memorandum No. 31 War. April 1940*. A canvas letter rack with a stitched section for every officer was one of the pieces of furniture which, with hired arm-chairs, a wireless set and other amenities, had lately appeared in the mess of the Second Battalion. Returning from an afternoon of 'company schemes', each of them found a copy of the tract protruding from his pouch. General Ironside commended it with the words: '*I direct all commanding officers to ensure that every junior officer is thoroughly examined in the questions set in Part 1 of this Memorandum and not to rest content until the answers are satisfactory.*'

Colonel Tickeridge said: 'You chaps had better take a dekko at the ATM this month. It seems to be important for some reason or other.'

There were one hundred and forty-three questions in the tract.

April 21st; the nine o'clock news announced that General Paget was at Lillehammer and that all was going well in Norway. When the news was over, music began. Guy found an arm-chair as far from the wireless as possible and in an atmosphere in which the scents of trodden grass, gin and roast beef were subdued by paraffin and hot iron, he began to study the '*life and death responsibilities of a sub. unit commander*'.

Many of the questions related either to the regular routine, of which no Halberdier officer could conceivably be negligent, or to abstruse technicalities quite outside his ken.

'I say, have *you* acquired – out of your grant – an old motorcar chassis and engine parts to assist M.T. training?'

'No. How many men in *your* platoon have you earmarked for signallers?'

'None.'

It was like a game of 'Happy Families'.

'Can you tell me why camouflage done late is more dangerous than no camouflage at all?'

'I suppose you might get stuck on the wet paint.'

'Are your men's arrangements for drying their clothes as good as yours?'

'They couldn't possibly be worse.'

'I say, Uncle, have you tested whether your platoon can cook in their mess-tins?'

'Yes. We did it last week.'

'What are the advantages during training of beginning night operations an hour before dawn?'

'They can only last an hour, I suppose.'

'No, seriously.'

'It seems a great advantage to me.'

The camp seemed to whisper and chatter with the questionnaire like Apthorpe's home-jungle at sundown.

Guy dreamily turned the pages. It was all rather like the advertisement of a correspondence course in Business Efficiency. 'How to catch the boss's eye in five lessons.' 'Why didn't *I* get promoted?' ... But a question here and there set him thinking about the last three weeks.

Are you trying to make yourself competent to take over the job of the next senior man to you?

Guy had no respect for Hayter. He was confident he could now do his job much better than Hayter. Moreover, he had lately learned that when he did take over another job, it would not be Hayter's.

Major Erskine had arrived on the same day as the National Service men. His 'braininess' was not oppressive. The imputation derived chiefly from the facts that he read Mr J. B. Priestley's novels, and was strangely dishevelled in appearance. His uniform was correct and clean but it never seemed to fit him, not through any fault of the tailor's, but rather because the major seemed to change shape from time to time during the day. One moment his tunic seemed too long, the next, too short. His pockets were too full. His anklets got twisted. He was more like a Sapper than a Halberdier. But he and Guy got on well together. Major Erskine did not talk much, but when he did it was with great simplicity and frankness.

One evening when Hayter had been more cocky than usual, Major Erskine and Guy walked back together from the company lines to the mess.

'That little tick wants his bottom kicked,' said Major Erskine. 'I think I *shall* kick it. Good for him and pleasant for me.'

'Yes. I can see that.'

Major Erskine then said: 'I shouldn't talk to you like that about your superior officer. Did anyone ever tell you why you're only commanding a platoon, Uncle?'

'No. I didn't think any explanation necessary.'

'They ought to have. You see, you were down for a company. Then the Brig. said he wouldn't have anyone commanding a *fighting* company who hadn't had a platoon first. I see his point. Headquarters is different. Old Uncle Apthorpe will stay there until he becomes GSO2(Q) or something wet like that. None of the temporary officers who've started high will ever get a rifle company. You will, before we go into action, unless you blot your copy-book in a pretty sensational way. I thought I'd tell you, in case you felt depressed about it.'

'I did rather.'

'Yes, I thought as much.'

Who runs the platoon – you or your platoon sergeant?

Guy's platoon sergeant was named Soames. Neither found the other *simpatico*. The normal relationship in the Halberdiers between platoon commander and sergeant was that of child and nannie. The sergeant should keep his officer out of mischief. The officer's job was to sign things, to take the blame and quite simply to walk ahead and get shot first. And, as an officer, he should have a certain intangibility belonging, as in old-fashioned households, to the further side of the baize-doors. All this was disordered in the relationship of Guy and Sergeant Soames. Soames reverenced officers in a more modern way, as men who had been sharp and got ahead; moreover he distinguished between regulars and temporaries. He regarded Guy as a nannie might some child, not of 'the family' but of inferior and suspicious origin, suddenly, by a whim of the mistress of the house, dumped, as a guest of indefinite duration, in her nursery. Moreover he was far too young, and Guy far too old, for him to be a nannie at all. Soames had signed on for long service in 1937. He had been a corporal for three months when the declaration of war and the formation of the brigade had precociously exalted him. He often bluffed and was exposed. Guy ran the platoon, but not in easy cooperation. Sergeant Soames wore his moustache in a gangster's cut. There was a great deal in him that reminded Guy of Trimmer.

How many men have you earmarked in your mind as possible candidates for a commission?

One. Sergeant Soames. Guy had done more than earmark him in his mind. He had presented a slip of paper bearing Sergeant Soames's name, number and history, to Major Erskine at the Company Office some days ago.

Major Erskine had said: 'Yes. I can't blame you. I have this morning sent in Hayter's name as an officer suitable for special training in Air Liaison, whatever Air Liaison may be. I expect it means he will be a full colonel in a year. Now you want to make Soames an officer just because *he's* a nasty bit of work. Jolly sort of army we're going to have in two years time when all the shits have got to the top.'

'But Soames won't come back to the Corps if he's commissioned.'

'That's exactly why I'm sending his name up. The same with Hayter, if he gets through his course on whatever it is.'

How many of your men do you know by name and what do you know of their characters?

Guy knew every name. The difficulty was to identify them. Each had three faces: an inhuman and rather hostile mask when he stood at attention; a vivacious and variable expression, mostly clownish, sometimes furious, sometimes heartsore, as he saw the men amongst themselves off duty or at stand-easies, going to the N.A.A.F.I. or arguing in the company lines; and thirdly a guarded but on the whole amiable grin when he spoke to them personally at these times or at stand-easies. Most English gentlemen at this time believed that they had a particular aptitude for endearing themselves to the lower classes. Guy was not troubled by this illusion, but he believed he was rather liked by these particular thirty men. He did not greatly care. He liked them. He wished them well. He did well by them so far as his limited knowledge of 'the ropes' allowed. He was perfectly ready, should need arise, to sacrifice himself for them – throw himself on a grenade, give away the last drop of water – anything like that. But he did not distinguish between them as human beings, any more or less than he did between his brother officers; he preferred Major Erskine to the young man, Jervis, with whom he shared a tent; he nursed a respect and slight suspicion for de Souza. For his platoon and company and battalion and for all Halberdiers everywhere he had a warmer sentiment than for anyone outside his family. It was not much but it was something to thank God for.

And at the very opening of this heterogeneous catechism stood the question that was quintessential to his very presence among those unchosen companions.

What are we fighting for?

The Training Memorandum mentioned with shame that many private soldiers had been found to entertain hazy ideas on the subject. Could Box-Bender have given a clear answer? Guy wondered. Could Ritchie-Hook? Had he any idea what all this biffing was for? Had General Ironside himself?

Guy believed he knew something of this matter that was hidden from the mighty.

England had declared war to defend the independence of Poland. Now that country had quite disappeared and the two strongest states in the world guaranteed her extinction. Now General Paget was at Lillehammer and it was announced that all was going well. Guy knew things were going badly. They had no well-informed friends, here in Penkirk, they had access to no intelligence files, but the smell of failure had been borne to them from Norway on the east wind.

But Guy's spirit was as high as on the day he had bade farewell to St Roger.

He was a good loser, but he did not believe his country would lose this war; each apparent defeat seemed strangely to sustain it. There was in romance great virtue in unequal odds. There were in morals two requisites for a lawful war, a just cause and the chance of victory. The cause was now, past all question, just. The enemy was exorbitant. His actions in Austria and Bohemia had been defensible. There was even a shadow of plausibility in his quarrel with Poland. But now, however victorious, he was an outlaw. And the more victorious he was the more he drew to himself the enmity of the world and the punishment of God.

Guy thought of this as he lay in his tent that night. He clasped Gervase's medal as he said his night prayers. And, just before sleep, came a personal comforting thought. However inconvenient it was for the Scandinavians to have Germans there, it was very nice for the Halberdiers. They had been assigned their special role of Hazardous Offensive Operations, but until last month there seemed little opportunity for playing it. Now a whole new coastline was open for biffing.

8

On the day that Mr Churchill became Prime Minister, Apthorpe was promoted Captain.

He had been forewarned by the adjutant and his servant was standing by in the Headquarter Company's office. As the first note of Battalion orders sounded from the orderly-room – before the cyclostyled sheets announcing the appointment had been collected, much less distributed – Apthorpe's pips were up. The rest of the forenoon passed in solemn ecstasy. He sauntered round the transport lines, called on the medical officer, ostensibly to inquire about a tonic he thought he needed, he flushed the quartermaster drinking tea in his store, but no one seemed to notice the new constellation. He was content to bide.

At midday the companies could be heard marching into camp from their training areas and dismissing. Apthorpe was waiting serenely in the mess-tent to welcome his brother officers.

'Ah, Crouchback, what can I offer you to drink?'

Guy was surprised, for Apthorpe had almost ceased to speak to him in the last few weeks.

'Oh, that's very nice of you. I've marched miles this morning. Can I have a glass of beer?'

'And you Jervis? de Souza?'

This was more surprising still, since Apthorpe had never at any stage of incubation spoken to de Souza or Jervis.

'Hayter, old man, what's yours?'

Hayter said: 'What's this? A birthday?'

'I understand it's usual in the Halberdiers to stand drinks on these occasions.'

'What occasions?'

It was unfortunate that he had chosen Hayter. Hayter thought nothing of temporary officers and was himself still a lieutenant.

'Good God,' said Hayter. 'You don't mean to say they've made you a captain?'

'With effect from April 1st,' said Apthorpe with dignity.

'Quite a suitable date. Still I don't mind taking a pink gin off you.'

There were moments, as in the gym barracks, when Apthorpe rose above the ridiculous. This was one of them.

'Give these young officers what they require, Crock,' he said and royally turned to new arrivals at the bar: 'Draw up, Adj. Drinks are on me. Colonel, I hope you'll join us.'

The mess-tent was filled for luncheon. Apthorpe dispensed hospitality. No one but Hayter much grudged him his elevation.

There was less interest in the change of Prime Ministers. Politics were considered an unsoldierly topic among the Halberdiers. There had been some rejoicing and dispute at Mr Hore-Belisha's fall in the winter. Since then Guy had not heard a politician's name mentioned. Some of Mr Churchill's broadcasts had been played on the mess wireless-set. Guy had found them painfully boastful and they had, most of them, been immediately followed by the news of some disaster, as though in retribution from the God of Kipling's *Recessional*.

Guy knew of Mr Churchill only as a professional politician, a master of sham-Augustan prose, a Zionist, an advocate of the Popular Front in Europe, an associate of the press-lords and of Lloyd George. He was asked:

'Uncle, what sort of fellow is this Winston Churchill?'

'Like Hore-Belisha except that for some reason his hats are thought to be funny.'

'Well, I suppose they had to make someone carry the can after the balls-up in Norway.'

'Yes.'

'He can't be much worse than the other fellow?'

'Better, if anything.'

Here Major Erskine leant across the table.

'Churchill is about the only man who may save us from losing this war,' he said.

It was the first time that Guy had heard a Halberdier suggest that any result, other than complete victory, was possible. They had had a lecture, it is true, from an officer lately returned from Norway, who had spoken frankly about the incompetent loading of ships, the disconcerting effect of dive-bombing, the activities of organized traitors and such matters. He had even hinted at the inferior fighting qualities of British troops. But he had made little impression. Halberdiers always assumed that 'the Staff' and 'the Q side' were useless, that all other regiments were scarcely worthy of the name of soldier, that foreigners let one down. Naturally things were going badly in the absence of the Halberdiers. No one thought of losing the war.

Apthorpe's promotion was a matter of more immediate interest.

Brigadier Ritchie-Hook could disappear behind his Victorian battlements, and lose his personality. Not so Apthorpe. That afternoon, the day of his promotion, Guy happened to pass him on the battalion parade ground and with one of those pathetic spasms of fourth-form fun that came easily in military life, Guy solemnly saluted him. Apthorpe as solemnly returned the attention. He was a little unsteady on his pins after the morning's celebrations, his face was oddly grave, but the incident passed off cheerfully.

Later that evening, just before dark, they met again. Apthorpe had evidently stuck close to the bottle, and was now in the state he called 'merry' – a state recognizable by his air of preternatural solemnity. As he approached, Guy with amazement saw him go through all the motions they used to practise in barracks before passing a senior officer. He put his stick under his left arm, he swung his right with exaggerated zest and he fixed his glassy eyes straight before him. Guy walked on with a genial 'Evening, Captain' and too late noticed that Apthorpe's hand was shoulder high, in the rudimentary stage of a salute. The hand fell, the eyes fixed themselves far ahead on the other side of the valley and Apthorpe passed, stumbling over a night bucket.

Somehow the memory of Guy's first, jocular salute had fixed itself indelibly in Apthorpe's mind; it survived his evening's merriment. Next day he was out of the clouds, slightly disturbed internally, but with a new *idée fixe*.

Before the first parade he said to Guy: 'I say, old man, I'd greatly appreciate it if you'd salute me when we pass one another in the camp area.'

'What on earth for?'

'Well, I salute Major Trench.'

'Of course you do.'

'The difference between him and me is only the same as between you and me if you see what I mean.'

'My dear fellow, it was all explained to us when we first joined, whom we saluted and when.'

'Yes, but don't you see that I am an exceptional case. There is no precedent for *me* in regimental customs. We all started equal not so long ago. I happen to have forged ahead a bit so naturally I have to do more to assert my authority than if I had years of seniority. Please, Crouchback, salute me. I am asking you as a friend.'

'I'm sorry, Apthorpe, I simply can't. I should feel such an ass.'

'Well, anyway, you might tell the other chaps.'

'You really mean that? You've thought the matter out?'

'I've thought of nothing else.'

'All right, Apthorpe, I'll tell them.'

'I can't order them, of course. Just say it is my wish.'

Apthorpe's 'wish' became quickly known and for some days he suffered a concerted persecution. He could always be seen approaching yards off, tensely self-conscious preparing for he knew not what. Sometimes his junior officers would salute him with unsmiling correctness; sometimes they would stroll past ignoring him; sometimes they would give a little flick of the cap and say: 'Hello, Uncle.'

The cruellest technique was devised by de Souza. On sighting Apthorpe he would put his stick under his left arm and march at attention gazing straight into Apthorpe's eyes with an expression of awe. Then two paces away he would suddenly relax, switch negligently at a weed, or on one occasion, drop suddenly on one knee and, still fixing the captain with his worshipping stare, fiddle with a bootlace.

'You know you'll drive that unhappy man stark mad,' said Guy to him.

'I think I shall, Uncle; I honestly think I shall.'

The fun came to an end one evening when Colonel Tickeridge summoned Guy to the orderly room.

'Sit down, Guy. I want to speak to you unofficially. I'm getting worried about Apthorpe. Frankly, is he quite right in the head?'

'He has his peculiarities, Colonel. I don't think he's likely to do anything dangerous.'

'I hope you're right. I'm getting the most extraordinary report of him from all sides.'

'He had a rather nasty accident the morning we left Southsand.'

'Yes, I heard about it. Surely that could not have affected his *head*? Let me tell you his latest. He's just formed up and asked me to put it in orders that the junior officers should salute him. That's not quite normal you'll admit.'

'No, Colonel.'

'Either that, he says, or will I put it in orders that you're *not* to salute him. That's not normal either. What exactly has been going on?'

'Well, I think he's been ragged a bit.'

'I'm bloody sure he has and it's gone far enough. Just pass it round that it's got to stop. You may find yourself in his shoes before long. Then you'll find you have plenty on your hands without being ragged by a lot of young asses.'

This happened, though the news did not reach Penkirk for some time, on the day when the Germans crossed the Meuse.

9

Guy passed the colonel's order round the mess and the affair, which de Souza preciously dubbed 'The Matter of the Captain's Salutation', came to an abrupt end. But in other ways, too, Apthorpe had been showing marked abnormality.

There was the question of the Castle. From the first day of his appointment, while still a lieutenant, Apthorpe took to dropping in there two or three times a week without ostensible cause, at the eleven-o'clock break, when tea was drunk in various ante-rooms and dens. Apthorpe would join the staff-captain and his peers and they, supposing he was on an errand from his battalion, entertained him. In this way he heard much 'shop' and was often able to surprise the adjutant with prior information on matters of minor policy. When tea was over and the staff went back to their rooms Apthorpe would saunter into the chief clerk's room and say: 'Anything special today about the Second Battalion, Staff?' After the third of these visits the sergeant clerk reported to the brigade major and asked whether these inquiries were authorized. The result was an order reminding all officers that they must not approach Brigade Headquarters except through the proper channels.

When this was posted Apthorpe said to the adjutant: 'I take this to mean that they come to me for permission?'

'For Christ's sake, why to *you*?'

'Well, after all I *am* the Headquarters commander here, am I not?'

'Apthorpe, are you tight?'

'Certainly not.'

'Well, come and see the C.O. about this. He can explain it better than I.'

'Yes, I suppose it *is* rather a nice point.'

It was not often that Colonel Tickeridge 'went off the handle'. That morning the whole camp heard the roars in his orderly room. But Apthorpe emerged as bland as ever.

'My God, Uncle, that was a rocket. We could hear it on the parade ground. What was it about?'

'Just a bit of red tape, old man.'

Since the loss of his thunder-box Apthorpe was impervious to shock.

The army was not then troubled, as it was later, by psychiatrists. Had it been, Apthorpe would no doubt have been lost to the Halberdiers. He remained – to the great comfort of his fellows.

Apthorpe's wildest aberration was his one-man war with the Royal Corps of Signals. This campaign was his predominant obsession during all his difficult days at Penkirk and from it he emerged with the honours of war.

It began by a simple misunderstanding.

Studying his duties by the light of his incandescent lamp, Apthorpe learned that the regimental signallers of his battalion came under his command for administrative purposes.

From the first this statement bulked over-large in Apthorpe's imagination. It was plain to him that this was where he joined, indeed controlled, the battle. There were ten of these signallers on the fateful 1st of April, volunteers for what they had supposed was a light duty, little trained, equipped with nothing but flags. Apthorpe was a man of certain odd accomplishments, among them a mastery of Morse. Accordingly for several days he made these men his special care and spent many chilly hours wagging a flag at them.

Then brigade signals arrived under their own officer, laden with radio telegraphy sets. These were men of the Royal Corps of Signals. By chance they were allotted lines next to the Second Battalion. Their officer was invited to mess with the battalion, rather than at the Castle a mile distant; their quartermaster was instructed to draw rations from the Second Battalion quartermaster. They thus became accidentally, but quite closely, associated with the battalion.

The situation was clear enough to all except Apthorpe, who conceived that they were under his personal command. He was still a lieutenant at this time. The Signals Officer was also a lieutenant, much younger than Apthorpe and younger than his age in looks. His name was Dunn. On his first appearance in the mess Apthorpe took him in charge, introducing him with courtly patronage as 'my latest subaltern'. Dunn did not quite know what to make of this, but since it involved many free drinks and since he was by nature shy to the point of gaucherie, he submitted cheerfully.

Next morning Apthorpe sent an orderly to the brigade signallers' lines.

'Mr Apthorpe's compliments and will Mr Dunn kindly report when his lines are ready for inspection.'

'What inspection? Is the Brigadier coming round? No one told me.'

'No, sir, Mr Apthorpe's inspection.'

Dunn was a shy man but this was too much for him.

'Tell Mr Apthorpe that when I have finished inspecting my own lines I shall be quite ready to come and inspect Mr Apthorpe's head.'

The Halberdier, a regular, showed no emotion. 'Could I have that message in writing, please, sir?'

'No. On second thoughts I'll see his adjutant.'

This first skirmish was treated lightly and unofficially.

'Don't be an ass, Uncle.'

'But, Adj. it's in my establishment. *Signallers.*'

'Battalion signals, Uncle. Not brigade signals.' Then, speaking as he supposed Apthorpe spoke to his men in Africa: 'No savvy? These boys, Royal Corps of Signals boys. Your boys, Halberdier boys. Damn it, d'you want me to draw you the badges?'

But the adjutant, in his haste, had made things too simple, for in fact the battalion signallers, though Halberdiers for all purposes except signalling, came under the Brigade Signals Officer for training. This fact, Apthorpe could not or would not, and certainly never did, grasp. Whenever Dunn ordered a training exercise, Apthorpe devised camp duties for all his signal section. He did more. He paraded his Halberdiers and told them they were never to accept orders from anyone but himself. The matter was moving up to an official level.

Apthorpe's case, though untenable, was strengthened by the fact that no one liked Dunn. When he formed up at the Second Battalion Orderly Room, the adjutant told him coldly that he was merely a guest in their mess and that for all official purposes he was at the Castle. Any complaints against his hosts should be addressed to the brigade major. Dunn tramped to the Castle and was told by the brigade major to settle the thing sensibly with Colonel Tickeridge. Colonel Tickeridge duly told Apthorpe that his men must work with brigade signals. Apthorpe immediately sent them all away on urgent compassionate leave. Back to the Castle went Dunn, all shyness shed. The Brigadier was then absent on one of his trips to London. The brigade major was the busiest man in Scotland. He said he would raise the matter at the next Battalion Commanders' Conference.

Apthorpe, meanwhile, withdrew his friendship from Dunn, and refused to speak to him. This quarrel in high places quickly spread to the men. There were hard words in the N.A.A.F.I. and between lines. Dunn put six Halber-diers on a charge of prejudicial conduct. In the orderly room they drew on the limitless pool of fellow Halberdiers who were always ready to give false witness in defence of the Corps, and Colonel Tickeridge dismissed the case.

So far it had been a feud of a normal military kind, differing from others only in the fact that Apthorpe had no case at all. In the middle of it he got his captaincy. In Apthorpe's story that event corresponds to Alexander's visit to Siwa. It was an illumination that changed all the colours and shapes about him. Fiends like de Souza lurked in black shadow, but a shining path led upward to the conquest of Dunn.

On the afternoon following the day of his promotion he proceeded to inspect the signallers' lines. Dunn found him there and stood momentarily confounded by what he saw.

It was Apthorpe's old interest, boots. He had found one that was in need of repair, and there he stood in the centre of a curious circle of signalmen, carefully dismembering it with a clasp knife.

'Apart from the quality of the leather,' he was saying, 'this boot is a disgrace to the Service. Look at the stitching. Look how the tongue has been fitted. Look at the construction of the eyeholes. Now in a well-made boot' . . . and he raised his foot placing it where all might admire it, on the nearby gas-detector.

'What the devil are you doing?' asked Dunn.

'Mr Dunn, I think you forget you are addressing a superior officer.'

'What are you doing in my lines?'

'I am verifying my suspicion that your boots are in need of attention.'

Dunn realized that for the moment he was beaten. Nothing short of physical violence would suit the occasion and that way lay endless disasters.

'We can discuss that later. At the moment they ought to be on parade.'

'You mustn't blame your sergeant. He reminded me of that fact more than once. It was I detained them.'

The two officers separated, Dunn to the Castle to lay his case before the brigade major, Apthorpe with a much stranger purpose. He sat down in his company office and penned a challenge to Dunn to meet him, armed with a heliograph, before their men, for a Trial by Combat in proficiency in Morse.

The Brigadier was at the Castle. He had just returned from London on the night train, hag-ridden by the news from France.

The brigade major said: 'I am afraid I've a serious disciplinary problem for you, sir. It will probably involve an Officer's Court Martial.'

'Yes,' said the Brigadier, 'yes.' He was gazing out of the window. His mind was far away, still trying to comprehend the unspeakable truths he had learned in London.

'An officer of the Second Battalion,' continued the brigade major, in rather louder tones, 'has been accused of entering Brigade Headquarters' lines and deliberately destroying the men's boots.'

'Yes,' said the Brigadier. 'Drunk?'

'Sober, sir.'

'Any excuse?'

'He considered the workmanship defective, sir.'

'Yes.'

The Brigadier stared out of the window. The brigade major gave a lucid account of the Dunn-Apthorpe campaign. Presently the Brigadier said:

'Were the boots good enough to run away in?'

'I haven't asked about that yet. It will no doubt come out when the Summary of Evidence is taken.'

'If they're good enough to run away in, they're good enough for our army. Damn it, if they lost their boots, they might have to meet the enemy. It's, as you say, a very serious matter.'

'Then shall I carry on with the preliminaries of a court martial, sir?'

'No. We've no time for that. Do you realize that the whole of our army and the French are on the run leaving everything behind them, half of them without firing a shot? Make these young idiots work together. Lay on a Brigade Exercise for the signallers. Let's see if they can work their instruments with or without boots. That's all that matters.'

So two days later, after feverish work at the Castle and in the orderly rooms, the Halberdier Brigade marched out into the dripping Midlothian countryside.

That day was memorable for Guy as the most futile he had yet spent in the army. His platoon lay on a rain-swept hillside doing absolutely nothing. They were quite near one of the brigade signalling posts and from it there rose from dawn to noon a monotonous, liturgical incantation: ... 'Hullo Nan, Hullo Nan. Report my signals. Over Hullo Nan, Hullo Nan. Are you hearing me. Over. Hullo King, Hullo King. Are you hearing me. Over. Hullo Nan. Hullo King. Nothing heard. Out. Hullo Able. Hullo Able. Am hearing you strength one, interference five. Out. Hullo all stations. Able. Baker. Charlie. Dog. Easy. Fox. Are you hearing me. Over ...' Throughout the chill forenoon the prayer rose to the disdainful gods.

The men rolled themselves in their anti-gas capes and ate their sodden rations. At length, walking very slowly, a signalman appeared out of the haze. He was greeted derisively by the platoon. He approached the signal station and from the depths of his clothing produced a damp piece of paper. The corporal brought it to Guy. '*Able Dog Yoke,*' it read. '*Close down R T stop signals will be by runner stop ack.*'

Another two hours passed. Then a 'runner' stumbled up the hill with a message for Guy. '*From OC D Coy to OC 2 pl. Exercise terminated. Rally forthwith road junction 643202.*' Guy saw no reason to inform the signallers. He fell in the platoon and marched off, leaving them quite alone where they had been lying.

'Well,' said Colonel Tickeridge in the mess, 'I've written my report on today's nonsense. I have recommended that brigade signals go away and get trained.'

It was generally recognized as being a personal success for Apthorpe. There had been a general attempt to be pleasant to him in the last two days since ragging had ceased. That evening he was the centre of hospitality. Next morning two commandeered civilian buses arrived near the Second Battalion lines. The signallers piled in and drove away.

'Brigade really showed some pace for once,' said de Souza.

The Halberdiers congratulated themselves on a triumph.

But the departure of the signalmen had been ordered the day before, far away in London, while at Penkirk they were first erecting their aerials into the rain, and for a reason quite unconnected with the failure of their apparatus.

Had they known it, the Halberdiers would have been even more jubilant. This was, for them, the start of the war.

10

This was Friday; pay day. Every Friday after Pay Parade Major Erskine lectured his company on the progress of the war. Lately there had been much detail of 'dents' and 'bulges' in the Allied line, of 'armour breaking through and fanning out', of 'pincers' and 'pockets'. The exposition was lucid and grave but most men's thoughts were on the week-end leave which began when he ceased speaking.

This Friday was different. An hour after the signalmen left an order was issued cancelling all leave and Major Erskine had an attentive and resentful audience. He said:

'I am sorry that your leave has been cancelled. This is not an order that applies only to us. All leave has been stopped throughout the Home Forces. You may form your own conclusion that there is a state of unusual danger. This morning, as you know, the brigade signallers were withdrawn. Some of you may think this was a consequence of yesterday's unsuccessful exercise. It was not. This afternoon we shall lose all our transport and carriers. The reason is this. We are not, as you know, fully equipped or trained. All specialists and all equipment is needed at once in France. That may give you some further idea of the seriousness of the situation there.'

He continued with his customary explanation of dents and bulges and of armour breaking through and fanning out. For the first time these things seemed to his hearers to have become a force in their own lives.

That evening a report, emanating from the clerks, filled the camp that the brigade was going immediately to the Orkneys. The Brigadier was known to be back in London and the Castle to be surrounded by cars from the Scottish Command.

Next day Guy's servant called him with the words: 'Sounds like I shan't be doing this many more days, sir.'

Halberdier Glass was a regular soldier. Most of the conscripts had been shy of volunteering as batmen, holding that 'that wasn't what they'd joined the bloody army for'. Old soldiers knew that menial duties brought numerous comforts and privileges, and competed for the job. Halberdier Glass was a surly man who liked to call his master with bad news. 'Two of our platoon overstayed their leave this morning'; 'Major Trench made a visit to the lines last night. Went on something awful about the bread in the swill tubs'; 'Corporal Hill shot himself just down by the bridge. They're bringing the body in now'; some small titbit of gossip of the kind calculated to make Guy start the day in low spirits. But this announcement was more serious.

'What d'you mean, Glass?'

'Well, that's the buzz, sir. Jackson got it in the sergeants' mess last night.'

'What's happening?'

'All regulars standing by to move, sir. Nothing said about the National Service men.'

When Guy reached the mess-tent everyone was talking about this rumour. Guy asked Major Erskine: 'Is there anything in it, sir?'

Major Erskine answered: 'You'll hear soon enough. The C.O. wants all officers in here at eight-thirty.'

The men were set to Physical Training and fatigue duties under their non-commissioned officers and the officers duly assembled. In every Halberdier battalion at that moment the Commanding Officers were breaking bad news, each in his way. Colonel Tickeridge said:

'What I have to say is most unpleasant for most of you. In an hour's time I shall be telling the men. It is all the harder for me to tell you because, for myself, I cannot help being glad. I had hoped we should have gone into action together. That is what we have all been working for. I think we should have given a good account of ourselves. But you know as well as I do that we aren't ready. Things are pretty sticky in France, stickier than most of you realize. Fully trained reinforcements are needed at once to make a decisive counter-attack. It has therefore been decided to send a regular battalion of Halberdiers to France *now*. I expect you can guess who will lead us. The Brigadier has been in London two days and has persuaded them to let him go down a step and command a battalion. I am very proud to say he's picked me to go down a step too and join him as second-in-command. We are taking most of the regular officers and other ranks now in camp. Those of you who are being left behind will naturally want to know what is to become of you. That, I am afraid, I can't answer. You realize, of course, that you will be enormously weakened, particularly in senior NCOs. You also realize that for the moment at any rate the brigade ceases to exist as a separate formation with a special role. It's just one of those things you have to accept in army life. You may be sure that the Captain-Commandant will do all he can to see that you keep your identity as Halberdiers and don't get pushed about too much. But at a time of national danger even regimental tradition has to go by the board. If I knew what was going to happen to you, I'd tell you. I hope we all join up together one day. Don't count on it or feel a grievance if you find yourselves attached elsewhere. Just show the Halberdier spirit wherever you are. Your duty now, as always, is to your men. Don't let their *morale* drop. Get some football going. Organize concerts and housey-housey. All ranks are confined to camp until further notice.'

The temporary officers left the tent, went out into the brilliant sunshine, in deep gloom.

Apthorpe's comment was: 'Wheels within wheels, old man. It's all the work of these signallers.'

Later the battalion paraded. Colonel (now Major) Tickeridge made much the same speech as he had made to the officers, but that simple man contrived to give a slightly different impression. They would all join up together again soon, he seemed to say; the Expeditionary Battalion was merely an advance party. They would all be united for the final biff.

In these conditions Guy at last got command of a company.

Chaos prevailed. The order was always to stand by for orders. The regulars who were leaving attended the medical officers for final examination. Venerable figures emerged from their places of concealment, were pronounced unfit, and sent back to store. The conscripts played football and under the chaplain's aegis sang '*We'll hang out the washing on the Siegfried Line*'.

In order, it was supposed, to avoid confusion, the remaining battalions were named X and Y. Guy sat in a tent in X Battalion lines attended by a sergeant major with fallen arches. All through the afternoon he received requests for week-end leave on urgent compassionate grounds from men whom neither he nor his decrepit assistant had ever seen before. 'My wife's expecting, sir', 'My brother's on embarkation leave, sir', 'Trouble at home, sir', 'My mother's been evacuated, sir'.

'We know nothing about them, sir,' said the sergeant major.

'If you give in to one you'll only have trouble.'

Guy miserably refused them all.

It was his first experience of that common military situation, 'a general flap'.

Not until 'Retreat' had been sounded, did a move-order arrive for the Expeditionary Battalion.

At reveille that Sunday morning X and Y Battalions turned out to see the battalion off. The call for breakfast sounded and they dispersed. At length a fleet of buses appeared up the valley. The battalion embussed. The remnants of the brigade cheered as they left and then turned back to the part-deserted camp and an empty day.

Chaos remained, without animation. Guy's commander in X Battalion was a major whom he did not know. At this season of prodigies Apthorpe emerged as second-in-command of Y Battalion with Sarum-Smith as his adjutant.

The week-end yawned before them.

On Sunday mornings at Penkirk a priest came out from the town and said mass at the Castle. He came that Sunday too, untroubled by the 'flap', and for three-quarters of an hour all was peace.

When Guy returned he was asked: 'You didn't by any chance pick up any orders at the Castle?'

'Not a word. Everything seemed dead quiet.'

'I expect everyone has forgotten about us. The best thing would be to send everyone on long leave.'

The company office, all company offices, were besieged with applications for leave. The remnant who were, for want of another name, still called 'Brigade Headquarters' were standing by for orders.

Rumours spread everywhere that they were to return to the Barracks and the Depot; that they were to be broken up and sent to Infantry Training Centres; that they were to be brigaded with a Highland regiment and sent to guard the docks; that they were to be transformed into Anti-Aircraft units. The men kicked footballs about and played mouth-organs. Not for the first time Guy was awed by their huge patience.

Halberdier Glass, who, despite his prognostications, had contrived to remain with Guy, reported these 'buzzes' to him at intervals throughout the day.

At last, late at night, orders were issued.

They were preposterous.

An enemy landing by parachute was imminent in the neighbourhood of Penkirk. All ranks were confined to camp. Each battalion was to keep a company, night and day, in immediate readiness to repel the attack. These would sleep in their boots, their rifles beside them with charged magazines; they would stand to at dusk, at dawn and once during the night. Guards were doubled. A platoon would ceaselessly patrol the perimeter of the camp. Other platoons would stop all traffic, day and night, on all roads within a five-mile radius and examine civilian identity cards. All officers would carry loaded revolvers, anti-gas capes, steel helmets and maps at all hours.

'I have *not* received these orders,' said the unknown major, giving his first, indeed his only, hint of character. 'I'll have them brought with my tea tomorrow morning. If Germans land tonight they will have no opposition from X Battalion. That, I think, is called the Nelson touch.'

Monday passed in the defence of Penkirk and two cowmen were arrested whose strong Scottish accents gave colour to the suspicion that they were conversing in German.

It was fine parachuting weather. The storm had quite passed and pre-mature summer bathed the valley. On Monday night Guy's company was on emergency duty. He had an outlying patrol on the hill above the camp which he visited at midnight. Later he sat gazing into the stars, with the men bivouacked round him. The regular battalion was probably in France, by now, he reflected; perhaps in the battle. Halberdier Glass had it for certain that they were in Boulogne. Suddenly from below came the sound of bugles and whistles. The platoon doubled back and found the whole camp astir. Apthorpe had distinctly seen a parachute land a few fields distant. Patrols, pickets and duty-companies rushed to the scene. Two or three rounds were waywardly fired.

'They always bury their parachutes,' said Apthorpe. 'Look for newly dug ground.'

All night they trampled down the young wheat until at reveille they handed over the duty to their reliefs. Several busloads of kilted soldiers had meanwhile arrived from a neighbouring camp. These were seasoned men who were sceptical of Apthorpe's vision. An indignant farmer spent most of the morning at the Castle computing the damage done him.

On Wednesday a move-order arrived. X and Y Battalions were to stand by at two hours' notice. Late that evening buses again appeared. There was no 'unconsumed portion of the day's ration' to encumber them. Halberdier Glass reported that the whole brigade staff were moving too.

'Iceland,' he said; 'that's where we're off to. I got it straight from the Castle.'

Guy asked his Commanding Officer where they were going.

'Aldershot Area. No information about what happens when we get there. What does it sound like to you?'

'Nothing.'

'It doesn't sound like a Halberdier establishment, does it? If you want to know what I think it sounds like, it sounds like Infantry Training Centres. I don't suppose *they* sound like anything to you?'

'Not much.'

'They sound like hell on earth to me. You fellows have had a raw deal. You've been in the Halberdiers, you've lived with us and been one of us. Now you'll probably find yourself in the Beds and Herts or the Black Watch. But you've only had six months of us. Look at me. God knows when I shall get back to the Corps, and it's been my whole life. All the fellows I entered with are at Boulogne now. D'you know why I'm left behind? One bad mark, my second year as a subaltern. That's the army all over. One bad mark follows you wherever you go till you die.'

'The battalion is definitely in Boulogne, sir?' asked Guy, anxious to stem these confidences.

'Definitely. And there's the hell of a fight going on there now, from all I hear.'

They were driven to Edinburgh and put into a lightless train. Guy shared a compartment with a subaltern he hardly knew. Almost at once the fatigue of the last days overcame him. He slept long and heavily, not waking until another brilliant day was creeping through the blackout. He raised a blind. They were still in Edinburgh station.

There was no water on that train and all the doors were locked. But Halberdier Glass appeared, mysteriously provided with a jug of shaving water and a cup of tea, carried Guy's belt into the corridor and began polishing. Presently they started and very slowly jolted their way south.

At Crewe the train stopped for an hour. Base little men with bands on their arms trotted about the platform bearing lists. Then a hand-wagon from Movement Control deposited a tank of warm cocoa in each coach, some tins of bully beef and a number of cardboard packets of sliced bread.

The journey continued. Guy could hear mouth-organs and singing above the roll of the wheels. He had nothing to read. The young officer opposite him whistled when he was awake, but mostly he slept.

Another stop. Another night. Another dawn. They were travelling now through an area of red brick and carefully kept little gardens. They passed a red London omnibus.

'This is Woking,' said his companion.

Soon the train stopped.

'Brookwood,' said the knowledgeable subaltern.

There was a Railway Transport Officer on the platform with lists. The Commander of X Battalion, redolent of anonymity, came down the platform peering anxiously through the steamy windows, looking for his officers.

'Crouchback,' he said. 'Davidson. We're getting out here. Fall in by companies in the station yard. Tell off a platoon to handle stores. Call the roll and inspect the men. They can't shave, of course, but see they are respectable otherwise. We've two miles march to camp.'

Somehow the dishevelled, comatose figures transformed themselves into Halberdiers. No one seemed lost. Everyone had a rifle. The kit-bags came bouncing out.

X Battalion moved off first. Guy marched at the head of his company, following the company in front, through the suburban lanes and delicious morning air. Presently they came to a field gate and the familiar smell of Soyer stoves. He followed the company commander in front in calling his men to attention. He heard the command ahead: 'Eyes left.' His turn came. He gave the command, saluting, and saw a Halberdier guard fallen in at the guard-house.

He gave the command: 'C Company, eyes front.'

From the distance of a hundred marching men he heard ahead: 'B Company, eyes right.'

What was it this time? he wondered.

'C Company, eyes right.'

He swung his head and found himself gazing straight into a single, glittering eye.

It was Ritchie-Hook.

A guide had been posted to lead the battalion to their parade ground. They formed close column of companies, ordered arms, stood easy. Brigadier Ritchie-Hook was standing beside the major.

'Glad to see you all again,' he roared. 'I expect you want breakfast. Get cleaned up first. You are all confined to camp. We're at two hours' notice to go overseas.'

The major saluted and turned to face the battalion he had so briefly dominated.

'For the time being this is our battalion area.' He said: 'I gather it won't be long. Guides will show you where to clean up. Battalion, shun. Slope arms. Fall out the officers.'

Guy marched forward, ranged himself with the other officers, saluted and marched off the parade ground. The battalion was dismissed. He heard the non-commissioned officers break out in a babble of orders. He was dazed. So was the major with the black mark against him.

'What does it mean, sir?'

'I only know what the Brigadier said as we marched in. Apparently there's a complete as-you-were. He's been fighting the War Office for days to keep the brigade in existence. As usual, he's won. That's all there is to it.'

'Does that mean things are better in France?'

'No. They're so bloody well worse that the Brigadier has got us all accepted as fully trained and ready for action.'

'D'you mean we're off to France too?'

'I shouldn't get too excited about that if I were you. The Regular Battalion got turned off their ship just as they were sailing. I rather feel in my bones that it may be some time yet before we go to France. There's been a lot happening over there while we were hunting parachutists in Scotland. It appears, among other things, that the Germans took Boulogne yesterday.'

BOOK THREE

Apthorpe Immolatus

I

Nine weeks of 'flap', of alternating chaos and order.

The Halberdiers were far from the battle, out of sight and hearing, but delicate nerves stretched to them from the front where the Allied armies were falling apart; each new shock carried its small painful agitation to the extremities. Chaos came from without in sudden, unexplained commands and cancellations; order grew from within as company, battalion and brigade each rearranged itself for the new unexpected task. They were so busy in those weeks with their own home-building, repairing, rearranging, improvising, that the great storm that was shaking the world passed overhead unnoticed until the crash of a bough set all the hidden roots again vibrating.

First, the task was Calais. No secret was made of their destination. Maps of that *terra incognita* were issued and Guy studied the street names, the approaches, the surrounding topography of the town he had crossed countless times, settling down to an aperitif in the Gare Maritime, glancing idly at the passing roofs from the windows of the restaurant-car; windy town of Mary Tudor, and Beau Brummel, and Rodin's Burghers; the most frequented, least known town in all the continent of Europe. There, perhaps, he would leave his bones.

But it was only at night that there was time for study or speculation. The days were spent in ceaseless, ant-like·business. In the move from Penkirk much had been lost, objects such as anti-tank rifles and aiming stands which no man could covet or conceal; among them Hayter, who went on his course of Air Liaison and was not seen again among the Halberdiers. Various regular officers, too, had proved medically unfit and left for Barracks or the Training Depot. Guy found himself back in the Second Battalion and still in command of a company.

It was far different from 'taking over' in normal conditions. When Ritchie-Hook spoke of his brigade as being at two hours' readiness to move into action, he was, indeed, 'shooting a line'. It was two days before it could take over its routine duties in the Area. These were arduous, for parachutists were hourly expected at Aldershot as at Penkirk. Standing Orders kept almost every man on duty every hour of the day. And first the men had to be collected. None had deserted but most were lost.

'You don't know what your battalion was?'

'First it was one and then another, sir.'

'Well, which was the first?'

'Can't say, sir.'

'Do you know who commanded it?'

'Oh yes, sir. C.S.M. Rawkes.'

Few of the conscripts knew the names of their officers.

When they joined, Rawkes had said: 'I am Company Sergeant-Major Rawkes. Take a good look so you'll know me again. I'm here to help you if you behave yourselves right. Or I'm here to make your life hell if you don't. It's for you to choose.'

They remembered that. Rawkes drew up the leave roster and detailed the fatigues. Officers, for men who had not yet been in battle, were as indistinguishable as Chinese. Few men, regular or conscript, had associations beyond their company. They knew of the Earl of Essex's Honourable Company of Free Halberdiers, they were proud to be dubbed 'Copper Heels' and 'Applejacks', but the brigade was a complex and remote conception. They did not know where the biffs came from; they were one of the hindmost wagons in a shunting train. A Kingdom was lost in Europe and somewhere in the Home Counties a Halberdier found himself with his leave stopped, manhandling stores for another move.

Guy in D Company was short of a second-in-command and a platoon commander, but he had Sergeant Major Rawkes and Quartermaster-Sergeant Yorke, both elderly, experienced and, above all, calm assistants. Ten men were unaccounted for; one man had broken camp; the company roll had been sent to Records; G.1098 Stores were arriving.

'Carry on, Sergeant Major.' 'Carry on, Colour Sergeant.' And they carried on.

Guy felt giddy but protected, as though the victim of an accident, dozing in bed, scarcely aware of how he had got there. Instead of medicine and grapes they brought him at regular intervals sheafs of paper that required his signature. A great forefinger, capped by what looked like a toe-nail, would point out the place for his name. He felt like a constitutional monarch of tender years, living in the shadow of world-respected, inherited councillors-of-state. He felt like a confidence trickster when at last, at noon the second day, he reported D Company as all present and correct.

'Good work, Uncle,' said Colonel Tickeridge. 'You're the first to report in.'

'The senior NCOs really did everything, sir.'

'Of course they did. You don't have to tell me that. But you'll have to take all the rockets when things go wrong, whether it's your fault or not. So take the occasional dewdrop in the same spirit.'

Guy was a little shy of giving orders to the two platoon commanders who had so lately been his fellows. They took them with perfect correctitude. Only when he said: 'Any questions?' de Souza's drawl would sometimes break in with: 'I don't quite understand the *purpose* of the order. What exactly are we looking for, when we stop civilian cars and ask for their identity cards?'

'Fifth columnists, I understand.'

'But, surely, they would have identity cards? They were issued compulsorily, you know, last year. I tried to refuse mine but the policeman positively pressed it on me.'

Or: 'Could you please explain why we have to have both a lying-in fire-picket *and* an anti-parachute platoon? I mean to say if I was a parachutist and I saw all the gorse on fire underneath I should take jolly good care to jump somewhere else.'

'Damn it, I didn't invent these orders. I'm just passing them on.'

'Yes, I know that. I just wondered if they make any sense to you. They don't to me.'

But whether orders made sense or not de Souza could be trusted to carry them out. Indeed he seemed to find a curious private pleasure in doing something he knew to be absurd, with minute efficiency. The other officer, Jervis, needed constant supervision.

The sun blazed down, withering the turf until it was slippery as a dance-floor and starting fires in the surrounding scrub. Routine was resumed. On the fourth evening of his command, Guy marched his company at nightfall into the training area where the place-names are incongruously taken from Central Africa, the memorial to a long-departed explorer; 'the heart of the Apthorpe country' as de Souza called it. They performed an exercise of 'company in the attack', became entirely intermixed, extricated themselves and bivouacked under the stars. A warm night, smelling of dry furze. Guy made a round of the sentries and then lay awake. Dawn came quickly, bringing momentary beauty even to that sorry countryside. They fell in and marched back to camp. Rather light-headed after his sleepness night Guy marched in front beside de Souza. From behind them came the songs: 'Roll out the barrel'; 'There are rats, rats, rats as big as cats in the quartermaster's stores'; 'We'll hang out the washing on the Siegfried Line'.

'That sounds a little out of date at the moment,' said Guy.

'Do you know what it always makes me think of, Uncle? A drawing of the last war, in one of the galleries, of barbed wire and a corpse hanging across it like a scarecrow. Not a very good drawing. I forget who did it. A sort of sham Goya.'

'I don't think the men really like it. They hear it at Ensa concerts and pick it up. I suppose as the war goes on, some good songs will grow out of it, as they did last time.'

'Somehow I rather doubt it,' said de Souza. 'There's probably a department of martial music in the Ministry of Information. Last-war songs were all eminently lacking in what's called morale-building qualities. "We're here because we're here, because we're here, because we're here", and "Take me back to dear old Blighty", "Nobody knows how bored we are and nobody seems to care". Not at all the kind of thing that would get official approval today. This war has begun in darkness and it will end in silence.'

'Do you say these things simply to depress me, Frank?'

'No, Uncle, simply to cheer myself up.'

When they reached camp, they found all the evidences of another 'flap'.

'Report at once to the orderly-room, sir.'

Guy found the battalion clerk and Sarum-Smith packing papers; the adjutant, telephoning, waved him into the presence of Colonel Tickeridge.

'What the devil do you mean by taking your company out at night without establishing a signal link with Headquarters? Do you realize that if it wasn't for Movement Control having made their usual balls-up, the whole brigade would have up-sticked and off and you'd have found the whole camp empty and bloody well serve you right? Don't you know that any training scheme has to be sent in to the adjutant with full map references?'

Guy had done this. Sanders was out at the time and he had given it to Sarum-Smith. He said nothing.

'Nothing to say?'

'I'm sorry, sir.'

'Well, see that D Company is ready to move by twelve hundred hours.'

'Very good, sir. May we know where we're going?'

'Embarking at Pembroke Dock.'

'For Calais, sir?'

'That's about the wettest question I've ever heard asked. Don't you even follow the news?'

'Not last night or this morning, sir.'

'Well, they've chucked in at Calais. Now go back to your company and get a move on.'

'Very good, sir.'

As he returned to his lines he remembered that, when last he heard, Tony Box-Bender's regiment was at Calais.

2

For a fortnight the Halberdier Brigade got no mail. When Guy at length heard news of Tony it was in two letters from his father written at an interval of ten days.

Marine Hotel, Matchet,
2nd June

My dear Guy,

I do not know where you are and I suppose you are not allowed to tell me, but I hope this letter will reach you wherever you are to tell you that you are always in my thoughts and prayers.

You may have heard that Tony was at Calais and that none of them came back. He is posted as missing. Angela has made up her mind he is a prisoner but I think you and I know him and his regiment too well to think of them giving themselves up.

He was always a good and happy boy and I could not ask a better death for anyone I loved. It is the *bona mors* for which we pray.

If you get this, write to Angela.

Ever your affec. father,
G. Crouchback.

Marine Hotel, Matchet,
12th June

My dear Guy,

I know you would have written to me if you could.

Have you heard the news of Tony? He is a prisoner and Angela, naturally I suppose, is elated simply that he is alive. It is God's will for the boy but I cannot rejoice. Everything points to a long war – longer perhaps than the last. It is a terrible experience for someone of Tony's age to spend years in idleness, cut off from his own people – one full of temptation.

It was not the fault of the garrison that they surrendered. They were ordered to do so from higher up.

Well, now our country is quite alone and I feel that that is good for us. An Englishman is at his best with his back to the wall and often in the past we have had quarrels with our allies which I believe were our own fault.

And last Tuesday was Ivo's anniversary, so that he has been much in my thoughts.

I am not quite useless yet. A boys' preparatory school (Catholic) has moved here from the East Coast. I can't remember whether I told you. A charming headmaster and his wife stayed here while they moved in. They were very short of masters and to my great surprise and delight they asked me to take a form for them. The boys are very good and I even get paid! which is a help as they have had to put their prices up in the hotel. It has been interesting brushing up my rusty Greek.

Ever your affec. father,
G. Crouchback.

These letters arrived together on the day when the Germans marched into Paris. Guy and his company were then quartered in a seaside hotel in Cornwall.

Much had happened since they left Aldershot eighteen days before. For those who followed events and thought about the future, the world's foundations seemed to shake. For the Halberdiers it was one damned thing after another. An urgent order came through Area Headquarters on the morning of their departure that the men were to be fortified for bad news. It was bad news enough that they were moving to Wales. They embarked in three ancient heterogeneous merchantmen, and hung hammocks in their dusty holds. They ate hard tack. During the warm night they lay anywhere about the decks. Steam was up; all communication with the shore forbidden.

Colonel Tickeridge said: 'I have no idea where we are going. I had a talk with the E.S.O. He seemed surprised we were here at all.'

Next morning they disembarked and saw the three ships sail away empty. The brigade split up and went into billets by battalions in neighbouring market towns, in shops and warehouses that had stood empty for nine years since the slump. The units and sub-units began home-building, training, playing cricket.

Then the brigade reassembled at the docks, re-embarked in the same ships, shabbier still now, for in the meantime they had been ferrying a broken army across the Channel from Dunkirk. There was a battery of Dutch gunners, without their guns, ensconced in one of them. Somehow they had got on board at Dunkirk. No one seemed to have a place for them in England. There they remained, sad and stolid and very polite.

The ships resembled blocks of slum tenements. Guy was occupied mainly in the effort of keeping his stores and men together. They disembarked for an hour's Physical Training, a company at a time. For the rest of the day they sat on their kitbags. A staff officer arrived from far away and produced a proclamation which was to be read to all troops, contradicting reports spread by the enemy, that the Air Force had been idle at Dunkirk. If British planes had not been noticed there, it was because they were busy on the enemy's lines of communication. The Halberdiers were more interested in the rumour that a German army had landed in Limerick and that their own role was to dislodge it.

'Hadn't we better dispel that rumour, sir?'

'No,' said Colonel Tickeridge. 'It's quite true. Not that the Germans are there yet. But our little operation is to meet them there if they do land.'

'Just us?'

'Just us,' said Colonel Tickeridge. 'So far as anyone seems to know – except, of course, for our Dutch chums.'

They were at two hours' notice to sail. After two days orders were relaxed to allow troops in formed bodies ashore for training and recreation. They had to remain within sight of the mast of their ship, which would hoist a flag to summon them in case of immediate sailing orders.

Colonel Tickeridge had an officers' conference in the saloon where he explained the details of the Limerick campaign. The Germans were expected with a fully equipped mechanized corps and ample air support and probably some help from the natives. The Halberdier Brigade would hold them off as long as possible.

'As to how long that will be,' said Colonel Tickeridge, 'your guess is as good as mine.'

Provided with a map of Limerick and this depressing intelligence, Guy returned to his huddled company.

'Halberdier Shanks, sir, has put in a request for leave,' said Rawkes.

'But he must know it's no use.'

'Urgent compassionate grounds, sir.'

'What are they, Sergeant-Major?'

'Won't say, sir. Insists, as his right, on seeing the Company Commander in private, sir.'

'Very well. He's a good man, isn't he?'

'One of the best, sir. That is to say of the National Service men.'

Halberdier Shanks was marched up. Guy knew him well, a handsome, capable, willing man.

'Well, Shanks, what is the trouble?'

'Please, sir, it's the competition. I *must* be at Blackpool tomorrow night. I've promised. My girl will never forgive me if I'm not.'

'Competition for what, Shanks?'

'The slow valse, sir. We've practised together three years now. We won at Salford last year. We'll win at Blackpool, sir. I know we will. And I'll be back in the two days, honest, sir.'

'Shanks, do you realize that France has fallen? That there is every likelihood of the invasion of England? That the whole railway system of the country is disorganized for the Dunkirk men? That our brigade is on two hours' notice for active service? Do you?'

'Yes, sir.'

'Then how can you come to me with this absurd application?'

'But, sir, we've been practising three years. We got a first at Salford last year. I can't give up now, sir.'

Was it 'the spirit of Dunkirk'?

'Request dismissed, Sergeant-Major.'

In accordance with custom C.S.M. Rawkes had been waiting within view in case the applicant for a private interview attempted personal violence on his officer. He now took over.

'Request dismissed. About turn, quick march.'

And Guy remained to wonder: was this the already advertised spirit of Dunkirk? He rather thought it was.

The days 'in the hulks', as de Souza called them, were few in number but they formed a distinct period of Guy's life in the Halberdiers; real discomfort for the first time, beastly food, responsibility in its most irksome form, claustrophobia, all these oppressed him; but he was free of all sense of national disaster. The rising and falling in the tides in the harbour, the greater or smaller number of daily sick, the men up on charges, the indications more or fewer, of failing temper – these were the concerns of the day. Sarum-Smith was appointed 'Entertainments Officer' and organized a concert at which three senior non-commissioned officers performed a strange piece of mummery traditional in the Halberdiers and derived, de Souza said, from a remote folk ceremony, dressed in blankets, carrying on a ritual dialogue under the names of 'Silly Bean', 'Black Bean' and 'Awful Bean'.

He organized a debate on the question: 'Any man who marries under thirty is a fool' which soon became a series of testimonies. 'All I can say is my father married at twenty-two and I never wish to see a happier homier house or a better mother nor I've had.'

He organized boxing matches.

Apthorpe was asked to lecture on Africa. He chose, instead, an unexpected subject: 'The Jurisdiction of Lyon King of Arms compared with that of Garter King of Arms.'

'But, Uncle, do you think it will interest the men?'

'Not all of them perhaps. Those that *are* interested will be very much interested indeed.'

'I believe they would greatly prefer something about elephants or cannibals.'

'Take it or leave it, Sarum-Smith.'

Sarum-Smith left it.

Guy lectured on the Art of Wine Making and had a surprising success. The men relished information on any technical subject.

Extraneous figures came to add to the congestion. An odd, old captain like a cockatoo in the gaudy service dress of a defunct regiment of Irish cavalry. He said he was the cipher officer and was roped in to lecture on 'Court Life at St Petersburg'.

Dunn and his men turned up. They had got to France and travelled in a great arc of insecurity behind the breaking lines from Boulogne to Bordeaux, without once leaving their railway coach. This experience of foreign travel, within sound of the guns, under fire once when an agitated airman passed their way, added perceptibly to Dunn's self-confidence. Sarum-Smith tried to induce him to give a lecture on 'the lessons learned in combat' but Dunn explained that he had spent the journey in holding a Court of Inquiry under the authority of the senior officer in the train, to examine the case of the carved boot. The verdict had been one of deliberate damage but since he had parted company with the convening officer he was not sure where the papers should be sent. He was reading the matter up in his Manual of Military Law.

A sinister super-cargo labelled 'Chemical Warfare (Offensive)' was delivered to the quay and left there for all to see.

Guy got a second-in-command, a dull young regular named Brent, and a third subaltern. So the days passed. Suddenly there was a warning order and another move. They disembarked. The Dutch gunners waved them a farewell as their train steamed away into the unknown. The maps of County Limerick were collected. They jolted slowly for ten hours, with many stops at sidings and many altercations with Transport Officers. They detrained at night, a magnificent, moonlit, scented night, and bivouacked in the woods surrounding a park, where all the paths glowed underfoot with phosphorescent deadwood. They were put into buses and dispersed along the sounding coast where Guy received the news of his cousin Tony.

He had two miles of cliff to defend against invasion. When de Souza was shown his platoon front he said: 'But, Uncle, it doesn't make sense. The Germans are mad as hatters but not in quite this way. They aren't going to land here.'

'They might put agents ashore. Or some of their landing craft might drift off course.'

'I think we've been sent here because we aren't fit for the likely beaches.'

After two days an inspecting general arrived with several staff officers and Ritchie-Hook, sulking; three car-loads of them. Guy showed them his gun pits, which were sited to cover every bather's path from the shore. The general stood with his back to the sea and gazed inland.

'Not much field of fire,' he said.

'No, sir. We expect the enemy from the other direction.'

'Must have all-round defence.'

'Don't you think they're a bit thin on the ground for that?' said Ritchie-Hook. 'They're covering a battalion front.'

'Parachutes,' said the general, 'are the very devil. Well, remember. The positions are to be held to the last man and the last round.'

'Yes, sir,' said Guy.

'Do your men understand that?'

'Yes, sir.'

'And remember, you must never speak of "*If* the enemy comes" but "*When* they come". They are coming *here, this* month. Understand?'

'Yes, sir.'

'All right, I think we've seen everything.'

'May I say a word?' asked a neat young staff officer.

'Carry on, I.O.'

'Fifth columnists,' said the Intelligence Officer, 'will be your special concern. You know what they did on the Continent. They'll do the same here. Suspect everyone – the vicar, the village grocer, the farmer whose family have lived here a hundred years, all the most unlikely people. Look out for signalling at night – lights, short-wave transmitters. And here's a bit of information for your ears alone. It mustn't go below platoon-commander level. We happen to know that the telegraph posts have been marked to lead the invading units to their rendezvous. Little metal numbers. I've seen them myself. Remove them and report to headquarters when you find them.'

'Very good, sir.'

The three cars drove on. Guy had been with de Souza's platoon when the final words of encouragement were spoken. Here the high road ran almost on the edge of the cliff. He and Brent walked to the next platoon position. On the way they counted a dozen telegraph poles, each marked with a metal number.

'All telegraph poles are,' said Brent, 'by the Post Office.'

'Sure?'

'Perfectly.'

Local Defence Volunteers helped patrol the area at night and reported frequent lamp-signals from fifth columnists. One story was so well told that Guy spent a night alone with Halberdier Glass, armed to the teeth, on the sands of a little cove; a boat was said to beach there often in darkness. But no one came their way that night. The only incident was a single tremendous flash which momentarily lit the whole coast. Guy remembered afterwards that in the momentary stillness he foolishly said: 'Here they come.' Then from far away came the thump and tremor of an explosion.

'Land-mine,' said Glass. 'Plymouth probably.'

In his vigils Guy thought often of Tony, with three, four, perhaps five years cut clean out of his young life just as those eight had been cut from his own.

Once on an evening of dense sea-mist a message came that the enemy were attacking with arsenical smoke. That was Apthorpe, momentarily left in charge at Headquarters. Guy took no action. An hour later a message came cancelling the alarm. That was Colonel Tickeridge, back at his post.

3

At the end of August Guy was sitting in his company office in the hotel when two captains of a county regiment entered and saluted.

'We're A Company, 5th Loamshires.'

'Good morning. What can I do for you?'

'You're expecting us, aren't you?'

'No.'

'We've come to take over from you.'

'First I've heard of it.'

'Damn. I suppose we've come to the wrong place again. You aren't D Company, 2nd Halberdiers?'

'Yes.'

'That's all right then. I expect the orders will get through in time. My chaps are due to arrive this afternoon. Perhaps you wouldn't mind showing us round?'

For weeks they had waited for fifth columnists. Here they were at last.

There was a field telephone, which sometimes worked, connecting D Company with Battalion Headquarters. Guy, as he had seen done in the films, wrote on a piece of paper *Ask Bn. H.Q, if these chaps are genuine* and turned to Brent: 'Just attend to this will you, Bill? I'll see to our visitors,' and to the Loamshires: 'Come outside. It's rather a good billet, isn't it?'

They stepped out to the hotel terrace; bright blue overhead and before them; warm gravel underfoot; roses all round them; at his side, the enemy. Guy studied the two men. They were in service uniforms. They should have been in battledress. The junior had not yet spoken – a German accent perhaps; the senior was altogether too good to be true, clipped voice, clipped moustache, a Military Cross.

'You want to see my L.M.G. positions, I expect?'

'Well, I suppose we ought to some time. At the moment I'm more interested in accommodation and messing arrangements. Is the bathing good? How do you get down to the beach? As far as I'm concerned this is going to be my summer holidays. We'd no sooner got straightened out after Dunkirk than they put us on defence duty on the invasion coast.'

'Would you like a bathe now?'

'Sound scheme, eh, Jim?'

The junior officer gave a grunt which might have been Teutonic.

'We usually undress up here and go down in great-coats. I can fit you out.'

Brent joined them to say that he had not been able to get an answer from Headquarters.

'Never mind,' said Guy. 'I'll see to it. I want you now to take our visitors bathing. Show them up to my room. They'll leave their things there. Find them a couple of great-coats and towels.'

As soon as the Loamshires had gone Guy turned back and found Sergeant-Major Rawkes.

'Sergeant-Major,' he said. 'Did you see anything odd about those two officers who came in just now?'

'We have never had much of an opinion of the Loamshires, sir.'

'I suspect them. They've just gone down to bathe with Mr Brent. I want you to relieve the man at the gun covering the bathing place.'

'Me, sir? At the gun?'

'Yes. This is a security matter. I can't trust anyone else. I want you to keep them covered all the time, on the way down, in the water, on the way up. If they try anything funny, fire.'

Sergeant-Major Rawkes, who had in recent weeks formed a good opinion of Guy, looked at him with mild despair.

'Shoot Mr Brent, sir?'

'No, no. Those fellows who say they are in the Loamshires.'

'What exactly would you mean by funny, sir?'

'If they attack Mr Brent, try to drown him, or push him over the cliffs.'

Rawkes shook his head sadly. He had let himself be taken in. He should never have come near trusting a temporary officer.

'That's orders, sir?'

'Yes, of course. Get on with it quick.'

'Very good, sir.'

He walked slowly to the gun pit.

''Op it, you two,' he said to the men on duty. 'Don't ask me why. Just 'op it and be grateful.'

Then he lowered himself to the Bren, stiffly, in protest. But as he put the weapon to his shoulder, he relaxed a little. This was a rare sport, officer-shooting.

Guy ran to his room and examined the intruders' kit. One of them instead of a service revolver was carrying a Luger. Guy pocketed the cartridge-clips of both weapons. There was no other suspicious feature; everything else in their pockets was English including a very correct move-order. Guy tried to telephone again and got through to Sarum-Smith.

'I must speak to the C.O.'

'He's at a conference at Brigade.'

'Well, the second-in-command or the adjutant then.'

'They're out. There's only me and the quartermaster left.'

'Can you get a message through to the C.O. at Brigade?'

'I don't think so. Is it important?'

'Yes. Take it down.'

'Wait a jiffy till I get a pencil.'

There was a pause and then the voice of Apthorpe spoke. 'Hullo, old man, something up?'

'Yes, will you get off the line. I'm trying to pass a message to Sarum-Smith.'

'He's gone off to find a razor blade to sharpen his pencil.'

'Well, will you take it? Message begins: "D Coy to 2 Bn via Bde HQ." '

'I'm not sure that's the correct form.'

'Damn the correct form. Tell the C.O. that I've got two men here who claim to be Loamshires. They say they have orders to take over my positions. I want to know if they're genuine.'

'I say, old man, that sounds a bit hot. I'll come right over myself.'

'Don't do anything of the sort. Just get my message to the C.O.'

'I could be with you in twenty minutes on my motor-bike.'

'Just pass my message to the C.O., there's a good chap.'

Huffily: 'Well, if you don't want me, that's your look-out. But it seems to me far too serious a matter to settle single-handed.'

'I'm not single-handed. I've a hundred men here. Just pass the message.'

Very huffily: 'Here is Sarum-Smith. It's his pigeon to pass messages. I'm very busy here, I can tell you, on pretty confidential business.'

Sarum-Smith, back at the telephone, took the message.

'Sure you've got it clear?'

'Yes. But I think there's an order that has some bearing on your query. It came just as the adjutant was leaving. He told me to pass it on but I've not got round to it. Wait a sec. It's somewhere here. Yes. Second Battalion will hand over their positions to Fifth Loamshires and concentrate forthwith at Brook Park with full stores and equipment. That's the place we first arrived at. Sorry for the delay.'

'Damn.'

'Do you want that message sent to the C.O.?'

'No.'

'It's all been rather a flap about nothing, hasn't it?'

As Guy rang off he saw the bathers return up the cliff under the sights of the entrenched Bren gun. They had enjoyed their swim, they said. They lunched with Guy, slept, and bathed again, then drove back to their unit. It would surprise them, Guy supposed, when they found their pistols unloaded. They would never know they had been as near death that sunny first day of their holidays as on the dunes at Dunkirk. One untimely piece of horse-play and they might have been goners.

*

Another series of jolts, buffer on buffer down the train.

The brigade assembled and went under canvas at Brook Park. 'Dispersal' was the prevailing fashion now. Instead of the dressed lines which had given Penkirk the airs and some of the graces of a Victorian colour-print, there was now a haphazard litter of tents, haunting the shadows round the solitary oaks of the park, or shrinking in the immature surrounding coverts. A great taboo fell on the making of tracks. Special sentries were posted to shout at men approaching Brigade Headquarters across the lawn, directing them to creep through the shrubberies.

The nature of Apthorpe's 'confidential business' was soon revealed. He had been helping the quartermaster arrange an unexpected consignment of tropical uniforms. In the first two days at Brook Park the Halberdiers paraded company by company and were issued with sun helmets and ill-fitting khaki drill. Few looked anything but absurd. The garments were then put away and nothing was said about them. They aroused little curiosity. In the past months they had moved so suddenly, so often and so purposelessly, they had been alternately provided with, deprived of, and reprovided with so many different military objects, that speculation about their future had become purely facetious.

'I suppose we're going to reconquer Somaliland' (which had just been precipitately abandoned), said de Souza.

'It's just part of a fully equipped Halberdier's normal kit,' said Brent.

However it produced one climax in the process which de Souza called 'the Languishing of Leonard'.

During their defence of the Cornish cliffs the Second Battalion had seen very little of one another. Now they were reunited and Guy found a sad change evident in Leonard. Mrs Leonard had planted herself and her baby in lodgings near him and she had worked hard on his divided loyalty. Bombs were beginning to fall in appreciable numbers. An invasion was confidently predicted for the middle of September. Mrs Leonard wanted a man about the house. When Leonard moved from the coast with his company, Mrs Leonard came too and settled in the village inn.

She asked Guy to dinner and explained her predicament.

'It's all right for you,' she said. 'You're an old bachelor. You'll make yourself very comfortable, I daresay, in India with native servants and all you want to eat. What's going to happen to me, that's what I'd like to know?'

'I don't think there's any prospect of our going to India,' said Guy.

'Then what's Jim's new hat for then?' asked Mrs Leonard. 'That's an Indian hat, isn't it? Don't you tell me they've given him that hat and those size six shorts to wear here in the winter.'

'It's just part of a fully equipped Halberdier's normal kit,' said Guy.

'D'you believe that?'

'No,' said Guy. 'Frankly, I don't.'

'Well then?' said Mrs Leonard triumphantly.

'Daisy won't understand it's what a soldier's wife has to put up with,' said Leonard. He had said this often obviously.

'I didn't marry a soldier,' said Mrs Leonard. 'If I'd known you were going to be a soldier I'd have married into the R.A.F. *Their* wives live comfortable and what's more they're the people who are winning the war. It says so on the wireless, doesn't it? It isn't as though it was only me; there's the baby to think of.'

'I don't think that in case of invasion, you could expect to have Jim expressly detailed for the defence of your baby, you know, Mrs Leonard.'

'I'd see he stayed around; anyway, he wouldn't go surf-bathing and lying about under palm trees and playing the ukulele.'

'I don't think those would be his duties if we went abroad.'

'Oh, come off the perch,' said Mrs Leonard. 'I've asked you here to help. You're in with the high-ups.'

'Lots of men have young babies, too.'

'But not *my* baby.'

'Daisy, you're being unreasonable. Do make her see sense, Uncle.'

'It isn't as though the whole army was going abroad. Why should they pick on Jim?'

'I suppose you *could* apply for transfer to barrack duties,' said Guy at last. 'There must be a lot of chaps there who'd be eager to come with us.'

'I bet there would,' said Mrs Leonard. 'It's just evacuation, that's what it is, sending you off thousands of miles from the war, with bearers and sahibs and chota pegs.'

It was a sad little party. As Leonard walked back to camp with Guy, he said: 'It's getting me down. I can't leave Daisy in the state she's in. Isn't it true women sometimes go off their heads for a bit just after having a baby?'

'So I've heard.'

'Perhaps that's the trouble with Daisy.'

Meanwhile the sun-helmets were laid aside and long, hot days were spent in biffing Brook House from every possible direction.

Some days later Leonard met Guy and said gloomily: 'I went to see the colonel this morning.'

'Yes.'

'About what Daisy has been saying.'

'Yes?'

'He was awfully sporting about it.'

'He's an awfully sporting man.'

'He's going to send my name in for transfer to the Training Depot. It may take some time, but he thinks it'll go through.'

'I hope your wife will feel relieved.'

'Uncle, do you think I'm behaving pretty poorly?'

'It's not my business.'

'I can see you do. Well, so do I.'

But he had not long in which to face whatever shame attached to his decision. That night, a warning-order arrived and everyone was sent on forty-eight hours' embarkation leave.

4

Guy went for a day to Matchet. It was summer holidays for the school. He found his father busy with North and Hillard's *Latin Prose* and a pale blue *Xenophon* 'brushing up' for the coming term.

'I can't read a word of it unseen,' said Mr Crouchback almost gleefully. 'I bet the little blighters will catch me out. They did last term again and again, but they were very decent about it.'

Guy returned a day early to see that everything was well with his company's arrangements. Walking through the almost empty camp at dusk, he met the Brigadier.

'Crouchback,' he said, peering. 'Not a captain yet?'

'No, sir.'

'But you've got your company.'

They walked together some way.

'You've got the best command there is,' said the Brigadier. 'There's nothing in life like leading a company in action. Next best thing is doing a job on your own. Everything else is just bumf and telephones.' Under the trees, in the failing light, he was barely visible. 'It's not much of a show we're going to. I'm not supposed to tell you where, so I shall. Place called Dakar. I'd never heard of it till they started sending me "Most Secret" intelligence reports, mostly about ground-nuts. A French town in West Africa. Probably all boulevards and brothels if I know the French colonies. We're in support. Worse really – we're in support of the supporting brigade. They're putting the Marines in before us, blast them. Anyway it's all froggy business. They think they'll get in without opposition. But it'll help training. Sorry I told you. They'd court-martial me if they found out. I'm getting too old for courts martial.'

He turned away abruptly and disappeared into the woodland.

Next day the move-order was issued to entrain for Liverpool. Leonard was left behind with the rear-party 'pending posting'. No one except Guy and the colonel knew why. Most supposed him ill. He had been looking like a ghost for some time.

Something of this kind had happened in Captain Truslove's regiment. A showy polo-player named Congreve sent in his papers when they were under orders for foreign service. The colonel announced at mess: 'Gentlemen, I must request that Captain Congreve's name shall never again be mentioned in my presence.' Congreve's fiancée returned his ring. From colonel to drummer-boy all felt tainted and many of their subsequent acts of heroism were prompted by the wish to restore the regiment's honour. (Not until the penultimate chapter did Congreve turn up again, elaborately disguised as an Afghan merchant with the keys of the Pathan fortress where Truslove himself awaited execution by torture.) But Guy had no shame about the defection of Leonard. It seemed, rather, as their train moved spasmodically towards Liverpool, that it was they who were deserting him. Their destination was not the Honolulu-Algiers-Quetta station of Mrs Leonard's film-clouded imagination, but it was a warm, highly coloured, well-found place far from bombs and gas and famine and enemy occupation; far from the lightless concentration-camp which all Europe had suddenly become.

Chaos in Liverpool. Quays and ships in absolute darkness. Bombs falling somewhere not far distant. Embarkation staff officers scanning nominal-rolls with dimmed torches. Guy and his company were ordered into one ship, ordered out again, stood-to on the dockside for an hour. An all-clear siren sounded and a few lamps glowed here and there. Embarkation officers who had gone to earth emerged and resumed their duties. At last, at dawn they numbly climbed on board and found their proper quarters. Guy saw them bedded down and went in search of his cabin.

This was in the first-class part of the ship, unchanged from peace time when it had been filled with affluent tourists. This was a chartered ship with the Merchant Marine crew. Already Goanese stewards were up and about in their freshly laundered white and red livery. They padded silently about their work, arranging ashtrays symmetrically in the lounges, drawing the curtains for another day. They were quite at peace. No one had told them about submarines and torpedoes.

But not all were at peace. Turning a corner in search of his cabin Guy found a kind of pugnacious dance being performed in and out of his cabin by Halberdier Glass and a Goanese of distinguished appearance – thin, elderly, with magnificent white moustaches spanning his tear-wet nut-brown face.

'Caught this black bastard in the very act, sir. Mucking about with your kit, sir.'

'Please, sir, I am the cabin boy, sir. I do not know this rude soldier.'

'That's all right, Glass. He's just doing his job. Now clear out both of you, I want to turn in.'

'You aren't surely going to have this native creeping round your quarters, sir?'

'I am no native, sir. I am a Christian Portuguese boy. Christian mama, Christian papa, six Christian children, sir.'

He produced from his starched blouse a gold medal, strung round his neck, much worn with the long swing and plunge of the ship rubbing it year by year to and fro on his hairless dark chest.

Guy's heart suddenly opened towards him. Here was his own kin. He yearned to show the medal he wore, Gervase's souvenir from Lourdes. There were men who would have done exactly that, better men than he; who would perhaps have said 'Snap' and drawn a true laugh from the sullen Halberdier and so have made true peace between them.

But Guy, with all this in his mind to do, merely felt in his pocket for two half-crowns and said: 'Here. Will this make things better?'

'Oh yes, sir, thank you. Very much better, sir,' and the Goanese turned and went on his way rejoicing a little, but not as a fellow man at peace; merely as a servant unexpectedly over-tipped.

To Glass Guy said: 'If I hear of you laying hands on the ship's company again, I'll send you to the guardroom.'

'Sir,' said Glass, looking at Guy as though at Captain Congreve who let down the regiment.

The men were given a 'long lie' that morning. At eleven o'clock Guy paraded his company on deck. An unusually large and varied breakfast – the normal third-class fare of the line – had dissipated the annoyances of the night. They were in good heart. He handed them over to their platoon commanders to check stores and equipment and went to explore. The Second Battalion had done better than the others, who were close packed in the ship moored next to them. They had their transport to themselves except for Brigade Headquarters and a medley of strangers – Free French liaison officers, Marine gunners, a naval beach-party, chaplains, an expert on tropical hygiene and the rest. A small smoking-room was labelled OPERATIONAL PLANNING. OUT OF BOUNDS TO ALL RANKS.

Lying out in the stream might be descried the huge inelegant colourless bulk of an aircraft carrier. All contact with the shore was forbidden. Sentries stood at the gangways. Military police patrolled the quay. But the object of the expedition was not long kept secret for at midday an airman jauntily swinging a parcel charged '*Most Secret. By hand of officer only*' allowed it to fall asunder as he approached his launch and a light breeze caught, bore up and scattered abroad some thousands of blue, white and red leaves printed with the slogan:

FRANÇAIS DE DAKAR*!*
Joignez-vous à nous pour délivrer la France!
GENERAL DE GAULLE.

No one, except one of the chaplains who was new to military life, seriously expected that these preparations would bring anything about. The

Halberdiers had been too much shifted, exhorted and disappointed during recent weeks. They accepted as part of their normal day the series of orders and cancellations and mishaps. Shore leave was given and then stopped; censorship of letters was raised and reimposed; the ship cast off, fouled an anchor, returned to the quayside; the stores were disembarked and re-embarked in 'tactical order'. And then quite suddenly one afternoon, they sailed. The last newspaper to come aboard told of heavier air-raids. De Souza called their transport 'the refugee ship'.

It seemed barely possible that they would not turn back but on they steamed into the Atlantic until they reached a rendezvous where the whole wide circle of grey water was filled with shipping of every size from the carrier and the battleship *Barham*, to a little vessel named *Belgravia*, which was reputed to carry champagne and bath-salts and other comforts for the garrison of Dakar. Then the whole convoy altered course and sailed south, destroyers racing round them like terriers, an occasional, friendly aeroplane swooping overhead and gallant little *Belgravia* wallowing on behind.

They practised doubling to 'action stations' twice a day. They carried 'Mae West' life-belts wherever they went. But they took their tone from the smooth seas and the Goanese stewards who tinkled their musical gongs up and down the carpeted passages. All was peaceful and when the cruiser *Fiji* was torpedoed in full sight of them a mile or two ahead, and all the naval detachment became busy with depth-charges, the incident barely disturbed their Sunday afternoon repose.

Dunn and his signalmen had reappeared and were on board with Brigade Headquarters, but Apthorpe ignored them, perhaps never was aware of their presence, so deep were his colloquies with the specialist on tropical medicine. The men did Physical Training and boxed and listened to lectures about Dakar and General de Gaulle and malaria and the importance of keeping clear of native women; they lay about on the forward deck and in the evenings the chaplains organized concerts for them.

Brigadier Ritchie-Hook, alone, was unhappy. His brigade had a minor and conditional role. It was thought that the Free French would find the town beflagged for them. The only opposition expected was from the battleship *Richelieu*. This the Royal Marines and a unit of unknown character called a 'commando' would deal with. The Halberdiers might not land at all; if they did it would be for 'cleaning up' and relieving the Marines on guard duty. Little biffing. In his chagrin he quarrelled with the ship's captain and was ordered off the bridge. He prowled about the decks alone, sometimes carrying a weapon like a hedging implement which he had found valuable in the previous war.

Presently the heat grew oppressive, the air stagnant and misty. There was an odd smell, identified as that of ground-nuts, borne to them from the near but invisible coast. And word went round that they were at their destination.

The Free French were said to be in parley with their enslaved compatriots. There was some firing somewhere in the mist. Then the convoy withdrew out of range and closed in. Launches went to and fro among the ships. A conference was held on the flagship from which Brigadier Ritchie-Hook returned grinning. He addressed the battalion, telling them that an opposed landing would take place next day, then went to the transport carrying his other battalions and gave them the stirring news. Maps were issued. The officers sat up all night studying their beaches, boundaries, second and third waves of advance. During the night the ships moved near inland and dawn disclosed a grey line of African coast across the steamy water. The battalion stood to, at their bomb-stations, bulging with ammunition and emergency rations. Hours passed. There was heavy firing ahead and a rumour that *Barham* was holed. A little Unfree French aeroplane droned out of the clouds and dropped a bomb very near them. The Brigadier was back on the bridge, on the best of terms with the captain. Then the convoy steamed out of range once more and at sundown another conference was called. The Brigadier returned in a rage and called the officers together.

'Gentlemen, it's all off. We are merely awaiting confirmation from the War Cabinet to withdraw. I'm sorry. Tell your men and keep their spirit up.'

There was little need for this order. Surprisingly a spirit of boisterous fun suddenly possessed the ship. Everyone had been a little more apprehensive than he had shown about the opposed landing. Troop decks and mess 'danced and skylarked'.

Immediately after dinner Guy was called to the room marked 'Out of Bounds to all Ranks'.

He found the Brigadier, the captain and Colonel Tickeridge all looking gleeful and curiously naughty. The Brigadier said: 'We are going to have a little bit of very unofficial fun. Are you interested?'

The question was so unexpected that Guy made no guess at the meaning and simply said: 'Yes, sir.'

'We tossed up between the companies. Yours won. Can you find a dozen good men for a reconnaissance patrol?'

'Yes, sir.'

'And a suitable officer to lead them?'

'Can I go myself, sir?' he said to Colonel Tickeridge.

This was true Truslove-style.

'Yes. Go off now and warn the men to be ready in an hour. Tell them it's an extra guard. Then come back here with a map and get your orders.'

When Guy returned he found the conspirators very cheerful.

'I've been having a little disagreement with the Force Commander,' said Ritchie-Hook. 'There was some discrepancy between the naval and military intelligence about Beach A. Got it marked?'

'Yes, sir.'

'In the final plan it was decided to leave Beach A alone. Some damn fool had reported it wired and generally impracticable. My belief is that it's quite open. I won't go into the reasons. But you can see for yourself that if we got ashore on Beach A we could have taken the frogs in the rear. They had some damn fool photographs and pretended to see wire in them and got windy. I saw no wire. The Force Commander said some offensive things about two eyes being better than one with a stereoscope. The discussion got a bit heated. The operation is cancelled and we've all been made to look silly, but I'd just like to make my point with the Force Commander. So I am sending a patrol ashore just to make certain.'

'Yes, sir.'

'Very well, that is the intention of the operation. If you find the place wired or get shot at come back quickly and we will say no more about it. If it's open, as I think it is, you might bring back some little souvenir that I can send the Force Commander. He's a suspicious fellow. Any little thing that will make him feel foolish – a coco-nut or something like that. We can't use the naval landing craft but the Captain here has played up like a sportsman and is lending a launch for the trip. Well, I'm turning in now. I shall be glad to hear your report in the morning. Settle the tactical details with your C.O.'

Ritchie-Hook left them. The captain explained the position of the launch and the sally-port.

'Any other questions?' asked Colonel Tickeridge.

'No, sir,' said Guy. 'It all seems quite clear.'

5

Two hours later Guy's patrol paraded in the hold from which the sally-port opened. They were dressed in rubber-soled shoes, shorts, and tunic-shirts; no caps; no gas-masks; their equipment stripped down to the belt. Each had a couple of hand grenades and his rifle, except for the Bren pair who would set up their gun on the first suitable spot and be ready to cover the retreat if they were opposed. All had blackened faces. Guy carefully gave them their instructions. The sergeant would board the boat first and land last, seeing everyone safely ashore. Guy would land first and the men fan out on either side. He would carry a torch stuffed with pink tissue paper which he would flash back from time to time to give the direction. Wire, if it existed, would be above high water. They would advance inland far enough to discover whether there was wire or not. The first man to come on wire was to pass the word up to him. They would investigate the extent of the wire. A single blast of his whistle meant withdrawal to the boat ... and so on.

'Remember,' he concluded, 'we're simply on reconnaissance. We aren't trying to conquer Africa. We only fire if we have to cover our withdrawal.'

Presently they heard the winch over their head and they knew that their boat was being lowered.

'There's an iron ladder outside. It'll be about six foot to the water level. See that the man before you has got into place before you start going down. All set?'

The lights were all turned off in the hold before the sally-port was opened by one of the crew. It revealed a faintly lighter square and a steamy breath of the sea.

'All set below?'

'Aye, aye, sir.'

'Then carry on, Sergeant.'

One by one the men filed from the darkness into the open night. Guy followed last and took his place in the bow. There was barely room to squat. Guy experienced the classic illusion of an unknown, unsought, companion among them. The sally-port shut noisily above them. A voice said: 'Any more for the *Skylark*?' Skylark was the *mot juste*, thought Guy. They cast off. The engine started with what seemed a great noise and the launch bounced gently away in the direction of Beach A.

It was nearly an hour's run for the beach lay on the north of the town in a position which, if captured, might have secured the landing to the south. The reek of the engine, the tropic night, the cramped bodies, the irregular smack of little waves on the bows. At last the man at the wheel said: 'We must be getting in now, sir.'

The engine slowed. The line of the shore was plain to see, quite near them. The clearer eyes of the seamen searched and found the wide gap of the beach. The engine was shut down and in complete silence they drifted gently inshore under their momentum. Then they touched sand. Guy was standing with his hands on the gunwale, ready. He vaulted overboard and found himself breast-high in the tepid water. He stumbled straight ahead uphill, waist-deep, knee-deep, then clear of the sea on firm sand. He was filled by the most exhilarating sensation of his life; his first foothold on enemy soil. He flashed his torch behind him and heard splashing; the boat was drifting out again and the last men had to swim a few strokes to get into their depth. He saw shadowy figures emerge and spread out on either side of him. He gave the two flashes which means 'Forward'. He could just see and hear the gun pair move off to the side flank to find a position. The patrol moved on uphill. First hard wet sand, then soft dry sand, then long spiky grass. They

kept on quietly. Palm trunks rose suddenly immediately in front. The first
thing he met was a fallen coco-nut. He picked it up and gave it to Halberdier
Glass, next to him on the left.

'Take this back to the boat and wait for us there,' he whispered.

Halberdier Glass had shown signs of respect during the early stages of the
expedition and an unwonted zeal.

'What me, sir? This here nut, sir? Back to the boat?'

'Yes, don't talk. Get on with it.'

He knew then that he had lost all interest in whether he held or forfeited
Glass's esteem.

The second thing he met was wire, loosely tangled between the palm
trunks. He gave the three flashes that meant: 'Go carefully. 'Ware wire.'

He heard stumbling on both sides of him and whispered messages came
up to him: 'Wire on the left.' 'Wire on the right.'

Casting a dim light forward now, and exploring with hands and feet, he
discovered a low, thin, ill-made defensive belt of wire. Then he was aware
of a dark figure, four paces from him, plunging forward across it.

'Stand still, that man,' he said.

The figure continued forward, clear of the wire and noisily pushing
through scrub and grass and thorn.

'Come back, damn you,' Guy shouted.

The man was out of sight but still audible. Guy blew his whistle. The men
obediently turned about and made off downhill for the beach. Guy stood
where he was, waiting for the delinquent. He had heard that men who ran
amok had sometimes been brought to their senses by an automatic response
to command.

'That half-file in front,' he shouted as though in the barrack square.
'About turn. Quick march.'

The only response, quite near to his left, was a challenge. 'Halte-là! Qui
vive?' Then the explosion of a grenade. And then suddenly firing broke out
on all sides, the full span of the beach; nothing formidable, a few ragged rifle
shots whistling between the palms. At once his own Bren on the flank opened
up with three bursts which fell alarmingly near him. It seemed to Guy rather
likely that he would soon be killed. He repeated the words which are
dignified by the name 'act' of contrition; words so familiar that he used them
in dreams when falling from a height. But he also thought: what a preposterous way in which to get oneself killed!

He ran back to the beach. The boat was there, two men in the water held
it in to the shore. The remainder of the patrol stood near it.

'Get aboard,' said Guy.

He ran across to the gunners and called them in.

There was still a lot of shouting in French and some wild shooting inland.

'All present and correct, sir,' reported the sergeant.

'No, there's a man adrift up there.'

'No, sir, I've counted them. All present. Jump in, sir, we'd better be off while we can.'

'Wait one minute. I must just have another look.'

The R.N.V.R. lieutenant in command of the boat said: 'My orders are to push off as soon as the operation is completed, or sooner if I think the boat is being put into excessive danger.'

'They haven't seen you yet. They're firing quite wild. Give me two minutes.'

Men, Guy knew, in the excitement of their first battle were liable to delusions. It would be highly convenient to suppose that he had imagined that dark, disappearing figure. But he went up the beach again and there saw his missing man crawling towards him.

Guy's one emotion was anger and his first words were: 'I'll have you court-martialled for this,' and then: 'Are you hit?'

'Of course I am,' said the crawling figure. 'Give me a hand.'

This was no German defence with searchlights and automatic weapons, but there had plainly been some reinforcement and the rifle shots were thicker. In his haste and anger Guy did not notice the man's odd tone. He pulled him up, no great weight, and staggered with him to the boat. The man was clutching something under his free arm. Not until they had both been hoisted aboard and the boat was running full speed out to sea did he give his attention to the wounded man. He turned his torch to the face and a single eye flashed back at him.

'Get my leg out straight,' said Brigadier Ritchie-Hook. 'And give me a field-dressing someone. It's nothing much but it hurts like the devil and it's bleeding too much. And take care of the coco-nut.'

Then Ritchie-Hook busied himself with his wound but not before he had laid in Guy's lap the wet, curly head of a Negro.

And Guy was so weary that he fell asleep, nursing the trophy. The whole patrol was asleep by the time they reached the ship. Only Ritchie-Hook groaned and swore sometimes in semi-coma.

6

'Would you want to be eating this nut now, sir, or later?'

Halberdier Hall looked down at Guy's bedside.

'What time is it?'

'Eleven sharp, sir, as was your orders.'

'Where are we?'

'Steaming along, sir, with the convoy, *not* towards home. Colonel wants to see you as soon as you're ready.'

'Leave the nut here. I'm taking it for a souvenir.'

Guy still felt weary. As he shaved he recalled the final events of the previous night.

He had woken much refreshed, bobbing under the high walls of the ship with the head of a Negro clasped in both hands.

'We've a wounded man here. Can you pass down a loop for hoisting?'

There was some delay above and then from the blind black door above a light flashed down.

'I'm the ship's surgeon. Will you come up and make way for me?'

Guy climbed aboard into the hold. The surgeon descended. He and two orderlies had a special apparatus for such occasions, a kind of cradle which was swung down, fastened to the Brigadier and tenderly drawn up again.

'Take him straight along to the sick bay and prepare him. Anyone else injured?'

'That's the only one.'

'No one warned me to expect wounded. Luckily we had everything ready this morning. No one told me to expect anything tonight,' the surgeon grumbled, out of sight and out of earshot behind the laden orderlies.

The men came aboard.

'You've all done jolly well,' said Guy. 'Fall out now. We'll talk about it tomorrow. Thanks, sailors. Good night.'

He woke Colonel Tickeridge to report.

'Reconnaissance successful, sir. One coco-nut' – and placed the head beside Colonel Tickeridge's ash-tray on the edge of his bunk.

Colonel Tickeridge came slowly awake.

'For Christ's sake what's that thing?'

'French colonial infantry, sir. No identifications.'

'Well for God's sake take it away. We'll talk about it in the morning. Everyone back safe?'

'All my patrol, sir. One supernumerary casualty. Stretcher case. He's been put in the sick bay.'

'What the devil do you mean by "supernumerary"?'

'The Brigadier, sir.'

'*What?*'

Guy had assumed that Colonel Tickeridge was in the secret; had been party to making him look a fool. Now he dropped something of his stiffness.

'Didn't you know he was coming, Colonel?'

'Of course I didn't.'

'He must have hidden in the hold and crashed the party in the dark, sir, with his face blacked.'

'The old devil. Is he badly hurt?'

'The leg.'

'That doesn't sound too bad.' Colonel Tickeridge, fully awake now, began to chuckle, then turned grave. 'I say, though, this is going to be the hell of a mess. Well, we'll talk about it tomorrow. Go to bed now.'

'And this?'

'For Christ's sake throw it in the drink.'

'Do you think I ought to, Colonel, without consulting the Brigadier?'

'Well, get it out of here.'

'Very good, sir. Good night.'

Guy took a firm grip of the wool and walked down the breathless corridor. He met a Goanese night steward and showed him the face. The man gave a squeal and fled. Guy was light-headed now. Apthorpe's cabin? No. He tried the door of the Operations Room. It was unlocked and unguarded. All the maps and confidential papers had been tidied away. He put his burden in the Brigadier's 'In' tray and, suddenly weary again, turned to his own cabin, threw down his bloody shirt, washed his bloody chest and hands, and fell deep asleep.

'How's the Brigadier, Colonel?' Guy asked when he reported to the orderly-room.

'Very cheerful. He's not been round from the chloroform long. He's asking for his coco-nut.'

'I left it on his desk.'

'You'd better take it to him. He wants to see you. From his account you seem to have put up rather a good show last night. It's jolly bad luck.' This was not quite the form Guy had expected congratulations to take. 'Sit down, Uncle, you aren't on a charge – yet.'

Guy sat silent while Colonel Tickeridge paced the carpet.

'It's only once or twice in a chap's life he gets the chance of a gong. Some chaps never get it. You got yours last night and did all right. By all justice I ought now to be drafting a citation for your M.C. Instead of which we're in the hell of a fix. I can't think what possessed us last night. We can't even keep the thing quiet. If it was just the battalion involved we might conceivably have tried, but the ship's full of odds and sods and the thing just isn't on. If the Brigadier hadn't stopped one, we might have made you carry the can. "Over-zealous young officer … mild reprimand", you know. But there'll have to be a medical report and an inquiry. You simply can't do things like that at his age and get away with it. If I'd had any idea what was in his head, I'd have refused cooperation. At least I think I should have done this morning. It won't look too good for the ship's captain either. It won't do you any good. Of course you were acting under orders. You're in the clear legally. But it'll be a black mark. For the rest of your life when your name comes up, someone is bound to say: "Isn't he the chap who blotted his copy-book at Dakar in 40?" Not, I suppose, that it matters to you. You'll be out of the Corps and your name won't crop up, will it? Come on, let's take the head to the Brig.'

They found him in the sick bay, alone in the officers' ward, his machete, freshly scoured, beside him.

'It wasn't a clean stroke,' he said. 'The silly fellow saw me first so I had to bung a grenade at him, then look for the head and trim it up tidy. Well, Crouchback, how d'you like having a brigadier under your command?'

'I found him most insubordinate, sir.'

'It was a potty little show, but you didn't do too badly for a first attempt. Did I hear you threaten me with a court-martial at one stage of the proceedings?'

'Yes, sir.'

'Never do that, Crouchback, particularly in the field, unless you've got a prisoner's escort handy. I've known a promising young officer shot with a Lee-Enfield for threatening things in the field. Where's my coco-nut?' Guy handed him the swaddled head. 'My word he's a beauty, isn't he? Look at his great teeth. Never saw a better. I'm damned if I give him to the Force Commander. I'll shrink and pickle him; it'll give me an interest while I'm laid up.'

When they left Guy asked: 'Does he know what you told me, Colonel? I mean about his being in for a row?'

'Of course he does. He's got out of more rows than anyone in the Service.'

'So you think he'll be all right this time?'

Colonel Tickeridge answered sadly and solemnly:

'He's the wrong age. You can be an *enfant terrible* or you can be a national figure no one dares touch. But the Brig's neither of those things. It's the end for him – at least he thinks it is and he ought to know.'

The convoy sailed down the coast and then began to break up, first one ship turning aside, then another. The men-o'-war steamed away to another rendezvous – all save the damaged ships who limped down to dry docks at Simonstown. The Free French pursued their mission of liberation elsewhere, the faithful little *Belgravia* with them. The two ships containing the Halberdier Brigade berthed at a British port. Since the night at Dakar a rare delicacy had kept everyone from questioning Guy. They knew something had happened, that all was not right. They pretended not to be curious. It was the same in the sergeants' mess and on the troop deck, Guy's sergeant told him. The Brigadier was carried ashore to hospital. The Brigade resumed its old duty of standing by for orders.

7

Three weeks later the brigade was still standing by for orders. Their transports had steamed out to sea and they were in camp on shore. The doctrine of 'dispersal' had not reached West Africa. The tents stood in neat lines on a stretch of sandy plain, five miles from the town, a few yards from the sea. The expert on tropical diseases had flown away and the rigorous, intolerably irksome hygienic precautions he had imposed fell into desuetude. Local leave to up-country stations was given to officers for sporting purposes. Apthorpe was one of the first to go. The town was out of bounds to all ranks. No one wished to go there. Later when he came to read *The Heart of the Matter* Guy reflected, fascinated, that at this very time 'Scobie' was close at hand, demolishing partitions in native houses, still conscientiously interfering with neutral shipping. If they had not the services of the new Catholic chaplain, Guy might have gone to Father Rank to confess increasing sloth, one dismal occasion of drunkenness, and the lingering resentment he felt at the injustice he had suffered in the exploit to which he had given the private name of 'Operation Truslove'.

Wireless news from England was all of air raids. Some of the men were consumed with anxiety; most were consoled by a rumour, quite baseless, which was travelling the whole world in an untraceable manner, that the invasion had sailed and been defeated, that the whole Channel was full of charred German corpses. The men paraded, marched, bathed, constructed a rifle range and were quite without speculation about their future. Some said they were to spend the rest of the war here keeping fit, keeping up their morale, firing on the new range; others said they were bound for Libya, round the Cape; others that they were to forestall the German occupation of the Azores.

Then, after three weeks, an aeroplane arrived bringing mail. Most of it had been posted before the expedition even sailed but there was a more recent, official bag. Leonard was still on the strength of the Second Battalion, pending posting. It was now announced that he was dead, killed by a bomb, on leave in South London. There was also a move-order for Guy. His presence was required at an inquiry into the doings on Beach A, which was to be held in England as soon as Brigadier Ritchie-Hook was fit to move.

There was also a new Brigadier. He sent for Guy on the day of his arrival. He was a youngish, thick, mustachioed, naturally genial man, plainly ill at ease in the present case. Guy had not seen him before, but he would have recognized him as a Halberdier without studying his corps buttons.

'You're Captain Crouchback?'

'Lieutenant, sir.'

'Oh, I've got you down here as captain. I must look into it. Perhaps your promotion came through after you left U.K. Anyway it doesn't matter now. It was only an Acting Rank of course while you had a company. I'm afraid you'll be losing your company for the time being.'

'Does that mean I'm under arrest, sir?'

'Good God, no. At least not exactly. I mean to say this is simply an inquiry not a court-martial. The Force Commander made a great fuss about it. I don't suppose it'll ever come to a court-martial. The Navy are being rather stiff too, but they do things their own way. I should say myself you're in the clear – unofficially, mind. As far as I understand the case you were simply acting under orders. You'll be attached here at my headquarters for general duties. We'll get you all off as soon as Ben – your Brigadier, I mean – can move. I'm trying to get them to lay on a flying-boat. Meanwhile just hang about until you're wanted.'

Guy hung about. He had had his captaincy without knowing it, and had now lost it.

'That means six or seven pounds more pay, anyway,' said the staff captain. 'It shouldn't take long to straighten out. Or I'd take a chance and give it to you now if you're short.'

'Thanks awfully,' said Guy. 'I can manage.'

'Nothing much to spend money on here certainly. You can be sure of getting it somewhere, sometime. Army pay follows you up, like income tax.'

The battalion wanted to 'dine' him 'out', but Tickeridge forbade it.

'You'll be back with us in a day or two,' he said.

'Shall I?' Guy asked when they were alone.

'I wouldn't bet on it.'

Meanwhile there had been a series of disturbing bulletins from and about Apthorpe.

Messages from up-country passed by telephone from one semi-literate native telephonist to another. The first message was: *'Captain Apthorpe him very sorry off collar requests extension leaves.'*

Two days later there was a long and quite unintelligible message to the Senior Medical Officer demanding a number of drugs. After that was the request that the specialist in tropical diseases (who had left them some time before) should come up-country immediately. Then silence. At last a day or two before the mail arrived, Apthorpe appeared.

He was slung in a sheeted hammock between two bearers, looking like a Victorian woodcut from a book of exploration. They deposited him on the hospital steps and at once began an argument about their 'dash', they talking very loudly in Mende, Apthorpe feebly in Swahili. He was carried indoors protesting: 'They understand perfectly. They're only pretending. It's their lingua franca.'

The boys remained like vultures day after day, disputing over their 'dash' and admiring the passing pageant of metropolitan life.

Everyone in the brigade mess was particularly pleasant to Guy, even Dunn who was genuinely delighted to have the company of someone of more ignominious position than himself.

'Tell me all about it, old chap. Is it true you went off and started a battle on your own?'

'I'm not allowed to talk. The matter is *sub judice*.'

'Like that matter of the boot. You've heard the latest? The lunatic Apthorpe has taken refuge in the hospital. I bet he's shamming.'

'I don't think so. He looked pretty sick when he came back from his leave up-country.'

'But he's used to this climate. Anyway, we'll catch him when he comes out. If you ask me I'd say he was in worse trouble than you are.'

This talk of Apthorpe brought back tender memories of Guy's early days in barracks. He asked permission of the brigade major to visit him.

'Take a car, Uncle.' Everyone was anxious to be agreeable. 'Take a bottle of whisky. I'll make it all right with the mess president.' (They were rationed to one bottle a month in this town.)

'Will that be all right with the hospital?'

'Very much all wrong, Uncle. That's your risk. But it's always done. Not worth while calling on a chap in hospital unless you bring a bottle. But don't say I told you. It's your responsibility if you're caught.'

Guy drove up the laterite road, past the Syrian stores and the vultures, noticing nothing except the dawdling natives who obstructed his way; later a few printed pages would create, not recall, the scene for him and make it forever memorable. People would say to him in eight years time: 'You were there during the war. Was it like that?' and he would answer: 'Yes. It *must* have been.'

Then out of the town by a steep road to the spacious, whitish hospital, where there was no wireless to aggravate the suffering, no bustle; fans swung to and fro, windows were shut and curtained against the heat of the sun.

He found Apthorpe alone in his room, in a bed near the window. When Guy entered he was lying doing nothing, staring at the sun-blind with his hands empty on the counterpane. He immediately began to fill and light a pipe.

'I came to see how you were.'

'Rotten, old man, rotten.'

'They don't seem to have given you much to do.'

'They don't realize how ill I am. They keep bringing me jigsaws and Ian

Hay. A damn fool woman, wife of a box-wallah here, offered to teach me crochet. I ask you, old man, I just ask you.'

Guy produced the bottle he had been concealing in the pocket of his bush-shirt.

'I wondered if you'd like some whisky.'

'That's very thoughtful. In fact I would. Very much. They bring us one medicine-glassful at sundown. It's not enough. Often one wants more. I told them so, pretty strongly, and they just laughed. They've treated my case all wrong from the very first. I know more about medicines than any of those young idiots. It's a wonder I've stayed alive as long as I have. Toughness. It takes some time to kill an old bush hand. But they'll do it. They wear one down. They exhaust the will to live and then – phut. You're a goner. I've seen it happen dozens of times.'

'Where shall I put the whisky?'

'Somewhere I can reach it. It'll get damned hot in the bed, but I think it's the best place.'

'How about the locker?'

'They're always prying in there. But they're slack about bed-making. They just pull the covers smooth before the doctor's round. Tuck it in at the bottom, there's a good chap.'

There was only a thin sheet and a thin cotton counterpane. Guy saw Apthorpe's large feet, bereft of their 'porpoises', peeling with fever. He tried to interest Apthorpe in the new brigadier and in his own obscure position, but Apthorpe said fretfully: 'Yes, yes, yes, yes. It's all another world to me, old man.'

He puffed at his pipe, let it go out, tried with a feeble hand to put it on the table beside him, dropped it, noisily in that quiet place, on the bare floor. Guy stooped to retrieve it but Apthorpe said: 'Leave it there, old man. I don't want it. I only tried to be companionable.'

When Guy looked up he saw tears on Apthorpe's colourless cheeks.

'I say, would you like me to go?'

'No, no. I'll feel better in a minute. Did you bring a corkscrew? Good man. I think I could do with a nip.'

Guy opened the bottle, poured out a tot, recorked and replaced the spirit under the sheet.

'Wash out the glass, old man, do you mind? I've been hoping you'd come – you especially. There's something worrying me.'

'Not the signalman's boot?'

'No, no, no, no. Do you suppose I'd let a little tick like Dunn worry me? No, it's something on my conscience.'

There was a pause during which the whisky seemed to perform its beneficent magic. Apthorpe shut his eyes and smiled. At last he looked up and said: 'Hullo, Crouchback, you here? That's lucky. There's something

I wanted to say to you. Do you remember years ago, when we first joined, I mentioned my aunt?'

'You mentioned two.'

'*Exactly*. That's what I wanted to tell you. There's only one.'

'I *am* sorry.' All the talk lately had been about people killed by bombs. 'Was it an air-raid? Leonard caught one . . .'

'No, no, no: I mean, there never was more than one. The other was an invention. I suppose you might call it a little joke. Anyway, I've told you.'

After a pause Guy could not resist asking: 'Which did you invent, the one at Peterborough or the one at Tunbridge Wells?'

'The one at Peterborough, of course.'

'Then where did you hurt your knee?'

'At Tunbridge Wells.' Apthorpe giggled slightly at his cleverness like Mr Toad in *The Wind in the Willows*.

'You certainly took me in thoroughly.'

'Yes. It was a good joke, wasn't it? I say, I think I'd like a drop more whisky.'

'Sure it's good for you?'

'My dear fellow, I've been just as ill as this before and pulled through – simply by treating it with whisky.'

He sighed happily after this second glass. He really did seem altogether better and stronger.

'There's another point I want to talk about. My will.'

'You needn't start thinking about that for years yet.'

'I think about it *now*. A great deal. I haven't much. Just a few thousand in "gilt-edged" my father left me. I've left it all back to my aunt of course. It's family money, after all, and ought to go back. The one at Tunbridge Wells not' – roguishly – 'the good lady at Peterborough. But there's someone else.'

Guy thought: could this inscrutable man have a secret, irregular ménage? Little dusky Apthorpes, perhaps?

'Look here, Apthorpe, please don't go telling me anything about your private affairs. You'll be awfully embarrassed about it later, if you do. You're going to be perfectly fit again in a week or two.'

Apthorpe considered this.

'I'm tough,' he admitted. 'I'll take some killing. But it's all a question of the will to live. I must set everything in order just in case they wear me down. That's what keeps worrying me so.'

'All right. What is it?'

'It's my gear,' said Apthorpe. 'I don't want my aunt to get hold of it. Some of it's at the Commodore's at Southsand. The rest is at that place in Cornwall, where we last camped. I left it in Leonard's charge. He was a trustworthy sort of chap, I always thought.'

Guy wondered: should he make it plain about Leonard? Better leave it till later. He had probably left Apthorpe's treasure at the inn when they went to London. It might be traced eventually. This was no time to add to Apthorpe's anxieties.

'If my aunt got it, I know exactly what she'd do. She'd hand the whole thing over to some High Church boy-scouts she's interested in. I don't want High Church boy-scouts playing the devil with my gear.'

'No. It would be most unsuitable.'

'Exactly. You remember Chatty Corner?'

'Vividly.'

'I want him to have it all. I haven't mentioned it in my will. I thought it might hurt my aunt's feelings. I don't suppose she really knows it exists. Now I want you to collect it and hand it over to Chatty on the quiet. I don't suppose it's strictly legal but it's quite safe. Even if she did get wind of it, my aunt is the last person to go to law. You'll do that for me, won't you, old man?'

'Very well. I'll try.'

'Then I can die happy – at least if anyone ever does die happy. Do you think they do?'

'We used to pray for it a lot at school. But for goodness' sake don't start thinking of dying *now*.'

'I'm a great deal nearer death now,' said Apthorpe, suddenly huffy, 'than you ever were at school.'

There was a rattle at the door and a nurse came in with a tray.

'Why! Visitors! You're the first he's had. I must say you seem to have cheered him up. We have been down in the dumps, haven't we?' she said to Apthorpe.

'You see, old man, they wear me down. Thanks for coming. Good-bye.'

'I smell something I shouldn't,' said the nurse.

'Just a drop of whisky I happened to have in my flask, nurse,' Guy answered.

'Well, don't let the doctor hear about it. It's the *very* worst thing. I ought really to report you to the S.M.O., really I ought.'

'Is the doctor anywhere about?' Guy asked. 'I'd rather like to speak to him.'

'Second door on the left. I shouldn't go in if I were you. He's in a horrid temper.'

But Guy found a weary, foolish man of his own age.

'Apthorpe? Yes. You're in the same regiment, I see. The Applejacks, eh?'

'Is he really pretty bad, doctor?'

'Of course he is. He wouldn't be here if he wasn't.'

'He talked a lot about dying.'

'Yes, he does to me, except when he's delirious. Then he seems worried about a bomb in the rears. Did he ever have any experience of the kind, do you know?'

'I rather think he did.'

'Well, that accounts for that. Queer bird, the mind. Hides things away and then out they pop. But I mustn't get too technical. It's a hobby-horse of mine, the mind.'

'I wanted to know, is he on the danger list?'

'Well, I haven't actually put him there. No need to cause unnecessary alarm and despondency. His sort of trouble hangs on for weeks often and just when you think you've pulled them through, out they go, you know.

'Apthorpe's got the disadvantage of having lived in this God-forsaken country. You chaps who come out fresh from England have got stamina. Chaps who live here have got their blood full of every sort of infection. And then, of course, they poison themselves with whisky. They snuff out like babies. Still, we're doing the best for Apthorpe. Luckily we're rather empty at the moment so everyone can give him full attention.'

'Thank you, sir.'

The R.A.M.C. man was a colonel but he was seldom called 'sir' by anyone outside his own staff. 'Have a glass of whisky?' he said gratefully.

'Thanks awfully, but I must be off.'

'Any time you're passing.'

'By the way, sir, how is our Brigadier Ritchie-Hook?'

'He'll be out of here any day now. Between ourselves he's rather a difficult patient. He made one of my young officers pickle a Negro's head for him. Most unusual.'

'Was the pickling a success?'

'Must have been, I suppose. Anyway he keeps the thing by his bed grinning at him.'

8

Next morning at dawn a flying-boat landed at Freetown.

'That's for you,' said Colonel Tickeridge. 'They say the Brig. will be fit to move tomorrow.'

But there was other news that morning. Apthorpe was in a coma.

'They don't think he'll ever come out of it,' Colonel Tickeridge said. 'Poor old Uncle. Still there are worse ways of dying and he hasn't got a madam or children or anything.'

'Only an aunt,' said Guy.

'Two aunts, I think he told me.'

Guy did not correct him. Everyone at Brigade Headquarters remembered Apthorpe well. He had been a joke there. Now the mess was cast into gloom, less at the loss of Apthorpe than at the thought of death so near, so unexpected.

'We'll lay on full military honours for the funeral.'

'He'd have liked that.'

'A good opportunity to show the flag in the town.'

Dunn fussed about his boot.

'I don't see how I'll be able to recover now,' he said. 'It seems rather ghoulish somehow, applying to the next of kin.'

'How much is it?'

'Nine shillings.'

'I'll pay.'

'I say, that's very sporting of you. It'll keep my books in order.'

The new brigadier went to the hospital that morning to inform Ritchie-Hook of his imminent departure. He returned at lunch-time.

'Apthorpe is dead,' he said briefly. 'I want to talk to you, Crouchback, after lunch.'

Guy supposed the summons was connected with his move-order and went to the brigadier's office without alarm. He found both the brigadier and the brigade major there, one looking angrily at him, the other looking at the table.

'You heard that Apthorpe was dead?'

'Yes, sir.'

'There was an empty whisky bottle in his bed. Does that mean anything to you?'

Guy stood silent, aghast rather than ashamed.

'I asked: "Does that mean anything to you?" '

'Yes, sir. I took him a bottle yesterday afternoon.'

'You knew it was against orders?'

'Yes, sir.'

'Any excuse?'

'No, sir, except that I knew he liked it and I didn't realize it would do him any harm. Or that he'd finish it all at once.'

'He was half delirious, poor fellow. How old are you, Crouchback?'

'Thirty-six, sir.'

'Exactly. That's what makes everything so hopeless. If you were a young idiot of twenty-one I could understand it. Damn it, man, you're only a year or two younger than I am.'

Guy stood still saying nothing. He was curious how the brigadier would deal with the question.

'The S.M.O. of the hospital knows all about it. So do most of his staff, I expect. You can imagine how he feels. I was with him half the morning before I could get him to see sense. Yes, I've begged you off, but please understand that what I've done was purely for the Corps. You've committed too serious a crime for me to deal with summarily. The choice was between hushing it up and sending you before a court martial. There's nothing would give me more personal satisfaction than to see you booted out of the army altogether. But we've one sticky business on our hands already – in which incidentally you are implicated. I persuaded the medico that we had no evidence. You were poor Apthorpe's only visitor but there are orderlies and native porters in and out of the hospital who *might* have sold him the stuff' (he spoke as though whisky, which he regularly and moderately drank, were some noxious distillation of Guy's own). 'Nothing's worse than a court martial that goes off half-cock. I also told him what a slur it would be on poor Apthorpe's name. It would all have had to come out. I gather he was practically a dipsomaniac and had two aunts who think the world of him. Pretty gloomy for them to hear the truth. So I got him to agree in the end. But don't thank me, and, remember, I don't want to see you again ever. I shall apply for your immediate posting out of the brigade as soon as they've finished with you in England. The only hope I have for you is that you're thoroughly ashamed of yourself. You can fall out now.'

Guy left the office unashamed. He felt shaken, as though he had seen a road accident in which he was not concerned. His fingers shook but it was nerves not conscience which troubled him; he was familiar with shame; this trembling, hopeless sense of disaster was something of quite another order; something that would pass and leave no mark.

He stood in the ante-room sweating and motionless and was presently aware of someone at his elbow.

'I see you aren't busy.'

He turned and saw Dunn. 'No.'

'Perhaps you wouldn't mind my mentioning it then? This morning you very kindly offered to settle that matter of the boot.'

'Yes, of course. How much was it? I forget. Nine pounds, wasn't it?'

'Good Lord, no. Nine shillings.'

'Of course. Nine shillings.' Guy did not want to show Dunn his trembling hands. 'I've no change now. Remind me tomorrow.'

'But you're off tomorrow, aren't you?'

'So I am. I forgot.'

His hands when he took them out of his pockets trembled less than he had feared. He counted out nine shillings.

'I'll make out the receipt in Apthorpe's name if it's all the same to you.'

'I don't want a receipt.'

'Must keep my books straight.'

Dunn left to put his books straight. Guy remained standing. Presently the brigade major came out of the office.

'I say, I'm awfully sorry about this business,' he said.
'It was a damned silly thing to do. I see that now.'
'I did say it was your responsibility.'
'Of course. Of course.'
'There was nothing I could possibly have said.'
'Of course not. Nothing.'

They took Ritchie-Hook out of the hospital before Apthorpe. Guy had half an hour to wait on the quay. The flying-boat lay out. All round the bum-boats floated selling fruit and nuts.

'Have you got my nut packed up safely, Glass?'

'Yes, sir.'

Halberdier Glass was in a black mood. Ritchie-Hook's servant was travelling home with his master. Glass had to stay behind.

Colonel Tickeridge had come down to the quay.

He said: 'I don't seem to bring luck to the officers I pick for promotion. First Leonard, then Apthorpe.'

'And now me, sir.'

'And now you.'

'Here comes the party.'

An ambulance drove up followed by the Brigadier's car. Ritchie-Hook, one leg huge, as though from elephantiasis, in plaster. The brigade major took his arm and led him to the edge of the quay.

'No prisoners' escort?' said Ritchie-Hook. 'Morning, Tickeridge. Morning, Crouchback. What's all this I hear about you poisoning one of my officers? The damn nurses couldn't stop talking about it all yesterday. Now jump to it. Junior officers into the boat first, out of it last.'

Guy jumped to it and sat as far as he could out of everyone's way. Presently they hoisted Ritchie-Hook down. Before the boat had reached the aircraft, the brigade car was honking its way through the listless, black crowds; they had run things pretty close for the funeral parade.

The flying-boat was a mail carrier. The after half of the cabin was piled high with bags among which the Halberdier servant luxuriously disposed himself for sleep. Guy remembered the immense boredom of censoring those letters home. Here and there one came across a man who through some oddity of upbringing had escaped the state schools. These wrote with wild phonetic mis-spellings straight from the heart. The rest strung together clichés which he supposed somehow communicated some exchange of affection and need. The old soldiers wrote SWALK on the envelope, meaning 'sealed with a loving kiss'. All these missives served as a couch for Ritchie-Hook's batman.

The flying-boat climbed in a great circle over the green land, then turned over the town. Already it was much cooler.

It had been the heat, Guy thought, all the false emotions of the past twenty-four hours. In England where winter would be giving its first hints of sharpness, where the leaves would be falling among the falling bombs, fire-gutted, shattered, where the bodies were nightly dragged half-clothed, clutching pets, from the rubble and glass splinters – things would look very different in England.

The flying-boat made another turn over White Man's Grave and set its course across the ocean, bearing away the two men who had destroyed Apthorpe.

White Man's Grave. The European cemetery was conveniently near the hospital. Six months of changing stations and standing by for orders had not corroded the faultless balance of the Halberdier slow march. The Second Battalion had called a parade the moment the news of Apthorpe's death arrived and the regimental sergeant-major had roared under the fiery sun and the boots had moved up and down the blistering road. This morning it was perfect. The coffin bearers were exactly sized. The bugles sounded Last Post in perfect unison. The rifles fired as one.

As a means of 'showing the flag' it was not greatly appreciated. The civil population were *aficionados* of funerals. They liked more spontaneity, more evident grief. But as a drill parade it was something that the Colony had never seen before. The flag-covered coffin descended without a hitch. The vital earth settled down. Two Halberdiers fainted, falling flat and rigid, and were left supine.

When it was all over Sarum-Smith, genuinely moved, said: 'It was like the burial of Sir John Moore at Corunna.'

'Sure you don't mean the Duke of Wellington at St Paul's?' said de Souza.

'Perhaps I do.'

Colonel Tickeridge asked the adjutant: 'Ought we to pass the cap round to put up a stone or something?'

'I imagine his relations in England will want to fix that.'

'They're well off?'

'Extremely, I believe. And High Church. They'd probably want something fancy.'

'Both Uncles gone the same day.'

'Funny, I was thinking the same. I rather preferred Crouchback on the whole.'

'He seemed a nice enough fellow. I could never quite make him out. Pity he made an ass of himself.'

Already the Second Battalion of the Halberdiers spoke of Guy in the past tense. He had momentarily been of them; now he was an alien; someone in their long and varied past, but forgotten.

OFFICERS
AND
GENTLEMEN

CONTENTS

Book One HAPPY WARRIORS   197

Interlude   275

Book Two IN THE PICTURE   283

Epilogue   387

BOOK ONE

Happy Warriors

I

The sky over London was glorious, ochre and madder, as though a dozen tropic suns were simultaneously setting round the horizon; everywhere the searchlights clustered and hovered, then swept apart; here and there pitchy clouds drifted and billowed; now and then a huge flash momentarily froze the serene fireside glow. Everywhere the shells sparkled like Christmas baubles.

'Pure Turner,' said Guy Crouchback, enthusiastically; he came fresh to these delights.

'John Martin, surely?' said Ian Kilbannock.

'No,' said Guy firmly. He would not accept correction on matters of art from this former sporting-journalist. 'Not Martin. The sky-line is too low. The scale is less than Babylonian.'

They stood at the top of St James's Street. Half-way down Turtle's Club was burning briskly. From Piccadilly to the Palace the whole jumble of incongruous façades was caricatured by the blaze.

'Anyway, it's too noisy to discuss it here.'

Guns were banging away in the neighbouring parks. A stick of bombs fell thunderously somewhere in the direction of Victoria Station.

On the pavement opposite Turtle's a group of progressive novelists in firemen's uniform were squirting a little jet of water into the morning-room.

Guy was momentarily reminded of Holy Saturday at Downside; early gusty March mornings of boyhood; the doors wide open in the unfinished butt of the Abbey; half the school coughing; fluttering linen; the glowing brazier and the priest with his hyssop, paradoxically blessing fire with water.

'It was never much of a club,' said Ian. 'My father belonged.'

He relit his cigar and immediately a voice near their knees exclaimed: 'Put that light out.'

'A preposterous suggestion,' said Ian.

They looked over the railings beside them and descried in the depths of the area a helmet, lettered ARP.

'Take cover,' said the voice.

A crescent scream immediately, it seemed, over their heads; a thud which raised the paving-stones under their feet; a tremendous incandescence just north of Piccadilly; a pentecostal wind; the remaining panes of glass above them scattered in lethal splinters about the street.

'You know, I think he's right. We had better leave this to the civilians.'

Soldier and airman trotted briskly to the steps of Bellamy's. As they reached the doors, the engines overhead faded and fell silent and only the crackling flames at Turtle's disturbed the midnight hush.

'Most exhilarating,' said Guy.

'Ah, you're new to it. The bore is that it goes on night after night. It can be pretty dangerous too with these fire-engines and ambulances driving all over the place. I wish I could have an African holiday. My awful Air Marshal won't let me go. He seems to have taken a fancy to me.'

'You can't blame yourself. It wasn't to be expected.'

'No indeed.'

In the front hall Job, the night-porter, greeted them with unnatural unction. He had had recourse to the bottle. His was a lonely and precarious post, hemmed in with plate glass. No one at that season grudged him his relaxation. Tonight he was acting – grossly over-acting – the part of a stage butler.

'Good evening, sir. Permit me to welcome you to England, home and safety. Good evening, my lord. Air Marshal Beech is in the billiard-room.'

'Oh, God.'

'I thought it right to apprise you, my lord.'

'*Quite* right.'

'The gutters outside are running with whisky and brandy.'

'No, Job.'

'So I was informed, sir, by Colonel Blackhouse. All the spirit store of Turtle's, gentlemen, running to waste in the streets.'

'We didn't see it.'

'Then we may be sure, my lord, the fire brigade have consumed it.'

Guy and Ian entered the back-hall.

'So your Air Marshal got into the club after all.'

'Yes, it was a shocking business. They held an election during what the papers call "the Battle of Britain", when the Air Force was for a moment almost respectable.'

'Well, it's worse for you than for me.'

'My dear fellow, it's a *nightmare* for *everyone*.'

The windows of the card-room had been blown out and bridge-players, clutching their score sheets, filled the hall. Brandy and whisky were flowing here, if not in the gutters outside.

'Hullo, Guy. Haven't seen you about lately.'

'I only got back from Africa this afternoon.'

'Odd time to choose. I'd have stayed put.'

'I've come home under a cloud.'

'In the last war we used to *send* fellows to Africa when they were under a cloud. What will you drink?'

Guy explained the circumstances of his recall.

More members came in from the street.

'All quiet outside.'

'Job tells me it's overrun with drunk firemen.'

'Job's drunk himself.'

'Yes, every night this week. Can't blame him.'

'Two glasses of wine, Parsons.'

'Some of the servants ought to be sober some of the time.'

'There's a fellow under the billiard-table now.'

'One of the servants?'

'Not one I've ever seen before.'

'Whisky, please, Parsons.'

'I say, I hope we don't have to take Turtle's in.'

'They come here sometimes when they're cleaning. Timid little fellows. Don't give any trouble.'

'Three whiskies and soda, please, Parsons.'

'Heard about Guy's balls-up at Dakar? Tell him, Guy. It's a good story.'

Guy told his good story again and many times that night.

Presently his brother-in-law, Arthur Box-Bender, appeared in shirt-sleeves from the billiard-room, accompanied by another Member of Parliament, a rather gruesome crony of his named Elderbury.

'D'you know what put me off that lost shot?' said Elderbury. 'I trod on someone.'

'Who!'

'No one I know. He was under the table and I trod on his hand.'

'Extraordinary thing. Passed out?'

'He said: "Damn".'

'I don't believe it. Parsons, is there anyone under the billiard-table?'

'Yes, sir, a new member.'

'What's he doing there?'

'Obeying orders, he says, sir.'

Two or three bridge-players went to investigate the phenomenon.

'Parsons, what's all this about the streets running with wine?'

'I haven't been out myself, sir. A lot of the members have been talking about it.'

The reconnaissance party returned from the billiard-room and reported:

'It's perfectly true. There *is* a fellow under the table.'

'I remember poor old Binkie Cavanagh used to sit there sometimes.'

'Binkie was mad.'

'Well, I daresay this fellow is too.'

'Hullo, Guy,' said Box-Bender, 'I thought you were in Africa.'

Guy told him his story.

'How very awkward,' said Box-Bender.

Tommy Blackhouse joined them.

'Tommy, what's all this you told Job about the streets running with wine?'

'*He* told *me*. Just been out to look. Not a drop in sight.'

'Have you been in to the billiard-room?'

'No.'

'Go and have a look. There's something worth seeing.'

Guy accompanied Tommy Blackhouse. The billiard-room was full but no one was playing. In the shadows under the table lurked a human shape.

'Are you all right down there?' Tommy asked kindly. 'Want a drink or anything?'

'I am perfectly all right, thank you. I am merely obeying the regulations. In an air raid it is the duty of every officer and man not on duty to take the nearest and safest cover wherever he may be. As the senior officer present I thought I should set an example.'

'Well, there's not room for us all, is there?'

'You should go under the stairs or into the cellar.'

The figure now revealed itself as Air Marshal Beech. Tommy was a professional soldier with a career ahead. It was his instinct to be agreeable to the senior officers of all services.

'I think it's pretty well over now, sir.'

'I have not heard the All Clear.'

As he spoke the siren sounded and the sturdy grey figure scrambled to its feet.

'Good evening.'

'Ah, Crouchback, isn't it? We met at Lady Kilbannock's.'

The Air Marshal stretched and dusted himself.

'I want my car. You might just call Air Headquarters, Crouchback, and have it sent round.'

Guy rang the bell.

'Parsons, tell Job that Air Marshal Beech wants his car.'

'Very good, sir.'

The Air Marshal's small eyes looked suspicious. He began to say one thing, thought better of it, said 'Thanks,' and left.

'You never were a good mixer, were you, Guy?'

'Oh, dear. Was I beastly to that poor wretch?'

'He won't look on you as a friend in future.'

'I hope he never did.'

'Oh, he's not such a bad fellow. He's putting in a lot of useful work at the moment.'

'I can't imagine his ever being much use to me.'

'It's going to be a long war, Guy. One may need all the friends one can get before it's over. Sorry about your trouble at Dakar. I happened to see the file yesterday. But I don't think it will come to much. There were some damn silly minutes on it, though. You ought to see it gets to the top level at once before too many people commit themselves.'

'How on earth can I do that?'

'Talk about it.'

'I have.'

'Keep talking. There are ears everywhere.'

Then Guy asked: 'Is Virginia all right?'

'As far as I know. She's left Claridge's. Someone told me she'd moved out of London somewhere. Didn't care for the blitz.'

From the way Tommy spoke, Guy thought that, perhaps, Virginia was not entirely all right.

'You've come up in the world, Tommy.'

'Oh, I'm just messing round with HOO. As a matter of fact there's something rather attractive in the air I can't talk about. I'll know for certain in a day or two. I might be able to fit you in. Have you reported to your regiment yet?'

'Going tomorrow. I only landed today.'

'Well, be careful or you'll find yourself part of the general parcel-post. I should stick around Bellamy's as much as you can. This is where one gets the amusing jobs nowadays. That is, if you want an amusing job.'

'Of course.'

'Well, stick around.'

They returned to the hall. It was thinning out since the All Clear. Air Marshal Beech was on the fender talking to the two Members of Parliament.

'. . . You back-benchers, Elderbury, can do quite a lot if you set yourselves at it. Push the Ministries. Keep pushing . . .'

As in a stage farce Ian Kilbannock's head emerged cautiously from the wash-room, where he had taken refuge from his chief. He withdrew hastily but too late.

'Ian. Just the man I want. Tool off to Headquarters and get the gen about tonight's do and ring through to me at home.'

'The air raid, sir? I think it's over. They got Turtle's.'

'No, no. You must know what I mean. The subject I discussed yesterday with Air Marshal Dime.'

'I wasn't there when you discussed it, sir. You sent me out.'

'You should keep yourself in the picture . . .'

But the rebuke never took full shape; the strip, as he would have preferred it, was not torn off, for at that moment there appeared from the outer hall the figure of Job, strangely illuminated. In some strictly private mood of his high drama Job had possessed himself of one of the six-branched silver candelabra from the dining-room; this he bore aloft, rigid but out of the straight so that six little dribbles of wax bespattered his livery. All in the back-hall fell silent and watched fascinated as this fantastic figure advanced upon the Air Marshal. A pace distant he bowed; wax splashed on the carpet before him.

'Sir,' he announced sonorously, 'your carriage awaits you.' Then he turned, and, moving with the confidence of a sleep-walker, retreated whence he had come.

The silence endured for a moment. Then: 'Really,' began the Air Marshal, 'that man –' but his voice was lost in the laughter. Elderbury was constitutionally a serious man, but when he did see a joke he enjoyed it extravagantly. He had felt resentful of Air Marshal Beech since missing an easy cannon through stepping on him. Elderbury chortled.

'Good old Job.'

'One of his very best.'

'Thank heaven I stayed on long enough to see that.'

'What would Bellamy's be without him?'

'We must have a drink on that. Parsons, take an order all round.'

The Air Marshal looked from face to happy face. Even Box-Bender's was gleeful. Ian Kilbannock was laughing more uproariously than anyone. The Air Marshal rose.

'Anyone going my way want a lift?'

No one was going his way.

As the doors, which in the past two centuries had welcomed grandee and card sharper, duellist and statesman, closed behind Air Marshal Beech, he wondered, not for the first time in his brief membership, whether Bellamy's was all it was cracked up to be.

He sank into his motor-car; the sirens sounded another warning.

'Home,' he ordered. 'I think we can just make it.'

2

Bombs were falling again by the time that Guy reached his hotel, but far away now, somewhere to the east among the docks. He slept fitfully and when the All Clear finally woke him the rising sun was disputing the sky with the sinking fires of the raid.

He was due in barracks that morning and he set out as uncertainly as on the day he first joined.

At Charing Cross trains were running almost to time. Every seat was taken. He jammed his valise across the corridor with his suitcase a few yards from him, making for himself a seat and a defence.

There were Halberdier badges in most of the carriages and the traffic at his destination was all for the barracks. The men hoisted their kit bags and climbed on board a waiting lorry. The handful of young officers squeezed together into two taxis. Guy took the third alone. As he passed the guard-room he had a brief, vague impression that there was something rather odd about the sentry. He drove to the Officers' House. No one was about. The preceding taxis disappeared in the direction of New Quarters. Guy left his luggage in the ante-room hall and crossed the square to the offices. A squad approached bearing buckets, their faces transformed as though by the hand of Circe from those of men to something less than the beasts. A muffled voice articulated: 'Eyes right.'

Ten pig-faces, visions of Jerome Bosch, swung towards him. Unnerved, automatically, Guy said: 'Eyes front, please, Corporal.'

He entered the adjutant's office, stood to attention and saluted. Two obscene fronts of canvas and rubber and talc were raised from the table. As though from beneath layers of bedclothes a voice said: 'Where's your gas-mask?'

'With the rest of my gear, sir, at the Officers' House.'

'Go and put it on.'

Guy saluted, turned about and marched off. He put on his gas-mask and straightened his cap before the looking-glass, which just a year ago had so often reflected his dress cap and high blue collar and a face full of hope and purpose. He gazed at the gross snout, then returned to the Adjutant. A company had fallen-in on the square; normal, pink young faces. In the orderly-room the Adjutant and Sergeant-Major sat undisguised.

'Take that thing off,' said the Adjutant. 'It's past eleven.'

Guy removed his mask and let it hang, in correct form, across his chest to dry.

'Haven't you read the Standing Orders?'

'No, sir.'

'Why the hell not?'

'Reporting back today, sir, from overseas.'

'Well, remember in future that every Wednesday from 1000 to 1100 hours all ranks take anti-gas precautions. That's a Command Standing Order.'

'Very good, sir.'

'Now, who are you and what do you want?'

'Lieutenant Crouchback, sir. Second Battalion Royal Halberdiers Brigade.'

'Nonsense. The Second Battalion is abroad.'

'I landed yesterday, sir.'

And then slowly, after all the masquerade with the gas-masks, old memories revived.

'We've met before.'

It was the nameless major, reduced now to captain, who had appeared at Penkirk and vanished three days later at Brookwood.

'You had the company during the great flap.'

'Of course. I say, I'm awfully sorry for not recognizing you. There have been so many flaps since. So many chaps through my hands. How did you get here? Oughtn't you to be in Freetown?'

'You weren't expecting me?'

'Not a word. I dare say your papers have gone to the Training Depot. Or up to Penkirk to the Fifth Battalion. Or down to Brook Park to the Sixth. Or to H O O. We've been expanding like the devil in the last two months. Records can't keep up. Well, I've about finished here. Carry on, Sergeant-Major. I shall be at the Officers' House if you want me. Come along, Crouchback.'

He and Guy went to the ante-room. It was not the room Guy had known, where he had sprained his knee on Guest Night. A dark rectangle over the fireplace marked the spot where 'The Unbroken Square' had hung; the bell from the Dutch frigate, the Afridi banner, the gilt idol from Burma, the Napoleonic cuirasses, the Ashanti drum, the loving-cup from Barbados, Tipu Sultan's musket, all were gone.

The Adjutant observed Guy's roving, lamenting eyes.

'Pretty bloody, isn't it? Everything has been stored away underground since the blitz.' Then from the bleakest spot in the universal desolation: 'I've lost a pip, too.'

'So I saw. Bad luck.'

'I expected it,' said the Adjutant. 'I wasn't due for promotion for another two years in the regular way. I thought the war might hurry things along a bit. It has for most chaps. It did for me for a month or two. But it didn't last.'

There was no fire.

'It's cold in here,' said Guy.

'Yes. No fires until evening. No drinks either.'

'I suppose it's the same everywhere?'

'No, it's *not*,' said the Adjutant crossly. 'Other regiments still manage to live quite decently. The Captain-Commandant is a changed character. Austerity is the order now. Trust the Corps to do it in a big way. We're sleeping four in a room and the mess subscription has been halved. We practically live on rations – like wild beasts,' he specified woefully but inaptly. 'I wouldn't stay here long if I were you. By the way, why *are* you here?'

'I came home with the Brigadier.' That seemed at the moment the most convenient explanation. 'You know he's back, of course?'

'First I've heard of it.'

'You know he got wounded?'

'No. Nothing ever seems to come to us here. Perhaps they've lost our address. The Corps got on very nicely the size it was. All this expansion has been the devil. They've taken my servant away – a man I'd had eight years. I have to share an old sweat with the Regimental Surgeon. That's what we've come to. They've even taken the band.'

'It's too cold to sit here,' said Guy.

'There's a stove in my office but the telephone keeps ringing. Take your choice.'

'What am I to do now?'

'My dear chap, as far as I'm concerned you're still in Africa. I'd send you on leave but you aren't on our strength. D'you want to see the Captain-Commandant? That could be arranged.'

'A changed character?'

'Horribly.'

'I don't see any reason to bother him.'

'No.'

'Well, then?'

They gazed hopelessly at one another across the empty grate.

'You must have had a move order.'

'No. I was just packed off like a parcel. The Brigadier left me at the aerodrome saying I'd be hearing from him.'

The Adjutant had exhausted all his meagre official repertoire.

'It couldn't have happened in peace-time,' he said.

'That is certainly true.'

Guy observed that this unknown soldier was collecting all his resolution for a desperate decision; at length: 'All right, I'll take a chance on it. You can use some leave, I suppose?'

'I promised to do something for Apthorpe – you remember him at Penkirk?'

'Yes, I do. Very well.' Exhilarated to find at last a firm mental foothold: 'Apthorpe. Temporary officer who somehow got made second-in-command of the Battalion. I thought him a bit mad.'

'He's dead now. I promised I'd collect his possessions and hand them over to his heir. I could do that in the next few days.'

'Excellent. If there's any bloodiness, that catches them two ways. We can call it compassionate or disembarkation leave, just as the cat jumps. Staying to lunch in the mess? I shouldn't.'

'I won't,' said Guy.

'If you hang about, there may be some transport going to the station. Two months ago I could have laid it on. That's all been stopped.'

'I'll get a taxi.'

'You know where to find the telephone? Don't forget to leave twopence in the box. I think I'll get back to my office. As you say, it's too cold here.'

Guy lingered. He entered the mess under the gallery which had lately resounded with 'The Roast Beef of Old England'. The portraits were gone from the walls, the silver from the side tables. There was little now to distinguish it from the dining-hall of Kut-al-Imara House. An AT came in from the serving door whistling; she saw Guy and continued to whistle as she rubbed a cloth over the bare boards of a table.

There was a click of balls from the billiard-room. Guy looked in and saw chiefly a large khaki behind. The player struck and widely missed an easy cannon. He stood up and turned.

'Wait for the shot,' he said with a stern but paternal air which purged the rebuke of all offence.

He was in his shirt-sleeves, revealing braces striped with the Halberdier colours. A red-tabbed tunic hung on the wall. Guy recognized him as an elderly colonel who had pottered about the mess a year ago. 'Care for a hundred up?' and 'Not much news in the papers today,' had been his constant refrain.

'I'm very sorry, sir,' said Guy.

'Puts a fellow off, you see,' said the Colonel. 'Care for a hundred up?'

'I'm afraid I am just going.'

'Everyone here is always going,' said the Colonel.

He padded round to his ball and studied the position. It seemed hopeless to Guy.

The Colonel struck with great force. All three balls sped and clicked and rebounded and clicked until finally the red trickled slower and slower towards a corner, seemed to come to a dead stop at the edge of the pocket, mysteriously regained momentum and fell in.

'Frankly,' said the Colonel, 'that was something of a fluke.'

Guy slipped away and gently closed the door. Glancing back through the glazed aperture he observed the next stroke. The Colonel put the red on its spot, studied the uncongenial arrangement and then with plump finger and thumb nonchalantly moved his ball three inches to the left. Guy left him to his solitary delinquency. What used the regulars to call him? Ox? Tiny? Hippo? The nickname escaped him.

With sterner thoughts he turned to the telephone and called for his taxi.

So Guy set out on the second stage of his pilgrimage, which had begun at the tomb of Sir Roger. Now, as then, an act of *pietas* was required of him; a spirit was to be placated. Apthorpe's gear must be retrieved and delivered before Guy was free to follow his fortunes in the King's service. His road lay backward for the next few days, to Southsand and Cornwall. 'Chatty' Corner, man of the trees, must be found, somewhere in the trackless forests of war-time England.

He paused in the ante-room and turned back the pages of the Visitors' Book to the record of that Guest Night last December. There, immediately below Tony Box-Bender's name, he found 'James Pendennis Corner'. But the column where his address or regiment should have stood, lay empty.

3

The last hour of the day at Our Lady of Victory's Preparatory School, temporarily accommodated at Matchet. Selections from Livy in Mr Crouchback's form-room. Black-out curtains drawn. Gas fire hissing. The customary smell of chalk and ink. The Fifth Form drowsy from the football field, hungry for high tea. Twenty minutes to go and the construe approaching unprepared passages.

'Please, sir, it is true, isn't it, that the Blessed Gervase Crouchback was an ancestor of yours?'

'Hardly an ancestor, Greswold. He was a priest. His brother, from whom I am descended, didn't behave quite so bravely, I'm sorry to say.'

'He didn't *conform*, sir?'

'No, but he kept very quiet – he and his son after him.'

'Do tell us how the Blessed Gervase was caught, sir.'

'I'm sure I've told you before.'

'A lot of us were absent that day, sir, and I've never quite understood what happened. The steward gave him away, didn't he?'

'Certainly not. Challoner misread a transcript from the St Omers records and the mistake has been copied from book to book. All our own people were true. It was a spy from Exeter who came to Broome asking for shelter, pretending to be a Catholic.'

The Fifth Form sat back contentedly. Old Crouchers was off. No more Livy.

'Father Gervase was lodged in the North turret of the forecourt. You have to know Broome to understand how it happened. There is only the forecourt, you see, between the house and the main road. Every good house stands on a road or a river or a rock. Always remember that. Only hunting-lodges belong in a park. It was after the Reformation that the new rich men began hiding away from the people. ...'

It was not difficult to get old Crouchers talking. Greswold major, whose grandfather he had known, was adept at it. Twenty minutes passed.

'... When he was examined by the Council the second time he was so weak that they gave him a stool to sit on.'

'Please, sir, that's the bell.'

'Time? Oh, dear, I'm afraid I've let myself run on, wasting your time. You ought to stop me, Greswold. Well, we'll start tomorrow where we left off. I shall expect a long, thorough construe.'

'Thank you, sir; good night. It was jolly interesting about the Blessed Gervase.'

'Good night, sir.'

The boys clattered away. Mr Crouchback buttoned his great-coat, slung his gas-mask across his shoulder and, torch in hand, walked downhill towards the lightless sea.

The Marine Hotel which had been Mr Crouchback's home for nine years was as full now as though in the height of summer. Every chair in the Residents' Lounge was held prescriptively. Novels and knitting were left to mark the squatters' rights when they ventured out into the mist.

Mr Crouchback made straight for his own rooms, but, encountering Miss Vavasour at the turn of the stairs, he paused, pressing himself into the corner to let her pass.

'Good evening, Miss Vavasour.'

'Oh, Mr Crouchback, I have been waiting for you. May I speak to you for a moment?'

'Of course, Miss Vavasour.'

'It's about something that happened today.' She spoke in a whisper. 'I don't want Mr Cuthbert to overhear me.'

'How very mysterious! I'm sure I have no secrets from the Cuthberts.'

'They have from you. There is a plot, Mr Crouchback, which you should know about.'

Miss Vavasour had turned about and was now making for Mr Crouchback's sitting-room. He opened the door and stood back to admit her. A strong smell of dog met their nostrils.

'Such a nice manly smell,' said Miss Vavasour.

Felix, his golden retriever, rose to meet Mr Crouchback, stood on his hind legs and pawed Mr Crouchback's chest.

'Down, Felix, down, boy. I hope he's been out.'

'Mrs Tickeridge and Jenifer took him for a long walk this afternoon.'

'Charming people. Do sit down while I get rid of this absurd gasbag.'

Mr Crouchback went into his bedroom, hung up his coat and haversack, peered at his old face in the looking-glass and returned to Miss Vavasour.

'Well, what is this sinister plot?'

'They want to turn you out,' said Miss Vavasour.

Mr Crouchback looked round the shabby little room, full of his furniture and books and photographs. 'I don't think that's possible,' he said; 'the

Cuthberts would never do a thing like that – after all these years. You must have misunderstood them. Anyway, they can't.'

'They can, Mr Crouchback. It's one of these new laws. There was an officer here today – at least he was dressed as an officer – a dreadful sort of person. He was counting all the rooms and looking at the register. He talked of taking over the whole place. Mr Cuthbert explained that several of us were permanent residents and that the others had come from bombed areas and were the wives of men at the front. Then the so-called officer said: "Who's this man occupying two rooms?" and do you know what Mr Cuthbert said? He said, "He works in the town. He's a school-teacher." *You*, Mr Crouchback, to be described like that!'

'Well, it's what I am, I suppose.'

'I very nearly interrupted them then and there, to tell them *who you are*, but of course I wasn't really part of the conversation. In fact I don't think they realized I was within hearing. But I *boiled*. Then this officer asked: "Secondary or Primary?" and Mr Cuthbert said: "Private" and then the officer laughed and said: "Priority nil." And after that I simply could not restrain myself any more so I simply got up and looked at them and left the room without a word.'

'I'm sure you did much the wisest thing.'

'But the impertinence of it!'

'I'm sure nothing will come of it. There are all sorts of people all over the place nowadays making inquiries. I suppose it's necessary. Depend upon it, it was just routine. The Cuthberts would never do a thing like that. Never. After all these years.'

'You are too trustful, Mr Crouchback. You treat everyone as if he were a gentleman. That officer definitely was *not*.'

'It was very kind of you to warn me, Miss Vavasour.'

'It makes me boil,' she said.

When Miss Vavasour had gone Mr Crouchback took off his boots and socks, his collar and his shirt and standing before the wash-hand-stand in trousers and vest washed thoroughly in cold water. He donned a clean shirt, collar and socks, shabby pumps and a slightly shabby suit made of the same cloth as he had worn throughout the day. He brushed his hair. And all the time he thought of other things than Miss Vavasour's disclosure. She had cherished a chivalrous devotion for him since she first settled at Matchet. His daughter Angela joked of it rather indelicately. For the six years of their acquaintance he had paid little heed to anything Miss Vavasour said. Now he dismissed the Cuthbert plot and considered two problems that had come to him with the morning's post. He was a man of regular habit and settled opinion. Doubt was a stranger to him. That morning, in the hour between Mass and school, he had been confronted with two intrusions from an unfamiliar world.

The more prominent was the parcel; bulky and ragged from the investigations of numberless clumsy departmental hands. It was covered with American stamps, customs declarations, and certificates of censorship.

'American parcel' was just beginning to find a place in the English vocabulary. This was plainly one of these novelties. His three Box-Bender granddaughters had been sent to a place of refuge in New England. Doubtless it came from them. 'How kind. How very extravagant,' he had thought and had borne it to his room for later study.

Now he cut the string with his nail scissors and spread the contents in order on his table.

First came six tins of 'Pullitzer's Soup'. They were variously, lusciously named but soup was one of the few articles of diet in which the Marine Hotel abounded. Moreover, he had an ancient conviction that all tinned foods were made of something nasty. 'Silly girls. Well, I daresay we shall be glad of it one day.' Next there was a transparent packet of prunes. Next a very heavy little tin labelled '*Brisko. A Must in every home.*' There was no indication of its function. Soap? Rat poison? Boot polish? He would have to consult Mrs Tickeridge. Next a very light larger tin named 'Yumcrunch'. This must be edible for it bore the portrait of an obese and badly brought-up little girl waving a spoon and fairly bawling for the stuff. Last and oddest of all a bottle filled with what seemed to be damp artificial pearls, labelled 'Cocktail Onions'. Could it be that this remote and resourceful people who had so generously (and, he thought, so unnecessarily) sheltered his grandchildren; this people whose chief concern seemed to be the frustration of the processes of nature – could they have contrived an alcoholic onion?

Mr Crouchback's elation palled; he studied his gift rather fretfully. Where in all this exotic banquet was there anything for Felix? The choice seemed to lie between Brisko and Yumcrunch.

He shook Yumcrunch. It rattled. Broken biscuits? Felix stood and pointed his soft muzzle.

'Yumcrunch?' said Mr Crouchback seductively. Felix's tail thumped the carpet.

And then suspicion darkened Mr Crouchback's contentment: suppose this were one of those new patent foods he had heard described, something 'dehydrated' which, eaten without due preparation, swelled enormously and fatally in the stomach.

'No, Felix,' he said. 'No Yumcrunch. Not until I have asked Mrs Tickeridge,' and at the same time he resolved to consult that lady about his other problem: the matter of Tony Box-Bender's odd postcard and Angela Box-Bender's odd letter.

The postcard had been enclosed in the letter. He had taken both to school with him and reread them often during the day. The letter read:

                                    Lower Chipping Manor,
                                         Nr Tetbury

Dearest Papa,

 News at last from Tony. Nothing very personal poor boy but such a joy to know
he is safe. Until this morning I didn't realize how anxious I have been. After all the
man who got away and wrote to us that he had seen Tony in the POW column might
have been mistaken. Now we know.

 He seems to think we can send him anything he needs but Arthur has been into
it and says no, that isn't the arrangement. Arthur says he can't approach neutral
embassies and I mustn't write to America either. Only regular Red Cross parcels may
be sent and they get those anyhow apparently whether we pay for them or not. Arthur
says the parcels are scientifically chosen so as to have all the right calories and that
there can't be one law for the rich and one for the poor when it comes to prison. I
see he's quite right in a way.

 The girls seem to be enjoying America tremendously.

 How is Dotheboys Hall?

                                         Love,
                                         Angela.

Tony's card read:

 Was not allowed to write before. Now in permanent camp. A lot of our chaps here.
Can daddy arrange parcels through neutral embassies? This is most important and
everyone says safest quickest way. Please send cigarettes, chocolates, golden syrup,
cocoa, tinned meat and fish (all kinds). Glucose 'D'. Hard biscuits (ships), cheese,
toffee, condensed milk, camel hair sleeping bag, air-cushion, gloves, hair brush. Could
girls in US help? Also Boulestin's Conduct of Kitchen. Trumper's Eucris. Woolly
slippers.

 There had been one other letter in Mr Crouchback's post, which saddened
him though it presented no problem. His wine merchants wrote to say that
their cellars had been partly destroyed by enemy action. They hoped to
maintain diminished supplies to their regular customers but could no longer
fulfil specific orders. Monthly parcels would be made up from whatever stock
was available. Pilfering and breakages were becoming frequent on the
railways. Customers were requested to report all losses immediately.

 Parcels, thought Mr Crouchback. Everything that day seemed to be
connected with parcels.

 After dinner, according to the custom of more than a year, Mr Crouchback joined Mrs Tickeridge in the Residents' Lounge.

 Their conversation began, as always, with the subject of Felix's afternoon
exercise. Then:

 'Guy's home. I hope we shall see him here soon. I don't know what he's
up to. Something rather secret, I expect. He came back with his Brigadier
– the man you call "Ben".'

 Mrs Tickeridge had that day received a letter from her husband in which certain plain hints informed her that Brigadier Ritchie-Hook had got into another of his scrapes. Well trained in service propriety she changed the subject.

'And your grandson?'

'That's just what I wanted to ask about. My daughter has had this postcard. May I show it to you – and her letter? Aren't they puzzling?'

Mrs Tickeridge took the documents and perused them. At length she said: 'I don't think I ever read Trumper's *Eucris*.'

'No, no. It's not that I'm puzzled by. That's hair-stuff. Used to use it myself when I could afford it. But don't you think it very peculiar that in his first postcard home he should only be asking for things for himself? It's most unlike him.'

'I expect he's hungry, poor boy.'

'Surely not? Prisoners of war have full army rations. There's an international agreement about it, I know. You don't suppose it's a code. "Glucose D" – whoever heard of "Glucose D"? I'm sure Tony has never seen the stuff. Someone put him up to it. You would think that a boy writing to his mother for the first time, when he must know how anxious she has been, would have something better to say than "Glucose D".'

'Perhaps he's *really* hungry.'

'Even so, he ought to consider his mother's feelings. You've read her letter?'

'Yes.'

'I'm sure she's got quite the wrong end of the stick. My son-in-law is in the House of Commons and of course he picks up some rather peculiar ideas there.'

'No, it's been on the wireless.'

'*The wireless*,' said Mr Crouchback in a tone as near bitterness as he possessed. 'The wireless. Just the sort of thing they would put about. It seems to me the most improper idea. Why should we not send what we want to those we love – even "Glucose D"?'

'I suppose in wartime it's only fair to share things equally.'

'Why? Less in wartime than ever I should have thought. As you say, the boy may be really hungry. If he wants "Glucose D" why can't I send it to him? Why can't my son-in-law get foreigners to help? There's a man in Switzerland who used to come and stay at Broome year after year. I know he'd like to help Tony. Why shouldn't he? I don't understand.'

Mrs Tickeridge saw the gentle, bewildered old man gaze earnestly at her, seeking an answer she could not give. He continued:

'After all, *any* present means that you want someone to have something someone else hasn't got. I mean even if it's only a cream jug at a wedding. I shouldn't wonder if the Government didn't try and stop us praying for people next.' Mr Crouchback sadly considered this possibility and then added: 'Not that anyone really *needs* a cream-jug and apparently Tony needs these things he asks for. It's all *wrong*. I'm not much of a dab at explaining things, but I *know* it's all *wrong*.'

Mrs Tickeridge was mending Jenifer's jersey. She darned silently. She was not much of a dab herself at explaining things. Presently Mr Crouchback spoke again, from the tangle of his perplexities.

'And what is Brisko?'

'Brisko?'

'And Yumcrunch? Both these things are in my room at the moment and I don't for the life of me know what to do with them. They're American.'

'I know just what you mean. I've seen them advertised in a magazine. Yumcrunch is what they eat for breakfast instead of porridge.'

'Would it suit Felix? Wouldn't blow him up?'

'He'd love it. And the other thing is what they use instead of lard.'

'Pretty rich for a dog?'

'I'm afraid so. I expect Mrs Cuthbert will be very grateful for it in the kitchen.'

'There's nothing you don't know.'

'Except Trumper's whatever-it-was.'

Presently Mr Crouchback took his leave, fetched Felix and let him out into the darkness. He brought down with him the tin of Brisko and carried it to the proprietress of the hotel in her 'Private Parlour'.

'Mrs Cuthbert, I have been sent this from America. It is lard. Mrs Tickeridge seems to think you might find it useful in the kitchen.'

She took it and thanked him rather awkwardly.

'There was something Mr Cuthbert wanted to see you about.'

'I am here.'

'Everything is getting so difficult,' she said; 'I'll fetch Mr Cuthbert.'

Mr Crouchback stood in the Private Parlour and waited. Presently Mrs Cuthbert returned alone.

'He says, will I speak to you. I don't know quite how to begin. It's all because of the war and the regulations and the officer who came today. He was the Quartering Commandant. You know it's nothing personal, don't you, Mr Crouchback? I'm sure we've always done all we can to oblige, making all sorts of exceptions for you, not charging for the dog's meals and your having your own wine sent in. Some of the guests have mentioned it more than once how you were specially favoured.'

'I have never made any complaint,' said Mr Crouchback. 'I am satisfied that you do everything you can in the circumstances.'

'That's it,' said Mrs Cuthbert, 'circumstances.'

'I think I know what you wish to say to me, Mrs Cuthbert. It is really quite unnecessary. If you fear I'll desert you now when you are going through difficult times, after I have been so comfortable for so many years, you may put your mind quite at rest. I know you are both doing your best and I am sincerely grateful.'

'Thank you, sir. It wasn't quite that ... I think Mr Cuthbert had better speak to you.'

'He may come to me whenever he likes. Not now. I am just going to take Felix off to bed. Good night, I hope that tin will be of help.'

'Good night and thank you, sir.'

Miss Vavasour met him on the stairs.

'Oh, Mr Crouchback, I couldn't help seeing you go into the Private Parlour. Is everything all right?'

'Yes, I think so. I had a tin of lard for Mrs Cuthbert.'

'They didn't say anything about what I told you about?'

'The Cuthberts seemed to be worried about the falling off of the service. I think I was able to reassure them. It is a difficult time for both of them – for all of us. Good night, Miss Vavasour.'

4

Meanwhile the talk in Bellamy's had drifted irresistibly upward. That very morning in a deep bed in a deep shelter a buoyant busy personage had lain, apportioning the day's work of an embattled Empire in a series of minutes.

'Pray inform me today on one half sheet of paper why Brig. Ritchie-Hook has been relieved of the command of his Brigade.'

And twenty-fours hours later, almost to the minute, while Mr Crouchback's form was beginning to construe the neglected passage of Livy, from the same heap of pillows the ukase went out:

P.M. to Secretary of State for War.
I have directed that no commander be penalized for errors in discretion *towards the enemy*. This directive has been flouted in a grievous and vexatious manner in the case of Col. late Brig. Ritchie-Hook, Royal Corps of Halberdiers. Pray assure me that suitable employment has been found for this gallant and resourceful officer as soon as he is passed fit for active service.

Telephones and typewriters relayed the trumpet note. Great men called to lesser men, and they to men of no consequence at all. Somewhere on the downward official slope Guy's name too appeared, for Ritchie-Hook, in his room at Millbank Hospital, had not forgotten his companion in guilt. Papers marked '*Passed to you for immediate action*' went from 'In' tray to 'Out' tray, until at length they found sea level with the Adjutant of the Halberdier Barracks.

'Sergeant-Major, we have Mr Crouchback's leave address?'

'Marine Hotel, Matchet, sir.'

'Then make out a move order for him to report forthwith to HOO HQ.'

'Am I to give the address, sir?'

'That wouldn't do. It's on the Most Secret list.'

'Sir.'

Ten minutes later the Adjutant remarked: 'Sergeant-Major, if we with-hold the address, how will Mr Crouchback know where to report?'

'Sir.'

'We could refer it back to HOO HQ.'

'Sir.'

'But it is marked "Immediate Action".'

'Sir.'

These two men of no consequence at all sat silent and despairing.

'I take it, sir, the correct procedure would be to send it by hand of officer?'

'Can we spare anyone?'

'There's one, sir.'

'Colonel Trotter?'

'Sir.'

'Jumbo' Trotter, as his nickname suggested, was both ponderous and popular; he retired with the rank of full colonel in 1936. Within an hour of the declaration of war he was back in barracks and there he had sat ever since. No one had summoned him. No one cared to question his presence. His age and rank rendered him valueless for barrack duties. He dozed over the newspapers, lumbered round the billiard-table, beamed on his juniors' scrimmages on Guest Nights, and regularly attended Church Parade. Now and then he expressed a wish to 'have a go at the Jerries'. Mostly he slept. It was he whom Guy had disturbed in the billiard-room on his last visit to the barracks.

Once or twice a week the Captain-Commandant, in his new role of martinet, resolved to have a word with Jumbo, but the word was never spoken. He had served under Jumbo in Flanders and there learned to revere him for his sublime imperturbability in many dangerous and disgusting circumstances. He readily gave his approval to the old boy's outing and left him to make his own arrangements.

It was a hundred and fifty miles to Matchet. Jumbo's few indispensable possessions could be contained in one japanned-tin uniform case and a pig-skin Gladstone. But there was his bedding. Never move without your bed and your next meal; that was a rule, said Jumbo. Altogether his luggage comprised rather a handful for Halberdier Burns, his aged servant; too much to take by train, he explained to the Barrack Transport Officer. Besides, it was the duty of everyone to keep off the railways. The wireless had said so. Trains were needed for troop movements. The Transport Officer was a callow, amenable, regular subaltern. Jumbo got a car.

Early next day, in that epoch of mounting oppression, it stood at the steps of the Officers' House. The luggage was strapped behind. Driver and servant stood beside it. Presently Jumbo emerged, well buttoned up against the morning chill, smoking his after-breakfast pipe, carrying under his arm the ante-room's only copy of *The Times*. The men jumped to the salute. Jumbo beamed benignantly on them and raised a fur-lined glove to the peak of his red hat. He conferred briefly with the driver over the map, ordering a detour which would bring him at lunch-time to a friendly mess, then settled himself in the rear-seat. Burns tucked in the rug and leapt to his place beside the driver. Jumbo glanced at the Deaths in the paper before giving the order to move.

The Adjutant, watching these sedate proceedings from his office window, suddenly said: 'Sergeant-Major, couldn't we have recalled Mr Crouchback here and given him the address ourselves?'

'Sir.'

'Too late to change now. Order, counter order, disorder, eh?'

'Sir.'

The car moved across the gravel towards the guard-house. It might have been carrying an elderly magnate from a London square to a long week-end in the Home Counties, in years before the Total War.

Mrs Tickeridge knew Colonel Trotter of old. She found him dozing in the hall of the Marine Hotel when she and Jenifer returned from their walk with Felix. He opened his pouchy eyes and accepted their presence without surprise.

'Hullo, Vi. Hullo, shrimp. Nice to see you again.'

He began to raise himself from his chair.

'Sit down, Jumbo. What on earth are you doing here?'

'Waiting for my tea. Everyone seems half asleep here; said tea was "off". Ridiculous expression. Had to send my man Burns into the kitchen to brew up. Met opposition from some civilian cook, I gather. Soon settled that. Had some opposition about quarters, too, from the woman in the office. Said she was full up. Soon settled that. Had my bed made up and my things laid out in a bathroom. Woman didn't seem too pleased about that either. Poor type. Had to remind her there was a war on.'

'Oh, Jumbo, there's only two baths between the whole lot of us.'

'Shan't be here long. All have to rough it a bit these days. Burns and the driver fixing themselves up in the town. Trust an old Halberdier to make himself comfortable. No camp-bed in a bathroom for Burns.'

Burns appeared at that moment with a laden tray and put it beside the colonel.

'Jumbo, what a tea! We never get anything like that. Hot buttered toast, sandwiches, an egg, cherry cake.'

'Felt a bit peckish. Told Burns to scrounge round.'

'Poor Mrs Cuthbert. Poor us. No butter for a week.'

'I'm looking for a fellow called Crouchback. Woman in the office said he was out. Know him?'

'He's a heavenly old man.'

'No. Young Halberdier officer.'

'That's his son, Guy. What d'you want with him? You're not taking him under arrest?'

'Lord, no.'

A look of elephantine cunning came into his eyes. He had no idea of the contents of the sealed envelope buttoned up below his medals.

'Nothing like that. Just a friendly call.'

Felix sat with his muzzle on Jumbo's knee gazing at him with devotion. Jumbo cut a corner of toast, dipped it in jam and placed it in the gentle mouth.

'Take him away, Jenifer, there's a good girl, or he'll have all my tea off me.'

Presently Jumbo fell into a doze.

He woke to the sound of voices near him. The woman from the office, the poor type, was in converse with a stout, upright Major wearing RASC badges.

'I've hinted,' the woman was saying. 'Mr Cuthbert as good as told him outright. He won't seem to understand.'

'He'll understand all right when he finds his furniture on the doorstep. If you can't move him quietly, I shall use my powers.'

'It does seem a shame rather.'

'You should be grateful, Mrs Cuthbert. I could have taken the whole hotel if I'd cared, and I would have but for Mr Cuthbert being on the square. I've taken over the Monte Rosa boarding-house instead. The people from there have to sleep somewhere, don't they?'

'Well, it's your responsibility. He'll be very upset, poor old gentleman.'

Jumbo studied the man carefully and suddenly said very loudly: 'Grigshawe.'

The effect was immediate. The Major swung round, stamped, stood to attention and roared back: 'Sir.'

'Bless my soul, Grigshawe, it *is* you. Wasn't sure. I'm very pleased to see you. Shake hands.'

'You're looking very well, sir.'

'You've had quick promotion, eh?'

'Acting-rank, sir.'

'We missed you when you put in for a commission. You shouldn't have left the Halberdiers, you know.'

'I wouldn't have but for the missus and it being peace-time.'

'What are you up to now?'

'Quartering Commandant, sir. Just clearing a little room here.'

'Excellent. Well, carry on. Carry on.'

'I've about finished, sir.' He stood to attention, nodded to Mrs Cuthbert and left, but there was no peace for Jumbo that afternoon. The room was hardly empty of Mrs Cuthbert before an elderly lady raised her head from a neighbouring chair and coughed. Jumbo regarded her sadly.

'Excuse me,' she said, 'I couldn't help overhearing. You know that officer?'

'What, Grigshawe? One of the best drill-sergeants we had in the Corps. Extraordinary system taking first-rate NCOs and making second-rate officers of them.'

'That's dreadful. I had quite made up my mind he must be some sort of criminal, dressed up – a blackmailer or burglar or something. It was our last hope.'

Jumbo had little curiosity about the affairs of others. It seemed to him vaguely odd that this pleasant-looking lady should so ardently desire Grigshawe to be an imposter. From time to time in his slow passage through life Jumbo had come up against things that puzzled him and had learned to ignore them. Now he merely remarked: 'Known him twenty years' and was preparing to leave his seat for a sniff of fresh air, when Miss Vavasour said: 'You see, he is trying to take Mr Crouchback's sitting-room.'

The name gave Jumbo pause and before he could disengage himself Miss Vavasour had begun her recital.

She spoke vehemently but furtively. In the Marine Hotel, scorn of the Quartering Commandant had quickly given place to dread. He came none knew whence, armed with unknown powers, malevolent, unpredictable, implacable. Miss Vavasour would with relish have thrown herself on any German paratrooper and made short work of him with poker or bread-knife. Grigshawe was a projection of the Gestapo. For two weeks now the permanent residents had lived in a state of whispering agitation. Mr Crouchback followed his routine, calmly refusing to share their alarm. He was the symbol of their security. If he fell, what hope was there for them? And his fall, it seemed, was now encompassed.

Jumbo listened restively. It was not for this he had driven all day with his Most Secret missive. He was out for a treat. There had been a number of jokes lately in the papers about selfish old women in safe hotels. He had chuckled over them often. He was on the point of reminding Miss Vavasour that there was a war on, when Mr Crouchback himself appeared before them, back from school with a pile of uncorrected exercise books, and suddenly the whole evening was changed and became a treat again.

Miss Vavasour introduced them. Jumbo, slow in some of his perceptions, was quick to recognize 'a good type'; not only the father of a Halberdier but a man fit to be a Halberdier himself.

Mr Crouchback explained that Guy was at Southsand, many miles away, collecting the possessions of a brother-officer who had died on active service. These were unexpectedly good tidings. Jumbo saw days, perhaps weeks, of pleasant adventure ahead. He had no objection to prolonging his tour of the seaside resorts indefinitely.

'No, no. Don't telephone him. I'll go there tomorrow myself.'

Then Mr Crouchback showed immediate solicitude for Jumbo's comfort. He must not think of sleeping in a bathroom. Mr Crouchback's sitting-room was at his disposal. Then Mr Crouchback gave him some excellent sherry and later, at dinner, burgundy and port. He did not mention that this was the last bottle of a little store which he could never hope to replenish.

They touched lightly on public affairs and found themselves in close agreement. Jumbo mentioned that in his latter years he had made a modest collection of old silver. Mr Crouchback knew a lot about that. They talked of fishing and pheasant-shooting, not competitively but in placid accord.

Mrs Tickeridge joined them later and gossiped about the Halberdiers. They did two-thirds of the crossword together. It was exactly Jumbo's idea of a pleasant evening. Nothing was said of Grigshawe and grievances, and in the end it was he who brought the matter up.

'Sorry to hear there's been trouble about your room here.'

'Oh, no trouble really. I've never even seen this Major Grigshawe they all talk about. I think he must rather have muddled the Cuthberts, and you know how rumours spread and get exaggerated in a little place like this. Poor Miss Vavasour seems to think we shall all be put into the street. I don't believe a word of it myself.'

'I've known Grigshawe for twenty years. Dare say he's got a bit too big for his boots. I'll have a word with him in the morning.'

'Not on *my* account, please. But it would be kind to put Miss Vavasour's mind at rest.'

'Perfectly simple matter if he handles it in the proper service way. All he has to do is put in a report that on the relevant date the room was occupied by a senior officer. You won't have any more trouble with Grigshawe, I can promise.'

'He's been no trouble to me, I assure you. He seems to have been a little brusque with the Cuthberts. I expect he thought he was only doing his duty.'

'I'll show him his duty.'

Mr Crouchback had already left the hotel when Jumbo came down next morning, but Jumbo did not forget. Before his leisurely departure he had a few words with Major Grigshawe.

Two days later Mr and Mrs Cuthbert sat in their Private Parlour. Major

Grigshawe had just left them with the assurance that their pensionnaires would be left undisturbed. The news was not welcome.

'We could have let that room of old Crouchback's for eight guineas a week,' said Mr Cuthbert.

'We could let every room in the house twice over.'

'Permanent residents were all very well before the war. They kept us going nicely in the winter months.'

'But there's a war on now. We can put the rates up again, I suppose.'

'We ought to make a clean sweep and take people only by the week. That's where the money comes. Keep people moving. Keep them anxious where they're going next. Some of these people with their houses blitzed are grateful for anything. Grigshawe's let us down, that's the truth of the matter.'

'Funny his giving up like that just when everything seemed so friendly.'

'You can't trust the army, not in business.'

'It was old Crouchback did it. I don't know how, but he did. He's an artful old bird if you ask me. Talks so that butter wouldn't melt in his mouth. "I do appreciate your difficulties, Mrs Cuthbert." "So grateful for your trouble, Mrs Cuthbert." '

'He's seen better days. We all know that. There's something about people like him. They were brought up to expect things to be easy for them and somehow or other things always *are* easy. Damned if I know how they manage it.'

There was a knock at the door and Mr Crouchback entered. His hair was rough from the wind and his eyes watery, for he had been sitting outside in the dark.

'Good evening. Good evening. Please don't get up, Mr Cuthbert. I just wanted to tell you something I've just decided. A week or so ago you said there was someone in need of a room here. I dare say you've forgotten, but I hadn't. Well, you know, thinking it over it seems to me that it's rather selfish keeping on both my rooms at a time like this. There's my grandson in a prison camp, people homeless from the towns, all those residents from Monte Rosa turned out with nowhere to go. It's all wrong for one old man like myself to take up so much space. I asked at the school and they're able to store my few sticks of furniture. So I came to give a week's notice that I shan't need the sitting-room in future, not in the immediate future, that is. After the war I shall be very pleased to take it on again, you know. I hope this isn't inconvenient. I'll stay, of course, until you find a suitable tenant.'

'We'll do that easy enough. Much obliged to you, Mr Crouchback.'

'That's settled then. Good night to you both.'

'Talk of the devil,' said Mrs Cuthbert, when Mr Crouchback had left. 'What d'you make of that?'

'Maybe he's feeling the pinch.'

'Not him. He's worth much more than you'd think. Why, he *gives* it away, right and left. I know because I've done his room sometimes. Letters of thanks from all over the shop.'

'He's a deep one and no mistake. I never have understood him, not properly. Somehow his mind seems to work different than yours and mine.'

5

The Times. 2 November 1940
Personal.
In the breakfast room of the Grand Hotel, Southsand, Guy sought his advertisement in the Agony Column, and at length found it.

CORNER, James Pendennis, popularly known as 'CHATTY', late of Bechuanaland or similar territory, please communicate with Box 108 when he will learn something to his advantage.

The grammar, he noted with chagrin, was defective but the call was as unambiguous as the Last Trump. It sounded a despairing note, as though from the gorge of Roncesvalles, for he had done his utmost in the matter of Apthorpe's gear and could now merely wait.

It was the sixteenth day since he had left barracks, his eleventh at Southsand. The early stages of his quest had been easy. Brook Park, where Apthorpe had jettisoned all that final residuum of the possessions which he regarded as the bare necessaries of life, was still in Halberdier hands. The stores left there were intact and accessible. An amiable Quartermaster was ready to part with anything that was 'signed for' in triplicate. Guy signed. He was received at the strange mess with fraternal warmth; with curiosity also for he was the first Halberdier to bring news from Dakar. They induced him to lecture the battalion on 'the lessons of an opposed landing'. He stayed mum on the subject of Ritchie-Hook's wound. They gave him transport and he was sent on his way with honour.

At Southsand he found the Commodore of the Yacht Club eager to disencumber himself. In his small spare bedroom Apthorpe had left what, at a pinch, might be regarded as superfluities. Three journeys by taxi were required to move them. The Commodore helped with his own hands to carry them downstairs and load them. When it was accomplished and the hotel porter had wheeled everything into the vaults, the Commodore asked: 'Staying here long?' and Guy had been obliged to answer: 'I really don't know.'

And still he did not know. Suddenly he found himself alone. The ener-gizing wire between him and the army was cut. He was as immobile as Apthorpe's gear. Various cryptic prohibitions had lately been proclaimed on the movement of goods. Guy sought aid of the R T O and was rebuffed.

'No can do, old boy. Read the regulations. Officers proceeding on, or returning from, leave may take only a haversack and one suitcase. You'll have to get a special move order for that stuff.'

Guy telegraphed to the Adjutant in barracks and after two days received in reply, merely: *Extension of leave granted.*

Here he was still, all animation suspended, while autumn turned sharply to winter, and gales shook the double windows of the hotel and great waves broke over the pill-boxes and barbed wire on the promenade.

Here it seemed he was doomed to remain forever, standing guard over a heap of tropical gadgets, like the Russian sentry he had once been told of, the Guardsman who was posted daily year in, year out, until the revolution, in the grounds of Tsarskoe Selo on the spot where Catherine the Great had once wished to preserve a wild-flower.

Southsand, though unbombed, was thought to be dangerous and had attracted no refugees of the kind who filled other resorts. It was just as he had known it nine months earlier, spacious and desolate and windy and shabby. One change only was apparent; the Ristorante Garibaldi was closed. Mr Pelecci, he learned, had been 'taken away' on the day Italy declared war, consigned in a ship to Canada and drowned in mid-Atlantic, sole spy among a host of innocents. Guy visited Mr Goodall and found him elated by the belief that a great rising was imminent throughout Christian Europe; led by the priests and squires, with blessed banners, and the relics of the saints borne ahead, Poles, Hungarians, Austrians, Bavarians, Italians and plucky little contingents from the Catholic cantons of Switzerland would soon be on the march to redeem the times. Even a few Frenchmen, Mr Goodall conceded, might join this Pilgrimage of Grace but he could promise no part in it for Guy.

The days passed. Ever prone to despond, Guy became sure that his brief adventure was over. He had his pistol. Perhaps, finally, he would get a shot at an invading Storm Trooper and die unrecognized, but sweetly and decorously. More probably he would still be sitting years hence in the Yacht Club and hear on the wireless that the war was won. Ever prone to elaborate his predicament rather fancifully, Guy saw himself make a hermitage of Apthorpe's tent and end his days encamped on the hills above Southsand, painfully acquiring the skills of 'Chatty' Corner, charitably visited once a week by Mr Goodall, a gentler version of poor mad Ivo, who had starved to death in the slums of North-West London.

So Guy mused while even at that moment, in the fullness of his time, 'Jumbo' Trotter was on the move to draw him back into the life of action.

It was All Souls' Day. Guy walked to church to pray for his brothers' souls – for Ivo especially; Gervase seemed far off that year, in Paradise perhaps, in the company of other good soldiers. Mr Goodall was there, popping in and down and up and out and in again assiduously, releasing *toties quoties* soul after soul from Purgatory.

'Twenty-eight so far,' he said. 'I always try and do fifty.'

The wings of the ransomed beat all about Mr Goodall, but as Guy left church he was alone in the comfortless wind.

'Jumbo' arrived after luncheon and found Guy re-reading *Vice Versa* in the winter garden. Guy recognized him at once and jumped to his feet.

'Sit down, my dear boy. I've just been making friends with your father.' He unbuttoned himself and took the letter from his breast pocket.

'Something important for you,' he said. 'I don't know what you're up to and I won't ask. I am a mere messenger. Better take it up to your room and read it there. Then burn it. Crumple the ash. Well, I expect in your job, whatever it is, you know more than I do about that sort of thing.'

Guy did as he was told. There was an outer envelope marked in red *By hand of officer* and an inner one marked *Most Secret*. He drew out a simple orderly-room chit on which was typed:

T/y Lt Crouchback, G. Royal Corps of Halberdiers
The above named officer will report forthwith to Flat 211 Marchmain House, St James's, SWI.
Capt. for Captain-Commandant Royal Corps of Halberdiers.

An undecipherable trail of ink preceded the last line. Even in the innermost depths of military secrecy the Adjutant continued to maintain his anonymity.

The ashes needed no crumbling; they fell in dust from Guy's fingers.

He returned to Jumbo.

'I've just had orders to report in London.'

'Tomorrow will do, I suppose?'

'It says "forthwith".'

'We couldn't get there before dark. Everyone packs up when the sirens go. I can run you up to London tomorrow morning.'

'That's very good of you, sir.'

'It's a pleasure. I like to look in at "the Senior" every so often to hear how the war's going. Plenty of room for you. Have you much luggage?'

'About a ton, sir.'

'Have you, by God? Let's have a look at it.'

Together they visited the baggage store and stood in silence before the heap of steel trunks, leather cases, brass-bound chests, shapeless canvas sacks, buffalo-hide bags. Jumbo was visibly awed. He himself believed in ample provision for the emergencies of travel. Here was something quite beyond his ambition.

'Nearer two tons than one,' he said at length. 'I say, you *must* be up to something? This needs organization. Where are Area Headquarters?'

'I'm afraid I don't know, sir.'

Such an admission would have earned any other subaltern a rebuke from 'Jumbo', but Guy was now enveloped in an aura of secrecy and importance.

'Lone wolf, eh?' he said. 'I'd better get to work on the blower.'

By this expression Jumbo and many others meant the telephone. He telephoned and presently reported that a lorry would call for them next morning.

'It's a small world,' he said. 'I found the fellow I was talking to at Area was a fellow I used to know well. Junior to me, of course. On old Hamilton-Brand's staff at Gib. Said I'd go along and look him up. Probably dine there. See you in the morning. No point in getting away too early. I told them to have our lorry loaded by ten. All right?'

'Very good, sir.'

'Lucky I knew the fellow at Area. Didn't have to tell him anything about you and your affairs. I just said "Mum's the word" and he twigged.'

All went smoothly next day; they drove to London with the lorry behind them and reached the Duke of York's Steps at one o'clock.

'No use your going to see your fellow now,' said Jumbo. 'Bound to be out. We can lunch here. Must see the men fed too. Problem is to find a place for your gear.'

At this moment a Major-General appeared up the steps, clearly bound for the club. Guy saluted him. Jumbo embraced him by both elbows.

'Beano.'

'Jumbo. What are you up to, old boy?'

'Looking for lunch.'

'Better hurry. Everything decent is off the table by one. Awful greedy lot, the young members.'

'Can you find me a guard, Beano?'

'Impossible, old boy. War House these days. Can't even find a batman.'

'Got a lot of hush-hush stuff here.'

'Tell you what,' said Beano after a pause for thought. 'There's a parking place at the War House, CIGS only. He's away today. I should put your stuff there. No one will touch it. Say it's the CIGS's personal baggage. I'll give your driver a chit. Then he and your other fellow can use the canteen.'

'Good for you, Beano.'

'Not at all, Jumbo.'

Guy accompanied these two senior officers into the club and found himself swept into the dining-room in a surge of naval and military might. Bellamy's had its sprinkling of distinguished officers but here everyone in sight was aflame with red tabs, gold braid, medal ribbons, and undisguised hunger. Guy diffidently stood back from the central table round which, as though at a hunt ball, they were struggling for food.

'Go in and fight for it,' said Beano. 'Every man for himself.'

Guy got the last leg of chicken but a Rear-Admiral deftly whisked it off his plate. Presently he emerged victualled in accordance with his rank with bully beef and beetroot.

'Sure that's all you want?' asked Jumbo hospitably. 'Doesn't look much to me.'

He himself had half a steak pie before him.

Throughout the meal Beano talked of a bomb which had narrowly missed him an evening or two earlier.

'I went down flat on my face, old boy, and got up covered in plaster. A narrow squeak, I can tell you.'

Eventually they left the table.

'Back to the grindstone,' Beano said.

'I'll wait here,' said Jumbo. 'I shan't desert you till I've seen my mission safely accomplished.'

On the steps of the club Guy turned aside from the main stream of members who were making for Whitehall, and walked the quarter-mile to Marchmain House, a block of flats in St James's, where his appointment lay.

Hazardous Offensive Operations Headquarters, that bizarre product of total war which later was to proliferate through five acres of valuable London property, engrossing the simple high staff officers of all the Services with experts, charlatans, plain lunatics and every unemployed member of the British Communist Party – HOO HQ, at this stage of its history, occupied three flats in a supposedly luxurious modern block.

Guy, reporting there, found a Major of about his own age, with the D.S.O., M.C. and a slight stammer. The interview lasted a bare five minutes.

'Crouchback, Crouchback, Crouchback, Crouchback,' he said, turning over a sheaf of papers on his table. 'Sergeant, what do we know of Mr Crouchback?'

The Sergeant was female and matronly.

'Ritchie-Hook file,' she said. 'General Whale had it last.'

'Go and get it, there's a good girl.'

'I daren't.'

'Well, it doesn't matter. I remember all about it now. You've been wished on us with your former Brigadier for "special duties". What are your "special duties"?'

'I don't know, sir.'

'Nor does anyone. You've come whistling down from a very high level. Do you know all about Commandos?'

'Not much.'

'You shouldn't know anything They're supposed to be a secret, though from the security reports we get from Mugg, they've made themselves pretty conspicuous there. I've had a letter from someone whose signature I can't read, complaining in strong terms that they've been shooting his deer with tommy-guns. Don't see how they get near enough. Remarkably fine stalking if true. Anyway that's where you're going – temporary attachment for training purposes X Commando, Isle of Mugg. All right?'

'Very good, sir.'

'Sergeant Trenchard here will make out your travel warrant. Have you got a batman with you?'

'At the moment,' said Guy, 'I have a service car, a three-ton lorry, an RASC driver, a Halberdier servant and a full Colonel.'

'Ah,' said the Major who was fast founding the HOO HQ tradition of being surprised at nothing. 'You ought to be all right, then. Report to Colonel Blackhouse at Mugg.'

'Tommy Blackhouse?'

'Friend of yours?'

'Yes. He married my wife.'

'Did he? *Did* he? I thought he was a bachelor.'

'He is, now.'

'Yes, I thought so. I was at the Staff College with him. Good chap; got some good chaps in his Commando too. Glad he's a friend of yours.'

Guy saluted, turned about and departed only very slightly disconcerted. This was the classic pattern of army life as he had learned it, the vacuum, the spasm, the precipitation, and with it all the peculiar, impersonal, barely human geniality.

Jumbo was asleep in the morning-room when Guy reached him.

'To horse, to horse,' he said, when fully awake and aware of the long road ahead. 'We ought to get clear of London before those bombs begin. Anything that puts the wind up Beano, is better avoided. Besides, we've got your stores to think of.'

Their lorry when they reached it bore marks of promotion. An efficient guard had plastered it with printed notices: *CIGS.*

'Shall I remove those, sir, before starting?'

'Certainly not. They can do no harm and may do a lot of good.'

'Shall I get one for the car too, sir?'

Jumbo paused. He was rather light-headed from his outing, breathing once more the bracing air of his youth when as an irresponsible subaltern he had participated in many wild extravagancies.

'Why not?' he said.

But he thought again. Reason regained its sway. He drew from the deep source of his military experience and knew to a finger's breadth how far one could go.

'No,' he said regretfully. 'That wouldn't do.'

They drove away from the stricken city. At St Albans they turned on the dim little headlights and almost immediately the first sirens wailed around them.

'No point in going much farther tonight,' said Jumbo. 'I know a place where we can put up about thirty miles north.'

6

The Isle of Mugg has no fame in song or story. Perhaps because whenever they sought a rhyme for the place, they struck absurdity, it was neglected by those romantic early-Victorian English ladies who so prodigally enriched the balladry, folklore and costume of the Scottish Highlands. It has a laird, a fishing fleet, an hotel (erected just before the First World War in the unfulfilled hope of attracting tourists) and nothing more. It lies among other monosyllabic protuberances. There is seldom clear weather in those waters, but on certain rare occasions Mugg has been descried from the island of Rum in the form of two cones. The crofters of Muck know it as a single misty lump on their horizon. It has never been seen from Eigg.

It is served twice weekly by steamer from the mainland of Inverness. The passenger rash enough to stay on deck may watch it gradually take shape, first as two steep hills; later he can recognize the castle – granite 1860, indestructible and uninhabitable by anyone but a Scottish laird, the quay, cottages and cliffs, all of granite, and the unmellowed brick of the hotel.

Guy and his entourage arrived at the little port a few hours before this steamer was due to sail. The sky was dark and the wind blowing hard. Jumbo made a snap decision.

'I shall remain here,' he said. 'Mustn't on any account hazard our stores. You go ahead and make your number with your CO. I will follow when the weather clears.'

Guy set out alone to find X Commando.

When the exotic name, 'Commando', was at length made free to the press it rapidly extended its meaning to include curates on motor bicycles. In 1940 a Commando was a military unit, about the size of a battalion, composed of volunteers for special service. They kept the badges of their regiments; no flashes or green berets then, nothing to display in inns. They were a secret force whose only privilege was to find their own billets and victuals. Each unit took its character from its commander.

Tommy Blackhouse declared: 'It's going to be a long war. The great thing is to spend it among friends.'

Tommy's friends inhabited his own ample world. Some were regular soldiers; others had spent a year or two of adolescence in the Brigade of Guards, to satisfy the whim of parents and trustees, before taking to other activities or to inactivity. To these he turned when at last his patiently awaited appointment was confirmed. Bellamy's rallied to him. He sent his troop leaders on a recruiting tour of their regiments. Too soon for some the Commando came into existence and was dispatched to train at Mugg. There Guy found them. He was directed from the quay to the hotel.

At three o'clock he found it empty except for a Captain of the Blues who reclined upon a sofa, his head enveloped in a turban of lint, his feet shod in narrow velvet slippers embroidered in gold thread with his monogram. He was nursing a white pekinese; beside him stood a glass of white liqueur.

The sofa was upholstered in Turkey carpet. The table which held the glass and bottle was octagonal, inlaid with mother-of-pearl. The pictorial effect was of a young prince of the Near East in his grand divan in the early years of the century.

He did not look up on Guy's entry.

Guy recognized Ivor Claire, a young show-jumper of repute, the owner of a clever and beautiful horse named Thimble. Guy had seen them in Rome at the Concorso Ippico; Claire leaning slightly forward in the saddle with the intent face of a pianist, the horse precisely placing his feet in the tan, leaping easily, without scuffle or hesitation, completing a swift, faultless round, in dead silence which broke at last into a tumult of appreciation. Guy knew him, too, as a member of Bellamy's. He should have known Guy for they had often sat opposite one another in the listless days of the preceding year and had stood together in the same group at the bar.

'Good afternoon,' said Guy.

Claire looked up, said, 'Good afternoon,' and wiped his dog's face with a silk handkerchief. 'The snow is very bad for Freda's eyes. Perhaps you want Colonel Tommy. He's out climbing.' Then, after a pause, politely: 'Have you seen last week's paper?'

And he held out the *Rum, Muck, Mugg and Eigg Times*.

Guy gazed about him at the heads of deer, the fumed oak staircase, the vast extent of carpet woven in the local hunting tartan.

'I think I've seen you about in Bellamy's.'

'How one longs for it.'

'My name is Crouchback.'

'Ah.' Claire had the air of having very shrewdly elicited this piece of information, of having made a move, early in a game of chess, which would later develop into mate. 'I should have some Kümmel if I were you. We've unearthed a cache of Wolfschmidt. You just score it up on that piece of paper over there.'

There were glasses on the central table and bottles and a list of names, marked with their potations.

'I'm here for training,' Guy volunteered.

'It's a death-trap.'

'Have you any idea where my quarters will be?'

'Colonel Tommy lives here. So do most of us. But it's full up now. Recent arrivals are at the coastguard station, I believe. I looked in once. It smells awfully of fish. I say, do you mind much if we don't talk? I fell fifty feet on the ice the other morning.'

Guy studied last week's *Rum, Muck, Mugg and Eigg Times*. Claire plucked Freda's eyebrows.

Soon, as in an old-fashioned, well-constructed comedy, other characters began to enter Left: first a medical officer.

'Is the boat in?' he asked of both indiscriminately.

Claire shut his eyes, so Guy answered: 'I came in her a few minutes ago.'

'I must telephone the harbour-master and have her held. Anstruther-Kerr has had a fall. They're bringing him down as fast as they can.'

Claire opened his eyes.

'Poor Angus. Dead?'

'Certainly not. But I must get him to the mainland at once.'

'That is your opportunity,' Claire said to Guy. 'Angus had a room here.'

The doctor went to the telephone, Guy to the reception office.

The manageress said: 'Poor Sir Angus, and he a Scot too. He should know better than to go scrambling about the rocks at his age.'

As Guy returned, an enormous Grenadier Captain in the tradition of comedy hustled into the hall. He was dressed in damp dungarees and panting heavily.

'Thank God,' he said. 'Just made it. Angus's fall has started a stampede. I was half-way up the cliff when we got the news and slid down fast.'

The medical officer returned.

'They'll hold the steamer another fifteen minutes. They say they can't make port in the dark.'

'Well,' said the breathless Captain, 'I'll cut along and get his room.'

'Too late, Bertie,' said Claire. 'It's gone.'

'Not possible.' Then he noticed Guy. 'Oh,' he said. 'Damn.'

The stretcher party arrived and a comatose figure, covered in great-coats, was gently laid on the tartan floor while the stretcher-bearers went up to pack his belongings.

Another gasping officer arrived.

'Oh, God, Bertie,' he said, seeing the Grenadier, 'have you got his room?'

'I have not, Eddie. You should be out with your troop.'

229

'I just thought I should come and make arrangements for Angus.'

'Don't make such a noise,' said the doctor. 'Can't you see there's a sick man here?'

'Two sick men,' said Claire.

'Isn't he dead?'

'They say not.'

'*I* was told he was.'

'Perhaps you will allow me to know better,' said the doctor.

As though to resolve the argument, a muffled voice from the stretcher said: 'Itching, Eddie. Itching all over like hell.'

'Formication,' said the doctor. 'Morphia often has that effect.'

'How very odd,' said Claire, showing real interest for the first time. 'I've an aunt who takes quantities of it. I wonder if she itches.'

'Well, if you haven't got it, Bertie,' said Eddie, 'I think I'll just cut along and get that room fixed up for myself.'

'Too late. It's gone.'

Eddie looked incredulously around the hall, saw Guy for the first time and like Bertie said: 'Damn.'

It occurred to Guy that he had better make sure of his claim. He carried his valise and suitcase upstairs and before Anstruther-Kerr's hair brushes were off the dressing-table, his were on it. He unpacked fully, waited until the stretcher-bearers had finished their work, then followed them, locking the door behind him.

More damp and snowy officers were gathered below, among them Tommy Blackhouse. No one took any notice of Guy, except Tommy, who said:

'Hullo, Guy. What on earth brings you here?'

There was a very slight difference between the Tommy whom he had known for twelve years and Tommy the commanding officer, which made Guy say: 'I've orders to report to you, Colonel.'

'Well, it's the first I've heard about it. I looked for you when we were forming, but that ass Job said you'd gone to Cornwall or somewhere. Anyway, we're losing chaps so fast that there's room for anyone. Bertie, have we had any bumpf about this Applejack – Guy Crouchback?'

'May be in the last bag, Colonel. I haven't opened it yet.'

'Well, for Christ's sake do.'

He turned again to Guy. 'Any idea what you're supposed to be here for?'

'Attached for training.'

'For you to train us, or for us to train you?'

'Oh, for you to train me.'

'Thank God for that. The last little contribution from HOO HQ came to train us. And that reminds me, Bertie, Kong must go.'

'Very good, Colonel.'

'Can you get him on Angus's boat?'

'Too late.'

'Everything always seems to be too late in this bloody island. Keep him away from my men anyhow, until we find somewhere to hide him. I'll see you later, Guy, and sort you out. *Very* pleased you're here. Come on, Bertie. We've got to open that bag and get some signals off.'

The melting men in dungarees began to fill their glasses.

Guy said to Eddie: 'I take it Bertie is the Adjutant?'

'In a sort of way.'

'Who is Kong?'

'Difficult to say. He looks like a gorilla. They caught him somewhere in HOO HQ and sent him here to teach us to climb. We call him King Kong.'

Presently the medical officer returned.

Everyone except Guy, who felt that his acquaintance was too small to justify solicitude, asked news of Angus.

'Quite comfortable.'

'Not itching?' asked Claire.

'He's as comfortable as possible. I've arranged for his reception the other end.'

'Well, in that case, doc, will you come and have a look at that chap of mine, Cramp, who took a toss today?'

'And I wish you'd see Corporal Blake, the fellow you patched up yesterday.'

'I'll see them at sick parade tomorrow.'

'Blake doesn't look fit to walk. No, come on, doc, and I'll stand you a drink. I don't like the look of him.'

'And Trooper Eyre,' said another officer. 'He's either tight or delirious. He landed on his head yesterday.'

'Probably tight,' said Claire.

The doctor looked at him with loathing. 'Rightho. You'll have to show me their billets.'

Soon Guy and Claire were left alone once more.

'I'm glad you beat Bertie and the rest to that room,' said Claire. 'Of course you can't expect it to make you popular. But perhaps you won't be here very long.' He shut his eyes and for some minutes there was silence.

The final entry was a man in the kilt and uniform of a Highland regiment. He carried a tall shepherd's staff and said in a voice that had more of the Great West Road in it than of the Pass of Glencoe, 'Sorry to hear about Angus.'

Claire looked at him. 'Angus who?' he asked with distaste that was near malevolence.

'Kerr, of course.'

'You are referring to Captain Sir Angus Anstruther-Kerr?'

'Who do you think?'

'I did not speculate.'

'Well, how is he?'

'He is said to be comfortable. If so, it must be the first occasion for weeks.'

During this conversation Guy had been studying the newcomer with growing wonder. At length he said:

'Trimmer.'

The figure, bonnet, sporran, staff and all, swung round.

'Why, if it isn't my old uncle!'

Claire said to Guy, 'Are you in fact related to this officer?'

'No.'

'On the occasions he has been here, we have known him as McTavish.'

'Trimmer is a sort of nickname,' said Trimmer.

'Curious. I remember your lately asking me to call you "Ali".'

'That's another nickname – short for Alistair, you know.'

'So I supposed. I won't ask you what "Trimmer" is short for. "Trimles-town" hardly seems probable. Well, I will leave you two old friends together. Good-bye, *Trimmer*.'

'So long, Ivor,' said Trimmer unabashed.

When they were alone, Trimmer said:

'You musn't mind old Ivor. He and I are great pals and chaff each other a bit. Did you spot his M.C.? Do you know how he got it? At Dunkirk, for shooting three territorials who were trying to swamp his boat. Great chap old Ivor. Care to give me a drink, uncle? That was the object of the exercise.'

'Why are you called McTavish?'

'That's rather a long story. My mother is a McTavish. Chaps often sign on under assumed names, you know. After I left the Halberdiers I didn't want to hang about waiting to be called up. My firm had been bombed out and I was rather at a loose end. So I went to Glasgow and joined up, no questions asked. McTavish seemed the right sort of name. I fairly whizzed through OCTU. None of that pomp and ceremony of the Halberdiers. I get a good laugh when I remember those guest nights and the snuff and all that rot. So here I am with the Jocks.' He had already helped himself to whisky. 'One for you? I'll sign Angus's name for both. It is a good system they have here. I often drop in and if there isn't a pal about, I sign another bloke's name. Only chaps I know would give me a drink if they were in, of course. Chaps like Angus, who's a Scot too.'

'You can sign my name,' said Guy. 'I belong here.'

'Good for you, uncle. Cheers. I've sometimes thought of joining the Commando myself, but I am sitting pretty snug at the moment. The rest of my battalion went off to Iceland. We had a roughish farewell party and I got a wrist sprained, so they left me behind with the other odds and sods and then we got sent here on defence duties.'

'Bad luck.'

'I don't imagine I'm missing much fun in Iceland. I say, talking of roughish parties, do you remember how you sprained a knee at that guest night with the Halberdiers?'

'I do.'

'Well, the chap they call King Kong was there.'

'Chatty Corner?'

'Never heard the name. Bloke who passed out.'

'The very man I am looking for.'

'No accounting for tastes. He's got himself quite a reputation in these parts as a killer. He lives round the point near our gun. A mean sort of billet. Never been inside. I'll take you there now if you like.'

It was deadly cold out of doors and the light fading. Beyond the quays lay a stone track, iced over now, in the shadows of the cliff. Guy envied Trimmer his shepherd's staff. They made slow time towards the point.

Trimmer pointed out local places of interest.

'That's where Angus came down.'

They paused, then made slowly forward until, rounding the cape, they met the biting wind.

'There's my gun,' said Trimmer.

Through tear-filled eyes Guy saw something sheeted, pointing out to sea.

'Salvage, off an armed trawler that got sunk near shore. We've got twenty rounds with her too.'

'I'll see it another day.'

'At the moment one of the twenty rounds is stuck half in and half out of the breech. Can't move it one way or the other. Tried everything. My men aren't used to artillery. Why should they be?'

Presently they came to a cluster of huts with some dim, golden windows.

'That's where the natives hang out. One can't make them understand black-out. Got Mugg to lecture them. No good.'

'Mugg?'

'That's what he calls himself. Stuffy old goat but he seems to be God almighty in these parts. Lives in the Castle.'

At last they reached a high, solitary building. What few and small windows it had were deep shadows. Not a chink showed.

'They call that the Old Castle. The factor lives there and Kong with him. I'll leave you here, if you don't mind. Kong and I don't hit it off and the factor's always making dirty cracks about my being Scotch.'

They parted with words of friendliness which froze like their breath in the wind and Guy approached the unfriendly place alone – *Child Roland to the dark tower*, he thought.

Whatever the age of the building – its outline seemed medieval – the entrance was Victorian and prosaic; a small granite porch, with brass on the door, which was embellished with small stained-glass panels. Guy, in obedience to the instructions dimly legible by torch light on the brass plate, knocked and rang. Soon there was a glimmer of light, footsteps, the turning of a lock and the door stood three inches open on its chain. A female voice challenged him, as plain in meaning and as obscure in vocabulary as the bark of a dog. Guy answered firmly: 'Captain James Pendennis Corner.'

'The Captain?'

'Corner,' said Guy.

The door shut and firm feet in loose slippers wandered away and the light in the glass panels with them.

Guy huddled in the lee of the little granite column. The wind blew harder, deafening him to the sounds of lock and chain within, so that when the door suddenly opened, he stumbled and nearly fell into the lightless hall. He was aware of the door being banged to and of the presence of another human being, first quite near him, then retreating and mounting. He stood where he was until a door above him opened and cast a golden light over the hall and a stone spiral staircase which rose immediately in front of him. A female figure stood black in the doorway. The structure no doubt was medieval but the scene might have been a set by Gordon Craig for a play of Maeterlinck's.

'Who the devil is it?' said a deep voice from within.

Guy climbed as cautiously as he had walked the track. The granite steps were smoother and harder than the ice outside. The female withdrew upwards into the shadows as he approached.

'Come in, whoever you are,' said the voice within.

Guy entered.

Thus he attained Chatty Corner's lair.

It had been a day of diverse happenings; the warm breakfast with Jumbo, the long drive over the frozen moorland, the sea-crossing during which Guy had sat below, gripping the corner of the teak table – receiving whenever he relaxed his hold a tremendous buffet backward and forward into one corner of the little saloon; the Kümmel at tea time, the drugged, sheeted figure of Anstruther-Kerr, whisky with Trimmer, the agonizing stumbling march against the wind, the villa door which opened into the dark tower – it had been an unnerving day and its climax found Guy so confounded between truth and fantasy that he was prepared, as he entered the room, to find a *tableau* from some ethnographic museum, some shaggy, prognathous hypothetical ancestor, sharpening a flint spear-head among a heap of gnawed bones between walls scrawled with imitation Picassos. Instead he found a man, bulky and hirsute indeed, but a man made in the same image as himself, and plainly far from well, wrapped in army blankets, seated before a peat fire on a commonplace upright chair, with his feet in a steaming bucket of mustard and water. At his hand stood a whisky bottle and on the hob a kettle of water.

'Chatty,' said Guy; tears of emotion filled his eyes (the lachrymatory glands being already over-stimulated by the cold wind). 'Chatty, is it really you?'

Chatty stared under his lowering brow, sneezed and drank hot whisky. Plainly his memories of the night with the Halberdiers were less vivid than Guy's.

'They called me that in Africa,' he said at last. 'Here they call me "Kong". Can't think why.'

He stared and sipped and sneezed. 'Can't think why they called me "Chatty" in Africa. My names are James Pendennis.'

'I know. I have been advertising for you in *The Times*.'

'*Rum, Muck, Mugg and Eigg Times*?'

'No, the London *Times*.'

'Well, that wouldn't be much good, would it? Not,' he added in fairness, 'that I often read the *Rum, Muck, Mugg and Eigg Times*, either. I'm not much of a reading man.'

Guy saw that the conversation must be brought sharply to its point.

'Apthorpe,' he said.

'Yes,' said Chatty. 'He's one for reading papers. Reads anything he picks up. He's a very well-informed man, Apthorpe. There's nothing he doesn't know about. He's told me a lot of things you'd never believe, Apthorpe has. Do you know him?'

'He's dead.'

'No, no. I dined with him less than a year ago in his mess. I'm afraid I got a bit tight that evening. Apthorpe used to hit the bottle a bit, you know.'

'Yes, I know. And now he's dead.'

'I'm very sorry to hear it.' He sneezed, drank and silently pondered the news. 'A man who knew everything. No age either. Years younger than me. What did he die of?'

'I suppose you might call it Bechuana tummy.'

'Beastly complaint. Never heard of anyone dying of it before. Very well off, too.'

'Not *very*, surely?'

'Private means. *Everyone* with *any* private means is well off. That's what has always held *me* back. Parson's son. No private means.'

It was like the game Guy used to play when he was an undergraduate and stayed at country houses – the game in which two contestants strove to introduce a particular sentence into their conversation in a natural manner. This was Guy's opening.

'Whatever money he had, he left to his aunt.'

'He used to talk a lot about his aunts. One lived ...'

'But,' said Guy inexorably, 'he left all his tropical gear to you. I've got it here – on the mainland, at least – to hand over.'

Chatty refilled his glass. 'Decent of him,' said Chatty. 'Decent of you.'

'There's an awful lot of it.'

'Yes. He was always collecting more and more. He used to show it to me whenever I dropped in. He was the soul of hospitality, Apthorpe. He used to put me up, you know, when I was in from the bush. We used to drink a lot at the club and then he'd show me his latest purchases. It was quite a routine.'

'But wasn't he in the bush, too?'

'Apthorpe! No, he had his job to look after in town. I took him for a day or two's shooting now and then – repaying hospitality, you know. But he was such an awful bad shot and got in the way, poor chap, and he never had long enough leave to travel any distance. They work them jolly hard in the tobacco company.'

Chatty sneezed.

'This is the hell of a place to send a man like me,' he continued. 'I offered my services as a tropical expert when the war began. They put me in charge of a jungle warfare school. Then, after Dunkirk, that was abolished and they somehow got my name on a list of mountaineers. Never been out of the bush in my life. I don't know a thing about rocks, still less ice. No wonder we get casualties.'

'About your gear,' said Guy firmly.

'Oh, don't worry about that. There's nothing I should need here, I don't suppose. I'll look it over some time. There's a perfectly awful fellow called McTavish lives next door. He goes across to the mainland now and then. I'll go with him, one of these days.'

'Chatty, you don't understand. I've legal obligations. I must hand over your legacy to you.'

'My dear chap, I shan't sue you.'

'There are moral obligations, too. Please. I can't explain, but it's most important to me.'

The wind howled and Chatty began:

'Queer old place this. Used to be the laird's castle before they built the present edifice. His agent lives here now.'

'Chatty, I think I can get your stuff over. I have connexions on the mainland.'

'They say it's haunted. I suppose it is in a way, but I tell them if they'd seen a few of the things I've seen in Africa ...'

'Plenty of storage here. I expect there's a cellar. All the gear will fit in without being in the way of anyone ...'

'There was a village just north of Tambago ...'

'Chatty,' said Guy. 'Will you do this? Will you sign for it?'

'Unseen?'

'Unseen and in triplicate.'

'I don't know much about the law.'

Guy folded the carbon paper in his field notebook and wrote: *Received 7 November 1940 Apthorpe's gear.*

'Sign here,' he said.

Chatty took the book and studied it with his head first on one side and then on the other. Till the final moment Guy feared he would refuse. Then Chatty wrote, large and irregularly, *J. P. Corner.*

Suddenly the wind dropped. It was a holy moment. Guy rose in silence and ritually received the book.

'Come back when you've time for a pow-wow,' said Chatty. 'I'd like to tell you about that village near Tambago.'

Guy descended and let himself out. It was cold but the wind had lost all its hostility. The sky was clear. There was even a moon. He calmly made his way back to the hotel which was full of the Commando.

Tommy greeted him.

'Guy, I've bad news. You've got to dine out tonight at the Castle. The old boy had been making a lot of complaints so I sent Angus round to make peace. He couldn't see the laird but it turned out he was some kind of cousin, so next day I got a formal invitation to dine there with Angus. I can't chuck now. No one else wants to come. You're the last to join, so go and change quick. We're off in five minutes.'

In his room Guy superstitiously deposited each copy of Chatty's acquittal in a separate hiding-place.

7

The seat of Colonel Hector Campbell of Mugg was known locally as 'the New Castle', to distinguish it from the ancient and more picturesque edifice occupied by the factor and Chatty Corner. The Campbells of Mugg had never been rich but at some moment in the middle of the nineteenth century a marriage, or the sale of property on the mainland which was being transformed from moorland to town, or a legacy from emigrant kinsmen in Canada or Australia – by an accession of fortune of some kind common among lairds, the Mugg of the time got money in his hands and proceeded to build. The fortune melted, but the new castle stood. The exterior was German in character, Bismarckian rather than Wagnerian, of moderate size but designed to withstand assault from all but the most modern weapons. The interior was pitch-pine throughout and owed its decoration more to the taxidermist than to sculptor or painter.

Before Guy and Tommy had left their car, the double doors of the New Castle were thrown open. A large young butler, kilted and heavily bearded, seemed to speak some words of welcome but they were lost in a gale of music. A piper stood beside him, more ornately clothed, older and shorter; a square man, red bearded. If it had come to a fight between them the money would have been on the piper. He was in fact the butler's father. The four of them marched forward and upward to the great hall.

A candelabrum, consisting of concentric and diminishing circles of tarnished brass, hung from the rafters. A dozen or so of the numberless cluster of electric bulbs were alight, disclosing the dim presence of a large circular dinner table. Round the chimney-piece, whose armorial decorations were obscured by smoke, the baronial severity of the rest of the furniture was mitigated by a group of chairs clothed in stained and faded chintz. Everywhere else were granite, pitch-pine, tartan and objects of furniture constructed of antlers. Six dogs, ranging in size from a couple of deer-hounds to an almost hairless pomeranian, gave tongue in inverse proportion to their size. Above all from the depths of the smoke cloud a voice roared.

'Silence, you infernal brutes. Down, Hercules. Back, Jason. Silence, sir.'

There were shadowy, violent actions and sounds of whacking, kicking, snarling and whining. Then the piper had it all to himself again. It was intensely cold in the hall and Guy's eyes wept anew in the peat fumes. Presently the piper, too, was hushed and in the stunning silence an aged lady and gentleman emerged through the smoke. Colonel Campbell was much bedizened with horn and cairngorms. He wore a velvet doublet above his kilt, high stiff collar and a black bow tie. Mrs Campbell wore nothing memorable.

The dogs fanned out beside them and advanced at the same slow pace, silent but menacing. His probable destiny seemed manifest to Guy, to be blinded by smoke among the armchairs, to be frozen to death in the wider spaces, or to be devoured by the dogs where he stood. Tommy, the perfect soldier, appreciated the situation and acted promptly. He advanced on the nearest deerhound, grasped its muzzle and proceeded to rotate its head in a manner which the animal appeared to find reassuring. The great tail began to wave in the fumes. The hushed dogs covered their fangs and advanced to sniff first at his trousers, then at Guy's. Meanwhile Tommy said:

'I'm awfully sorry we couldn't let you know in time. Angus Anstruther-Kerr had an accident today on the rocks. I didn't want to leave you a man short, so I've brought Mr Crouchback instead.'

Guy had already observed the vast distances that separated the few places at table and thought this explanation of his presence less than adequate to the laird's style of living. Mrs Campbell took his hand gently.

'Mugg will be disappointed. We make more of kinship here than you do in the south, you know. He's a little deaf, by the way.'

But Mugg had firmly taken his hand.

'I never met your father,' he said. 'But I knew his uncle, Kerr of Gellioch, before his father married Jean Anstruther of Glenaldy. You resemble neither the one or the other. Glenaldy was a fine man, though he was old when I knew him, and it was a sorrow having no son, to pass the place of Gellioch to.'

'This is Mr Crouchback, dear.'

'Maybe, maybe, I don't recollect. Where's dinner?'

'Katie's not here yet.'

'Is she dining down tonight?'

'You know she is, dear. We discussed it. Katie is Mugg's great-niece from Edinburgh, who's paying us a visit.'

'Visit? She's been here three years.'

'She worked too hard at her exams,' said Mrs Campbell.

'We'll not wait for her,' said Mugg.

As they sat at the round table the gulf that should have been filled by Katie, lay between Guy and his host. Tommy had at once begun a brisk conversation about local tides and beaches with Mrs Campbell. The laird looked at Guy, decided the distance between them was insurmountable and contentedly splashed about in his soup.

Presently he looked up again and said:

'Got any gun-cotton?'

'I'm afraid not.'

'Halberdier?'

'Yes.'

He nodded towards Tommy.

'Coldstreamer?'

'Yes.'

'Same outfit?'

'Yes.'

'Extraordinary thing.'

'We're rather a mixed unit.'

'Argyll myself, of course. No mixture there. They tried cross-posting at the end of the last war. Never worked.'

Fish appeared. Colonel Campbell was silent while he ate, got into trouble with some bones, buried his head in his napkin, took out his teeth and at last got himself to rights.

'Mugg finds fish very difficult nowadays,' said Mrs Campbell during this process.

The host looked at Tommy with a distinctly crafty air now and said:

'Saw some sappers the day before yesterday.'

'They must have been ours.'

'They got gun-cotton?'

'Yes, I think so. They've got a lot of stores marked "Danger".'

The laird now looked sternly at Guy.

'Don't you think it would have been a more honest answer to admit it in the first place?'

Tommy and Mrs Campbell stopped talking of landing-places and listened.

'When I asked you if you had gun-cotton, do you suppose I imagined you were carrying it on your person now? I meant, have you brought any gun-cotton on to my island?'

Here Tommy intervened. 'I hope you've no complaint about it being misused, sir?'

'Or dynamite?' continued the laird disregarding. 'Any explosive would do.'

At this moment the piper put an end to the conversation. He was followed by the butler bearing a huge joint which he set before the host. Round and round went the skirl. Colonel Campbell hacked away at the haunch of venison. The butler followed his own devious course with a tray of red-currant jelly and unpeeled potatoes. Not before the din was over and a full plate before him did Guy realize that a young lady had unobtrusively slipped into the chair beside him. He bowed as best he could from the intricate framework of antlers which constituted his chair. She returned his smile of greeting liberally.

She was, he judged, ten or twelve years younger than himself. Either she was freckled, which seemed unlikely at this place and season, or else she had been splashed with peaty water and had neglected to wash, which seemed still less likely in view of the obvious care she had taken with the rest of her toilet. An hereditary stain perhaps, Guy thought, suddenly appearing in Mugg to bear evidence of an ancestral seafaring adventure long ago among the Spice Islands. Over the brown blotches she was richly rouged, her short black curls were bound with a tartan ribbon, held together by a brooch of the kind Guy had supposed were made only for tourists, and she wore a dress which in that hall must have exposed her to an extremity of frigeration. Her features were regular as marble and her eyes wide and splendid and mad.

'You aren't doing very well, are you?' she remarked suddenly on a note of triumph.

'This is Mr Crouchback, dear,' said Mrs Campbell, frowning fiercely at her husband's great-niece. 'Miss Carmichael. She comes from Edinburgh.'

'And a true Scot,' said Miss Carmichael.

'Yes, of course, Kate. We all know that.'

'Her grandmother was a Campbell,' said the laird, in a tone of deepest melancholy, 'my own mother's sister.'

'My mother was a Meiklejohn and her mother a Dundas.'

'No one is questioning your being a true Scot, Katie,' said the great-aunt; 'eat your dinner.'

During this exchange of genealogical information, Guy had pondered on Miss Carmichael's strange preliminary challenge. He had not distinguished himself, he fully realized, in the preceding conversation, though it would have taken a master, he thought, to go right. And, anyway, how did this beastly girl know? Had she been hiding her freckles in the smoke, or, more likely, was she that phenomenon, quite common, he believed, in these parts – the seventh child of a seventh child? He had had a hard day. He was numb and choked and under-nourished. An endless procession marched across his mind, Carmichaels, Campbells, Meiklejohns, Dundases, in columns of seven, some kilted and bonneted, others in the sober, durable garb of the Edinburgh professions, all dead.

He steadied himself with wine, which in contrast to soup or fish was excellent. 'Doing well', of course, was an expression of the nursery. It meant eating heavily. Hitherto instinct and experience alike had held him back from the venison. Now, openly rebuked, he put a fibrous, rank lump of the stuff into his mouth and began desperately chewing. Miss Carmichael turned back to him.

'Six ships last week,' she said. 'We can't get Berlin, so we have to go by your wireless. I expect it's a lot more really, ten, twenty, thirty, forty ...'

The laird cut across this speculation by saying to Tommy, 'That's what sappers are for, aren't they? – blowing things up.'

'They built the Anglican Cathedral in Gibraltar,' said Guy, in a stern effort to 'do better' but rather indistinctly, for the venison seemed totally unassimilable.

'No,' said the laird. 'I went to a wedding there. They didn't blow that up. Not at the time of the wedding anyhow. But rocks, now.' (He looked craftily at Tommy.) 'They could blow rocks up, I dare say, just as easily as you and I would blow up a wasps' nest.'

'I should keep a long way off if they tried,' said Tommy.

'I always told my men that the nearer you are to the point of an explosion, the safer you are.'

'That's not the orthodox teaching nowadays, I'm afraid.'

Miss Carmichael had stopped counting and said:

'We have quite grown out of the Bonnie Prince Charlie phase, you know. Edinburgh is the heart of Scotland now.'

'A magnificent city,' said Guy.

'It's *seething*.'

'Really?'

'Absolutely seething. It is time I went back there. But I'm not allowed to talk about it, of course.'

She produced from her bag a gold pencil and wrote on the tablecloth, guarding her message with her forearm.

'Look.'

Guy read: 'POLLITICAL PRISNER' and asked with genuine curiosity:
'Did you *pass* your exams at Edinburgh, Miss Carmichael?'
'Never. I was far too busy with more important things.'

She began vigorously rubbing the cloth with breadcrumbs and suddenly, disconcertingly, assumed party manners saying:

'I miss the music so. All the greatest masters come to Edinburgh, you know.'

While she wrote, Guy had managed to remove the venison from his mouth to his plate. He took a draught of claret and said clearly:

'I wonder if you came across a friend of mine at the University. Peter Ellis – he teaches Egyptology or something like that. He used to seethe awfully when I knew him.'

'He did not seethe *with us*.'

The laird had finished his plateful and was ready to resume the subject of explosives.

'They need practice,' he roared, interrupting his wife and Tommy who were discussing submarines.

'We all do, I expect,' said Tommy.

'I will show them just the place. I *own* the hotel, of course,' he added without apparent relevance.

'You think it spoils the view? I'm inclined to agree with you.'

'Only one thing wrong with the hotel. Do you know what?'

'The heating?'

'It doesn't pay. And d'you know why not? No bathing beach. Send those sappers of yours up to me and I can show them the very place for their explosion. Shift a few tons of rock and what do you find? Sand. There was sand there in my father's time. It's marked as sand on the Survey and the Admiralty chart. Bit of the cliff came down; all it needs is just lifting up again.'

The laird scooped the air as though building an imaginary sand-castle.

With the pudding came the nine-o'clock news. A wireless-set was carried to the centre of the table, and the butler tried to adjust it.

'Lies,' said Miss Carmichael. 'All lies.'

There was a brief knock-about turn such as Scots often provide for their English guests, between the laird and his butler, each displaying feudal loyalty, independence, pure uncontrolled crossness and ignorance of the workings of modern science.

Sounds emerged but nothing which Guy could identify as human speech.

'Lies,' repeated Miss Carmichael. 'All lies.'

Presently the machine was removed and replaced with apples.

'Something about Khartoum, wasn't it?' said Tommy.

'It will be retaken,' announced Miss Carmichael.

'But it was never lost,' said Guy.

242

'It was lost to Kitchener and the Gatling-gun,' said Miss Carmichael.

'Mugg served under Kitchener,' said Mrs Campbell.

'There was something I never liked about the fellow. Something fishy, if you know what I mean.'

'It is a terrible thing,' said Miss Carmichael, 'to see the best of our lads marched off, generation after generation, to fight the battles of the English for them. But the end is upon them. When the Germans land in Scotland, the glens will be full of marching men come to greet them, and the professors themselves at the universities will seize the towns. Mark my words, don't be caught on Scottish soil on that day.'

'Katie, go to bed,' said Colonel Campbell.

'Have I gone too far again?'

'You have.'

'May I take some apples with me?'

'Two.'

She took them and rose from her chair.

'Good night, all,' she said jauntily.

'It was those exams,' said Mrs Campbell. 'Far too advanced for a girl. I will leave you to your port,' and she followed Miss Carmichael out, perhaps to chide her, perhaps to calm her with a glass of whisky.

Colonel Campbell was not by habit a drinker of port. The glasses were very small indeed and it did not need the seventh child of a seventh child to detect that the wine had been decanted for some time. Two wasps floated there. The laird, filling his own glass first, neatly caught one of them. He held it up to his eye and studied it with pride.

'It was there when the war began,' he said solemnly. 'And I was hoping it could lie there until we pledged our victory. Port, you understand, being more a matter of ceremony here than of enjoyment. Gentlemen, the King.'

They swallowed the noxious wine. At once Mugg said:

'Campbell, the decanter!'

Heavy cut-glass goblets were set before the three men; a trumpery little china jug of water and a noble decanter of almost colourless, slightly clouded liquid.

'Whisky,' said Mugg with satisfaction. 'Let me propose a toast. The Coldstream, the Halberdiers *and* the Sappers.'

They sat round the table for an hour or more. They talked of military matters with as much accord as was possible between a veteran of Spion Cop and tyros of 1940. They reverted in their talk, every few minutes, to the subject of high explosive. Then Mrs Campbell returned to them. They stood up. She said:

'Oh dear, how quickly the evening goes. I've barely seen anything of you. But I suppose you have to get up so early in the mornings.'

Mugg put the stopper in the whisky decanter.

Before Tommy or Guy could speak, the piper was among them. They mouthed their farewells and followed him to the front door. As they got into their car they saw a storm-lantern waving wildly from an upper window. Tommy made the gesture of taking a salute, the piper turned about and blew away up the corridor. The great doors shut. The lantern continued to wave and in the silence came the full and friendly challenge: 'Heil Hitler.'

Tommy and Guy did not exchange a word on the road home. Instead they laughed, silently at first, then loud and louder. Their driver later reported that he had never seen the Colonel like it, and as for the new Copper Heel, he was 'well away'. He added that his own entertainment below stairs had been 'quite all right too'.

Tommy and Guy were indeed inebriated, not solely, nor in the main, by what they had drunk. They were caught up and bowled over together by that sacred wind which once blew freely over the young world. Cymbals and flutes rang in their ears. The grim isle of Mugg was full of scented breezes, momentarily uplifted, swept away and set down under the stars of the Aegean.

Men who have endured danger and privation together often separate and forget one another when their ordeal is ended. Men who have loved the same woman are blood brothers even in enmity; if they laugh together, as Tommy and Guy laughed that night, orgiastically, they seal their friendship on a plane rarer and loftier than normal human intercourse.

When they reached the hotel Tommy said:

'Thank God you were there, Guy.'

They moved from the heights of fantasy into an unusual but essentially prosaic scene.

The hall had become a gaming-house. On the second day of the Commando's arrival Ivor Claire had ordered the local carpenter, a grim Calvinist with an abhorrence of cards, to make a baccarat shoe on the pretext that it was an implement of war. He now sat at the central table, which was now neatly chalked into sections, paying out a bank. At other tables there was a game of poker and two couples of backgammon. Tommy and Guy made for the table of drinks.

'Twenty pounds in the bank!'

Without turning round Tommy called 'Banco', filled his glass and joined the large table.

Bertie from the poker table asked Guy:

'Want a hand? Half-crown ante and five-bob raise.'

But the cymbals and flutes were still sounding faintly in Guy's ears. He shook his head and wandered dreamily upstairs to a dreamless sleep.

'Tight,' said Bertie. 'Tight as a drum.'

'Good luck to him.'

Next morning at breakfast Guy was told: 'Ivor cleaned up more than £150 last night.'

'They weren't playing a big game when I saw them.'

'Things always tend to get bigger when Colonel Tommy is about.'

It was still dark outside at breakfast-time. The heating apparatus was not working yet; the newly rekindled peat fire sent a trickle of smoke into the dining-room. It was intensely cold.

Civilian waitresses attended them. Presently one of them approached Guy.

'Lieutenant Crouchback?'

'Yes.'

'There's a soldier outside asking for you.'

Guy went to the door and found the driver from last night. There was something indefinably cheeky about the man's greeting.

'I found these in the car, sir. I don't know whether they are the Colonel's or yours.'

He handed Guy a bundle of printed papers. Guy examined the top sheet and read, in large letters:

CALL TO SCOTLAND.
ENGLANDS PERIL IS SCOTLANDS HOPE.
WHY HITLER MUST WIN.

This, he realized, was Katie's doing.

'Have you ever seen anything like these before?'

'Oh, yes, sir. All the billets are full of them.'

'Thank you,' Guy said: 'I'll take charge.'

The driver saluted, Guy turned about and his feet slipped on the frozen surface of the steps. He dropped the papers, breaking the frail bond of knitting-wool which held them together and saved himself from falling only by clutching at the departing driver. A great gust of wind came as they stood embracing and bore away the treasonable documents, scattering them high in the darkness.

'Thank you,' said Guy again and returned more cautiously indoors.

The Regimental orderly room was upstairs, two communicating bedrooms. Grey dawn had broken when Guy went to report officially to his Commanding Officer.

Bertie, the large Grenadier whom Eddie had described as being 'in a sort of way' the Adjutant, was in the outer room smoking a pipe. Guy saluted. Bertie said:

'Oh, hullo. D'you want to see Colonel Tommy? I'll see if he's busy.'

He put down his pipe on an ash tray which advertised a sort of soda-water and went next door. Presently his head appeared.

'Come in.'

Guy saluted at the door, as he had been taught in the Halberdiers, marched to the centre of Tommy's table and stood to attention until Tommy said: 'Good morning, Guy.'

245

'That was a surprisingly funny evening we had last night,' Tommy said, and then to Bertie: 'Have you found out anything about this officer, Bertie?'

'Yes, Colonel.'

Tommy took a paper from his Adjutant.

'Where was it?'

'On my table, Colonel.'

Tommy read the letter carefully. 'See the reference CP oblique R X? That's the same reference as they used when they sent Kong here if I'm not mistaken. It looks as though HOO HQ have got into a muddle with their filing system. We at least leave our bumf handy on the table.' He flicked the paper into a wire tray.

'Well, Guy, you aren't to be one of us, I'm afraid. You're the personal property of Colonel Ritchie-Hook, Royal Halberdiers, sent here until he's passed fit. I'm sorry. I could have used you to take over Ian's section. But it's not fair on the men to keep switching officers about. We'll have to get a proper replacement for Ian. The question now is, what's to be done with you?'

In all his military service Guy never ceased to marvel at the effortless transitions of intercourse between equality and superiority. It was a figure which no temporary officer ever learned to cut. Some of them were better than the regulars with their men. None ever achieved the art of displaying authority over junior officers without self-consciousness and consequent offence. Regular soldiers were survivals of a happy civilization where differences of rank were exactly defined and frankly accepted.

In the thirteen years of Guy's aquaintance with Tommy he had spent few hours in his company, yet their relationship was peculiar. He had known him first as an agreeable friend of his wife's; then, when momentarily she took him as her lover, as some kind of elemental which had mindlessly sent all Guy's world spinning in fragments; later, without bitterness, as an odd uncomfortable memory, someone to be avoided for fear of embarrassment; Tommy had lost as much as he by his adventure.

Then the war came, collecting, as it seemed, the scattered jigsaw of the past and setting each piece back into its proper place. At Bellamy's he and Tommy were amiable acquaintances, as they had been years before. Last night they had been close friends. Today they were Colonel and Subaltern.

'Is there no chance of the Halberdiers seconding me to you?'

'None by the look of this letter. Besides, you're getting a bit long in the tooth for the kind of job we're going to do. Do you think you could climb those cliffs?'

'I could try.'

'Any damn fool can try. That's why I'm five officers short. Do you think you could handle the office bumf better than Bertie?'

'I am sure he could, Colonel,' said Bertie.

Tommy looked at them both sadly. 'What I want is an administrative officer. An elderly fellow who knows all the ropes and can get round the staff. Bertie doesn't fit; I'm afraid you don't either.'

Suddenly Guy remembered Jumbo.

'I think I've got the very thing for you, Colonel,' he said, and described Jumbo in detail.

When he finished Tommy said: 'Bertie, go and get him. People like that are joining the Home Guard in hundreds. Catch him before they do. He'll have to come down in rank, of course. If he's all you say he is, he'll know how to do it. He can transfer to the navy or something and come here as an RNVR Lieutenant. For Christ's sake, Bertie, why are you standing there?'

'I don't know how to fetch him, Colonel.'

'All right, go out to C troop and take over Ian's section. Guy, you're assistant adjutant. Go and get your man. Don't stand there like Bertie. See the harbour-master, get a lifeboat, get moving.'

'I've also got a three-ton lorry, shall I bring that?'

'Yes, of course. Wait.'

Guy recognized the look of the professional soldier, as he had seen it in Jumbo, overclouding Tommy's face. The daemon of caution by which the successful are led, was whispering: 'Don't go too far. You won't get away with a lorry.'

'No,' he said. 'Leave the lorry and bring the naval candidate.'

8

Neither character nor custom had fitted Trimmer to the life of a recluse. For a long time now he had been lying low doing nothing to call himself to the notice of his superiors. He had not reported the condition of his piece of artillery. So far there had been no complaints. His little detachment were well content; Trimmer alone repined as every day his need for feminine society became keener. He was in funds, for he was not admitted to the gambling sessions at the hotel. He was due for leave and at last he took it, seeking what he called 'the lights'.

Glasgow in November 1940 was not literally a *ville lumière*. Fog and crowds gave the black-out a peculiar density. Trimmer, on the afternoon of his arrival, went straight from the train to the station hotel. Here too were fog and crowds. All its lofty halls and corridors were heaped with luggage and thronged by transitory soldiers and sailors. There was a thick, shifting mob at the reception office. To everybody the girl at the counter replied: 'Reserved rooms only. If you come back after eight there may be some cancellations.'

Trimmer struggled to the front, leered and asked: 'Have ye no a wee room for a Scottish laddie?'

'Come back after eight. There may be a cancellation.'

Trimmer gave her a wink and she seemed just perceptibly responsive, but the thrust of other desperate and homeless men made further flirtation impossible.

With his bonnet on the side of his head, his shepherd's crook in his hand and a pair of major's crowns on his shoulders (he had changed them for his lieutenant's stars in the train lavatory), Trimmer began to saunter through the ground floor. There were men everywhere. Of the few women each was the centre of a noisy little circle of festivity, or else huddled with her man in a gloom of leave-taking. Waiters were few. Everywhere he saw heads turned and faces of anxious entreaty. Here and there a more hopeful party banged the table and impolitely shouted: 'We want service.'

But Trimmer was undismayed. He found it all very jolly after his billet on Mugg and experience had taught him that anyone who really wants a woman, finds one in the end.

He passed on with all the panache of a mongrel among the dustbins, tail waving, ears cocked, nose a-quiver. Here and there in his passage he attempted to insinuate himself into one or other of the heartier groups, but without success. At length he came to some steps and the notice: *CHÂTEAU de MADRID. Restaurant de grand luxe.*

Trimmer had been to this hotel once or twice before but he had never penetrated into what he knew was the expensive quarter. He took his fun where he found it, preferably in crowded places. Tonight would be different. He strolled down rubber-lined carpet and was at once greeted at the foot of the stairs by a head waiter.

'*Bon soir, monsieur.* Monsieur has engaged his table?'

'I was looking for a friend.'

'How large will monsieur's party be?'

'Two, if there is a party. I'll just sit here a while and have a drink.'

'*Pardon, monsieur.* It is not allowed to serve drinks here except to those who are dining. Upstairs . . .'

The two men looked at one another, fraud to fraud. They had both knocked about a little. Neither was taken in by the other. For a moment Trimmer was tempted to say: 'Come off it. Where did you get that French accent? The Mile End Road or the Gorbals?'

The waiter was tempted to say: 'This isn't your sort of place, chum. Hop it.'

In the event Trimmer said: 'I shall certainly dine here if my friend turns up. You might give me a look at the menu while I have my cocktail.'

And the head waiter said: '*Tout de suite, monsieur*.'

Another man deprived Trimmer of his bonnet and staff.

He sat at the cocktail bar. The decoration here was more trumpery than in the marble and mahogany halls above. It should have been repainted and re-upholstered that summer, but war had intervened. It wore the air of a fashion magazine, once stiff and shiny, which too many people had handled. But Trimmer did not mind. His acquaintance with fashion magazines had mostly been in tattered copies.

Trimmer looked about and saw that one chair only was occupied. Here in the corner was what he sought, a lonely woman. She did not look up and Trimmer examined her boldly. He saw a woman equipped with all the requisites for attention, who was not trying to attract. She was sitting still and looking at the half-empty glass on her table and she was quite unaware of Trimmer's brave bare knees and swinging sporran. She was, Trimmer judged, in her early thirties; her clothes – and Trimmer was something of a judge – were unlike anything worn by the ladies of Glasgow. Less than two years ago they had come from a *grand couturier*. She was not exactly Trimmer's type but he was ready to try anything that evening. He was inured to rebuffs.

A sharper eye might have noted that she fitted a little too well into her surroundings – the empty tank which had lately been lit up and brilliant with angel fish; the white cordings on the crimson draperies, now a little grimy, the white plaster sea-horses, less gay than heretofore – the lonely woman did not stand out distinctly from these. She sat, as it were, in a faint corroding mist – the exhalation perhaps of unhappiness or ill health, or of mere weariness. She drained her glass and looked past Trimmer to the barman who said: 'Coming up right away, madam,' and began splashing gin of a previously unknown brand into his shaker.

When Trimmer saw her face he was struck by a sense of familiarity; somewhere, perhaps in those shabby fashion-magazines, as he had seen it before.

'I'll take it over,' he said to the barman, quickly lifting the tray with the new cocktail on it.

'Excuse me, sir, *if* you please.'

Trimmer retained his hold. The barman let go. Trimmer carried the tray to the corner.

'Your cocktail, madam,' he said jauntily.

The woman took the glass, said 'Thank you' and looked beyond him. Trimmer then remembered her name.

'You've forgotten me, Mrs Troy?'

She looked at him slowly, without interest.

'Have we met before?'

'Often. In the *Aquitania*.'

'I'm sorry,' she said. 'I'm afraid I don't remember. One meets so many people.'

'Mind if I join you?'

'I am just leaving.'

'You could do with a rinse and set,' said Trimmer, adding in the tones of the *maître d'hôtel*, 'Madam's hair is *un peu fatigué, n'est-ce pas*? It is the sea-air.'

Her face showed sudden interest, incredulity, welcome.

'Gustave! It can't be you?'

'Remember how I used to come to your cabin in the mornings? As soon as I saw your name on the passenger list I'd draw a line through all my eleven-thirty appointments. The old trouts used to come and offer ten-dollar tips but I always kept eleven-thirty free in case you wanted me.'

'Gustave, how awful of me! How could I have forgotten? Sit down. You must admit you've changed a lot.'

'You haven't,' said Trimmer. 'Remember that little bit of massage I used to give you at the back of the neck. You said it cured your hangovers.'

'It did.'

They revived many fond memories of the Atlantic.

'Dear Gustave, how you bring it all back. I always loved the *Aquitania*.'

'Mr Troy about?'

'He's in America.'

'Alone here?'

'I came to see a friend off.'

'Boy friend?'

'You always were too damned fresh.'

'You never kept any secrets from me.'

'No great secret. He's a sailor. I haven't known him long but I liked him. He went off quite suddenly. People are always going off suddenly nowadays, not saying where.'

'You've got me for a week if you're staying on.'

'I've no plans.'

'Nor me. Dining here?'

'It's very expensive.'

'My treat, of course.'

'My dear boy, I couldn't possibly let you spend your money on me. I was just wondering whether I could afford to stand you dinner. I don't think I can.'

'Hard up?'

'Very. I don't quite know why. Something to do with Mr Troy and the war and foreign investments and exchange control. Anyway, my London bank manager has suddenly become very shifty.'

Trimmer was both shocked and slightly exhilarated by this news.

The barrier between hairdresser and first-class passenger was down. It was important to start the new relationship on the proper level – a low one. He did not fancy the idea of often acting as host at the Château de Madrid.

'Anyway, Virginia, let's have another drink here?'

Virginia lived among people who used Christian names indiscriminately. It was Trimmer's self-consciousness which called attention to his familiarity.

'Virginia?' she said, teasing.

'And I, by the way, am Major McTavish. My friends call me "Ali" or "Trimmer".'

'They know about your being a barber, then?'

'As a matter of fact they don't. The name Trimmer has nothing to do with that. Not that I'm ashamed of it. I got plenty of fun on the *Aquitania*, I can tell you – with the passengers. You'd be surprised, if I told you some of the names. Lots of your own set.'

'Tell me, Trimmer.'

For half an hour he kept her enthralled by his revelations, some of which had a basis of truth. The restaurant and foyer began to fill up with stout, elderly civilians, airmen with showy local girls, an admiral with his wife and daughter. The head waiter approached Trimmer for the third time with the menu.

'How about it, Trimmer?'

'I wish you'd call me "Ali".'

'Trimmer to me, every time,' said Virginia.

'How about a Dutch treat as we're both in the same boat?'

'That suits me.'

'Tomorrow we may find something cheaper.'

Virginia raised her eyebrows at the word 'tomorrow', but said nothing. Instead she took the menu card and without consultation ordered a nourishing but economical meal.

'*Et pour commencer*, some oysters? A little *saumon fumé*?'

'No,' she said firmly.

'Not keen on them myself,' said Trimmer.

'I am, but we're not having any tonight. Always read the menu from right to left.'

'I don't get you.'

'Never mind. I expect there are all sorts of things we don't "get" about one another.'

Virginia was looking her old self when she entered the restaurant: 'class written all over her' as Trimmer inwardly expressed it, and, besides, she gleamed with happy mischief.

At dinner Trimmer began to boast a little about his military eminence.

'How lovely,' said Virginia: 'all alone on an island.'

'There are some other troops there in training,' he conceded, 'but I don't have much to do with them. I command the defence.'

'Oh, damn the war,' said Virginia. 'Tell me more about the *Aquitania*.'

She was not a woman who indulged much in reminiscence or speculation. Weeks passed without her giving thought to the past fifteen years of her life – her seduction by a friend of her father's, who had looked her up, looked her over, taken her out, taken her in, from her finishing-school in Paris; her marriage to Guy, the Castello Crouchback and the endless cloudy terraces of the Rift Valley; her marriage to Tommy, London hotels, fast cars, regimental point-to-points, the looming horror of an Indian cantonment; fat Augustus with his cheque book always handy; Mr Troy and his taste for 'significant people' – none of this, as Mr Troy would say, 'added up' to anything. Nor did age or death. It was the present moment and the next five minutes which counted with Virginia. But just now in this shuttered fog-bound place, surrounded by strangers in the bright little room, surrounded by strangers in the blackness outside, miles of them, millions of them, all blind and deaf, not 'significant people'; now while the sirens sounded and bombs began to fall and guns to fire far away among the dockyards – now, briefly, Virginia was happy to relive, to see again from the farther side of the looking-glass, the ordered airy life aboard the great liner. And faithful Gustave who always kept his crowded hour for her, with his false French and his soothing thumb on the neck and shoulders and the top of the spine, suddenly metamorphosed beside her into a bare-kneed major with a cockney accent, preposterously renamed – Gustave was the guide providentially sent on a gloomy evening to lead her back to the days of sun and sea-spray and wallowing dolphins.

At that moment in London Colonel Grace-Groundling-Marchpole, lately promoted head of his most secret department, was filing the latest counter-intelligence:

Crouchback, Guy, temporary Lieutenant Royal Corps of Halberdiers, now stationed with undefined duties at Mugg at HQX Commando. This suspect has been distributing subversive matter at night. Copy attached.

He glanced at *Why Hitler must win.*

'Yes, we've seen this before. Ten copies have been found in the Edinburgh area. This is the first from the islands. Very interesting. It links up the Box case with the Scottish Nationalists – a direct connexion from Salzburg to Mugg. What we need now is to connect Cardiff University with Santa Dulcina. We shall do it in time, I've no doubt.'

Colonel Marchpole's department was so secret that it communicated only with the War Cabinet and the Chiefs of Staff. Colonel Marchpole kept his information until it was asked for. To date that had not occurred and he rejoiced under neglect. Premature examination of his files might ruin his private, undefined Plan. Somewhere in the ultimate curlicues of his mind, there was a Plan. Given time, given enough confidential material, he would succeed in knitting the entire quarrelsome world into a single net of conspiracy in which there were no antagonists, merely millions of men working, unknown to one another, for the same end; and there would be no more war.

Full, Dickensian fog enveloped the city. Day and night the streets were full of slow-moving, lighted trams and lorries and hustling coughing people. Sea-gulls emerged and suddenly vanished overhead. The rattle and shuffle and the hooting of motor-horns drowned the warnings of distant ships. Now and then the air-raid sirens rose above all. The hotel was always crowded. Between drinking hours soldiers and sailors slept in the lounges. When the bars opened they awoke to call plaintively for a drink. The mêlée at the reception counter never diminished. Upstairs the yellow lights burned by day against the whitish-yellow lace which shut out half the yellow-brown obscurity beyond; by night against a frame of black. This was the scene in which Trimmer's idyll was laid.

It ended abruptly on the fourth day.

Trimmer had ventured down about midday into the murky hall to engage tickets for the theatre that evening. One of the suppliant figures at the reception-counter disengaged himself and jostled him.

'Sorry. Why, hullo, McTavish. What are you doing here?'

It was the second-in-command of his battalion, a man Trimmer believed to be far away in Iceland.

'On leave, sir.'

'Well, it's lucky running into you. I'm looking for bodies to take up north. Just landed at Greenock this morning.'

The Major looked at him more closely and fixed his attention on the badges of rank.

'Why the devil are you dressed like that?' he asked.

Trimmer thought quickly.

'I was promoted the other day, sir. I'm not with the regiment any more. I'm on special service.'

'First I've heard of it.'

'I was seconded some time ago to the Commandos.'

'By whose orders?'

'HOO HQ.'

The Major looked doubtful.

'Where are your men?'

'Isle of Mugg.'

'And where are you when you're not on leave?'

'Isle of Mugg, too, sir. But I'm nothing to do with the men now. I think they are expecting an officer to take over any day. I am under Colonel Blackhouse.'

'Well, I suppose it's all right. When is your leave up?'

'This afternoon, as a matter of fact.'

'I hope you've enjoyed it.'

'Thoroughly, thank you.'

'It's all very rum,' said the Major. 'Congratulations on your promotion, by the way.'

Trimmer turned to go. The Major called him back. Trimmer broke into a sweat.

'You're leaving your room here? I wonder if anyone else has got it.'

'I'm rather afraid they have.'

'Damn.'

Trimmer pushed his way forward to the hall porter. Instead of theatre tickets, it was train and ship he wanted now.

'Mugg? Yes, sir. You can just do it. Train leaves at 12.45.'

Virginia was sitting at the dressing-table. Trimmer seized his hair-brushes from under her hands and began filling his sponge-bag at the wash-hand-stand.

'What are you doing? Did you get the tickets all right?'

'I'm sorry, it's off.'

'Gustave!'

'Recalled for immediate service, my dear. I can't explain. War on, you know.'

'Oh God!' she said. 'Another of them.'

Slowly she took off her dressing-gown and returned to bed.

'Aren't you coming to see me off?'

'Not on your life, Trimmer.'

'What are you going to do?'

'I'll be all right. I'm going to sleep again. Good-bye.'

So Trimmer returned to Mugg. He had enjoyed his leave beyond all expectation, but it had left him with a problem of which he could see only one solution, and that a most unwelcome one.

While Trimmer was in Glasgow Tommy Blackhouse had been called to London. In his absence a lassitude fell on the Commando. In the brief hours of daylight the troops marched out to uninhabited areas and blazed away their ammunition into the snowy hillside and the dark sea. One of them killed a seal. Card playing languished and in the evenings the hotel lounge was full of silent figures reading novels – *No Orchids for Miss Blandish, Don't, Mr Disraeli*, the *Chartreuse de Parme* and other oddly assorted works of fiction passed from hand to hand.

Jumbo Trotter completed his work of filing and indexing the waste paper in the orderly-room. He had transformed himself for the time being into a Captain of the Home Guard, pending 'posting' to RNVR.

He and Guy sat in the orderly-room on the morning after Trimmer's return. They both wore their greatcoats and gloves. Jumbo was further muffled in a balaclava helmet. He had *Don't, Mr Disraeli* that morning and was visibly puzzled by it.

Presently he said:

'Did you see the letter from the laird?'

'Yes.'

'He seems to think the Colonel promised to give him some explosives. Doesn't sound likely.'

'I was there. Nothing was promised.'

'I rather like a bit of an explosion myself.'

He resumed his reading.

After a few minutes Guy shut *No Orchids for Miss Blandish*.

'Unreadable,' he said.

'Other fellows seemed to enjoy it. Claire recommended this book. Can't make it out at all. Is it a sort of skit on something?'

Guy turned over the papers in the 'pending' tray.

'What about Dr Glendening-Rees?' he asked. 'I don't think Colonel Tommy is going to be much interested in him.'

Jumbo took the letter and re-read it.

'Can't do anything until he comes back. Can't do very much then. This reads like an order to me. HOO HQ seem to send us every crank in the country. First Chatty Corner, now Dr Glendening-Rees. "Eminent author-ity on dietetics" ... "original and possibly valuable proposal concerning emergency food supplies in the field" ... "afford every facility for research under active service conditions". Can't we put him off?'

'He seems to have started. I dare say he'll liven things up a bit.'

A letter had lain on the table all the morning addressed in sprawling unofficial writing. The envelope was pale violet in colour and flimsy in texture.

'Do you think this is private?'

'It's addressed "OC X Commando", not to the Colonel by name. Better open it.'

It was from Trimmer.

'McTavish has put in an application to see Colonel Tommy.'

'The fellow who was chucked out of the Halberdiers? What does he want?'

'To join the Commando apparently. He seems very eager about it suddenly.'

'Of course,' said Jumbo tolerantly, 'there are lots of fellows who aren't quite up to the mark for *us*, who are quite decent fellows all the same. If you ask me, there are several fellows here already who wouldn't quite do in the

Corps. Decent fellows, mind you, but not up to the mark.' Jumbo gazed before him, sadly, tolerantly, considering the inadequacy of No. X Commando.

'You know,' he said, 'they've issued NCOs with binoculars.'

'Yes.'

'I call that unnecessary. And I'll tell you something. There's one of them – Claire's CSM – queer looking fellow with pink eyes – they call him a "Corporal-Major" I believe. I overheard him the other day refer to these binoculars of his as his "opera glasses". Well, I mean to say –' He paused for effect and continued on the original topic.

'I gather McTavish wasn't a great success in his own regiment. Sergeant Bane got it from his Sergeant that they threw him out of a window the day before embarking for Iceland.'

'I heard it was a horse-trough. Anyway, they knocked him about a bit. There was a lot of that sort of thing when I joined. Ink baths and so forth. No sense in it. Only made bad fellows worse.'

'Colonel Tommy's coming back tonight. He'll know what to do with him.'

Tommy Blackhouse returned as expected. He immediately called for the troop-leaders and said:

'Things are beginning to move. There's a ship coming for us tomorrow or the day after. Be ready to embark at once. She's fitted with ALCs. What are they, Eddie?'

'I don't know, Colonel.'

'Assault landing craft. These are the first lot made. You may have seen some of them on your Dakar jaunt, Guy. We start full-scale landing exercises at once. HOO HQ are sending observers so they had better be good. Issue maps to everyone down to Corporals. I'll give details of the scheme tomorrow.

'I haven't been so lucky with replacements. OCs don't seem as ready to play now as they were six weeks ago, but HOO have promised to bring us up to strength somehow. That's all. Guy, I shall want you.'

When the troop leaders had left, Tommy said:

'Guy, have you ever wondered why we are here?'

'No. I can't say I have.'

'I dare say nobody has. This place wasn't chosen simply for its bloodiness. You'll all know in good time. If you'd ever studied *Admiralty Sailing Directions* it might occur to you that there is another island with two hills, steep shingle beaches and cliffs. Somewhere rather warmer than this. The name doesn't matter now. The point is that these exercises aren't just a staff college scheme for Northland against Southland. They're the dress rehearsal for an operation. It won't do any harm if you pass that on. We've been playing about too long. Anything happen while I was away?'

'McTavish is very anxious to see you. He wants to join.'

'The wet Highlander who jammed his gun?'

'Yes, Colonel.'

'Right. I'll see him tomorrow.'

'He's no good, you know.'

'I can use anyone who's really keen.'

'He's keen all right. I don't quite know why.'

Ivor Claire occupied himself during the 'flap' in making elaborate arrangements for the safe-conduct of his pekinese, Freda, to his mother's care.

9

The promised ship did not come next day or the day after or for many days, while the nights lengthened until they seemed continuous. Often the sun never appeared and drab twilight covered the island. The fishermen sat at home over the peat and the streets of the little town were as empty at noon as at midnight. Once or twice the mist lifted, the two hills appeared and a cold glare on the horizon cast long shadows across the snow. No one looked for the ship. Officers and men began to wish themselves back with their regiments.

There should be a drug for soldiers, Guy thought, to put them to sleep until they were needed. They should repose among the briar like the knights of the Sleeping Beauty; they should be laid away in their boxes in the nursery cupboard. This unvarying cycle of excitement and disappointment rubbed them bare of paint and exposed the lead beneath.

Now that Jumbo was installed in the orderly-room, Guy's position became that of an ADC. Tommy kept him busy. He acquired a certain status in the unit as someone likely to be in the know about Christmas leave, as a mediator for the troop-leaders in their troubles and squabbles. His age was unremarkable here. Jumbo set a high standard of antiquity. Half a dozen of the troop-leaders were also in their middle thirties. No one called him 'Uncle'. Indeed, he was not one of the family at all, merely a passing guest. He knew, now, the name of the Mediterranean island they were planning to take, but he would not be with them on the night. There was here none of the exhilaration of a year ago, of Brigadier Ritchie-Hook's: 'These are the men you will lead in battle.' His work was solely among the officers; notoriously a deleterious form of soldiering. For relaxation he collected the poorest men in the mess and played poker with them for low stakes. He was slightly better off than they and he played a reasonably good game. Whenever one of his party showed too much confidence, Guy advised him to join the big game. After a night with the rich, he invariably returned crestfallen and cautious. Thus Guy made a regular five or six pounds a week.

The assault of the island was rehearsed, first by day, the troops marching to their beaches and from there scrambling inland to objectives which in Mugg were merely map-references, but, in the Mediterranean, were gun-emplacements and signal-posts. Guy acted as intelligence officer and observer and umpire. All went well.

They tried it again on a night of absolute blackness. Tommy and Guy stood by their car on the road near the old Castle. The RSM sent up the rocket which announced the start of the exercise. Bertie's troop stumbled through the glow of the dimmed motor lamps and disappeared noisily into the blackness beyond. A civilian bus passed them. All was silent. Tommy and Guy sat in the car waiting while the headquarters signallers huddled in blankets at the road-side like a group of Bedouin. Wireless silence was being observed until the objectives were gained.

'We might as well be in bed,' said Tommy. 'Nothing can happen for two hours or more and then we can't do anything about it.'

But within twenty minutes of the start there was a twinkle in the sky.

'Verey light, sir,' reported the RSM.

'Can't be.'

Another tiny spark appeared from the same direction. Guy consulted the map.

'Looks like D Troop.'

'Dammit, they've got the farthest to go of anyone. I specially gave it to them to make Ivor do some work for a change.'

There was a mutter from the signallers and presently one of them reported.

'D Troop in position, sir.'

'Give me the damn thing,' said Tommy. He took the instrument.

'Headquarters to D Troop. Where are you? Over ... I can't hear you. Speak up. Over ... Colonel Blackhouse here. Give me Captain Claire. Over ... Ivor, where are you? ... You can't be ... Damn. Out.' He turned to Guy. 'All I can get is a request to return. Go and see them, Guy.'

On the island of Mugg there were two routes to the site of D Troop's objective. Their orders sent them across four miles of moorland to a spot twelve miles distant by the main coast-road and just off it. In the future operation this road led through a populous and heavily garrisoned village. Guy, in the car, now took this route. He followed the track on foot where it diverged.

He was soon challenged by a sentry.

Claire's voice came from nearby. 'Hullo. Who's that?'

'Colonel Tommy sent me.'

'You're very welcome, we're getting frozen. Position occupied and defence consolidated. That I think was the object of the exercise.'

The troop were established in the comparative comfort of a sheep-pen. There was a perceptible smell of rum all about them. Claire held a mug.

'How the hell did you get here, Ivor?'

'I hired a bus. You might call it "captured transport". Can I take the troop back and dismiss? They're getting cold.'

'Not as cold as most.'

'I make their comfort my first concern. Well, can we go?'

'I suppose so. Colonel Tommy will want to talk about this.'

'I am expecting congratulations.'

'Congratulations, Ivor, from myself. I don't know what anyone else is going to say about it.'

Every other troop lost itself that night. After three hours Tommy ordered rockets to be fired, ending the exercise, and sections appeared out of the darkness until dawn, shuffling, soaked and spiritless as stragglers on the road from Moscow.

'I'll see Ivor first thing tomorrow,' said Tommy grimly as he and Guy finally separated.

But Claire's case was unanswerable. The Commandos were expressly raised for irregular action, for seizing tactical advantages on their own initiative. In the operation, Claire explained, there would probably be a bus lying about somewhere.

'In the operation that road leads through a battalion of light infantry.'

'Nothing about that in orders, Colonel.'

Tommy sat silent for some time. At last he said: 'All right, Ivor, you win.'

'Thank you, Colonel.'

The episode greatly endeared Claire to his own troop. The rest of the Commando were very angry about it indeed. Among the men it led to a feud; among the officers to marked coldness. And thus unexpectedly it drew Claire and Guy closer together. Claire required someone to talk to, and was limited in his choice by his sudden unpopularity. Moreover, he had observed with respect Guy's conduct of his poker table. As for Guy, he had recognized from the first a certain remote kinship with this most dissimilar man, a common aloofness, differently manifested – a common melancholy sense of humour; each in his way saw life *sub specie aeternitatis*; thus with numberless reservations they became friends, as had Guy and Apthorpe.

One man who remained in nervous expectation of the ship's arrival was Trimmer. Nemesis, in the shape of 'a spot of awkwardness', seemed very near. Once on the high seas, bound for a secret destination; better still torpedoed and cast up on a neutral shore, Trimmer would be all right. Meanwhile there was the danger that the second-in-command of his battalion had made inquiries about his rank and posting and that somewhere between the Headquarters of Scottish Command and the Adjutant-General's Office in London papers were slowly passing from tray to tray which might at any moment bring his doom.

There was also the danger that his detachment might become restive, but this he solved by sending them all on fourteen days' leave. The men looked doubtful. Trimmer looked confident. He emptied his book of travel-vouchers, giving each man of his plenty. In the case of his Sergeant-Major he added five one-pound notes.

'Where do we report back after leave, sir?'

Trimmer considered this. Then an inspiring thought came to him.

'India,' he said: 'report to the Fourth Battalion.'

'Sir?'

'Climate a great change from Mugg. I leave the detachment in your charge, Sergeant-Major. Enjoy your leave. Then report to Sea Transport. They'll find you a ship.'

'What, without a move order, sir?'

'But you see I am no longer in command. I've been seconded. I can't sign a move order in any case.'

'Should we go back to regimental headquarters, sir?'

'Perhaps that might be more strictly correct. But I should mess about at the docks first a bit. We must try and cut red-tape where we can.'

'Which docks, sir?'

That was easy. 'Portsmouth,' said Trimmer with decision.

'Must have something in writing, sir.'

'I've just explained to you, I'm not in a position to give any orders. All I know is that the Fourth Battalion want you in India. I saw our battalion second-in-command in Glasgow and he gave me the order verbally.' He looked in his note-case and reluctantly produced another two pounds. 'That's all I have,' he said.

'Very good, sir,' said the Sergeant-Major.

He was not the best of soldiers nor the brightest but there was a look in his eyes which made Trimmer fear that seven pounds had been wasted. That man would make for the depot like a homing pigeon, the day his leave expired.

It fell to Guy to find employment for Trimmer himself. It was easy for Tommy in the exhilarating prospect of immediate embarkation to take Trimmer on; it was a different matter to impose him on a disillusioned troop-leader.

The trouble was that three of the four troops who were short of officers, were volunteers from the Household Brigade. Their commanders protested that it was impossible for guardsmen to serve under an officer from a line regiment, and Tommy, a Coldstreamer, agreed. There was a Scottish Troop to which Trimmer should properly go, but that was up to strength. The composite troop of Rifle Brigade and 60th needed an officer, but here the huge hostility that had subsisted underground between them and the Foot Guards came at once to the surface. Why should a rifleman accept Trimmer, when a guardsman would not? It had not occurred to Tommy that he could be suspected of personal bias in the matter; he had merely followed what seemed to him the natural order of things. His own brief service in a line regiment he regarded as a period of detention, seldom remembered. For the first and last time in his career he had made a minute military *gaffe*.

'If they don't want McTavish, I can give them Duncan. He's HLI. Dammit, all light infantry drill is much the same, isn't it?'

But Duncan would not do, nor would the leader of the Scottish troop surrender him. Generations of military history, the smoke of a hundred battlefields darkened the issue.

Guy and Jumbo, Halberdiers, serenely superior to such squabbles, solved the problem.

There existed in a somewhat shadowy form a sixth troop, named 'Specialists'. It comprised a section of Marines skilled with boats and ropes and beaches, two interpreters, a field-security policeman, heavy machine gunners, and a demolition squad. The commander was an Indian cavalryman chosen for his experience in mountain warfare. This officer, Major Graves, had been playing Achilles from days before Guy landed on Mugg. He had taken Chatty Corner's arrival as a deliberate slight on his own hardily acquired skills. He made no protest but he brooded. The dark mood was only lighted by the tale of Chatty's casualties, one of the first of whom was his sapper Subaltern who commanded the demolition squad.

Guy had warmed to this disgruntled, sandy little man whose heart was in the North-West Frontier and he had more than once cajoled him to the poker table. He found him, now, at the time of crisis, playing patience in his troop office.

'I wonder if you've met McTavish, who's just joined us?'

'No.'

'You're short of an officer, aren't you?'

'I'm short of a bloody lot of things.'

'Colonel Tommy wants to send McTavish to you.'

'What's his particular line?'

'Well, nothing *particular*, I think.'

'A specialist in damn-all?'

'He seems a fairly adaptable chap. He might make himself generally helpful, Colonel Tommy thought.'

'He can have the sappers if he wants them.'

'Do you think that's a good thing?'

'I think it's a bloody silly thing. I had a perfectly good chap. Then the CO sent a sort of human ape with orders to break his neck. Since then I've barely seen the sappers. I don't know what they do. I'm sick of them. McTavish can have them.'

Thus, Trimmer first set foot upon the path to glory, little knowing his destination.

That afternoon Tommy left the island once more on a summons from London.

A few days later Jumbo said to Guy: 'Busy?'

'No.'

'It wouldn't be a bad thing if you went up to the Castle. Colonel Campbell has been writing again. Always keep in with the civilian population if you can.'

Guy found the laird at home, indeed in carpet slippers, and in a genial mood. They sat in a circular turret room full of maps and the weapons of sport. He maundered pleasantly for some minutes about 'a ranker fellow! ... Not a Scot at all ... Nothing against rankers except they will stick by the book ... Nothing against English regiments. A bit slow to get moving, that was all ... Have to give commissions to all sorts now of course ... Same in the last war ... Met him when he first came to the island. ... Didn't think much of him ... Didn't know he was one of yours. Not a bad fellow when you got to know him ...' Until gradually Guy realized that the laird was talking of Trimmer.

'Had him up after lunch yesterday.'

To bring matters to the point Guy said: 'McTavish now commands the demolition squad.'

'*Exactly.*'

Mugg rose and began fumbling under his writing-table. At length he produced a pair of boots.

'You know what we were talking about the other evening. I'd like you to come and see.'

He donned his boots and an inverness cape and selected a tall stick from the clutter of rods, gaffs and other tall sticks. Together he and Guy walked into the wind until they stood on the cliff half a mile from the house, overlooking a rough shore of rocks and breakers.

'There,' Mugg said. 'The bathing beach. McTavish says it may be a long job.'

'I'm no expert but I should rather think he is right.'

'We have a proverb here, "What's gone down has to come up." '

'In England we have one like that only the other way round.'

'*Not* quite the same thing,' said Mugg severely.

They looked down on the immense heap of granite.

'It came down all right,' said Mugg.

'Evidently.'

'It was rather a mistake.'

An odd look, a Mona Lisa smirk under the moustache, came into the laird's weather-beaten face.

'I blew it down,' said the laird at length.

'You, sir?'

'I used to do a lot of blowing,' said the laird, 'up and down. Come over here.'

They walked back a quarter of a mile along the headland in the direction of the castle and looked inland.

'Over there,' said the laird. 'It's hard to see in the snow. Where there's that hollow. You can see thistle tops round the edge. You'd not think there had been a stable there, would you?'

'No sir.'

'Stabling for ten, a coach-house, harness-rooms?'

'No.'

'There *was*. Place wasn't safe, woodwork all rotten, half the tiles gone. Couldn't afford to repair it and no reason to. I hadn't any horses. *So up it went*. They heard the bang at Muck. It was a wonderful sight. Great lumps of granite pitching into the sea and all the cattle and sheep on the island stampeding in every direction. That was on 15 June 1923. I don't suppose anyone on the island has forgotten that day. I certainly haven't.' The laird sighed. 'And now I haven't a stick of gelignite on the place. I'll show you what I have got.'

He led Guy into the crater to a little hut, hitherto invisible. It was massively built of granite.

'We made that from part of the stable which didn't go up for some reason or other. The rest of the stone went on the roads. I sold it to the government. It's my only explosion so far that has shown a profit. Something very near £18 after everything was paid, including the labour on the magazine. This is the magazine.'

The snow, which had drifted high round the hut, had been dug clear to make a narrow passage to the door.

'Must have ready access. You never know when you'll need a bit of gun-cotton, do you? But I don't bring many people here. There was a sort of inspector from the mainland came last summer. Said there had been a report that I was storing explosives. I showed him a few boxes of cartridges. Told him to look anywhere. He never found the magazine. You know how reports get about in a small place like this. Everyone knows everyone and then you get grudges. My factor has grudges with almost everyone on the island, so they try and take it out of him by making reports. Let me lead the way.'

The laird took a key from his pocket and opened the door on a single, lightless chamber. He lit an end of candle and held it high with the air of an oenophilist revealing his most recondite treasure. There was in fact a strong resemblance to a wine-cellar in the series of stone bins which lined the walls – a cellar sadly depleted.

'My gelignite once,' said the laird, 'from here to here. . . . Now this is gun-cotton. I'm still fairly well-off for that, as you can see. That's all that's left of the nitro-glycerine. I haven't used any for fifteen years. It may have deteriorated. I'll get some up soon and try it out. . . . This is all empty, you see. In fact, you might say there's nothing much worth having now. You have to keep filling up, you know, or you soon find yourself with nothing. My main shortages are fuses and detonators. . . . Hullo, here's a bit of luck.' He put his candle down so that huge shadows filled the magazine. 'Catch.'

He tossed something out of the farther darkness into the darkness where Guy stood. It passed for a moment through the candle light, hit Guy on the chest and fell to the ground.

'Butter fingers,' said the laird. 'That's dynamite. Didn't know I had any left. Throw it back, there's a good fellow.'

Guy groped and at last found the damp paper-wrapped cylinder. He held it out cautiously.

'That won't hurt you. Thousand-to-one-chance of trouble with dynamite. Not like some things I've had in my time.'

They turned to the door. Guy was sweating in the bitter cold. At last they were in the open air, between the walls of snow. The door was locked.

'Well,' said the laird, 'I've let you spy out the poverty of the land. You understand now why I'm appealing for help. Now let me show you some of the things that need doing.'

They walked for two hours, examining falls of rock, derelict buildings, blocked drains, tree stumps and streams which needed damming.

'I couldn't get the ranker fellow really interested. I don't suppose he ever caught a fish in his life.'

For every problem the laird had a specific, drawn from a simple range of high or slow explosive.

When they parted the laird seemed to wait for thanks, as might an uncle who has been round Madame Tussaud's with a nephew and put himself out to make the tour amusing.

'Thank you,' said Guy.

'Glad you enjoyed it. I shall expect to hear from your Colonel.'

They were standing at the Castle gates.

'By the way,' said the laird. 'My niece, whom you met the other evening. She doesn't know about the magazine. It's not really any business of hers. She's just here on a visit.' He paused and regarded Guy with his fine old blue, blank eyes and then added, 'Besides, she might waste it, you know.'

But the prodigies of the island were not yet exhausted.

As Guy returned to the hotel, he paused to observe a man with a heavy load on his back who stood on the edge of the sea, bent double among the rocks and clawing at them, it appeared, with both hands. He rose when he saw Guy, and advanced towards him carrying a dripping mass of weed; a tall wild man, hatless and clothed in a suit of roughly dressed leather; his grey beard spread in the wind like a baroque prophet's; the few exposed portions of skin were as worn and leathery as his trousers; he wore gold-rimmed pince-nez and spoke not in the accents of Mugg but in precise academic tones.

'Do I, perhaps, address Colonel Blackhouse?'

'No,' said Guy. 'No, not at all. Colonel Blackhouse is in London.'

'He is expecting me. I arrived this morning. The journey took me longer than I expected. I came North on my bicycle and ran into some very rough weather. I was just getting my lunch before making myself known. Can I offer you some?'

He held out the seaweed.

'Thank you,' said Guy. 'No, I am just going to the hotel. You must be Dr Glendening-Rees!'

'Of course.' He filled his mouth with weed and chewed happily, regarding Guy with fatherly interest. 'Lunch at the hotel?' he said. 'You won't find hotels on the battlefield, you know.'

'I suppose not.'

'Bully beef,' said the doctor. 'Biscuit, stewed tea. Poison. I was in the first war. I know. Nearly ruined my digestion for life. That's why I've devoted myself to my subject.' He reached into his pocket and produced a handful of large limpets. 'Try these. Just picked them. Every bit as agreeable as oysters and *much* safer. There's everything a man can want here,' he said, gazing fondly at the desolate fore-shore. 'A rare banquet. I can warrant your men will miss it when they get inland. Things aren't made quite so easy for them there, particularly at this time of year. Not much showing above ground. You have to grub for it and know what you're looking for. It's all a matter of having a *flair*. The young roots of the heather, for instance, are excellent with a little oil and salt, but get a bit of bog myrtle mixed with them and you're done. I don't doubt we can train them.'

He sucked greedily at the limpets.

'I'm attached to headquarters. We heard you were coming. The Colonel will be very sorry to miss you.'

'Oh, I can start without him. I have a schedule prepared. Now don't let me keep you. Go along to your hotel lunch. I shall be a little time here. One of the lessons you will have to learn is to eat slowly in the natural, rational way. Where shall I find someone in authority?'

'At the hotel' – it was not a word to placate Dr Glendening-Rees – 'I'm afraid.'

'There were no hotels in Gallipoli.'

Some two hours later, when he had completed his natural and rational luncheon, Dr Glendening-Rees sat opposite Jumbo and Guy in the regimental office, explaining his plan of action.

'I shall want a demonstration squad from you. Half a dozen men will be enough at this stage. Pick them at random. I don't want the strongest or the youngest or the fittest – just a cross-section. We will be out five days. The essential thing is to make a thorough inspection first. My last experiment was ruined by bad discipline. The men were loaded with concealed food. Their officer even had a bottle of whisky. As a result their whole diet was unbalanced and instead of slowly learning to enjoy natural foods, they broke camp at night, killed a sheep and made themselves thoroughly sick. The only supplement they can possible need is a little olive oil and barley sugar. I shall keep that and dole it out if I detect any deficiency in the roots. At the end of five days I suggest we hold a little tug-of-war between my squad and six men who have been normally victualled and I'll guarantee my men give a good account of themselves.'

'Yes,' said Jumbo. 'Yes. That should be most interesting. A pity the CO isn't here.'

'No doubt he will be here to see the tug-of-war. I've been studying the map of Mugg. It is ideal for our purpose. On the west coast there is a large tract that seems quite uninhabited. There will be no temptation for them to pilfer from farms. Eggs, for instance, would be fatal to the whole conception. I have a full training routine worked out for them – marching, PT, digging. They will get invaluable experience in making a snow bivouac. Nothing more snug if you go the right way about it.'

'Well,' said Jumbo. 'The thing to do is just to stand by, eh? The CO will be back tomorrow or the next day.'

'Oh, but I've got my orders, direct from HOO HQ. I'm to start "forthwith". Didn't they notify you?'

'We had a chit to say you were coming.'

'This, was it not?' The doctor produced from his fleecy bosom a carbon copy of the letter that lay in the pending tray. 'Correct me if I am wrong, but I read that as a direct order to give me every facility for my research.'

'Yes,' conceded Jumbo. 'It could be read in that sense. Why not go out and make a recce on your own? I've never been across to the west coast. Map may be out of date, you know. Often are. I daresay the whole place has been built over now. Why not take a few days off and make sure?'

Jumbo was replete with unnatural and irrational foods; he was drowsy and no match for an opponent exhilarated with rare marine salts and essences.

'That's not how I read my orders,' said the doctor, 'or yours.'

Jumbo looked anxiously at Guy. 'I can't see any of the troop leaders playing on this one.'

'Except Major Graves.'

'Yes, it's a case for the Specialists, plainly.'

'For Trimmer and the sappers.'

'They constitute a cross-section?'

'Yes, Dr Glendening-Rees. I think that would be a very fair description.'

Major Graves seemed to take a fierce relish in relaying these instructions.

'From tomorrow you cease to be under my command. Your section will report in full marching order to a civilian medico, under whose orders you will remain until further notice. You will live in the open on heather and seaweed. I can tell you no more than that. HOO HQ has spoken.'

'I take it, sir, that I shall not be required to go with them?'

'Oh yes, McTavish. There's a job of work for you, quite a job. You have to see that your men get nothing to eat, and of course set them an example yourself.'

'Why us, sir?'

'Why, McTavish? Because we aren't the Guards or the Green Jackets, that's why. Because we're a troop of odds and sods, McTavish. That's why *you* are here.'

Thus with no kind word to speed him Trimmer led his detachment into the unknown.

10

'A familiar sight surely?' said Ivor Claire.

Guy examined the yacht through his field-glasses.

'*Cleopatra*,' he read.

'Julia Stitch,' said Claire. 'Too good to be true.'

Guy also remembered the ship. She had put into Santa Dulcina not many summers ago. It was a tradition of the Castello, which Guy rather reluctantly observed, to call on English yachts. He dined on board. Next day the yacht-party, six of them, had climbed up to lunch with him, lightly, hyperbolically, praising everything.

A large dish of spaghetti had been fomented. A number of fleshless fowls had been dismembered and charred; some limp lettuces drenched in oil and sprinkled with chopped garlic. It was a depressing luncheon which even Mrs Stitch's beauty and gaiety could barely enliven. Guy told the story of the romantic origin of the 'Castello Crauccibac'. The *vino scelto* began its soporific work. Conversation lapsed. Then as they sat rather gloomily in the loggia, while Josefina and Bianca were removing the meat-plates, there rose from above them the wild tocsin: '*C'e scappata la mucca.*'* It was the recurring drama of Santa Dulcinese life, the escape of the cow, more pit-pony than minotaur, from her cellar under the farmhouse.

Josefina and Bianca took up the cry: '*Accidente!*' '*Porca miseria. C'e scappata la mucca,*' dropped everything and bounded over the parapet.

'*C'e scappata la mucca,*' cried Mrs Stitch, precipitately following.

The dazed animal tumbled from low terrace to terrace among the vines. Mrs Stitch was up with her first. Mrs Stitch was the one to grasp the halter and lead her back with soothing words to her subterranean stall.

'I was on board once,' Guy said.

'I sailed in her. Three weeks of excruciating discomfort. The things one did in peace-time!'

'It seemed a lap of luxury to me.'

'Not the bachelors' cabins, Guy. Julia was brought up in the old tradition of giving hell to bachelors. There was mutiny brewing all the time. She used to drag one out of the casino like a naval picket rounding up a red-light quarter. But there's no one, no one in the world I'd sooner see at the moment.' In the weeks of their acquaintance Guy had never seen Claire so moved with enthusiasm. 'Let's go down to the quay.'

'Can she know you're here?'

'Trust Julia to keep in touch with chums.'

'No chum of mine, alas.'

'Everyone is a chum of Julia's.'

But as the *Cleopatra* drew alongside, a chill struck the two watchers.

'Oh God,' said Claire, '*uniforms.*'

Half a dozen male figures stood at the rail. Tommy Blackhouse was there beside a sailor deeply laced with gold; General Whale was there; Brigadier Ritchie-Hook was there. Even, preposterously, Ian Kilbannock was there. But not Mrs Stitch.

The newcomers, even the Admiral, looked unwell. Guy and Claire stood to attention and saluted. The Admiral raised a feeble hand. Ritchie-Hook bared his teeth. Then, as if by previous arrangement, the senior officers went below to seek the repose which had been denied them on their voyage. The *Cleopatra* rudely commandeered, had taken her revenge; she had been built for more friendly waters.

Tommy Blackhouse and Ian Kilbannock came ashore. Tommy's servant, grey ghost of a guardsman, followed with luggage.

* 'The cow has got out.'

268

'Is Jumbo in the office?'

'Yes, Colonel.'

'We've got to lay on that exercise for tomorrow night.'

'Shall I come too?'

'This is where we part company, Guy. Your Brigadier is taking you over now. Our Brigadier. For your information we are now part of "Hookforce", Brigadier Ritchie-Hook commanding. Why the hell aren't you with your troop, Ivor?'

'We're training by sections today,' said Claire.

'Well, you can come and help get out tomorrow's orders.'

Ian said: 'I think Tommy might have done something about my suitcase. The RAF does not understand about servants.'

'What have you done with your Air Marshal?'

'I got him down,' said Ian. 'I got him right down in the end. All the preliminary symptoms of persecution mania. He had to let me go – like Pharaoh and Moses if you appreciate the allusion. I didn't actually have to slay his first-born, but I made him break out in boils and blains from social inferiority – literally. A dreadful sight. So now I'm at Hostile Offensive Operations, appropriately enough. Have you got a man you can send for my luggage?'

'No.'

'You may have noticed I've gone up in rank.' He showed his cuff.

'I'm afraid I don't know what that means.'

'But surely you can count? I don't expect people to know the names of RAF ranks, but you must notice there is one more of these things. It looks newer than the others. I rather think I equal a Major. It's monstrous I should have to carry my own bag.'

'You won't need your bag. There's nowhere to sleep on the island. What are you doing here, anyway?'

'There was to have been a conference on board – most secret operational planning. Sea-sickness intervened. Like a lunatic,' said Ian, 'I came for the trip. I thought it would be a nice change from the blitz, God help me. I've had no sleep or food. An awful inside cabin over the screw.'

'The bachelors' quarters?'

'Slave quarters, I should think. I had to share with Tommy. He was disgustingly sick. As a matter of fact I think I might be able to eat something now.'

Guy took him to the hotel. Food was found, and while Ian ate he explained his new appointment.

'It might have been made for me. In fact, I rather think it *was* made for me, on Air Marshal Beech's entreaty. I liaise with the Press.'

'You haven't come to write *us* up?'

'Good God, no. You're a deadly secret still. That's the beauty of my job.

Everything at HOO is secret, so all I have to do is drink with the American journalists at the Savoy from time to time and refuse information. I tell them I'm a newspaper-man myself and know how they feel. They say I'm a regular guy. And so I am, dammit.'

'Are you, Ian?'

'You've never seen me with my fellow journalists. I show them the democratic side of my character – not what Air Marshal Beech saw.'

'I should awfully like to see it too.'

'You wouldn't understand.' He paused, drank deeply and then added: 'I've been pretty red ever since the Spanish war.'

Guy had nothing to do that morning. He watched Ian eat and drink and smoke. As an illusion of well-being returned, Ian became confidential.

'There's a ship coming for you today.'

'We've heard that before.'

'My dear fellow, I *know*. Hookforce sails in the next convoy. The three other Commandos are on board their ships already. You'll be quite an army if you aren't sunk on the way out.' He progressed from confidence to indiscretion. 'This exercise is all a blind. Tommy doesn't know, of course, but the moment you're all safely below the hatches, you up stick and away.'

'There was some loose talk about an island.'

'Operation Bottleneck? That was off weeks ago. Since then there's been Operation Quicksand and Operation Mousetrap. They're both off. It's Operation Badger now, of course.'

'And what is that?'

'If you don't know, I oughtn't to tell you.'

'Too late to go back now.'

'Well, frankly it's simply Quicksand under another name.'

'And they tell you all this, Ian, at HOO HQ?'

'I pick things up. Journalist's training.'

That afternoon, as on every preceding afternoon, the troopship failed. Tommy devised his orders for the exercise and issued them to the troop-leaders; troop-leaders relayed them to section commanders. The *Cleopatra* held her own secrets of recuperation and planning. At evening the hotel filled. X Commando was always the gayer for Tommy's presence. Most of the mess were old acquaintances of Ian's. They welcomed him with profusion until at length after midnight he sought assistance in finding his way back to the yacht. Guy led him.

'Delightful evening,' he said. 'Delightful fellows.' His voice was always slower and higher when he was in liquor. 'Just like Bellamy's without the bombing. How right you were, Guy, to fix yourself up with this racket. I've been round the other Commandos. Not at all the same sort of fellows. I should like to write a piece about you all. But it wouldn't do.'

'No, it would not. Not at all.'

'Don't misunderstand me,' – the night air was taxing his residue of self-command – 'I don't refer to security. There's an agitation now from the Mystery of Information to take you off the secret list. Heroes are in strong demand. Heroes are urgently required to boost civilian morale. You'll see pages about the Commandos in the papers soon. But not about your racket, Guy. They just won't do, you know. Delightful fellows, heroes too, I dare say, but the Wrong Period. Last-war stuff, Guy. Went out with Rupert Brooke.'

'You find us poetic?'

'No,' said Ian, stopping in his path and turning to face Guy in the darkness. 'perhaps not poetic, exactly, but Upper Class. Hopelessly upper class. You're the "Fine Flower of the Nation". You can't deny it and *it won't do*.'

In the various stages of inebriation, facetiously itemized for centuries, the category, 'prophetically drunk', deserves a place.

'This is a People's War,' said Ian prophetically, 'and the People won't have poetry and they won't have flowers. Flowers stink. The upper classes are on the secret list. We want heroes of the people, to or for the people, by, with and from the people.'

The chill air of Mugg completed its work of detriment. Ian broke into song:

> 'When wilt thou save the people?
> Oh, God of Mercy! When?
> The People, Lord, the People!
> Not thrones and crowns, but men!'

He broke into a trot and breathlessly repeating the lines in a loud tuneless chant, reached the gangway.

Out of the night the voice of Ritchie-Hook rang terribly: 'Stop making that infernal noise, whoever you are, and go to bed.'

Guy left Ian cowering among the quayside litter, waiting a suitable moment to slip on board.

Next morning at first light to Guy's surprise the troopship at last emerged from the haze of myth and was seen to be solidly at anchor beyond the mouth of the harbour.

'Guy, if the Brigadier doesn't want you, you can make yourself useful to me. Jumbo and I have got to get out embarkation orders. You might go on board and fix up accommodation with the navy. It'll be the hell of a business getting everything on board. I hope to God they'll give us another day before the exercise.'

'According to Ian there isn't going to be an exercise.'

'Oh, rot. They've sent half HOO HQ down to watch it.'

'Ian says it's a blind.'

'Ian doesn't know what he's talking about.'

'There's that section of McTavish's I mentioned,' said Jumbo, 'out in the wilds.'

'Call them in.'

'No signal link.'

'Hell. Where are they?'

'No information. They're due back the day after tomorrow.'

'They'll have to miss the exercise, that's all.'

This was not Guy's first embarkation. He had been through it all before at Liverpool with the Halberdiers. This ship was not 'hired transport'. She was manned by a new naval crew. Guy conscientiously inspected mess decks and cabins. After two hours he said: 'There simply isn't room, sir.'

'There must be,' said the First Officer. 'We're fitted out to army specifications to carry one infantry battalion. That's all I know about it.'

'We aren't quite a normal battalion.'

'That's your pigeon,' said the First Officer.

Guy returned to report. He found Jumbo alone.

'Well, you and the Brigadier and whatever other headquarters he's taking had better go in another ship,' said Jumbo. 'I think everyone would have a happier voyage without the Brigadier.'

'That doesn't solve the problem of the Sergeants. Can't they muck in with the men for once?'

'Impossible. Trouble's begun already with the Sergeants. The Grenadiers formed up to Colonel Tommy. All their NCOs carry three stripes and claim to mess apart. Then the Green Jackets formed up to say that in that case their Corporals must too. By the way, I hope you've got me a decent cabin?'

'Sharing with Major Graves and the doctor.'

'I expected something rather better than that, you know.'

At luncheon Guy found himself the object of persecution.

'You've got to realize,' said Bertie with unusual severity, 'that my men are big men. They need space.'

'My servant must have quarters next door to me,' said Eddie. 'I can't go shouting down to the troop deck every time I want anything.'

'But, Guy, we *can't* sleep with the Coldstream.'

'I won't be responsible for the heavy machine-guns, Crouchback, unless I have a lock-up,' said Major Graves. 'And what's this about doubling up with the MO? I mean to say, that's a bit thick.'

'I can't possibly share the sick-bay with the ship's surgeon,' said the doctor. 'I'm entitled to a cabin of my own.'

'It doesn't seem to me you've done *anything* for us.'

'What they need is Julia Stitch to keep them in order,' said Claire sympathetically.

Tommy Blackhouse meanwhile was preparing himself for a disagreeable interview which he could no longer postpone. Tommy, like most soldiers, sought when possible to delegate unkindness. He now realized that he and only he must break bad news to Jumbo.

'Jumbo,' he said when they were alone in the office, 'I shouldn't bother to come on board tonight. We don't really need you for the exercise and there's a lot of stuff here to clear up.'

'Everything in the office is clear up to date, Colonel.'

'The ship's cram-full. You'll be more comfortable on shore.'

'I'd like to get settled in for the voyage.'

'The trouble is, Jumbo, that there's not going to be room for you.'

'Crouchback has found me a berth. Tight quarters, but I shall manage.'

'You see, you aren't really part of operational headquarters.'

'Not really part of the Commando?'

'You know our establishment. No administration officer. Supernumerary.'

'As far as that goes,' said Jumbo, 'I think it can be regularized.'

'It isn't only that, I'm afraid. I want to take you, of course. I don't know what I shall do without you. But the Brigadier's orders are that we only take combatant soldiers.'

'Ben Ritchie-Hook? I've known him for more than twenty years.'

'That's the trouble. The Brigadier thinks you're a bit senior for our sort of show.'

'Ben thinks that?'

'I'm afraid so. Of course I dare say if we set up a permanent headquarters in the Middle East you could come out and join us later. Meanwhile they want you at HOO HQ.'

Jumbo was a Halberdier, trained from first manhood in the giving and taking of orders. He was hard hit, but he excluded all personal feelings.

'I shall have to adjust my posting,' he said. 'It will be rather complicated. Back to barracks.'

'They can use you at HOO HQ.'

'They must apply in the proper quarter, in the proper form. My place is in barracks.' He sat among his files before his empty trays, his old heart empty of hope. 'You don't think it might help if I saw Ben Ritchie-Hook?'

'Yes,' said Tommy, rather eagerly. 'I should do that. You'll have plenty of time. He'll be in London for at least three weeks. They're flying him out to join us in Egypt. I dare say you can get him to take you with him.'

'Not if he doesn't want me. I've never known Ben do anything he doesn't want to do. You're taking Crouchback?'

'He's going to be Brigade Intelligence Officer.'

'I'm glad you'll have at least one Halberdier. He'll make a useful officer. A lot to learn, of course, but the right stuff in him.'

'I don't know when we sail. You'll stay here until then, of course.'

'Of course.'

It was a relief to both of them when Major Graves came to complain about the sappers' stores. None of his troop could be trusted to handle explosives. Was there a suitable magazine on board?

'Oh, leave them where they are until the sappers get back.'

'Unguarded?'

'They'll be safe enough.'

'Very good, sir.'

When Major Graves left, Tommy communed further with his orders for the exercise. The secret of their futility was kept from him until all were embarked. Then the party from the *Cleopatra* came aboard and it was announced that there was to be no exercise. Major-General Whale from HOO HQ had intended to address a full parade of all ranks but deck-space was lacking. Instead he told the officers. No embarkation leave. No last letters. The ship would join others carrying other Commandos under escort at a rendezvous on the high seas.

'Shanghaied, by God,' said Claire.

Jumbo could not know that Tommy had been kept in the dark too. To his sad old sense of honour it was the final betrayal. He watched from the icy fore-shore as the troopship and the yacht sailed away; then heavily returned to the empty hotel. His jaunt was over.

On his desert island Mugg crept out to pilfer the sapper stores, and the sappers themselves, emaciated and unshaven, presently lurched in carrying Dr Glendening-Rees on a wattle hurdle.

INTERLUDE

'I must say,' said Ivor Claire, 'the local inhabitants are uncommonly civil.'

He and Guy sat at sundown in the bar of the hotel. Light shone out into the dusk unscreened to join the headlamps of the cars, passing, turning and stopping on the gravel, and the bright shop windows in the streets beyond. Cape Town at the extremity of two dark continents was a *ville lumière* such as Trimmer had sought in vain.

'Three ships in and a reception committee for each. Something laid on for everybody.'

'It's partly to tease the Dutch, partly to keep the soldiery out of mischief. I gather they had trouble with the last Trooper.'

'Partly good nature too, I fancy.'

'Oh, yes, partly that, I've no doubt.'

'It didn't do B Commando much good. They've been taken on a route march, poor devils.'

'Probably the best thing for them.'

An upright elderly man came across the room. 'Good evening, gentlemen,' he said. 'Forgive my butting in. I'm secretary of the club here. I don't know whether you've been there yet.'

'Yes, indeed,' said Guy, 'thank you very much. I was taken to luncheon there today.'

'Ah, good. Do use it as your own if you want a game of billiards or bridge or anything. Remember the way? Next door to the post office.'

'Thank you very much.'

'There's usually a small gathering about this time. I'll look out for you if you drop in, and introduce you to some fellows.'

'Thanks awfully.'

'You've set us wondering, you know – the different regimental badges. Are you all replacements?'

'We're a mixed lot,' said Claire.

'Well, I know we mustn't ask questions. Are you both fixed up for dinner?'

'Yes, thank you very much.'

'Uncommonly civil fellows,' said Claire when they were again alone. 'Anyway, I've had the most satisfactory day.'

'I too.'

'I took my time going ashore but there were still friendly natives hanging about. A nice ass of a woman came up and said: "Is there anything special you'd like to do or see?" and I said: "Horses." I haven't thought of anything much except horses – and of course Freda – for the last six weeks, as you may imagine. "That may be a bit difficult," she said. "Are you safe on one?" So I pointed out I was in a cavalry regiment. "But aren't you all mechanized now?" I said I thought I could still keep up and she said: "There's Mr Somebody, but he's rather special. I'll see." So she got hold of Mr Somebody and as luck would have it, he'd seen Thimble win at Dublin and was all over me. He had a very decent stable indeed somewhere down the coast and let me pick my horse and we spent the morning hacking. After luncheon I took a jumper he's schooling over the fences. I feel a different and a better man. What happened to you?'

'Eddie and Bertie and I went to the Zoo. We persecuted the ostriches, tried to make them put their heads in the sand, but they wouldn't. Eddie got into the cage and chased them all over the place with a black keeper pleading through the wire. Bertie said one kick of an ostrich can kill three horses. Then we got picked up by a sugar-daddy who took us to the club. Excellent food and you know there's nothing really much the matter with South African wine.'

'I know nothing of wine.'

'The sugar-daddy explained they only send their bad vintages abroad and keep all the good to drink themselves. Bertie and Eddie went off with him afterwards to see vineyards. I went to the Art Gallery. They've two remarkable Noel Patons.'

'I know nothing of art.'

'Nor did Noel Paton. That's the beauty of him.'

Bertie and Eddie came into the bar, huge, unsteady, rosy and smiling.

'We've been sampling wine all the afternoon.'

'Eddie's tight.'

'We're both tight as owls.'

'We've got to take some girls dancing, but we're too tight.'

'Why not lie down for a bit?' said Claire.

'Exactly what I thought. That's why I brought Eddie here – to have a bath.'

'Might drown,' said Eddie.

'Charming girls,' said Bertie. 'Husbands away at the war. Must sober up.'

'Sleep would be the thing.'

'Sleep and bath and then dance with the girls. I'll get some rooms.'

'It's odd,' said Ivor Claire, 'I feel absolutely no urge to get tight now I'm allowed to. In that ship I hardly drew a sober breath.'

'Let's walk.'

They sauntered out into the town.

'I suppose one or more of those absurd stars is called the Southern Cross,' said Claire, gazing up into the warm and brilliant night.

'It's the kind of thing one ought to know, I suppose, for finding one's way in the dark.'

'The dark,' said Claire, 'the black-out. That's the worst thing about the ship. It's the worst thing about the whole war.'

Here everything was ablaze. Merchandise quite devoid of use or beauty shone alluringly in the shop windows. The streets were full of Hookforce. Car-loads of soldiers drove slowly past laden with the spoils of farms and gardens, baskets of oranges and biblical bunches of grapes.

'Fair-day,' said Guy.

Then there was a sterner sound. The soldiers on the pavement, reluctant to lose their holiday mood, edged into doorways and slipped down side turnings. A column of threes in full marching order, arms swinging high, eyes grimly fixed to the front, tramped down the main street towards the docks. Guy and Claire saluted the leading officer, a glaring, fleshless figure.

'B Commando,' said Guy. 'Colonel Prentice.'

'Awfully mad.'

'I was told that he always wears the stockings his great-great-grandfather had at Inkermann. Can that be true?'

'I heard it. I think so.'

'Enclosing every thin man, there's a fat man demanding elbow-room.'

'No doubt he's enjoying himself in his own fashion. One way and another, Guy, Cape Town seems to have provided each of us with whatever we wanted.'

'Ali Baba's lamp.'

'We needed it. Where to now?'

'The club?'

'Too matey. Back to the hotel.'

But when they got there Claire said: 'Too many soldiers.'

'Perhaps there's a garden.'

There was. Guy and Claire sat on a wicker seat looking across an empty illumined tennis lawn. Claire lit a cigarette. He smoked rather seldom. When he did so, it was with an air of conscious luxury.

'What a voyage,' he said. 'Nearly over now. How one longed for a torpedo at times. I used to stand on deck at night and imagine one, a beautiful streak of foam, a bang, and then the heads all round bobbing up for the third time and myself, the sole survivor, floating gently away to some nearby island.'

277

'Wishful thinking. They cram you into open boats, you go mad from drinking sea-water.'

'What a voyage,' said Claire again. 'We're told, and we tell our men, that we have to hold Egypt so as to protect the Suez Canal. And to reach Suez we go half-way to Canada and Trinidad. And when we do get there we shall find the war's over. According to the chap I had lunch with, they can't build cages quick enough to hold the Italian prisoners coming in. I dare say we shall be turned on to guard duties.'

This was February 1941. English tanks were cruising far west of Benghazi; bankers, labelled 'AMGOT', were dining nightly at the Mohamed Ali Club in Cairo, and Rommel, all unknown, was even then setting up his first headquarters in Africa.

Of the nine weeks which had passed since X Commando sailed from Mugg, five only had been spent on the high seas. In the war of attrition which raged ceaselessly against the human spirit, anticlimax was a heavy weapon. The Commando, for all the rude haste and trickery of departure, sailed exultingly. By noon on the second day rumour had it that the rendezvous with the navy was off. Rumour was right. At the second dawn they sailed into Scapa Flow and lay-to beside the sister ships which carried their fellow Commandos. There had been sinkings and diversions and counter-orders; a German capital ship was haunting the Western Approaches. Brigadier Ritchie-Hook appeared and for a month his force relentlessly 'biffed' the encircling hills, night after long night. He brought with him a Halberdier Brigade Major who instructed Guy in the otiose duties of Intelligence Officer. Guy chalked the nightly wanderings of the Commandos on the talc face of his map and recorded them next day in the War Diary. On these exercises the Brigadier seldom spent long at his 'battle headquarters'. Guy and the Brigade Major shivered alone on the beaches, while Ritchie-Hook roamed the moors alone with a haversack full of 'thunder-flashes'.

Guy was sorrowfully conscious that his old hero cut a slightly absurd figure in the eyes of X Commando. They were quick with injurious nick-names in that group. Someone dubbed Ritchie-Hook 'the Widow Twankey' and the preposterous name stuck.

Trimmer and his section were absent. They had momentarily slipped through one of the cracks in the military floor.

Hookforce remained at twelve hours' notice for service overseas. There was no leave; no private communication with the shore. Christmas and New Year passed in dire gloom. The RN officers stood aloof from the RNVR, touchy young men in beards. The bar, which might have been a place of sympathy, proved the centre of contention, for the navy were limited by rank in their wine bills, while the army were not. Below decks there was no wet canteen and gross rumours circulated there of orgies among the officers. It was not a happy ship. At length they sailed on their huge detour. Brigadier and Brigade Major returned for further conferences in London, to join them by air in the Middle East. Trimmer and his sappers arrived at Hoy two days later.

'I wonder,' said Guy, 'were we rather bloody to the navy?'

'They are such awful pip-squeaks,' said Claire without animosity. 'The little ones with beards particularly.'

'It didn't help when Bertie referred to the Captain as "that booby on the roof".'

'The name stuck. It didn't help, of course, when the Pay-Master took Eddie's place in the ward-room and Eddie told him he didn't expect to find a ticket collector in a restaurant car.'

'Eddie was tight that evening.'

'Colonel Tommy messing with the Booby-on-the-Roof had no idea what we had to suffer.'

'He always took our side when there were complaints.'

'Well, naturally. We are his chaps. The pip-squeaks complained altogether too much.'

'The sergeants have been awful.'

'All successful mutinies have been led by NCOs.'

'I shouldn't be surprised if Corporal-Major Ludovic turned out to be a communist.'

'He's all right,' said Claire, automatically defending his own man.

'His eyes are horrible.'

'They're colourless, that's all.'

'Why does he wear bedroom slippers all day?'

'He says it's his feet.'

'Do you believe him?'

'Of course.'

'He's a man of mystery. Was he ever a trooper?'

'I suppose so, once.'

'He looks like a dishonest valet.'

'Yes, perhaps he was that too. He hung about Knightsbridge Barracks and no one knew what to make of him. He just reported at the beginning of the war as a reservist and claimed the rank of Corporal of Horse. His name was on the roll all right, but no one seemed to know anything about him, so naturally they wished him on me when the troop formed.'

'He was the *éminence grise* behind the complaint that "Captain's rounds" violated the sanctity of the sergeants' mess.'

'So they do. I wonder,' said Claire, changing the subject delicately, 'how the other Commandos got on with their sailors?'

'Quite well, I believe. Prentice makes his officers keep to the same drink ration as the navy.'

'I bet that's against King's Regulations.' Then he added: 'I shouldn't be surprised if I didn't get rid of Ludovic when we reach Egypt.'

They sat in silence for some time. Then Guy said:

'It's getting cold. Let's go inside and forget the ship for one evening.'

They found Bertie and Eddie in the bar.

'We're quite sober now,' said Eddie.

'So we're just having one drink before joining the girls. Good evening, Colonel.'

Tommy had entered behind them.

'Well,' he said, 'well. I thought I'd find some of my officers here.'

'A drink, Colonel?'

'Yes, indeed. I've had the hell of a day at Simonstown and I've got some rather disturbing news.'

'I suppose,' said Claire, 'we're going to turn round now and sail back.'

'Not that, but about our Brigadier.'

'*La veuve?*'

'He and the Brigade Major. Their aeroplane left Brazzaville last week and hasn't been heard of since. It seems Hookforce may have to change its name.'

'Your friend, Guy,' said Eddie.

'I love him. He'll turn up.'

'He'd better hurry if he's going to command our operation.'

'Who's in charge now?'

'It seems I am, at the moment.'

'Ali Baba's lamp,' said Claire.

'Eh?'

'Nothing.'

Later that night Guy and Tommy and Claire returned to the ship. Eddie and Bertie were walking the decks; 'walking ourselves sober,' they explained. They carried a bottle and refreshed themselves every second circuit.

'Look,' Eddie said. 'We had to buy it. It's called "Kommando".'

'It's brandy,' said Bertie. 'Rather horrible. Do you think, Colonel, we might send it up to the Booby?'

'No.'

'The only other thing I can think of is to throw it overboard before it makes us sick.'

'Yes, I should do that.'

'No lack of *esprit de corps?* It's called Kommando.'

Eddie dropped the bottle over the rail and leant gazing after it.

'I think I'm going to be sick, all the same,' he said.

Later, in the tiny cabin he shared with the two deeply sleeping companions, Guy lay awake. He could not yet mourn Ritchie-Hook. That ferocious Halberdier, he was sure, was even then biffing his way through the jungle on a line dead straight for the enemy. Guy thought instead with deep affection of X Commando. 'The Flower of the Nation', Ian Kilbannock had ironically called them. He was not far wrong. There was heroic simplicity in Eddie and Bertie. Ivor Claire was another pair of boots entirely, salty, withdrawn, incorrigible. Guy remembered Claire as he first saw him in the Roman spring in the afternoon sunlight amid the embosoming cypresses of the Borghese Gardens, putting his horse faultlessly over the jumps, concentrated as a man in prayer. Ivor Claire, Guy thought, was the fine flower of them all. He was quintessential England, the man Hitler had not taken into account, Guy thought.

BOOK TWO

In the Picture

I

Major-General Whale held the appointment of Director of Land Forces in Hazardous Offensive Operations. He was known in countless minutes as the DLFHOO and to a few old friends as 'Sprat'. On Holy Saturday 1941 he was summoned to attend the ACIG's weekly meeting at the War Office. He went with foreboding. He was not fully informed of the recent disasters in the Middle East but he knew things were going badly. Benghazi had fallen the week before. It did not seem clear where the retreating army intended to make its stand. On Maundy Thursday the Australians in Greece had been attacked on their open flank. It was not clear where they would stand. Belgrade had been bombed on Palm Sunday. But these tidings were not Sprat's first concern that morning. The matter on the ACIG's agenda which accounted for Sprat's presence was '*Future of Special Service Forces in UK*'.

The men round the table represented a galaxy of potent initials, DSD, AG, QMG, DPS, and more besides. These were no snowy-headed, muddled veterans of English tradition but lean, middle-aged men who kept themselves fit; men on the make; a hanging jury, thought Sprat, greeting them heartily.

The Lieutenant-General in the chair said:

'Just remind us – will you, Sprat? – what precisely is your present strength?'

'Well, sir, there *were* the Halberdiers.'

'Not since last week.'

'And Hookforce.'

'Yes, Hookforce. What's the latest from them?' He turned to a Major-General who sat in a cloud of pipe-smoke on his left.

'No one seems to have found any use for them in ME. "Badger", of course, was cancelled.'

'Of course.'

'Of course.'

'Of course.'

'That is hardly their fault, sir,' said Sprat. 'First they lost their commander. Then they lost their assault ships. The canal was closed when they reached Suez, you remember. They were put into temporary camps in Canal Area. Then when the canal was cleared the ships were needed to take the Australians to Greece. They moved by train to Alex.'

'Yes, Sprat, we know. Of course it's not their fault. All I mean is, they don't seem to be exactly pulling their weight.'

'I rather think, sir,' said a foxy Brigadier, 'that we shall soon hear they've been broken up and used as replacements.'

'Exactly. Anyway, they are MEF now. What I want to get at is: what land forces do you command at this moment in UK?'

'Well, sir, as you know, recruiting was suspended after Hookforce sailed. That left us rather thin on the ground.'

'Yes?'

Hands doodled on the agenda papers.

'At the moment, sir, I have one officer and twelve men, four of whom are in hospital with frost-bite and unlikely to be passed fit for active service.'

'Exactly. I merely wanted your confirmation.'

Outside, in the cathedral, whose tower could be seen from the War Office windows; far beyond in the lands of enemy and ally, the Easter fire was freshly burning. Here for Sprat all was cold and dark. The gangmen of the departments closed in for the kill. The representative of the DPS drew a series of little gallows on his agenda.

'Frankly, sir, I don't think the DPS has even quite understood what function the Commandos have which could not be performed by ordinary regimental soldiers or the Royal Marines. The DPS does not like the volunteer system. Every fighting man shall be prepared to undertake any task assigned him, however hazardous.'

'Exactly.'

The staff officers pronounced judgement by turn.

'... I can only say, sir, that the special postings have put a considerable extra strain on our department. ...'

'... As we see it, sir, either the Commandos become a *corps d'élite*, in which case they seriously weaken the other arms of the service, or they become a sort of Foreign Legion of throw-outs, in which case we can hardly see them making very much contribution to the war effort. ...'

'I don't want to say anything against your chaps, Sprat. Excellent raw material, no doubt. But I think you must agree that the experiment of relaxing barrack discipline hasn't quite worked out. That explosion at Mugg ...'

'I think, if you'll allow me, I can explain ...'

'Yes, yes, no doubt. It's really quite beside the point. I'm sorry it was brought up.'

'The security precautions at the embarkation ...'

'Yes, yes. Someone put a foot wrong. No blame attaches to HOO HQ.'

'If we could start another recruiting drive I am sure the response ...'

'That is just what Home Forces do *not* want.'

'The Ministry of Information ...' began Sprat desperately, most infelicitously. The doodling hands were still. Breaths were momentarily caught, then sharply, with clouds of smoke, expelled. 'The Ministry of Information,' said Spray defiantly, 'have shown great interest. They are only waiting for a successful operation to release the whole story to the press. Civil morale,' he faltered, '... American opinion ...'

'That, of course,' said the chairman, 'does not concern this committee.'

In the end a minute was drafted to the CIGS recommending that no steps were desirable with regard to Special Service Forces.

Sprat returned to his own office. All over the world, unheard by Sprat, the *Exultet* had been sung that morning. It found no echo in Sprat's hollow heart. He called his planners to him and his liaison officer.

'They're out to do us down,' he reported succinctly. He need not name the enemy. No one thought he meant the Germans. 'There's only one thing for it. We must mount an operation at once and call in the press. What have we got that's suitable for one rather moderate officer and eight men?'

The planners at HOO HQ were fertile. In their steel cupboards lay in various stages of elaboration and under a variety of sobriquets projects for the assault of almost every feature of the enemy's immense coastline.

A pause.

'There's "Popgun", sir.'

' "Popgun"? "Popgun"? That was one of yours, wasn't it, Charles?'

'No one was much interested. I always thought it had possibilities.'

'Remind me.'

'Popgun' was the least ambitious of all the plans. It concerned a tiny, uninhabited island near Jersey on which stood, or was believed to stand, a disused light-house. Someone on the naval side, idly scanning a chart, had suggested that supposing the enemy had tumbled to the tricks of RDF this island and this ruin might be a possible choice of station. Charles reminded Sprat of these particulars.

'Yes. Lay on "Popgun". Ian, you'll be up to the neck in this. You'd better get into touch with McTavish at once. You'll be going with him.'

'Where is he?' asked Ian Kilbannock.

'He must be somewhere. Someone must know. You and Charles find him while I collect a submarine.'

While the first bells of Easter rang throughout Christendom, the muezzin called his faithful to prayer from the shapeless white minaret beyond the barbed wire; South, West and North the faithful prostrated themselves towards the rising sun. His voice fell unheeded among the populous dunes of Sidi Bishr.

Already awake, Guy rose from his camp-bed and shouted for shaving-water. He was brigade duty-officer, nearing the end of his tour of duty beside the office telephone. During the night there had been one air-raid warning. GHQ Cairo had been silent.

The brigade, still named 'Hookforce', occupied a group of huts in the centre of the tented camp. Tommy Blackhouse was Deputy Commander with the acting rank of full colonel. He had returned from Cairo on the third day of their sojourn in Egypt with red tabs and a number of staff officers, chief among them a small, bald, youngish man named Hound. He was the Brigade Major. Neither in the Halberdiers nor in the Commandos had Guy met a soldier quite like Major Hound, nor had Major Hound met a force like Hookforce.

He had chosen a military career because he was not clever enough to pass into the civil service. At Sandhurst in 1925 the universal assumption was that the British army would never again be obliged to fight a European war. Young Hound had shown an aptitude for administration and his failures in the riding-school were compensated by prizes at Bisley. Later in the drift of war he was found in the pool of unattached staff officers in Cairo when Hookforce arrived leaderless at Suez. To them he came and he did not disguise his distaste for their anomalies. They had no transport, they had no cooks, they had far too many officers and sergeants, they wore a variety of uniforms and followed a multitude of conflicting regimental customs, they bore strange arms, daggers and toggle-ropes and tommy-guns. B Commando was ruled by a draconic private law and a code of punishment unauthorized by King's Regulations. X Commando might have seemed lawless but for the presence of fifty Free Spaniards who had drifted in from Syria and been inexplicably put under command; beside their anarchy all minor irregularities became unremarkable. The camp police were constantly flushing women in the Spanish lines. One morning they dug up the body of an Egyptian cab-driver, just beyond the perimeter, lightly buried in sand with his throat cut.

When Major Hound left Cairo he had been told:

'There's no place here for private armies. We've got to get these fellows, whoever they are, reorganized as a standard infantry brigade.'

Later a recommendation was made that Hookforce should be disbanded and distributed as replacements. An order followed from London to hold fast pending a decision at the highest level as to the whole future of Special Service Forces. Major Hound kept his own counsel about these matters. They were not communicated to him officially. He learned them in Cairo on his frequent trips to the Turf Club and to Shepheard's Hotel in conversation with cronies from GHQ. He mentioned the state of discipline in camp, also unofficially. And Hookforce remained at Sidi Bishr declining from boredom to disorder and daily growing more and more to justify the suspicions of GHQ.

Guy remained Intelligence Officer. Five spectacled men, throw-outs from the Commandos, were attached to him as his section. In the employment of these men he waged a deadly private war with the Brigade Major. Lately he had shed them, attaching them to the Signals Officer for instruction in procedure.

Breakfast was brought him at the office table; a kind of rissole of bully beef gritty with sand, tea that tasted of chlorine. At eight the office clerks appeared; at a quarter past Corporal-Major Ludovic, whom Ivor Claire had succeeded in promoting to headquarters. He gazed about the hut with his pale eyes, observed Guy, saluted him in a style that was ecclesiastical rather than military, and began ponderously moving papers from tray to tray; not thus the Brigade Major, who arrived very briskly at twenty past.

'Morning, Crouchback,' said Major Hound. 'Nothing from GHQ? Then we can take it that the last cancellation stands. The units can get out into the country. How about your section? They've finished their signalling course, I think. How do you propose to exercise them today?'

'They're doing PT under Sergeant Smiley.'

'And after?'

'Infantry drill,' said Guy, crossly improvising, 'under me.'

'Good. Smarten 'em up.'

At nine Tommy arrived.

'More trouble with X Commando,' said Major Hound.

'Damn.'

'Graves is on his way to see you.'

'Damn. Guy, have you still got those obliques of "Badger"?'

'Yes, Colonel.'

'Bung 'em back to GHQ. They won't be wanted now.'

'You needn't stay in the office while Major Graves is here,' said the Brigade Major to Guy. 'Better get on with that drill parade.'

Guy went in search of his section. Sergeant Smiley called them hastily to their feet on his approach. Six cigarettes smouldered in the sand at their feet.

'Fall them in in a quarter of an hour with rifles and drill order, outside the brigade office,' he ordered.

For an hour he drilled them in the powdery sand. It all came back to him from the barrack square. He stood by the Brigade Major's window, opened his mouth wide and roared like a Halberdier. Inside the hut Major Graves was telling his tale of injustice and neglect. Corporal-Major Ludovic was typing his journal.

'*Man is what he hates,*' he wrote. '*Yesterday I was Blackhouse. Today I am Crouchback. Tomorrow, merciful heaven, shall I be Hound?*'

'... The odd numbers of the front rank will seize the rifles of the even numbers of the rear rank with the left hand crossing the muzzles, magazines turned outward, at the same time raising the piling swivels with the forefinger and thumb of both hands ...'

He paused, aware of an obvious anomaly.

'In the present instance,' he continued, falling into a parody of his old drill-sergeant, 'number two being a blank file, there are no even numbers in the rear rank. Number three will therefore for the purpose of this exercise regard himself as even....'

He concluded his exposition.

'Squad, pile arms. As you were. Listen to the detail. The odd numbers of the front rank – that's you, number one – will seize the rifles of even numbers of the rear rank – that's you, number three ...'

The Brigade Major's head appeared at the window.

'I say, Crouchback, could you move your men a bit farther away?'

Guy spun on his heel and saluted.

'Sir.'

He spun back.

'Squad will retire. About turn. Quick march. Halt. About turn. As you were. About turn. As you were. About turn.' They were now fifty yards from him but his voice carried.

'I will give you the detail once more. The odd numbers of the front rank will seize the rifles of the even numbers of the rear rank ...'

Behind their steamy goggles the men glimpsed that this performance was being played not solely for their own discomfort. Sergeant Smiley began to join his powerful tones to Guy's.

After half an hour Guy gave them a stand-easy. Tommy Blackhouse called him in.

'Most impressive, Guy,' he said. 'First rate. But I must ask you to dismiss now. I've got a job for you. Go into town and see Ivor and find out when he's coming back.'

For a fortnight Ivor Claire had been absent from duty. He had led a party armed with tent mallets in pursuit of Arab marauders, had tripped on a guy-rope and twisted his knee. Eschewing the services of the RAMC he had installed himself in a private nursing-home.

Guy went to the car-park and found a lorry going in for rations. The road ran along the edge of the sea. The breeze was full of flying sand. On the beaches young civilians exposed hairy bodies and played ball with loud, excited cries. Army lorries passed in close procession, broken here and there by new, tight-shut limousines bearing purple-lipped ladies in black satin.

'Drop me at the Cecil,' said Guy, for he had other business in Alexandria besides Ivor Claire. He wished to make his Easter duties and preferred to do so in a city church, rather than in camp. Already, without deliberation, he had begun to dissociate himself from the army in matters of real concern.

Alexandria, ancient asparagus bed of theological absurdity, is now somewhat shabbily furnished with churches. Guy found what he sought in a side street, a large unobtrusive building attached to a school, it seemed, or a hospital. He entered into deep gloom.

A fat youth in shorts and vest was lethargically sweeping the aisle. Guy approached and addressed him in French. He seemed not to hear. A bearded, skirted figure scudded past in the darkness. Guy pursued and said awkwardly:

'*Excusez-moi, mon père. Y a-t-il un prêtre qui parle anglais ou italien?*'

The priest did not pause.

'*Français,*' he said.

'*Je veux me confesser, en français si c'est nécessaire. Mais je préfère beaucoup anglais ou italien, si c'est possible.*'

'*Anglais,*' said the hasty priest. '*Par-là.*'

He turned abruptly into the sacristy pointing as he went towards a still darker chapel. Khaki stockings and army boots protruded from the penitents' side of the confessional. Guy knelt and waited. He knew what he had to say. The mutter of voices in the shadows seemed to be prolonged inordinately. At length a young soldier emerged and Guy took his place. A bearded face was just visible through the grille; a guttural voice blessed him. He made his confession and paused. The dark figure seemed to shrug off the triviality of what he had heard.

'You have a rosary? Say three decades.'

He gave the absolution.

'Thank you, father, and pray for me.' Guy made to go but the priest continued:

'You are here on leave?'

'No, father.'

'You have been here long?'

'A few weeks.'

'You have come from the desert?'

'No, father.'

'You have just come from England? You came with new tanks?'

Suddenly Guy was suspicious. He was shriven. The priest was no longer bound by the seal of confession. The grille still stood between them. Guy still knelt, but the business between them was over. They were man and man now in a country at war.

'When do you go to the desert?'

'Why do you ask?'

'To help you. There are special dispensations. If you are going at once into action I can give you communion.'

'I'm not.'

Guy rose and left the church. Beggars thronged him. He walked a few steps towards the main street where the trams ran, then turned back. The boy with the broom had gone. The confessional was empty. He knocked on the open door of the sacristy. No one came. He entered and found a clean tiled floor, cupboards, a sink, no priest. He left the church and stood once more among the beggars, undecided. The transition from the role of penitent to that of investigating officer was radical. He could not now remember verbatim what had occurred. The questions had been impertinent; were they necessarily sinister? Could he identify the priest? Could he, if called to find a witness, identify the young soldier?

Two palm trees in a yard separated the church from the clergyhouse. Guy rang the bell and presently the fat boy opened the door, disclosing a vista of high white corridor.

'I would like to know the name of one of your fathers.'

'The fathers have this moment gone to rest. They have had very long ceremonies this morning.'

'I don't want to disturb him – merely to know his name. He speaks English and was hearing confessions in the church two minutes ago.'

'No confessions now until three o'clock. The fathers are resting.'

'I have been to confession to this father. I want to know his name. He speaks English.'

'I speak English. I do not know what father you want.'

'I want his name.'

'You must come at three o'clock, please, when the fathers have rested.'

Guy turned away. The beggars settled on him. He strode into the busy street and the darkness of Egypt closed on him in the dazzling sunlight. Perhaps he had imagined the whole incident, and if he had not, what profit was there in pursuit? There were priests in France working for the allies. Why not a priest in Egypt, in exile, doing his humble bit for his own side? Egypt teemed with spies. Every troop movement was open to the scrutiny of a million ophthalmic eyes. The British order of battle must be known in minute detail from countless sources. What could that priest accomplish except perhaps gain kinder treatment for his community if Rommel reached Alexandria? Probably the only result, if Guy made a report, would be an order forbidding H M forces to frequent civilian churches.

Ivor Claire's nursing-home overlooked the Municipal Gardens. Guy walked there through the crowded streets so despondently that the touts looking at him despaired and let him pass unsolicited.

He found Claire in a wheeled-chair on his balcony.

'*Much* better,' he said in answer to Guy's inquiry. 'They are all very pleased with me. I may be able to get up to Cairo next week for the races.'

'Colonel Tommy is getting a little restive.'

'Who wouldn't be at Sidi Bishr? Well, he knows where to find me when he wants me.'

'He seems rather to want you now.'

'"Oh, I don't think I'd be much use to him until I'm fit, you know. My troop is in good hands. When Tommy kindly relieved me of Corporal-Major Ludovic my anxieties came to an end. But we must keep touch. I can't have you doing a McTavish on me.'

'Two flaps since you went away. Once we were at two hours' notice for three days.'

'I know. Greek nonsense. When there's anything really up I shall hear from Julia Stitch before Tommy does. She is a mine of indiscretion. You know she's here?'

'Half X Commando spend their evenings with her.'

'Why don't you?'

'Oh, she wouldn't remember me.'

'My dear Guy, she remembers everyone. Algie has some sort of job keeping his eye on the King. They're very well installed. I thought of moving in on them but one can't be sure that Julia will give an invalid quite all he needs. There's rather too much coming and going, too – generals and people. Julia pops in most mornings and brings me the gossip.'

Then Guy recounted that morning's incident in the church.

'Not much to shoot a chap on,' said Claire. 'Even a clergyman.'

'Ought I to do anything about it?'

'Ask Tommy. It might prove a great bore, you know. Everyone is a spy in this country.'

'That's rather what I thought.'

'I'm sure the nurses here are. They walk out with the Vichy French from that ship in the harbour. What's the news from Sidi Bishr?'

'Worse. A little worse every day. B Commando are on the verge of mutiny. Prentice has confined them to camp until every man has swum a hundred yards in boots and equipment. They'll shoot him when they go into action. Major Graves still thinks he ought to command X Commando.'

'He must be insane to want to.'

'Yes. Tony is having a bad time. The Grenadiers are all down with Gyppy tummy. Five Coldstreamers put in to be returned to their regiment. Corporal-Major Ludovic is suspected of writing poetry.'

'More than probable.'

'Our Catalan refugees have even got Tommy worried. An Arab mess waiter went off with A Commando's medical stores. We've got four courts-martial pending and ten men adrift. God knows how many arms stolen. The NAAFI till has been burgled twice. Someone tried to set the camp cinema on fire. Nothing has been heard of the Brigadier.'

'That at least is good news.'

'Not to me, Ivor.'

They were interrupted by a shrill guttersnipe whistle from the street below.

'Julia,' said Claire.

'I'd better go.'

'Don't.'

A minute later Mrs Algernon Stitch was with them. She wore linen and a Mexican sombrero; a laden shopping basket hung over one white arm. She inclined the huge straw disc of her hat over Claire and kissed his forehead.

'Why are your nurses so disagreeable, Ivor?'

'Politics. They all claim to have lost brothers at Oran. You remember Guy?'

She turned her eyes, her true blue, portable and compendious oceans upon Guy, absorbed him and then very loudly, in rich Genoese accents, proclaimed:

'*C'e scappata la mucca.*'

'You see,' said Ivor, as though displaying a clever trick of Freda's, 'I told you she would remember.'

'Why wasn't I told you were here? Come to lunch?'

'Well, I don't know exactly. It's awfully kind of you ...'

'Good. Are you coming, Ivor?'

'Is it a party?'

'I forget who.'

'Perhaps I'm best where I am.'

Mrs Stitch gazed over the balcony into the gardens.

'Forster says they ought to be "thoroughly explored",' she said. 'Something for another day.' To Guy. 'You've got his *Guide*?'

'I've always wanted a copy. It's very scarce.'

'Just been reprinted. Here, take mine. I can always get another.'

She produced from her basket a copy of E. M. Forster's *Alexandria*.

'I didn't know. In that case I can get one for myself. Thanks awfully, though.'

'Take it, fool,' she said.

'Well, thanks awfully. I know his *Pharos and Pharillon,* of course.'

'Of course; the *Guide* is topping too.'

'Have you brought me anything, Julia?' Claire asked.

'Not today, unless you'd care for some Turkish delight.'

'Yes, please.'

'Here you are. I haven't finished shopping yet. In fact, I must go now.' To Guy. 'Come on.'

'Not much of a visit.'

'You should come to lunch when you're asked.'

'Well, thank you for the sweets.'

'I'll be back. Come on.'

She led Guy down and out. He tried to circumvent her at the door of her little open car but was peremptorily ordered away.

'Other side, fool. Jump in.'

Off she drove, darting between camels and trams and cabs and tanks, down the Rue Sultan, spinning left at the Nebi Daniel, stopping abruptly in the centre of the crossing and saying: 'Just look. The Soma. In the days of Cleopatra the streets ran from the Gate of the Moon to the Gate of the Sun and from the lake harbour to the sea harbour with colonnades all the way. White marble and green silk awnings. Perhaps you knew.'

'I didn't.'

She stood up in the car and pointed. 'Alexander's tomb,' she said. 'Somewhere under that monstrosity.'

Motor-horns competed with police whistles and loud human voices in half a dozen tongues. A uniformed Egyptian armed with a little trumpet performed a ritual dance of rage before her. A gallant RASC driver drew up beside her.

'Stalled has she, lady?'

Two guides attempted to enter the car beside them.

'I show you mosky. I show you all moskies.'

'Forster says the marble was so bright that you could thread a needle at midnight. Why are they making such a fuss? There is all the time in the world. No one here ever lunches before two.'

Mrs Stitch, Guy reflected, did not seem to require much conversation from him. He sat silent, quite soaked up by her.

'I'd never set foot in Egypt until now. It's been a great disappointment. I can't get to like the people,' she said sadly, drenching the rabble in her great eyes. 'Except the King – and it's not policy to like him much. Well, we must get on. I've got to find some shoes.'

She sat down, sounded her horn, and thrust the little car relentlessly forward.

Soon she turned off into a side street marked OUT OF BOUNDS TO ALL RANKS OF H.M. FORCES.

'Two Australians were picked up dead here the other morning,' Guy explained.

Mrs Stitch had many interests but only one interest at a time. That morning it was Alexandrian history.

'Hypatia,' she said, turning into an alley. 'I'll tell you an odd thing about Hypatia. I was brought up to believe she was murdered with oyster shells, weren't you? Forster says tiles.'

'Are you sure we can get down this street?'

'Not sure. I've never been here before. Someone told me about a little man.'

The way narrowed until both mudguards grated against the walls.

'We'll have to walk the last bit,' said Mrs Stitch, climbing over the windscreen and sliding down the hot bonnet.

Contrary to Guy's expectation they found the shop. The 'little man' was enormous, bulging over a small stool at his doorway, smoking a hubble-bubble. He rose affably and Mrs Stitch immediately sat in the the place he vacated.

'Hot sit-upon,' she remarked.

Shoes of various shapes and colours hung on strings all about them. When Mrs Stitch did not see what she wanted, she took a pad and pencil from her basket and drew, while the shoemaker beamed and breathed down her neck. He bowed and nodded and produced a pair of crimson slippers which were both fine and funny, with high curling toes.

'Bang right,' said Mrs Stitch. 'Got it in one.'

She removed her white leather shoes and put them in her basket. Her toe nails were pale pink and brilliantly polished. She donned the slippers, paid and made off. Guy followed at her side. After three steps she stopped and leaned on him, light and balmy, while she again changed shoes.

'Not for street wear,' she said.

When they reached the car they found it covered with children who greeted them by sounding the horn.

'Can you drive?' asked Mrs Stitch.

'Not awfully well.'

'Can you back out from here?'

Guy gazed over the little car down the dusty populous ravine.

'No,' he said.

'Neither can I. We'll have to send someone to collect it. Algie doesn't like my driving myself anyhow. What's the time?'

'Quarter to two.'

'Damn. We'll have to take a taxi. A tram might have been fun. Something for another day.'

The villa provided for the Stitches lay beyond Ramleh, beyond Sidi Bishr, among stone-pine and bougainvillaea. The white-robed, red-sashed Berber servants alone were African. All else smacked of the Alpes Maritimes. The party assembled on the veranda was small but heterogeneous. Algernon Stitch lurked in the background; in front were two little local millionairesses, sisters, who darted towards Mrs Stitch a-tiptoe with adulation.

'*Ah, chère madame, ce que vous avez l'air star, aujourd'hui.*'

'Lady Steetch, Lady Steetch, your hat. *Je crois bien que vous n'avez pas trouvé cela en Egypte.*'

'*Chère madame, quel drôle de panier.* I find it original.'

'Lady Steetch, your shoes.'

'Five piastres in the bazaar,' said Mrs Stitch (she had changed again in the taxi), leading Guy on.

'*Ça, madame, c'est génial.*'

'Algie, you remember the underground cow?'

Algernon Stitch looked at Guy with blank benevolence. His wife's introductions were more often allusive than definitive. 'Hullo,' he said. 'Very glad to see you again. You know the Commander-in-Chief, I expect.'

The rich sisters looked at one another, on the spot yet all at sea. Who was this officer of such undistinguished rank? *Son amant, sans doute.* How had their hostess described him? *La vache souterraine? Ou la vache au Métro?* This, then, was the new chic euphemism. They would remember and employ it with effect elsewhere. '. . . My dear, I believe her chauffeur is her underground cow . . .' It had the tang of the great world.

Besides the Commander-in-Chief there were in the party a young Maharaja in the uniform of the Red Cross, a roving English cabinet minister, and an urbane pasha. Mrs Stitch, never the slave of etiquette, put Guy on her right at table, but thereafter talked beyond him at large. She started a topic.

'Mahmoud Pasha, explain Cavafy to us.'

Mahmoud Pasha, a sad exile from Monte Carlo and Biarritz, replied with complete composure:

'Such questions I leave to His Excellency.'

'Who is Cavafy? What is he?' passed from dark eye to dark eye of the sisters as they sat on either side of their host, but they held their little scarlet tongues.

The roving minister, it appeared, had read the complete works in the Greek. He expounded. The lady on Guy's right said:

'Do they perhaps speak of Constantine Cavafis?' pronouncing the name quite differently from Mrs Stitch. 'We are not greatly admiring him nowadays in Alexandria. He is of the past, you understand.'

The Commander-in-Chief was despondent as he had good reason to be. Everything was out of his control and everything was going wrong. He ate in silence. At length he said:

'I'll tell you the best poem ever written in Alexandria.'

'Recitation,' said Mrs Stitch.

' "They told me, Heraclitus, they told me you were dead . . ." '

'I find it so sympathetic,' said the Greek lady. 'How all your men of affairs are poetic. And they are not socialist, I believe?'

'Hush,' said Mrs Stitch.

' ". . . For death he taketh all away, but them he cannot take." '

'Very prettily spoken,' said Mrs Stitch.

'I can do it in Greek,' said the cabinet minister.

'To be Greek, at this moment,' said the lady next to Guy, 'is to live in mourning. My country is being murdered. I come here because I love our hostess. I do not love parties now. My heart is with my people in my own country. My son is there, my two brothers, my nephew. My husband is too old. He has given up cards. I have given up cigarettes. It is not much. It is all we can do. It is – would you say emblematic?'

'Symbolic?'

'It is symbolic. It does not help my country. It helps us a little *here*.' She laid her jewelled hand upon her heart.

The Commander-in-Chief listened in silence. His heart, too, was in the passes of Thessaly.

The Maharaja spoke of racing. He had two horses running next week at Cairo.

Presently they all left the table. The Commander-in-Chief moved across the veranda to Guy.

'Second Halberdiers?'

'Not now, sir. Hookforce.'

'Oh, yes. Bad business about your Brigadier. I'm afraid you fellows have got rather left out of things. Shipping is the trouble. Always is. Well, I'm supposed to be on my way to Cairo. Where are you going?'

'Sidi Bishr.'

'Right on my way. Want a lift?'

The ADC was put in front with the driver. Guy sat in the back with the Commander-in-Chief. They very quickly reached the gates of the camp. Guy made to get out.

'I'll take you in,' said the Commander-in-Chief.

The Catalan refugees were duty-troop that day. They crowded round the Commander-in-Chief's great car with furious, unshaven faces. They poked tommy-guns through the open windows. Then, satisfied that these were temporary allies, they fell back, opened the gates and raised their clenched fists in salutation.

The Brigade Major was smoking in a deck-chair at the flap of his tent when he recognized the flag on the passing car. He leaped to his looking-glass, buckled himself up, pulled himself together, crowned himself with a sun helmet, armed himself with a cane and broke into a double as he approached the sandy space where Guy had that morning drilled his section. The big car was driving away. Guy strolled towards him holding his guidebook.

'Oh, it's you back at last, Crouchback. Thought for a moment that was the C-in-C's car?'

'Yes. It was.'

'What was it doing here?'

'Gave me a lift.'

'The driver had no business to fly the C-in-C's flag without the C-in-C being inside. You should know that.'

'He *was* inside.'

Hound looked hard at Guy.

'You aren't by chance trying to pull my leg, are you, Crouchback?'

'I should never dare. The C-in-C asked me to apologize to the Colonel. He would have liked to stop but he had to get on to Cairo.'

'Who's mounting guard today?'

'The Spaniards.'

'Oh, God. Did they turn out properly?'

'No.'

'Oh, God.'

Hound stood suspended, anguished by conflicting pride and curiosity. Curiosity won.

'What did he say?'

'He recited poetry.'

'Nothing else?'

'We spoke of the problems of shipping,' said Guy. 'They plague him.' The Brigade Major turned away. 'By the way,' Guy added, 'I think I detected an enemy agent in church today.'

'Most amusing,' said Hound over his shoulder.

Holy Saturday in Matchet; Mr Crouchback broke his Lenten fast. He had given up, as he always did, wine and tobacco. During the preceding weeks two parcels had come from his wine merchant, badly pilfered on the railway, but still with a few bottles intact. At luncheon Mr Crouchback drank a pint of burgundy. It was what his merchant cared to send him, not what he would have ordered, but he took it gratefully. After luncheon he filled his pipe. Now that he had no sitting-room, he was obliged to smoke downstairs. That afternoon seemed warm enough for sitting out. In a sheltered seat above the beaches, he lit the first pipe of Easter, thinking of that morning's new fire.

2

No. 6 Transit Camp, London District, was a camp in name only. It had been a large, unfashionable, entirely respectable hotel. The air was one of easy well-being. No bomb had yet broken a window-pane. Here Movement Control sent lost detachments. Here occasionally was brought a chaplain under close arrest. In this green pasture Trimmer and his section for a time lay down. Here Kerstie Kilbannock elected to do her war-work.

Kerstie was a good wife to Ian, personable, faithful, even-tempered and economical. All the pretty objects in their house had been bargains. Her clothes were cleverly contrived. She was sometimes suspected of fabricating the luncheon *vin rosé* by mixing the red and white wines left over from dinner; no more damaging charge was ever brought against her. There were nuances in her way with men which suggested she had once worked with them and competed on equal terms. Point by point she was the antithesis of her friend Virginia Troy.

On his going into uniform Ian's income fell by £1,500. Kerstie did not complain. She packed her sons off to their grandmother in Ayrshire and took two friends named Brenda and Zita into her house as paying guests. She took them also, unpaid, into her canteen at No. 6 Transit Camp, London District. Kerstie was paid, not much but enough. The remuneration was negative; wearing overalls, eating free, working all day, weary at night, she spent nothing. When Virginia Troy, casually met during an air-raid at the Dorchester Hotel, confided that she was hard up and homeless – though still trailing clouds of former wealth and male subservience – Kerstie took her into Eaton Terrace – 'Darling, don't breathe to Brenda and Zita that you aren't paying' – and into her canteen – 'Not a word, darling, that you're being paid.'

Working as waitresses these ladies, so well brought up, giggled and gossiped about their customers like real waitresses. Before she began work Virginia was initiated into some of their many jokes. Chief of these, by reason of his long stay, was the officer they called 'Scottie'. Scottie's diverse forms of utter awfulness filled them with delight.

'Wait till you see him, darling. Just wait.'

Virginia waited a week. All the ladies preferred the 'other ranks' canteen by reason of the superior manners which prevailed there. It was Easter Monday, after Virginia had been there a week, that she took her turn beside Kerstie at the officers' bar.

'Here comes our Scottie,' said Kerstie and, nosy and knowing, Trimmer sauntered across the room towards them. He was aware that his approach always created tension and barely suppressed risibility and took this as a tribute to his charm.

'Good evening, beautiful,' he said in his fine, free manner. 'How about a packet of Players from under the counter?' and then, seeing Virginia, he fell suddenly silent, out of it, not up to it, on this evening of all evenings.

Fine and free, nosy and knowing, Trimmer had seemed, but it was all a brave show, for that afternoon the tortoise of total war had at last overtaken him. A telephone message bade him report next day at HOO HQ at a certain time, to a certain room. It boded only ill. He had come to the bar for stimulus, for a spot of pleasantry with 'les girls' and here, at his grand climacteric, in this most improbable of places, stood a portent, something beyond daily calculation. For in his empty days he had given much thought to his escapade with Virginia in Glasgow. So far as such a conception was feasible to Trimmer, she was a hallowed memory. He wished now Virginia were alone. He wished he were wearing his kilt. This was not the lovers' meeting he had sometimes adumbrated at his journey's end.

On this moment of silence and uncertainty Virginia struck swiftly with a long, cool and cautionary glance.

'Good evening, Trimmer,' she said.

'You two know each other?' asked Kerstie.

'Oh, yes. Well. Since before the war,' said Virginia.

'How very odd.'

'Not really, is it, Trimmer?'

Virginia, as near as is humanly possible, was incapable of shame, but she had a firm residual sense of the appropriate. Alone, far away, curtained in fog – certain things had been natural in Glasgow in November which had no existence in London, in spring, amongst Kerstie and Brenda and Zita.

Trimmer recovered his self-possession and sharply followed the line.

'I used to do Mrs Troy's hair,' he said, 'on the *Aquitania*.'

'Really? I crossed in her once. I don't remember you.'

'I was rather particular in those days what customers I took.'

'That puts you in your place, Kerstie,' said Virginia. 'He was always an angel to me. He used to call himself Gustave then. His real name's Trimmer.'

'I think that's rather sweet. Here are your cigarettes, Trimmer.'

'Ta. Have one?'

'Not on duty.'

'Well, I'll be seeing you.'

Without another glance he sauntered off, disconcerted, perplexed but carrying himself with an air. He wished he had been wearing his kilt.

'You know,' said Kerstie, 'I think that rather spoils our joke. I mean there's nothing very funny about his being what he is when one knows what he is – is there? – if you see what I mean.'

'I see what you mean,' said Virginia.

'In fact, it's all rather sweet of him.'

'Yes.'

'I must tell Brenda and Zita. He won't mind, will he? I mean he won't disappear from our lives now we know his secret?'

'Not Trimmer,' said Virginia.

Next morning at 1000 hours General Whale looked sadly at Trimmer and asked:

'McTavish, what is your state of readiness?'

'How d'you mean, sir?'

'Is your section all present and prepared to move immediately?'

'Yes, sir, I suppose so.'

'Suppose so?' said GSO II (Planning). 'When did you last inspect them?'

'Well, we haven't exactly had any actual inspection.'

'All right, Charles,' interposed General Whale, 'I don't think we need go into that. McTavish, I've some good news for you. Keep it under your hat. I'm sending you on a little operation.'

'Now, sir? Today?'

'Just as soon as it takes the navy to lay on a submarine. They won't keep you hanging about long, I hope. Move to Portsmouth tonight. Make out your own list of demolition stores and check it with Ordnance there. Tell your men it's routine training. All right?'

'Yes, sir. I suppose so, sir.'

'Good. Well, go with Major Albright to the planning-room and he'll put you in the picture. Kilbannock will be with you, but purely as an observer, you understand. You are in command of the operation. Right?'

'Yes, I think so, sir, thank you.'

'Well, in case I don't see you again, good luck.'

When Trimmer had followed GSO II (Planning) and Ian Kilbannock from the room, General Whale said to his ADC, 'Well, he took that quite quietly.'

'I gather there's not much prospect of opposition.'

'No. But McTavish didn't know that, you know.'

Trimmer remained quiet while he was 'put in the picture'. It was significant, Ian Kilbannock reflected while he listened to the exposition of GSO II (Planning) that this metaphoric use of 'picture' had come into vogue at the time when all the painters of the world had finally abandoned lucidity. GSO II (Planning) had a little plastic model of the objective of 'Popgun'. He had air photographs and transcripts of pilots' instructions. He spoke of tides, currents, the phases of the moon, charges of gun-cotton, fuses and detonators. He drafted a move order. He designated with his correct initials the naval authority to whom Popgun Force should report. He gave the time of the train to Portsmouth and the place of accommodation there. He delivered a stern warning about the need for 'security'. Trimmer listened agape but not aghast, in dreamland. It was as though he were being invited to sing in Grand Opera or to ride the favourite in the Derby. Any change from No. 6 Transit Camp, London District, was a change for the worse, but he had come that morning with the certainty that those paradisal days were over. He had expected, at the best, to be sent out to rejoin Hookforce in the Middle East, at the worst to rejoin his regiment in Iceland. Popgun sounded rather a lark.

When the conference was over Ian said: 'The Press will want to know something of your background when this story is released. Can you think up anything colourful?'

'I don't know. I might.'

'Well, let's get together this evening. Come to my house for a drink before the train. I expect you've got a lot to do now.'

'Yes, I suppose I have.'

'You haven't by any chance lost that section of yours, have you?'

'Not exactly. I mean, they must be somewhere around.'

'Well, you'd better spend the day finding them, hadn't you?'

'Yes, I suppose I ought,' said Trimmer gloomily.

This was the day when the ladies in Eaton Terrace kept their weekly holiday. Kerstie had arranged substitutes so that all four could be at liberty together. They slept late, lunched in hotels, did their shopping, went out with men in the evenings. At half past six all were at home. The black-out was up; the fire lighted. The first sirens had not yet sounded. Brenda and Zita were in dressing-gowns. Zita's hair was in curling-pins and a towel. Brenda was painting Kerstie's toe-nails. Virginia was still in her room. Ian intruded on the scene.

'Have we anything to eat?' he asked. 'I've brought a chap I've got to talk to and he's catching a train at half past eight.'

'Well, well, well,' said Trimmer, entering behind him. 'This *is* a surprise for all concerned.'

'Captain McTavish,' said Ian, 'of No. X Commando.'

'Oh, we know him.'

'Do you? Do they?'

'Behold a hero,' said Trimmer. 'Just off to death or glory. Do I understand one of you lovelies is married to this peer of the realm?'

'Yes,' said Kerstie, 'I am.'

'What is all this?' asked Ian, puzzled.

'Just old friends meeting.'

'There's nothing to eat,' said Kerstie, 'except some particularly nasty-looking fish. Brenda and Zita are going out and Virginia says she doesn't want anything. There's some gin.'

'Does Mrs Troy live here too, then?' asked Trimmer.

'Oh yes. All of us. I'll call her.' Kerstie went to the door and shouted: 'Virginia, look what's turned up.'

'There's something here I don't understand,' said Ian.

'Never mind, darling. Give Trimmer some gin.'

'Trimmer?'

'That's what we call him.'

'I think perhaps I won't stay,' said Trimmer, all the bounce in him punctured suddenly at the thought of Virginia's proximity.

'Oh rot,' said Ian. 'There's a lot I want to ask you. We may not have time at Portsmouth.'

'What on earth are you and Trimmer going to do at Portsmouth?'

'Oh, nothing much.'

'Really, how odd they are being.'

Then Virginia joined them, modestly wrapped in a large bath-towel.

'What's this?' she said. 'Guests? Oh, you again? You do get around, don't you?'

'I'm just going,' said Trimmer.

'Virginia, you must be nicer to him. He's off to death or glory, he says.'

'That was just a joke,' said Trimmer.

'Obviously,' said Virginia.

'*Virginia*,' said Kerstie.

'I can get something to eat at the canteen,' said Trimmer. 'I ought to go and make sure that none of my fellows has given me the slip, anyway.'

Ian concluded that he was in the presence of a mystery which like so many others, come war, come peace, was beyond his comprehension.

'All right,' he said. 'If you must. We'll meet at the sea-side tomorrow. I'm afraid you'll never get a taxi here.'

'It isn't far.'

So Trimmer went out into the darkness and the sirens began to wail.

'Well, I must say,' said Ian, returning to them. 'That was all very awkward. What was the matter with you all?'

'He's a friend of ours. We somehow didn't expect him here, that's all.'

'You weren't awfully welcoming.'

'He's used to our little ways.'

'I give up,' said Ian. 'How about this horrible fish?'

But later when he and Kerstie were alone in their room, she came clean.

'. . . and what's more,' she concluded, 'if you ask me, there's something rum between him and Virginia.'

'How do you mean rum?'

'Darling, how is anything ever rum between Virginia and anyone?'

'Oh, but that's impossible.'

'If you say so, darling.'

'Virginia and McTavish?'

'Well, didn't they seem rum to you?'

'Something was rum. You all were, it seemed to me.'

After a pause Kerstie said: 'Weren't those bombs rather near?'

'No, I don't think so.'

'Shall we go down?'

'If you think that you'd sleep better.'

They carried their sheets and blankets into the area kitchen where iron bedsteads stood along the walls. Brenda and Zita and Virginia were already there, asleep.

'It's important about his having been a hairdresser. A first-class story.'

'Darling, you surely aren't going to write about our Trimmer?'

'I might,' said Ian. 'You never know. I might.'

At Sidi Bishr camp in the brigade office, Tommy Blackhouse said:

'Guy, what's all this about your consorting with spies?'

'What indeed?' said Guy.

'I've a highly confidential report here from Security. They have a suspect, an Alsatian priest, they've been watching. They've identified you as one of his contacts.'

'The fat boy with the broom?' said Guy.

'No, no, an RC priest.'

'I mean was it a fat boy with a broom who reported me?'

'They do not as a rule include portraits of their sources of information.'

'It's true I went to confession in Alexandria on Saturday. It's one of the things we have to do now and then.'

'So I've always understood. But this report says that you went round to the house where he lives and tried to get hold of him out of school.'

'Yes, that's true.'

'What a very odd thing to do. Why?'

'Because as a matter of fact I thought he was a spy.'

'Well, he *was*.'

'Yes, I thought so.'

'Look here, Guy, this may be a serious matter. Why the devil didn't you report it?'

'Oh, I did, at once.'

'Who to?'

'The Brigade Major.'

Major Hound, who was sitting at a neighbouring table relishing what he took to be Guy's discomfiture, started sharply.

'I received no report,' he said.

'I made one,' said Guy. 'Don't you remember?'

'No. I certainly don't.'

'I told you myself.'

'If you had, there would be a note of it in my files. I checked them this morning before you came in, as a matter of fact.'

'The day the C-in-C gave me a lift home.'

'Oh,' said Hound, disconcerted. 'That? I thought that you were trying to pull my leg.'

'For Christ's sake,' said Tommy. 'Did Guy make a report to you or didn't he?'

'I think he did say something,' said Major Hound, 'in the most irregular fashion.'

'And you took no action?'

'No. It was not an official report.'

'Well, you'd better draft an official report to these jokers, letting Guy out '

'Very good, Colonel.'

So Major Hound wrote in the finest of Staff College language that Captain Crouchback had been investigated and the Deputy-Commander of Hookforce was satisfied that there had been no breach of security on the part of that officer. And this letter, together with the original report, was photographed and multiplied and distributed and deposited in countless tin boxes. In time a copy reached Colonel Grace-Groundling-Marchpole in London.

'Do we file this under "Crouchback"?'

'Yes, and under "Box-Bender" too, and "Mugg". It all ties in,' he said gently, sweetly rejoicing at the underlying harmony of a world in which duller minds discerned mere chaos.

Trimmer and his section lay long at Portsmouth. The navy were hospitable, incurious, not to be hurried. Ian travelled up and down to London as the whim took him. The ladies in his house were full of questions. Trimmer had become a leading topic among them.

'You'll hear in good time,' said Ian, further inflaming their interest.

Trimmer's Sergeant knew something about demolition. He made a successful trial explosion in an enclosed fold of the hills. The experiment was repeated a day or two later in the presence of GSO II (Planning) HOO HQ and one of the men was incapacitated. One day Popgun Force was embarked in a submarine and Trimmer explained the projected operation. An hour later they were put ashore again, on a report of new minelaying in the Channel. From that time they were placed virtually under close arrest in the naval barracks. Trimmer's batman, a man long manifestly mutinous, took the occasion to desert. This information was badly received at HOO HQ.

'Strictly speaking of course, sir,' said GSO II (Planning), 'Popgun should be cancelled. Security has been compromised.'

'This is no time for strict speaking,' said DLFHOO, '– security.'

'Quite, sir. I only meant McTavish will look pretty silly if he finds the enemy waiting for him.'

'He looks pretty silly to me now.'

'Yes, sir. Quite.'

So eventually Popgun Force re-embarked, comprising Trimmer, his Sergeant, five men, and Ian. Even thus depleted they seemed too many.

They sailed at midday. The ship submerged and immediately all sense of motion, all sense of being at sea, utterly ceased. It was like being in a tube train, Ian thought, stuck in the tunnel.

He and Trimmer were invited to make themselves comfortable in the comfortless little cell that was called the ward-room. The Sergeant was in the Petty Officers' mess. The men disposed among the torpedoes.

'We shan't be able to surface until after dark,' said the Captain. 'You may find it a bit close by then.'

After luncheon the Third Hand distributed a specific against carbon dioxide poisoning.

'I should try and get some sleep,' he said.

Ian and Trimmer lay on the hard padded seats and presently slept.

Both awoke with headaches when the ship's officers came in for dinner.

'We ought to be at your island in about four hours,' said the Captain.

After dinner the sailors went back to the control-room and the engines. Ian drank. Trimmer composed a letter.

Writing did not come easily to him and this was not an easy letter to write.

I am leaving this to be sent to you in case I do not come back. When I said death or glory it wasn't just a joke you see. I want you to know that I thought of you at the last. Ever since we met I've known I had found the real thing. It was good while it lasted.

He filled three pages of his message pad. He signed it, after cogitation, 'Gustave'. He read it through. As he did so he conjured up the image of Virginia, as he had seen her on the afternoon of his flight from Glasgow, as he had met her again in London; of Virginia not so much as he had seen her, but rather as she had seemed to see him. He re-read the letter under the imagined wide stare of those contemptuous eyes and that infinitesimal particle of wisdom that lay in Trimmer's depths asserted itself. It just would not do, not for Virginia. He folded it small, tore it across and let the pieces fall to the steel deck.

'I think I could do with a spot,' he said to Ian.

'No, no. Later. You have responsibilities ahead.'

Time passed slowly. At last there came a sudden exhilaration. 'What's this?'

'Fresh air.'

Presently the Captain came in and said: 'Well, this is the time we ought to be coming in.'

'Shall I go and stir my chaps up?'

'No, leave them. I doubt if you'll be able to land tonight.'

'Why on earth not?' asked Ian.

'I seem to have lost your bloody island.'

He left them.

'What the hell's he up to?' said Trimmer. 'We can't go back now. They'll all desert if they try and lock us up in those barracks again.'

The Third Hand came into the wardroom.

'What's happening?' asked Ian.

'Fog.'

'Surely with all the gadgets you can find an island?'

'You might think so. We may yet. We can't be far off.'

The ship was on the surface and the trap open. The night had been chosen with the best meteorological advice. The little empty island should have shone out under a gibbous moon. But there was no moon visible that night, no stars, only mist curling into the flats.

Half an hour passed. The ship seemed to be nosing about very slowly in the calm waters. The Captain returned to the wardroom.

'Sorry. It looks as though we've got to pack it up. Can't see anything. It may lift of course as quick as it came down. We've got some time in hand.'

Ian filled his glass. Soon he began to yawn. Then to doze. The next thing he knew the Captain was with them again.

'O.K.', he said. 'We're in luck. Everything is clear as day and here's your island straight ahead. I reckon you've an hour and a half for the job.'

Trimmer and Ian awoke.

Sailors dragged four rubber dinghies into the open night and inflated them on deck from cylinders of compressed air. The demolition stores were lowered. Popgun Force sat two and two, bobbing gently at the ship's side. Low cliffs were clear before them, a hundred yards distant. Popgun Force paddled inshore.

Orders were detailed and lucid, drafted at HOO HQ. Two men, the beach-party, were to remain with the boats. The Sergeant was to land the explosives and wait while Trimmer and Ian reconnoitred for the tower which, in the model, stood on the summit of the island half a mile inland. They would all be in sight of one another's signalling-lamps all the time.

As Ian climbed awkwardly over the rubber gunwale and stood knee deep in the water, which gently lapped the deep fringe of bladder-wrack, he felt the whisky benevolently stirring within him. He was not a man of strong affections. Hitherto he had not greatly liked Trimmer. He had been annoyed at the factitious importance which seemed to surround him in Eaton Terrace. But now he felt a comradeship in arms.

'Hold up, old boy,' he said loudly and genially, for Trimmer had fallen flat.

He gave a heave. Hand in hand he and Trimmer landed on enemy territory. Popgun Force stood on the beach.

'All right to carry on smoking, sir?' asked the Sergeant.

'I suppose so,' said Trimmer. 'I don't see why not. I could do with a fag myself.'

Little flames spurted on the beach.

'Well, carry on according to plan, Sergeant.'

The cliffs presented no problem. They had fallen in half a dozen places and grassy slopes led up between them. Trimmer and Ian walked briskly forward and up.

'We ought to be able to see the place on the skyline,' said Trimmer rather plaintively. 'It all seems much flatter than the model.'

'"Very flat Norfolk,"' said Ian in an assumed voice.

'What on earth do you mean?'

'Sorry. I was quoting from my favourite play.'

'What's that got to do with it?'

'Nothing really, I suppose.'

'It's all very well to be funny. This is serious.'

'Not to me, Trimmer.'

'You're drunk.'

'Not yet. I daresay I shall be before the evening's out. I thought it a wise precaution to bring a bottle ashore.'

'Well, give me a go.'

'Not yet, old boy. I have only your best interests at heart. Not yet.'

He stood in the delusive moonlight and swigged. Trimmer stared anxiously about him. The gentle sound-effects of Operation Popgun, the susurrus of the beach, the low mutter of the demolition party, the heavy breathing of the two officers as they resumed their ascent, were suddenly horrifically interrupted by an alien voice, piercing and not far distant. The two officers stopped dead. 'For Christ's sake,' said Trimmer. 'What's that? It sounds like a dog.'

'A fox perhaps.'

'Do foxes bark like that?'

'I don't think so.'

'It can't be a dog.'

'A wolf?'

'Oh, do try not to be funny.'

'You're allergic to dogs? I had an aunt . . .'

'You don't find dogs without people.'

'Ah. I see what you mean. Come to think of it I believe I read somewhere that the Gestapo use bloodhounds.'

'I don't like this at all,' said Trimmer. 'What the hell are we going to do?'

'You're in command, old boy. In your place I'd just push on.'

'Would you?'

'Certainly.'

'But you're drunk.'

'Exactly. If I was in your place I'd be drunk too.'

'Oh God. I wish I knew what to do.'

'Push on, old boy. All quiet now. The whole thing may have been a hallucination.'

'D'you think so?'

'Let's assume it was. Push on.'

Trimmer drew his pistol and continued the advance. They reached the top of a grassy ridge, and saw half a mile to their flank a dark feature that stood out black against the silver landscape.

'There's your tower,' said Ian.

'It doesn't look like a tower.'

' "Moonlight can be cruelly deceptive, Amanda," ' said Ian in his Noël Coward voice. 'Push on.'

They moved forward cautiously. Suddenly the dog barked again and Trimmer as suddenly fired his pistol. The bullet struck the turf a few yards ahead but the sound was appalling. Both officers fell on their faces.

'What on earth did you do that for?' asked Ian.

'D'you suppose I meant to?'

A light appeared in the building ahead. Ian and Trimmer lay flat. A light appeared downstairs. A door opened and a broad woman stood there, clearly visible, holding a lamp in one hand, a shotgun under her arm. The dog barked with frenzy. A chain rattled.

'God. She's going to let it loose,' said Trimmer. 'I'm off.'

He rose and bolted, Ian close behind.

They came to a wire fence, tumbled over it and ran on down a steep bank.

'*Sales Boches!*' roared the woman and fired both barrels in their direction. Trimmer dropped.

'What's happened?' asked Ian, coming up with him where he lay groaning. 'She can't have hit you.'

'I tripped over something.'

Ian stood and panted. The dog seemed not to be in pursuit. Ian looked about him.

'I can tell you what you tripped over. A railway line.'

'A railway line?' Trimmer sat up. 'By God, it is.'

'Shall I tell you something else? There aren't any railways where we ought to be.'

'Oh God,' said Trimmer, 'where are we?'

'I rather think we're on the mainland of France. Somewhere in the Cherbourg area, I daresay.'

'Have you still got that bottle?'

'Of course.'

'Give it to me.'

'Steady on, old boy. One of us ought to be sober and it's not going to be me.'

'I believe I've broken something.'

'Well, I shouldn't sit there too long. A train's coming.'

The rhythm of approaching wheels swelled along the line. Ian gave Trimmer a hand. He groaned, hobbled and sank to the ground. Very soon the glow and spark of the engine came into view and presently a goods-train rolled slowly past. Ian and Trimmer buried their faces in the sooty verge.

Not until it was out of sight and almost out of hearing did either speak. Then Ian said: 'D'you know it's only sixteen minutes since we landed?'

'Sixteen bloody minutes too long.'

'We've got plenty of time to get back to the beach. Take it easy. I think we ought to make a slight detour. I didn't like the look of that old girl with the gun.'

Trimmer stood up, resting on Ian's shoulder.

'I don't believe anything is broken.'

'Of course it isn't.'

'Why "of course". It might easily have been. I came the hell of a cropper.'

'Listen, Trimmer, this is no time for argument. I am greatly relieved to hear that you are uninjured. Now step out and perhaps we shall get home.'

'I ache all over like the devil.'

'Yes, I'm sure you do. Step out. Soon over. Damn it, one might think it was you that was drunk, instead of me.'

It took them twenty-five minutes to reach the boats. Trimmer's shaken body seemed to heal with use. Towards the end of the march he was moving fast and strongly but he suffered from cold. His teeth chattered and only a stern sense of duty prevented Ian from offering him whisky. They passed the place where they had left the demolition party but found it deserted.

'I suppose they did a bunk when they heard that shot,' said Trimmer. 'Can't blame them really.'

But when they came to the beach all four dinghies were there with their guards. There was no sign of the rest of the force.

'They went inland, sir, after the train passed.'

'*Inland?*'

'Yes, sir.'

'Oh.' Trimmer drew Ian aside and asked anxiously: 'What do we do now?'

'Sit and wait for them, I suppose.'

'You don't think we can go back to the ship and leave them to follow?'

'No.'

'No. I suppose not. Damn. It's bloody cold here.'

Every two minutes Trimmer looked at his watch, shivering and sneezing.

'Orders are to re-embark at zero plus sixty.'

'Plenty of time to go yet.'

'Damn.'

The moon set. Dawn was still far distant.

At length Trimmer said: 'Zero plus fifty-two. I'm frozen. What the hell does the Sergeant mean by going off on his own like this? His orders were to wait for orders. It's his own look-out if he's left behind.'

'Give him till zero plus sixty,' said Ian.

'I bet that woman's given the alarm. They've probably been captured.

There's probably a howling mob of Gestapo looking for us at the moment
– with bloodhounds ... zero plus fifty-nine.'

He sneezed. Ian took a final swig.

'Here, my dear Watson,' he said, 'if I am not mistaken, come our clients
– one side or the other.'

Footsteps softly approached. A dimmed torch winked the signal.

'Off we go then,' said Trimmer, not pausing to greet his returning men.

There was a flash and a loud explosion inland behind them.

'Oh God,' said Trimmer. 'We're too late.'

He scrambled for the boat.

'What was that?' Ian asked the Sergeant.

'Gun-cotton, sir. When we saw the train go by, not having heard anything
from the Captain, I went up myself and laid a charge. Hop in quiet,
lads.'

'Splendid,' said Ian. 'Heroic.'

'Oh, I wouldn't say that, sir. I just thought we might as well show the
Jerries we'd been here.'

'In a day or two's time,' said Ian, 'you and Captain McTavish and your
men are going to wake up and find yourselves heroes. Can you do with some
whisky?'

'Much obliged, sir.'

'For God's sake, come on,' said Trimmer from the boat.

'I'm coming. Be of good comfort, Master Trimmer, and play the man.
We shall this day light such a candle by God's grace in England as I trust
shall never be put out.'

A signal was made just before dawn briefly announcing the success of the
expedition. The submarine dived and the Captain in his cabin began to
draft his account of the naval operation. In the wardroom Ian coached
Trimmer in the military version. High spirits do not come easily under
water. All were content.

Major Albright, GSO II (Planning) HOO HQ, was at Portsmouth to
meet them when they came ashore that afternoon. He was effusive, almost
deferential.

'What can we do for you? Just say.'

'Well,' said Trimmer, 'how about a spot of leave? The chaps are pretty
browned off with Portsmouth.'

'You'll have to come to London.'

'Don't mind if I do.'

'General Whale wants to see you. He'll want to hear your own story, of
course.'

'Well, it's more Kilbannock's story really.'

'Yes,' said Ian. 'You'd better leave all that side of it to me.'

And later that night he told the DLF HOO all that he had decided the General should know.

'Jolly good show. Just what was needed. Jolly good,' said the General. 'We must get an M.M. for the Sergeant. McTavish ought to have something. Not quite a D.S.O. perhaps but certainly an M.C.'

'You don't think of putting me in for anything, sir?'

'No. All I want from you is a citation for McTavish. Go and write it now. Tomorrow you can see about a release to the Press.'

In his life in Fleet Street Ian had undertaken many hard tasks for harder masters. This was jam. He returned to General Whale in ten minutes with a typewritten sheet.

'I've pitched it pretty low, sir, for the official citation. Confined myself strictly to the facts.'

'Of course.'

'When we give it to the Press, we might add a little colour, I thought.'

'Certainly.'

General Whale read:

Captain McTavish trained and led a small raiding force which landed on the coast of occupied France. On landing he showed a complete disregard of personal safety which communicated itself to his men. While carrying out his personal reconnaissance he came under small-arms fire. Fire was returned and the enemy post silenced. Captain McTavish pushed farther inland and identified the line of the railways. Observation was kept and heavy traffic in strategic materials was noted. A section of the permanent way was successfully demolished, thereby gravely impeding the enemy's war effort. Captain McTavish, in spite of having sustained injuries in the course of the action, successfully re-embarked his whole force, without casualties, in accordance with the time-table. Throughout the latter phases of the operation he showed exemplary coolness.

'Yes,' said General Whale. 'That ought to do it.'

3

'Not out,' said Mr Crouchback.

The small batsman at the other end rubbed his knee. Greswold, the fast bowler, the captain of Our Lady of Victory, looked at the umpire in agony.

'Oh, sir.'

'I'm sorry. I just wasn't looking, I'm afraid. Have to give the other fellows the benefit of the doubt, you know.'

He was wearing the fast bowler's sweater, the sleeves knotted round his throat, the body hanging over his thin shoulders, and was glad of the protection against the chill evening wind.

Greswold walked back, tossing the ball crossly from hand to hand. He took a long run; came up at a great pace; Mr Crouchback could not quite see the position of his foot as he delivered the ball. It seemed well over the line. He considered giving a 'no ball' but before he spoke the wicket was down. The little chap was out this time and no mistake. In fact, the whole side was out and the first match of the term was won. Our Lady of Victory's champions returned to the pavilion, gathering round Greswold and thumping him on the back.

'He was out the first time,' said the wicket-keeper.

'Oh, I don't know; Croucher didn't think so.'

'Croucher was watching an aeroplane.'

'Anyway, what's the odds?'

Mr Crouchback walked home to the Marine Hotel with Mrs Tickeridge, who had brought Jenifer and Felix to the match. They walked round by the beach and Jenifer threw sticks into the sea for Felix. Mr Crouchback asked:

'You saw the paper this morning?'

'You mean about the raid on the French railway?'

'Yes. What a splendid young fellow this Captain McTavish must be. You saw he had been a hairdresser?'

'Yes.'

'That's what's so heartening. That's where we've got the Germans beaten. It was just the same in the first war. We've got no junker class in this country, thank God. When the country needs them, the right men come to the fore. There was this young fellow curling women's hair on a liner, calling himself by a French name; odd trade for a Highlander, you might think. There he was. No one suspected what he had in him. Might never have had the chance to show it. Then war comes along. He downs his scissors and without any fuss carries out one of the most daring exploits in military history. It couldn't happen in any other country, Mrs Tickeridge.'

'It wasn't a very attractive photograph of him, was it?'

'He looks what he is – a hairdresser's assistant. And all honour to him. I expect he's a very shy sort of fellow. Brave men often are. My son never mentioned him and they must have been together in Scotland for quite a time. I daresay he felt rather out of it up there. Well, he's shown them.'

When they reached the hotel Miss Vavasour said:

'Oh, Mr Crouchback, I've been waiting to ask you. Would you mind if I cut something out of your newspaper when you've quite finished with it?'

'Of course. Not at all. Delighted.'

'It's the photograph of Captain McTavish. I've got a little frame that will just take it.'

'He deserves a frame,' said Mr Crouchback.

The news of Operation Popgun reached Sidi Bishr first on the BBC news, later in the form of a signal of congratulation to Force HQ from the C-in-C.

'I suppose I'd better pass this on to X Commando?' said Major Hound.

'Of course. To all the units. Have it read out on parade.'

'To the Spaniards too?'

'Particularly the Spaniards. They're always boasting about convents they blew up in their civil war. This'll show 'em we can play the same game. Get that fat interpreter to work.'

'You knew this chap McTavish, Colonel?'

'Certainly. I took him on when I had X Commando. You remember, Guy?'

'Yes, indeed.'

'You and Jumbo Trotter tried to keep him out. Remember? I wish I had a few more officers like McTavish out here. I'd like to have seen old Jumbo Trotter's face when he read the news.'

*

Jumbo in fact had beamed. He had proclaimed to the ante-room of the Halberdier Barracks:

'Poor old Ben Ritchie-Hook; no judge of men. A first-class fighting man, but he had his blind spots, you know. If he took a down on a man, he could be unreasonable. He turned McTavish out of the Corps, you know. Fellow had to join a Highland regiment in the ranks. *I* spotted him at once. Not a peacetime soldier, mind you, but no more was Ben. If you ask me, the two of them were a chip off the same block. That's why they never could hit it off. Often happens like that. Seen it dozens of times.'

When Ivor Claire heard the news he merely said: 'Some nonsense of Brendan's, obviously.'

The ladies of Eaton Terrace said:

'What about our Scottie now?'

'What indeed?'

'Were we beastly to him?'

'Not really.'

'Not often.'

'I always had a soft spot.'

'Shall we ask him round?'

'D'you think he'd come?'

'We can try.'

'It would jolly well serve us right if he despised us.'

'I despise myself rather.'

'Virginia. You haven't said anything. Shall we try and get hold of Scottie?'

'Trimmer? Do what you like, my dears, only count me out.'

'Virginia, don't you *want* to make amends?'

'I don't,' said Virginia and left them.

Ty.Lt.A/g Capt. McTAVISH, H.M.C. Future employment of.

'Really,' said the chairman, 'I don't understand why this is a matter for our committee.'

'Minute from the War Cabinet, sir.'

'Extraordinary. I should have thought they had more important things on their minds. What's it all about?'

'Well, sir, you remember McTavish?'

'Yes, yes, of course. Nice bit of work. Excellent young officer.'

'You haven't seen the *Daily Beast*?'

'Of course not.'

'Exactly, sir. You know that Lord Copper has always had it in for the regular army – old school tie, and that sort of rot.'

'I did not,' said the General, filling his pipe. 'I never see the rag.'

'Anyway, they've dug up the story that McTavish began the war as an officer on probation in the Halberdiers and got turned down. They say it was because he'd been a barber.'

'Nothing wrong with that.'

'No, sir. But all the Halberdiers who had anything to do with him are in the Middle East. We've asked for a report, but it will take some time and if, as I presume it is, it's an adverse one, we can't very well use it.'

'What a lot of fuss about nothing.'

'Exactly, sir. The *Daily Beast* are making McTavish an example. Saying the army is losing its best potential leaders through snobbery. You know the kind of thing.'

'I do not,' said the General.

'One of the Labour members has put down a question about him.'

'Oh Lord, has he? That's bad.'

'The Minister wants an assurance that McTavish has been found employment suitable to his merits.'

'Well, that oughtn't to be difficult. It was decided last week to raise three more Commandos. Can't he be given one of those?'

'I don't think he's quite up to it.'

'Really, Sprat, I should have thought he was just the kind of young officer you're always trying to poach. *You* don't object to his having been a barber, do you?'

'Of course not, sir.'

'You were full of his praises last week. Make a note that he is to be found suitable employment in your outfit.'

'Very good, sir.'

'And by suitable I don't mean your ADC.'

'God forbid,' Sprat breathed.

'I mean something that will satisfy those Labour fellows in the House of Commons that we know how to use good men when we find them.'

'Very good, sir.'

DLFHOO returned to his headquarters, as he usually returned from attendance at the War Office, in black despair. He sent for Ian Kilbannock.

'You overdid it,' he said.

Ian knew what he meant.

'Trimmer?'

'Trimmer. McTavish. Whatever he's called. You've gone and got the politicians interested. We're stuck with him now for the rest of the war.'

'I've been giving some thought to the matter.'

'Decent of you.'

'You know,' said Ian, who, since he and his General had become, as it were, accomplices in fraud, had adopted an increasingly familiar tone in the office, 'you'll never get the best out of your subordinates by being sarcastic. I've been thinking about Trimmer and I've learned something. He's got sex appeal.'

'Nonsense.'

'I've seen evidence of it in my own immediate circle – particularly since his outing to France. I've had the Ministries of Information, Supply, Aircraft Production and the Foreign Office after him. They want a hero of just Trimmer's specifications to boost civilian morale and Anglo-American friendship. You can give him any rank you please and second him indefinitely.'

Major-General Whale was silent.

'It's an idea,' he said at length.

'It's particularly important to get him out of London. He's always hanging round my house these days.'

4

Corporal-Major Ludovic's journal comprised not only *pensées* but descriptive passages which reviewers in their season later commended.

Major Hound is bald and both his face and scalp shine. Early in the morning after shaving there is a dry shine. After an hour he begins to sweat and there is a greasy shine. Major Hound's hands begin to sweat before his face. The top of his head is always dry. The sweat starts two inches above his eyebrows and never extends to his scalp. Does he use a cigarette-holder in order to protect his teeth and fingers from stain, or in order to keep smoke from his eyes? He often tells the orderly to empty his ash-tray. Captain Crouchback despises Major Hound but Colonel Blackhouse finds him useful. I am barely aware of Major Hound's existence. It is in order to fix him in my mind that I have set down these observations.

The defeat in Greece was kept secret until the remnants of the army arrived in Alexandria. They were collected and dispersed for reorganization and equipment. '*We live,*' wrote Corporal-Major Ludovic, '*in the Age of Purges and Evacuation. To empty oneself, that is the task of contemporary man. Cultivate the abhorred vacuum. "The earth is the Lord's and the emptiness thereof."*' Every available unit in the area was sent west into Cyrenaica. Hookforce were the only fighting troops in Alexandria. They found themselves called on to find guards for government buildings and banks. They were assigned a role in the defence of the city in the event of a German breakthrough. Early in May Tommy Blackhouse, Major Hound and Guy drove out with a Brigadier from Area Command to inspect the sandy ridge between Lake Mariout and the sea where they were expected to hold Rommel's armour with their knives and toggle-ropes and tommy-guns.

'What's to stop him coming round the other side?' asked Tommy.

'According to the plan – the Gyppos,' said the Brigadier.

He laughed, Tommy laughed, they laughed all four.

Guy spent long hours in the club library with bound copies of *Country Life*. Sometimes he joined his old friends of X Commando at the Cecil Hotel or the Union Bar. X Commando had not gone to the trouble of organizing an officers' mess. B Commando dined as punctually and solemnly as Halberdiers in barracks, with Colonel Prentice's great-great-grandfather's sabre displayed on the table. X Commando kept a pile of hard-boiled eggs, oranges and sardines in their tent; they roared at their scuttling and giggling Berber servants for tea and gin, threw down cigar-ends and cigarette-packets and matches and corks and peel and tins round their feet.

'One might be on the Lido,' said Ivor Claire, regarding with disgust the littered sand of the tent floor.

Half a dozen wealthy Greek houses opened their doors to them. And there was Mrs Stitch. Guy did not repeat his visit but her name was everywhere. X Commando felt her presence as that of a beneficent, alert deity, their own protectress. Things could not go absolutely wrong with them while Mrs Stitch was about.

Guy set his intelligence section to make a map of the camp, for Major Hound had returned from one of his trips to Cairo with a case labelled 'intelligence stores' which proved to contain a kindergarten outfit of coloured inks and drawing materials. He fought a daily battle with Major Hound to preserve his men from guard-duties.

So the days passed until in the third week of May war came to Major Hound.

It was heralded by the customary ceremonial fanfare of warning-orders and counter-orders, but before the first of these notes sounded, Mrs Stitch had told Ivor Claire and he had told Guy.

'I hear we're off to Crete at any moment,' Guy said to Major Hound.

'Nonsense.'

'Well. Wait and see,' said Guy.

Major Hound pretended to be busy at his desk. Then he sat back and fitted a cigarette into his holder.

'Where did you hear this rumour?'

'X Commando.'

'Both attacks in Crete have been held,' said Major Hound. 'The situation is well under control. I *know* this.'

'Good,' said Guy.

There was another pause during which Major Hound pretended to read his files. Then:

'It doesn't occur to you, I suppose, that we have a priority commitment in the defence of Alexandria?'

'I gathered that Crete was first priority at the moment.'

'The garrison there is larger than they can supply as it is.'

'Well, I dare say I'm wrong.'

'Of course you're wrong. You should know better than to listen to rumours.'

Another pause; this was the witching hour, noted by Corporal-Major Ludovic, when the shine on the Brigade Major's face changed from dry to greasy.

'Besides,' he said, 'this brigade hasn't the equipment for defensive action.'

'Then why are we defending Alexandria?'

'That would be an emergency.'

'Perhaps there's an emergency in Crete.'

'I'm not arguing with you, Crouchback. I'm telling you.'

Silence; then:

'Why doesn't that orderly empty the ash-trays? What do you know about the shipping situation, Crouchback?'

'Nothing.'

'Exactly. Well, for your information we aren't in a position to reinforce Crete even if we wanted to.'

'I see.'

Another pause. Major Hound was not at ease that day. He resorted to his old method of attack.

'How, by the way, is your section employed this morning?'

'Ruling thin red lines. The map of Crete is a straight off-print from the Greek issue, so I am having a half-inch grid put on for our own use.'

'Maps of Crete? Who authorized anyone to draw maps of Crete?'

'I fetched them myself yesterday evening from Ras-el-Tin.'

'You had no business to. That's exactly how rumours start.'

Presently Tommy came into the office. Guy and Major Hound stood up.

'Anything through from Cairo yet?' he asked.

'The mail has gone to the registry, Colonel. Nothing of immediate importance.'

'No one at GHQ starts work before ten. The wires will start buzzing in a few minutes. Meanwhile get out a warning order to the units. I suppose you know we're off?'

'Back to Canal Area for reorganization?'

'Christ, no. Where's that Staff Captain? We must work out a loading table. I met the Flag Officer in command of destroyers at Madame Kaprikis's last night. He's all ready for us. Guy, collect some maps of Crete for issue down to section leaders.'

'That's all laid on, Colonel,' said the Brigade Major.

'Well done.'

At quarter-past ten the telephone from GHQ Cairo began its day-long litany of contradictions. Major Hound listened, noted, relayed with the animation of a stockbroker.

'Yes, sir. Very good, sir. All understood. All informed,' he said to GHQ. 'Get cracking,' he said to the units.

But this show of zeal did not deceive Ludovic.

'*Major Hound seems strangely lacking in the Death-Wish*,' he noted.

It was Major Hound's first operational embarkation, Guy's third. He callously watched the transactions, first earnest, then anxious, then embittered, between Brigade Major, Staff Captain and ESO, the lines of overburdened, sulky soldiers moving on and off the narrow decks, the sailors fastidiously picking their way among the heaps of military equipment. He knew it all of old and he kept out of it. He talked to a Marine AA gunner who said:

'No air cover. The RAF have packed up in Crete. If we don't make the run in and out in darkness we haven't a hope of getting through. Your chaps will have to be a lot quicker getting ashore than they are coming aboard.'

A mine-laying cruiser and two destroyers were lying in for Hookforce; all bore the scars of the evacuation of Greece. The ship detailed for brigade headquarters was the most battered.

'She needs a month in dock,' said the Marine. 'We'll be lucky if she makes the trip, enemy action apart.'

They sailed at dusk. On board the destroyer with headquarters were three troops of B Commando. The men lay about on the flats and mess decks, the officers in the wardroom. Tommy Blackhouse was invited to the bridge. Peace of a kind reigned.

'Crouchback,' said Major Hound, 'has it occurred to you that Ludovic is keeping a diary?'

'No.'

'It's contrary to regulations to take a private diary into the front line.'

'Yes.'

'Well, you'd better warn him. He's writing something unofficial I'm pretty sure.'

At eight o'clock the Maltese steward laid the table for dinner, setting a bowl of roses in the centre. The captain remained on the bridge. The first officer apologized for him and for the accommodation.

'We aren't equipped for hospitality on this scale,' he said. 'Not enough of anything I'm afraid.'

The soldiers took out their mugs and canteens and knives and forks. The batmen helped the steward. Dinner was excellent.

'No cause for alarm until dawn,' said the first officer cheerfully as he left them.

The captain had given up his cabin to Tommy and Major Hound and the second-in-command of B Commando. Valises and bedrolls had been left in camp. The army officers arranged themselves on chairs and benches and floor in the wardroom. Soon they were all asleep.

Guy awoke at dawn and went up into the fresh air; a delicious morning after the breathless night, a calm sea, no other ship in sight, no land, the destroyer steaming rather slowly, it seemed, into the luminous void. Guy met the Marine gunner.

'Is this where our troubles begin?' he asked.

'Not here.' Then as Guy seemed surprised he added: 'Notice anything odd about the sun?'

Guy looked. It was well above the horizon now, ahead on their left, cool and brilliant.

'No,' he said.

'Just where you expected to see it?'

'Oh,' said Guy. 'I see what you mean. It ought to be on the other side.'

'Exactly. We shall be back in Alex in an hour. Engine trouble.'

'That's going to be awkward.'

'She was overdue for an overhaul, as I told you, and she caught a packet in the Aegean. Suits me all right. I haven't had any shore leave this year.'

At breakfast Tommy scowled silently, not so Major Hound who was openly jubilant. He put the nozzle of his Mae West in his mouth and made a little pantomime of playing the bagpipes.

'This is the hell of a thing,' Tommy said to Guy. 'But there's a good chance of their laying on another destroyer in Alexandria.'

'I should rather doubt that, Colonel,' said Major Hound. 'The navy is fully committed.'

'We're one of their commitments. I've made a signal to Prentice on board the cruiser putting him in command until we turn up. I've told him his main job is to keep the brigade intact as a formation. The danger is that they'll try and lump the units into the general reserve of Creforce. Then there'll be trouble winkling them out and getting them together again for our proper role. I hope Prentice is up to it. He hasn't much experience of the tricks of GOCs.'

'Did you mention that matter to Ludovic, Crouchback?'

'Not yet.'

'This will be a good time.'

'What matter?' asked Tommy.

'Just a matter of routine security, Colonel.'

They were in sight of land when Guy found Corporal-Major Ludovic.

'It has come to my ears that you are keeping a diary,' he said.

Ludovic regarded him with his disconcerting grey-pink stare.

'I should hardly call it that, sir.'

'You realize that anything written which is liable to fall into the enemy's hands is subject to censorship.'

'So I have always understood, sir.'

'I'm afraid I must ask to see what it is.'

'Very good, sir.' He took his message-pad from the pocket of his shorts. 'I have left the typewriter in camp, sir, with the rest of the office equipment. I don't know if you'll be able to read it.'

Guy read:

'Captain Crouchback has gravity. He is the ball of lead which in a vacuum falls no faster than a feather.'

'That's all you've written?'

'All I have written since we left camp, sir.'

'I see. Well, I don't think that compromises security in any way. I wonder how *I'm* meant to take it.'

'It was not intended for your eyes, sir.'

'As a matter of fact I have never believed that theory about feathers in a vacuum.'

'No, sir. It sounds totally against nature. I merely employed it figuratively.'

When the ship berthed Tommy and Major Hound went ashore. There were high staff-officers, naval and military, awaiting them on the quay and they went with them to one of the port-offices to confer. The troops leant over the rails, spat and swore.

'Back to Sidi Bishr,' they said.

Quite soon Tommy and Hound returned on board, Tommy cheerful.

'Off again,' he said to Guy. 'They've laid on another destroyer. Here's the latest intelligence. Everything in Crete is under control. The navy broke up the sea landings and sunk the lot. The enemy only hold two pockets and the New Zealanders have got them completely contained. Reinforcements are rolling in every night for the counter-attack. The BGS from Cairo says it's in the bag. We've got a very nice role, raiding lines of communications on the Greek mainland.'

Tommy believed all this. So did Major Hound; no part of his training or previous experience had made him a sceptic. But he remained glum.

The change of ships was quickly done. Like a line of ants the laden men followed one another down one gang plank and up another, swearing quietly. They found quarters indistinguishable from those they had left. New naval officers gave the old greetings and the old apologies. By sunset everyone had settled in.

'We sail at midnight,' said Tommy. 'They don't want to reach the Karso channel until after dark tomorrow. No reason why we shouldn't dine ashore.'

He and Guy went to the Union Bar. It did not occur to them to ask Major Hound to join them. The restaurant seemed as full as ever, despite the notorious crisis in man-power. They ate lobster pilaff and a great dish of quail cooked with Muscat grapes.

'It may be our last decent meal for some time,' Tommy remarked. 'The BGS heard from someone that fresh food is rather short in Crete.'

They ate six birds each and drank a bottle of champagne. Then they had green artichokes and another bottle.

'I dare say in a day or two we shall think of this dinner,' said Tommy, gazing fondly at the leaves which littered their plates, 'and wish we were back here.'

'Not really,' said Guy, washing the butter from his fingers.

'No, not really. Not for all the quail in Egypt.'

They were gay as they drove down to the lightless docks. They found their ship and were asleep before she sailed.

Major Hound awoke to feel his bunk rise and fall, to hear the creaking of plates and the roll and thump of shifting stores. He began to shiver and sweat and swallow. He lay flat on his back, gripping the blankets, open eyed in the darkness, desperately sad. His servant found him thus at seven o'clock when he lurched in with a mug of tea in one hand, a mug of shaving water in the other and a cheerful greeting. Major Hound remained rigid. The man began to polish the boots which still shone from his labours of the previous morning.

'For God's sake,' said Major Hound, 'do that outside.'

321

'Hard to find anywhere to move, sir.'

'Then leave them.'

'Very good, sir.'

Major Hound cautiously raised himself on one elbow and drank the tea. Immediately the nausea which he had fought through the long small hours returned irresistibly. He reached the wash-basin, clung there and remained for ten minutes with his head resting on the heavy rim. At length he ran some water, dried his eyes and breathing heavily returned to his bed; not, however, before he had seen his face in the little looking-glass. It gave him a further fright.

Rain and spray swept the decks all day, keeping the men below. The little ship wallowed in a heavy long swell.

'This low cloud is a godsend,' said the captain. 'We're near the spot where *Juno* copped it.'

Guy was not often troubled by sea-sickness. He had, however, drunk a quart of wine the previous evening and that, with the movement of the ship, subdued him; not so Tommy Blackhouse, who was in high spirits, now in the wardroom, now on the bridge, now on the troop decks; nor Corporal-Major Ludovic, who early in the afternoon attracted respect in the petty-officers' mess as with a travelling manicure set he prepared his toe-nails for whatever endurances lay ahead.

Lassitude settled on the soldiers.

An hour after dark Tommy Blackhouse fell. He was returning from the bridge when the ship took an unusually heavy plunge; his nailed boots slipped on the steel ladder and he fell to the steel deck with a crash that was clearly heard in the wardroom. Then he was heard shouting and after a minute the first officer announced:

'Your Colonel's hurt himself. Can someone come and help?'

The two troop-leaders of B Commando carried him awkwardly to the sick-bay where the surgeon gave him morphia. He had broken his leg.

From then on Guy went between the prostrate figures of the Brigade Major and the deputy commander. There was little to choose between them as far as ill-looks went.

'That puts the lid on it,' was Major Hound's immediate response to the news. 'There's no point in brigade headquarters landing at all.'

Tommy Blackhouse, in pain, and slightly delirious dictated orders. 'You will be met by liaison officers from Hookforce and Creforce. On disembarkation brigade will immediately set up rear headquarters under Staff Captain, and establish W/T links with units ... Staff Captain will make contact with the force DQMG and arrange for supplies ... Forward headquarters consisting of BM and IO will report to Lt-Col. Prentice at B Commando HQ and give him the written orders from GHQ ME defining the special role of Hookforce in harassing enemy L of C ... Lt-Col. Prentice will report to GOC Creforce and present these orders ... His primary task is to prevent Commando units being brigaded with infantry in Creforce reserve ... Deputy commander Hookforce will immediately mount operations under command GOC Creforce ...'

He repeated himself often, dozed, woke and summoned Guy once more to repeat his orders.

The sea abated as the ship rounded the eastern point of Crete and steamed along the north coast. When they came into Suda Bay it was quite calm. A young moon was setting. The first sign of human activity they saw was a burning tanker lying out in the harbour and brightly illuminating it. The destroyer dropped anchor and Major Hound gingerly left his bunk and climbed to the bridge. Guy remained with Tommy. Captain Slimbridge, the signaller, and the officers of B Commando were putting their men in readiness to disembark. Captain Roots the Staff Captain and Corporal-Major Ludovic were in conference. Tommy became fretful.

'What's happening? They've only got two hours to turn round in. A lighter ought to have come out the moment we berthed.' Presently there was a hail alongside. 'There it is. Go and see, Guy.'

Guy went on the dark deck. It was crowded with troops standing-to, heaped with stores, motor-cycles, signalling equipment. A small pulling boat lay alongside and a single figure came aboard. Guy went back to report.

'Go up to the captain and see what's going on.'

Guy found the captain in his cabin with Major Hound and a haggard, unshaven, shuddering Lieutenant-Commander wearing a naval greatcoat and white shorts.

'I've got my orders to pull out and by God I'm pulling out,' the sailor was saying. 'I got my orders this morning. I ought to have gone last night. I've been waiting all day on the quay. I had to leave all my gear behind. I've only got what I stand up in.'

'Yes,' said the captain, 'so we see. What we want to know is whether a lighter is coming out for us.'

'I shouldn't think so. The whole place is a shambles. I'm pulling out. I got my orders to pull out. Got them in writing.' He spoke in a low monotone. 'I could do with a cup of tea.'

'Wasn't there an ESO on the quay?' asked Major Hound.

'No. I don't think so. I found this boat and rowed out. I've got my orders to pull out.'

'We don't seem to get any acknowledgment of our signals,' said the captain.

'It's a bloody shambles,' said the man from Crete.

'Well,' said the captain. 'I wait here two hours. Then I sail.'

'You can't sail too soon for me.' Then he turned to Major Hound and said with an awful personal solicitude. 'You've got to know the password, you know. You can't go anywhere on shore unless you know that. They'll shoot you as soon as look at you, some of these sentries, if you don't know the password.'

'Well, what is it?'

'Changes every night.'

'Exactly; what is it?'

'That I *do* know. That I *can* tell you. I know it as well as I know my own name.'

'What is it?'

The sailor looked with blank, despairing eyes. 'Sorry,' he said. 'It's slipped my mind at the moment.'

Guy and Major Hound left.

'It looks like another false alarm,' said the Major quite cheerfully.

Guy went to report to Tommy.

'God almighty,' he said. 'Christ all bloody mighty. What's come over them all? Has everyone gone to sleep?'

'I don't think it's that,' said Guy.

Three-quarters of an hour passed and then word went crackling over the ship: 'Here it comes.'

Guy went on deck. Sure enough a large dark shape was approaching across the water. The men all round him began to hoist their burdens. The sailors had already thrown a rope net over the side. The troops crowded to the rail. A voice from below called:

'Two hundred walking wounded coming aboard.'

Major Hound cried, 'Who's there? Is there anyone from Movement Control?'

No one answered him.

'I must see the captain,' said Major Hound. 'That MLC must go back, land the wounded, come back empty for us, land us and then take on the wounded. That's the way it should be done.'

No one heeded him. Very slowly bearded and bandaged figures began to appear along the side of the ship.

'Get back,' said Major Hound. 'You can't possibly come aboard while we're here.'

'Passengers off the car first, please,' said a facetious voice in the darkness.

The broken men clambered on deck and thrust a passage through the waiting troops. Someone in the darkness said: 'For God's sake get this gear out of the way' and the word was taken up: 'Ditch all gear. Ditch all gear.'

'What on earth are they doing?' cried Major Hound. 'Stop them.'

The three troops of B Commando were under control. Headquarters troops were on the other side of the ship. The signallers began throwing their wireless sets overboard. A motor-cycle followed.

Guy found the officer in command of the MLC.

'I cast off fifteen minutes after the last of this party gets on board. You've got to look slippy,' said the sailor. 'I've another journey after this. Two hundred more wounded and a Greek general. Then I sink the boat and come aboard myself and it's good-bye to Crete for yours truly.'

'What's going on?' asked Guy.

'It's all over. Everyone's packing up.'

Guy went below to make a final, brief report to his commander.

'Things have a way of turning out lucky for you, Tommy,' he said without any bitterness.

The sick-bay was crowded now. Two army doctors and the ship's surgeon were dealing with urgent cases. While Guy stood there beside Tommy's bunk a huge, bloody, grimy, ghastly Australian sergeant appeared in the door. He grinned like a figure of death and said: 'Thank God we've got a navy,' then sank slowly to the deck and on the instant passed into the coma of death. Guy stepped over his body and fought his way past the descending line of men; there were many unwounded among them, ragged, unshaven, haggard, but seemingly whole.

'What are you?' he asked one of them.

'Records,' said the man.

Presently without any clear order given Hookforce began climbing down the rope net into the MLC.

The moon was down. The only light was the burning tanker a mile distant.

'Major Hound,' Guy called. 'Major Hound.'

A soft voice beside him said: 'The Major is safely aboard. I found him. He came with me, Corporal-Major Ludovic.'

The MLC chugged up to the quay, a structure so blasted that it seemed like rough, natural rock. Before they could get ashore wounded and stragglers began scrambling into the boat.

'Get back, you bastards,' shouted the captain. 'Cast off there.' The seamen pushed the craft away from the sea-wall. 'I'll shoot any man who tries to come aboard till I'm ready for him. Get back the lot of you. Get the hell off the quay.'

The ragged mob began pushing back in the darkness. 'Now, you pongoes,' said the captain of the MLC, 'jump to it.'

He ran the craft in again and at last the party landed. This event so large to Guy and Major Hound and the rest of them, would be recorded later in the official history:

'A further encouragement was given to the hard-pressed garrison of Crete when at midnight on 26th May HMS *Plangent* (Lt.-Comdr Blake-Blakiston) landed HQ Hookforce plus remainder of B Commando at Suda and took off 400 wounded without incident.'

The MLC captain shouted: 'Can't take any more. Get back, the rest of you. Cast off.'

The crowd of disappointed men sat among the broken stones. The laden boat moved off towards the ship. The newly landed party pushed through the stragglers and fell in.

'Find the liaison officers,' said Major Hound. 'They must be here.'

Guy shouted: 'Anyone from Hookforce?'

A bundle of bandages groaned: 'Oh, pipe down.'

Then two figures emerged from the crowd and identified themselves as troop-leaders from B Commando.

'Ah,' said Major Hound. 'At last. I was beginning to wonder. You're from Colonel Prentice?'

'Well, not exactly,' said one of the officers. He spoke in the same dull undertone as the fugitive sailor. It was a voice which Guy was to recognize everywhere in the coming days; the accent of defeat. 'He's dead, you see.'

'Dead?' said Major Hound crossly as though officiously informed of the demise of an aunt who, he had every reason to suppose, was in good health. 'He can't be. We were in communication with him the day before yesterday.'

'He was killed. A lot of the Commandos were.'

'We should have been informed. Who is in command now?'

'I believe I am.'

'What are you doing here?'

'We heard a ship was coming to take us off. But it seems we were wrong.'

'You *heard*? Who gave orders for your embarkation?'

'We haven't had any orders from anyone for twenty-four hours.'

'Look here,' said the second-in-command of B Commando, 'hadn't we better go somewhere where you can put us in the picture?'

'There's an office over there. We've been sitting in it since the bombing stopped.'

He and Guy and Major Hound and the B Commando second-in-command stumbled among the pits and loose cobbles to a hut marked 'SNO'. Guy laid his map-case on the table and turned his torch on it.

'We've sixty men and four officers, counting me. There may be others straggling. This is all I could collect. They're down here in the port area. You can't move on the roads. And I've got a couple of trucks. Everyone's pinching transport. But they're safe enough down here under guard. All the traffic is moving south to Sphakia.'

'I think you'd better tell us what's happened.'

'I don't know much. It's a shambles. They were moving out last night when we arrived – all the odds and sods, that is. The line was up on what they call 42nd Street. We were put under command of A Commando and rushed straight out to counter-attack at dawn. That was when Prentice was killed. We got right on to the aerodrome. Then we discovered that the Spaniards who were supposed to be on our flank, hadn't shown up. And there was no sign of the people who were supposed to come through and relieve us. So we sat there for an hour being shot at from all directions. Then we moved off again. We lost A Commando. Stukas got most of our transport. We lay in the fields all day being dive-bombed. Then after dark we came down here and here we are.'

'I see,' said Major Hound. 'I see.'

He was turning the problem in his clouded mind, finding no staff solution. At length he said: 'I suppose you know where Creforce headquarters are?'

'They might be anywhere now. They *were* in a monastery building somewhere off the main road.'

'And the other Commandos?'

'C was in the counter-attack with us. I think they're lying up somewhere near HQ. I haven't seen X since we landed. They were sent off on a different job somewhere else.'

Major Hound's good habits began to take control. He took the map.

'*That*,' he said, pointing blindly into the contours behind Suda, 'is assembly point. Rendezvous there forthwith. *That* is brigade headquarters. I will now go forward to Creforce. The GOC must see our orders from C-in-C at once. I shall need a guide. I will see unit commanders at headquarters at 0900 hours. Are you in W/T communication with A, C, and X?'

'No.'

'Pass the message by runner. Any questions?'

The second-in-command of B Commando seemed about to speak. Then his shoulders sagged and he turned about and left.

'You've made a note of those orders, Crouchback?'

'Yes. Do you think they'll be carried out?'

'I presume so. Anyway, they have been given. One can't do more.'

Major Hound dispatched Captains Roots and Slimbridge and the rear headquarters to their map reference in the hills. Then he and Guy with their servants climbed into the three-ton lorry and drove off. A guide from B Commando sat in front with the driver.

As they left the port area they turned into the main road that led from Canea. They drove without lights. The sky was clear and full of stars. They could see a fair way and as far as they could see and as far as they went the road was densely filled with walking men interspersed with motor-vehicles of all kinds, lightless also, moving at walking pace. Some of the men were in short columns of threes, fully equipped, some were wounded, supporting one another, some wandered without arms. The lorry moved against all this traffic, clearing a passage. Occasionally a man would shout at them. One said: 'Wrong way, mate.' Most of the men did not look up. Some walked straight into the bonnet and mudguards. For some miles the flow of men never changed. Then they turned up a lane and a sentry halted them. The driver opened the bonnet and began to work on the engine with a flash-lamp.

'Put out that light,' said the sentry.

'What are you doing?' asked Major Hound.

'Taking the distributor. We don't want this truck pinched.'

The guide led them into a peaceful vineyard. They were challenged again and at length reached some dark buildings. Guy looked at his watch. Half past two.

The batmen sat down outside. Guy and Major Hound pushed back the two blankets which hung over the door of a peasant's two-roomed house. Inside a storm lantern and maps lay on the table. Two men were asleep, sitting on chairs, their heads in their arms on the table. Major Hound saluted. One of the men raised his head.

'Yes?'

'Brigade Headquarters, Hookforce, reporting, sir, with orders from C-in-C M E.'

'What? Who?' The face of the BGS was blank with weariness. 'The GOC is not to be disturbed. We're moving in an hour. Just leave whatever it is you've got. I'll attend to it.'

GSO I slowly sat up.

'Did you say "Hookforce"? The GOC has been waiting for a report from you all day.'

'It's very urgent I should see him.'

'Yes, yes, of course. But not just now. He can't see anyone now. This is the first sleep he's had for two days and we've got to make our move before dawn. Is Colonel Blackhouse with you?'

Major Hound began to explain the situation, to put BGS and GSO I in the picture. It was plain to Guy that they understood nothing. For Major Hound it was enough that the words should be spoken, the correct sounds made even into the void of their utter weariness.

'... Based on Canea ... Raiding tasks on enemy of L of C in conjunction with SNO ...'

'Yes,' said BGS. 'Thank you. Leave it here. The GOC shall see it. Ask Colonel Blackhouse to report at eight.'

He pointed to the map on the talc cover of which the new headquarters were neatly marked in chalk. It was conveniently near the place chosen by Major Hound, Guy noticed, on the forward slopes just off the road where it turned inland for the mountains and the south coast.

They returned to the lorry and as they drove into the main road, going with the stream now, a New Zealand officer stopped them. 'Can you take on some wounded?'

'I don't know where the ADS is,' said Major Hound.

'Nor do I. These are men from the Canea hospital. The Jerries turned them out.'

'That hardly sounds likely.'

'Well, here they are.'

'Oh. Where do they want to go?'

'Anywhere.'

'We're only going three miles.'

'That'll be some help.'

The wounded men began climbing and pulling one another up until the lorry was full.

'Thanks,' said the New Zealander.

'Where are you going yourself?'

'Sphakia, if I can make it.'

Presently they came to a part of the road where the walking and marching men had somehow been directed into the side and there was a clear way ahead. They began bumping along at a fair speed, the wounded men often groaning as they were thrown about.

Guy was being painfully pressed against the backboard. He dug forward with his knees and the man in front edged forward, then turned and peered at him in the darkness. A curious sound emerged:

'Sorry and all that. Bit on the tight side, what?'

It was a preposterous accent, the grossly exaggerated parody of the hot-potato, haw-haw voice; something overheard from Christmas charades. Guy flashed his torch and discerned a youngish man incongruously clothed in service-dress, Sam Browne, and the badges of a Lieutenant-Colonel.

'Are you wounded?' Guy asked.

'Hardly. Jolly sporting of you to give me a lift.'

'Where are you going?'

'Following the jolly old crowd, don't you know. It's *sauve qui peut* now, as the French say.'

'Do they? Is it? May I ask who you are?'

'I'm OC Transit Camp. Or rather I was, what? Nothing *we* could do, don't you know? Our orders are to find our own way to the coast.'

The lorry slowed among another block of walking men. Guy began to wonder about this man next to him. It was a device of German parachute troops, he had been told, to infiltrate in enemy uniforms and spread subversive rumours.

'Was it part of your orders to tell everyone it's *sauve qui peut?*'

'Hardly.'

Major Hound was separated from them by half a dozen hunched and prostrate men. Guy crawled and pushed towards him.

'Who's this chap at the back?' he whispered. 'Do you think he's all right?'

'I don't know why not.'

'He's got a very odd way of speaking and he's saying some very odd things.'

'He seems perfectly normal to me. Anyway, this is as far as we can take him.'

They had reached the high ground where Major Hound had sited his headquarters. All was in order here. A signaller stood at the side of the road as sentry and guide. As they stopped, stragglers gathered round. 'Room for another, mate?'

'Get out. Everyone out,' said Major Hound.

Sergeant Smiley joined them.

'Move to it,' he shouted.

Uncomplaining, unquestioning, the wounded men managed their descent and silently limped off among the moving crowd.

'Thanks no end,' said the O C Transit Camp.

The lorry was driven off the road among boulders and trees; its distributor was again removed, its camouflage-net correctly spread.

Corporal-Major Ludovic appeared in the glimmer.

'Everything in order, Corporal-Major?'

'Sir.'

'Captain Roots here?'

'He went in the truck with Captain Slimbridge to look for rations.'

'Good. All-round defence posted?'

'Sir.'

'Well, I think I'll turn in. It'll be light in an hour. Then we shall know better how we stand.'

Whatever strange tides were flowing round him, Major Hound still kept afloat, like Noah, sure in his own righteousness. But he did not sleep.

Guy made his bed behind a boulder among thorny sweet shrubs. He too lay awake. That strange man in service dress, he decided, was not a German paratrooper; merely a private soldier who had stolen officer's uniform the better to effect his escape.

And quarter of a mile distant on the road to the mountains the silent men stumbled and the blind cars rattled.

Major Hound had eaten nothing since he put to sea. His first thought, as headquarters came to life at dawn, was of food.

'Time we were brewing up, Corporal-Major.'

'Captain Roots and his ration-party have not returned, sir.'

'No tea?'

'No tea, sir. No water except what's in our bottles. I was advised not to light a fire, sir, on account of the hostile aircraft.'

Major Hound's second thought was of his personal appearance. He opened his haversack, propped a looking-glass against a boulder, smeared his face with sticky matter from a tube and began to shave.

'Crouchback, are you awake?'

'Yes.'

'We've got a conference this morning.'

'Yes.'

'Better spruce up a bit. Have you any shaving-cream?'

'Never use it.'

'I can lend you some of mine. You don't need much.'

'Thanks awfully, I'll wait for hot water. From what I could see last night there isn't a great deal of shaving done on this island.'

Major Hound wiped his face and razor, and handed it and his towel to his batman. He studied the crowded road through his binoculars.

'I can't think what's happened to Roots.'

'While we were waiting last night, sir,' said Corporal-Major Ludovic, 'I got into conversation with an Australian Sergeant. Apparently in the last day or two there have been many cases of men shooting officers and stealing their motor-vehicles. In fact, he suggested that he and I should adopt the practice, sir.'

'Don't talk nonsense, Corporal-Major.'

'I rejected the suggestion, sir, with scorn.'

Major Hound looked hard at Ludovic, then he rose and strolled slowly towards the risen sun.

'Crouchback,' he called. 'Would you come over here a minute?'

Guy joined him and walked behind up the little white goat-track until they were out of earshot, when Major Hound said:

'Does Ludovic strike you as queer?'

'He always has.'

'Was he trying to be insolent just now?'

'I think perhaps he was trying to be funny.'

'It's going to be awkward if he cracks up.'

'Very.'

They stood silent among a little group of umbrella pines watching the procession on the road. It had thinned now, no longer the solid block of the hours of darkness; men trudged along apart in pairs and clusters. One lorry only was in sight, slowly climbing the slope towards them.

Hound said rather quickly as though he had been rehearsing the question: 'I say, do you mind if I call you "Guy"?'

'Not particularly.'

'My friends usually call me "Fido".'

'Philo?'

'Fido.'

'Oh. Yes. I see.'

A pause.

'I don't altogether like the look of things, Guy.'

'Neither do I, Fido.'

'What's more, I'm damned hungry.'

'So am I.'

'You don't really think they can have murdered Roots and gone off with our lorry?'

'No.'

As they spoke in low confidential tones there came to them from the bright morning sky the faint, crescent hum of an aeroplane and with it a nearer, louder, more doleful, scarcely more human sound, echoed from man to man along the dusty road: 'Aircraft. Take cover. Take cover. Take cover. Aircraft.'

At once the whole aspect was transformed. All the men stumbled off the road, flung themselves down face forward and totally disappeared among the scrub and rock. The dust subsided behind them. The lorry drove straight to the cover of the pines where Guy and Fido stood, stopped when it could go no deeper. A dozen men climbed out and ran from it, falling flat among the tactically dispersed elements of Hookforce headquarters.

'This won't do,' said Fido.

He walked towards them.

'Look here, you men, this is Brigade Headquarters area.'

'Aircraft,' they said. 'Take cover.'

The little, leisurely reconnaissance plane grew from a glint of silver to a recognizable machine. It flew low above the road, dwindled, turned, grew again, turned its attention to the lorry and fired a burst, wide by twenty yards, circled, mounted and at length disappeared to seawards into the silent quattrocento heaven.

Guy and Fido had lain down when the bullets fell. They stood up and grinned at one another, accomplices in indignity.

'You'd better move on now,' said Fido to the men from the truck.

None of them answered.

'Who's in command of this party?' asked Fido. 'You, Sergeant?'

The man addressed said sulkily, 'Not exactly, sir.'

'Well, you'd better take command and move on.'

'You can't move, not in daytime. There's Jerries over all the time. We've had a week of it.'

All round now heads were bobbing up in the bushes but no one moved on the road. The Sergeant swung his pack forward and took out a tin of biscuits and a tin of bully-beef. He hacked the meat open with his bayonet and began carefully dividing it.

Fido watched. He craved. Not Guy nor the ragged, unshaven Sergeant, not Fido himself who was dizzy with hunger and lack of sleep, nor anyone on that fragrant hillside could know that this was the moment of probation. Fido stood at the parting of the ways. Behind him lay a life of blameless professional progress; before him the proverbial alternatives: the steep path of duty and the heady precipice of sensual appetite. It was the first great temptation of Fido's life. He fell.

'I say, Sergeant,' he said in an altered tone, 'have you any of that to spare?'

'Not to spare. Our last tin.'

Then one of the other men spoke, also gently:

'You don't happen to have a smoke on you, sir?'

Fido felt in his pocket, opened his cigarette case and counted.

'I might be able to spare a couple,' he said.

'Make it four and you can have my bully. I'm queer in the stomach.'

'And two biscuits.'

'No, I can eat biscuit. It's bully I never have fancied.'

'One biscuit.'

'Five fags.'

The deal was done. Fido took his price of shame in his hand, the little lump of the flaky, fatty meat and his single biscuit. He did not look at Guy, but went away out of sight to eat. It took a bare minute. Then he returned to the centre of his group and sat silent with his map and his lost soul.

5

The 'tactical dispersal' of Hookforce headquarters, modified by the defection of Captains Roots and Slimbridge and their ration-party and the incursion of various extraneous elements, had an appearance of being haphazard: The 'all-round defence' comprised four signallers outlying with rifles at the points of the compass. Under their guard little groups rested among scrub and boulder. The Brigade Major sat alone in the centre, Guy some distance away. The warmth of the early sun comforted them all.

Guy's servant approached with a mess-tin containing cold baked beans, biscuits and jam.

'All I could scrounge, sir.'

'Splendid. Where did it come from?'

'Our section, sir. Sergeant Smiley had a look round on the quay last night.'

Guy joined his men who were eating with caution, out of sight of the improvident clerks and signallers. They greeted him cheerfully. This was their picnic, he their guest; it was not for him officiously to ordain a general distribution of their private spoils.

'I don't see any immediate intelligence task,' he said. 'The best thing we can do is to make a recce for water. There ought to be a spring in one of these gullies.'

Sergeant Smiley handed round cigarettes.

'Go carefully with those,' said Guy. 'We may find them valuable for barter.'

'I got ten tins off the navy, sir.'

Guy sent two men to look for water. He marked his map. He noted on his pad. '*28/6/41. Adv. Bde HQ established on track west of road 346208 0500 hrs. Enemy recce plane 0610.*' It occurred to him on that morning of uncertainty that he was behaving pretty much as a Halberdier should. He wished that Colonel Tickeridge could be there to see him, and even as he cherished this remote whim, Colonel Tickeridge in fact appeared.

Not recognizably at first; a mere speck in the empty road, then, as he drew nearer, two specks. In the words of the *Manual of Small Arms*, at six hundred yards the heads were dots, the bodies tapered; at three hundred yards the faces were blurred; at two hundred yards all parts of the body were distinctly seen; his old commander's great moustache was unmistakable.

'Hi,' Guy shouted, hastening towards the road, 'Colonel Tickeridge, sir. Hi.'

The two Halberdiers halted. They were as cleanshaven as Fido, all their equipment in place, just as they had appeared during battalion exercises at Penkirk.

'Uncle. Well, I'll be damned! What are you up to? You aren't Creforce headquarters by any happy chance?'

It was no time for detailed remniscence. They exchanged some essential military information. The Second Halberdiers had come out of Greece without firing a shot and lived in billets between Retino and Suda, waiting for orders. At last Colonel Tickeridge had been summoned to headquarters. He was in complete ignorance of the progress of the battle. Nor had he yet heard of the loss of Ben Ritchie-Hook. Guy began to put him in the picture.

Fido was not yet so sunk in dishonour that he could bear to see a junior officer speak to a senior without intervening. He bustled up and saluted.

'You're looking for Force Headquarters, sir? They should be on the reverse slope. I'm reporting there at eight myself.'

'I was called for eight but I'm going while things are quiet. The Germans work a strict time-table. At eight o'clock sharp they start throwing things. They knock off for lunch, then carry on until sunset. Never varies. What's the GOC doing back here? Who are all these frightful-looking fellows I see all over the shop? What's going on?'

'They say it's *sauve qui peut* now,' said Fido.

'Don't know the expression,' said Colonel Tickeridge.

It was twenty past seven.

'I'm pushing on. They never by any chance hit anyone with their damned bombs, but they make me nervous.'

'We'll come too,' said Fido.

No one else moved over the roads. The men who had tramped all night lay deep in the scrub, feeling the sun, breathing the spicy air, hungry and thirsty and dirty, waiting for the long dangerous day to bring another laborious night.

Punctually at eight the sky filled with aeroplanes. The GOC's conference was just beginning. A dozen officers squatted round him in a booth of blankets and boughs and camouflage-net. Some of them, who had been heavily bombed in the last week, hunched their shoulders and, as a machine approached, seemed deaf to other sounds. No bombs or bullets came near them.

'I regret to inform you, gentlemen,' said the GOC, 'that the decision has been taken to abandon the island.' He proceeded to give a summary of the situation ... 'This brigade and that brigade have borne the brunt of the fighting and are severely mauled ... I have therefore withdrawn them from the action and ordered them to embarkation points on the south coast.' That was the rabble of the previous night, Guy thought; those are the drowsy, footsore men in the bushes ... 'I have withdrawn them from the action ...'

The General proceeded to the details of a rear-guard. Hookforce and the Second Halberdiers, it appeared, were the only units now capable of fighting. The General indicated lines to be held.

'Is this a last-man, last-round defence?' asked Colonel Tickeridge cheerfully.

'No. No. A planned withdrawal ...' So-and-so was to fall back through such-and-such ... This bridge and that were to be blown behind the last sub-unit.

'I don't seem to have much on my flanks,' said Colonel Tickeridge presently.

'You needn't worry about them. The Germans never work off the roads.'

At length he said: 'It must be accepted that administration has to some extent broken down ... Dumps of ammunition and rations will be established at various points on the road ... It is hoped that more may be flown in tonight ... Some improvisation may be necessary ... I will move my headquarters tonight to Imbros ... Traffic to present headquarters must be kept to a minimum. You will leave singly, avoiding making tracks ...'

By nine o'clock Guy and Fido were back where they had started. Twice on the return journey they took cover as an aeroplane swooped low over their heads. Once or twice as they walked the open road voices from the bush admonished them: 'Keep down, can't you,' but mostly they moved through a land seemingly devoid of human life. When they reached their headquarters Fido busied himself in transcribing the General's orders. Then he said:

'Guy, do you think the unit commanders will turn up at my conference?'

'No.'

'It's their own fault if they don't.' He looked hopelessly about him with his keen eyes. 'No one moving anywhere. I think you'd better take the truck and distribute orders personally.'

'Where?'

'Here,' said the Brigade Major, pointing to the chalk marks on his map, 'and here, and here. Or somewhere,' he added in blank despair.

'Corporal-Major, where's our driver?'

The driver could not be found. No one remembered seeing him that morning. He was not a Commando man, but one of the transport pool attached to them in this island of disillusion.

'What the devil can have happened to him, Corporal-Major?'

'I conclude, sir, that finding it impossible to drive away, he preferred to walk. The moment I saw him, sir, I formed the impression that his heart was not in the fight and, fearing to lose another vehicle, I took possession of the distributor.'

'Excellent work, Corporal-Major.'

'Transport of all kinds being, sir, in the cant expression of the Australian I mentioned, gold dust, sir.'

'I'm worried about Roots,' said the Brigade Major. 'Keep an eye out for him.'

A Stuka came near them, spotted the intruders' truck, circled, dived and dropped three bombs on the farther side of the road among the invisible stragglers, then lost interest and soared away to the west. Guy, Fido and Ludovic rose to their feet.

'I shall have to move headquarters,' said Fido. 'They'll see that damned truck.'

'Why not move the truck?' said Guy.

Ludovic, without waiting for an order, mounted the vehicle, got it going, backed into the road and drove half a mile. The stragglers roused themselves to shout abusively after him. As he returned on foot carrying a tin of petrol in each hand another Stuka appeared, dived on the truck and, luckier than its predecessor, toppled it over with a near miss.

'There goes your —ing transport,' said Ludovic to the straggler Sergeant. He had the manservant's gift of tongues, speaking now in strong plebeian tones; when he turned to the Brigade Major he was his old fruity self. 'May I suggest, sir, that I take a couple of men and go with Captain Crouchback? We might be able to pick up some rations somewhere.'

'Corporal-Major,' said Guy, 'you don't by any chance suspect I might make off alone with our truck?'

'Certainly not, sir,' said Ludovic demurely.

Fido said: 'No. Yes. Well. Whatever you think best. Only get on with it, for God's sake.'

Guy found a volunteer driver from his section and soon they set off, he in the cab, Ludovic and two men in the back, down the road they had travelled in darkness.

Sea and land seemed empty; the sky alone throbbed with life. But the enemy had lost interest in trucks for the moment. The aeroplanes were no longer roaming at large. Instead they had some insect-plan a mile or more away in the hills south of the harbour. They followed an unvarying course, coming in from the sea at five-minute intervals, turning, diving, dropping bombs, machine-gunning, circling, diving, bombing, firing, three times each along the same line, then out to sea again to their base on the mainland. As they performed this rite Guy and his truck went about their business undisturbed.

Trampled gardens, damaged and deserted villas gave place to gutted terraces along the road; then villas again into the country beyond Suda.

'Stop here a moment,' said Guy. 'We ought to be near X Commando.'

He studied the map, he studied the surviving landmarks. There was a domed church on the left among olive trees, some of them burned and splintered, most of them full and placid as the groves of Santa Dulcina.

'This must be it. Draw into cover and wait here.'

He got down and walked alone into the plantation. It was full, he found, of trenches and the trenches were full of men. They sat huddled, half asleep, and few looked up when Guy questioned them. Sometimes one or another said, in the flat undertone of Creforce: 'Keep down, for God's sake. Take cover, can't you?' They were pay-clerks and hospital-orderlies and aerodrome ground-staff, walking-wounded, RASC, signallers, lost sections of infantry, tank-crews without tanks, gunners without guns; a few dead bodies. They were not X Commando.

Guy returned to his truck.

'Drive on slowly. Keep a look-out at the back. They'll have a sentry posted on the road.'

They drove on and presently came to two men in foreign uniforms working with spades at the side of the road, one old, one young. The old man was rather small, very upright, very brown, very wrinkled, with superb white moustaches and three lines of decorations. The young man threw down his spade and ran into the road to stop the lorry while the old man stood looking at the heap they had made and then crossed himself three times in the Greek manner.

'It is General Miltiades,' said the young man in clear English. 'We have been separated from the Household a week now. Would you be so kind as to take us to the harbour? The General is to take an English ship to Egypt. We should have been there last night, but an aeroplane shot our car and wounded the driver. The General would not leave him. He died two hours ago and we have just buried him. Now we must go on.'

'That was the last ship from Suda. He must go to Sphakia.'

'Can you take us?'

'I can take you a few miles. Jump in, if you don't mind my doing a few errands on the way.'

They began to drive on but the interpreter beat on the back of the cab, saying: 'That is the wrong way. Only Germans that way,' and in confirmation of his opinion a motor-cyclist suddenly appeared and stopped in front of them. He wore a grey uniform and a close-fitting helmet. He stared at Guy through his goggles with blank young eyes, then hastily turned about and drove off.

'I say,' said Guy to his driver, 'what do you imagine that was?'

'Looked like a Jerry, sir.'

'We *have* come too far. About turn.'

Unmolested they backed and turned and drove away. After half a mile Guy said: 'I ought to have had a shot at that man.'

'Didn't give us much time, sir.'

'He ought to have had a shot at us.'

'I reckon he was taken by surprise same as we were. I never thought somehow to see a Jerry so close.'

Ludovic could not have seen the cyclist; that, in a way, was a comfort. They passed the Greek staff-car; they passed the church.

'The stragglers seem to be in front of the firing-line in this battle,' Guy remarked.

They drove slowly, looking for signs of Hookforce. Soon there was a beating on the back of the cab.

'Sir,' said Ludovic, 'this General knows where there are rations, and petrol.'

Directed from behind they drove back into Suda and near the port stopped at a warehouse. Most of it was burned, but on the far side of the yard stood a pile of petrol tins and two Greek soldiers guarding a little heap of provisions. They greeted the general staff with warmth. There was wine among the stores and many empty flasks lying about.

'You can give these good men a lift also?' asked the interpreter. 'They are a little drunk, I believe, and not able to march.'

'Jump in,' said Guy.

Ludovic examined the provisions. There were bales of hay, sacks of rice and macaroni and sugar and coffee, some dried but reeking fish, huge, classical jars of oil. These were not army rations but the wreckage of private enterprise. He chose a cheese, two boxes of ice-cream cornets and a case of sardines. These and wine alone were useful without the aid of fire.

They drove slowly back. The aeroplanes still pounded away at their

338

invisible target in the hills. The Greek soldiers fell asleep. The General changed his boots.

The sun was high and hot, and as Guy's truck reached the point where the road turned inland the succession of aeroplanes ceased. The last of them dwindled and vanished, a hush fell, perceptible even in the rattling cab, and suddenly all over the roadside figures appeared, stretching and strolling. This was the luncheon recess.

'That looks like our lot,' said the driver, pointing to two men with an anti-tank rifle at the side of the road.

Here at last was Hookforce, in slit trenches interspersed with stragglers in a wide vineyard. The trees were old and gnarled and irregular, full of tiny green fruit just formed. The COs were together squatting in the shade of a cart-house, A, C, and X Commandos and the Major from B Commando who had landed from the destroyer the night before.

Guy approached and saluted.

'Good morning, sir; good morning, sir. Good morning, Tony.'

Since Tommy's promotion, X had been commanded by a Coldstreamer named Tony Luxmore, a grave, cold young man consistently lucky at cards. He greeted Guy crossly.

'Where the hell have you been? We've just sweated up to brigade head-quarters and back looking for you.'

'Looking for *me*, Tony?'

'Looking for orders. What's happened to your Brigade Major? We woke him up but we couldn't get any sense out of him. He kept repeating that everything was laid on. Orders were being distributed by hand of officer.'

'He's hungry.'

'Who isn't?'

'He hasn't had any sleep.'

'Who has?'

'He had a bad crossing. Anyway, here are your orders.'

Tony Luxmore took the pencilled sheets and while he and the other commanders studied them, Guy filled his water-bottle at the well. Cistus and jasmine flowered among the farm buildings, but there was a sour smell in the air, exhaled by the dirty men.

'These don't make any sense,' said the CO of A Commando.

Guy tried to elucidate the planned withdrawal. Hookforce, he learned, had done their own regrouping that morning, dissolving the remains of B Commando and attaching them by troops and sections to replace the losses of A and C. X Commando alone was up to strength. The orders were amended. Guy made notes in his pocket-book and marks on his map-cover, taking a dry relish in punctiliously observing the forms of procedure. Then he prepared to leave the weary men, deeply weary himself and out of temper with them.

339

General Miltiades meanwhile had been sitting calmly in the back of the truck. Suddenly Tony Luxmore noticed him. He was a man who, once seen, was not easily forgotten.

'General Miltiades,' he cried. 'Hullo, sir. You wouldn't remember me. You came with the King to stay with my parents at Wrackham.'

The General smiled in all his wrinkles. He did not remember Tony or Tony's parents, the wintry pillared house where he had slept, the farm where he had eaten Irish-stew, or the high bare coverts where in another age not long ago he had shot pheasant. He was past seventy. In youth he had fought the Turks and been often wounded. In middle life the politicians had often sent him into exile. In old age he was homeless again, finally it might seem, still following his king. Barracks, boarding-houses, palaces, English country houses, stricken battlefields – all were the same to General Miltiades.

He climbed down with agility. His liaison officer followed, carrying a straw-covered flask in each hand.

'The General asks you to take wine with him.'

Mugs were filled. The General had some English. He proposed a toast; with no shade of irony in his steady, pouchy eyes; the single word: 'Victory.'

'How about you, Corporal-Major?' Guy asked.

'Thank you, sir. I have already refreshed myself.'

There was saluting and hand-shaking. Then Guy's party boarded the lorry again and drove away.

'*Captain Crouchback,*' Corporal-Major Ludovic noted, '*is pleased because General Miltiades is a gentleman. He would like to believe that the war is being fought by such people. But all gentlemen are now very old.*'

Ludovic sat on a hot boulder some little distance apart. The cheese, the wafers, the sardines had been divided. Some men ravenously ate all at once. Ludovic had stowed away a substantial part – 'The unexpired portion' of how many days' ration? Everyone had had a mug of wine. Now they spread blankets to protect their knees against the fierce sun and were one by one falling asleep. General Miltiades had tried to explain, with map and interpreter, various peculiarities of the terrain which might be exploited to the enemy's discomfort. Major Hound proved an inattentive audience. He said petulantly to Guy, when the General briefly pottered away alone into the cover, 'What did you want to bring him here for? How are we going to get rid of him?'

'I suggest we give him a lift to the GOC later in the day.'

'I've got to think about moving headquarters.'

Guy tried to explain the readjustments among the units. Major Hound said: 'Yes, yes. It's their responsibility.'

He had taken in nothing.

Then Guy, too, lay down to sleep. The General returned and lay down. Ludovic slept. Fido alone kept open his keen bewildered eyes.

They did not sleep long. Sharp at two o'clock came the drone of engines and the dismal cry repeated across the hillside. 'Aircraft. Take cover. Take cover. Take cover.'

Major Hound became suddenly animated.

'Cover all metal objects. Put away all maps. Hide your knees. Hide your faces. Don't look up.'

The Stukas came over in formation. They had another insect-plan for the afternoon. Just below Hookforce headquarters lay a circular fertile pocket of young corn, such as occur unaccountably in Mediterranean hills. This green patch had been chosen by the airmen as a landmark. Each machine flew straight to it, coming very low, then swung east to a line a mile away off the road, dropped bombs, fired its machine-gun, turned again and headed for the sea. It was the same kind of operation as Guy had watched on the other side of the road that morning. One after another the aeroplanes roared down.

'What on earth are they after?' Guy asked.

'For God's sake keep quiet,' said Fido.

'They can't possibly hear us.'

'Oh, do keep quiet.'

'Fido, if we stuck a Bren on a tripod we couldn't miss.'

'Don't move,' said Fido. 'I forbid you to move.'

'I'll tell you what they're doing. They're clearing a way for their infantry to come round our flanks.'

'Oh, do shut up.'

The General slept on. Everyone else was awake, motionless, numb, as though mesmerized by the monotonous mechanical procession.

Hour after hour the bombs thumped. When to the cowering and torpid men the succession seemed interminable, it abruptly ceased. The drone of the last aeroplane faded into silence and the hillside came to life. Everywhere men began lacing their boots and collecting whatever equipment they still had with them. The stragglers in headquarters area silently took the road. Fido raised his muzzle.

'I've been thinking,' he said. 'I don't believe we're going to see Roots and Slimbridge again, or their lorry. We're simply left in the air with no rear headquarters.'

'Well, we've no Brigade Commander either. I don't know why you want an advanced headquarters, for that matter.'

'No,' said Fido, 'neither do I.'

His tail was right down. Now he was not fair game.

'I dare say we can be some help coordinating,' said Guy in an attempt to console.

'I don't know exactly what you mean by that.'

'Neither do I, Fido. Neither do I. I'm going to sleep.'

'I think I'd better send the General to the General, don't you?'

'Whatever you like.

'In the lorry?'

'Yes. It can come back for us.'

Guy moved away and found a place with few thorns. He lay looking up into the sky. The sun was not yet down but the moon rode clear above them, a fine, opaque, white brush-stroke on the rim of her disc of shadow. Guy was aware of the movement round him, of the Greeks and the lorry and Ludovic, and then was deep asleep.

When he awoke the moon had travelled far among the stars. Fido was scratching and snuffling at him.

'I say, Guy, what's the time?'

'For Christ's sake, Fido, haven't you got a watch?'

'I must have forgotten to wind it.'

'Half past nine.'

'Only that. I thought it was much later.'

'Well, it isn't. D'you mind if I go to sleep again?'

'Ludovic isn't back yet with the truck.'

'Then there's no point in waking up.'

'What's more, he's taken my batman with him.'

Guy slept again, it seemed very briefly. Then Fido was pawing him again.

'I say, Guy, what's the time?'

'Didn't you put your watch right when I told you last time?'

'I can't have, somehow I must have forgotten. It's ticking but it says seven fifteen.'

'Well, it's a quarter past ten.'

'Ludovic's not back yet.'

Guy turned over and slept again, more lightly this time. He kept waking and turning. His ears caught an occasional truck on the road. Later he heard rifle-fire some distance away and a motor-cycle stop; then loud excited conversation. He looked at his watch; just on midnight. He needed more sleep but Fido was standing beside him shouting, 'Where's Sergeant Smiley? Get brigade headquarters fallen in on the road. Get cracking, everyone.'

'What on earth's the matter?'

'Don't bother me with questions. Get cracking.'

Hookforce headquarters comprised eight men now. Fido looked at them in the starlight.

'Where's everyone else?'

'Went with the Corporal-Major, sir.'

'We shan't see them again,' said Fido bitterly. 'Forward.'

It was not forward they went but backward; back a long way, Fido ahead setting a strenuous pace over the rough road. Guy was at first too dazed to do more than keep step beside him; after a mile he tried to talk.

'What on earth's happened?'

'The enemy. All round us. Closing in on the road from both flanks.'

'How do you know?'

'The Commandos are engaging them lower down.'

Guy asked no further questions then. All his breath was needed for the march. Sleep had brought no refreshment. The past twenty-four hours had wearied and weakened them all, and Guy was ten years older than most of the men. Fido was putting out all his strength, staring straight ahead into the uncertain star-gloaming. The young moon had set. The pace was slower than a route march, faster than anything else on the road that night. They passed ghostly limping couples, and the ghosts of formed bodies of troops dragging slowly in the same blind flight. They passed peasants with donkeys. After an hour by Guy's watch, he said: 'Where are we going to halt, Fido?'

'Not here. We must get as far as we can before day-break.'

They passed an empty village.

'How about here?'

'No. An obvious target. We must push on.'

The men were beginning to drop behind.

'I must rest for ten minutes,' said Guy. 'Let the men catch up.'

'Not here. There's no cover.'

The road at this point was a scratched contour round the side of a hill, with precipitous slopes up and down on either hand.

'Once we halt we shan't get on again tonight.'

'There's something in that, Fido. Anyway, take it easy a bit.'

But Fido would not take it easy. He led on through another deserted village; going slow, but with all his powers, then there were trees at the roadside and a suggestion of open country beyond. It was nearly four o'clock.

'For God's sake let's stop here, Fido.'

'We've a good hour of darkness still. We must push on while we can.'

'Well, I can't. I'm stopping here with my section.'

Fido did not demur. He turned abruptly off the road and sat down in what seemed to be an orchard. Guy waited on the road while the men one by one came up.

'We're setting up headquarters here,' he said fatuously.

The men stumbled off the road, over the wall, into the grove of fruit trees. Guy lay down and slept fitfully.

Fido did not sleep until dawn; in a dream untroubled of hope, he brooded, clasping his knees. He had fallen among thieves. He considered the plain treachery of Ludovic, the suspected treachery of Roots and Slimbridge and he began framing the charges for a court-martial. He considered the probabilities of such a court ever being convened, of himself ever being available to give evidence and found them nugatory. Presently the sun rose, the wayfarers, much sparser now, sought cover, and Fido snoozed.

He awoke to a strange spectacle. The road beside him was thronged with hairy men – not merely unshaven but fully bearded with fine dark locks – a battalion of them in numbers, waving a variety of banners, shirts and scraps of linen on sticks; some of them bore whole sheets of bed linen as canopies over their heads. They were dressed in motley. Guy Crouchback was talking to the leading man in a foreign language.

Fido raised his head over the wall and called: 'Guy, Guy. Who are they?'

Guy went on talking and presently returned, smiling.

'Italian prisoners,' he explained. 'Not a happy party. They surrendered to the Greeks weeks ago on the Albanian frontier. Since then they've been marched from place to place until they managed to infiltrate into the retreat and got here. Now they've been told to join up with the Germans and they're full of indignation that we won't transport them to Egypt. They've got a very fierce doctor in charge who says it's contrary to international convention to turn unwounded prisoners loose until the end of hostilities. What's more, he has an idea that the island is full of furious Australians who will murder them if they catch them. He was demanding an armed escort.'

Fido was not amused. He merely said:

'I don't know of any international convention which prescribes that.'

In a year or two of war 'Liberation' would acquire a nasty meaning. This was Guy's first meeting with its modern use.

The procession shuffled dismally past and was still in sight when the first aeroplane of the day roared down on them. Some stood their ground and waved their white flags; others scattered. These were the wiser. The German fired a line of bullets through them; several fell; the remainder scattered for cover as the airman returned and fired again.

'The Australians *will* murder them if they start attracting attention,' said Guy.

Then the German roared away to seek other targets. The irate doctor returned to the road and examined the fallen. He shouted for help and presently two Italians and an Englishman joined him. Together they moved the wounded and dying into the shade. The white flags lay unregarded in the dust.

Guy sat down beside Fido.

'We came a long way last night.'

'Twelve miles, perhaps, I ought to find the GOC and report.'

'Report what? Don't you think we'd better know what's really happening?'

'How can we?'

'I can go and find out.'

'Yes. Did you eat all your rations yesterday? I did.'

'I too. What's more, I'm thirsty.'

'Perhaps there might be something in that village we passed, eggs or something. I believe I heard a cock crowing once. Why not take your servant and Sergeant Smiley and send them back with anything you find.'

'I'd sooner go alone.'

Fido did not find it in his heart to order a foraging party.

Guy left him in command of a clerk, three signallers and the intelligence section. There seemed to be no orthodox tactical disposal for this force which was scattered and asleep. Fido gazed about him. At a short distance the ground fell away to a gully in which lay a stagnant pool. Two or three men – not his – were bathing their feet there. Fido joined them and dabbled in the night-cool stagnant water.

'I shouldn't drink that,' he said to one of the men who was lapping near him.

'Got to, chum. Threw my bottle away yesterday when it was empty. How far is it now?'

'To Sphakia? Not more than twenty miles, I think.'

'That's not so bad.'

'There's a biggish climb ahead.'

The man examined his boots carefully.

'I think they'll hold out,' he said. 'I can if they do.'

Fido let his feet dry. He threw away his socks and put on a clean pair which he had kept in his pack. He then examined his boots; nothing wrong with them; they would last for weeks more; but would Fido? He felt dizzy and inert. Every movement required forethought, decision and effort. He looked about him and saw quite close a culvert which ran under the road and in time of rain carried the stream of which this puddle was a relic. It was wide, clean, dry now and keenly inviting. Carrying his boots, Fido padded to the mouth on his clean socks. He could see at the far end a deliciously remote, framed picture of a green and dun valley; between him and it everything was dark and empty. Fido crept in. He went half-way until both bright landscapes were the same size. He unbuckled his equipment and put it beside him. He found the curve of the drain comfortable to his aching back; like a hunted fox, like an air marshal under a billiard-table, he crouched in torpor.

Nothing disturbed him. The Germans were busy that day landing re-inforcements and searching for rescue-ships. There were no bombs or bullets here. All that was left of Hookforce rolled down the road overhead, but Fido did not hear. No sound penetrated to his kennel and in the silence two deep needs gnawed at him – food and orders. He must have both or perish. The day wore on. Towards evening an intolerable restlessness possessed him; hoping to stay his hunger, he lit his last cigarette and smoked it, slowly, greedily sucking until the glowing stub began to burn the tips of his fingers.

Then he took one last deep breath and, as he did so, the smoke touched some delicate nerve of his diaphragm and he began to hiccup. The spasms tortured him in his cramped position; he tried lying full length; finally he crawled into the open. For all his agitation he moved laboriously and crazily like a man photographed in 'slow motion'; thus he climbed to the road and sat beside it on the wall. Men were on the move again, trudging past, some with their eyes in the dust, some fixed on the mountains ahead. It was the moment of evening when the milky wisp of moon became sharp and luminous. Fido saw none of this; each regular hiccup took him by surprise and was at once forgotten; between hiccups his mind was dull and empty, his eyes dazzled and fogged; there was a continuous faint shrilling in his ears as though from distant grasshoppers.

Presently there was an intrusion from the exterior world. A car approached. It came very slowly, and when Fido stood in the road, waving, it stopped. It was a small shabby sports-car, once doubtless the pride of some gilded Cretan youth. Sprawled in the back, upheld by a kneeling orderly, as though in gruesome parody of a death scene from grand opera, lay a dusty and bloody New Zealand officer. In front sat a New Zealand Brigadier and a young officer driving, both haggard. The Brigadier opened his eyes and said:

'Drive on. Can't stop.'

'I've got to get to Headquarters,' said Fido.

'No room. My Brigade Major's in a bad way. Must get him to a dressing-station.'

'I'm a Brigade Major. Hookforce. I've an urgent personal report for the GOC.'

The Brigadier blinked and squinnied and collected his powers of thought.

'Hookforce?' he said. 'Hookforce. You're finding the rear-guard?'

'Yes, sir. I know the GOC wants my report at once.'

'That makes a difference,' said the Brigadier. 'I reckon that gives you priority. Hop out, Giles; I'm sorry but you'll have to walk from here.'

The haggard young officer said nothing. He looked desperate. He climbed out and the Brigadier moved into his place at the wheel. He leaned against the warm stone wall and watched the car drive slowly towards the mountains.

For a time no one spoke except the wounded man who babbled in delirium. Fatigue had brought the Brigadier to a condition resembling senility, in which comatose periods alternated with moments of sharp vexation. For the moment his effort of decision had exhausted him. One tiny patch in his mind remained alive, and with this he steered, braked, changed gear. The road ran zigzag and the darkness deepened.

Fido as though in bed between the opening of the door and the drawing of the curtains recalled the nightmare march of the preceding night and measured each slow mile in terms of blisters and sweat and hunger and thirst and lassitude. He was moving effortlessly in the right direction, passing the ragged men who had gone by as he sat on the wall. Every minute he hiccuped.

Suddenly the Brigadier said: 'Shut up.'

'Sir?'

'How can I drive when you keep making that infernal noise?'

'I'm sorry, sir.'

The other Brigade Major kept saying: 'The returns aren't in from the units. Why aren't the returns in?'

The Brigadier fell silent again. Hie mind seemed to gape and close like the mouth of a goldfish. Presently he said:

'Bloody good rear-guard. We got caught with our trousers down all right. Before we'd even had breakfast there were fellows shooting at us with a damned mortar. That's how Charlie copped it. Where was your bloody rear-guard? What's happening? Put me in the picture.'

Fido roused himself from his happy trance. He said whatever came to mind.

'The situation is fluid,' he said; he hiccuped and continued. 'Out-flanked. Infiltrated. Patrol activity. Probing. Break through in strength. Element of surprise. Coordinated withdrawal.'

The Brigadier was not listening.

'Oh,' he said, 'so that's the long and short of it?'

Two miles of dreamland. Then: 'What exactly are you going to report to the General?'

'Sitrep,' said Fido simply. 'Every hour at the hour; orders,' he continued, 'reporting for orders. Information. Intention. *Method*,' he suddenly shouted.

'Quite correct,' said the Brigadier. 'Quite correct.'

He was leaning heavily on the steering-wheel, staring into the darkness. They were climbing steeply now, back and forward along the face of the precipice, with groups of shadowy men straggling everywhere. The Brigadier enjoyed the peculiar immunity from accident that is granted to sleep-walkers.

It seemed to Fido that the moment of unpleasantness was past, but when at length the Brigadier spoke it was with unmistakable malevolence.

'Get out, bastard,' he said.

'Sir?'

'Who in hell d'you think you are, taking Giles's place? Giles is worth six of you. Get out and walk, bastard.'

'Me, sir?'

'You are a bastard, aren't you?'

'No, sir.'

Fido's hiccups ceased suddenly.

'Oh,' The Brigadier seemed disconcerted by this denial. 'My mistake. Sorry. Still, you can bloody well get out and walk, just the same – bastard.'

But he did not stop and soon he began to whistle through his teeth. Fido dozed. Thus they came to the head of the pass where they were suddenly jolted into consciousness. They had collided with something large and black and solid.

'What the hell?' said the Brigadier.

They had not been travelling fast enough to incur much damage. The horn at least was working and the Brigadier pierced the fastness with its ignoble note.

'Aw, pipe down,' came in feeble protest from the darkness.

'What the devil have they stopped for? Go and move them on.'

Fido climbed out and felt his way round the obstruction. It was an empty lorry. Another stood in front of it and beyond that another. Fido groped forward, finding himself one of an ant-line of toiling men who were climbing off the road into the rugged mountain-side. He discerned that the cliff was down on one side and on the other the road had fallen away into the valley leaving a single steep, precarious mass of broken rock. Beyond it the road led down. An officer was rolling stones down the precipice, calling: 'I want men for a working-party. We've got to get this clear. I want volunteers.'

No one heeded him.

Fido stopped and said, 'What's this? A bomb?'

'Sappers. Blew the road without orders and cleared out. I'll have 'em court-martialled if it's the last thing I do. If I have to wait the whole bloody war in prison to do it. I'll get their names. Lend a hand, for Christ's sake.'

'You'll never do it,' said Fido.

'I must. There's five thousand men got to come through.'

'I'll report it,' said Fido. 'I'm on my way to headquarters now. I'll see the General hears about it personally.'

'You'd do better to stay and help.'

'Must push on,' said Fido.

He pushed on, over the landslide, down the road to the plain, to the plain which led to the sea, and as he pushed he left behind him all memory of the frantic, forlorn road-mender, of the irascible New Zealand Brigadier and the dying Major. His mind curled up and slept and the swing of his body carried him from one numb foot to the other, one after the other, on and down towards the sea.

Creforce HQ was a line of caves. Fido found them soon after midnight. Good order prevailed there and military discipline; a sentry challenged him and having heard his account of himself directed him where to go. Fido paused on the goat-track like a drunkard composing himself before entering sober company. Now that his weary quest was at length accomplished it was borne in on him that he had nothing to report, nothing to ask, no reason to be there at all. He had been led by instinct, nosing out his master. He brought no propitiatory rat. He was a bad dog; he had been off on his own, rolling in something nasty. He wanted to fawn and lick the correcting hand.

This would not do. Gradually Fido's slumbrous mind came alive with humanity as the Cretan hillsides had done when the last aeroplane departed.

The mouths of the caves had been roughly walled with loose stones and screens of blankets propped against them. He peered into the first and found a section of signallers round a storm lantern and a wireless set, vainly calling Cairo. The next was in darkness. Fido flashed his torch and saw half a dozen sleeping men and beyond them on a natural shelf of rock a tin of familiar aspect. Cautiously and, it seemed to him, very courageously, Fido stepped across and stole six biscuits – all that remained. He ate them luxuriously in the star-light and wiped the crumbs from his lips. Then he entered the presence of the GOC.

The roof of the cave was too low to allow Fido to stand to attention. He struck his head painfully, then bent and saluted the dust before his feet.

The headmen of the defeated tribe huddled on their haunches like chimps in a zoo. The paramount-chief seemed to recognize Fido.

'Come in,' he said. 'Everything going well?'

'Yes, sir,' said Fido desperately.

'They'll be able to take off their full thousand tonight? The check points are functioning satisfactorily? Priorities being observed as laid down, eh?'

'I've come from Hookforce, sir.'

'Oh. I thought you were from the beach. I want a report from the beach.'

The BGS said: 'We got a sitrep from the Halberdiers three hours ago. As you know, they are holding the line the line at Babali Inn. They fall back through you before dawn. Your men all in position?'

'Yes, sir,' Fido lied.

'Good. The navy landed stores tonight. They're dumped at the approaches to Sphakia. The DQMG will issue chits for you to draw on them. There ought to be plenty to see you through until the Germans have taken over the job of feeding you.'

'But aren't *we* being taken off, sir?'

'No,' said the General. 'No. I'm afraid that won't be possible. The navy are doing what they can, doing magnificently. Someone's got to stay behind and cover the final withdrawal. Hookforce were last on, so I'm afraid you're the last off. Sorry, but there it is.'

This was not a people among whom toothless elders were held in honour. Strong yellow fangs gnawed the human sacrifice.

One of the staff said: 'Are you all right for money?'

'Sir?'

'Some of you may be able to make your own ways in small parties to Alexandria. Buy boats along the coast. "Caiques" they call them. You'll need drachmas.' He opened a suitcase and revealed what might have been the spoils of a bank robbery. 'Help yourself.'

Fido took two great bundles of 1,000-drachma notes.

'Remember,' continued the staff officer, 'wherever the enemy shows his head, give him a bloody nose.'

'Yes, sir.'

'Sure you have enough drachmas?'

'Yes, I think so, sir.'

'Well, good luck.'

'Good luck. Good luck. Good luck,' echoed the headmen as Fido saluted his toes and made his way into the open air.

As he passed the sentry he left the world of good order and military discipline and was on his own in the wilderness. Somewhere not far away, in easy walking distance, lay the sea and the navy. He had only to keep moving downhill. His torch was dying. He lit his footsteps with occasional flickers, provoking protests from the surrounding scrub. 'Put that bloody light out.'

He plunged on and down.

'Put that bloody light out.'

Suddenly quite near him there was a rifle shot. He heard the crack and smack and whistling ricochet among the rocks behind him. He dropped his torch and began feebly to trot. He lost the path and stumbled from boulder to boulder until treading on something which seemed smooth and round and solid in the starlight he found himself in the top of a tree which grew twenty feet below. Scattering Greek currency among the leaves, he subsided quite gently from branch to branch and when he reached ground continued to roll over and over, down and down, caressed and momentarily stayed by bushes until at length he came to rest as though borne there by a benevolent Zephyr of classical myth, in a soft, dark, sweet-smelling, empty place where the only sound was the music of falling water. And there for a time his descent ended. Out of sight, out of hearing, the crowded boats put out from the beach; the men-o'-war sailed away and Fido slept.

Sage and thyme, marjoram and dittany and myrtle grew all about Fido's mossy bed and, as the sun mounted over the tufted precipice, quite overcame the sour sweat of his fear.

The spring had been embellished, consecrated and christianized; the water glittered and bubbled through two man-made basins and above it an arch had been cut in the natural rock. Above the arch, in a flat panel, the head of a saint, faded and flaked, was still discernible.

Fido awoke in this Arcadian vale to find standing near him and gazing fiercely down a figure called straight from some ferocious folk-tale. His bearing was patriarchal, his costume, to Fido's eyes, phantasmagoric – a goat-skin jacket, a crimson sash stuck full of antique weapons, trousers in the style of Abdul the Damned, leather puttees, bare feet. He carried a crooked staff.

'Good morning,' said Fido. 'I am English, an ally. I fight the Germans. I am hungry.'

The Cretan made no answer. Instead he reached forward with his crosier, deftly hooked Fido's pack from beside him and drew it away.

'Here. I say. What d'you think you're doing?'

The old man removed and examined Fido's possessions, transferring them one by one to his own pouch. He took even the safety-razor and the tube of soap. He turned the pack upside down and shook it, made as though to throw it away, thought better and hung it round his massive neck. Fido watched, fascinated. Then he shouted: 'Stop that, damn you. Give those things back.'

The old man regarded him as though he were a fractious great-grandson. Fido drew his pistol.

'Give those back or I'll shoot,' he cried wildly.

The Cretan studied the weapon with renewed interest, nodded gravely and stepped forward.

'Stop,' cried Fido. 'I'll shoot.'

But his finger lay damp and limp on the trigger. The old man leant forward. Fido made no movement. The horny hand touched his and gently loosened his grip on the butt. The old man studied the pistol for a moment, nodding, then tucked it beside his daggers in the red sash. He turned and silently, surely, climbed away up the hillside.

Fido wept.

He lay there all the morning long, quite devoid of the power and will to move. Sometimes he dreamed horribly, sometimes through his waking maze he tried to consider his situation. Enemies encompassed him. Someone had tried to shoot him the night before – German, Australian, Cretan, it did not signify; every hand was against him. At noon he crawled to the fountain and put his bald head under the jet. It brought him sharply to a realization of his hunger. There had been talk last night of dumps of food on the beaches. The stream must lead to the sea, to the beaches, to the dumps of food. He had somewhere about him a chit from the DQMG. He did not, even in his extremity, quite abandon his faith in the magic of official forms. In bumf lay salvation. He stood and groggily pursued his course.

Soon the way narrowed and became a gorge, with the path straying in and out of the water. He moved very slowly, often pausing to lean against the rock-wall. Into the stillness of one of these pauses struck a horripilant sound. Someone was coming. There was no escape on either hand; the cliffs rose sheer. He could only turn or stand and wait his fate. Fido stood. The steps came very close. Fido could wait no longer. He ran forward to meet whatever was coming, his hands up, crying: 'I surrender. I am unarmed. I'm a non-combatant. Don't shoot.'

He shut his eyes. Then a voice said: 'Major Hound, sir. You're not yourself. Try some of this, sir.'

Fido subsided. He was dimly aware of an icy sit-upon and a burning head. It seemed to him that he was squatting in the brook while over him there stood the phantasm of Corporal-Major Ludovic proffering a bottle. Tart, tepid wine poured down his throat and dribbled on his chin and chest. He gulped and panted and blubbed a little and gradually recovered some possession of himself while Ludovic, a firmer image with each passing moment, leaned on the opposing wall and watched.

'A fortunate meeting, if I may say so, sir. Can you manage another mile? Dinner's ready.'

Dinner. Fido felt in the pockets of his bush-shirt. Forty or fifty thousand drachmas fluttered between his trembling fingers. Then he found what he wanted, his chit from the DQMG.

'Dinner,' he affirmed.

Ludovic examined it, smoothed it and tucked it away. He collected the bank-notes. He held out a hand and drew Fido firmly to his feet. Then he turned and led.

The gorge soon widened and became a little cultivated plain bounded by receding cliffs and opening on the sea. Ludovic's way led off the path and the stream, following the rocky margin. It was hard going and Fido lagged and staggered until after half an hour he whispered, 'Corporal-Major. Wait for me. I can't go on,' so faintly that the words were lost in the sound of his stumbling boots. Ludovic strode on. Fido stood with hanging head and closed eyes, out on his feet. And in that moment of prayerless abandonment, succour was vouchsafed. Tiny, delicious, doggy perceptions began to flutter in the void. He raised his bowed nose and sniffed. Clear as the horn of Roland a new note was recalling him to life. Unmistakable and compelling, above the delicate harmony of bee-haunted flower and crushed leaf a great new smell was borne to him; the thunderous organ-tones of Kitchen. Fido was suffused, inebriated, transported. He pressed forward, he overtook Ludovic, he passed him, wordlessly, following his nose in and out of boulders, up treacherous screes, the scent stronger with every frantic step; until at length he came to a wide cave high in the cliff face and he stumbled into the cool gloom where amid steam and wood-smoke a group of shadowy men sat round an iron cauldron; in it there seethed chickens and hares and kids, pigs and peppers and cucumbers and garlic and rice and crusts of bread and dumplings and grated cheese and pungent roots and great soggy nameless white tubers and wisps of succulent green and sea-salt and a good deal of red wine and olive oil.

Fido was bereft of knife, fork, spoon, and tin. He squinnied round the congregation and discerned the semblance of his batman about to tuck in. He snatched. The man held fast.

'Here, what's the idea?'

Fido pulled, the man pulled back, their thumbs deep in the hot grease. Then from behind them Ludovic, in the voice of comradeship, said persuasively: 'Give over, Syd. Anyone with eyes in his head can see the Major's all in. We can't have him going sick on us now we've found him, can we, Syd?'

So Fido took possession of the tin and silently feasted.

The cave was commodious; from its modest mouth it opened into a spacious chamber and branched into dim, divergent passages; from somewhere in its depths came the sound of running water. It held without overcrowding three women, some assorted live-stock and more than fifty men, mostly Spaniards.

These wanderers had got away to a good start. They were familiar with defeat in all its aspects, versed in its stratagems, sharp to recognize its portents. Before their lighter touched shore they had sniffed the air of disaster and twelve hours before the rout began had resumed their migration, passing through villages still unravaged by war, looting with practised hands. Theirs was the cauldron and its rich contents, theirs the women, theirs the brass bedstead and other pieces of domestic furniture which gave an impression of cosy settled occupation to their place of refuge. But they were heirs of a tradition of hospitality. Fiercely resistant of other intruders, they had greeted their old comrades of Hookforce, when out foraging they fortuitously met, with happy smiles raised fists and sentiments of proletarian solidarity.

They retained their arms but had shed all but the rudiments of their British uniforms in favour of a variety of Cretan hats, scarves and jackets. When Fido paused in his eating and looked about him, he took them for local brigands, but he was known to them. He had not been a favourite of theirs at Sidi Bishr. Had he come possessed of any pretence of authority or equipped with any desirable property they would have made short work of him. But destitute, he was their kin and their guest. They watched him benevolently.

Presently Ludovic said: 'I shouldn't eat any more just at present, sir.' He rolled a cigarette and handed it to Fido. 'I've always considered it a mystery, sir, that one immediately revives after eating. According to science, several hours of digestion must pass before any real physical nourishment is obtained.'

The speculation did not interest Fido. Replete and fortified, he began to resume the habits of his calling.

'I'm not quite clear, Corporal-Major, how you come to be here?'

'Much the same way as yourself, I think, sir.'

'I expected you to report back to headquarters.'

'There, sir, we both made a miscalculation. I thought I should be safely back in Egypt by this time, but I encountered difficulties, sir. I found check points at all the approaches to the beach. Only formed bodies of men under their officers were allowed through. There was what you might call a shambles last night in the dark. Men looking for officers, officers looking for men. That was why I was so particularly pleased to meet you today. I was looking for an unattached officer. I hardly hoped it would be you, sir. With your help we shall get off very nicely, I believe. I've got the men all lined up for parade tonight – rather a motley crowd, I fear, sir, representing all arms of the service. Not quite what we're used to at Knightsbridge or Windsor. But they'll pass in the dark. The Spaniards have decided to stay on.'

'What you're suggesting is entirely irregular, Corporal-Major.'

Ludovic regarded him softly.

'Come, come, Major Hound, sir. Don't you think we might drop all that? Just between ourselves, sir. Tonight when we embark our party, later when we get back to Alex – it will be quite appropriate then; but just at the moment, as we are here, after what's happened, sir, don't you think it will be more suitable,' and his voice changed suddenly from its plummy to its plebeian mode – 'to shut your bloody trap.'

Suddenly, for no human reason, a great colony of bats came to life in the vault of the cave, wheeled about, squeaking in the smoke of the fire, fluttered and blundered and then settled again, huddled head-down, invisible.

6

Guy was weary, hungry and thirsty, but he had fared better than Fido in the last four days and, compared with him, was in good heart, almost buoyant, as he tramped alone, eased at last of the lead weight of human company. He had paddled in this lustral freedom on the preceding morning when he caught X Commando among the slit trenches and olive trees. Now he wallowed.

Soon the road ran out and round the face of a rocky spur – the place where Fido had found no cover – and here he met a straggling platoon of infantry coming fast towards him, a wan young officer well ahead.

'Have you seen anything of Hookforce?'

'Never heard of them.'

The breathless officer paused as his men caught up with him and formed column. They still had their weapons and equipment.

'Or the Halberdiers?'

'Cut off. Surrounded. Surrendered.'

'Are you sure?'

'Sure? For Christ's sake, there are parachutists everywhere. We've just been fired on coming round that corner. You can't get up the road. A machine-gun, the other side of the valley.'

'Where exactly?'

'Believe you me, I didn't wait to see.'

'Any casualties?'

'I didn't wait to see. Can't wait now. I wouldn't try that road if you know what's healthy.'

The platoon scuffled on. Guy looked down the empty exposed road and then studied his map. There was a track over the hill which rejoined the road at a village two miles on. Guy did not greatly believe in the machine-gun but he chose the short cut and painfully climbed until he found himself on the top of the spur. He could see the whole empty, silent valley. Nothing moved anywhere except the bees. He might have been standing in the hills behind Santa Dulcina any holiday morning of his lonely boyhood.

Then he descended to the village. Some of the cottage doors and windows were barred and shuttered, some rudely broken down. At first he met no one. A well stood before the church, built about with marble steps and a rutted plinth. He approached thirstily but found the rope hanging loose and short from its bronze staple. The bucket was gone and leaning over he saw far below a little shaving-glass of light and his own mocking head, dark and diminished.

He entered an open house and found an earthenware jar of classic shape. As he removed the straw stopper he heard and felt a hum and, tilting it to the light, found it full of bees and a residue of honey. Then looking about in the gloom he saw an old woman gazing at him. He smiled, showed his empty water-bottle, made signs of drinking. Still she gazed, quite blind. He searched his mind for vestiges of Greek and tried: '*Hudor. Hydro. Dipsa.*' Still she gazed, quite deaf, quite alone. Guy turned back into the sunlight. There a young girl, ruddy, bare-footed and in tears, approached him frankly and took him by the sleeve. He showed her his empty bottle, but she shook her head, made little inarticulate noises and drew him resolutely towards a small yard on the edge of the village, which had once held livestock but was now deserted except by a second, similar girl, a sister perhaps, and a young English soldier who lay on a stretcher motionless. The girls pointed helplessly towards this figure. Guy could not help. The young man was dead, undamaged it seemed. He lay as though at rest. The few corpses which Guy had seen in Crete had sprawled awkwardly. This soldier lay like an effigy on a tomb – like Sir Roger in his shadowy shrine at Santa Dulcina.

Only the bluebottles that clustered round his lips and eyes proclaimed that he was flesh. Why was he lying here? Who were these girls? Had a weary stretcher-party left him in their care and had they watched him die? Had they closed his eyes and composed his limbs? Guy would never know. It remained one of the countless unexplained incidents of war. Meanwhile, lacking words the three of them stood by the body, stiff and mute as figures in a sculptured Deposition.

To bury the dead is one of the corporal works of charity. There were no tools here to break the stony ground. Later, perhaps, the enemy would scavenge the island and tip this body with others into a common pit and the boy's family would get no news of him and wait and hope month after month, year after year. A precept came to Guy's mind from his military education: 'The officer in command of a burial party is responsible for collecting the red identity discs and forwarding them to Records. The green disc remains on the body. If in doubt, gentlemen, remember that green is the colour of putrefaction.'

Guy knelt and took the disc from the cold breast. He read a number, a name, a designation, *RC*. 'May his soul and the souls of all the faithful departed, in the mercy of God, rest in peace.'

Guy stood. The bluebottles returned to the peaceful young face. Guy saluted and passed on.

The country opened and soon Guy came to another village. Toiling beside Fido in the darkness, he had barely noticed it. Now he found a place of some size, other roads and tracks converged on a market square; the houses had large barns behind them; a domed church stood open. Of the original inhabitants there was no sign; instead, English soldiers were posted in doorways – Halberdiers – and at the cross-roads sat Sarum-Smith, smoking a pipe.

'Hullo, uncle. The CO said you were about.'

'I'm glad to find you. I met a windy officer on the road who said you were all in the bag.'

'It doesn't look like it, does it? There was something of a schemozzle last night but we weren't in that.'

Since Guy last saw him in West Africa, Sarum-Smith had matured. He was not a particularly attractive man, but man he was. 'The CO's out with the Adj, going round the companies. You'll find the second-in-command at battalion headquarters, over there.'

Guy went where he was directed, to a farmhouse beside the church. Everything was in order. One notice pointed to the regimental aid post, another to the battalion-office. Guy passed the RSM and the clerks and in the further room of the house found Major Erskine. An army blanket had been spread on the kitchen table. It was, in replica, the orderly room at Penkirk.

Guy saluted.

'Hullo, uncle, you could do with a shave.'

'I could do with some breakfast, sir.'

'Lunch will be coming up as soon as the CO gets back. Brought us some more orders?'

'No, sir.'

'Information?'

'None, sir.'

'What's headquarters up to then?'

'Not functioning much at the moment. I came to get information from you.'

'We don't know much.'

He put Guy in the picture. The Commandos had lost two troops somehow during the night. An enemy patrol had wandered in from the flank during the morning and hurriedly retired. The Commandos were due to come through them soon and take up positions at Imbros. They had motor transport and should not have much difficulty in disengaging. The Second Halberdiers were to hold their present line till midnight and then fall back behind Hookforce to the beach perimeter. 'After that we're in the hands of the navy. Those are the orders as I understand them. I don't know how they'll work out.'

A Halberdier brought Guy a cup of tea.

'Crock,' said Guy, 'I hope you remember me?'

'Sir.'

'Rather different from our last meeting.'

'Sir,' said Crock.

'The enemy aren't attacking in any strength yet,' Major Erskine continued. 'They're just pushing out patrols. As soon as they bump into anything, they stop and try working round. All quite elementary. We could hold them for ever if those blasted Q fellows would do their job. What are we running away for? It's not soldiering as I was taught it.'

A vehicle stopped outside and Guy recognized Colonel Tickeridge's large commanding voice. He went out and found the Colonel and the Adjutant. They were directing the unloading from a lorry of three wounded men, two of them groggily walking, the third lying on a stretcher. As this man was carried past him he turned his white face and Guy recognized one of his former company. The man lay under a blanket. His wound was fresh and he was not yet in much pain. He smiled up quite cheerfully.

'Shanks,' said Guy. 'What have you been doing to yourself?'

'Must have been a mortar bomb, sir. Took us all by surprise, bursting right in the trench. I am lucky, considering. Chap next to me caught a packet.'

This was Halberdier Shanks who, Guy remembered, used to win prizes for the Slow Valse. In the days of Dunkirk he had asked for compassionate leave in order to compete at Blackpool.

'I'll come and talk when the MO's had a look at you.'

'Thank you, sir. Nice to have you back with us.'

The other two men had limped off to the RAP. They must be from D Company too, Guy supposed. He did not remember them; only Halberdier Shanks, because of his Slow Valse.

'Well, uncle, come along in and tell me what I can do for you.'

'I was wondering if there was anything *I* could do for *you*, Colonel.'

'Yes, certainly. You will lay on hot dinners for the battalion, a bath for me, artillery support and a few squadrons of fighter aircraft. That's about all we want this morning, I think.' Colonel Tickeridge was in high good humour. As he entered his headquarters he called: 'Hi, there. Bring on the dancing-girls. Where's Halberdier Gold?'

'Just coming up, sir.'

Halberdier Gold was an old friend, since the evening at Matchet when he had carried Guy's bag from the station, before the question even arose of Guy's joining the corps. He smiled broadly.

'Good morning, Gold; remember me?'

'Good morning, sir. Welcome back to the battalion.'

'Vino,' called Colonel Tickeridge. 'Wine for our guest from the higher formation.'

It was said with the utmost geniality but it struck a slight chill after the men's warmer greeting.

Gold laid a jug of wine on the table with the biscuits and bully beef. While they ate and drank, Colonel Tickeridge told Major Erskine:

'Quite a bit of excitement on the left flank. We were up with D Company and I was just warning Brent to expect fireworks in half an hour or so when the Commandos pull out, when I'm blessed if the blighters didn't start popping off at us with a heavy mortar from the other side of the rocks. De Souza's platoon caught it pretty hot. Lucky we had the truck there to bring back the pieces. We just stopped to watch Brent winkle the mortar out. Then we came straight home. I've made some nice friends out there – a company of New Zealanders who rolled up and said please might they join in our battle – first-class fellows.'

This seemed the moment for Guy to say what had been in his mind since meeting Shanks.

'That's exactly what I want to do, Colonel,' he said. 'Isn't there a platoon you could let me take over?'

Colonel Tickeridge regarded him benevolently. 'No, uncle, of course there isn't.'

'But later in the day, when you get casualties?'

'My good uncle, you aren't under my command. You can't start putting in for a cross-posting in the middle of a battle. That's not how the army works, you know that. You're a Hookforce body.'

'But, Colonel, those New Zealanders –'

'Sorry, uncle. No can do.'

And that, Guy knew from of old, was final.

Colonel Tickeridge began to explain the details of the rear-guard to Major Erskine. Sarum-Smith came to announce that the Commandos were coming through and Guy followed him out into the village and saw a line of dust and the back of the last Hookforce lorry disappearing to the south. There was a little firing, rifles and light machine-guns, and an occasional mortar bomb three-quarters of a mile to the north where the Halberdiers held their line. Guy stood between his friends, isolated.

A few hours earlier he had exulted in his loneliness. Now the case was altered. He was a 'guest from the higher formation', a 'Hookforce body', without place or function, a spectator. And all the deep sense of desolation which he had sought to cure, which from time to time momentarily seemed to be cured, overwhelmed him as of old. His heart sank. It seemed to him as though literally an organ of his body were displaced, subsiding, falling heavily like a feather in a vacuum jar; Philoctetes set apart from his fellows by an old festering wound; Philoctetes without his bow. Sir Roger without his sword.

Presently Colonel Tickeridge cheerfully intruded on his despondency.

'Well, uncle, nice to have seen you. I expect you want to get back to your own people. You'll have to walk, I'm afraid. The Adj and I are going round the companies again.'

'Can I come too?'

Colonel Tickeridge hesitated, then said: 'The more the merrier.'

As they went forward he asked news of Matchet. 'You staff wallahs get all the luck. We've had no mail since we went into Greece.'

The Second Halberdiers and the New Zealanders lay across the main road, their flanks resting on the steep scree that enclosed the valley. D Company were on the far right flank, strung out along a water-course. To reach them there was open ground to be crossed. As Colonel Tickeridge and his party emerged from cover a burst of fire met them.

'Hullo,' he said, 'the Jerries are a lot nearer than they were this morning.'

They ran for some rocks and approached cautiously and circuitously. When they finally dropped into the ditch they found Brent and Sergeant-Major Rawkes. Both were preoccupied and rather grim. They acknowledged Guy's greeting and then turned at once to their CO.

'They've brought up another mortar.'

'Can you pin-point it?'

'They keep moving. They're going easy with their ammunition at present but they've got the range.'

Colonel Tickeridge stood and searched the land ahead through his field-glasses. A bomb burst ten yards behind; all crouched low while a shower of stone and metal rang overhead.

'We haven't anything to spare for a counter-attack,' said Colonel Tickeridge. 'You'll have to give a bit of ground.'

In training Guy had often wondered whether the exercises at Penkirk bore any semblance to real warfare. Here they did. This was no Armageddon, no torrent of uniformed migration, no clash of mechanical monsters; it was the conventional 'battalion in defence', opposed by lightly armed, equally weary small forces. Ritchie-Hook had done little to inculcate the arts of withdrawal, but the present action conformed to pattern. While Colonel Tickeridge gave his orders, Guy moved down the bank. He found de Souza and his depleted platoon. He had a picturesque bandage round his head. Under it his sallow face was grave.

'Lost a bit of my ear,' he said. 'It doesn't hurt. But I'll be glad when today is over.'

'You're retiring at midnight, I gather.'

' "Retiring" is good. It sounds like a maiden aunt going to bed.'

'I dare say you'll be in Alexandria before me,' said Guy. 'Hookforce is last out, covering the embarkation. I don't get the impression that the Germans are anxious to attack.'

'D'you know what I think, uncle? I think they want to escort us quietly into the ships. Then they can sink us at their leisure from the air. A much tidier way of doing things.'

A bomb exploded short of them.

'I wish I could spot that damned mortar,' said de Souza.

Then an orderly summoned him to company headquarters. Guy went with him and rejoined Colonel Tickeridge.

It took little time to mount the withdrawal on the flank. Guy watched the battalion adjust itself to its new line. Everything was done correctly. Colonel Tickeridge gave his orders for the hours of darkness and for the final retreat. Guy made notes of times and lines of march in which the Halberdiers and New Zealanders would pass through Hookforce. Then he took his leave.

'If you run across any blue jobs,' said Colonel Tickeridge, 'tell them to wait for us.'

For the third time Guy followed the road south. Night fell. The road filled with many men. Guy found the remnants of his headquarters where he had left them. He did not inquire for Major Hound. Sergeant Smiley offered no information. They fell in and set out into the darkness. They marched all night, one silent component of the procession of lagging, staggering men.

Another day; another night.

*

'Night and day,' crooned Trimmer, 'you are the one. Only you beneath the moon and under the sun, in the roaring traffic's boom –'

'Listen,' said Ian Kilbannock severely, 'you are coming to the Savoy to meet the American Press.'

'In the silence of my lonely room I think of you.'

'*Trimmer.*'

'I've met them.'

'Not these. These are Scab Dunz, Bum Schlum, and Joe Mulligan. They're great fellows, Scab, Bum, and Joe. Their stories are syndicated all over the United States. Trimmer, if you don't stop warbling I shall recommend your return to regimental duties in Iceland. Bum and Scab are naturally antifascist. Joe is more doubtful. He's Boston Irish and he doesn't awfully care for us.'

'I'm sick of the Press. D'you see what the *Daily Beast* are calling me – "The Demon Barber"?'

'Their phrase, not ours. I wish I'd thought of it.'

'Anyway, I'm lunching with Virginia.'

'I'll get you out of that.'

'It isn't exactly a hard date.'

'Leave it to me.'

Ian picked up the telephone and Trimmer lapsed into song.

'There's oh such a burning, yearning, churning under the hide of me.'

'Virginia? Ian. Colonel Trimmer regrets he's unable to lunch today, madam.'

'The demon barber? It never occurred to me to lunch with him. Ian, do something, will you? for an old friend. Persuade your young hero that he utterly nauseates me.'

'Is that quite kind?'

'There are dozens of girls eager to go out with him. Why must he pick on me?'

'He says there's a voice within him keeps repeating, "You, you, you."'

'Cheek. Tell him to go to hell, Ian, like an angel.'

Ian rang off.

'She says you're to go to hell,' he reported.

'Oh.'

'Why don't you lay off Virginia? There's nothing in it for you.'

'But there is, there was. She can't put on this stand-offish turn with me. Why, in Glasgow –'

'Trimmer, you must have seen enough of me to know that I'm the last man in the world you should choose to confide in – particularly on questions of love. You must forget all about Virginia, all about all these London girls you've been going about with lately. I've got a great treat in store for you. I'm going to take you round the factories. You're going to boost production.

Lunch-hour talks. Canteen dances. We'll find you all kinds of delicious girls. You're in for a lovely time, Trimmer, in the midlands, in the north, far away from London. But meanwhile you must do your bit for Anglo-American relations with Scab and Bum and Joe. There's a war on.'

In the staff-car which took them to the Savoy, Ian tried to put Trimmer in the picture.

'. . . You won't find Joe much interested in military operations, I'm glad to say. He's been brought up to distrust the "red coats". He looks on us all as feudal colonial oppressors, which, I will say for you, Trimmer, you definitely are not. We've got to sell him the new Britain that is being forged in the furnace of war. Dammit, Trimmer, I don't believe you're listening.'

Nor was he. A voice within him kept forlornly repeating, 'You, you, you.'

Ian Kilbannock, like Ludovic, had a gift of tongues. He spoke one language to his friends, another to Trimmer and General Whale, another to Bum, Scab, and Joe.

'Hiya, boys,' he cried, entering the room. 'Look what the cat's brought in.'

It was not for economy that these three fat, untidy men lived cheek by jowl together; their expense accounts were limitless. Nor was it, as sometimes in the past, for motives of professional rivalry; in this city of communiqués and censorship there were no scoops to be had, no need to watch the opposition. It was the simple wish for companionship; their common condition of exile; the state of their nerves. Low diet, deep drinking and nightly alarms had transformed them, or rather had greatly accelerated processes of decay that were barely noticeable in the three far-feared ace reporters who had jauntily landed in England more than a year ago. They had covered the fall of Addis Ababa, of Barcelona, of Vienna, of Prague. They were here to cover the fall of London and the story had somehow gotten stale. Meanwhile they were subject to privations and dangers which, man and boy, they had boastfully endured for days at a time, but which, prolonged indefinitely and widely shared, became irksome.

Their room overlooked the river but the windows had been criss-crossed with sticking plaster and few gleams of sunshine penetrated them. Inside, the electric light burned. There were three typewriters, three cabin-trunks, three beds, a tumbled mass of papers and clothes, numberless cigarette-ends, dirty glasses, clean glasses, empty bottles, full bottles. Three pairs of bloodshot eyes gazed at Trimmer from three putty-coloured faces.

'Bum, Scab, Joe, this is the boy you've all been wanting to meet.'

'Is that a fact?' asked Joe.

'Colonel McTavish, I'm pleased to meet you,' said Bum.

'Colonel Trimmer, I'm pleased to meet you,' said Scab.

'Hey,' said Joe. 'Who is this joker? McTavish? Trimmer?'

'That is still being discussed at a high level,' said Ian. 'I'll let you know for certain before your story is released.'

'What story?' asked Joe balefully.

Scab came to the rescue.

'Don't mind Joe, Colonel. Let me fix you a drink.'

'Joe isn't feeling too hot this morning,' said Bum.

'I just asked what's the guy's name and what's the story. What's not too hot about that?'

'What say we all have a drink?' said Bum.

Of Trimmer's abounding weaknesses hard drinking was not one. He did not enjoy whisky before luncheon. He refused the glass thrust upon him.

'What's wrong with the guy?' asked Joe.

'Commando training,' said Ian.

'Is that so? Well, I'm just a goddam newsman and I don't train. When a guy won't drink with me, I drink alone.'

Scab was the most courtly of the trio.

'I can guess where you want to be right now, Colonel,' he said.

'Yes,' said Trimmer, 'Glasgow, in the station hotel, in a fog.'

'No, sir. Where you want to be right now is in Crete. Your boys are putting up a wonderful fight there. You heard the Old Man on the radio last night? There is no question, he said, of evacuating Crete. The attack has been held. The defence is being reinforced. It's a turning-point. There's going to be no more withdrawal.'

'We're with you in this,' said Bum generously, 'all the way. I don't say there haven't been times I've hated you limeys' guts. Abyssinia, Spain, Munich, that's all done with, Colonel. What wouldn't I give to be in Crete. That's where the news is today.'

'You may remember,' said Ian, 'you asked me to bring Colonel McTavish to lunch. You thought he could give you a story.'

'That's right. We did, didn't we? Well, how about we have another drink first, even if the Colonel can't join us?'

They drank and they smoked. The hands which lit the cigarettes became steadier with each glass, the genial tones more emotional.

'I like you, Ian, even if you are a lord. Hell, a man can't help it if he's a lord. You're all right, Ian, I like you.'

'Thank you, Bum.'

'I like the Colonel too. He don't say much and he don't drink any but I like him. He's a regular guy.'

Even Joe softened enough to say: 'Anybody says the Colonel isn't all right, I'll punch his teeth in.'

'Everyone says the Colonel's all right, Joe.'

'They better.'

Presently the time for luncheon passed.

'There isn't anything fit to eat around here, anyway,' said Joe.

'I'm not hungry right now myself,' said Bum.

'Food? I can take it or leave it,' said Scab.

'Now, boys,' said Ian. 'Colonel McTavish is a pretty busy man. He's here to give you his story. How about asking him anything you want now?'

'All right,' said Joe. 'What else have you done, Colonel? That raid of yours was good copy. They ate it up back home. You got decorated. You got made Colonel. So what? Where else have you been? Tell us what you did this week and the week before. How come you're not in Crete?'

'I've been on leave,' said Trimmer.

'Well, that's a hell of a story.'

'Here's the angle, boys,' said Ian. 'The Colonel here is a portent – the new officer which is emerging from the old hide-bound British Army.'

'How do I know he's not high-bound?'

'Joe, you don't have to be so suspicious,' said Scab. 'Anyone with eyes in his head can see he isn't hide-bound.'

'He doesn't *look* high-bound,' Joe conceded, 'but how do I know he *isn't*. Are you high-bound?'

'He's not hide-bound,' said Ian.

'Why don't you let the Colonel answer for himself? I put it to you, Colonel, are you or are you not high-bound?'

'No,' said Trimmer.

'That's all I wanted to know,' said Joe.

'You asked him. He told you,' said Bum.

'Now I know. So what the hell?'

Presently through the fumes of tobacco and whisky a great earnestness enveloped Scab.

'You're not hide-bound, Colonel, and I'll tell you why. You've had advantages these stuff-shirts haven't had. You've worked, Colonel. And where have you worked? On an ocean liner. And who have you worked for? For American womanhood. Am I right or am I right? It all ties in. I can make a great piece out of this. How it's the casual personal contacts that make international alliances. The beauty parlour as the school of democracy. You must have had some very very lovely contacts on that ocean liner, Colonel.'

'I had the pick of the bunch,' said Trimmer.

'Tell them,' said Ian, 'about your American friends.'

A small pink gleam of professional interest broke in the journalists' eyes while Trimmer by contrast lapsed into trance.

'There was Mrs Troy,' he began.

'I don't think that's quite what the boys want,' said Ian.

'Not every voyage, of course, but two or three times a year. Four times in 1938 when half our regulars were keeping away because of the situation in Europe. *She* wasn't afraid,' mused Trimmer. 'I always looked for her name on the passenger list. Before it was printed I used to slip into the office and take a dekko. There was something about her – well, you know how it is – like music. When she had a hangover I was the only one who could help. There was something about me, she said, the way I massaged the back of her neck.'

'But you must have met other, more typical Americans?'

'She isn't typical. She isn't American except she married one and she hadn't any use for him. She's something quite apart.'

'They aren't interested in Mrs Troy,' said Ian. 'Tell them about the others.'

'Old trouts mostly,' said Trimmer. 'Mrs Stuyvesant Oglander. There were smart ones too, of course, Astors, Vanderbilts, Cuttings, Whitneys – they all came to me, but nobody was like Mrs Troy.'

'What I had in mind for my readers, Colonel, was something a little more homy.'

Trimmer had his pride. He awoke now from his reverie, sharply piqued.

'I never touched the homy ones,' he said.

'Goddammit,' cried Joe in triumph. 'What d'you know? The Colonel *is* high-bound.'

Then Ian abandoned this phase of Anglo-American friendship and within a few minutes he and Trimmer stood in the Strand vainly searching for a taxi. It was the moment of Guy's despair at Babali Hani. Their prospect, too, was dismal. The London crowd shuffled past, men in a diversity of drab uniforms, women in the strange new look of the decade – trousered, turbaned, cigarettes adhering and drooping from grubby weary faces; all of them surfeited with tea and Woolton pies, all of them bearing gas-masks which bumped and swung to their ungainly tread.

'You didn't do very well,' said Ian severely.

'I'm hungry.'

'You won't find anything to eat at this time of day. I'm going home.'

'Shall I come with you?'

'No.'

'Will Virginia be there?'

'I shouldn't think so.'

'She was when you telephoned.'

'She was just going out.'

'I haven't seen her for a week. She's given up her job at the Transit Camp. I've asked the other girls. They won't say where she's working. You know how girls are.'

Ian looked sorrowfully at his protégé. It was in his mind to offer some sort of exhortation, to remind him of the coming delights of the armament industry, but Trimmer looked so sorrowfully back at him that he merely said: 'Well, I'm walking to HOO HQ. You'll be hearing from me,' and turning, set off towards Trafalgar Square.

Trimmer followed as far as the Tube station, then broke off without a word and descended, a sad little song in his heart, to a platform lined with bunks where he waited long for a crowded train.

At Marchmain House HOO HQ, revitalized by the new exalted enthusiasm for Special Service troops, was expanding. More flats were added and more faces. It was here, in Ian's office, that Virginia Troy had taken refuge.

'Have you shaken off the Demon?' she asked.

'He just melted away, humming horribly. Virginia, I've got to talk to you seriously about Trimmer. The welfare of the department is at stake. Do you realize that he constitutes our sole contribution to the war effort to date? I have never seen a man so changed by success. A month ago he was all bounce. With that accent, that smile and that lock of hair he was absolutely cut out to be a great national figure. Look at him today. I doubt if he'll last the summer. I've already seen Air Marshal Beech break up under my eyes. I know the symptoms. It mustn't happen again. I shall get a bad name in the service and this time it isn't my fault at all. As the victim has remarked, it's you, you, you. Do I have to remind you that you came to me with tears and made my home life hideous until I got you this job? I expect a little loyalty in return.'

'But, Ian, why d'you suppose I wanted to leave the canteen except to get away from Trimmer?'

'I thought you were bored with Brenda and Zita.'

'Only because they always had Trimmer around.'

'Ah,' said Ian. 'Oh.' He twiddled with things on his desk. 'What's all this about Glasgow?' he asked.

'Oh, *that*,' she said. 'That was nothing. That was fun. Not a bit like what's going on now.'

'Now the poor beast thinks he's in love.'

'Yes, it's too indecent.'

On 31 May, Guy sat in a cave overhanging the beach of Sphakia where the final embarkation was shortly to begin. By his watch it was not yet ten o'clock but it seemed the dead of night. Nothing stirred in the moonlight. In the crowded ravine below the Second Halberdiers stood in column of companies, every man in full marching order, waiting for the boats. Hookforce was deployed on the ridge above, holding the perimeter against an enemy who since sunset had fallen silent. Guy had brought his section here late that afternoon. They had marched all the previous night and most of that day, up the pass, down to Imbros, down a gully to this last position. They dropped asleep where they halted. Guy had sought out and found Creforce headquarters and brought from them to the Hookforce commanders the last grim orders.

He dozed and woke for seconds at a time, barely thinking.

There were footsteps outside. Guy had not troubled to post a look-out. Ivor Claire's troop was a few hundred yards distant. He went to the mouth of the cave and in the moonlight saw a familiar figure and heard a familiar voice: 'Guy? Ivor.'

Ivor entered and sat beside him.

They sat together, speaking between long pauses in the listless drawl of extreme fatigue.

'This is a damn fool business, Guy.'

'It will all be over tomorrow.'

'Just beginning. You're sure Tony Luxmore hasn't got the wrong end of the stick? I was at Dunkirk, you know. Not much fuss about priorities there. No inquiries afterwards. It doesn't make any sense, leaving the fighting troops behind and taking off the rabble. Tony's all in. I bet he muddled his orders.'

'I've got them all in writing from the GOC. Surrender at dawn. The men aren't supposed to know yet.'

'They know all right.'

'The General's off in a flying-boat tonight.'

'No staying with the sinking ship.'

'Napoleon didn't stay with his army after Moscow.'

Presently Ivor said: 'What does one *do* in prison?'

'I imagine a ghastly series of concert parties – perhaps for years. I've a nephew who was captured at Calais. D'you imagine one can do anything about getting posted where one wants?'

'I presume so. One usually can.'

Another pause.

'There would be no sense in the GOC sitting here to be captured.'

'None at all. No sense in any of us staying.'

Another pause.

'Poor Freda,' said Ivor. 'Poor Freda She'll be an old dog by the time I see her again.'

Guy briefly fell asleep. Then Ivor said: 'Guy, what would you do if you were challenged to a duel?'

'Laugh.'

'Yes, of course.'

'What made you think of that now?'

'I was thinking about honour. It's a thing that changes, doesn't it? I mean, a hundred and fifty years ago we would have had to fight if challenged. Now we'd laugh. There must have been a time a hundred years or so ago when it was rather an awkward question.'

'Yes. Moral theologians were never able to stop duelling – it took democracy to do that.'

'And in the next war, when we are completely democratic, I expect it will be quite honourable for officers to leave their men behind. It'll be laid down in King's Regulations as their duty – to keep a *cadre* going to train new men to take the place of prisoners.'

'Perhaps men wouldn't take kindly to being trained by deserters.'

'Don't you think in a really modern army they'd respect them the more for being fly? I reckon our trouble is that we're at the awkward stage – like a man challenged to a duel a hundred years ago.'

Guy could see him clearly in the moonlight, the austere face, haggard now but calm and recollected, as he had first seen it in the Borghese Gardens. It was his last sight of him. Ivor stood up saying: 'Well, the path of honour lies up the hill,' and he strolled away.

And Guy fell asleep.

He dreamed continuously, it seemed to him, and most prosaically. All night in the cave he marched, took down orders, passed them on, marked his map, marched again, while the moon set and the ships came into the bay and the boats went back and forth between them and the beach, and the ships sailed away leaving Hookforce and five or six thousand other men behind them. In Guy's dreams there were no exotic visitants among the shades of Creforce, no absurdity, no escape. Everything was as it had been the preceding day, the preceding night, night and day since he had landed at Suda, and when he awoke at dawn it was to the same half-world; sleeping and waking were like two airfields, identical in aspect though continents apart. He had no clear apprehension that this was a fatal morning, that he was that day to resign an immeasurable piece of his manhood. He saw himself dimly at a great distance. Weariness was all.

'They say the ships left food on the beach,' said Sergeant Smiley.

'We'd better have a meal before we go to prison.'

'It's true then, sir, what they're saying, that there's no more ships coming?'

'Quite true, Sergeant.'

'And we're to surrender?'

'Quite true.'

'It don't seem right.'

The golden dawn was changing to unclouded blue. Guy led his section down the rough path to the harbour. The quay was littered with abandoned equipment and the wreckage of bombardment. Among the scrap and waste stood a pile of rations – bully beef and biscuit – and a slow-moving concourse of soldiers foraging. Sergeant Smiley pushed his way through them and passed back half a dozen tins. There was a tap of fresh water running to waste in the wall of a ruined building. Guy and his section filled their bottles, drank deep, refilled them, turned off the tap; then breakfasted. The little town was burned, battered and deserted by its inhabitants. The ghosts of an army teemed everywhere. Some were quite apathetic, too weary to eat; others were smashing their rifles on the stones, taking a fierce relish in this symbolic farewell to their arms; an officer stamped on his binoculars; a motor bicycle was burning; there was a small group under command of a sapper Captain doing something to a seedy-looking fishing-boat that lay on its side, out of the water, on the beach. One man sat on the sea-wall methodically stripping down his Bren and throwing the parts separately far into the scum. A very short man was moving from group to group saying: 'Me surrender? Not bloody likely. I'm for the hills. Who's coming with me?' like a preacher exhorting a doomed congregation to flee from the wrath to come.

'Is there anything in that, sir?' asked Sergeant Smiley.

'Our orders are to surrender,' said Guy. 'If we go into hiding the Cretans will have to look after us. If the Germans found us we should only be marched off as prisoners of war – our friends would be shot.'

'Put like that, sir, it doesn't seem right.'

Nothing seemed right that morning, nothing seemed real.

'I imagine a party of senior officers have gone forward already to find the right person to surrender to.'

An hour passed.

Ths short man filled his haversack with food, slung three water-bottles from his shoulders, changed his rifle for the pistol which an Australian gunner was about to throw away, and bowed under his load, sturdily strutted off out of their sight. Out to sea, beyond the mouth of the harbour, the open sea calmly glittered. Flies everywhere buzzed and settled. Guy had not taken off his clothes since he left the destroyer. He said: 'I'll tell you what I'm going to do, Sergeant. I'm going to bathe.'

'Not in *that*, sir?'

'No. There'll be clean water round the point.'

Sergeant Smiley and two men went with him. There was no giving of orders that day. They found a cleft in the rocky spur that enclosed the harbour. They strolled through and came to a little cove, a rocky foreshore, deep clear water. Guy stripped and dived and swam out in a sudden access of euphoria; he turned on his back and floated, his eyes closed to the sun, his ears sealed to every sound, oblivious of everything except physical ease, solitary and exultant. He turned and swam and floated again and swam; then he struck out for the shore, making for the opposite side. The cliffs here ran down into deep water. He stretched up and found a handhold in a shelf of rock. It was already warm with the sun. He pulled up, rested luxuriously on his forearms with his legs dangling knee deep in water, paused, for he was feebler than a week ago, then raised his head and found himself staring straight into the eyes of another, a man who was seated above him on the black ledge and gazing down at him; a strangely clean and sleek man for Creforce; his eyes in the brilliant sunshine were the colour of oysters.

'Can I give you a hand, sir?' asked Corporal-Major Ludovic. He stood and stooped and drew Guy out of the sea. 'A smoke, sir?'

He offered a neat, highly pictorial packet of Greek cigarettes. He struck a light. Guy sat beside him, naked and wet and smoking.

'Where on earth have you been, Corporal-Major?'

'At my post, sir. With rear headquarters.'

'I thought you'd deserted us?'

'Did you, sir? Perhaps we both made a miscalculation.'

'Have you seen Major Hound?'

'Oh yes, sir. I was with him until – as long as he needed me, sir.'

'Where is he now? Why have you left him?'

'Need we go into that, sir? Wouldn't you say it was rather too early or rather too late for inquiries of that sort?'

'What are you doing here?'

'To be quite frank, sir, I was considering drowning myself. I am a weak swimmer and the sea is most inviting. You know something of theology, I believe, sir, I've seen some of your books. Would moralists hold it was suicide if one were just to swim out to sea, sir, in the fanciful hope of reaching Egypt? I haven't the gift of faith myself, but I have always been intrigued by theological speculation.'

'You had better rejoin Sergeant Smiley and the remains of headquarters.'

'You speak as an officer, sir, or as a theologian?'

'Neither really,' said Guy.

He stood up.

'If you aren't going to finish that cigarette, may I have it back?' Corporal Ludovic carefully pinched off the glowing end and returned the half to its packet. 'Gold-dust,' he said, relapsing into the language of the barracks. 'I'll follow you round, sir.'

Guy dived and swam back. By the time he was dressed, Corporal-Major Ludovic was among them. Sergeant Smiley nodded dully. Without speaking, they strolled together into Sphakia. The crowd of soldiers had grown and was growing as unsteady files shuffled down from their hiding-places in the hills. Nothing remained of the ration dump. Men were sitting about with their backs against the ruined walls eating. The point of interest now was the boating party who were pushing their craft towards the water. The sapper Captain was directing them in a stronger voice than Guy had heard for some days.

'Easy ... All together, now, heave ... steady ... keep her moving ...' The men were enfeebled but the boat moved. The beach was steep and slippery with weed. '... Now then, once more all together ... she's off ... let her run ... What ho, she floats ...'

Guy pushed forward in the crowd.

'They're barmy,' said a man next to him. 'They haven't a hope in hell.'

The boat was afloat. Three men, waist deep, held her; the Captain and the rest of his party climbed on board and began bailing out and working on the engine. Guy watched them.

'Anyone else coming?' the sapper called.

Guy waded to him.

'What are your chances?' he asked.

'One in ten, I reckon, of being picked up. One in five of making it on our own. We're not exactly well found. Coming?'

Guy made no calculation. Nothing was measurable that morning. He was aware only of the wide welcome of the open sea, of the satisfaction of finding someone else to take control of things.

'Yes. I'll just talk to my men.'

The engine gave out a puff of oily smoke and a series of small explosions.

'Tell them to make up their minds. We'll be off as soon as that thing starts up.'

Guy said to his section: 'There's one chance in five of getting away. I'm going. Decide for yourselves.'

'Not for me, sir, thank you,' said Sergeant Smiley. 'I'll stick to dry land.'

The other men of his Intelligence section shook their heads.

'How about you, Corporal-Major? You can be confident that no moral theologian would condemn this as suicide.'

Corporal-Major Ludovic turned his pale eyes out to sea and said nothing.

The sapper shouted: 'Liberty boat just leaving. Anyone else want to come?'

'I'm coming,' Guy shouted.

He was at the side of the boat when he noticed that Ludovic was close behind him. The engine started up, drowning the sound which Ludovic had heard. They climbed on board together. One of the watching crowd called, 'Good luck, chums,' and his words were taken up by a few others, but did not carry above the noise of the engine.

The sapper steered. They moved quite fast across the water, out of the oil and floating refuse. As they watched they saw that the crowd on shore had all turned their faces skyward.

'Stukas again,' said the sapper.

'Well, it's all over now. I suppose they've just come to have a look at their spoils.'

The men on shore seemed to be of this opinion. Few of them took cover. The match was over, stumps drawn. Then the bombs began to fall among them.

'Bastards,' said the sapper.

From the boat they saw havoc. One of the aeroplanes dipped over their heads, fired its machine-gun, missed and turned away. Nothing further was done to molest them. Guy saw more bombs burst on the now-deserted waterfront. His last thoughts were of X Commando, of Bertie and Eddie, most of all of Ivor Claire, waiting at their posts to be made prisoner. At the moment there was nothing in the boat for any of them to do. They had merely to sit still in the sunshine and the fresh breeze.

So they sailed out of the picture.

7

Silence was all. Ripeness was all. Silence swelled lusciously like a ripening fig, while through the hospital the softly petulant north-west wind, which long ago delayed Helen and Menelaus on that strand, stirred and fluttered.

This silence was Guy's private possession, all his own work.

There were exterior sounds in plenty, a wireless down the corridor, another wireless in the block beyond the window, the constant jingle of trolleys, footsteps, voices; that day as each preceding day people came into Guy's room and spoke to him. He heard them and understood and was as little tempted to answer as to join in the conversation of actors on a stage; there was an orchestra pit, footlights, a draped proscenium, between him and all these people. He lay like an explorer in his lamp-lit tent while in the darkness outside the anthropophagi peered and jostled.

There had been a silent woman in Guy's childhood named Mrs Barnet. He was often taken to visit her by his mother. She lay in the single upper room of a cottage which smelled of paraffin and geraniums and of Mrs Barnet. Her niece, a woman of great age by Guy's standards, stood and answered his mother's inquiries. His mother sat on the only chair by the bedside and Guy stood beside her, watching them all and the pious plaster statues which clustered everywhere round Mrs Barnet's bed. It was the niece who said thank you for the provisions Guy's mother brought and said, when they left: 'Auntie does so appreciate your coming, ma'am.'

The old woman never spoke. She lay with her hands on the patchwork quilt and gazed at the lamp-stained paper on the ceiling, a paper which, where the light struck it, revealed a sheen of pattern like the starched cloth on the dining-room table at home. Her head lay still but she moved her eyes to follow the movements in her room. Her hands turned and twitched, ceaselessly but very slightly. The stairs were precipitous and enclosed top and bottom by thin, grained doors. The old niece followed them down into the parlour and into the village street, thanking them for their visit.

'Mummy, why do we visit Mrs Barnet?'

'Oh, we have to. She's been like that ever since I came to Broome.'

'But does she know us, Mummy?'

'I'm sure she'd miss it, if we didn't come.'

His brother Ivo had been silent, too, Guy remembered, in the time before he went away, sitting all day sometimes in the long gallery doing nothing, sitting aloof at the table while others were talking, quite alert and quite speechless.

In the nursery Guy had had his own periods of silence. 'Swallowed your tongue, have you?' Nannie would ask. It was in similar tones that the Sister addressed him, coming in four or five times in the day with a cheerful rallying challenge. 'Nothing to say to us today?'

The lame Hussar who brought round the whisky-and-soda at sundown lost patience sooner. At first he had tried to be friendly. 'Tommy Blackhouse is two doors down asking for you. I've known Tommy for years. Wish I could have joined his outfit. Rotten show their all getting put in the bag ... I caught my little packet at Tobruk ...' and so on. But when Guy lay mute, he gave it up and now stood equally silent with his tray of glasses waiting while Guy drank.

Once the Chaplain had come.

'I've got you listed as Catholic – is that right?'

Guy did not answer.

'I'm sorry to hear you aren't feeling too good. Anything you want? Anything I can do? Well, I'm always about. You've only to ask for me.' Still Guy did not answer. 'I'll just leave this with you,' said the priest, putting a rosary into his hands, and that was relevant to Guy's thoughts for the last thing he remembered was praying. They had all prayed in the boat in the days of extremity, some offering to do a deal: 'Get me out of here, God, and I'll live different. Honest I will,' others repeating lines of hymns remembered from childhood; all save Ludovic, godless at the helm.

There was one clear moment of revelation between great voids when Guy discovered himself holding in his hand, not, as he supposed, Gervase's medal, but the red identity disc of an unknown soldier, and heard himself saying preposterously: 'Saint Roger of Waybroke defend us in the day of battle and be our safeguard against the wickedness and snares of the devil ...'

After that all was silence.

Guy lay with his hands on the cotton sheet rehearsing his experiences.

Could there be experience without memory? Could there be memory where fact and fancy were indistinguishable, where time was fragmentary and elastic, made up of minutes that seemed like days, of days like minutes? He could talk if he wished to. He must guard that secret from them. Once he spoke he would re-enter their world, he would be back in the picture.

There had been an afternoon in the boat, in the early days of anxiety and

373

calculation, when they had all sung 'God save the King'. That was in thanksgiving. An aeroplane with RAF markings had come out of the sky, had changed course, circled and hurtled over their heads, twice. They had all waved and the machine had soared away to the south towards Africa. Deliverance seemed certain then. The sapper ordered watches; all next day they kept a look-out for the boat which must be on its way, which never came. That night hope died and soon the pain of privation gave place to inertia. The sapper who had been so brisk and busy lapsed into a daze. Fuel had given out. They had hoisted the sail. It needed little management. Sometimes it hung slack, sometimes it filled to the breeze. The men sprawled comatose, muttering and snoring. Suddenly the sapper shouted frantically, 'I know what you're up to.' No one answered him. He turned to Ludovic and cried, 'You thought I was asleep, but I heard you. I heard everything.'

Ludovic gazed palely and silently. The sapper said with intense malevolence:

'Understand this. If I go, you go with me.'

Then, exhausted, he sank his head on his blistered knees. Guy between dozing and waking, prayed.

Later – that day? the next? the day after? – the sapper moved to a place beside Guy and whispered: 'I want your pistol, please.'

'Why?'

'I threw mine away before I found this boat. I'm skipper here. I'm the only man entitled to arms.'

'Nonsense.'

'Are you in this too?'

'I don't know what you're talking about.'

'No, that's right isn't it? You were asleep. But I heard them, while you were asleep. I know their plans, *his* plan,' he said, nodding towards Ludovic. 'So, you see, don't you, I *must* have your pistol, *please*.'

Guy looked into the wild eyes and took the pistol from his holster.

'If you fall asleep again *he*'ll get hold of it. That's his plan. I'm the only man who can stay awake. I've got to keep awake. If I go to sleep, *he*'s got us all.' The mad eyes were full of pleading. 'So you see, please, I must have the pistol.'

Guy said: 'That's the best place for it,' and dropped the weapon over the side of the boat.

'Oh, you fool, you bloody fool. He's got us now.'

'Lie down,' said Guy. 'Keep quiet. You'll make yourself ill.'

'One against the lot of you,' said the sapper. 'All alone.'

And that night between moonset and sunrise he disappeared. At dawn the sail hung limp. There was no fixed point anywhere on the horizon to tell them whether they were motionless or drifting with the current and there was no sign of the sapper.

What else was real? The bugs. They were a surprise at first. Guy had always thought of the sea as specially clean. But all the old timbers of the boat were full of bugs. At night they swarmed everywhere, stabbing and stinking. By day they crawled into the shady places of the body, behind the knees, on the back of the neck, on the under cheek. They were real. But what of the whales? There was an hour of moonlight quite clear in Guy's mind when he had awoken to hear all the surrounding water singing with a single low resonant note and to see all round them huge shining humps of meat heaving and wallowing. Had they been real? Had the fog been real that descended and enclosed them and vanished again as swiftly as it came? And the turtles? That night or another, after the moon had set, Guy saw the calm plain fill with myriads of cats' eyes. There was some life still, which Guy was husbanding, in the battery of his torch. He cast a dim beam outward and saw the whole surface of the water encrusted with carapaces gently bobbing one against the other and numberless ageless lizard-faces gaping at him as far as his light reached.

Guy still cogitated these dubious episodes while his health waxed as though the sap were rising vernally in a dry twig. They had tended him carefully. At first while he was still dazed with morphia, they suspended a jar of salts above him and ran a rubber tube from it into the vein of his arm just as gardeners fatten vegetable marrows for the Flower Show, and his horrible tongue had become small and red and wet once more as the liquid surged through him. They had oiled him like a cricket-bat and his old, wrinkled skin grew smooth. Very soon the hollow eyes that glared so fiercely from the shaving-glass had resumed their habitual soft melancholy. The wild illusions of his mind had given place to intermittent sleep and vague, calm consciousness.

In his first days he had gratefully drunk the fragrant cups of malty beverages and the tepid rice-water. Appetite lagged behind his physical advance. They put him on 'light diet', boiled fish and sago, and he ate nothing. They promoted him to tinned herrings, bully beef and great boiled potatoes, blue and yellow, and cheese.

'How's he eating?' the inspecting Colonel always asked.

'Only fair,' the Sister reported.

Guy was a nuisance to this stout, kindly and rather breathless officer. He knew it and was sorry.

The Colonel tried many forms of appeal from the peremptory, 'Come along, Crouchback. Snap out of it,' to the solicitous: 'What you need is sick leave. You could go anywhere – Palestine if you liked. Feed yourself up. Just make the effort.' The Colonel sent a psychiatrist to him, a neurotic whom Guy easily baffled by his unbroken silence. At last the Colonel said: 'Crouchback, I have to tell you that your papers have come through. Your temporary appointment ceased on the day of the capitulation in Crete. As from the first of this month you revert to Lieutenant. Can't you understand, man,' he cried in exasperation; 'you're losing *money* lying there?'

There was real urgency in the appeal. Guy would have liked to reassure him, but by now he had lost the knack, just as once on a visit to England before the war, when he was very tired, he had unaccountably found himself impotent to tie his bow tie. He had repeated what seemed to be the habitual movements; each time the knot either fell apart or else produced a bow that stood rigidly perpendicular. For ten minutes he had struggled at his glass before ringing for help. Next evening and on all subsequent evenings he had performed the little feat of dexterity without difficulty. So now, moved by the earnestness of the senior medical officer, he wished to speak and could not.

The senior medical officer examined the charts on which were recorded Guy's normal temperature, his steady pulse and the regular motions of his body.

The senior officer handed the charts to a Sister in a red cape, who handed them to a Sister in a striped cape, and the procession left him alone.

Outside the door he spoke anxiously and reluctantly about moving Guy to an 'observation ward'.

But mad or sane, Guy offered no scope for an observer. He lay like Mrs Barnet with his hands on the cotton sheet, scarcely moving.

When release came it was not through official channels.

Quite suddenly one morning a new clear voice called Guy irresistibly to order.

'*C'e scappato il Capitano.*'

Mrs Stitch, a radiant contrast to the starched and hooded nurses who had been Guy's only visitants, stood at his door. Without effort or deliberation Guy replied: '*No Capitano oggi, signora, Tenente.*'

She came and sat on the bed and immediately plunged into the saga of a watch which the King of Egypt had given her and how Algie Stitch had doubted whether she should accept it and how the Ambassador had been in no doubts at all and what the Commander-in-Chief's sister had said. 'I can't help it, I *like* the King.' And she produced the watch from her bag – not the basket today, something fresh and neat from New York – and set it to do its tricks. It was a weighty, elaborately hideous mechanism of the Second Empire, jewelled and enamelled and embellished with cupids which clumsily gavotted as the hours struck, and Guy found himself answering easily.

Presently Mrs Stitch said: 'I've just been talking to Tommy Blackhouse. He's down the passage with his leg strung up to the roof. I wanted to take him home with me but they won't let him move. He sent you all sorts of messages. He wants your help writing to next-of-kin of his Commando. That was an awful business.'

'Yes, Tommy was lucky to be out of it.'

'Eddie and Bertie – all one's friends.'

'And Ivor.'

Guy had thought long of Ivor in his silent days, that young prince of Athens sent as sacrifice to the Cretan labyrinth.

'Oh, Ivor's all right,' said Mrs Stitch. 'Never better. He's just been staying with me.'

'*All right?* How? In a boat like me?'

'Well, not quite like you. More comfortable. Trust Ivor for that.'

Like the saline solution which had dripped through the rubber tube into his punctured arm, this news of Ivor oozed through Guy, healing and quickening.

'That's lovely,' he said. 'That's really delightful. It's the best thing that's happened.'

'Well, of course *I* think so,' said Mrs Stitch. 'I'm on Ivor's side always.'

Guy did not notice any qualification in her tone. He was too much exhilarated by the thought of his friend's escape.

'Is he about? Make him come and see me.'

'He's not about. He left yesterday, in fact, for India.'

'Why India?'

'He was sent for. The Viceroy is a sort of cousin. He claimed him.'

'I can't imagine Ivor being made to do anything he didn't want.'

'I think he wanted to go, all right – after all, it's about the only place left where there's plenty of horses.'

At that moment the Sister brought in the tray.

'I say, is that what they give you to eat? It looks revolting.'

'It is.'

Mrs Stitch took a spoon and sampled the luncheon.

'You can't eat this.'

'Not very well. Tell me about Ivor. When did he get out?'

'More than a week ago. With all the others.'

'What others? *Did* any of Hookforce get away?'

'I think so. Tommy told me there were some signallers and a Staff Captain.'

'But X Commando?'

'No. I don't think there were actually any others of them.'

'But I don't quite understand. What was Ivor doing?'

'It's a saga. I can't embark on it now.' She rang a chime on her watch and set the cupids dancing. 'I'll come back. It's lovely seeing you so well. They gave me quite a different account of you.'

'I was with Ivor the last evening in Crete.'

'Were you, Guy?'

'We had a long gloomy talk about the surrender. I can't understand what happened after that.'

'I imagine everything was pretty complete chaos.'

'Yes.'

'And everyone too tired and hungry to remember anything.'

'More or less everyone.'

'No one making much sense.'

'Not many.'

'No one with much reason to be proud of themselves.'

'Not a great many.'

'Exactly what I've said all along,' said Mrs Stitch triumphantly. 'Obviously, by the end there *weren't* any orders.'

It was Guy's first conversation since his return to consciousness. He was a little dizzy, but it came to him, nevertheless, that an attempt was being made at – to put it in its sweetest form – cajolery.

'There were orders, all right,' he said, 'perfectly clear ones.'

'Were there, Guy? Are you sure?'

'Quite sure.'

Mrs Stitch seemed to have lost her impatience to leave. She sat very still, with the funny watch in her hands. 'Guy,' she said, 'I think I'd better tell you, there are a lot of beastly people about at the moment. They aren't all being awfully nice about Ivor. As you remember them, there wasn't anything in those orders to give the impression Ivor was meant to stay behind and be taken prisoner, was there?'

'Yes.'

'Oh ... I don't suppose you remember them very well.'

'I've got them written down.'

Her splendid eyes travelled over the poor little room and came to rest on the locker which held all Guy's possessions.

'In there?'

'Presumably. I haven't looked.'

'I suppose they were countermanded.'

'I don't know who by. The General had left.'

'What happened,' said Julia as though at repetition in the schoolroom, 'was an order from the beach for Hookforce to embark immediately. Ivor was sent down to verify it. He met the naval officer in charge who told him that guides had been sent back and that Hookforce was already on its way. His ship was just leaving. There was another staying for Hookforce. He ordered him into the boat straight away. Until Ivor reached Alexandria he thought the rest of Hookforce was in the other cruiser. When he found it wasn't, he was in rather a jam. That's what happened. So you see no one can blame Ivor, can they?'

'Is that his story?'

'It's our story.'

'Why did he run off to India?'

'That was my idea. It seemed just the ticket. He had to go somewhere. Tommy's Commando doesn't exist any more. Ivor's regiment's not here. He couldn't spend the rest of the war in the Mohamed Ali Club, I mean. It was seeing him so much about, made people gossip. Of course,' she added, 'there was no reason then to expect anyone from Hookforce to turn up until after the war. What are you going to do with those notes of yours?'

'I suppose someone will want to see them.'

'Not Tommy.'

She was right in that. After she left, Guy walked down the passage to Tommy's room. He passed the Sister on the way.

'I was just going to talk to Colonel Blackhouse.'

'*Talk?*' she said. '*Talk?* It's plain to see *you've* had a visitor.'

Tommy lay with his leg in plaster, suspended on a line from a pulley. He greeted Guy with delight.

'They ought to recommend you for an MC or something,' he said. 'Trouble is, of course, Crete wasn't all that successful. They prefer handing out decorations after a victory. Were you ever actually in command of the party?'

'No. There was a sapper who did everything at first. After we lost him, we more or less drifted I think.'

'What became of Hound?'

'I've no idea. Ludovic is the only man who can tell you that.'

'I gather Ludovic turned out well.'

'Did he?'

'First class. It was he who carried you ashore at Sidi Barani, you know.'

'I didn't know.'

'He must be strong as a horse. He was only in hospital two days. I've put him in for a commission. I can't say I ever liked the fellow much, but clearly I was wrong, as usual. The nurses told me you were off your head, Guy. You seem all right to me.'

'Julia Stitch called this morning.'

'Yes, she told me on her way out. She's going to try and get you moved up to her house.'

'She told me about Ivor.'

'Yes. So she said.' The professional wariness which Guy well knew in Tommy now clouded his frank and friendly expression. 'Ivor was in great form. They wouldn't let him go and see you. He was full of congratulations on your getting away. Pity he had to go off so soon.'

'Did he tell you the story of his own escape?'

'One version of it.'

'You didn't believe it?'

'My dear Guy, what d'you take me for? No one believes it, least of all Julia.'

'You aren't going to do anything about it?'

'*I*? It's nothing to do with me, thank God. My position at the moment is Major, waiting re-posting on discharge from hospital. Ivor's put up a pretty poor show. *We* know that – you won't find me applying for him a second time. Julia's got him out of the way. She had to work hard to do it, I can tell you. Now the best thing is for everyone to keep quiet and forget the whole business. It's far too big a thing for anyone to *do* anything about. He might have to stand court-martial for desertion in the face of the enemy. That would be the bloody hell of a thing. They shot people for it in the last war. Of course no one's going to *do* anything. Come to think of it, it's a lucky thing for Ivor we haven't your Brigadier Ritchie-Hook with us. *He*'d do something.'

Guy did not mention the notes in his locker. Instead they talked of the future.

'It looks as if Commandos are off as far as the Middle East is concerned,' said Tommy. 'We're both lucky. We shan't get pushed about. We've got battalions of our own regiments out here. You'll go back to the Halberdiers, I take it?'

'I hope so. There's nothing I ask better.'

That afternoon Guy was transported to Mrs Stitch's. The hospital sent him there in an ambulance. Indeed, they insisted on carrying him in and out of that vehicle on a stretcher, but before leaving he walked from place to place making his farewells.

'You'll be in clover up there,' said the senior medical officer, signing him off the strength. 'Nothing like a bit of home comfort to pull you round.'

'What it is to have influence!' said the Sister.

'She tried to kidnap me,' said Tommy. 'I love Julia, but you have to be jolly well to stay with her.'

Guy had heard this warning on Ivor's lips and discounted it. Coming from the sturdier Tommy it made him hesitate, but it was then too late. The stretcher-bearers stood remorsely at his side. Within half an hour he was at Mrs Stitch's luxurious official residence.

Her grandparents had spent their lives in the service of Queen Victoria and in that court had formed standards of living which projected themselves over another generation and determined Mrs Stitch's precocious but impressionable childhood. Mrs Stitch grew up with the conviction that comfort was rather common. She enjoyed the sumptuous and, within certain incalculable limits, the profuse – no one at her table could ever be quite sure which course of a seemingly classic dinner might not disconcertingly prove to be the last; she enjoyed change and surprise, crisp lettuce-freshness and hoary antiquity, but she did not like male guests to live soft.

This was apparent when she led the stretcher-party down to the room prepared for Guy; down it was, well below ground-level. Mrs Stitch danced lightly from cockroach to cockroach across the concrete floor, squashing six on her way to the window. This she threw open on the kitchen yard. At eye level the bare feet of Berber servants passed to and fro. One squatted near, plucking a goose whose feathers caught by the north-west breeze floated in among them.

'There,' she said. 'Lovely. What more could anyone ask? – I know, flowers.' She was gone. She was back, laden with tuberoses. 'Here,' she said, putting them in the basin. 'If you want to wash, use Algie's loo.' She surveyed the room with unaffected pleasure. 'All yours,' she said. 'Join us when you feel like it.' She was gone. She was back. 'Fond of cats? Here's some. They'll keep down the beetles.' She threw in two tiger-like animals and shut the door. They stretched and scornfully left by the window.

Guy sat on the bed feeling that things had been too much for him that day. He still wore the pyjamas and dressing-gown which seemed to be the correct rig for this move. The stretcher-bearers now returned with his luggage.

'Can we help with your gear, sir? There doesn't seem anywhere to put anything much, does there, really?'

No cupboard, no drawer; a peg. One of the men hung up his equipment; they saluted and left.

Guy's kit had followed him – much pilfered, it transpired – from camp to hospital. There was also the bundle containing the laundered rags he had worn in Crete and the neat packet of possessions taken from his pockets and haversack; with the red identity disc lay his manumission from Chatty Corner and the pocket-book in which he had kept the notes for his War Diary. The elastic band had gone. The covers were blistered and limp and creased and tattered, some of the pages stuck together. Guy carefully separated them with a razor-blade. It was all there. On the blotched maths-paper he could follow in the deterioration of his writing the successive phases of exhaustion. As he grew feebler he had written larger and more heavily. The last entry was a deep scrawl, covering a sheet, recording the appearance of an aeroplane over the boat. This was his contribution to History; this perhaps the evidence in a notorious trial.

Guy lay on his bed, too much shaken by the physical events of the day to concentrate on the moral issues. For Julia Stitch there was no problem. An old friend was in trouble. Rally round. Tommy had his constant guide in the precept: never cause trouble except for positive preponderant advantage. In the field, if Ivor or anyone else were endangering a position, Tommy would have had no compunction in shooting him out of hand. This was another matter. Nothing was in danger save one man's reputation. Ivor had behaved abominably but he had hurt no one but himself. He was now out of the way. Tommy would see to it that he was never again in a position to behave as he had done in Crete. His troop was out of the way too, until the end of the war. It did not much matter, as far as winning the war went, what they said in their prison camp. Perhaps in later years when Tommy met Ivor in Bellamy's he might be a shade less cordial than of old. But to instigate a court-martial on a capital charge was inconceivable; in the narrowest view it would cause endless professional annoyance and delay; in the widest it would lend comfort to the enemy.

Guy lacked these simple rules of conduct. He had no old love for Ivor, no liking at all, for the man who had been his friend had proved to be an illusion. He had a sense, too, that all war consisted in causing trouble without much hope of advantage. Why was he here in Mrs Stitch's basement, why were Eddie and Bertie in prison, why was the young soldier lying still unburied in the deserted village of Crete, if it was not for Justice?

So he lay pondering until Mrs Stitch called him up to cocktails.

Days passed while Guy lay in the chaise-longue beside the strutting and preening peacocks. Guests came and went singly and in large parties, pashas, courtiers, diplomats, politicians, generals, admirals, subalterns, Greek and Egyptian and Jewish and French, but Mrs Stitch never neglected Guy. Three or four times a day she was at his side with the hypodermic needle of her charm.

'Isn't there anybody you'd like me to ask?' she said one day, planning dinner.

'Well, there is one. Colonel Tickeridge. I hear he's in camp at Mariout. You won't know him but you couldn't help liking him.'

'I'll find him for you.'

That was early in the morning of 22 June – a day of apocalypse for all the world for numberless generations, and for Guy among them, one immortal soul, a convalescent Lieutenant of Halberdiers.

Algernon Stitch brought the news of the invasion of Russia when he returned for luncheon. Only Mrs Stitch and Guy and two secretaries were there.

'Why couldn't the silly fellow have done it to start with?' Algernon Stitch asked, 'instead of landing the lot of us in the soup first.'

'Is it a Good Thing?' Mrs Stitch asked the simple question of the schoolroom.

'Can't tell. The experts don't believe the Russians have a chance. And they've got a lot of things the Germans will find useful.'

'What's Winston going to say?'

'Welcome our new allies, of course. What else can he?'

'It's nice to have one ally,' said Mrs Stitch.

Nothing else was spoken of at luncheon – the Molotov pact, the partition of Poland, the annexation of the Baltic republics, the resources of the Ukraine, the numbers of aeroplanes, of divisions, transport and oil, Tilsit and Tolstoi, American popular opinion, Japan and the Anti-Comintern Pact – all the topics that were buzzing everywhere in the world at that moment. But Guy remained silent.

Mrs Stitch briefly held his hand on the tablecloth. 'Feeling low today?'

'Awfully.'

'Cheer up. Your chum is coming to dinner.'

But Guy needed more than Colonel Tickeridge.

It was just such a sunny, breezy Mediterranean day two years before when he read of the Russo-German alliance, when a decade of shame seemed to be ending in light and reason, when the Enemy was plain in view, huge and hateful, all disguise cast off; the modern age in arms.

Now that hallucination was dissolved, like the whales and turtles on the voyage from Crete, and he was back after less than two years' pilgrimage in a Holy Land of illusion in the old ambiguous world, where priests were spies and gallant friends proved traitors and his country was led blundering into dishonour.

That afternoon he took his pocket-book to the incinerator which stood in the yard outside the window, and thrust it in. It was a symbolic act; he stood like the man at Sphakia who dismembered his Bren and threw its parts one by one out into the harbour, splash, splash, splash, into the scum.

Colonel Tickeridge was cheerful that evening, unworried by issues of right and wrong. The more fellows shooting Germans the better, obviously. Rotten sort of government the Russian. So it had been last time. And the Russians changed it. Probably they would again. He explained these points to Guy before dinner. Colonel Tickeridge was content and only slightly bemused. He supposed so large a party must be celebrating something; what, he never learned. He was a little awed by the eminence of some of his fellow guests, the generals in particular. He was not attracted by the lady on either side. He couldn't understand it when they broke into French. But he tucked in. It was decent of Uncle Crouchback to get him brought here. And later in the evening as he and Guy sat together under the palm trees Mrs Stitch joined them.

'Have you your pistols?' she quoted. 'Have you your sharp-edged axes? Halberdiers! O Halberdiers!'

'Eh?' said Colonel Tickeridge. 'Sorry, I'm not quite there.'

'What have you been talking about?'

'I've been arranging my future,' said Guy. 'Very satisfactorily. The Colonel is taking me back.'

'We lost a lot of good fellows over there, you know. We're busy re-forming at the moment. Don't want to take replacements out of the pool, if we can help it. Glad to have one of the old lot back again. Only hope the Brigadier won't snap him up.'

'The Brigadier?' asked Mrs Stitch, politely, vaguely. 'Who is he?'

'Ben Ritchie-Hook. You must have heard of him.'

Mrs Stitch was suddenly alert. 'I think I have. Isn't he dead? I thought that was how Tommy Blackhouse came to command whatever it was.'

'He was lost. Not dead. Far from it. He turned up in western Abyssinia leading a group of wogs. Wanted to go on with them, of course, but the powers that be wouldn't stand for that. They winkled him out and got him to Khartoum. He's due in Cairo this week. We only just heard. It's been a day of all-round good news, hasn't it?'

'Isn't he something of a martinet?'

'Oh, I wouldn't say that exactly. I'd say more of a fizzer, really.'

'Tommy mentioned him the other day, talking about – about something. Hasn't he rather the reputation of a trouble-maker?'

'Only for those who need it,' said Colonel Tickeridge.

'I think I know what you mean,' said Guy.

'There was some fellow in the last war let him down,' said Colonel Tickeridge. 'Not one of ours, of course. Ben was only a company commander then and this fellow was on the staff. Ben got hit immediately after and was in hospital for months. By the time he came out the fellow had got posted into an entirely different show. But Ben never let up on him. He hounded him down and got him broken. It's the big-game hunter in him.'

'I see. I see,' said Mrs Stitch. 'And he's really been in command of Tommy's force all the time?'

'On paper.'

'And he's due when?'

'Before the end of the week, I gather.'

'I see. Well now, I must go and help Algie.'

Two days later Guy and Mrs Stitch sat in the sunlight with orange-juice and melon and coffee and crescent rolls when the peace of the early morning was broken by a motor-bicycle and the odorous garden was affronted with a cloud of greasy smoke. A military dispatch-rider presented a letter. It was a move order, posting Guy to a transit camp at Suez for immediate return to the United Kingdom. It emanated from Movement Control, District Headquarters. He passed it over the table to Mrs Stitch.

'Oh, dear,' she said. 'We shall miss you.'

'But I don't understand. I was due for a medical at the end of the week. They would have passed me fit to join the battalion.'

'Don't you *want* to go home?'

'Of course not.'

'Everybody else seems to.'

'There's been some mistake. D'you think I could have the car for half an hour and straighten it out?'

'Do. If you really think it's worth while.'

Guy drove to headquarters and found the Major who had signed the letter. Guy explained. '... Medical on Saturday ... CO 2nd Halberdiers has applied for posting ... Ritchie-Hook on the way ...'

'Yes,' said the Major. 'it looks as though something's gone wrong. Most of my day is spent arguing with chaps who *want* to go back. Homes bombed, wives unfaithful, parents insane – they'll throw any line. It ought to be easy enough to *keep* someone here. I don't quite see,' he said, turning the file, 'where this order originated. Officially you're simply on sick leave. This seems to have come from GHQ Cairo. What's it got to do with them? It isn't as though they were in any hurry to have you at home. You're booked for the slowest possible route. *Canary Castle*. She's unloading at Suez now. Awful old hulk. She's going into dry dock in Durban on the way back. You'll be weeks. Have you been blotting your copybook by any chance?'

'Not that I know of.'

'Got TB or anything?'

'No.'

'Well, it can't be anything we can't straighten out. Ring me back this afternoon.' He gave Guy the number of his extension.

Julia was still at home when he returned.

'Everything fixed?'

'I think so.'

'Good. No one's in to luncheon. Like to be dropped at the Union Bar?'

Later that afternoon Guy succeeded in speaking to the Major whose number had until then been engaged.

'I asked about you, Crouchback. Nothing I can do, I'm afraid. That order came from right up at the top.'

'But why?'

'That's a thing you probably know more about than I do.'

'Anyway, I can wait until my Brigadier arrives, can't I? He'll be able to do something.'

'Sorry, old boy. Your orders are to embus for Suez 0700 hours tomorrow. Report here at 0615. I shan't be here myself but there'll be someone about. Hope you have a good trip. The old *Canary*'s quite steady. You'll find her full of wop prisoners.'

That night there was a large party. Most of the Greek royal family were there. Guy found it unusually difficult to get a word alone with Mrs Stitch. When he did, he said: 'Julia, you can do anything. Fix this thing for me.'

'Oh, no, Guy, I never interfere with the military. Algie wouldn't like it at all.'

Later that night, as Guy packed, he found the red identity disc he had carried out of Crete. He did not know the correct procedure, where he should send it, how addressed. Finally he wrote on a sheet of Mrs Stitch's thick paper: '*Taken from the body of a British soldier killed in Crete. Exact position of grave unknown,*' folded it unsigned and addressed the envelope simply *GHQME*. Eventually, he supposed, it would reach the right department.

But next morning when he found Mrs Stitch up and dressed and waiting to see him off, he thought of a more satisfactory way of paying his debt.

'Julia,' he said, 'do you think Algie could possibly get one of his staff to deal with this for me?'

'Of course. What is it?'

'Just a bit of unfinished business from Crete. I don't know the right man to send it to. Algie's secretary will know.'

Mrs Stitch took the envelope. She noted the address. Then she fondly kissed Guy.

As he drove away she waved the envelope; then turned indoors and dropped it into a waste-paper basket. Her eyes were one immense sea, full of flying galleys.

EPILOGUE

'Good evening, Job.'

'Good evening, sir. Very glad to see you back.'

'Things seem pretty quiet.'

'Oh, I wouldn't say that, sir.'

'No air raids, I mean.'

'Oh, no, sir. That's all over now. Hitler needs all he's got for the Russians.'

'Has Mr Box-Bender arrived yet?'

'Yes, sir. Inside.'

'Hullo, Guy, you back?'

'Hully, Guy, where have you been?'

'I say, Guy, weren't you with Tommy? Awful business about Eddie and Bertie.'

'Bad luck Tony Luxmore got caught.'

'Anyway, you got away.'

'And Tommy?'

'And Ivor?'

'I was awfully pleased to hear Ivor was all right.'

'Did you see Algie and Julia?'

'Ah, there you are, Guy,' said Box-Bender. 'I've been waiting for you. We'll go straight up and start dinner, if you don't mind. I've got to get back to the House. Besides, everything gets eaten these days if you don't look sharp.'

Guy and his brother-in-law struggled through and up to the coffee-room. Under the chandeliers waitresses distributed the meagre dinner. It was barely half past seven, but already most of the tables were taken. Guy and Box-Bender had to sit in the middle of the room.

'I hope we keep this to ourselves. There's something I particularly want to talk to you about. Better have the soup. The other thing is made of dried eggs. Good trip home?'

'Eight weeks.'

'*Eight weeks*. Did you bring anything back with you?'

'I had some oranges. They went bad on the voyage.'

'Oh. Don't look. Elderbury's trying to find somewhere to sit ... Hullo, Elderbury, you joining us?'

Elderbury sat with them.

'Heard the results of the Tanks for Russia Week?'

'Yes,' said Box-Bender.

'Great idea of Max's.'

'I should like to have seen Harold Macmillan standing to attention while they sang the Red Flag.'

'I saw it on the news-reel. And Mrs Maisky unveiling the picture of Stalin.'

'Well, it's worked,' said Box-Bender. 'Production was up twenty per cent. Twenty per cent – and they were supposed to be working all-out before.'

'And that strike in Glasgow. "Aid to Russia" stopped that.'

'So the *Express* said.'

'Tanks for Russia?' asked Guy. 'I'm afraid all this is new to me. They want tanks pretty badly in the desert.'

'They'll get them, too, don't you worry,' said Box-Bender. 'Naturally the workers are keen to help Russia. It's how they've been educated. It doesn't do any harm to let them have a pot of red paint and splash round with hammers and sickles and "Good old Uncle Joe". It'll wash off. The tanks will get to the place they're most needed. You can be sure of that.'

'Mind you, I'm all for the Russians,' said Elderbury. 'We've had to do a lot of readjustment in the last few weeks. They're putting up a wonderful fight.'

'Pity they keep retreating.'

'Drawing them on, Guy, drawing them on.'

Neither Elderbury nor the dinner conduced to lingering.

'Look,' said Box-Bender briskly, when he and Guy were alone in a corner of the billiard-room. 'I haven't much time. This is what I wanted to show you.' He took a typewritten paper from his pocket-book and handed it to Guy. 'What d'you make of that?'

Guy read:

The Spiritual Combat by Francis de Sales.

Christ the Ideal of the Monk by Abbot Marmion.

Spiritual Letters of Don John Chapman.

The Practice of the Presence of God by Lawrence.

'I think it ought to be "Dom John" not "Don John",' he said.

'Yes, yes, very likely. My secretary copied them. But what d'you make of it?'

'Most edifying. I can't say I've read them much myself. Are you thinking of becoming a monk, Arthur?'

The effect of the little quip was remarkable.

'*Exactly*,' said Box-Bender. 'That's exactly what I expected you to say. It's what other people have said when I showed them.'

'But what is this list?'

'They're the books Tony has sent for from prison. *Now*. What d'you to say to that?'

Guy hesitated. 'It's not like him,' he said.

'Shall I tell you what I think? *Religious mania*. It's as plain as a pikestaff the poor boy's going off his head.'

'Why "mania", Arthur? Lots of quite sane people read books like that.'

'Not Tony. At his age. Besides, you know, one's got to remember Ivo.'

There it was, out in the open for a moment's airing, the skeleton from Box-Bender's cupboard. Box-Bender remembered Ivo every day of his busy prosperous life.

Tension quickly resolves in Bellamy's.

'Mind if I join you again?' said Elderbury, carrying a cup of coffee. 'Nowhere else to sit.' And shortly afterwards Guy saw Ian Kilbannock and made his escape.

'What's all this about Ivor Claire?' he asked.

'I've no idea. I've been at sea for eight weeks. The last I heard of him, he'd gone to India.'

'Everyone's saying he ran away in Crete.'

'We all did.'

'They say Ivor ran much the fastest. I thought you might know.'

'I don't, I'm afraid. How's HOO HQ?'

'Seething. We've moved into new premises. Look at these.'

He showed the rings on his cuff.

'There seem more of them.'

'They keep coming. I've got a staff of my own – including Virginia, incidentally. She'll be delighted to hear you're back. She's always talking of you. She's away with Trimmer at the moment.'

'Trimmer?'

'You remember him. McTavish. He's officially named Trimmer now. They couldn't decide for weeks. In the end it went to the Minister. He decided there were too many Scots heroes. Also, of course, Trimmer's so tremendously not Scottish. But he's doing a great job. We've had our noses out of joint a bit this last week. There's a female Soviet sniper going the rounds and getting all the applause. That's why I sent poor Virginia to put some ginger into our boy. He was pining rather. Now things are humming again – except for Virginia, of course. She was sick as mud at having to go – Scunthorpe, Hull, Huddersfield, Halifax . . .'

Next day Guy reported at the Halberdier barracks. His old acquaintance was still in the office, promoted Major once more.

'Back again,' he said. 'Quite an annual event. You come with the fall of the leaf, ha ha.' He was much jollier now he was a Major. 'Everything in order, too, this time. We've been expecting you for weeks. I expect you'd like a spot of leave?'

'Really,' said Guy, 'I don't think I would. I've been sitting about in a ship since the end of June. I might as well get to work.'

'The Captain-Commandant said something about putting you on the square for a fortnight to smarten up.'

'That suits me.'

'Sure? It seemed a bit rough to me. Returned hero and all that. But the Captain-Commandant says people forget everything on active service. I'd better take you to him this morning. Haven't you any gloves?'

'No.'

'We can probably find a pair in the Officers' House.'

They did. They also found Jumbo.

'I've read about your escape,' he said. 'It got in the papers.'

He spoke with gentle, genial reproof. It was not the business of a Halberdier officer to get his name in the papers, but Guy's exploit had been wholly creditable.

At noon, gloved, Guy was marched in to the Captain-Commandant. Colonel Green had aged. 'Mr Crouchback reporting from Middle East, sir,' said the Adjutant.

Colonel Green looked up from his table and blinked.

'I remember you,' he said. 'One of the first batch of young temporary officers. I remember you very well. Apthorpe, isn't it?'

'Crouchback,' said the Adjutant more loudly, putting the relevant papers into the hands of the Captain-Commandant.

'Yes, yes, of course . . .' He reviewed the papers. He remembered the good things he knew of Guy . . . 'Crouchback. Middle East . . . Bad luck you couldn't stay out there and join the second battalion. They wanted you, I know. So did your Brigadier. Old women, these medicos. Still, one has to go by what they say. I've got their report here. They as good as say you're lucky to be alive . . . change of climate essential . . . well, you look fit enough now.'

'Yes, sir, thank you. I'm quite fit now.'

'Good. Excellent. We shall be seeing something of one another, I hope . . .'

That afternoon Guy paraded on the square with a mixed squad of recruits and officers in training under Halberdier Colour-Sergeant Oldenshaw.

'. . . I'll just run through the detail. The odd numbers of the front rank will seize the rifles of the even numbers of the rear rank with the left hand crossing the muzzles – all right? – magazines turned outward – all right? – at the same time raising the piling swivels with the forefinger and thumb of both hands – all right? . . .'

All right, Halberdier Colour-Sergeant Oldenshaw. All right.

UNCONDITIONAL
SURRENDER

To my daughter
MARGARET
Child of the Locust Years

CONTENTS

Synopsis of Preceding Volumes   395

Prologue LOCUST YEARS   397

Book One STATE SWORD   403

Book Two FIN DE LIGNE   429

Book Three THE DEATH WISH   505

Epilogue FESTIVAL OF BRITAIN   571

Synopsis of Preceding Volumes

'The enemy at last was in plain view, huge and hateful, all disguise cast off. It was the Modern Age in arms. Whatever the outcome there was a place for him in that battle.'

This was the belief of Guy Crouchback in 1939 when he heard the news of the Molotov–Ribbentrop Treaty. What follows is the story of his attempt to find his 'place in that battle'.

He is 35 years old, rising 36, the only surviving son of his father, Gervase. For some years he has lived alone in Italy in the villa built by his grandfather. Of his brothers one was killed in the war, the other died insane. He has a sister Angela married to an MP, Arthur Box-Bender. The Crouchbacks are a family of old-established, west-country, Catholic gentry allied to most of the other historic recusant families of the country. One of them was martyred under Elizabeth I. Their estates have been sold. The family house, Broome, remains in their possession but is let to a convent. Gervase Crouchback lives in a small seaside hotel at Matchet. He has a bachelor brother, Peregrine, a notorious bore.

Guy married a wife named Virginia who quickly deserted him for a soldier, Tommy Blackhouse. At the time the story opens, she is in process of separation from a third husband, an American named Troy. For eight years she has lived in the world of rich, gay, cosmopolitan society. Guy has grown lonely and joyless. His Church does not allow him to seek a second wife. He sees the war as an opportunity to re-establish his interest in his fellow men and to serve them.

After many difficulties he is commissioned in the Royal Corps of Halberdiers, an unfashionable regiment of infantry, proud of its achievements and peculiarities; he proves himself a reasonably efficient officer. In the Halberdiers he serves under Ritchie-Hook, a ferocious hero of the first war. Among his batch of officers in training are De Souza, a cynic, and Trimmer, a former hairdresser, whose probationary commission is speedily terminated.

Virginia has returned to England at the moment when many are leaving it. One evening on leave Guy attempts to make love to her in Claridge's Hotel but is repulsed with mild ridicule.

He sails on the Dakar expedition, comes under official disapprobation for an escapade arranged by Ritchie-Hook and is indirectly responsible for the death of another officer, by the injudicious gift of a bottle of whisky when he is down with fever. All this time he has ludicrously aroused the suspicions of a secret department of counter-espionage presided over by Grace-Groundling-Marchpole. He returns to England, and becomes attached to the newly formed Commandos, one of which is commanded by Blackhouse. Here he makes friends with Ivor Claire, a dandy. 'Jumbo' Trotter, an ancient

Halberdier, deeply versed in service lore, is also temporarily attached to the Commando. Claire has a Corporal of Horse named Ludovic, a mysterious reservist recalled to the regiment, who keeps a volume of *pensées*. Ludovic rises to be Brigade Corporal Major. The Commando, as part of 'Hookforce', sails to Egypt. Here a brigade-major is attached to them from the staff pool named 'Fido' Hound. Mrs Stitch, a beauty, is in Alexandria with her husband, who holds a cabinet appointment in the Middle East.

Hookforce – without Blackhouse, who has broken his leg – goes to Crete at the moment when the defence is falling. 'Fido' Hound and Ludovic severally desert and meet in a cave on the south cast where an irregular body of Spanish refugees have taken shelter. Nothing more is ever heard of Hound. It is to be supposed that Ludovic perpetrated or connived at his murder. Blackhouse's commando is ordered to provide the rearguard for the disembarkation and surrender on the following morning. That night Claire deserts his troop and insinuates himself into the disembarkation. On the morning of the surrender Guy meets Ludovic on the beach. They join a small party escaping by boat. They suffer acutely from privation and exposure. Ludovic alone remains capable. The delirious sapper officer who was originally in command, disappears overboard during the night. It is to be supposed that Ludovic precipitated him. Finally they reach the African coast. Ludovic carries Guy ashore, and while he is half-conscious in hospital, is sent back to England to be decorated and commissioned. Ludovic believes that Guy knows the truth of the disappearance of 'Fido' Hound. He does know, and has the proof in the written orders to the rearguard, the full culpability of Claire's desertion. Mrs Stitch, in order to save Claire's reputation, gets Guy sent back to England by slow convoy to rejoin the Halberdier Depot.

Virginia meanwhile is in difficulties. Troy no longer remits her allowance. Trimmer is used by Lord Kilbannock, who is Press Officer in Hazardous Offensive Operations HQ, an organization which from small beginnings becomes one of the busiest departments of war, to carry out a raid for publicity purposes. He becomes a national hero and falls deeply in love with Virginia, whom he knew professionally, and with whom he had a brief affair in Glasgow. At Kilbannock's instigation, in order to keep Trimmer in heart for his public appearances, Virginia falls into a prolonged and, to her, distasteful liaison with Trimmer.

As Guy, in the late autumn of 1941, rejoins his regiment he believes that the just cause of going to war has been forfeited in the Russian alliance. Personal honour alone remains.

'The hallucination was dissolved, like the whales and turtles on the voyage from Crete, and he was back after less than two years' pilgrimage in a Holy Land of illusion in the old ambiguous world, where priests were spies and gallant friends proved traitors and his country was led blundering into dishonour.'

PROLOGUE

Locust Years

When Guy Crouchback returned to his regiment in the autumn of 1941 his position was in many ways anomalous. He had been trained in the first batch of temporary officers, had commanded a company, had been detached for special duties, had been in action and acquitted himself with credit; he had twice put up captain's stars and twice removed them; their scars were plainly visible on his shoulder straps. He had been invalided home on an order direct from GHQ ME and the medical authorities could find nothing wrong with him. There were rumours that he had 'blotted his copybook' in West Africa. When he was commissioned in 1939 his comparative old age had earned him the sobriquet of 'uncle'. Now he was two years older and the second batch of officers in training were younger than those who had joined with him. To them he seemed a patriarch; to him they seemed a generation divided by an impassable barrier. Once he had made the transition, had thrown himself into the mêlée on the ante-room floor, had said 'cheerioh' when he drank with them, and had been accepted as one of themselves. He could not do it a second time. Nor were there any longer mêlées and guest nights, nor much drinking. The new young officers were conscripts who liked to spend their leisure listening to jazz on the wireless. The first battalion, his battalion, followed Ritchie-Hook biffing across the sands of North Africa. A draft of reinforcements were sent out to them. Guy was not posted with them. Hookforce, all save four, had been taken prisoner in Crete. He had no comrades in arms in England except Tommy Blackhouse who returned to raise another Special Service Force. They met Tommy in Bellamy's and he offered him a post on his staff, but the shadow of Ivor Claire lay dark and long over Commandos, and Guy answered that he was content to soldier on with the Halberdiers.

This he did for two blank years. A Second Brigade was formed, and Guy followed its fortunes in training, with periodic changes of quarters from Penkirk in Scotland to Brook Park in Cornwall. Home Forces no longer experienced the shocks, counter-orders, and disorders of the first two years of war. The army in the Far East now suffered as they had done. In Europe the initiative was now with the Allies. They were laboriously assembled and equipped and trained. Guy rose to be second-in-command of his battalion with the acting rank of major.

Then in August 1943 there fell on him the blow that had crushed Jumbo at Mugg: 'I'm sorry, uncle, but I'm afraid we shan't be taking you with us when we go to foreign parts. You've been invaluable in training. Don't know what I should have done without you. But I can't risk taking a chap of your age into action.'

'Am I much older than you, colonel?'

'Not much, I suppose, but I've spent my life in this job. If I get hit, the second-in-command will have to take over. Can't risk it.'

'I'd gladly come down in rank. Couldn't I have a company? Or a platoon?'

'Be your age, uncle. No can do. This is an order from brigade.'

The new brigadier, lately arrived from the Eighth Army, was the man to whom, briefly, Guy had been attached in West Africa when he encompassed the death of Apthorpe. On that occasion the brigadier had said: 'I don't want to see you again ever.' He had fought long and hard since then and won a DSO, but throughout the dust of war he remembered Guy. Apthorpe, that brother-uncle, that ghost, laid, Guy had thought, on the island of Mugg, walked still in his porpoise boots to haunt him; the defeated lord of the thunder-box still worked his jungle magic. When a Halberdier said: 'No can do', it was final.

'We shall need you for the embarkation, of course. When you've seen us off, take a spot of leave. After that you're old enough to find yourself something to do. There's always "barrack duties", of course, or you might report to the War House to the pool of unemployed officers. There's plenty of jobs going begging for chaps in your position.'

Guy took his leave and was at Matchet when Italy surrendered. News of the king's flight came on the day the brigade landed at Salerno. It brought Guy some momentary exhilaration.

'That looks like the end of the Piedmontese usurpation,' he said to his father. 'What a mistake the Lateran Treaty was. It seemed masterly at the time – how long? Fifteen years ago? What are fifteen years in the history of Rome? How much better it would have been if the Popes had sat it out and then emerged saying: "What was all that? Risorgimento? Garibaldi? Cavour? The House of Savoy? Mussolini? Just some hooligans from out of town causing a disturbance. Come to think of it wasn't there once a poor little boy whom they called King of Rome?" That's what the Pope ought to be saying today.'

Mr Crouchback regarded his son sadly. 'My dear boy,' he said, 'you're really talking the most terrible nonsense, you know. That isn't at all what the Church is like. It isn't what she's *for*.'

They were walking along the cliffs returning at dusk to the Marine Hotel with Mr Crouchback's retriever, ageing now, not gambolling as he used but loping behind them. Mr Crouchback had aged too, and for the first time showed concern with his own health. They fell silent, Guy disconcerted by his father's rebuke, Mr Crouchback still, it seemed, pondering the question he had raised; for when at length he spoke it was to say: 'Of course it's reasonable for a soldier to rejoice in victory.'

'I don't think I'm interested in victory now,' said Guy.

'Then you've no business to be a soldier.'

'Oh, I want to stay in the war. I should like to do some fighting. But it doesn't seem to matter now who wins. When we declared war on Finland . . .'

He left the sentence unfinished, and his father said: 'That sort of question isn't for soldiers.'

As they came into sight of the hotel, he added: 'I suppose I'm getting like a schoolmaster. Forgive me. We mustn't quarrel. I used often to get angry with poor Ivo; and with Angela. She was rather a tiresome girl the year she came out. But I don't think I've ever been angry with you.'

Matchet had changed in the last two years. The army unit for whom Monte Rosa had been cleared, had gone as quickly as they came, leaving the boarding-house empty. Its blank windows, and carpetless floors stood as a symbol of the little town's brief popularity. Refugees from bombing returned to their former homes. Mrs Tickeridge moved to be near a school for Jenifer. The days when the Cuthberts could 'let every room twice over' were ended and they reluctantly found themselves obliged to be agreeable. It was not literally true, as Miss Vavasour claimed, that they 'went down on their knees' to keep their residents, but they did offer Mr Crouchback his former sitting room at its former price.

'No, thank you very much,' he had said. 'You'll remember I promised to take it again *after* the war, and unless things change very much for the worse I shall do that. Meanwhile my few sticks are in store and I don't feel like getting them out again.'

'Oh, we will furnish it for you, Mr Crouchback.'

'It wouldn't be quite the same. You make me very comfortable as I am.'

His former rent was now being paid as a weekly allowance to an unfrocked priest.

The Cuthberts were glad enough to accommodate parents visiting their sons at Our Lady of Victories and obscurely supposed that if they antagonized Mr Crouchback, he would somehow stop their coming.

Guy left next day and reported to the Halberdier barracks. He had little appetite for leave now.

Three days later a letter came from his father:

Marine Hotel
Matchet
20 September 1943

My Dear Guy,

I haven't been happy about our conversation on your last evening. I said too much or too little. Now I must say more.

Of course in the 1870s and 80s every decent Roman disliked the Piedmontese, just as the decent French now hate the Germans. They had been invaded. And, of course, most of the Romans we know kept it up, sulking. But that isn't the Church. The Mystical Body doesn't strike attitudes and stand on its dignity. It accepts suffering and injustice. It is ready to forgive at the first hint of compunction.

When you spoke of the Lateran Treaty did you consider how many souls may have been reconciled and have died at peace as the result of it? How many children may have been brought up in the faith who might have lived in ignorance? Quantitative judgements don't apply. If only one soul was saved that is full compensation for any amount of loss of 'face'.

I write like this because I am worried about you and I gather I may not live very much longer. I saw the doctor yesterday and he seemed to think I have something pretty bad the matter.

As I say, I'm worried about you. You seemed so much enlivened when you first joined the army. I know you are cut up at being left behind in England. But you mustn't sulk.

It was not a good thing living alone and abroad. Have you thought at all about what you will do after the war? There's the house at Broome the village calls 'Little Hall' – quite incorrectly. All the records refer to it simply as the 'Lesser House'. You'll have to live somewhere and I doubt if you'll want to go back to the Castello even if it survives, which doesn't seem likely the way they are bombing everything in Italy.

You see I am thinking a lot about death at the moment. Well that's quite suitable at my age and condition.

Ever your affec. father,
G. Crouchback

2

When Hookforce sailed without him, Jumbo Trotter abandoned all hope of active service. He became commandant of No. 6 Transit Camp, London District, a post which required good nature, sobriety, and little else except friends of influence – in all of which qualities Jumbo was rich. He no longer bore resentment against Ben Ritchie-Hook. He accepted the fact that he was on the shelf. The threat of just such a surrender of his own condition overcast Guy.

Jumbo often took a drive to the Halberdier barracks to see what was on. There in late September he found Guy disconsolately installed as PAD officer and assistant adjutant.

'Put in to see the Captain Commandant,' he advised. 'Say there is something coming through for you any day but you have to be in London. Get posted to the "unemployed pool" and come and stay at my little place. I can make you quite comfortable.'

So Guy moved to Jumbo's little place – Little Hall? Lesser House? – No. 6 Transit Camp, London District, and for a few days looked into the depths of the military underworld. There was a waiting-room in an outlying dependency of the War Office where daily congregated officers of all ages whose regiments and corps had no use for them.

There had been a 'Man-power Directive' from the highest source which enjoined that everyone in the country should be immediately employed in the 'war-effort'. Guy was interviewed by a legless major who said: 'You seem to have done all right. I don't know why they've sent you to this outfit. First Halberdier I've had through my hands. What have you been up to?'

He studied the file in which was recorded all Guy's official biography of the last four years.

'Age,' said Guy.

'Thirty-nine, just rising forty. Yes, that's old for your rank. You're back to captain now of course. Well all I can offer at the moment is a security job at Aden and almoner at a civilian hospital. I don't suppose either particularly appeals to you?'

'No.'

'Well, stick around. I may find something better. But they don't look for good fellows in my office. Look about outside and see what you can find.'

And, sure enough, one evening early in October, after his third attendance on the legless major (who offered him, with undisguised irony, an administrative post in Wales at a school of air photography interpretation) he met Tommy Blackhouse once more in Bellamy's. Tommy now had a brigade of Commandos. He was under orders to sail shortly for Italy to rehearse the Anzio landings and was keeping dead quiet about his movements. He only said, 'Wish you'd decided to come to me, Guy.'

'Too late now?'

'Far too late.'

Guy explained his predicament.

'That's the hell of a mess.'

'The fellow at the War Office has been very civil.'

'Yes, but you'll find he'll get impatient soon. There's a flap about man-power. They'll suddenly pitch you into something awful. Wish I could help.'

Later that evening he said: 'I've thought of something that might do as a stop-gap. I keep a liaison officer at HOO HQ. God knows what he does.

Anyway I'm taking him away somewhere else. There are a few odd bodies that have got attached to me. They came under HOO. You could liaise with them for a bit if you liked.'

When Jumbo heard of it, he said: 'Strictly speaking I suppose you aren't "in transit" any more.'

'I hope I am.'

'Well, anyway, stay on here as long as you like. We'll find a way of covering you in the returns. London District is never much trouble. All stock-brokers and wine-merchants from the Foot Guards. Awfully easy fellows to deal with.'

But it was not for this that he had dedicated himself on the sword of Roger of Waybroke that hopeful morning four years back.

BOOK ONE

State Sword

I

In all the hosts of effigies that throng the aisles of Westminster Abbey one man only, and he a sailor, strikes a martial attitude. The men of the middle ages have sheathed their swords and composed their hands in prayer; the men of the age of reason have donned the toga. A Captain Montagu alone, in Flaxman's posthumous statue, firmly grips his hilt, and, because they had so many greater treasures to protect, the chapter left him to stand there throughout the war unencumbered by sand bags, gazing across the lower nave as he had gazed at the ships of revolutionary France in the waters of Ushant on the day of victory and death.

His name is not well remembered and his portrait, larger than life and portly for his years, has seldom attracted the notice of sightseers. It was not his sword but another which on Friday, 29 October 1943, drew the column of fours which slowly shuffled forward from Millbank, up Great College Street, under a scarred brick wall, on which during the hours of darkness in the preceding spring a zealous, arthritic communist had emblazoned the words, SECOND FRONT NOW, until they reached the door under the blasted and bombed west window. The people of England were long habituated to queues; some had joined the procession ignorant of its end – hoping perhaps for cigarettes or shoes – but most were in a mood of devotion. In the street a few words were exchanged; no laughter.

The day was overcast, damp, misty, and still. Winter overcoats had not yet appeared. Each member of the crowd carried a respirator – valueless now, the experts secretly admitted, against any gas the enemy was likely to employ, but still the badge of a people in arms. Women predominated; here and there a service man – British, American, Polish, Dutch, French – displayed some pride of appearance; the civilians were shabby and grubby. Some, for it was their lunch hour, munched Woolton pies; others sucked cigarettes made of the sweepings of canteen floors. Bombing had ceased for the time being but the livery of air-raid shelter remained the national dress. As they reached the abbey church, which many were entering for the first time in their lives, all fell quite silent as though they were approaching a corpse lying in state.

The sword they had come to see stood upright between two candles, on a table counterfeiting an altar. Policemen guarded it on either side. It had been made at the King's command as a gift to 'the steel-hearted people of Stalingrad'. An octogenarian, who had made ceremonial swords for five sovereigns, rose from his bed to forge it; silver, gold, rock-crystal, and enamel had gone to its embellishment. In this year of the Sten gun it was a notable weapon and was first exhibited as a feat of craftsmanship at Goldsmith's Hall and at the Victoria and Albert Museum. Some few took comfort at this evidence that ancient skills survived behind the shoddy improvisation of the present. It was not thus that it affected the hearts of the people. Every day the wireless announced great Russian victories while the British advance in Italy was coming to a halt. The people were suffused with gratitude to their remote allies and they venerated the sword as the symbol of their own generous and spontaneous emotion.

The newspapers and the Ministry of Information caught on. *The Times* 'dropped into poetry'.

> ... I saw the Sword of Stalingrad,
> Then bow'd down my head from the Light of it,
> Spirit to my spirit, the Might of it
> Silently whispered – O Mortal, Behold ...
> I am the Life of Stalingrad,
> You and its people shall unite in me,
> Men yet unborn, in the great Light in me
> Triumphs shall sing when my Story is told.

The gossip-writer of the *Daily Express* suggested it should be sent round the kingdom. Cardiff, Birmingham, Sheffield, Manchester, Glasgow, and Edinburgh paid it secular honours in their Art Galleries and Guild Halls. Now, back from its tour, it reached its apotheosis, exposed for adoration hard by the shrine of St Edward the Confessor and the sacring place of the kings of England.

Guy Crouchback drove past the line of devotees on his way to luncheon. Unmoved by the popular enthusiasm for the triumphs of 'Joe' Stalin, who now qualified for the name of 'uncle', as Guy had done and Apthorpe, he was not tempted to join them in their piety. 29 October 1943 had another and more sombre significance for him. It was his fortieth birthday and to celebrate the occasion he had asked Jumbo Trotter to luncheon.

It was through Jumbo's offices that he now sat at east behind a FANNY driver instead of travelling by bus. After four years of war Jumbo preserved his immunity to sumptuary regulations. As also did Ruben. In a famine-stricken world the little fish-restaurant dispensed in their seasons Colchester oysters, Scotch salmon, lobsters, prawns, gulls' eggs, which rare foods were specifically exempt from the law which limited the price of hotel meals to five shillings, and often caviar, obtained, only Ruben knew how, through diplomatic channels. Most surprising of all there sometimes appeared cheeses from France, collected by intrepid parachutists and conveyed home by submarine. There was an abundance of good wine, enormously costly, at a time when the cellars of the hotels were empty and wine merchants dealt out meagre monthly parcels only to their oldest customers. Ruben had for some years enjoyed a small and appreciative clientèle. Once he had served in Bellamy's and there were always tables for its members. There was also an increasing dilution of odd-looking men who called the proprietor 'Mr Ruben' and carried large quantities of banknotes in their hip pockets. That restaurant was a rare candle in a dark and naughty world. Kerstie Kilbannock, who had made noxious experiments with custard powder and condiments, once asked: 'Do tell me, Ruben, how do you make your mayonnaise?' and received the grave reply: 'Quite simply, my lady, fresh eggs and olive oil.'

Guy led Jumbo to a corner table. He had spent little time in London since his return from Egypt and he could seldom afford to feast, but Ruben was loyal to old faces and familiar names.

'Rather a change from the Senior,' Jumbo remarked as he surveyed the company. 'A *great* change,' he added as he read the menu. They consumed great quantities of oysters. As they rose surfeited from their table, it was seized by a couple who had just come in; Kerstie Kilbannock and an American soldier. As though playing musical chairs, she was in Jumbo's warm place before he had taken his cap from the peg above him.

'Guy, how are you?'

'Forty.'

'We've been lunching with Ruby at the Dorchester and are so hungry we had to pop in here and fill up. You know the Lootenant?'

'Yes, indeed. How are you, Loot?'

Everyone knew Lieutenant Padfield; even Guy who knew so few people. He was a portent of the Grand Alliance. London was full of American soldiers, tall, slouching, friendly, woefully homesick young men who seemed always in search of somewhere to sit down. In the summer they had filled the parks and sat on the pavements round the once august mansions which had been assigned to them. For their comfort there swarmed out of the slums and across the bridges multitudes of drab, ill-favoured adolescent girls and their aunts and mothers, never before seen in the squares of Mayfair and Belgravia. These they passionately and publicly embraced, in the blackout and at high noon, and rewarded with chewing-gum, razor blades, and other rare trade-goods from their PX stores. Lieutenant Padfield was a horse of a different colour; not precisely, for his face, too, was the colour of putty; he too slouched; he, too, was a sedentary by habit. But he was not at all homesick; when not in a chair he must have been in rapid motion, for he was ubiquitous. He was twenty-five years old and in England for the first time. He had been one in the advanced party of the American army and there was no corner of the still intricate social world where he was not familiar.

Guy first met him when on leave he went reluctantly to call on his uncle Peregrine. This was during the Loot's first days in England.

'... Brought a letter from a fellow who used to come to Cowes. Wants to see my miniatures. ...'

Then during the same week Guy was asked to dinner at the House of Commons by his brother-in-law Arthur Box-Bender. '... Told we ought to do something about some of these Americans. They're interested in the House, naturally. Do come along and give a hand. ...' There were six young American officers, the Loot among them.

Very soon he had ceased to be a mere member of the occupying forces to whom kindness should be shown. Two or three widows survived from the years of hospitality and still tried meagrely to entertain. The Lieutenant was at all their little parties. Two or three young married women were staking claims to replace them as hostesses. The Loot knew them all. He was in every picture gallery, every bookshop, every club, every hotel. He was also in every inaccessible castle in Scotland, at the sick bed of every veteran artist and politician, in the dressing-room of every leading actress and in every university common-room, and he expressed his thanks to his hosts and hostesses not with the products of the PX stores but with the publications of Sylvia Beach and sketches by Fuseli.

When Guy went to have his hair cut the Loot seemed always to be in the next chair. One of the few places where he was never seen was HOO HQ. He had no apparent military function. In the years of peace he had been the junior member of an important firm of Boston lawyers. It was said that the Loot's duties were still legal. Either the American army was exceptionally law-abiding or they had a glut of advocates. The Loot was never known to serve on a court-martial.

Now he said: 'I was at Broome yesterday.'

'Broome? You mean our Broome? What on earth took you there, Loot?'

'Sally Sackville-Strutt has a daughter at the school. We went to see her play hockey. She's captain of "Crouchback". You knew the school was divided into two houses called "Crouchback" and the "Holy Family"?'

'The invidious distinction has been remarked on.'

' "Crouchback" won.' He began beckoning to Ruben. 'Do we meet tonight at the Glenobans?'

'No.'

'Did you go to see the Sword of Stalingrad? I went when it was first on view at the Goldsmiths' Hall. I think it is a very lovely gesture of your king's but there was a feature no one could explain to me – the escutcheon on the scabbard will be upside down when it is worn on a baldric.'

'I don't suppose Stalin will wear it on a baldric.'

'Maybe not. But I was certainly surprised at your College of Arms passing it. Well I'll be seeing you around.'

'Around' was the right word.

'Pretty fair cheek that young American finding fault with the sword,' said Jumbo as they left the restaurant. 'What's more *he* didn't discover the mistake. There was a letter about it in *The Times* weeks ago. I'll drop you back at your office. Can't have you using public transport on your birthday. I haven't anything much on this afternoon. That was the best lunch I've had for three years. I may take a little nap.'

In the autumn of 1943 Hazardous Offensive Operations Headquarters was a very different organization from the modest offices which Guy had visited in the winter of 1940. The original three flats remained part of their property – an important part, for they housed Ian Kilbannock's busy Press service – as did numerous mansions from Hendon to Clapham in which small bands of experts in untroubled privacy made researches into fortifying drugs, invisible maps, noiseless explosives, and other projects near to the heart of the healthy schoolboy. There was a Swahili witch-doctor in rooms off the Edgware Road who had been engaged to cast spells on the Nazi leaders.

'D'you know, Charles, I sometimes think that black fellow's something of a charlatan,' General Whale once remarked to Major Albright in a moment of confidence. 'He indents for the most extraordinary stores. But we know Hitler's superstitions and there's a good deal of evidence that with superstitious people these curses do sometimes work.'

Even Dr Glendening-Rees, fully recovered from the privations of Mugg, had a dietary team in Upper Norwood, from whose experiments batches of emaciated 'conscientious objectors' were from time to time removed to hospital. But the ostensible authority of these activities resided in the Venetian-Gothic brick edifice of the Royal Victorian Institute, a museum nobly planned but little frequented in the parish of Brompton. Its few valuable exhibits had been removed to safe storage. Other less portable objects had been left to the risks of bombardment and still stood amid the labyrinth of ply-board partitions with which the halls were divided.

The compartment assigned to the Special Service Forces Liaison Office – Guy's – was larger than most but there was little floor space for he shared it with the plaster reconstruction of a megalosaurus, under whose huge flanks his trestle table was invisible from the door. This table carried three wire trays, 'In', 'Out', and 'Pending', all empty that afternoon – a telephone, and a jig-saw puzzle. For the first few days of his occupancy he had had an AT secretary but she had been removed by a newly installed civilian efficiency-expert. Guy did not repine, but to fill his time, he prosecuted a controversy on the subject. Tommy had said he did not know what the liaison office was supposed to do; nor did Guy.

A captain of Marines peered round the giant carnivore and presented him with a file marked: *Operation Hoopla. Most Secret. By Hand of Officer only.*

'Will you minute this and pass it on to "Beaches"?'

'I thought "Hoopla" had been cancelled.'

'Postponed,' said the Marine. 'The party we had in training was sent to Burma. But we're still working on it.'

The intention of 'Hoopla' was to attack some prodigious bomb-proof submarine-pens in Brittany. A peremptory demand for Immediate Action against these strongholds had been received from the War Cabinet. 'If the Air Force can't destroy the ships, we can kill the crews,' General Whale had suggested. Twelve men were to perform this massacre after landing in a Breton fishing boat.

The latest minute read:

In view of Intelligence Report C/806/RT/12 that occupied France is being supplied with ersatz motor fuel which gives an easily recognizable character to exhaust fumes, it is recommended that samples of this fuel should be procured through appropriate agency, analysed, reproduced, and issued to Hoopla Force for use in auxiliary engine of fishing boat.

Someone before Guy had added the minute: *Could not a substance be introduced into standard fuel which would provide a characteristic odour of ersatz?*

Someone else, an admiral, had added: *It was decided (see attached minute) that auxiliary engine should be used only under a strong offshore wind. I consider risk of detection of odour negligible in such circumstances.*

Guy more modestly wrote: *Noted and approved. Guy Crouchback, Capt. for Brig. Commander S.S. Forces,* and squeezed past the megalosaurus to carry the file on its way.

'Beaches' was rather a jovial room. It housed an early Victorian locomotive engine, six sailors, and a library of naval charts. The reappearance of 'Hoopla' was here greeted with ironic applause. Some time back General Whale had forfeited the kindly sobriquet of 'Sprat' and was now known in the lower and more active regions of his command as 'Brides-in-the-bath'; for the reason that all the operations he sponsored seemed to require the extermination of all involved.

Next door to 'Beaches' there lived three RAF sergeants in what was called 'the studio'. Here beaches were constructed in miniature, yards and yards of them, reproducing from air-photographs miles and miles of the coast of occupied Europe. The studio was full of tools and odd scraps of material, woods, metals, pastes, gums, pigments, feathers, fibres, plasters, and oils many of them strongly aromatic. The tone was egalitarian in an antiquated, folky way distantly derived from the disciples of William Morris. Two of the sergeants were mature craftsmen; one, much younger, wore abundant golden curls such as the army would have cropped. He was addressed as 'Susie' and like his predecessors in the Arts and Crafts movement professed communism.

In their ample spare time these ingenious men were building a model of the Royal Victorian Institute. Guy took every opportunity to visit them and admire their work, as it daily grew in perfection. He paused there now.

'Been to see the Stalingrad sword?' Susie asked. 'Nice bit of work. But I reckon a few machine guns would be more to the point.'

He was addressing a tall, grey civilian dandy who stood nonchalantly posed beside him twirling a single eye-glass on its black cord. This was Sir Ralph Brompton, the diplomatic adviser to HOO HQ. He seemed a figure of obsolescent light comedy rather than of total war.

'It affords the People an opportunity for self-expression,' said Sir Ralph.

He was a retired ambassador who daily patrolled the building in the self-imposed task of 'political indoctrination'; an old man with a mission, but in no hurry.

He had called on Guy and after a very few words had despaired of him as a sympathetic subject. He did not now disguise his annoyance at being found with Susie.

'I just dropped in,' he said, half to Guy, half to the senior sergeant, 'to see if you were getting the *Foreign Affairs Summary* regularly.'

'I don't know,' said the senior sergeant. 'Are we, Sam?' He looked vaguely round the littered work-benches. 'We don't get bothered with much paper work here.'

'But you *should*,' said Sir Ralph. 'I make a special point of it being circulated to *all* ranks. Much devoted labour went into the last issue. You have to read between the lines sometimes. I'm at a disadvantage in saying quite all that needs saying in black and white. There is still a certain amount of prejudice to be cleared up – not in the highest quarters of course, or among the People. But *half way down*,' he said, gazing at Guy through his single eye-glass, without animosity seeing him with his back to a wall, facing a firing squad. 'One learns a certain amount of professional discretion in my absurd occupation. There will be no need for that after the war. Meanwhile one can only hint. I can tell you the main points: Tito's the friend, not Mihajlovic. We're backing the wrong horse in Malaya. And in China too. Chiang is a collaborationist. We have proof. The only real resistance is in the northern provinces – Russian trained and Russian armed, of course. They are the men who are going to drive out the Japs. It's all in the *Summary* if you read it attentively. I'll get you a copy. Don't forget this evening, Susie. I'm afraid I can't be there myself, but they are counting on you.'

He sauntered out twirling his eyeglass.

'What are you and that old geezer up to?' asked Sam.

'Party meeting,' said Susie.

'I know better things to do in the blackout than meetings.'

'So does the old geezer, it seems,' said the third sergeant.

'He's a bit of a bourgeois at heart for all his fine talk,' Susie admitted. All the time he spoke he was concentrating on his small lathe, turning tiny spiral columns with exquisite precision.

'You'll soon have that finished,' said Guy to the senior sergeant.

'Yes, barring interruptions. You can never tell when they'll come asking for more beaches. There isn't the same satisfaction in beaches.'

'They ought to have landed on them this summer,' said Susie. 'That's what was promised.'

'I didn't give no promises,' said Sam, busy with the fretsaw cutting little mahogany flagstones.

Guy left these happy, industrious men and paused in his progress at the room of Mr Oates, the civilian efficiency expert.

No one could be reasonably described as 'out of place' in HOO HQ, but Mr Oates, despite his unobtrusive appearance (or by reason of it), seemed bizarre to Guy. He was a plump, taciturn little man and he alone among all his heterogeneous colleagues proclaimed confidence. Of the others some toiled mindlessly, passing files from tray to tray, some took their ease, some were plotting, some hiding, some grousing; all quite baffled. But Mr Oates believed he was in his own way helping to win the war. He was a profoundly peaceful man and his way seemed clear before him.

'Any result of my application for the return of my typist?'

'Negative,' said Mr Oates.

'Kilbannock has three typists.'

'Not now. I have just withdrawn two of them. There is another, Mrs Troy, who is officially attached to him but her work seems mainly extramural. In fact her position is somewhat anomalous in this headquarters. I shall raise it at the next man-power conference.'

There had been a showy addition to Mr Oates's furniture since Guy's last visit; an elaborate machine of more modern construction than any permanent exhibit in the museum.

'What have you got there?'

Mr Oates made a little grimace of gratification.

'Ah! You have found my tender spot. You might call it my pet. Absolutely new. It's just been flown in from America. It took 560 man hours to install. The mechanics came from America, too. There isn't another like it in the country.'

'But what is it?'

'An Electronic Personnel Selector.'

'Have we any electronic personnel?'

'It covers every contingency. For example, suppose I want to find a lieutenant-colonel who is a long-distance swimmer, qualified as a barrister, with experience in catering in tropical countries, instead of going through all the records I just press these buttons, one, two, three, four, and . . .' there was a whirring noise from the depths of the engine, a series of clicks as though from a slot-machine telling fortunes on a pier, a card shot up. 'You see – totally blank – that means negative.'

'I think I could have guessed that.'

'Yes, I was illustrating an extreme example. Now here' – he picked up a chit from his tray – 'is a genuine inquiry. I've been asked to find an officer for special employment; under forty, with a university degree, who has lived in Italy, and had Commando training – one, two, three, four, five –' whirr, click, click, click, click, click. 'Here we are. Now that *is* a remarkable coincidence.'

The card he held bore the name of A/Ty. Captain Crouchback, G., RC, att. HOO HQ.

Guy did not attempt to correct the machine on the point of his age, or of the extent of his Commando training.

'I seem the only one.'

'Yes. I don't know what it's for, of course, but I will send your name in at once.'

2

Thirty-seven years old, six foot two in height, upright, powerful, heavier than he had been in the Middle East and paler, with a hint of flabbiness in the cheeks, wearing service dress, a well-kept Sam Browne belt, the ribbon of the MM and the badges of a Major in the Intelligence Corps; noticeable, if at all, for the pink-grey irises of his eyes; the man whom Hookforce had known as Corporal Major Ludovic paused reminiscently by the railings of St Margaret's, Westminster.

This was the place where he and others of his regiment had paraded twelve years and a few months ago, in King's Guard order as guard of honour for the wedding of one of their officers. Ludovic was a corporal then. The crowds had been enormous, less orderly and lighter of heart than those who now shuffled forward towards the Abbey, for the bride was a fashionable beauty and the bridegroom's name was familiar on advertisement hoardings and the labels of beer bottles.

They had lined the aisle; then while the register was being signed, had formed up along this path which led from the door to the motor car. Their finery had excited cries of admiration. As the organ sounded the first notes of the Wedding March they had drawn their swords and held them in a posture for which no drill-book has a name, forming an arch over the wedded couple. The bride had smiled right and left looking up at each of them in the eyes, thanking them. The bridegroom held his top hat in his hand and greeted by name those of his squadron he recognized. Two manikins carried the train clothed at enormous cost in replicas of Ludovic's own uniform; then the bridesmaids, plumper and plainer than the bride but flowery in full June. Then they had lowered their swords to the 'carry'; a royal party had passed between them smiling also; then parents, and after them a long stream of guests; scarcely visible under the peak of the helmet behind and all round them were reporters and photographers and a cheering, laughing London crowd.

It was after that wedding, in the tented yard behind a house in St James's Square (now demolished by a bomb), that Sir Ralph Brompton had first accosted Ludovic. The royal party sat in the ballroom on the first floor, where the young couple received their guests. A temporary wooden stair had been built from the ballroom balcony to the tent (for it was a rule that no member of the royal family should be in a room without an alternative egress) and the guests, after they had made their salutations, went below, leaving that still little pool of humble duty for the noisier celebrations under the canvas. Later, when they discussed the question, as they often did, neither Sir Ralph nor Ludovic was able to explain what distinguished the young corporal from his fellows, except that he stood a little apart from them. He did not like beer, and great jugs of special brew, made by the bridegroom's father for the occasion, were being pressed on the guard of honour, the tenants, and foremen and old servants who segregated themselves in their own corner of the marquee. Sir Ralph, as tall as any trooper and almost as splendid in grey tail suit and full cravat, had joined the convivial, plebeian group and said: 'You're much better off with the ale. The champagne is poison,' and so had begun an association which developed richly.

Sir Ralph was then doing a spell at the Foreign Office. When the time came for him to go abroad on post, he arranged for Ludovic's release from the regiment, who were sorry to lose him; he had lately been promoted corporal of horse at an early age. Then had begun five years' life abroad in Sir Ralph's company, as 'valet' at the embassy, as 'secretary' when they travelled on leave. Sir Ralph discreetly attended to his protégé's education, lending him books on psychology which he relished and on Marxist economics which he found tedious; giving him tickets for concerts and the opera, leading him, when they were on holiday, through galleries and cathedrals.

The marriage did not last long. There was an unusually early divorce. Ludovic, as he now was, constituted the sole progeny of that union.

It was 5 o'clock. At 5.30 the Abbey had to be shut for the night. Already the police were turning away the extremity of the queue saying: 'You won't get in today. Come back tomorrow morning – early,' and the people obediently drifted into the dusk to join other queues elsewhere.

Major Ludovic went straight to the Abbey entrance, laid his blank oyster gaze on the policeman and raised his gloved hand to acknowledge a salute that had not been given.

"Ere, just a moment, sir, where are you going?'

'The – er – King's present to the – er – Russians – they tell me it's on show here.'

'Got to wait your turn. There's others before you, sir.'

Ludovic spoke with two voices. He had tried as an officer; now he reverted to the tones of the barrack-room. 'That's all right, cock. I'm here on duty same as yourself,' and the puzzled man stood back to let him by.

Inside the Abbey it seemed already night. The windows gave no light. The two candles led the people forward, who, as they were admitted in twenties, broke their column of fours, advanced in a group and then fell into single file as they reached the sword. They knew no formal act of veneration. They paused, gazed, breathed, and passed on. Ludovic was the tallest of them. He could see the bright streak from above their heads. He held his cap and his cane behind his back and peered intently. He had a special interest there, but when he came to the sword and tried to linger he was pressed silently on, not jostled resentfully, but silently conscribed into the unseeing, inarticulate procession who were asserting their right to the fair share of everything which they believed the weapon symbolized. He had no time to study the detail. He glimpsed the keen edge, the sober ornament, the more luxurious scabbard, and then was borne on and out. It was not five minutes before he found himself once more alone, in the deepening fog.

Ludovic had an appointment with Sir Ralph for 5.30. He had to meet by appointment in these days. They were no longer on the old easy terms, but Ludovic did not lose touch. In his altered and exalted status he did not look for money, but there were other uses to which their old association could be put. Whenever he came to London he let Sir Ralph know and they had tea together. Sir Ralph had other companions for dinner.

They met at their old place of assignation. Once Sir Ralph had a house in Hanover Terrace, and his retreat in Ebury Street – rooms over a shop, which had something of the air of expensive undergraduate digs – had been a secret known to barely fifty men. Now these rooms were his home; he had moved the smaller pieces of his furniture there; but not many more people – fewer perhaps – knew the way there than in the old days.

Ludovic walked down Victoria Street, crossed the shapeless expanse at the bottom and reached the familiar doorstep at the same moment as his host. Sir Ralph opened the door and stood back for Ludovic to enter. He had never lacked devoted servants. 'Mrs Embury,' he called, 'Mrs Embury,' and his housekeeper appeared above them on the half landing. She had known Ludovic in other days.

'Tea,' he said, handing her a little parcel, 'Lapsang Suchong – half a pound of it. Bartered in what strange eastern markets, I know not. But the genuine article. I have a friend at our headquarters who gets me some from time to time. We must go easy with it, Mrs Embury, but I think we might "brew up" for "the Major".'

They went upstairs and sat in the drawing-room.

'No doubt you want to hear my opinion of your "*Pensées*".'

'I want to hear Everard Spruce's.'

'Yes, of course, I deserved that little snub. Well, prepare yourself for good news – Everard is *delighted* with them and wants to publish them in *Survival*. He is quite content to leave them anonymous. The only thing he doesn't quite like is the title.'

'*Pensées*,' said Ludovic. 'D'you know what they call our badge?' He tapped the floral device on the lapel of his tunic. '"A pansy sitting on its laurels".'

'Yes, yes. Very good. I have heard the witticism before. No; Everard thinks it dated. He suggests "Notes in Transit" or something of the sort.'

'I don't see it matters.'

'No. But he's definitely interested in you. Wants to meet. In fact, I tentatively accepted an invitation for you this evening. I shan't, alas, be able to introduce you. But you're expected. I'll give you the address. I am expecting another visitor here.'

'Curly?'

'They call him "Susie" at the headquarters. No, not Susie. He's a dear boy and a stalwart party member but a little earnest for the long blackout. I am packing him off to a meeting. No, I expect a very intelligent young American named Padfield – an officer, *like you*.'

Mrs Embury brought in the tea, and the little, over-furnished room was full of its fragrance.

'I can't offer you anything to eat I'm afraid.'

'I know better than come to London for food,' said Ludovic. 'We do all right at my billet.' He had learned his officer's voice from Sir Ralph but seldom used it when they were alone. 'Mrs Embury isn't very matey these days?'

'It's your high rank. She doesn't know how to take it. And you, what have you been up to?'

'I went to the Abbey before I came here – to see the sword.'

'Yes, I suppose like everyone else you are coming to appreciate the Soviet achievement. You usen't to have much share in my "red" sympathies. We nearly had a tiff once, remember? about Spain.'

'There were Spaniards in the Middle East – proper bastards.' Ludovic stopped short remembering what he resolutely strove to forget. 'It wasn't anything to do with politics. That sword is the subject of this week's literary competition in *Time and Tide* – a sonnet. I thought if I went to see it, I might get some ideas.'

'Oh dear, don't tell Everard Spruce about that. I'm afraid he would look down his nose at literary competitions in *Time and Tide*.'

'I just like writing,' said Ludovic. 'In different ways about different things. Nothing wrong with that, I suppose?'

'No, indeed. The literary instinct. But don't tell Everard. *Did* you get any ideas?'

'Not what I could use in a sonnet. But it set me thinking – about swords.'

'That wasn't quite their idea; not, as they say now, the object of the exercise. You were meant to think about tanks and bombers and the People's Army driving out the Nazis.'

'I thought of *my* sword,' said Ludovic stubbornly. 'Technically, I suppose, it was a sabre. *We* called them "swords" – "state swords". Never saw it again after I left the regiment. They weren't reissued when we were recalled. Took a lot of looking after, a sword. Every now and then the armourer had them in and buffed them; ordinary days it was Bluebell and the chain-burnisher. Mustn't leave a spot on it. You could always tell a good officer. On a wet day he didn't give the order "Return swords" but "With drawn swords, prepare to dismount". You took it half way up the blade in your left hand and transferred to the near side of the withers. That way you didn't get water into the scabbard. Some officers didn't think of that; the good ones did.'

'Yes, yes, most picturesque,' said Sir Ralph. 'Not much bearing on the conditions at Stalingrad.'

Then Ludovic suddenly assumed his officer's voice and said 'After all, it was the uniform first attracted you, don't you remember?'

Only a preternaturally astute reader of Ludovic's aphorisms could discern that their author had once been at heart – or rather in some vestigial repository of his mind – a romantic. Most of those who volunteered for Commandos in the spring of 1940 had other motives besides the desire to serve their country. A few merely sought release from regimental routine; more wished to cut a gallant figure before women; others had led lives of particular softness and were moved to re-establish their honour in the eyes of the heroes of their youth – legendary, historical, fictitious – that still haunted their manhood. Nothing in Ludovic's shortly to be published work made clear how he had seen himself. His early schooling had furnished few models of chivalry. His original enlistment in the Blues, so near the body of the king, so flamboyantly accoutred, had certainly not been prompted by any familiarity or affection for the horse. Ludovic was a townsman. The smell of stables brought no memories of farm or hunt. In his years with Sir Ralph Brompton he had lived soft; any instinct for expiation of which he was conscious, was unexpressed. Yet he had volunteered for special service at the first opportunity. His fellow volunteers now had ample leisure in their various prison camps to examine their motives and strip themselves of illusion. As also had Ludovic, at liberty; but his disillusionment (if he ever suffered from illusion) had preceded the débâcle at Crete. There was a week in the mountains, two days in a cave, a particular night in an open boat during the exploit that had earned him his MM and his commission, of which he never spoke. When questioned, as he had been on his return to Africa, he confessed that his memory of those events was almost blank; a very common condition, sympathetic doctors assured him, after a feat of extreme endurance.

His last two years had been as uneventful as Guy's.

After his rapid discharge from hospital he had been posted to the United Kingdom to be trained as an officer. At the board who interviewed him, he had expressed no preference for any arm of the service. He had no mechanical bent. They had posted him to the Intelligence Corps, then in process of formation and expansion. He had attended courses, learned to interpret air-photographs, to recognize enemy uniform, and compute an order of battle, to mark maps, to collate and summarize progress-reports from the field; all the rudimentary skills. At the end his early peace-time training as a trooper impressed the selection-board that he was a 'quartermaster type' and an appointment was found for him far from the battle, far from the arcane departments whose existence was barely hinted at in the lecture room; in a secret place, indeed, but one where no secrets were disclosed to Ludovic. He was made commandant of a little establishment where men, and sometimes women, of all ages and nations, military and civilian, many with obviously assumed names, were trained at a neighbouring aerodrome to jump in parachutes.

Thus whatever romantic image of himself Ludovic had ever set up was finally defaced.

In his lonely condition he found more than solace, positive excitement, in the art of writing. The further he removed from human society and the less he attended to human speech, the more did words, printed and written, occupy his mind. The books he read were books about words. As he lay unshriven, his sleep was never troubled by the monstrous memories which might have been supposed to lie in wait for him in the dark. He dreamed of words and woke repeating them as though memorizing a foreign vocabulary. Ludovic had become an addict of that potent intoxicant, the English language.

Not laboriously, luxuriously rather, Ludovic worked over his note-books, curtailing, expanding, polishing; often consulting Fowler, not disdaining Roget; writing and rewriting in his small clerkly hand on the lined sheets of paper which the army supplied; telling no one what he was up to, until at length there were fifty foolscap pages, which he sent to Sir Ralph, not asking his opinion, but instructing him to find a publisher.

It was in miniature a golden age for the book-trade; anything sold; the supply of paper alone determined a writer's popularity. But publishers had obligations to old clients and an eye to the future. Ludovic's *pensées* stirred no hopes of a sequel of best-selling novels. The established firms were on the look out for promise rather than accomplishment. Sir Ralph therefore sent the manuscript to Everard Spruce, the founder and editor of *Survival*; a man who cherished no ambitions for the future, believing, despite the title of his monthly review, that the human race was destined to dissolve in chaos.

The war had raised Spruce, who in the years preceding it had not been the most esteemed of his coterie of youngish, socialist writers, to unrivalled eminence. Those of his friends who had not fled to Ireland or to America had joined the Fire Brigade. Spruce by contrast had stood out for himself and in that disorderly period when Guy had sat in Bellamy's writing so many fruitless appeals for military employment, had announced the birth of a magazine devoted 'to the Survival of Values'. The Ministry of Information gave it protection, exempted its staff from other duties, granted it a generous allowance of paper, and exported it in bulk to whatever countries were still open to British shipping. Copies were even scattered from aeroplanes in regions under German domination and patiently construed by partisans with the aid of dictionaries. A member who complained in the House of Commons that so far as its contents were intelligible to him, they were pessimistic in tone and unconnected in subject with the war effort, was told at some length by the Minister that free expression in the arts was an essential of democracy. 'I personally have no doubt,' he said, 'and I am confirmed in my opinion by many reports, that great encouragement is given to our allies and sympathizers throughout the world by the survival' (laughter) 'in this country of what is almost unique in present conditions, a periodical entirely independent of official direction.'

Spruce lived in a fine house in Cheyne Walk cared for by secretaries to the number of four. It was there that Ludovic was directed by Sir Ralph. He went on foot through the lightless streets, smelling the river before him in the deepening fog.

He was not entirely unacquainted with men of letters. Several had been habitués of Ebury Street; he had sat at café tables with them on the Mediterranean coast; but always in those days he had been an appendage of Sir Ralph's, sometimes ignored, sometimes punctiliously brought into the conversation, often impertinently studied; never regarded as a possible confrère. This was the first time that Ludovic had gone among them in his own right. He was not the least nervous but he was proudly conscious of a change of status far more gratifying than any conferred by military rank.

Spruce was in his middle thirties. Time was, he cultivated a proletarian, youthful, aspect; not successfully; now, perhaps without design, he looked older than his years and presented the negligent elegance of a fashionable don. One of his friends, on joining the Fire Brigade, had left a trunk under Spruce's protection and when he was buried by a falling chimney Spruce had appropriated his wardrobe; the secretaries had adjusted the Charvet shirts and pyjamas; the suits were beyond their skill; Spruce was, thus, often seen abroad in a voluminous furlined overcoat, while at home, whenever the temperature allowed, he dispensed with a jacket. Tonight he wore a heavy silk, heavily striped shirt and a bow tie above noncommittal trousers. The secretaries were dressed rather like him though in commoner materials; they wore their hair long and enveloping in a style which fifteen years later was to be associated by the newspapers with the King's Road. One went bare-footed as though to emphasize her servile condition. They were sometimes spoken of as 'Spruce's veiled ladies'. They gave him their full devotion; also their rations of butter, meat, and sugar.

One of these opened the door to Ludovic and without asking his name said through a curtain of hair: 'Do come in quick. The blackout's not very efficient. They're all upstairs.'

There was a party in the drawing-room on the first floor.

'Which is Mr Spruce?'

'Don't you know? Over there, of course, talking to the Smart Woman.'

Ludovic looked round the room where, in a company of twenty or so, women predominated, but none appeared notably dressy, but the host identified himself by coming forward with an expression of sharp inquiry.

'I am Ludovic,' said Ludovic. 'Ralph Brompton said you were expecting me.'

'Yes, of course. Don't go until we have had the chance of a talk. I must apologize for the crowd. Two anti-fascist neutrals have been wished on me by the Ministry of Information. They asked me to collect some interesting people. Not easy these days. Do you speak Turkish or Portuguese?'

'No.'

'That's a pity. They are both professors of English Literature but not very fluent in conversation. Come and talk to Lady Perdita.'

He led Ludovic to the woman with whom he had been standing. She was wearing the uniform of an air-raid warden and had smudges of soot on her face. 'Smart', Ludovic perceived denoted rank rather than chic in this milieu.

'I was at your wedding,' said Ludovic.

'Surely not? No one was.'

'Your first wedding.'

'Oh, yes, of course, everyone was *there*.'

'I held my sword over your head when you left the church.'

'That was a long time ago,' said Lady Perdita. 'Think of it: *swords*.'

The bare-footed secretary approached with a jug and a glass.

'Will you have a drink?'

'What is it?'

'There's nothing else,' she said. 'I made it. Half South African Sherry and half something called "Olde Falstaffe Gin".'

'I don't think I will, thank you,' said Ludovic.

'Snob,' said Lady Perdita. 'Fill me up, Frankie, there's a dear.'

'There's hardly enough to go round.'

'I'll have this chap's ration.'

The host interrupted: 'Perdita, I want you to meet Dr Iago from Coimbra. He talks a bit of French.'

Ludovic was left with the secretary, who kept custody of her eyes. Addressing her bare toes she said: 'One thing about a party, it does warm the room. Who are you?' she asked.

'Ludovic. Mr Spruce has accepted something I wrote for *Survival*.'

'Yes, of course,' she said. 'I know all about you now. I read your manuscript too. Everard is awfully impressed with it. He said it was as though Logan Pearsall Smith had written Kafka. Do you know Logan?'

'Only by his writing.'

'You must meet him. He's not here tonight. He doesn't go out now. I say, what a relief to meet a real writer instead of all these smarties Everard wastes his time on' (this with a dark glance from her feet to the air-raid warden). 'Look; there *is* some whisky. We've only got one bottle so we have to be rather careful with it. Come next door and I'll give you some.'

'Next door' was the office, a smaller room austerely, even meanly furnished. Back-numbers of *Survival* were piled on the bare floorboards, manuscripts and photographs on the bare table; a black sheet was secured by drawing-pins to cover the window. Here, when they were not engaged on domestic tasks – cooking, queueing, or darning – the four secretaries stoked the cultural beacon which blazed from Iceland to Adelaide; here the girl who could type answered Spruce's numerous 'fan letters' and the girl who could spell corrected proofs. Here it seemed some of them slept for there were divan beds covered with blankets only and a large, much undenticulated, comb.

Frankie went to the cupboard and revealed a bottle. Many strange concoctions of the 'Olde Falstaffe' kind circulated in those days. This was not one of them.

'Not opened yet,' she said.

Ludovic was not fond of spirits nor was whisky any rarity at his well-found station; nevertheless he accepted the offered drink with a solemnity which verged on reverence. This was no mere clandestine treat. Frankie was initiating him into the occult company of Logan and Kafka. He would find time in the days to come to learn who Kafka was. Now he drained the glass swallowing almost without repugnance the highly valued distillation.

'You seemed to want that,' said Frankie. 'I daren't offer you another yet I'm afraid. Perhaps later. It depends who else turns up.'

'It was just what I wanted,' said Ludovic; '*all* that I wanted,' repressing a momentary inclination to retch.

3

The Kilbannocks' house in Eaton Terrace had suffered no direct damage from bombing; not a pane of glass had been broken, not a chimney-pot thrown down; but four years of war had left their marks on the once gay interior. Kerstie did her best, but paint, wallpapers, chintzes, and carpets were stained and shabby. Despite these appearances the Kilbannocks had in fact recovered from the comparative penury of 1939. Kerstie no longer took lodgers. She had moved from the canteen of the Transit Camp to a well paid job as cipher clerk; Ian's pay rose with the rings on his cuff; an aunt had died leaving him a modest legacy. And there was nothing in those days to tempt anyone to extravagance. Kerstie had had Ian's evening clothes cleverly adapted into a serviceable coat and skirt. The children were still confined to their grandmother in Scotland and came to London only on occasions.

On this October evening they were expecting Virginia Troy, once an inmate, now rather a rare visitor.

'You'd better go out to Bellamy's or somewhere,' said Kerstie, 'I gathered on the telephone that Virginia wants a heart-to-hearter.'

'Trimmer?'

'I suppose so.'

'I'm thinking of shipping him to America.'

'It will be much the best thing.'

'We've done pretty well all we can with him in this country. We've finished the film. The BBC don't want to renew "The Voice of Trimmer" Sunday evening postscripts.'

'I should think not.'

'It seemed a good idea. Somehow it didn't catch on. Trimmer has to be seen as well as heard. Besides, there are a lot of rival heroes with rather better credentials.'

'You think the Americans will swallow him?'

'He'll be something new. They're sick of fighter pilots. By the way, do you realize it was Trimmer who gave the monarch the idea for this Sword of Stalingrad? Indirectly, of course. In the big scene of Trimmer's landing I gave him a "commando dagger" to brandish. I don't suppose you've even seen the things. They were an idea of Brides-in-the-Bath's early on. A few hundred were issued. To my certain knowledge none was ever used in action. A Glasgow policeman got a nasty poke with one. They were mostly given away to tarts. But they were beautifully made little things. Well, you know how sharp the royal eye is for any detail of equipment. He was given a preview of the Trimmer film and spotted the dagger at once. Had one sent round to him. Then the royal mind brooded a bit and the final result was that thing in the Abbey. An odd item of contemporary history.'

'Are you going to Bellamy's?'

'Everard Spruce asked us to a party. I might look in.'

The bell of the front door sounded through the little house.

'Virginia, I expect.'

Ian let her in. She kissed with cold detestation and came upstairs.

'I thought you were sending him out,' she said to Kerstie.

'I am. Run along, Ian, we have things to talk about.'

'Do I have to remind you that I am your direct superior officer?'

'Oh God, how that joke bores me.'

'I see you've brought luggage.'

'Yes, can I stay for a bit, Kerstie?'

'Yes, for a bit.'

'Until Trimmer's out of the country. He says he's had a warning order to stand by for a trip – somewhere where he can't take me, thank God.'

'I always hoped,' said Ian, 'you might come to like him.'

'I've done two years.'

'Yes, you've been jolly good. You deserve a holiday. Well, I'll leave you two. I expect I'll be pretty late home.'

Neither woman showed any regret at this announcement. Ian went downstairs and out into the darkness.

'There's nothing in the house to drink,' said Kerstie. 'We could go out somewhere.'

'Coffee?'

'Yes, I can manage that.'

'Let's stay in then.'

'Nothing much to eat either. I've got some cod.'

'No cod, thanks.'

'I say, Virginia, you're pretty low.'

'Dead flat. What's happened to everyone? London used to be full of chums. Now I don't seem to know anyone. Do you realize that since my brother was killed I haven't a single living relation?'

'My dear, I am sorry. I hadn't heard. In fact I didn't know you had a brother.'

'He was called Tim – five years younger than me. We never got on. He was killed three years ago. You've such hundreds of children and parents and cousins, Kerstie. You can't imagine what it feels like to be quite alone. There's my step-mother in Switzerland. She never approved of me and I can't get at her now anyway. I'm scared, Kerstie.'

'Tell.'

Virginia was never one whose confidences needed drawing out.

'Money,' she said. 'I've never known what it was like to have *no* money.

It's a very odd sensation indeed. Tim made a will leaving all he had to some girl. Papa never left me anything. He thought I was well provided for.'

'Surely Mr Troy will have to cough up eventually. Americans are great ones for alimony.'

'That's what I thought. It's what my bank manager and lawyer said. At first they thought it was just some difficulty of exchange control. They wrote him a lot of letters polite at first, then firm, then threatening. Finally, about six months ago they hired a lawyer in New York to serve a writ. A fine move that turned out to be. Mr Troy has divorced me.'

'Surely he can't do that?'

'He's done it. All signed and sealed. Apparently he's had a man watching me and taking affidavits.'

'How absolutely disgusting.'

'It's just like Mr Troy. I ought to have suspected when he lay so low. We've sent for copies of the evidence in case there is any sort of appeal possible. But it doesn't sound likely. After all, I haven't been strictly faithful to Mr Troy all this time.'

'He could hardly expect that.'

'So not only no alimony, but an overdraft and a huge lawyer's bill. I did the only thing I could and sold jewels. The beasts gave me half what they cost; said no one was buying at the moment.'

'Just what they said to Brenda.'

'Then this morning a very awkward thing happened. One of the things I sold was a pair of clips Augustus gave me. I'd quite forgotten about them till they turned up in an old bag. What's more I'd forgotten that when I lost them years ago I had reported it to the insurance company and been paid. Apparently I've committed a criminal offence. They've been fairly decent about that. They aren't going to the police or anything but I've got to refund the money – £250. It doesn't sound much but I haven't got it. So this afternoon I've been hawking furs around. They say no one's buying *them* either, though I should have thought it's just what everyone *will* want with winter coming on and no coal.'

'I always envied your furs,' said Kerstie.

'Yours for £250.'

'What's the best offer you got?'

'Believe it or not, £75.'

'I happen to have a little money in the bank at the moment,' said Kerstie thoughtfully. 'I could go a bit higher than that.'

'I need three times as much.'

'You must have *some* other things left.'

'All I possess in the world is downstairs in your hall.'

'Let's go through it, Virginia. You always had so many things. I'm sure we can find something. There's that cigarette case you're using now.'

'It's badly knocked about.'

'But it was good once.'

'Mr Troy, Cannes, 1936.'

'I'm sure we can find enough to make up £250.'

'Oh Kerstie, you are a comfort to a girl.'

So the two of them, who had 'come out' the same year and led such different lives, the one so prodigal, the other so circumspect and sparing, spread out Virginia's possessions over the grubby sofa and spent all that evening like gypsy hucksters examining and pricing those few surviving trophies of a decade of desirable womanhood, and in the end went off to bed comforted, each in her way, and contented with their traffic.

4

Guy felt that he had been given a birthday present; the first for how many years? The card that had come popping out of the Electronic Personnel Selector bearing his name, like a 'fortune' from a seaside slot-machine, like a fortune indeed in a more real sense – the luck of the draw in a lottery or sweepstake – brought an unfamiliar stir of exhilaration, such as he had felt in his first days in the Halberdiers, in his first minutes on enemy soil at Dakar; a sense of liberation such as he had felt when he had handed over Apthorpe's legacy to Chatty Corner and when he broke his long silence in the hospital in Alexandria. These had been the memorable occasions of his army life; all had been during the first two years of war; of late he had ceased to look for a renewal. Now there was hope. There was still a place for him somewhere outside the futile routine of HOO HQ.

He came off duty at six and, at the Transit Camp, on an impulse, did what he had seldom done lately, changed into blue patrols. He then took the tube railway, where the refugees were already making up their beds, to Green Park Station and walked under the arcade of the Ritz towards St James's Street and Bellamy's. American soldiers leant against the walls every few paces hugging their drabs, and an American soldier of another kind greeted him in the front hall of the club.

'Good evening, Loot.'

'Are you going to Everard Spruce's party?'

'Haven't been asked. Don't know him really. I thought you were expected at the Glenobans'.'

'I shall visit them later. First I am taking dinner with Ralph Brompton. But I thought I should look in on Everard on the way.'

He returned to his task of letter writing at the table opposite Job's box, which Guy had never before seen used.

In the back hall Guy found Arthur Box-Bender.

'Just slipped away from the House for a breather. Everything is going merrily on the eastern front.'

'Merrily?'

'Wait for the nine o'clock news. You'll hear something then. Uncle Joe's fairly got them on the run. I shouldn't much care to be one of his prisoners.'

By a natural connexion of thought Guy asked: 'Have you heard from Tony?'

Gloom descended on Box-Bender. 'Yes, as a matter of fact, last week. He's still got that tom-fool idea in his head about being a monk. He'll snap out of it, I'm sure, as soon as he gets back to normal life, but it's worrying. Angela doesn't seem to mind awfully. She's worried about your father.'

'So am I.'

'She's at Matchet now. As you know he's stopped working at that school, which is something gained. He never ought to have taken it on at his age. He's got this clot you know. It might become serious any moment.'

'I know. I saw him last month. He seemed all right then but he wrote to me afterwards.'

'There's nothing one can do about it,' said Box-Bender. 'Angela thought she should be handy in case anything happened.'

Guy went on to the bar where he found Ian Kilbannock talking to an elderly Grenadier.

'. . . You know how sharp the royal eye is for any detail of equipment,' he was saying. 'The monarch sent for one of those daggers. That's what set the royal mind brooding about cutlery.'

'It's been a great success.'

'Yes, I claim a little indirect credit for it myself. Evening, Guy. Who do you think has just turned me out of my house? – Virginia.'

'How was she?'

'On the rocks. I only saw her for a second but she was palpably on the rocks. I'd heard some loose talk about her affairs before.'

'I'll give you a drink,' said Guy, 'it's my birthday. Two glasses of wine, Parsons.'

Guy did not speak about the Electronic Selector but the thought of it warmed him as they talked of other things. When their glasses were empty the Grenadier said: 'Did someone say it was his birthday? Three glasses of wine, Parsons.'

When it would have been Ian's turn to order, he said: 'They've put up the prices. Ten bob a glass for this champagne now and it's not good. Why don't you come to Everard Spruce's and drink free?'

'Will he have champagne?'

'Sure to. He enjoys heavy official backing and tonight he's got two distinguished foreigners to impress. It's pleasant to get into a completely civilian circle once in a while. D'you read his paper?'

'No.'

'Nor do I. But it's highly thought of. Winston reads it.'

'I don't believe you.'

'Well perhaps not personally. But a copy goes to the Cabinet Offices I happen to know.'

'I hardly know Spruce. The Loot's going.'

'Then anyone can. He'll be able to get a cab. They always stop for Americans.'

Lieutenant Padfield was still at work on his correspondence; he wrote rather laboriously; the pen did not come readily to him; in youth he had typed; in earliest manhood dictated. Ian sent him up to Piccadilly and, sure enough, he returned in a quarter of an hour with a taxi.

'Glad to have you come with me,' he said. 'I thought you were not acquainted with Spruce.'

'I changed my mind.'

'*Survival* is a very significant organ of opinion.'

'Signifying what, Loot?'

'The survival of values.'

'You think I need special coaching in that subject?'

'Pardon me.'

'You think I should read this paper?'

'You will find it very significant.'

It was nearly eight o'clock when they reached Cheyne Walk. Some of the party, including the neutral guests, had already sickened of Frankie's cocktail and taken their leave.

'The party's really over,' said one of the secretaries, not Frankie; she wore espadrilles and the hair through which she spoke was black. 'I think Everard wants to go out.'

Lieutenant Padfield was engaged in over-paying the taxi; he still, after his long sojourn, found English currency confusing and the driver sought to confuse him further. On hearing these mumbled words he said: 'My, is it that late? I ought to be in Ebury Street. If you don't mind I'll take the taxi on.'

Guy and Ian did not mind. The Lieutenant had fulfilled his manifest destiny in bringing them here.

Strengthened in her resolution by this defection the secretary, Coney by name, said: 'I don't believe there's anything left to drink.'

'I was promised champagne,' said Guy.

'Champagne,' said Coney, taken aback, not knowing who he was, not knowing either of these uniformed figures looming out of the lightless mist, but knowing that Spruce had, in fact, a few bottles of that wine laid down. 'I don't know anything about champagne.'

'Well, we'll come up and see,' said Ian.

Coney led them upstairs.

Though depleted the company was still numerous enough to provide a solid screen between the entrance and the far corner in which Ludovic was seated. For two minutes now he had been in enjoyment of what he had come for, the attention of his host.

'The arrangement is haphazard or planned?' Spruce was asking.

'Planned.'

'The plan is not immediately apparent. There are the more or less generalized aphorisms, there are the particular observations – which I thought, if I may say so, extremely acute and funny. I wondered: are they in any cases libellous? And besides these there seemed to me two poetic themes which occur again and again. There is the Drowned Sailor motif – an echo of the *Waste Land* perhaps? Had you Eliot consciously in mind?'

'Not Eliot,' said Ludovic. 'I don't think he was called Eliot.'

'Very interesting. And then there was the Cave image. You must have read a lot of Freudian psychology.'

'Not a lot. There was nothing psychological about the cave.'

'Very interesting – a spontaneous liberation of the unconscious.'

At this moment Coney infiltrated the throng and stood beside them.

'Everard, there are two men in uniform asking for champagne.'

'Good heavens, not the police?'

'One might be. He's wearing an odd sort of blue uniform. The other's an airman. I've never seen them before. They had an American with them but he ran away.'

'How very odd. You haven't given them champagne?'

'Oh no, Everard.'

'I'd better go and see who they are.'

At the door Ian had collided with the Smart Woman and kissed her warmly on each dusty cheek.

'Drinks have run out here,' she said, 'and I am due at my Warden's Post. Why don't you two come there? It's only round the corner and there's always a bottle.'

Spruce greeted them.

'I'm afraid we're a little late. I brought Guy. You remember him?'

'Yes, yes, I suppose so. Somewhere,' said Spruce. 'Everything is over here. I was just having a few words with a very interesting New Writer. We always particularly welcome contributions from service men. It's part of our policy.'

The central knot of guests opened and revealed Ludovic, his appetite for appreciation whetted but far from satisfied, gazing resentfully towards Spruce's back.

'Ludovic,' said Guy.

'That is the man I was speaking of. You know him?'

'He saved my life,' said Guy.

'How very odd.'

'I've never had a chance to thank him.'

'Well, do so now. But don't take him away. I was in the middle of a fascinating conversation.'

'I think I'll go off with Per.'

'Yes, do.'

The gap had closed again. Guy passed through and held out his hand to Ludovic who raised his oyster eyes with an expression of unmitigated horror. He took the hand limply and looked away.

'Ludovic, surely you remember me?'

'It is most unexpected.'

'Hookforce. Crete.'

'Oh yes, I remember.'

'I've always been hoping to run into you again. There's so much to say. They told me you saved my life.' Ludovic mutely raised his hand to the ribbon of the MM. It was as though he were beating his breast in penitence. 'You don't seem very pleased to see me.'

'It's the shock,' said Ludovic, resuming his barrack-room speech, 'not looking to find you here, not at Mr Spruce's. You of all people, here of all places.'

Guy took the chair where Spruce had sat.

'My memory's awfully vague of those last days in Crete and in the boat.'

'Best forgotten,' said Ludovic. 'Things happen that're best forgotten.'

'Oh, come. Aren't you rather overdoing the modest hero? Besides I'm curious. What happened to Major Hound?'

'I understand he was reported missing.'

'Not a prisoner?'

'Forgive me Mr – Captain Crouchback. I am not in Records.'

'And the sapper who got the boat going. I was awfully ill – so was he – delirious.'

'You were delirious too.'

'Yes. Did you rescue the sapper too?'

'I understand he was reported lost at sea.'

'Look,' said Guy, 'are you doing anything for dinner?'

It was as though Banquo had turned host.

'No,' said Ludovic. 'No,' and without apology or a word of farewell to Guy or Spruce or Frankie, he made precipitately for the stairs, the front door and the sheltering blackout.

'What on earth happened to him?' asked Spruce. 'He can't have been drunk. What did you say to him?'

427

'Nothing. I asked him about old times.'

'You knew him well?'

'Not exactly. We always thought him odd.'

'He has talent,' said Spruce. 'Perhaps a hint of genius. It's most annoying his disappearing like that. Well, the party's over. Will you girls shoo the guests away and then clear up? I have to go.'

Guy spent the remaining hours of his fortieth birthday at Bellamy's playing 'slosh'. When he returned to his room at the Transit Camp his thoughts were less on the past than on the future.

Unheard in Bellamy's the sirens sounded an alert at eleven o'clock and an 'all clear' before midnight.

Unheard too in Westminster Abbey where the Sword of Stalingrad stood unattended. The doors were locked, the lights all extinguished. Next day the queue would form again in the street and the act of homage would be renewed.

Ludovic was not successful in the *Time and Tide* literary competition. His sonnet was not even commended. He studied the winning entry:

> ... Here lies the sword. Ah, but the work is rare,
> Precious the symbol. Who has understood
> How close the evil or how dread the good
> Who scorns the vestures that the angels wear?

He could make no sense of it. Was the second 'who' a relative pronoun with 'good' as its antecedent? He compared his own lucid sonnet:

> Stele of my past on which engravéd are
> The pleadings of that long divorce of steel,
> In which was stolen that directive star,
> By which I sailed, expunged be. No spar,
> No mast, no halyard, bowsprit, boom or keel
> Survives my wreck ...

Perhaps, he reflected, the lines were not strictly appropriate to the occasion. He had failed to reflect the popular mood. It was too personal for *Time and Tide*. He would send it to *Survival*.

BOOK TWO

Fin de Ligne

I

Virginia Troy had not been in his house ten days before Ian Kilbannock began to ask: 'When is she going?'

'I don't mind having her,' said Kerstie. 'She's not costing us much.'

'But she isn't contributing anything.'

'I couldn't ask Virginia to do that. She was awfully decent to us when she was rich.'

'That's a long time ago. I've had Trimmer shipped to America. I just don't understand why she has to stay here. The other girls used to pay their share.'

'I might suggest it to her.'

'As soon as you can.'

But when Virginia returned that evening she brought news which put other thoughts out of Kerstie's head.

'I've just been to my lawyers,' she said. 'They've got the copy of all Mr Troy's divorce evidence. Who do you think collected it?'

'Who?'

'Three guesses.'

'I can't think of anyone.'

'That disgusting Loot.'

'It's not possible.'

'Apparently he's a member of the firm who works for Mr Troy. He still does odd jobs for them in his spare time.'

'After we've all been so kind to him! Are you going to give him away?'

'I don't know.'

'People ought to be warned.'

'It's all our own fault for taking him up. He always gave me the creeps.'

'A thing like this,' said Kerstie, 'destroys one's faith in human nature.'

'Oh, the Loot isn't human.'

'No, I suppose not really.'

'He made a change from Trimmer.'

'Would you say Trimmer was human?'

429

They fell back on this problem, which in one form or another had been fully debated between them for three years.

'D'you miss him at all?'

'Pure joy and relief. Every morning for the last four days I've woken up to the thought "Trimmer's gone".'

At length after an hour's discussion Kerstie said: 'I suppose you'll be looking for somewhere else to live now.'

'Not unless you want to get rid of me.'

'Of course it isn't that, darling, only Ian . . .'

But Virginia was not listening. Instead she interrupted with: 'Have you got a family doctor?'

'We always go to an old boy in Sloane Street called Puttock. He's very good with the children.'

'I've never had a doctor,' said Virginia, 'not one I could call *my* doctor. It comes of moving about so much and being so healthy. I've sometimes been to a little man in Newport to get him to sign for sleeping pills, and there was a rather beastly Englishman in Venice who patched me up that time I fell downstairs at the Palazzo Corombona. But mostly I've relied on chemists. There is a magician in Monte Carlo. You just go to him and say you have a pain and he gives you a *cachet* which stops it at once. I think perhaps I'll go and see your man in Sloane Street.'

'Not ill?'

'No. I just feel I ought to have what Mr Troy calls a "check-up".'

'There's a most luxurious sick-bay in HOO HQ. Every sort of apparatus and nothing to pay. General Whale goes there for "sun-rays" every afternoon. The top man is called Sir Somebody Something – a great swell in peace-time.'

'I think I'd prefer your man. Not expensive?'

'A guinea a visit I think.'

'I might afford that.'

'Virginia, talking of money: you remember Brenda and Zita used to pay rent when they lived here?'

'Yes, indeed. It's awfully sweet of you to take me in free.'

'I adore having you. It's only Ian; he was saying tonight he wondered if you wouldn't feel more comfortable if you paid something . . .'

'I couldn't be more comfortable as I am, darling, and anyway I couldn't possibly afford to. Talk him round, Kerstie. Explain to him that I'm broke.'

'Oh, he knows that.'

'*Really* broke. That's what no one understands. I'd talk to Ian myself only I think you'd do it better.'

'I'll *try*. . . .'

2

The processes of army postings were not yet adapted to the speed of the Electronic Personnel Selector. It was a week before Guy received any notification that his services might be needed by anyone for any purpose. Then a letter appeared in his 'In' tray addressed to him by name. It contained a summons to present himself for an interview with an officer who described himself as 'G I Liberation of Italy'. He was not surprised to learn that this man inhabited the same building as himself, and when he presented himself he met a nondescript lieutenant-colonel whom he had seen off and on in the corridors of the building; with whom indeed he had on occasions exchanged words at the bar of the canteen.

The Liberator gave no sign of recognition. Instead he said: 'Entrate e s'accomode.'

The noises thus issuing from him were so strange that Guy stood momentarily disconcerted, not knowing in what tongue he was being addressed.

'Come in and sit down,' said the colonel in English. 'I thought you were supposed to speak Italian.'

'I do.'

'Looks as though you needed a refresher. Say something in Italian.'

Guy said rapidly and with slightly exaggerated accent: 'Sono più abituato al dialetto genovese, ma di solito posso capire e farmi capire dapertutto in Italia fuori Sicilia.'

The colonel caught only the last word and asked desperately and fatuously: 'Siciliano lei?'

'Ah, no, no, no.' Guy gave a lively impersonation of an Italian gesture of dissent. 'Ho visitato Sicilia, poi ho abitato per un bel pezzo sulla costa ligure. Ho viaggiato in quasi ogni parte d'Italia.'

The colonel resumed his native tongue. 'That sounds all right. You wouldn't be much use to us if you only talked Sicilian. You'll be working the north, in Venetia probably.'

'Li per me tutto andrà liscio,' said Guy.

'Yes,' said the colonel, 'yes, I see. Well let's talk English. The work we have in mind is, of course, secret. As you probably know the advance in Italy is bogged down at the moment. We can't expect much movement there till the spring. The Germans have taken over in force. Some of the wops seem to be on our side. Call themselves "partisani", pretty left wing by the sound of them. Nothing wrong with that of course. Ask Sir Ralph Brompton. We shall be putting in various small parties to keep G H Q informed about what they're up to and if possible arrange for drops of equipment in suitable areas.

An intelligence officer and a signalman are the essentials of each group. You've done Commando training, I see. Did that include parachuting?'

'No, sir.'

'Well, you'd better take a course. No objection I suppose?'

'None whatever.'

'You're a bit old but you'll be surprised at the ages of some of our chaps. You may not have to jump. We have various methods of getting our men in. Any experience of small boats?'

Guy thought of the little sailing-craft he had once kept at Santa Dulcina, of his gay excursion to Dakar and the phantasmagoric crossing from Crete, and answered truthfully, 'Yes, sir.'

'Good. That may come in useful. You will be hearing from us in due course. Meanwhile the whole thing is on the secret list. You belong at Bellamy's, don't you? A lot of loose talk gets reported from there. Keep quiet.'

'Very good, sir.'

'A rivederci, eh?'

Guy saluted and left the office.

When he returned to the Transit Camp he found a telegram from his sister, Angela, announcing that his father had died suddenly and peacefully at Matchet.

3

All the railway stations in the kingdom displayed the challenge: IS YOUR JOURNEY REALLY NECESSARY?

Guy and his brother-in-law caught the early, crowded train from Paddington on the morning of the funeral.

Guy had a black arm band attached to his tunic. Box-Bender wore a black tie with a subfusc suit of clothes and a bowler.

'As you see, I'm not wearing a top hat,' said Box-Bender. 'Seems out of place these days. I don't suppose there'll be many people there. Peregrine went down the day before yesterday. He'll have fixed everything up. Have you brought sandwiches?'

'No.'

'I don't know where we'll get lunch. Can't expect the convent to do anything about us. I hope Peregrine and Angela have arranged something at the pub.'

It was barely light when they steamed out of the shuttered and patched station. The corridor was full of standing sailors travelling to Plymouth. The little bulbs over the seats had been disconnected. It was difficult to read the flimsy newspapers they carried.

'I always had a great respect for your father,' said Box-Bender. Then he fell asleep. Guy remained open-eyed throughout the three-hour journey to the junction at Taunton.

Uncle Peregrine had arranged for a special tram-like coach to be attached to the local train. Here were assembled Miss Vavasour, the priest from Matchet and the headmaster of the school of Our Lady of Victory. There were many others wearing mourning of various degrees of depth, whom Guy knew he should recognize, but could not. They greeted him with murmured words of condolence, and seeing it was necessary, reminded him of their names – Tresham, Bigod, Englefield, Arundell, Hornyold, Plessington, Jerningham, and Dacre – a muster of recusant names – all nearly or remotely cousins of his. Their journey was really necessary.

Out of his hearing Miss Vavasour said of Guy, sighing: *'Fin de ligne.'*

Noon was the hour appointed for the beginning of the Requiem Mass. The local train was due at Broome at half past eleven and arrived almost on time.

There is no scarcity of places of worship in this small village.

In penal times Mass had been said regularly in the house and a succession of chaplains employed there in the guise of tutors. This little chapel is preserved as a place of occasional pilgrimage in honour of the Blessed Gervase Crouchback.

The Catholic parish church is visible from the little station yard; a Puginesque structure erected by Guy's great-grandfather in the early 1860s at the nearer extremity of the village street. At the further end stands the medieval church of which the nave and chancel are in Anglican use while the north aisle and adjoining burying ground are the property of the lord of the manor. It was in this plot that Mr Crouchback's grave had been dug and in this aisle that his memorial would later stand among the clustered effigies and brasses of his forebears.

After the Act of Emancipation a wall had been built to divide the aisle from the rest of the church and for a generation it had served the Catholic parish. But the monuments left little room for worshippers. It was for this reason that Guy's great-grandfather had built the church (which in the old style the Crouchbacks spoke of as 'the chapel') and the presbytery and had endowed the parish with what was then an adequate stipend. Most of the village of Broome is Catholic, an isolated community of the kind that is found in many parts of Lancashire and the outer islands of Scotland, but is very rare in the west of England. The Anglican benefice has long been united with two of its neighbours. It is served by a clergyman who rides over

433

on his bicycle once a month and reads the service if he finds a quorum assembled. The former vicarage has been partitioned and let off as cottages.

Broome Hall stands behind iron gates, its drive a continuation of the village street. Mr Crouchback used often, and not quite accurately, to assert that every 'good house', by which he meant one of medieval foundation, stood on a road, a river, or a rock. Broome Hall had been on the main road to Exeter until the eighteenth century when a neighbour who sat for the county in the House of Commons obtained authority to divert it through his own property and establish a profitable toll pike. The old right of way still runs under the walls of the Hall but it carries little traffic. It is a lane which almost invisibly branches off the motor-road, swells into the village street, runs for half a mile as a gravelled carriage-drive and then narrows once more amid embowering hedge-rows which, despite a rough annual cutting, encroach more and more on the little frequented track.

When the convent came to Broome they brought their own chaplain and converted one of the long, panelled galleries into their chapel. Neither they nor their girls appeared in the parish church except on special occasions. Mr Crouchback's funeral was such a one. They had met the body when it arrived from Matchet on the previous evening, had dressed the catafalque and that morning had sung the dirge. Their chaplain would assist at the Requiem.

Angela Box-Bender was on the platform to meet the train. She had an air of gravity and sorrow.

'I say, Angie,' her husband asked, 'how long is this business going to take?'

'Not more than an hour. Father Geoghegan wanted to preach a panegyric but Uncle Peregrine stopped him.'

'Any chance of anything to eat? I left the flat at six this morning.'

'You're expected at the presbytery. I think you'll find something there.'

'They don't expect me to take any part, do they? I mean carry anything? I don't know the drill.'

'No,' said Angela. 'This is one of the times when no one expects anything of you.'

The little parlour of the presbytery was much crowded. Besides their host, Uncle Peregrine and the chaplain from the convent, there were four other priests, one with the crimson of a monsignore.

'His lordship the Bishop was unable to come. He sent me to represent him and convey his condolences.'

There was also a layman whom Guy recognized as his father's solicitor from Taunton.

Father Geoghegan was fasting, but he dispensed hospitality in the form of whisky and cake. Uncle Peregrine edged Guy into a corner. His fatuous old face expressed a kind of bland decorum.

'The hatchment,' he said. 'There was some difficulty about the hatchment. One can't get anything done nowadays. No heraldic painters available anywhere. There are quite a collection of old hatchments in the sacristy, none in very good condition. There was your grandfather's, but of course that was impaling Wrothman so it would hardly have done. Then I had a bit of luck and turned up what must have been made for Ivo. Rather rough work, local I should think. I was abroad at the time of his death, poor boy. Anyway, it is the simple blazon without quarterings. It is the best we can do in the circumstances. You don't think I did wrong to put it up?'

'No, Uncle Peregrine, I am sure you did quite right.'

'I think I'd better be going across. People are beginning to arrive. Someone will have to show them where to sit.'

The priest from Matchet said: 'I don't think your father has got long for purgatory.'

The solicitor said: 'We ought to have a word together afterwards.'

'No reading of the will?'

'No, that only happens in Victorian novels. But there are things we shall have to discuss some time and it's difficult to meet these days.'

Arthur Box-Bender was seeking to make himself agreeable to the domestic prelate '. . . not a member of your persuasion myself but I'm bound to say your Cardinal Hinsley did a wonderful job of work on the wireless. You could see he was an Englishman first and a Christian second; that is more than you can say of one or two of *our* bishops.'

Angela said: 'I've been dealing with letters as best I can. I've had hundreds.'

'So have I.'

'Extraordinary the number of people one's never heard of who were close friends of papa. I slept at the convent last night and shall go home tonight. The nuns are being awfully decent. Reverend Mother wants anyone to come back and have coffee afterwards. There's so many people we'll have to talk to. I had no idea so many people would get here.'

They were arriving on foot, by motor car and in pony traps. From the presbytery window Guy and Angela watched them. Angela said: 'I'm taking Felix home with me. They're keeping him at the inn at the moment.' Then the clergy withdrew to vest and Uncle Peregrine came to fetch the chief mourners.

'Prie-dieus,' he said, 'on the right in front.'

They crossed the narrow strip of garden and entered under the diamond-shaped panel cut by the house carpenter for poor mad Ivo. The sable and argent cross of Crouchback had not greatly taxed his powers of draughtsmanship. It was no ornament designed by the heralds to embellish a carriage door but something rare in English armoury – a device that had been carried into battle. They walked up the aisle with their eyes on the catafalque and the tall unbleached candles which burned beside it. The smell of beeswax and chrysanthemums, later to be permeated by incense, was heavy on the brumous air.

The church had been planned on a large scale when the Crouchback family were at the height of prosperity and the conversion of England seemed something more than a remote pious aspiration. Gervase and Hermione had built it; they who acquired the property of Santa Dulcina. It was as crowded for Mr Crouchback's funeral as for midnight Mass at Christmas. When the estate was bit by bit dispersed in the lean agricultural years, the farms had been sold on easy terms to the tenants. Some had changed hands since, but there were three pews full of farmers in black broadcloth. The village were there in force; many neighbours; the Lord Lieutenant of the county was in the front pew on the left next to a representative of the Knights of Malta. Lieutenant Padfield sat with the Anglican vicar, the family solicitor, and the headmaster of Our Lady of Victory. The nuns' choir was in the organ loft. The priests, other than the three who officiated, lined the walls of the chancel. Uncle Peregrine had seen that everyone was in his proper place.

Box-Bender kept his eyes on Angela and Guy, anxious to avoid any liturgical solecism. He genuflected with them, sat, then, like them, knelt, sat again, and stood as the three priests vested in black emerged from the sacristy, knelt again but missed signing himself with the cross. He was no bigot. He had been to Mass before. He wanted to do whatever was required of him. Across the aisle the Lord Lieutenant was equally undrilled, equally well disposed.

Silence at first; the Confiteor was inaudible even in the front pew. Just in time Box-Bender saw his relations cross themselves at the absolution. He hadn't been caught that time. Then the nuns sang the *Kyrie*.

Guy followed the familiar rite with his thoughts full of his father.

'*In memoria aeterna erit justus: ab auditione mala non timebit.*' The first phase was apt. His father had been a 'just man'; not particularly judicious, not at all judical, but 'just' in the full sense of the psalmist – or at any rate in the sense attributed to him by later commentators. Not for the first time in his life Guy wondered what was the *auditio mala* that was not to be feared. His missal gave the meaningless rendering 'evil hearing'. Did it mean simply that the ears of the dead were closed to the discords of life? Did it mean they were immune to malicious gossip? Few people, Guy thought, had ever spoken ill of his father. Perhaps it meant 'bad news'. His father had suffered as much as most men – more perhaps – from bad news of one kind or another; never fearfully.

'Not long for purgatory,' his confessor had said of Mr Crouchback. As the nuns sang the *Dies Irae* with all its ancient deprecations of divine wrath, Guy knew that his father was joining his voice with theirs:

Ingemisco, tamquam reus:
Culpa rubet vultus meus
Supplicanti parce, Deus;

That would be his prayer, who saw, and had always seen, quite clearly the difference in kind between the goodness of the most innocent of humans and the blinding, ineffable goodness of God. 'Quantitative judgements don't apply,' his father had written. As a reasoning man Mr Crouchback had known that he was honourable, charitable and faithful; a man who by all the formularies of his faith should be confident of salvation; as a man of prayer he saw himself as totally unworthy of divine notice. To Guy his father was the best man, the only entirely good man, he had ever known.

Of all the people in the crowded church, Guy wondered how many had come as an act of courtesy, how many were there to pray that a perpetual light should shine upon Mr Crouchback? 'Well,' he reflected, ' "The Grace of God is in courtesy"; in Arthur Box-Bender glancing sidelong to be sure he did the right thing, just as in the prelate who was holding his candle in the chancel, representing the bishop; in Lieutenant Padfield, too, exercising heaven knows what prodigy of ubiquity. "Quantitative judgements don't apply." '

The temptation for Guy, which he resisted as best he could, was to brood on his own bereavement and deplore the countless occasions of his life when he had failed his father. That was not what he was here for. There would be ample time in the years to come for these selfish considerations. Now, *praesente cadavere*, he was merely one of the guard who were escorting his father to judgement and to heaven.

The altar was censed. The celebrant sang: '. . . *Tuis enim fidelibus, Domine, via mutatur, non tollitur* . . .' 'Changed not ended,' reflected Guy. It was a huge transition for the old man who had walked with Felix along the cliffs at Matchet – a huge transition, even, for the man who had knelt so rapt in prayer after his daily Communion – to the 'everlasting mansion prepared for him in heaven'.

The celebrant turned the page of his missal from the Preface to the Canon. In the hush that followed the sacring bell Guy thanked God for his father and then his thoughts strayed to his own death, that had been so near in the crossing from Crete, that might now be near in the mission proposed for him by the nondescript colonel.

'*I'm worried about you,*' his father had written in the letter which, though it was not his last – for he and Guy had exchanged news since; *auditiones malae* of his father's deteriorating health and his own prolonged frustration – Guy regarded as being in a special sense the conclusion of their regular, rather reserved correspondence of more than thirty years. His father had been worried, not by anything connected with his worldly progress, but by his evident apathy; he was worrying now perhaps in that mysterious transit camp through which he must pass on his way to rest and light.

437

Guy's prayers were directed to, rather than for, his father. For many years now the direction in the *Garden of the Soul*, 'Put yourself in the presence of God', had for Guy come to mean a mere act of respect, like the signing of the Visitors' Book at an Embassy or Government House. He reported for duty saying to God: 'I don't ask anything from you. I am here if you want me. I don't suppose I can be any use, but if there is anything I can do, let me know,' and left it at that.

'I don't ask anything from you'; that was the deadly core of his apathy; his father had tried to tell him, was now telling him. That emptiness had been with him for years now even in his days of enthusiasm and activity in the Halberdiers. Enthusiasm and activity were not enough. God required more than that. He had commanded all men to *ask*.

In the recesses of Guy's conscience there lay the belief that somewhere, somehow, something would be required of him; that he must be attentive to the summons when it came. They also served who only stood and waited. He saw himself as one of the labourers in the parable who sat in the market-place waiting to be hired and were not called into the vineyard until late in the day. They had their reward on an equality with the men who had toiled since dawn. One day he would get the chance to do some small service which only he could perform, for which he had been created. Even he must have his function in the divine plan. He did not expect a heroic destiny. Quantitative judgements did not apply. All that mattered was to recognize the chance when it offered. Perhaps his father was at that moment clearing the way for him. 'Show me what to do and help me to do it,' he prayed.

Arthur Box-Bender had been to Mass before. After the Last Gospel, when the priest left the altar, he looked at his watch and picked up his bowler hat. Then when the priest appeared differently dressed and came within a few feet of him, he surreptitiously tucked his hat away again. The absolution was sung, then priest and deacon walked round the catafalque, first sprinkling it with holy water, then censing it. The black cope brushed against Box-Bender's almost black suit. A drop of water landed on his left cheek. He did not like to wipe it off.

The pall was removed, the coffin borne down the aisle. Angela, Uncle Peregrine and Guy fell in behind it and led the mourners out. Box-Bender modestly took a place behind the Lord Lieutenant. The nuns sang the Antiphon and then filed away from the gallery to their convent. The procession moved down the village street from the new church to the old in silence broken only by the tread of the horse, the creaking of harness, and the turning of the wheels of the farm cart which bore the coffin; the factor walked at the old mare's head leading her.

It was a still day; the trees were dropping their leaves in ones and twos; they twisted and faltered in the descent as their crumpled brown shapes directed, but landed under the boughs on which they had once budded. Guy thought for a moment of Ludovic's note-book, of the 'feather in the vacuum' to which he had been compared and, by contrast, remembered boisterous November days when he and his mother had tried to catch leaves in the avenue; each one caught insured a happy day? week? month? which? in his wholly happy childhood. Only his father had remained to watch the transformation of that merry little boy into the lonely captain of Halberdiers who followed the coffin.

On the cobbled pavements the villagers whose work had kept them from church turned out to see the cart roll past. Many who had come to the church broke away and went about their business. There was not room for many to stand in the little burying ground.

The nuns had lined the edges of the grave with moss and evergreen leaves and chrysanthemums, giving it a faint suggestion of Christmas decoration. The undertaker's men deftly lowered the coffin; holy water, incense, the few prayers, the silent Paternoster, the Benedictus; holy water again; the De Profundis. Guy, Angela, and Uncle Peregrine came forward, took the sprinkler in turn and added their aspersions. Then it was ended.

The group at the graveside turned away and, as they left the churchyard, broke into subdued conversation. Angela greeted those she had not met that morning. Uncle Peregrine made his choice of those who should come to the house for coffee. Guy encountered Lieutenant Padfield in the street.

'Nice of you to have come,' he said.

'It is a very significant occasion,' said the Lieutenant: 'Signifying what?' Guy wondered. The Lieutenant added, 'I'm coming back to the Hall. Reverend Mother asked me.'

When? How? Why? Guy wondered, but he said nothing except: 'You know the way?'

'Surely.'

The Lord Lieutenant had hung back, remaining in the public, Anglican graveyard, Box-Bender with him. Now he said: 'I won't bother your wife or your nephew. Just give them my sympathy, will you?' and, as Box-Bender saw him to his car, added: 'I had a great respect for your father-in-law. Didn't see much of him in the last ten years, of course. No one did. But he was greatly respected in the county.'

The funeral party walked back along the village street. Opposite the Catholic church and presbytery, the last building before the gates, was the 'Lesser House', a stucco façade and porch masking the much older structure. This was not in the convent's lease. It had fulfilled various functions in the past, often being used as a dower house. The factor lived there now. The blinds were in the windows, drawn down for the passing of the coffin. It was a quiet house; the street in front was virtually a cul-de-sac and at the back it was open to the park. It was here his father had suggested that Guy should end his days.

The convent school was prosperous and the grounds well kept even in that year when everywhere in the country box and yew were growing untrimmed and lawns were ploughed and planted with food-stuffs.

A gate tower guards the forecourt at Broome. Behind it lie two quadrangles, medieval in plan, Caroline in decoration, like a university college; as in most colleges there is a massive Gothic wing. Gervase and Hermione had added this, employing the same architect as had designed their church. At the main door stood the Reverend Mother and a circle of nuns. In the upper windows and in the turret where the Blessed Gervase Crouchback had been taken prisoner appeared the heads of girls, some angelic, some grotesque, like the corbels in the old church, all illicitly peeping down on the mourners.

The Great Hall had been given a plaster ceiling in the eighteenth century. Gervase and Hermione had removed it revealing the high timbers. In Guy's childhood the walls above the oak wainscot had been hung with weapons collected in many quarters and symmetrically arranged in great steely radiations of blades and barrels. These had been sold with the rest of the furniture. In their place hung a few large and shabby religious pictures of the kind which are bequeathed to convents, smooth German paintings of the nineteenth century portraying scenes of gentle piety alternating with lugubrious and extravagant martyrdoms derived at some distance from the southern baroque. Above the dais, where the panelling ran the full height of the room, a cinema screen held the place where family portraits had hung and in a corner were piles of tubular metal chairs and the posts of a badminton set. This hall was the school's place of recreation. Here the girls danced together in the winter evenings to the music of a gramophone and tender possessive friendships were contracted and repudiated; here in the summer was held the annual concert, and a costume play, chosen for its innocence of subject and for the multiplicity of its cast, was tediously enacted.

The nuns had spread a trestle table with as lavish a repast as the stringency of the times allowed. What was lacking in nourishment was compensated for by ingenuity of arrangement. Cakes compounded of dried egg and adulterated flour had been ornamented with nuts and preserved fruit that were part of the monthly bounty of their sister-house in America; the 'unsolicited gift' parcels which enriched so many bare tables at that time. Slices of spam had been cut into trefoils. The school prefects in their blue uniform dresses carried jugs of coffee already sweetened with saccharine. Box-Bender wondered if he might smoke and decided not.

With Uncle Peregrine beside him to identify them, Guy made a round of the guests. Most asked what he was doing and he answered: 'pending posting'. Many reminded him of occurrences in his childhood he had long forgotten. Some expressed surprise that he was no longer in Kenya. One asked after his wife, then realized she had made a gaffe and entangled herself further by saying: 'How idiotic of me. I was thinking for the moment you were Angela's husband.'

'She's over there. He's over there.'

'Yes, of course, how utterly foolish of me. Of course I remember now. You're Ivo, aren't you?'

'A very natural confusion,' said Guy.

Presently he found himself with the solicitor.

'Perhaps we could have a few words in private?'

'Let us go outside.'

They stood together in the forecourt. The heads had disappeared from the windows now; the girls had been rounded up and corralled in their classrooms.

'It always takes a little time to prove a will and settle up but I think your father left his affairs in good order. He chose to live very quietly but he was by no means badly off, you know. When he inherited, the estate was very large. He sold up at a bad time but he invested wisely and he never touched capital. He gave away most of the income. That is what I wanted to talk to you about. He made a large number of covenants, some to institutions, some to individuals. These of course terminate with his death. The invested money is left half to you and half to your sister for your lives and afterwards to her children and, of course, to your children if you have any. Death duties will have to be paid, but there will be a considerable residue. The total income which you will share has been in the last few years in the neighbourhood of seven thousand.'

'I had no idea it was so large.'

'No, he didn't spend seven hundred on himself. Now there is the question of the payments by covenant. Will you and your sister wish to continue them? There might be cases of real hardship if they were stopped. He was paying allowances to a number of individuals who, I believe, are entirely dependent on him.'

'I don't know about the institutions,' said Guy. 'I am sure my sister will agree with me in continuing the payments to individuals.'

'Just so. I shall have to see her about it.'

'How much is involved?'

'To individuals not more than two thousand; and, of course, many of the recipients are very old and unlikely to be a charge for many years more.

'There's another small point. He had some furniture at Matchet; nothing, I think, of any value. I don't know what you'll want to do with that. Some is at the hotel, some in store at the school. I should suggest selling it locally. There's quite a shortage of everything like that now. It was all well made, you will remember. It might get a fair price.'

The brass bedstead, the triangular wash-hand stand, the prie-dieu, the leather sofa, the object known to the trade as a 'club fender' of heavy brass upholstered on the top with turkey carpet, the mahogany desk, the book-case full of old favourites, a few chairs, the tobacco jar bearing the arms of New College, bought by Mr Crouchback when he was a freshman, the fine ivory crucifix, the framed photographs – all well made, as the lawyer said, and well kept – these were what Mr Crouchback had chosen from his dressing-room and from the smoking-room at Broome to furnish the narrow quarters of his retreat. Angela had taken the family portraits and a few small, valuable pieces to Box-Bender's house in the Cotswolds. And then in the six days' sale silver and porcelain and tapestries, canopied beds, sets of chairs of all periods, cabinets, consoles; illuminated manuscripts, suits of armour, stuffed animals; no illustrious treasures, not the collection of an astute connoisseur; merely the accumulations and chance survivals of centuries of prosperous, unadventurous taste; all had come down into the front court where Guy now stood, and had been borne away and dispersed, leaving the whole house quite bare, except for the chapel; there the change of ownership passed unrecorded and the lamp still burned; not, as it happened, a thing of great antiquity; something Hermione had picked up in the Via Babuino. The phrase, often used of Broome, that its sanctuary lamp had never been put out, was figurative.

All Guy's early memories of his father were in these spacious halls, as the central and controlling force of an elaborate régime which, for him, was typified by the sound of hooves on the cobbled forecourt and of the rake in the gravelled quadrangle; but in Guy's mind the house was primarily his mother's milieu; he remembered the carpet covered with newspaper and the flower petals drying for pot-pourri, his mother walking beside him by the lake under a sunshade, sitting beside him on winter afternoons helping him with his scrapbook. It was here that she had died leaving the busy house desolate to him and to his father. He had lost the solid image of his father as a man of possessions and authority (for even in his declining fortunes, up to the day of leaving Broome, Mr Crouchback had faithfully borne all his responsibili-ties, sitting on the bench and the county council, visiting prisons and hospitals and lunatic asylums, acting as president to numerous societies, as a governor of schools and charitable trusts, opening shows and bazaars and returning home after a full day to a home that usually abounded with guests) and saw him now only as the recluse of his later years in the smell of dog and tobacco in the small seaside hotel. It was to that image he had prayed that morning.

'No,' said Guy, 'I should like to keep everything at Matchet.'

Uncle Peregrine came down the steps.

'You should go and say goodbye to the Reverend Mother. Time to be moving off. The train leaves in twenty minutes. I wasn't able to reserve a coach for the return journey.'

On the way to the station Miss Vavasour came to Guy's side. 'I wonder,' she said, 'will you think it very impertinent to ask but I should so much like to have a keepsake of your father; any little thing; do you think you could spare something?'

'Of course, Miss Vavasour. I ought to have thought of it myself. What sort of thing? My father had so few personal possessions, you know.'

'I was wondering, if no one else wants it, and I don't know who would, do you think I could have his old tobacco-jar?'

'Of course. But isn't there anything more personal? One of his books? A walking stick?'

'The tobacco-jar is what I should *like*, if it's not asking too much. It seems somehow specially personal. You must think me very foolish.'

'Certainly. Please take it by all means if that is what you would really like.'

'Oh, thank you. I can't tell you how grateful. I don't suppose I shall stay on much longer at Matchet. The Cuthberts have not been considerate. It won't be the same place without your father and the tobacco-jar will remind me – the smell you know.'

Box-Bender did not return to London. He had an allowance of parliamentary petrol. Angela had used it to come to Broome. He and she and the dog, Felix, drove back to their house in the Cotswolds.

Later that evening, he said: 'Everyone had a great respect for your father.'

'Yes, that was rather the theme of the day, wasn't it?'

'Did you talk to the solicitor?'

'Yes.'

'So did I. Had you any idea your father was so well off? Of course it's your money, Angie, but it will come in very handy. There was something said about some pensions. You're not obliged to continue them you know.'

'So I gathered. But Guy and I will do so.'

'Mind you, one can't be sure they're all deserving cases. Worth looking into. After all your father was very credulous. Our expenses get heavier every year. When the girls come back from America, we shall have to meet all kinds of bills. It's a different matter with Guy. He hasn't anyone to support except himself. And he had his whack when he went to Kenya you know. He had no right to expect any more.'

'Guy and I will continue the pensions.'

'Just as you like, Angie. No business of mine. Just thought I'd mention it. Anyway, they'll all fall in one day.'

4

When Virginia Troy went to visit Dr Puttock for the second time, he received her cordially.

'Yes, Mrs Troy, I am happy to say that the report is positive.'

'You mean I *am* going to have a baby?'

'Without any doubt. These new tests are infallible.'

'But this is awful.'

'My dear Mrs Troy, I assure you that there is nothing whatever to worry about. You are thirty-three. Of course, it is generally advisable for a woman to enter her child-bearing period a little younger, but your general condition is excellent. I see no reason to anticipate any kind of trouble. Just carry on with your normal activities and come back to see me in three weeks so that I can see that everything is going along all right.'

'But it's all *wrong*. It's quite impossible for me to have a baby.'

'Impossible in what sense? I presume you had marital intercourse at the appropriate time.'

'"Marital?"' said Virginia. 'Isn't that something to do with marriage?'

'Yes, yes, of course.'

'Well, I haven't seen my husband for four years.'

'Ah, I see; well. That's a legal rather than a medical problem, is it not? Or should I say social? One finds a certain amount of this kind of thing nowadays in all classes. Husbands abroad in the army or prisoners of war; that sort of thing. Conventions are not as strict as they used to be – there is not the same stigma attached to bastardy. I presume you know the child's father.'

'Oh, I know him all right. He's just gone to America.'

'Yes, I see that that is rather inconvenient, but I am sure you will find things turn out well. In spite of everything the maternity services run very smoothly. Some people even think that a disproportionate attention is given to the next generation.'

'Dr Puttock, you *must* do something about this.'

'*I*? I don't think I understand you,' said Dr Puttock icily. 'Now I am afraid I must ask you to make way for my other patients. We civilian doctors are run off our feet, you know. Give my kind regards to Lady Kilbannock.'

Virginia was remarkable for the composure with which she had hitherto accepted the vicissitudes of domesticity. Whatever the disturbances she had caused to others, her own place in her small but richly diverse world had been one of coolness, light and peace. She had found that place for herself, calmly recoiling from a disorderly childhood and dismissing it from her thoughts. From the day of her marriage to Guy to the day of her desertion of Mr Troy and for a year after, she had achieved a *douceur de vivre* that was alien to her epoch; seeking nothing, accepting what came and enjoying it without compunction. Then, ever since her meeting with Trimmer in fog-bound Glasgow, chill shadows had fallen, deepening daily. 'It's all the fault of this damned war,' she reflected, as she went down the steps into Sloane Street. 'What good do they think they're doing?' she asked herself as she surveyed the passing uniforms and gasmasks. 'What's it all *for*?'

She went to her place of business in Ian Kilbannock's office and telephoned to Kerstie in 'Ciphers'.

'I've got to see you. How about luncheon?'

'I was going out with a chap.'

'You must chuck him, Kerstie. I'm in trouble.'

'Oh, Virginia, not again.'

'The first time. Surely you know what people mean when they say "in trouble"?'

'Not *that*, Virginia?'

'Just that.'

'Well, that is something, isn't it. All right. I'll chuck. Meet me in the club at one.'

The officers' club at HOO HQ was gloomier in aspect than the canteens at No. 6 Transit Camp. It had been designed for other purposes. The walls were covered with ceramic portraits of Victorian rationalists, whiskered, hooded and gowned. The wives and daughters of the staff served there under the wife of General Whale, who arranged the duties so that the young and pretty were out of sight in the kitchen and pantry. Mrs Whale controlled, among much else, the tap of a coffee urn. Whenever one of these secluded beauties appeared by the bar, Mrs Whale was able to raise a cloud of steam which completely concealed her. Mrs Whale had resisted the entry of the female staff but had been overborne. She made things as disagreeable for them as she could, often reprimanding them: 'Now you can't sit here coffee-housing. You're keeping the men from the tables and *they* have work to do.'

She said precisely this when Virginia set about expounding her situation to Kerstie.

'Oh Mrs Whale, we've only just arrived.'

'You've had plenty of time to eat. Here's your bill.'

The nondescript colonel who was liberating Italy was in fact looking for a place. He took Virginia's warm chair gratefully.

'I should like to boil that bitch in her own stew,' said Virginia as they left.

They found a dark corner outside and there she described her visit to Dr Puttock. Eventually Kerstie said: 'Don't worry, darling, I'll go and talk to him myself. He dotes on me.'

'Go soon.'

'This evening on the way home. I'll tell you what he says.'

Virginia was already at Eaton Terrace when Kerstie returned. She was wearing the clothes she wore all day and was sitting as she had first sat down, doing nothing, waiting.

'Well,' she said, 'how did it go?'

'We'd better both have a drink.'

'Bad news?'

'It was all rather disturbing. Gin?'

'What did he say, Kerstie? Will he do it?'

'*He* won't. He was frightfully pompous. I've never known him like it before. Most welcoming at first until I told him what I'd come about. Talked about professional ethics; said I was asking him to commit a grave crime; asked me, would I go to my bank manager and suggest he embezzled money for me. I said, yes, if I thought there was any chance of his doing it. That softened him a little bit. I explained about you and how you were broke. Then he said: "She won't find it a cheap operation." That rather gave him away. I said: "Come off it. You know there *are* doctors who do this kind of thing," and he said: "One has heard of such cases – in the police courts usually." And I said: "I bet you know one or two who haven't been caught. It goes on all the time. It just happens that Virginia and I have never had to inquire before." Then I sucked up to him a lot and reminded him how he had always looked after me when I had babies. I suppose it wasn't strictly *à propos* but it seemed to soften him; so at last he said he did know the name of someone who might help, and as a family friend, not as a doctor, he might give me the name. Well, I mean to say, he's always been a doctor to me not a family friend. He's never been in the house except to charge a guinea a time; but I didn't bring that up. I said: "Well, come on. Write it down," and then, Virginia, he rather shook me. He said: "No. *You* write it down," and I put out a hand to take a piece of paper off his desk and he said: "Just a minute," and he took out a pair of scissors and cut the address off the top. "Now," he said, "you can write this name and address. I haven't heard of the man for some time. I don't know if he's still practising. If your friend wants an appointment, she had better take a hundred pounds with her in notes. That's the best I can do. And remember I'm not doing it. I have no knowledge of this matter. I have never seen your friend." Do you know, he had me so nervous I could hardly write.'

'But you got the name?'

Kerstie took the slip of paper from her bag and handed it to her.

'Brook Street?' said Virginia. 'I thought it would be someone in Paddington or Soho. No telephone number. Let's look him up.'

They found the name and respectable address but when they tried to ring him up they were told the number was 'unobtainable'.

'I'm going round there now,' said Virginia. 'The hundred pounds will have to wait. I must have a look at him. You wouldn't like to come too?'

'No.'

'I wish you would, Kerstie.'

'No. The whole thing's given me the creeps.'

So Virginia went alone. There was no taxi in Sloane Square. She took the tube to Bond Street and picked her way through the American soldiers to the once quiet and fashionable street. When she reached the place where the house should have stood, she found a bomb crater flanked on either side with rugged cliffs of brick and plaster. Usually at such places there was a notice stating the new address of the former occupants. Virginia searched with her electric torch and learned that a neighbouring photographer and a hat shop had removed elsewhere. There was no spoor of the abortionist's passage. Perhaps he lay with his instruments somewhere under the rubble.

She was near Claridge's Hotel and from old habits sought refuge there in her despair. Lieutenant Padfield was standing by the fireplace straight before her. She turned away, seeming not to see him, and wearily walked down the corridor to Davies Street; then thought: 'What the hell? *I* can't start cutting people,' turned again and smiled.

'Loot, I didn't recognize you. One's like a pit-pony coming in from the blackout. Will you buy a girl a drink?'

'Just what I was about to suggest. I have to go out in a minute – to Ruby at the Dorchester.'

'Is that where she lives now? I used to go to her parties in Belgrave Square.'

'You should go see her. People don't go to see her as much as they used. She's a very significant and lovely person. Her memory is fantastic. Yesterday she was telling me all about Lord Curzon and Elinor Glyn.'

'I won't keep you, but I feel I need a drink.'

'It seems they were both interested in the occult.'

'Yes, Loot, yes. Just give me a drink.'

'It's not a thing that has ever greatly interested me, the occult. I'm interested in live people mostly. I mean, I'm interested in Ruby remembering, more than in what she remembers. Now some days back I was at a Catholic Requiem in Somerset county. It was the live people there I found significant. There were a lot of them. It was Mr Gervase Crouchback's funeral at Broome.'

'I saw he had died,' said Virginia. 'It's years since we met. I was fond of him once.'

'A lovely person,' said the Lieutenant.

'Surely you never knew him, Loot?'

'Not personally, only by repute. He was reputed as very fine indeed. I was glad to learn that he was so well off.'

'Not Mr Crouchback, Loot; you've got that wrong. He was ruined long ago.'

'There were people like that in the States twelve years ago. Wiped out in the crash. But they got it all back again.'

'Mr Crouchback wasn't like that, I assure you.'

'From what I hear he wasn't ever "ruined". It was just that the way things were over here after the first war, real estate didn't produce any income. Not only it didn't pay – it was a regular loss. When Mr Crouchback sold up, he not only got a price for the land; he saved himself all he had been paying out every year to keep things going. He wouldn't let the place run down. Sooner than that he'd clear out altogether. That was how he reckoned it. There were some valuable things, too, he sold out of the house. So he ended up a very substantial person.'

'What a lot you know about everyone, Loot.'

'Well, yes. I've been told before now I'm funny that way.'

Virginia was not a woman who left things unsaid.

'I know all about you and my divorce.'

'Mr Troy is an old and valued client of my firm,' said the Lieutenant. 'There was nothing personal about it. Business before friendship.'

'You still look on me as a friend?'

'Surely.'

'Then go and find a taxi.'

That aptitude never failed the Lieutenant. As Virginia drove back to Eaton Terrace, men and women emerged into the dim headlights signalling vigorously to the cab, waving bank-notes. She had a brief sense of triumph that she was sitting secure in the darkness; then the full weight of her failure bowed her, literally, so that she was crouched with her head near her knees when they drew up at the house where she lodged. Kerstie was on the doorstep.

'What luck. Keep the taxi,' and then: 'Everything all right?'

'No, nothing. I saw the Loot.'

'At the doctor's? I should have thought that's one place he wouldn't be.'

'At Claridge's. He came clean.'

'But how about the doctor?'

'Oh, he was no good. Blitzed.'

'Oh dear. I tell you what; I'll ask Mrs Bristow in the morning. She knows everything.' (Mrs Bristow was the charwoman.) 'Must go now. I'm going to poor old Ruby.'

'You'll find the Loot.'

'I'll give him socks.'

'He says we're friends. I expect I'll be in bed when you get back.'

'Good night.'

'Good night.'

Virginia went alone into the empty house. Ian Kilbannock was away for some nights conducting a party of journalists round an assault course in Scotland. The dining-room table was not laid. Virginia went down into the larder, found half a loaf of greyish bread, some margarine, a segment of imitation cheese and ate them at the kitchen table.

She was not a woman to repine. She accepted change, though she did not so express it to herself, as the evidence of life. A mile of darkness away, in her hotel sitting-room, Ruby repined. Her brow and the skin round her old eyes were taut with 'lifting'. She looked at the four unimportant people who sat round her little dinner-table and thought of the glittering guests in Belgrave Square; thirty years of them, night after night, the powerful, the famous, the promising, the beautiful: thirty years' work to establish and impose herself ending now with – what were their names? what did they do? – these people sitting with electric fires behind their chairs talking of what? 'Ruby, tell us about Boni de Castellane.' 'Tell us about the Marchesa Casati.' 'Tell us about Pavlova.' Virginia had never sought to impose herself. She had given parties, too; highly successful ones, all over Europe and in certain select parts of America. She could not remember the names of her guests; many she had not known at the time. As she ate her greasy bread in the kitchen she did not contrast her present lot with her past. Now, as it had been for the past month, she was aghast at the future.

Next morning Kerstie came early to Virginia's room.

'Mrs Bristow's here,' she said. 'I can hear her banging about. I'll go down and tackle her. You keep out of it.'

Virginia did not take long preparing herself for these days. There was no longer the wide choice in her wardrobe or the expensive confusion on her dressing-table. She was ready dressed, sitting on her bed waiting, fiddling with her file at a broken fingernail, when Kerstie at length came back to her.

'Well, that was all right.'

'Mrs Bristow can save me?'

'I didn't let on it was you. I rather think she suspects Brenda and she's always had a soft spot for her. She was most sympathetic. Not at all like Dr Puttock. She knows just the man. Several of her circle have been to him and say he's entirely reliable. What's more he only charges twenty-five pounds. I'm afraid he's a foreigner.'

'A refugee?'

'Well, rather more foreign than that. In fact he's black.'

'Why should I mind?' asked Virginia.

'Some people might. Anyway, here's the name and address. Dr Akonanga, 14 Blight Street, W2. That's off the Edgware Road.'

'Different from Brook Street.'

'Yes and quarter the price. Mrs Bristow doesn't think he has a telephone. The thing to do is go to his surgery early. He's very popular in his district, Mrs Bristow says.'

An hour later Virginia was on the doorstep of number fourteen. No bombs had fallen in Blight Street. It was a place of lodging houses and mean tobacconists, that should have been alive with children. Now the Pied Piper of the state schools had led them all away to billets and 'homes' in the country, and only the elderly and the slatternly remained of its inhabitants. The word 'Surgery' was lettered on what had once been a shop window. A trousered woman, with her hair in a turban, was smoking at the door.

'Do you know if Dr Akonanga is at home?'

'He's gone.'

'Oh dear.' Virginia suffered again all the despair of the previous evening. Her hopes had never been firm or high. It was Fate. For weeks now she had been haunted by the belief that in a world devoted to destruction and slaughter this one odious life was destined to survive.

'Been gone nearly a year. The government took him.'

'You mean he's in prison?'

'Not him. Work of national importance. He's a clever one, black as he may be. What it is, there's things them blacks know what them don't that's civilized. That's where they put him.' She pointed to a card on the jamb of the door which read: DR AKONANGA, *nature-therapeutist and deep psychologist, has temporarily discontinued his practice. Parcels and messages to* and there followed an address two doors from the bombed house where she had peered into the darkness the evening before.

'Brook Street? How odd.'

'Gone up in the world,' said the woman. 'What I say, it takes a war for the clever ones to be appreciated.'

Virginia found a cab in the Edgware Road and drove to the new address, once a large private house, now in military occupation. A sergeant sat in the hall.

'Can I see your pass, please?'

'I'm looking for Dr Akonanga.'

'Your pass, please.'

Virginia showed an identity card issued by HOO HQ.

'That's OK,' said the sergeant. 'You can't miss him. We always know when the doctor's at work. Hark.'

From high overhead at the top of the wide staircase came sounds which could only be the beat of a tom-tom. Virginia climbed towards it thinking of Trimmer who had endlessly, unendurably crooned 'Night and Day' to her. The beat of the drum seemed to be saying: 'You, you, you.' She reached the door behind which issued the jungle rhythm. It seemed otiose to add the feeble tap of her knuckles. She tried the handle and found herself locked out. There was a bell with the doctor's name above it. She pressed. The drumming stopped. A key turned. Virginia was greeted by a small, smiling, nattily dressed Negro, not in his first youth; there was grey in his sparse little tangle of beard; he was wrinkled and simian and what should have been the whites of his eyes were the colour of Trimmer's cigarette-stained fingers; from behind him there came a faint air blended of spices and putrefaction. His smile revealed many gold capped teeth.

'Good morning. Come in. How are you? You have the scorpions?'

'No,' said Virginia, 'no scorpions this morning.'

'Pray come in.'

She stepped into a room whose conventional furniture was augmented with a number of hand-drums, a bright statue of the Sacred Heart, a cock, decapitated but unplucked, secured with nails to the table top, its wings spread open like a butterfly's, a variety of human bones including a skull, a brass cobra of Benares ware, bowls of ashes, flasks from a chemical laboratory stoppered and holding murky liquids. A magnified photograph of Mr Winston Churchill glowered down upon the profusion of Dr Akonanga's war-stores, but Virginia did not observe them in detail. It was the fowl that caught her attention.

'You are not from HOO HQ?' asked Dr Akonanga.

'Yes, as a matter of fact I am. How did you guess?'

'I have been expecting scorpions for three days. Major Allbright assured me they were being flown from Egypt. I explained they are an essential ingredient for one of my most valuable preparations.'

'There's always a delay nowadays in getting what one wants, isn't there? I don't know Major Allbright I'm afraid. Mrs Bristow sent me to you.'

'Mrs Bristow? I am not sure I have the honour –'

'I've come as a private patient,' said Virginia. 'You've treated lots of her friends. Women like myself,' she explained with her high incorrigible candour, 'who want to get rid of babies.'

'Yes, yes. Perhaps a long time ago in what you would call the "piping days" of peace. All that is changed. I am now in the government service. General Whale would not like it if I resumed my private practice. Democracy is at stake.'

Virginia shifted her gaze from the headless fowl to the unfamiliar assembly of equipment. She noticed a copy of *No Orchids for Miss Blandish*.

'Dr Akonanga,' she asked, 'what can you think you are doing that is more important than me?'

'I am giving Herr von Ribbentrop the most terrible dreams,' said Dr Akonanga with pride and gravity.

What dreams troubled Ribbentrop that night, Virginia could not know. She dreamed she was extended on a table, pinioned, headless and covered with blood-streaked feathers, while a voice within her, from the womb itself, kept repeating: 'You, you, you.'

5

Ludovic's command was stationed in a large, requisitioned villa in a still desolate area of Essex. The owners had been ready to move out when they saw and heard, a few flat fields away, the bulldozers move in to prepare the new aerodrome; a modest enough construction, a single cross of runway, a dozen huts, but enough to annihilate the silence they had sought there. They left behind them most of their furniture, and Ludovic's quarters in what had been designed as the nurseries were equipped with all he required. He had never shared the taste of Sir Ralph and his friends for bric-à-brac. There was a certain likeness between his office and Mr Crouchback's sitting-room at Matchet without the characteristic smell of pipe and retriever. Ludovic did not smoke and he had never owned a dog.

When he was appointed, he was told: 'It's no business of yours who your "clients" are or where they are going. You simply have to see they're comfortable during the ten days they spend with you. Incidentally, you will be able to make yourself pretty comfortable too. I don't imagine the change will be unwelcome' – looking at his file – 'after your experiences in the Middle East.'

For all his tutelage under Sir Ralph Brompton in the arts of peace Ludovic lacked Jumbo Trotter's zest for comfort and his ingenuity in pursuing it. He shared a batman with his staff-captain, Fremantle; his belt and boots always shone. He cherished an old trooper's fetish for leather. His establishment drew a special scale of rations, for it catered for 'clients' who were taking vigorous physical exercise and suffering, most of them, from nervous anxiety. Ludovic ate heavily but without discrimination. His life was the life of the mind and there was little to occupy it in his official duties. The staff-captain had charge of administration; three athletic officers performed the training and these brave young men went in fear of Ludovic. They had less information even than he about the identity of their pupils. They did not know even the initial letters of the departments they served, and they believed, rightly, that when they visited the market town, security police in plain clothes offered them drinks and tried to draw them into indiscretion on the subject of their employment. They reported at the end of each course on the prowess of their 'clients'. Ludovic transcribed and where necessary paraphrased their verdicts and forwarded them in a nest of envelopes to the sponsors.

One morning at the end of November he settled to this, which was almost his only task. Training reports lay on his desk. *P T O K*, he read, *but a nervous type. Got worse. Had to be pushed out for last jump. N B G. – His excellent physique is not matched by psychological stamina*, he wrote. Then he consulted Roget and under the heading of Prospective Affections found: 'Cowardice, pusillanimity, poltroonery, dastardness, abject fear, funk, dunghill-cock, coistril, nidget, Bob Acres, Jerry Sneak.' 'Nidget' was a new word. He moved to the dictionary and found: '*Nidget*; an idiot. A triangular horse-shoe used in Kent and Sussex.' Not applicable. 'Dunghill-cock' was good, but perhaps too strong. Major Hound had been a dunghill-cock. He tried 'coistril' and found only: '*Coistrel*: a groom, knave, base fellow' and the quotation: 'the swarming rabble of our coistrell curates.'

His eyes followed the columns, like a prospector's panning for gold. Everywhere in the dross of 'coition ... cojuror ... colander' nuggets gleamed. '*Coke-upon-Littleton*: cant name of a mixed drink ...' – He seldom frequented the bar in the ante-room. He could hardly call for Coke-upon-Littleton. Perhaps it could be used in rebuke. 'Fremantle, it seemed to me you had had one too many Cokes-upon-Littleton last night.' – 'Coke' he noted was pronounced 'cook'. '*Colaphize*: to buffet and knock ...'; and so browsed happily until recalled to his duties by the entrance of his staff-captain with an envelope marked 'secret'. He hastily completed the report: *Failed to eradicate faults in training. Not recommended for active operations*, and signed at the foot of the sheet.

'Thank you, Fremantle,' he said. 'You can take the confidential reports, seal them and give them to the despatch rider to take back. What did you think of our last batch?'

'Not up to much.'

'A rabble of coistrell curates?'

'Sir?'

'Never mind.'

Each batch of 'clients' left early in the morning to be succeeded by the next in the late afternoon two days later. The intervening period was one of ease for the staff when, if they were in funds, they could go to London. Only the chief instructor, who was a man of few pleasures, remained on duty that day. He did not like to be long parted from the gymnastic apparatus in which the station abounded, and was resting in the ante-room from a vigorous hour on the trapeze when the staff-captain found him. He refused a drink. The staff-captain mixed himself a pink gin at a bar, scrupulously entered it in the ledger, and said after a pause:

'Don't you think the old man is getting rather rum lately?'

'I don't see much of him.'

'Can't understand half he says these days.'

'He had a bad time escaping from Crete. Weeks in an open boat. Enough to make anyone rum.'

'He was babbling about curates just now.'

'Religious mania, perhaps,' said the chief instructor. 'He doesn't give me any trouble.'

Upstairs Ludovic opened the envelope, removed the roll of the 'clients' arriving next day and scanned it cursorily. An all military batch he noted. He had only one slight cause of uneasiness. So much remained from his early training that he would not have liked to find an officer of the Household Cavalry under his command. This had not occurred yet, nor did it now. But there was a name of more evil omen. The list was alphabetically arranged and at its head stood: 'Crouchback, G. T/Y Capt. RCH.'

Even in the moment of horror his new vocabulary came pat. There was one fine word which exactly defined his condition: 'Colaphized'. It carried a subtle echo, unsupported by its etymology, of 'collapse'.

To be struck twice in a month after two years' respite; to be struck where he should have been most sheltered, in the ivory tower of *avant-garde* letters, in the keep of his own seemingly impregnable fastness, was a disaster beyond human calculation. He had read enough of psychology to be familiar with the word 'trauma'; to know that to survive injury without apparent scar gave no certainty of abiding health. Things had happened to Ludovic in the summer of 1941, things had been done by him, which, the ancients believed, provoked a doom. Not only the ancients; most of mankind, independently, cut off from all communications with one another, had discovered and proclaimed this grim alliance between the powers of darkness and justice. Who was Ludovic, Ludovic questioned, to set his narrow, modern scepticism against the accumulated experience of the species?

He opened his dictionary and read: '*Doom*: irrevocable destiny (usually of adverse fate), final fate, destruction, ruin, death.' He turned to Roget and found '*Nemesis*: Eumenides; keep the wound green; *lex talionis*; ruthless; unforgiving, inexorable; implacable, remorseless.' His sacred scriptures offered no comfort that morning.

At the same time as Ludovic was contemplating the arcane operation of Nemesis in the lowlands of Essex, Kerstie was causing dismay in Eaton Terrace by revealing the effects of causality in the natural order.

Ian had returned from his tour of the Highlands. He had dismissed his party of journalists on the platform at Edinburgh and delayed a night to visit his mother at the castellated dwelling on the Ayrshire coast which his grandfather, the first baron, had built as the family seat. The main building had been requisitioned and, though massive, was being eroded by soldiers. The Dowager Lady Kilbannock lived in the factor's house and there gratefully entertained Ian's sons in their school holidays. It was his first visit since the beginning of the war. He was still savouring the unaccustomed warmth of his welcome.

He had arrived in London that morning but had no intention of reporting back to his office until afternoon. Virginia was there to help his depleted secretariat deal with the telephone. He had bathed after his night journey, shaved, and breakfasted, lit a cigar from a box given him by his mother, and was prepared for an easy morning, when Kerstie had joined him. The cipher clerks worked irregular hours according to the press of business. She had been on night shift and returned home hoping for a bath. She was not pleased to find that Ian had used all the hot water. In her vexation she sprang the news of Virginia's predicament.

Ian's first words were: 'Good God. At her age. After all her experience'; and then: 'Well, she can't have it here.'

'She's in an odd mood,' said Kerstie. 'She seems to have lost all her spirit. The country must still be teeming with helpful doctors or for that matter midwives. I believe a lot of them make a bit on the side that way. She happens to have struck it unlucky twice. Now she's just given up trying. Talks about Fate.'

Ian drew deeply at his cigar, wondered why Scotland was still stocked with commodities that had long disappeared from the south, then turned gentler thoughts towards Virginia. He had momentarily seen himself as a figure of melodrama driving her from his door. Now he said:

'Has she thought of the Loot?'

'As a doctor?'

'No, no. As a husband. She should marry someone. That's what a lot of girls do, who funk an operation.'

'I don't think the Loot likes women.'

'He's always about with them. But he wouldn't really do. What she needs is a chap who's just off to Burma or Italy. Lots of chaps marry on embarkation leave. She needn't announce the happy event until a suitable time. When he comes home, if he does come home, he won't be likely to ask to see its birth certificate. He'll be proud as Punch to find a child to greet him. It happens all the time.' He smoked in silence before the gas fire, while Kerstie went up to change and wash in cold water. When she returned, wearing one of Virginia's 1939 suits, he was still thinking of Virginia.

'How about Guy Crouchback?' he asked.

'How about him?'

'I mean as a husband. He's off to Italy quite soon, I believe.'

'What a disgusting idea. I like Guy.'

'Oh, so do I. Old friends. But he's been keen on Virginia. She told me he made a pass at her when she first came back to London. They were saying in Bellamy's that he's been left a lot of money lately. Come to think of it, he was once married to Virginia in the remote ages. You'd better put the idea into her head. Let it lie there and fructify. She'll do the rest. But she must look sharp.'

'Ian, you absolutely nauseate me.'

'Well perhaps I'd better have a word with her at the office as her boss. Got to see to the welfare of one's command.'

'There are times I really detest you.'

'Yes, so does Virginia. Well, who else do you suggest for her? I dare say one of the Americans would be the best bet. The trouble is that, from the litter of contraceptives they leave everywhere, it looks as though they lacked strong philoprogenitive instincts.'

'You couldn't get Trimmer recalled?'

'And undo the work of months? Not on your life. Besides Virginia hates him more than anyone. She wouldn't marry him, if he came to her in his kilt escorted by bagpipes. He fell in love with her, remember? That was what sickened her. He used to sing "Night and Day" about her, to *me*. "Like the beat, beat, beat of the tom-tom, when the jungle shadows fall." It was excruciating.'

Kerstie sat close to Ian by the fireplace in the cloud of rich smoke. It was not affection that drew her but the warmth of the feeble blue flames.

'Why don't you go to Bellamy's,' she asked, 'and talk to your beastly friends there?'

'Don't want to run into anyone from HOO HQ. Officially I'm still in Scotland.'

'Well, I'm going to sleep. I don't want to talk any more.'

'Just as you like. Cheer up,' he added, 'if she can't qualify for a ward for officers' wives, I believe there are special state maternity homes now for unmarried factory-girls. Indeed, I know there are. Trimmer visited one during his Industrial Tour and was a great success there.'

'Can you imagine Virginia going to one of them?'.

'Better than her staying here. Far better.'

Kerstie did not sleep long but when she came downstairs at noon, she found that the lure of Bellamy's had proved stronger than Ian's caution and that the house was empty save for Mrs Bristow who was crowning her morning's labour with a cup of tea and a performance on the wireless of 'Music While You Work'.

'Just off, ducks,' she said using a form of address that had become prevalent during the blitz. 'I've got a friend says she can give me another doctor as might help your friend.'

'Thank you, Mrs Bristow.'

'Only he lives in Canvey Island. Still you can't find things where you want them now, can you ducks? Not with the war.'

'No, alas.'

'Well, I'll bring the name tomorrow. So long.'

Kerstie did not think Canvey Island a promising resort and was confirmed in this opinion when, a few minutes later, Virginia telephoned from her office.

'Canvey Island? Where's that?'

'Somewhere near Southend I think.'

'That's out.'

'It's Mrs Bristow's last hope.'

'*Canvey Island*. Anyway, that's not what I rang up about. Tell me, does Ian know about me?'

'I think he does.'

'You told him?'

'Well, yes.'

'Oh, I don't mind but, listen, he's just done something very odd. He's asked me to lunch with him. Can you explain that?'

'No, indeed not.'

'It's not as though he didn't see all too much of me every day at home and in the office. He says he wants to talk to me privately. Do you think it's about my trouble?'

'I suppose it might be.'

'Well, I'll tell you all about it when I come back.'

Kerstie considered the matter. She was a woman with moral standards which her husband did not share. Finally she tried to telephone to Guy but a strange voice answered from the shade of the megalosaurus saying that Captain Crouchback had been posted to another department and was inaccessible.

An aeroplane rising half a mile distant, and thunderously skimming the chimneys of the house, an obsolete bomber such as was adapted for parachute training, roused Ludovic from the near-stupor into which he had fallen. He rose from his deep chair and at his desk entered on the first page of a new notebook a *pensée*: *The penalty of sloth is longevity*. Then he went to the window and gazed blankly through the plate glass.

He had chosen these rooms because they were secluded from the scaffolds and platforms where the training exercises took place in front of the house. He faced, across half an acre of lawn, what the previous owners had called their 'arboretum'. Ludovic thought of it merely as 'the trees'. Some were deciduous and had now been stripped bare by the east wind that blew from the sea, leaving the holm oaks, yews, and conifers in carefully contrived patterns, glaucous, golden, and of a green so deep as to be almost black at that sunless noon; they afforded no pleasure to Ludovic.

Where, he asked himself, could he hide during the next ten days? It did not occur to him to go on leave. He had had all the leave that was due to him and his early training had left him with a superstitious regard for orders. Jumbo Trotter would have devised a dozen perfectly regular means of absenting himself. He would, if all else failed, have posted himself to a senior officers' 'refresher' course. Ludovic had never sought to master the byways of military movement. He stared at the arboretum and remembered the saw: 'The place to hide a leaf is in a tree.'

He went downstairs and across the hall to the ante-room. Captain Fremantle was still there with the chief instructor.

'Sit down. Sit down,' he said, for he had never experienced, and had not sought to introduce under his command, the easy manners of the Officers' House at Windsor or at the Halberdiers' Depot. 'Here is the nominal roll of tomorrow's batch.' He handed it over and then he lingered. 'Fremantle,' he said, 'does my name appear anywhere?'

'Appear, sir?'

'I mean are the men under instruction aware of my name?'

'Well, sir, you usually meet them and speak to them the first night, don't you? You begin: "I am the commandant. My name is Ludovic. I want you all to feel free to come to me with any difficulties."'

This had indeed been the custom which Ludovic had inherited from his more genial predecessor in office, and very unnerving his baleful stare, as he spoke these formalities of welcome, had proved to more than one apprehensive 'client'. None had ever come to him with any difficulty.

'Do I? Is that what I say?'

'Well, something like that usually, sir.'

'Ah, but if I *don't* meet them, could they find out who I am? Is there a list of the establishment posted anywhere? Does my name appear on standing orders? Or daily orders?'

'I think it does, sir. I'll have to check on that.'

'I want all orders in future to be signed by you "Staff captain for Commandant". And have any notices that need it retyped with my name omitted. Is that clear?'

'Yes, sir.'

'And I shan't be coming into the mess. I shall take all my meals in my office for the next week or so.'

'Very good, sir.'

Captain Fremantle regarded him with puzzled concern.

'You may think this rather strange, Fremantle. It's a question of security. They are tightening it up. As you know, this station is on the secret list. There have been some leaks lately. I received orders this morning that I was to go, as it were, "under-ground". You may think it all rather extravagant. I do myself. But those are our orders. I shall start the new régime today. Tell the mess corporal to serve my lunch upstairs.'

'Very good, sir.'

He left them and walked out of the french windows towards the trees.

'Well,' said the chief instructor, 'what d'you make of that?'

'He didn't get any orders this morning. I went through the mail. There was only one "secret" envelope – the nominal roll we always get.'

'Persecution mania,' said the chief instructor. 'It can't be anything else.'

Ludovic walked alone among the trees. What had been paths were ankle deep in dead leaves and cones and pine needles. His glossy boots grew dull. Presently he turned back and, avoiding the french windows, entered by a side door and the back stairs. On his table lay a great plate of roast meat – a week's ration for a civilian – a heap of potatoes and cold thick gravy, and beside it a pudding of sorts. He gazed at these things, wondering what to do. The bell did not work nor, had it done so, were the mess orderlies trained to answer it. He could not bear to sit beside this distasteful plethora waiting to see what would become of it. He took to the woods once more. Now and then an aeroplane came in to land or climbed roaring above him. Dusk began to fall. He was conscious of damp. When at last he returned to his room, the food was gone. He sat in his deep chair while the gathering dusk turned to darkness.

There was a knock at the door. He did not answer. Captain Fremantle looked in and the light from the passage revealed Ludovic sitting there, empty-handed, staring.

'Oh,' said Captain Fremantle, 'I'm sorry, sir. I was told you had gone out. Are you all right, sir?'

'Quite all right, thank you. Why should you fear otherwise? I like sometimes to sit and think. Perhaps if I smoked a pipe, it would seem more normal. Do you think I should buy a pipe?'

'Well, that's rather a matter of taste, isn't it, sir?'

'Yes, and to me it would be highly disagreeable. But I will buy a pipe, if it would make you easier in your mind about me.'

Captain Fremantle withdrew. As he shut the door he heard Ludovic switch on the light. He returned to the ante-room.

'The old man's stark crazy,' he reported.

It was part of the very light veil of secrecy which enveloped Ludovic's villa that its location was not divulged to the 'clients'. It was known officially as No. 4 Special Training Centre. Those committed to it were ordered to report at five in the afternoon to the Movement Control office in a London terminus, where they were mustered by a wingless Air Force officer and thence conveyed into Essex by motor bus. They did not see this airman again until the day of departure. His contribution to the war effort was to travel with them in the dark and see that none deserted or fell into conversation with subversive agents.

Foreign refugees who composed many of the training courses were obfuscated by this stratagem and when caught and tortured by the Gestapo could only give the unsatisfactory answer that they were taken in the dark to an unknown destination, but Englishmen had little difficulty in identifying their route.

When Guy arrived at the rendezvous he found a group of officers which grew to twelve in number. None was higher than captain in rank; all were older than the lean young athletes of the Parachute Regiment. Guy was the oldest of them by some five or six years. They came from many different regiments and like him had been chosen ostensibly for their knowledge of foreign languages and their appetite, if not for adventure, at least for diversity in the military routine. The last to report was a Halberdier, and Guy recognized his one-time subaltern, Frank de Souza.

'Uncle! What on earth are you doing here? Are you on the staff of this Dotheboys Hall they're taking us to?'

'Certainly not. I'm coming on the course with you.'

'Well, that's the most cheering thing I've heard about it yet. It can't be as arduous as they make out if they take old sweats like you.'

They sat together at the back of the bus and throughout the hour's drive talked of the recent history of the Halberdiers. Colonel Tickeridge was now brigadier; Ritchie-Hook a major-general. 'He can't bear it and he's not much use at it either. He's never to be found at his own headquarters. Always biffing about in front.' Erskine now commanded the 2nd Battalion; de Souza had had D Company until a few weeks ago; then he had put in for a posting, claiming a hitherto unrevealed proficiency in Serbo-Croat. 'I suppose they might call it "battle weariness", ' he said. 'Anyway, I wanted a change. Four years is too long in the same outfit for a man who's naturally a civilian. Besides it wasn't the same. There aren't many of the original battalion left. Not many casualties really. We had a suicide in the company. I never knew what about. A militia-man – perfectly cheerful all day and shot himself in his tent one evening. He left a letter to the CSM saying he hoped he would not cause any trouble. A few men got badly hit and sent home. Only one officer, Sarum-Smith, killed, but chaps got shunted about, first one, then another of the temporary officers were sent off on courses and never came back; half the senior NCO's were superannuated; the new young gentlemen were a dreary lot; until one suddenly realized the whole thing had changed. And then in Italy there were Americans all over the place clamouring for dough-nuts and Coca-Cola and ice-cream. So I decided to put my knowledge of Jugo-Slavia to use.'

'What do you know about it, Frank?'

'I once spent a month in Dalmatia, a most agreeable place, and I mugged up a bit of the language from a tourists' phrase book – enough to satisfy the examiners.'

Guy related his own drab history culminating in his meeting with the Electronic Selector in HOO HQ.

'Did you come across old Ralph Brompton there?'

'Do *you* know him, Frank?'

'Oh, rather. In fact it was he who told me about this Partisan Liaison Mission.'

'When you were in Italy?'

'Yes; he wrote. We're old friends.'

'How very odd. I thought all his friends were pansies.'

'Not at all. Nothing of the sort, I assure you. In fact,' de Souza added with an air of mystification, 'I shouldn't be surprised if half this bus load weren't friends of Ralph Brompton's one way or another.'

As he said this an unmilitary-looking man, in a beret and greatcoat, turned round in the seat in front of them and scowled at de Souza, who said in a voice of parody: 'Hullo, Gilpin. Did you see any good shows in town?'

Gilpin grunted and turned back, and then de Souza in fact began to talk about the theatre.

The welcome at their destination was cordial and efficiently organized. Orderlies were standing by to take their baggage up to their rooms. 'I've put you two Halberdiers together,' said Captain Fremantle. 'Here's the ante-room. I shall be saying a few words after dinner. Meanwhile I expect you can all do with a drink. Dinner will be in half an hour.'

Guy went up. De Souza remained below. As Guy returned he paused on the stairs, hearing his own name mentioned. De Souza and Gilpin were in conversation in what they took to be privacy; Gilpin was plainly rebuking de Souza, who with uncharacteristic humility was attempting to exculpate himself.

'Crouchback's all right.'

'That's as may be. You had no call to bring up Brompton's name. You've got to watch out who you talk to. You can't trust anyone.'

'Oh, I've known old Crouchback since 1939. We joined the Halberdiers on the same day.'

'Yes, and Franco plays a nice game of golf I've been told. What's the name "Halberdiers" got to do with it? I reckon you've been picking up a little too much free and easy, Eighth Army esprit de bloody corps.'

The two moved to the ante-room and Guy, puzzled, followed them after a minute. Seeing de Souza without his 'British warm' Guy noticed that he wore the ribbon of the MC.

That evening Captain Fremantle addressed them:

'I am the staff captain. My name is Fremantle. The commandant wishes you to feel free to come to me with any difficulties . . .' He read the standing orders, explained the arrangements of messing and security.

The chief instructor followed him giving them the programme of the course; five days' instruction and physical training; then the qualifying five jumps from an aeroplane at times to be determined by the conditions of the weather. He gave them some encouraging figures about the rarity of fatalities. 'Every now and then you get a "Roman candle". Then you've had it. We've had a few cases of men fouling their ropes and making a bad landing. On the whole it's a lot safer than steeple-chasing.'

Guy had never ridden in a steeple-chase and, looking about him, he reflected that no one in the audience, nor the speaker either, seemed likely to have done so.

They went to bed early. De Souza said: 'All army courses are like prep schools – all that welcoming of the new boys. But we seem to have struck one of the better-class establishments. Dinner wasn't at all bad. The programme sounds reasonable. Think we are going to be happy here.'

'Frank, who's Gilpin?'

'Gilpin? Chap in the Education Corps. I think he's a school teacher in civil life. A bit earnest.'

'What's he doing here?'

'The same as the rest of us, I expect. He wants a change.'

'How do you come to know him?'

'I know all sorts, uncle.'

'One of Sir Ralph's set?'

'Oh, I shouldn't suppose so. Would you?'

For two days the squad 'limbered up'. The PT instructor showed a solicitude for Guy's age which he did not at all resent.

'Take it easy. Don't do too much at first, sir. Anyone can see you've been at an office desk. Stop the moment you feel you've had enough. We take them all sizes and shapes here. Why last month we had a man so heavy he had to use two parachutes.'

On the third day they jumped off a six foot height and rolled on the grass when they landed. On the fourth day they jumped from ten foot and in the afternoon were sent up a scaffolding higher than the house from which in parachute harness they jumped at the end of a cable which, sprung and weighted, set them gently on their feet at the end of the drop. Here they were sharply scrutinized by the chief instructor for symptoms of hesitation in taking the plunge.

'You'll be all right, Crouchback,' he said. 'Rather slow off the mark, Gilpin.'

During these days Guy experienced a mild stiffness and was massaged by a sergeant specially retained for this service. There was no night-flying from the adjoining aerodrome. Guy slept excellently and enjoyed a sense of physical well-being. It did not irk him as it irked others of the squad, that they were confined to the grounds.

Early on de Souza showed curiosity about the head of their little school. 'The commandant, does he exist? Has anyone seen him? It's like one of those ancient oriental states where the viziers bring messages from an invisible priest-king.'

Later he said: 'I've seen food going up the back stairs. He's shut up somewhere on the top storey.'

'Perhaps he's a drunk.'

'More than likely. I came home in a ship where the O C Troops was a raging dipsomaniac, locked in his cabin for the entire voyage.'

Later he reported: 'It can't be drink. I've seen the plates coming down empty. Chap with the horrors can't eat. At least our O C Troops didn't.'

'I expect it's the warder's dinner.'

'That's what it is. He's either drunk or insane and he has to have a man sitting with him night and day to see he doesn't commit suicide.'

Later he said to a group in the ante-room: 'There's nothing wrong with the commandant. He's being held prisoner. There's been a palace plot and his staff are selling the rations on the black market. Or do you think the whole place has been taken over by the Gestapo? Where could parachutists most safely land? At a parachute training base. They shot everyone except the commandant. They have to keep him to sign the bumf. Meanwhile they get particulars of all our agents. There's that instructor who's always fooling about with a camera. Says he's making "action studies" to correct faulty positions in jumping. Of course what he's really doing is making records of us all. They'll be microfilmed and sent out via Portugal. Then the Gestapo will have a complete portrait gallery and they can pick us up as soon as we show our faces. We ought to organize a rescue party.' Gilpin snorted with contempt at this fantasy and left the room. 'An earnest fellow,' said de Souza, with, Guy thought he could detect, an infinitesimal *nuance* of bravado, 'just as I told you. What's more he's windy about tomorrow's jump.'

'So am I.'

'So am I,' said others of the group.

'I don't believe you are, Guy,' said de Souza.

'Oh yes,' said Guy untruthfully, 'I'm windy as hell.'

Part of the apparatus erected on the front lawn was the fuselage of an aeroplane. It was fitted with metal seats along the sides; an aperture had been cut in the floor; it was a replica of the machine from which they would jump and on the final afternoon of training they were drilled there by the 'despatching officer'.

He gave the warning order: 'Coming into target area,' removed the cover from the manhole. 'First pair ready.'

Two of the squad sat opposite one another with legs dangling. 'Number one. Jump.' His arm came down.

The first man precipitated himself on the grass and number three took his place. 'Number two jump.' And so on, again and again throughout the afternoon until they moved briskly and thoughtlessly. 'You don't have to think of anything. Just watch my hand. The parachute has a slip rope and opens automatically. Once you're out all you have to think about is keeping your legs together and rolling lightly when you land.'

But there was an air of apprehension in the ante-room that evening. De Souza worked his joke about the 'mystery man' in command for all it was worth.

'I saw a "face at the window",' he reported. 'A huge, horrible, pallid face. It stared straight down at me and then disappeared. Obviously seized by the guards. It was the face of a man totally abandoned to despair. I dare say they keep him under drugs.'

Gilpin said: 'What's this about "Roman Candles"?'

'When the parachute doesn't open and you fall plumb straight.'

'How does that happen?'

'Faulty packing, I believe.'

'And the packing is left to a lot of girls. You'd only need one fascist agent on the assembly line and she could kill hundreds of men – thousands probably. There would be no way of catching her and her "Roman candles". Why are they called "Roman candles", anyway, if it isn't a fascist trick? I'm as ready as the next man to take a reasonable risk. I don't like the idea of trusting my life to some girl in a packing station – so-called refugees perhaps – Polish and Ukrainian agents as likely as not.'

'You *are* windy, aren't you, Gilpin?'

'I'm calculating the risk, that's all.'

One of the younger 'clients' said: 'If these buggers think they're going to get me to jump out of an aeroplane sober, they'd better think again.'

De Souza said: 'Of course, it's perfectly possible that the commandant is the head of the organization. They won't let him appear because he can't speak English – only Ukrainian. But he comes out at night and repacks the parachutes so that they won't open. It takes hours, of course, so he has to sleep all day.'

But the joke was wearing thin.

'For Christ's sake,' said Gilpin in admonition, and they all fell silent. De Souza saw he had lost the sympathy of his audience.

'Uncle,' he said that night, 'I believe you and I are the only ones who aren't windy and I'm not so sure about myself.'

When all the lights were out, Ludovic emerged from his retreat and stumbled to the edge of the dark trees, breathed for a few minutes the scent of sodden leaves, which carried no fond memories for him, and then returned to his room to write: *Those who take too keen an interest in the outside world, may one day find themselves locked outside their own gates.*

It was not an entirely original *pensée*. He had come on it and vaguely remembered it, in an undergraduate magazine that Sir Ralph had received and left among his litter. It seemed to him apt.

Next morning, was almost windless; there was a pale suggestion of sunshine; jolly jumping weather.

'If it stays like this,' said the chief instructor as though offering a special, unexpected treat, 'we may be able to get in a night drop at the end of the course.'

He went early to the dropping-ground, a barren heath some miles distant, to see that it was suitably marked and to set up the loud-speaker apparatus through which he admonished his pupils as they fell towards him. The squad drove to the aerodrome, where their arrival seemed unexpected.

'It's always like this,' said the despatching officer. 'They've nothing else to do except lay on a flight for us, but at the last minute there's always difficulties.'

The dozen soldiers sat in the Nissen hut loud with jazz where a flying officer regarded them incuriously over the *Daily Mirror*. Presently he strolled out.

'Isn't there any way of turning off that music?' asked Guy. A knob was found. There was a brief respite of silence, then a blue-grey arm appeared from behind a door, manipulated the machine, and the music was resumed in even greater volume.

After half an hour the despatching officer returned. He was accompanied by the young man who had studied the *Daily Mirror*.

'I've ironed that out,' he said. 'All set?'

The flying officer wore some additions to his costume. 'The crate's really in for overhaul,' he said, 'but I dare say we can make it.'

They all trooped across the runway and climbed into the shabby old aeroplane. They put on their parachute harness and the despatching officer examined it cursorily. The rip-cords were clipped to a steel bar above the trap. There was very little light in the fuselage. Guy sat next to Gilpin, who was the man before him, No. 7 to his No. 8 in the order they had rehearsed. 'I wish they'd get on with it,' he said, but further conversation was obviated by the roar of the engines. Gilpin looked queasy.

It was one of the objects of the exercise to accustom the squad to flying conditions. They were not taken direct to the dropping-area but in a long circle, wheeling over the sea and then coming inshore again. Very little could be seen from the portholes. The harness was more uncomfortable than it had seemed on the ground. They sat bowed and cramped, in twilight, noise, and the smell of petrol. At length the despatching officer and his sergeant opened the man-hole. 'Coming into the target area,' he warned. 'First pair ready.'

De Souza was No. 1. He slipped out cleanly at the fall of the hand and No. 3 took his place.

'Wait for it,' said the despatching officer. There was an interval of a minute between each drop as the machine banked and returned to its target. Soon Gilpin and Guy sat face to face. The landscape below turned vertiginously. 'Don't look down. Watch my hand,' said the despatching officer. Gilpin did not raise his eyes to the signal. The despatching officer gave the command: 'No. 7. Jump.'

But Gilpin sat rigid, feet dangling over the abyss, hands gripping the edge, gazing down. The despatching officer said nothing until the machine had completed its steep little circle; then to Guy: 'You next. No. 8. Jump.'

Guy jumped. For a second, as the rush of air hit him, he lost consciousness. Then he came to himself, his senses purged of the noise and smell and throb of the machine. The hazy November sun enveloped him in golden light. His solitude was absolute.

He experienced rapture, something as near as his earthbound soul could reach to a foretaste of paradise, *locum refrigerii, lucis et pacis*. The aeroplane seemed as far distant as will, at the moment of death, the spinning earth. As though he had cast the constraining bonds of flesh and muscle and nerve, he found himself floating free; the harness that had so irked him in the narrow, dusky, resounding carriage now almost imperceptibly supported him. He was a free spirit in an element as fresh as on the day of its creation.

All too soon the moment of ecstasy ceased. He was not suspended motionless; he was falling fast. An amplified voice from below exhorted him: 'You're swinging No. 7. Steady yourself with the ropes. Keep your legs together.' At one moment he had the whole wide sky as his province; at the next the ground sprang to meet him as though he were being thrown by a horse. As his boots touched, he rolled as he had been taught. He felt a heavy blow on the knee as though he had landed on a stone. He lay in the sedge, dazed and breathless; then, as he had been taught, disengaged his harness. He attempted to stand, suffered a sharp pain in his knee and toppled once more to the ground. One of the instructions approached: 'That was all right, No. 7. Oh, it's you, Crouchback. Anything wrong?'

'I think I've hurt my knee,' said Guy.

It was the same knee he had twisted on guest night at the Halberdier barracks.

'Well, sit quiet till the jump's over. Then we'll attend to you.'

Again and again the aeroplane swooped overhead filling the sky with parachutes. Finally Gilpin landed quite near him, his qualms subdued. The sturdy, unmilitary figure joined him, infused with an unfamiliar jauntiness.

'Well, that wasn't so bad, was it?' he said.

'Highly enjoyable, up to a point,' said Guy.

'I missed my cue the first time,' said Gilpin. 'Don't know how it happened.

I was like that square-bashing. Never got the trick of "instinctive, un-questioning obedience to orders", I suppose.'

Guy wanted to ask whether he had been 'assisted' through the man-hole. He refrained and, since Gilpin was the last of the squad, there was never anyone to know except the readers of his confidential report.

'I expect we shall do another jump this afternoon,' said Gilpin. 'I feel quite ready for one now.'

'I'm damned if I do,' said Guy.

That evening Captain Fremantle reported to Ludovic: 'One casualty, sir. Crouchback.'

'Crouchback?' said Ludovic vaguely as though the name was new to him. 'Crouchback?'

'One of the Halberdiers, sir. We thought he was a bit old for the job.'

'Yes,' said Ludovic. 'One of those accidents with, how do you describe them – "Roman candles"?'

'Oh, no. Nothing as bad as that. Just a sprain, I think.' Ludovic dis-sembled his chagrin at this news. 'We've sent him over to the RAF hospital for an X-ray. They'll probably keep him there for a bit. Will you be going over to see him?'

'No, I can't manage that, I'm afraid. I have a lot of work on hand. Telephone and find the result of the X-ray. Perhaps later you or one of the instructors might visit him and see that he is comfortable.'

Captain Fremantle knew exactly how much work Ludovic had on hand. The former commandant had always made a point of visiting injured 'clients'; even, on rare occasions, attending their funerals.

'Very good, sir,' said Captain Fremantle.

'Oh, and, by the way, you might tell the mess-corporal I shall be dining down tonight.'

There was a mood of exuberance, almost of exultation, in the ante-room that evening. The eleven surviving members of the squad had made their second jump in weather of undisturbed tranquillity. They had overcome all their terrors of the air and were confident of finishing the course with honour. Some sprawled at their ease in the armchairs and sofas; some stood close together laughing loud and long. Even Gilpin was not entirely aloof from the general conviviality. He said: 'I don't mind admitting now I didn't quite like the look of it the first time,' and accepted a glass of bottled beer from the despatching officer who had that morning ignominiously bundled him into space and stepped firmly on his fingers as he clutched the edge of the man-hole in vain resistance to the force of the slip-stream.

Into this jolly company Ludovic entered like the angel of death. No one had believed the literal detail of de Souza's fantasies but their repetition and enlargement had created an aura of mystery and dread about the commandant who lurked overhead and was seen and heard by none, which Ludovic's appearance did nothing to dispel.

He overtopped the largest man in the room by some inches. There was at that time a well-marked contrast in appearance between the happy soldiers destined for the battlefield and those who endangered their digestions and sanity at office telephones. Standing before and above those lean and flushed young men, Ludovic's soft bulk and pallor suggested not so much the desk as the tomb. Complete silence fell. 'Present me,' Ludovic said, 'to these gentlemen.'

Captain Fremantle led him round. He laid a clammy hand in each warm, dry palm and repeated each name as Captain Fremantle uttered it '. . . de Souza . . . Gilpin . . .' as though he was reciting the titles of a shelf of books he had no intention of reading.

'Can I get you a drink, sir?' de Souza boldly asked.

'No, no,' said Ludovic from the depths of his invisible sarcophagus. 'I too have my rules of training to observe.' Then he surveyed the hushed circle. 'One of you has been incapacitated, I learn. You are now an eleven without a spare man, without A. N. Other. What is the news of Captain A. N. Other, Fremantle?'

'Crouchback, sir? Nothing new since I saw you. The X-ray is tomorrow.'

'Keep me informed. I am anxious about Captain A. N. Other. Pray continue with your festivities, gentlemen. They sounded hilarious from upstairs. Continue. My presence is entirely informal.'

But the young officers emptied their glasses and laid them aside.

Gilpin's eyes were on the level of Ludovic's breast.

'You are wondering,' Ludovic said sternly and suddenly, 'how I acquired the Military Medal.'

'No, I wasn't,' said Gilpin. 'I was just wondering what it was.'

'It is the award for valour given to "Other Ranks". I won it in flight – not in such a flight as you have enjoyed today. I won it by running away from the enemy.'

Had there been any suggestion of mirth in Ludovic's manner, his hearers would have been ready enough to laugh. As things were, they stood abashed. Ludovic took a large steel watch from the pocket below his ribbons. 'It is time for dinner,' he said. 'Lead on, Fremantle.'

Hitherto at this station it had been the habit to drop into the mess at any time up to half an hour of dinner being announced and to sit anywhere. Tonight Ludovic took the head of the table. The chief instructor took the foot and there was some competition to sit as near him as possible. At length two unhappy men found themselves obliged to take their places on either side of Ludovic.

'Do you say Grace in your mess?' Ludovic asked one of them.

'Only on guest nights, sir.'

'And this is not a guest night. It is the antonym. We are commemorating the absence of Captain A. N. Other. Do you know a Grace, Fremantle? Does no one know a Grace? Well, we will eat graceless.'

The dinner that night was particularly good. The oppression of Ludovic's presence could not keep the hungry young men from their food. A murmur of conversation spread from the foot of the table but did not quite reach the head where Ludovic ate copiously and with a peculiar precision and intent care in the handling of knife and fork – 'like a dentist', de Souza described it later – in his own simply constructed solitude, as remote and impenetrable as Guy's brief excursion in the skies. When he had finished he rose and without a word softly and heavily left the room. But his going did not appreciably raise the general spirits. Everyone discovered he was weary, and after the nine o'clock news went up to bed. De Souza was sorry Guy was not with him to discuss the evening's gruesome apparition. He had already dubbed the commandant 'Major Dracula' and his mind was teeming with necrophilic details which Gilpin, he knew, would condemn as bourgeois. Downstairs the staff lingered. They had been a cosy little band. The awe in which they held Ludovic had not seriously threatened their comfort. Now, it came to each of them, a dislocation impended, perhaps of absurdity, perhaps of enormity; something, at any rate, profoundly inimical to their easy routine.

'I'm not altogether sure of the form,' said the chief instructor. 'What does one do if one's commanding officer goes mad? I mean who reports it to whom?'

'He may get better.'

'He was a damn sight worse tonight.'

'Do you think the clients noticed?'

'I don't see how they could help it. After all, this batch aren't refugees.'

'He's not actually *done* anything yet.'

'But what will he do when he does?'

Next day was fine and the routine was repeated but that evening there was little exhilaration. Even the youngest and fittest were complaining of bruises and strains, and all found that familiarity did not entirely expunge the natural reluctance inherent in man, to fling himself into space. Ludovic appeared at luncheon and dinner, without éclat now. At dinner he introduced one topic only, and then to Captain Fremantle, saying: 'I think I shall get a dog.'

'Yes sir. Jolly things to have about.'

'I don't want a jolly dog.'

'Oh, no, I see, sir, something for protection.'

'*Not* for protection.' He paused and surveyed the stricken staff-captain, the curious and silent diners. 'I require something for *love*.'

No one spoke. A savoury, rather enterprising for the date, was brought to him. He ate it in a single, ample mouthful. Then he said: 'Captain Claire had a Pekinese.' After a pause he added: 'You would not know Captain Claire. He came out of Crete too – *without a medal*.' Another pause, a matter of seconds by their watches; of hours in the minds of his hearers. 'I require a loving Pekinese.'

Then as though impatient of a discussion on which his mind was already decided, he rose from the table as suddenly as he had done the night before, stalked out giving an impression that even then there was awaiting him on the further side of the oak door the animal of his choice, which he would gather to himself and bear away into the haunted shades that were his true habitat.

He shut the door behind him but through the heavy oak panels his voice could be heard singing a song, not of his own youth; one which a father or uncle must have sung reminiscently to the extraordinary little boy that was to become Ludovic:

> 'Father won't buy me a bow – wow – wow – wow.
> Father won't buy me a bow – wow – wow.
> I've got a little cat and I'm very fond of that
> But what I want's a bow – wow – wow – wow.'

'It might be a good thing,' the chief instructor later said to Captain Fremantle, 'to sound one of the more responsible of the clients and see what they make of the old man.'

Next day the wind was blowing hard from the east. All the morning the squad sat about waiting on weather reports until at noon the chief instructor announced that the exercise was cancelled. Captain Fremantle, who during the past thirty-six hours had become increasingly nervous in the contemplation of Ludovic's evident decline, welcomed the respite as an opportunity to carry out the chief instructor's plan.

He chose de Souza.

'Someone ought to go and call at the hospital. Care to come and see your fellow Halberdier? We might lunch out. There's quite a decent black-market road-house not far away.'

They went into the wind without a soldier-driver. As soon as they were clear of the villa Captain Fremantle said: 'Of course I know it's not strictly the thing to discuss a senior officer but you seem to me a sensible sort of fellow and I wanted to ask you unofficially and in confidence whether any of you chaps have noticed anything odd about the commandant.'

'Major Dracula?'

'Major Ludovic. Why do you call him that?'

'It's just the name he's got with our squad. I don't think anyone ever told us his real name. He is certainly singular. Has he not always been like this?'

'No. It's been coming on, especially the last few days. He was never exactly bonhomous; kept himself to himself; but there was nothing you could actually put your finger on.'

'And now there is?'

'Well, you saw him the last two nights.'

'Yes, but you see I didn't know him before. I had a theory but from what you tell me it seems I was wrong.'

'What did you think?'

'I thought he was dead.'

'I don't quite get you.'

'In Haiti they call them "Zombies". Men who are dug up and put to work and then buried again. I thought perhaps he had been killed in Crete or wherever it was. But clearly I was wrong.'

Captain Fremantle began to wonder if he had been wise in his choice of confidant.

'I wouldn't have mentioned the matter if I'd thought you would make a joke of it,' he said crossly.

'It was merely a hypothesis,' de Souza conceded airily; 'and of course it was based on the brief period I have had him under observation. I dare say the real explanation is quite prosaic. He's just going off his rocker.'

'You mean a case for the psychiatrist?'

'Oh, that's not what I mean at all. *They* never do any good. I should get him a Pekinese and keep him hidden as much as you can. In my experience the more responsible posts in the army are largely filled by certifiable lunatics. They don't cause any more trouble than the sane ones.'

'If you're going to treat it all as a joke . . .' Captain Fremantle began.

'It will certainly be a joke to Guy Crouchback,' said de Souza. 'I expect he's in need of one. Air Force jokes are deeply depressing.'

They reached the hospital, a temporary and unsightly structure. A flag of the R A F flapped furiously overhead. Crouched against the wind they mounted the concrete ramp and entered.

A long-haired youth in Air Force uniform sat at a table by the door with a cup of tea before him and a cigarette adhering to his lower lip.

'We have come to see Captain Crouchback.'

'D'you know where to find him?'

'No. Perhaps you can tell us.'

'I don't know, I'm sure. Did you say "captain"? We don't take army blokes here.'

'He came yesterday for an X-ray.'

'You can try Radiology.'

'Where's that?'

'It'll tell you on the board,' said the airman.

'I suppose it would be no good putting that man on a charge for insolence?' said Captain Fremantle.

'Not the smallest,' said de Souza. 'It isn't an offence in the Air Force.'

'Surely you're wrong there?'

'Not wrong; merely facetious.'

It was not a busy hospital and this was its least busy hour. The patients had been fed, and left, it was supposed, to sleep; the staff were feeding themselves. No one was in the room marked 'Radiology'. The two soldiers wandered down empty corridors whose floors were coated with some dark, slightly sticky substance designed to muffle their footsteps.

'There must be someone on duty somewhere.'

Seeing a door labelled 'No visitors', de Souza opened it and entered. He found an inflamed and apparently delirious man who broke into complaint that his bed was overrun with poisonous insects.

'DT's, I suppose,' said de Souza. 'Perhaps if we ring his bell someone will think he has taken a turn for the worse and come with sedatives.'

He rang and at length an orderly appeared.

'We're looking for an army officer named Crouchback.'

'This isn't him. This one's on the danger list. You'd better come out,' and when they were once more in the corridor he added: 'Never saw anything like it before. Some joker in Alex gave him a parcel "by hand of officer only" to take to London. It was full of scorpions and they escaped.'

'What risks you boys in blue do run for us! But how do we find Captain Crouchback?'

'You might ask at the registrar's.'

They found an office and an officer.

'Crouchback? No, never heard of him.'

'You keep a list of the inmates?'

'Of course we do. What d'you think?'

'No Crouchback on it? He came yesterday.'

'I wasn't on yesterday.'

'Could we see the officer who was?'

'He's off today.'

'It sounds like a plain case of abduction,' said de Souza.

'Look here, I don't know who the devil you two are or how you got in or what you think you're doing.'

'Security check up. Just routine,' said de Souza. 'We shall make our report to the proper quarter.'

When they left the building the wind blew so fiercely that speech was impossible until they reached the shelter of the car. Then Captain Fremantle said: 'I say, you know, you shouldn't have spoken to that chap like that. It might get us into trouble.'

'Not *us*. You perhaps. My identity, you must remember is a carefully guarded secret. Now for the black market.'

The road-house offered shelter from the gale but none of the luxuries of

Ruben's. Indeed, it differed from neighbouring hotels only in enjoying a larger share of the rations sold by Captain Fremantle's own quartermaster-sergeant. They were able to eat, however, with more zest than under Ludovic's sinister regard.

'Pity we didn't get to see Crouchback,' said Captain Fremantle at length. 'They must have moved him.'

'These oubliettes open and close constantly in army life. You don't think he was kidnapped on the commandant's orders? He harped rather, did he not, on the absence of Captain A. N. Other? You might almost call it "gloating".' Stirred by the heavy North African wine de Souza's imagination rolled into action as though at a 'story conference' of jaded script-writers. 'In assuming insanity we have been accepting altogether too simple an explanation of your commander's behaviour. We are in deep political waters, Fremantle. I was surprised to meet old Uncle Crouchback at the bus station; a man clearly far too old for fooling about with parachutes. I should have been suspicious but I was thinking of the simple, zealous officer I knew in 1939. Four years of total war can change a man. They have changed me. I left an unimportant but conspicuous part of my left ear in Crete. Uncle Crouchback was sent here with a purpose. Perhaps to watch Major Ludovic; perhaps to be watched by him. One or other is a fascist agent; perhaps both. Uncle Crouchback has been working at HOO HQ – a notorious nest of conspiracy. Perhaps sealed orders were sent to your Ludovic, giving no explanation; curtly remarking "the above-mentioned officer is expendable". Someone was remarking the other evening that it would not be difficult to arrange for a "Roman Candle". Crouchback's number in the squad was already known. No doubt Ludovic and his accomplices had arranged a trap of the kind.'

Captain Fremantle's simple mind, warmed, too, by the purple ferruginous vintage, was caught by the idea.

'As a matter of fact,' he said, 'that was the first thing the commandant asked when I reported Crouchback's accident. "A Roman Candle?" he asked as though it was the most natural thing in the world.'

'It would have seemed natural. The commandant was not to know the hour of the assassination. It might have been on the first afternoon; it might have been yesterday. But Crouchback's little accident saved him – for the time being. Now they have caught up with him. I don't think you or I will ever see my old comrade-in-arms again.'

They discussed and elaborated the possibilities of plot, counterplot, and betrayal. Captain Fremantle was a simple man. Before the war he had served in a lowly capacity in an insurance company. His post for the last three years had given him an occasional glimpse into arcane matters. Too many strange persons had briefly passed through his narrow field of vision for him to be totally unaware of the existence of an intricate world of deception and peril that lay beyond his experience. Roughly speaking he was ready to believe anything he was told. De Souza confused him only by suggesting so much.

Later, as they drove back, de Souza developed a new plot.

'Are we being too contemporary?' he asked. 'We are thinking in terms of the thirties. Both uncle Crouchback and your Major Dracula came to manhood in the twenties. Perhaps we should look for a love motive. Your commandant is plainly as queer as a coot and Uncle Crouchback's sex-life has always been something of a mystery. He never made his mark as a *coureur* when I served with him. This may well be a simple old-fashioned case of blackmail or, better still, of amorous jealousy.'

'Why "better still"?'

Captain Fremantle was far out of his depth.

'Altogether less sordid.'

'But how do you know the commandant has any connexion with Crouchback's disappearance?'

'It is our working hypothesis.'

'I simply don't know whether to take you seriously or not.'

'No, you don't, do you? But you must admit you have enjoyed our little outing. It's given you something to think about.'

'I suppose it has, in a way.'

It was a baffled and bemused staff-captain who returned in the early afternoon to his headquarters. He had been deputed to make tactful inquiries of the most responsible-seeming of the officers under instruction as to whether he and his fellow officers had noticed any little oddities in the behaviour of his commandant. He had found himself investigating a mystery, perhaps a murder, whose motives lay in the heights of international politics or the depths of unnatural vice. Captain Fremantle was not at his ease in such matters.

The house, when they reached it, seemed empty. It was certainly silent save for the howling of the wind in the chimneys. One RASC private was on duty at the garage. Everyone else, confined to quarters without employment, had gone to bed, except Major Ludovic who, Captain Fremantle was informed, had left by car while they were still in the aerodrome, taking a driver with him and remarking in the phase universally used by commanding officers to explain their absence from their posts, that he was 'called to a conference'.

'I think perhaps I'll go and lie down too,' said de Souza. 'Thank you for the outing.'

The staff captain looked at his tidy office where no new papers had arrived since morning. Then he, too, took his puzzled head to his pillow. The African wine gently asserted its drowsy powers. He slept until the batman came in to put up the blackout screen in his window.

'Sorry, sir,' said the man as he discovered the tousled figure; 'didn't know you was here.'

Captain Fremantle slowly came to himself.

'Time I showed a leg,' he said. Then: 'Is the commandant back?'

'Yessir,' said the man grinning.

'What's the joke, Ardingly?' There was a confidence and cordiality between these two to which Ludovic, who shared Ardingly's services, was a stranger. 'The major, sir. He's going on funny.'

'Funny?'

Phantasmagoric memories came into Captain Fremantle's quickening mind. 'Going on funny?'

'Yessir. He's been and got a little dog.'

'And he is going on funny with it?'

'Well, not a bit like the major, sir.'

'Perhaps I'd better go and see.'

'Perhaps you'd say "acting soft",' Ardingly conceded.

Captain Fremantle had lain down to rest with the minimum of preparation. He had removed his boots, anklets, and tunic. Now he arose and put on service dress and followed the corridor into Major Ludovic's part of the house. Pausing outside the door he heard from inside a clucking noise, as though a countrywoman were feeding poultry. He knocked and entered.

The floor of Ludovic's room was covered with saucers containing milk, gravy, spam, biscuits, Woolton sausage, and other items of diet, some rationed, some on points, some free to the full purse. Here and there the food had been rudely spilt; none of it seemed to have appealed to the appetite of the Pekinese puppy which crouched under Ludovic's bed in a nest of shredded paper. It was a pretty animal with eyes as prominent as Ludovic's own. Ludovic was on all fours making the noises which had been audible outside; he was, at first sight, all khaki trouser-seat, like Jumbo Trotter at the billiard-table; a figure from antiquated farce, 'caught bending', inviting the boot. He raised to Fremantle a face that was radiant with simple glee; there was no trace of embarrassment or of resentment at the intrusion. He wished to share with all the overflowing delight of his heart.

'Cor,' he said, 'just take a dekko at the little perisher. Wouldn't fancy anything I give him. Had me worried. Thought he was sick. Thought I ought to call in the MO. Then I turned me back for a jiffy and blessed if he hasn't polished off the last number of *Survival*. How d'you call that for an appetite?' Then falling into a fruity and, to Captain Fremantle, blood-curdling tone of infatuation, he addressed himself to the puppy: 'What'll kind staff-captain-man say if you won't eat his nice grub, eh? What'll kind editor-man say if you eat his clever paper?'

*

Guy meanwhile lay in bed less than a mile from Ludovic and his pet. There were, as de Souza has remarked, oubliettes which from time to time opened and engulfed members of His Majesty's forces. Thus it had happened to Guy. He was clothed in flannel pyjamas not his own; his leg was encased in plaster and it seemed to him that he had lost all rights of property over that limb. He was left alone in a hut so full of music that the wind swept over it unheard. It was the Emergency Ward of the aerodrome. Here he had been delivered in an ambulance from the RAF hospital, where a young medical officer had informed him that he required no treatment. 'Just lie up, old boy. We'll have another look at you in a few weeks and then take the plaster off. You'll be quite comfortable.'

Guy was not at all comfortable. There were no fellow patients in the ward. Its sole attendant was a youth who, sitting on Guy's bed, announced, as soon as the stretcher-party had left: 'I'm a CO.'

'Commanding Officer?' Guy asked without surprise.

Anything seemed possible among these inhabitants.

'Conscientious Objector.'

He explained his objections at length above the turmoil of jazz. They were neither political nor ethical but occult, being in some way based on the dimensions of the Great Pyramid.

'I could have lent you a book about it, but it got pinched.'

There was no malice in this youth nor was there the power to please. Guy asked for something to read. 'There was a welfare bloke came with some books once. I reckon someone must have flogged them. They weren't the sort of books anyone could read anyway. They don't take in any papers in the RAF. Any news they want they hear on the blower.'

'Can't you stop this infernal noise?'

'What noise was that?'

'The wireless.'

'Oh no. I couldn't do that. It's laid on special. Piped all through the camp. It isn't wireless anyway. Some of it's records. You'll find you get so you don't notice it.'

'Where are my clothes?'

The conscientious objector looked vaguely round the hut. 'Don't seem to be here, do they? Perhaps they got left behind. You'll have to see Admin about that.'

'Who's Admin?'

'He's a bloke comes round once a week.'

'Listen,' said Guy. 'I've got to get out of here. Will you telephone to the parachute school and ask Captain Fremantle to come here?'

'Can't hardly do that.'

'Why on earth not?'

'Only Admin's allowed to telephone. What's the number of this school?'

'I don't know.'

'Well, there you are.'

'Can I see Admin?'

'You'll see him when he comes round.'

For an excruciating day Guy lay staring at the corrugated iron roof while the sounds of jazz wailed and throbbed around him. Very frequently the attendant brought him cups of tea and plates of inedible matter. During the watches of the second night he formed the resolution to escape.

The wind had dropped in the night. His fellows, he reflected, would now be starting for their fifth jump. With pain and enormous effort he hobbled across the ward supporting himself by the ends of the empty beds. In a corner stood the almost hairless broom with which the attendant was supposed to dust the floor. Using this as a crutch, Guy stumbled into the open. He recognized the buildings; the distance across the asphalt yard to the officers' mess would have been negligible to a whole man. For the first time since his unhappy landing Guy felt the full pain of his injury. Sweating in the chill November morning he accomplished the fifty difficult paces. It was not an excursion which would have passed without notice at the Halberdier barracks. Here it was no one's business either to stop him or to help him.

At length he subsided in an armchair.

One or two pilots gaped but they accepted the arrival of this pyjama'd cripple with the same indifference as they had shown him when he had arrived in uniform with his batch of parachutists. He shouted to one of them above the noise of the music: 'I want to write a letter.'

'Go ahead. It won't disturb me.'

'Is there such a thing as a piece of paper and a pen?'

'Don't see any, do you?'

'What do you fellows do when you want to write a letter?'

'My old man taught me: "Never put anything in writing," he used to say.'

The pilots gaped. One went out; another came in.

Guy sat and waited; not in vain. After an hour the party of parachutists arrived, led on this occasion by Captain Fremantle.

The staff captain had slept (twice) on the problem of Guy's disappearance. He now gave no notional assent to any of de Souza's 'hypotheses', but an aura of mystery remained, and he was quite unprepared for the apparition of Guy in flannel pyjamas waving a broom. He came cautiously towards him.

'Thank God you've come,' said Guy with a warmth to which Captain Fremantle was little accustomed.

'Yes. I have to see the AO about a few things.'

'You've got to get me out of here.'

Captain Fremantle had more than three years' experience of the army and, as the facts of Guy's predicament were frantically explained, the staff-solution came pat: 'Not my pigeon. The SMO will have to discharge you.'

'There's no medical officer here. Only some kind of orderly.'

'He won't do. Must be signed for by the SMO.'

The eleven 'clients' were morose. Their former exhilaration had subsided with their fears. This last jump was merely a disagreeable duty. De Souza saw Guy and approached him.

'So you are safe and well, uncle,' he said.

Guy had served as the source of invention to beguile a wet day. That joke was over. De Souza now wished to finish his course early and get back to London and a waiting girl.

'I'm being driven insane, Frank.'

'Yes,' said de Souza, 'yes, I suppose you are.'

'The staff-captain says he can't do anything about me.'

'No. No. I don't suppose he can. Well, I'm glad to have seen you all right. It looks as if they wanted us to take off.'

'Frank, do you remember Jumbo Trotter in barracks?'

'No. Can't say I do.'

'He might be able to help me. Will you telephone to him as soon as you get back? Just tell him what's happened to me and where I am. I can give you his number.'

'But *shall* I get back? That is the question uppermost in my mind at the moment. We put our lives in jeopardy every time we go up in that aeroplane – or rather every time we leave it. Perhaps you'll find me in the next bed to you insensible. Perhaps I shall be dead. I am told you dig your own grave – those are the very words of the junior instructor – if the parachute doesn't open – burrow into the earth five feet deep and all they have to do is shovel the sides down on one. I keep reminding Gilpin of that possibility. In that rich earth a richer dust concealed. In my case a corner that shall be for ever Anglo-Sephardi.'

'Frank, will you telephone to Jumbo for me?'

'If I survive, uncle, I will.'

Guy stumbled back to his bed.

'Wasn't it a bit cold out there?' asked the conscientious objector.

'Bitterly.'

'I was wondering who'd got my brush.'

Guy lay on the bed, exhausted by his efforts. His plastered leg ached more than it had done at any time since his injury. Presently the conscientious objector came in with tea.

'Got some books out of the Squadron Leader's office,' he said, giving him two tattered pictorial journals which, from their remote origin in juvenile humour, were still dubbed 'comics'; but for their price they would have been more appropriately named 'penny-dreadfuls' for the incidents portrayed were uniformly horrific.

An aeroplane came in to land.

'Was that the parachute flight?' Guy asked.

'Couldn't say, I'm sure.'

'Be a good fellow. Go and find out. Ask if anyone was hurt.'

'They wouldn't tell me a thing like that. Don't suppose they'd know, anyway. They just drop them out and come back. Ground staff collect the bodies.'

Guy studied the Squadron Leader's 'comic'.

Wherever he went de Souza left his spoor of unreasonable anxiety.

Few things were better calculated to arouse Jumbo's sympathies than the news that a Halberdier had fallen into the hands of the Air Force. Those who knew him only slightly would not have recognized him as a man of swift action. In Guy's case his normal gentle pace became a stampede. Not Jumbo alone with his car, driver, and batman, but the Transit Camp Medical Officer in his car with his orderly, and an ambulance and its crew all sped out of London into Essex. The right credentials were produced, the right manumissions completed; Guy's clothes were collected from the hospital, his remaining baggage from the Training Centre, Guy himself from the emergency ward, and he was back in London in his quiet room before de Souza, Gilpin, and their fellows had been marshalled into the bus for their return to the 'dispersal centre'.

Next morning Captain Fremantle reported to his commandant with the customary sheaf of confidential reports. He found Ludovic at a desk clear of all papers. The Pekinese puppy was in sole occupation of that oaken surface on which had been indited so many of Ludovic's *pensées*; he gave intermittent attention to the efforts being made to divert him with a ping-pong ball, a piece of string, and an india-rubber.

'What are you going to call him, sir?' Captain Fremantle asked in the obsequious tones which usually provoked a rebuff. This afternoon he was received more kindly.

'I'm giving it a lot of thought. Captain Claire called his dog Freda. That name is precluded by the difference of sex. I knew a dog called Trooper once – but he was a much bigger animal of quite different character.'

'Something Chinese, perhaps?'

'I shouldn't like that at all,' said Ludovic severely. 'It would remind me of Lady Cripps's fund.' He looked with distaste at the documents offered him. 'Work,' he said. 'Routine. All right, leave them here.' He tenderly bore the puppy to its basket. 'Stay there,' he said. 'Daddy's got to earn you your din-din.'

Captain Fremantle saluted and withdrew. Ludovic found the necessary forms and began his work of editing.

'*De Souza O.K.*' he read, and baldly translated: *The above named officer has satisfactorily completed his course and is highly recommended for employment in the field.*

Of Gilpin he wrote: *Initial reluctance was overcome but with evident effort. It is recommended that further consideration should be given to the stability of this officer's character before he is passed as suitable.*

With deliberation he left Guy to the last. The chief instructor had written: *NBG. Too old. Spirit willing – flesh weak.* Ludovic paused, seeking the appropriate, the inevitable words for the sentence he was determined to pronounce. As a child he had been well grounded in Scripture and was familiar with the tale of Uriah the Hittite in its resonant Jacobean diction, but though tempted, he eschewed all archaisms in composing this *pensée*. *A slight accident*, he wrote, *in no way attributable to this officer's infirmity or negligence, prevented his completing the full course. However he showed such outstanding aptitude that he is recommended for immediate employment in action without further training.*

He folded the papers, marked them *Most Secret*, put them in a nest of envelopes and summoned his staff-captain.

'There,' he said to the puppy, 'Daddy's finished his horrid work. Did you think you'd been forgotten? Was you jealous of the nasty soldier-men?'

When Captain Fremantle reported, he found Ludovic with the puppy on his heart, buttoned into his tunic, only its bright white head appearing.

'I've decided what to call him,' Ludovic said. 'You may think it rather a conventional name but it has poignant associations for me. His name is Fido.'

6

The Transit Camp, despite all Jumbo's manifest will to give Guy a position of privilege there – he had come during the last year to regard him almost as a contemporary; no longer as an adventurous temporary officer but as a seasoned Halberdier cruelly but unjustly relegated like himself to an unheroic role – was not an ideal place for the bedridden. It had served well as a place to leave in the early morning for HOO HQ and as a place to return to late from Bellamy's. It was not the place to spend day and night – particularly such nights as Guy now suffered, made almost sleepless by the throb and dead weight of his plastered knee. For two days the relief from music and from the attentions of the conscientious objector was solace enough. Then a restless melancholy began to afflict him. Jumbo noticed it.

'You ought to see more fellows,' he said. 'It's awkward here in some ways. Can't have a lot of women coming in and out. Oughtn't really to have civilians at all. Isn't there anyone who'd take you in? Nothing easier than to draw lodging allowances.'

Guy thought: Arthur Box-Bender? He would not be welcome. Kerstie Kilbannock? Virginia was living there.

'No,' he said. 'I don't believe there is.'

'Pity. How would it be if I sent a message to your club? Your porter might send some fellows round. How's the knee today by the way?'

Guy was not seriously injured – something had been cracked, something else twisted out of place; he was in slightly worse condition than he had been after the Halberdier guest night; no more than that – but he was hampered and in pain. His calf and ankle were swollen by the constriction of the plaster.

'I believe I shall be a lot more comfortable without this thing on it.'

'Who put it on?'

'One of the Air Force doctors.'

'Soon get that off,' said Jumbo. 'I'll send my man up at once.'

Obediently the R A M C major attached to the camp – one of the lighter posts of that busy service – came to Guy's room with a pair of shears and laboriously removed the encumbrance.

'I suppose it's all right doing this,' he said. 'They ought to have sent me the X-ray pictures, but of course they haven't. Does it seem more comfortable like that?'

'Much.'

'Well, that's the important thing. I dare say a spot of heat might help. I'll send along a chap with a lamp.'

This reincarnation of Florence Nightingale did not appear. The swelling of calf and ankle slightly subsided; the knee grew huge. Instead of a continuous ache Guy suffered from frequent agonizing spasms when he moved in the bed. They were on the whole preferable.

The immediate result of Jumbo's appeal to Bellamy's was a visit from Lieutenant Padfield. He came in the morning, when most men and women in London were ostensibly busy, bearing the new number of *Survival* and a Staffordshire figure of Mr Gladstone; also a fine bunch of chrysanthemums, but these were not for Guy.

'I'm on my way to the Dorchester,' he explained. 'Ruby had rather a misfortune last night. One of our generals over here is a great admirer of *Peter Pan*. Ruby asked him to dinner to meet Sir James Barrie. She kindly asked me too. I was surprised to learn Barrie was still alive. Well, of course, he isn't. We waited an hour for him and when at last she rang for dinner they said room-service was off and that there was a red warning anyway. "That's what it is," she said. "He's gone down to a shelter. Ridiculous at his age." So we got no dinner and the general was upset and so was Ruby.'

'You do lead a complicated life, Loot.'

'The same sort of thing is happening all the time in New York, they tell me. All the social secretaries are in Washington. So I thought, a few flowers ...'

'You might take her Mr Gladstone too, Loot. It was a very kind thought but, you know, I've nowhere to put him.'

'Do you think Ruby would really like it? Most of her things are French.'

'Her husband was in Asquith's cabinet.'

'Yes, of course he was. I'd forgotten. Yes, that would make a difference. Well I must be going.' The Lieutenant dallied at the door uncertainly regarding the earthenware figure. 'The Glenobans sent you many messages of condolence.'

'I don't know them.'

'And so did your Uncle Peregrine – such an interesting man ... You know I don't really think this would go well in Ruby's room.'

'Give it to the Glenobans.'

'Are they Liberals?'

'I dare say. Lots of Scotch are.'

'I might change it for a Highlander. There was one in the same shop.'

'I'm sure the Glenobans would prefer Mr Gladstone.'

'Yes.'

At length the Lieutenant departed on his work of mercy, leaving Guy to *Survival*.

This was the issue on which little Fido had gorged. It had gone to press long before Everard Spruce received Ludovic's manuscript. Guy turned the pages without interest. It compared unfavourably in his opinion with the Squadron Leader's 'comic' particularly in the matter of draughtsmanship. Everard Spruce, in the days when he courted the Marxists, dissembled a discreditable, personal preference for Fragonard above Léger by denying all interest in graphic art, affirming stoutly and correctly that the Workers were solidly behind him in his indifference. 'Look at Russia,' he would say. But the Ministry of Information in the early days of *Survival*, before the Russian alliance, had pointed out that since Hitler had proclaimed a taste for 'figurative' painting, defence of the cosmopolitan *avant garde* had become a patriotic duty in England. Spruce submitted without demur and *Survival* accordingly displayed frequent 'art supplements', chosen by Coney and Frankie. There was one such in the current issue, ten shiny pages of squiggles. Guy turned from them to an essay by the pacific expatriate Parsnip, tracing the affinity of Kafka to Klee. Guy had not heard of either of these famous names.

His next caller was his uncle, Peregrine.

Uncle Peregrine, like the Lieutenant, had ample leisure. He brought no gift, supposing his attendance was treat enough. He sat holding his umbrella and soft, shabby hat and looked at his nephew reproachfully.

'You should take more care of yourself,' he said, 'now that you are the head of the family.'

He was five years younger than Guy's father but he looked rather older; an imperfect and ill-kept cast from the same mould.

When the Lieutenant spoke of Peregrine Crouchback as 'interesting' he was making a unique judgement. A man of many interests certainly, well read, widely travelled, minutely informed in many recondite subjects, a discerning collector of bibelots; a man handsomely apparelled and adorned when he did duty at the papal court; a man nevertheless assiduously avoided even by those who shared his interests. He exemplified the indefinable numbness which Guy recognized intermittently in himself; the saturnine strain which in Ivo had swollen to madness, terror of which haunted Box-Bender when he studied his son's letters from prison-camp.

In 1915 Uncle Peregrine contracted a complicated form of dysentery on his first day in the Dardanelles and was obliged to spend the rest of the war as ADC to a colonial governor who repeatedly but vainly cabled for his recall. In the nineteen twenties he had hung about the diplomatic service as honorary attaché. Once Ralph Brompton, as first secretary, had been posted to the same embassy, and had sought to make him the chancery butt; unsuccessfully; his apathetic self-esteem was impervious to ridicule; no spark could be struck from that inert element. For the last decade, after the decline in the value of the pound, Uncle Peregrine had made his home in London, in an old-fashioned flat near Westminster Cathedral, at whose great functions he sometimes assisted in various liveries. Perhaps he was a legitimate object of interest to an inquiring foreigner like the Lieutenant. He could have occured nowhere else but in England and in no period but his own.

Uncle Peregrine quite enjoyed the war. He was naturally frugal and welcomed the excuse to forgo wine and food, to wear his old clothes and to change his linen weekly. He was quite without fear for his own safety when the bombs were falling. He rejoiced to see so many of his gloomier predictions of foreign policy fulfilled. For a time he busied himself with the despatch of parcels to distressed civilians in enemy hands. Lately he had found more congenial work. There was a 'salvage drive' in progress in the course of which public-spirited citizens were exhorted to empty their shelves so that their books could be pulped to produce official forms and *Survival*. Many rare and beautiful volumes perished before it occurred to the ministry that they could more profitably be sold. A committee was then authorized to survey two centuries of English literature laid out, backs uppermost, in what had once been a school gymnasium; male and female, the old buffers poked among the bindings, making their choice of what should be saved, priced, and put into the market. They met two or three times a week for their business, in which, as in all matters, Uncle Peregrine was scrupulously honest; but he exercised the prerogative of pre-emption enjoyed by the stallholders of charitable bazaars. He invariably asked a colleague to decide the price of anything he coveted; if it fell within his means, he paid and bore it off. Not more than twenty items had been added to his little library in this way, but every one was a bibliophile's treasure. The prices were those which the old amateurs remembered to have prevailed in the lean last years of peace.

'A young American protégé of mine told me you were here,' he continued. 'You may remember meeting him with me. It doesn't seem much of a place,' he added critically surveying Guy's room. 'I don't think I ever heard of it before.'

He inquired into the condition of Guy's knee and into the treatment he was receiving. Who was his medical man? 'Major Blenkinsop? Don't think I've ever heard of him. Are you sure he understands the knee? Highly specialized things, knees.' He spoke of an injury he himself sustained many years before on a tennis-lawn at Bordighera. 'Fellow I had then didn't understand knees. It's never been quite the same since.'

He picked up *Survival*, glanced at the illustrations, remarked without hostility: 'Ah, *modern*', and then passed on to public affairs. 'Shocking news from the eastern front. The Bolshevists are advancing again. Germans don't seem able to stop them. I'd sooner see the Japanese in Europe – at least they have a king and some sort of religion. If one can believe the papers we are actually helping the Bolshevists. It's a mad world, my masters.'

Finally he said: 'I came with an invitation. Why don't you move into my flat until you are fit? There's plenty of room, I've still got Mrs Corner; she does what she can with the rations. The lift works – which is more than a lot of people can claim. There's a Dutch Dominican – not that I approve of Dominicans in the general way – giving a really interesting series of Advent conferences at the Cathedral. You can see he doesn't like the way the war's going. You'd be better off than you are here. I'm at home most evenings,' he added as though that constituted an inestimable attraction.

It was the measure of Guy's melancholy that he did not at once reject the offer; that in fact he accepted it.

Jumbo arranged for an ambulance to take him to his new address. The lift, as promised, bore him up to the large, dark, heavily furnished flat and Mrs Corner, the housekeeper, received him as an honourably wounded soldier.

Not very far away Colonel Grace-Groundling-Marchpole was studying a list submitted to him for approval.

'Crouchback?' he said. 'Haven't we a file on him?'

'Yes. The Box-Bender case.'

'I remember. *And* the Scottish nationalists.'

'And the priest in Alexandria. There's been nothing much on him since.'

'No. He may have lost contact with his headquarters. It's just as well we didn't pull him in at the time. If we let him go to Italy he may lead us into the neo-fascist network.'

'It won't be so easy keeping track of him there. The Eighth Army is not security conscious.'

'No. It's a moot point. On the whole, perhaps, the noes have it.'

He wrote: *This officer cannot be recommended for secret work in Italy*, and turned to the name of de Souza.

'Communist party member of good standing,' he said. 'Quite sound at the moment.'

The room in which Guy was to spend six weeks and make a momentous decision, had seldom been occupied during Uncle Peregrine's tenancy. Its window opened on a brick wall. It was furnished with pieces from the dispersal of Broome. Guy lay in a large old bed ornamented with brass knobs. Here Major Blenkinsop paid him a cursory visit.

'Still pretty puffy, eh? Well, the only thing is to keep it up.'

Through Jumbo's good offices Guy was able to lay in some gin and whisky. The circle of his acquaintances had widened in the last four years. During his first days at the flat he received several visitors, Ian Kilbannock among them. After twenty minutes of desultory gossip he said: 'You remember Ivor Claire?'

'Yes, indeed.'

'He's joined the Chindits in Burma. Surprising, don't you think?'

Guy thought of his first view of Ivor in the Borghese Gardens. 'Not altogether.'

'The whispering campaign took some time to reach the Far East. Or perhaps he got bored with viceregal circles.'

'Ivor doesn't believe in sacrifice. Who does nowadays? But he had the will to win.'

'I can't think of anything more sacrificial than plodding about in the jungle with those desperadoes. I don't know what he thinks he's going to win there.'

'There was a time I was very fond of Ivor.'

'Oh, I'm *fond* of him. Everyone is and everyone has forgotten his little *faux pas* in Crete. That's what makes it so rum his charging off to be a hero *now*.'

When Ian left, Guy brooded about the antithesis between the acceptance of sacrifice and the will to win. It seemed to have personal relevance, as yet undefined, to his own condition. He re-read the letter from his father which he carried always in his pocket book. '*The Mystical Body doesn't strike attitudes or stand on its dignity. It accepts suffering and injustice ... Quantitative judgements don't apply.*'

There was a congress at Teheran at the time entirely occupied with quantitative judgements.

7

At the end of the first week of that December, History records, Mr Winston Churchill introduced Mr Roosevelt to the Sphinx. Fortified by the assurances of their military advisers that the Germans would surrender that winter, the two puissant old gentlemen circumambulated the colossus and silently watched the shadows of evening obliterate its famous features. Some hours later that same sun set in London not in the harsh colours of the desert but fading into the rain where no lamps shone on the wet paving. At that hour, with something of the bland, vain speculation which had been expressed on the faces of the leaders of the Free World, Uncle Peregrine stood at his front-door and regarded the woman who had rung his bell.

'I've come to see Guy Crouchback,' she said.

There was no light on the landing. The light in the hall was a mere glimmer. Uncle Peregrine found the blackout congenial and observed the regulations with exaggerated rigour.

'Does he expect you?'

'No. I've only just heard he was here. You don't remember me, do you? Virginia.'

'Virginia?'

'Virginia Crouchback, when you knew me.'

'Oh,' he said. 'You are, are you?' Uncle Peregrine was never really disconcerted but sometimes, when a new and strange fact was brought to his notice, he took a little time to assimilate it. 'It is a terrible evening. I hope you did not get wet coming here.'

'I took a cab.'

'Good. You must forgive my failure to recognize you. It's rather dark and I never knew you very well, did I? Are you sure Guy will want to see you?'

'Pretty sure.'

Uncle Peregrine shut the front-door and said: 'I was at your wedding. Did we meet after that?'

'Once or twice.'

'You went to Africa. Then someone said you had gone to America. And now you want to see Guy?'

'Yes, please.'

'Come in here. I'll tell him.' He led Virginia into the drawing-room. 'You'll find plenty to interest you here,' he added as though presaging a long wait. 'That is, if you're interested in things.'

He shut the door behind him. He also shut Guy's before he announced in a low tone: 'There's a young woman here who says she's your wife.'

'Virginia?'

'So she claims.'

'Good. Send her in.'

'You *wish* to see her?'

'Very much.'

'If there's any trouble, ring. Mrs Corner is out, but I shall hear you.'

'What sort of trouble, Uncle Peregrine?'

'*Any* sort of trouble. You know what women are.'

'Do *you*, Uncle Peregrine?'

He considered this for a moment and then conceded: 'Well, no. Perhaps I don't.'

Then he went out, led Virginia back and left husband and wife together.

Virginia had taken trouble with her appearance. Kerstie was away, attending St Nicholas' Day festivities at her son's prep school, and Virginia had borrowed some of the clothes she had lately sold her. She bore no visible signs of her pregnancy, or, in Guy's eyes, of the many changes which had occurred in her since their last meeting. She came straight to his bed, kissed him, and said: 'Darling. What a long time it's been.'

'February 14th, 1940,' said Guy.

'As long as that? How can you remember?'

'It was a big day in my life, a bad day, a climacteric ... I've heard news of you. You work in Ian's office and live with him and Kerstie.'

'Did you hear something else, rather disgusting?'

'I heard rumours.'

'About Trimmer?'

'That was Ian's story.'

'It was all quite true.' Virginia shuddered. 'The things that happen to one! Anyway, that's all over. I've had a dreary war so far. I almost wish I'd stayed in America. It all seemed such fun at first, but it didn't last.'

'I found that,' said Guy. 'Not perhaps in quite the same way. The last two years have been as dull as peace.'

'You might have come and seen me.'

'I made rather an ass of myself at our last meeting, if you remember.'

'Oh, *that*,' said Virginia. 'If you only knew the asses I've seen people make of themselves. *That's* all forgotten.'

'Not by me.'

'Ass,' said Virginia.

She drew a chair up, lit a cigarette and asked fondly about his injuries. 'So brave,' she said. 'You know you really are brave. *Parachuting*. I'm scared even sitting in an aeroplane, let alone jumping out.' Then she said: 'I was awfully sorry to see your father's death.'

'Yes. I had always expected him to live much longer – until the last few months.'

'I wish I'd seen him again. But I dare say he wouldn't have wanted it.'

'He never came to London,' said Guy.

Virginia for the first time looked round the sombre room. 'Why are you here?' she asked. 'Ian and Kerstie say you're rich now.'

'Not *now*. The lawyers are still busy. But it looks as if I may be a bit better off eventually.'

'I'm dead broke,' said Virginia.

'That isn't at all like you.'

'Oh, you'll find I've changed in a lot of ways. What can I do to amuse you? We used to play piquet.'

'I haven't for years. I don't suppose there are any cards in the house.'

'I'll bring some tomorrow, shall I?'

'If you're coming tomorrow.'

'Oh, yes, I'll come. If you'd like me to, that's to say.'

Before Guy could answer the door opened and Uncle Peregrine entered. 'I just came to see you were all right,' he said.

What did he suspect? Assassination? Seduction? He stood studying the pair of them as the statesmen had studied the Sphinx, not really expecting an utterance, but dimly conscious of the existence of problems beyond his scope. Also, and more simply, he wanted to have another look at Virginia. He was unaccustomed to such visitors and she in particular had lurid associations for him. Well travelled, well read, well informed, he was a stranger in the world. He had understood few of the jokes which in bygone days Ralph Brompton used to devise at his expense. Virginia was a Scarlet Woman; the fatal woman who had brought about the fall of the House of Crouchback; and, what was more, to Uncle Peregrine she fully looked the part. Not for him to read the faint, indelible signature of failure, degradation, and despair that was written plain for sharper eyes than his. In the minutes which had passed since he had shown her in to Guy, he had not attempted to resume his reading. He had stood by his gas-fire considering what he had seen during his brief passage. He had returned to confirm his impression.

'I'm afraid I haven't any cocktails,' he said.

'Good gracious no. I should think not.'

'Guy often has some gin, I believe.'

'All gone,' said Guy, 'until Jumbo's next visit.'

Uncle Peregrine was fascinated. He could not bring himself to leave. It was Virginia who made the move.

'I must be off,' she said, though in fact she had nowhere at all to go. 'But I'll come back now I know what you need. Cards and gin. You won't mind having to pay for them, will you?'

Uncle Peregrine led her to the door; he followed her into the lift; he stood with her on the benighted steps and gazed with her into the rain.

'Will you be all right?' he asked. 'You might find a cab at Victoria.'

'I'm only going to Eaton Terrace. I'll walk.'

'It's a long way. Shall I see you home?'

'Don't be an ass,' said Virginia, stepping down into the rain. 'See you tomorrow.'

It was, as Uncle Peregrine observed, a long way. Virginia strode out bravely, flickering her torch at the crossings. Even on that inclement evening every doorway held an embraced couple. The house, when she reached it, was quite empty. She hung up her coat to dry. She washed her underclothes. She went to the cupboard where she knew Ian kept a box of sleeping pills. Kerstie never needed such things. Virginia took two and lay unconscious while the sirens gave warning of a distant, inconsiderable 'nuisance raid'.

At Carlisle Place Uncle Peregrine returned to Guy's room.

'I suppose it's quite usual nowadays,' he said, 'divorced people meeting on friendly terms?'

'It has been so for a long time, I believe, in the United States.'

'Yes. And, of course, she has lived there a lot, hasn't she? That would explain it. What's her name?'

'Troy, I think. It was when I last saw her.'

'Mrs Troy?'

'Yes.'

'Funny name. Are you sure you don't mean Troyte? There are people near us at home called Troyte.'

'No. Like Helen of Troy.'

'Ah,' said Uncle Peregrine. 'Yes. Exactly. Like Helen of Troy. A very striking woman. What did she mean about paying for the gin and the cards. Is she not well off?'

'Not at all, at the moment.'

'What a pity,' said Uncle Peregrine. 'You would never guess, would you?'

When Virginia came next evening she greeted Uncle Peregrine as 'Peregrine'; he bridled and followed her into Guy's room. He watched her unpack her basket, laying gin, angostura bitters, and playing-cards on the table by the bed. He insisted on paying for her purchases, seeming to derive particular pleasure from the transaction. He went to his pantry and brought glasses. He did not drink gin himself, nor did he play piquet, but he hung about the scene fascinated. When at length he left them alone, Virginia said: 'What an old pet. Why did you never let me meet him before?'

She came daily, staying sometimes for half an hour, sometimes for two hours, insinuating herself easily into Guy's uneventful routine so that her visits became something for him to anticipate with pleasure. She was like any busy wife visiting any bed-ridden husband. It was seldom that they saw one another alone. Uncle Peregrine played the part of duenna with an irksome assumption of archness. On Sunday Virginia came in the morning, and while Uncle Peregrine was at the cathedral, she asked Guy: 'Have you thought what you're going to do after the war?'

'No. It's hardly the time to make plans.'

'People are saying the Germans will collapse before the spring.'

'I don't believe it. And even if they do, that's only the beginning of other troubles.'

'Oh, Guy, I wish you were more cheerful. There's fun ahead, always. If I didn't think that, I couldn't keep going. How rich are you going to be?'

'My father left something like two hundred thousand pounds.'

'Goodness.'

'Half goes to Angela and a third to the government. Then for the next few years we have to find a number of pensions. I get the rent for Broome, that's another three hundred.'

'What does all that mean in income?'

'I suppose about two thousand eventually.'

'Not beyond the dreams of avarice.'

'No.'

'But better than a slap with a wet fish. And you had a pittance before. How about Uncle Peregrine? He must have a bit. Is that left to you?'

'I've no idea. I should have thought to Angela's children.'

'That could be changed,' said Virginia.

That day there was a pheasant for luncheon. Mrs Corner, who had come to accept Virginia's presence without comment, laid the dining-room table for two and Guy ate awkwardly on his tray while Virginia and Uncle Peregrine made a lengthy meal apart.

On the tenth day Uncle Peregrine did not return until after seven o'clock. Virginia was then on the point of leaving when he entered the room, a glint of roguish purpose in his eye.

'I haven't seen you,' he said.

'No. I've missed you.'

'I wonder whether by any possible, happy chance you are free this evening. I feel I should like to go out somewhere.'

'Free as the air,' said Virginia. 'How lovely.'

'Where would you like to go? I'm not much up in restaurants, I am afraid. There is a fish place near here, opposite Victoria Station, where I sometimes go.'

'There's always Ruben's,' said Virginia.

'I don't think I know it.'

'It will cost you a fortune,' said Guy from his bed.

'*Really*,' said Uncle Peregrine appalled at this breach of good manners. 'I should *hardly* have thought that a matter to discuss in front of my guest.'

'Of course it is,' said Virginia. 'Guy's quite right. I was only trying to think of somewhere cosy.'

'The place I speak of is certainly quiet. It has always struck me as discreet.'

'*Discreet?* Gracious. I don't think I've ever in my life been anywhere "discreet". How heavenly.'

'And since the sordid subject has been raised,' added Uncle Peregrine, looking reproachfully at his nephew, 'let me assure you it is *not* particularly cheap.'

'Come on. I can't wait,' said Virginia.

Guy watched the departure of this oddly-matched couple with amusement in which there was an element of annoyance. If Virginia was doing nothing that evening, he felt, her proper place was by his side.

They walked to the restaurant through the damp dark. Virginia took his arm. When, as happened at crossings and turnings, he tried with old-fashioned etiquette to change sides and put himself in danger of passing vehicles, she firmly retained her hold. At no great distance they found the fish shop and climbed the stairs at its side to the restaurant overhead. New to Virginia, well known to the unostentatious and discriminating, the long room with its few tables receded in a glow of Edwardian, rose-shaded lights. Peregrine Crouchback shed his old coat and hat and handed his umbrella to an ancient porter and then said with an effort: 'I expect you want, that's to say, I mean, wash your hands, tidy up, ladies' cloakroom, somewhere I believe up those stairs.'

'No thanks,' said Virginia, and then added, as they were being shown to a table: 'Peregrine, have you ever taken a girl out to dinner before?'

'Yes, of course.'

'Who? When?'

'It was some time ago,' said Uncle Peregrine vaguely.

They ordered oysters and turbot. Virginia said she would like to drink stout. Then she began: 'Why have you never married?'

'I was a younger son. Younger sons didn't marry in my day.'

'Oh rot. I know hundreds who have.'

'It was thought rather *outré* among landed people, unless of course they found heiresses. There was no establishment for them. They had a small settlement which they were expected to leave back to the family – to their nephews, other younger sons. There had to be younger sons of course in case the head of the family died young. They came in quite useful in the last war. Perhaps we are rather an old-fashioned family in some ways.'

'Didn't you ever want to marry?'

'Not really.'

Uncle Peregrine was not at all put out by these direct personal questions. He was essentially imperturbable. No one, so far as he could remember, had ever shown so much interest in him. He found the experience enjoyable, even when Virginia pressed further.

'Lots of affairs?'

'Good heavens, no.'

'I'm sure you aren't a pansy.'

'Pansy?'

'You're not homosexual?'

Even this did not disconcert Uncle Peregrine. It was a subject he had rarely heard mentioned by a man; never by a woman. But there was something about Virginia's frankness which struck him as childlike and endearing.

'Good gracious, no. Besides the "o" is short. It comes from the Greek not the Latin.'

'I knew you weren't. I can always tell. I was just teasing.'

'No one has ever teased me about *that* before. But I knew a fellow once in the diplomatic service who had that reputation. There can't have been anything in it. He ended up as an ambassador. They would hardly have appointed a fellow like *that*. He was rather a vain, dressy fellow. I dare say that was what made people talk.'

'Peregrine, have you never been to bed with a woman?'

'Yes,' said Uncle Peregrine smugly, 'twice. It is not a thing I normally talk about.'

'Do tell.'

'Once when I was twenty and once when I was forty-five. I didn't particularly enjoy it.'

'Tell me about them.'

'It was the same woman.'

Virginia's spontaneous laughter had seldom been heard in recent years; it had once been one of her chief charms. She sat back in her chair and gave full, free tongue; clear, unrestrained, entirely joyous, with a shadow of ridicule, her mirth rang through the quiet little restaurant. Sympathetic and envious faces were turned towards her. She stretched across the tablecloth and caught his hand, held it convulsively, unable to speak, laughed until she was breathless and mute, still gripping his bony fingers. And Uncle Peregrine smirked. He had never before struck success. He had in his time been at parties where others had laughed in this way. He had never had any share in it. He did not now know quite what it was that had won this prize, but he was highly gratified.

'Oh Peregrine,' said Virginia at last with radiant sincerity. 'I love you.'

He was not afraid to spoil his triumph with expatiation.

'I know most men go in for love affairs,' he said. 'Some of them can't help it. They can't get on at all without women, but there are plenty of others – I dare say you haven't come across them much – who don't really care about that sort of thing, but they don't know any reason why they shouldn't, so they spend half their lives going after women they don't really want. I can tell you something you probably don't know. There are men who have been great womanizers in their time and when they get to my age and don't want it any more and in fact can't do it, instead of being glad of a rest, what do they do but take all kinds of medicines to make them *want* to go on? I've heard fellows in my club talking about it.'

'Bellamy's?'

'Yes. I don't go there much except to read the papers. Awfully rowdy place it's become. I was put up as a young man and go on paying the subscription, I don't know why. I don't know many fellows there. Well, the other day I heard two of them who must have been about my age, talking of which doctor was best to make them *want* women. All manner of expensive treatments. You can't explain that, can you?'

'I knew a man called Augustus who did just that.'

'Did you? And he told you about it? Extraordinary.'

'Why is it different from going for a walk to get up an appetite for luncheon?'

'Because it's Wrong,' said Uncle Peregrine.

'You mean "wrong" according to your religion?'

'Why, how else could anything be wrong? asked Uncle Peregrine with perfect simplicity and continued his dissertation on the problems of sex: 'There's another thing. You only have to look at the ghastly fellows who are a success with women to realize there isn't much point in it.'

But Virginia was not attending. She began to make a little pagoda of the empty oyster-shells on her plate. Without raising her eyes, she said: '*I'm* rather thinking of becoming a Catholic.'

It has been said of Uncle Peregrine that he was never disconcerted. Exception must be made of the abrupt access of displeasure which now struck him. It is one of the established delights of celibacy to discourse frankly, even grossly, of the vagaries of lust to an attractive woman; it was one which Uncle Peregrine had never before experienced and he was enjoying it stupendously. Now she had rudely let drop the guillotine.

'Oh,' he said. 'Why?'

'Don't you think it would be a good thing?'

'It depends on your reasons.'

'Isn't it always a good thing?'

The waiter reproachfully rearranged the oyster-shells on Virginia's plate before removing it.

'Well, isn't it?' she pressed. 'Come on. Tell. Why are you so shocked suddenly? I've heard an awful lot one way and another about the Catholic Church being the church of sinners.'

'Not from me,' said Uncle Peregrine.

The waiter brought them their turbot.

'Of course, if you'd sooner not discuss it . . .'

'I'm not really competent to,' said the Privy Chamberlain, the knight of Devotion and Grace of the Sovereign Order of St John of Jerusalem. 'Personally I find it very difficult to regard converts as Catholics.'

'Oh, don't be so stuck up and snubbing. What about Lady Plessington? She is a pillar, surely?'

'I have never felt quite at ease with Eloise Plessington where religion is concerned. Anyway, she was received into the Church when she married.'

'Exactly.'

'And you, my dear, were not.'

'Do you think it might have made a difference – with Guy and me, I mean – if I had been?'

Uncle Peregrine hesitated between his acceptance in theory of the operation of divine grace and his distant but quite detailed observation of the men and women he had known, and relapsed to his former 'I'm really not competent to say.'

A silence fell on the pair; Uncle Peregrine deploring the turn the conversation had taken, Virginia considering how she could give further impetus in that direction. They ate their turbot and were brought coffee before their plates were removed. Diners were not encouraged to linger over their tables in those days. At length Virginia said: 'You see I rather hoped for your support in a plan of mine. I've got a bit tired of knocking about. I thought of going back to my husband.'

'To Troy?'

'No, no. To Guy. After all he is my real husband, isn't he? I thought becoming a Catholic might help. No amount of divorces count in your Church, do they? I suppose we shall have to go to some registry office to make it legal, but we're already married in the eyes of God – he's told me so.'

'Lately?'

'Not very lately.'

'Do you think he wants you back?'

'I bet I could soon make him.'

'Well,' said Uncle Peregrine, 'that alters everything.' He looked at her with eyes of woe. 'It was *Guy* you've been coming to see all these last days?'

'Of course. What did you think? ... Oh, Peregrine, did you think I had designs on *you*?'

'The thought had crossed my mind.'

'You thought perhaps I might provide your third—' She used a word, then unprintable, which despite its timeless obscenity did not make Uncle Peregrine wince. He even found it attractive on her lips. She was full of good humour and mischief now, on the verge of another access of laughter.

'That was rather the idea.'

'But surely that would have been Wrong?'

'Very Wrong indeed. I did not seriously entertain it. But it recurred often, even when I was sorting the books. You could have moved into the room Guy is now in. I don't think Mrs Corner would have seen anything objectionable. After all, you are my niece.'

Virginia's laughter came again, most endearing of her charms.

'Darling Peregrine. And you wouldn't have needed any of those expensive treatments your chums in Bellamy's recommend?'

'In your case,' said Uncle Peregrine with his cavalier grace, 'I am practically sure not.'

'It's perfectly sweet of you. You don't think I'm laughing *at* you, do you?'

'No, I don't believe you are.'

'Any time you want to try, dear Peregrine, you're quite welcome.'

The pleasure died in Peregrine Crouchback's sad old face.

'That wouldn't be quite the same thing. Put like that I find the suggestion embarrassing.'

'Oh dear, have I made a floater?'

'Yes. It was all a fancy really. You make it sound so practical. I found I looked forward to seeing you about the flat, don't you know? It wasn't much more than that.'

'And I want a husband,' said Virginia. 'You wouldn't consider that?'

'No, no. Of course that would be quite impossible.'

'Your religion again.'

'Well, yes.'

'Then it will have to be Guy. Don't you see now why I want to become a Catholic? He can't very well say no, can he?'

'Oh yes, he can.'

'But knowing Guy you don't think he will, do you?'

'I really know Guy very little,' said Uncle Peregrine rather peevishly.

'But you'll help me? When the point comes up, you'll tell him it's his duty?'

'He's not at all likely to consult me.'

'But if he does? And when it comes to squaring Angela?'

'No, my dear,' said Uncle Peregrine, 'I'll be damned if I do.'

The evening had not gone as either of them had planned. Uncle Peregrine saw Virginia to her door. She kissed him, for the first time, on their parting. He raised his hat in the darkness, paid off the taxi and walked despondently home, where he found Guy awake, reading.

'Have a good time?' he asked.

'It is always good, so far as anything is nowadays, at that restaurant. It cost more than two pounds,' he added, his memory still sore from the imputation of parsimony.

'I mean, did you enjoy yourself?'

'Yes and no. More no than yes perhaps.'

'I thought Virginia seemed in cracking form.'
'Yes and no. More yes than no. She laughed a lot.'
'That sounds all right.'
'Yes and no. Guy, I have to warn you. That girl has *Designs*.'
'On you, Uncle Peregrine?'
'On you.'
'Are you sure?'
'She told me.'
'Do you think you should repeat it?'
'In the circumstances, yes.'
'Not yes and no?'
'Just yes.'

Sir Ralph Brompton had been schooled in the old diplomatic service to evade irksome duties and to achieve power by insinuating himself into places where, strictly, he had no business. In the looser organization of total war he was able to trip from office to office and committee to committee. The chiefs of HOO considered they should be represented wherever the conduct of affairs was determined. Busy themselves in the highest circles, they willingly delegated to Sir Ralph the authority to listen and speak for them and to report to them, in the slightly lower but not much less mischievous world of their immediate inferiors.

Liberation was Sir Ralph's special care. Wherever those lower than the Cabinet and the Chiefs of Staff adumbrated the dismemberment of Christendom, there Sir Ralph might be found.

On a morning shortly before Christmas in an office quite independent of HOO Sir Ralph dropped in for an informal chat on the subject of liaison with Balkan terrorists. The man whom he was visiting had been rather suddenly gazetted brigadier. His functions were as ill-defined as Sir Ralph's; they were dubbed 'co-ordination'. There had been times in Sir Ralph's professional career when he had been aware that certain of his colleagues and, later, of his staff were engaged in secret work. Strange men not of the service had presented credentials and made use of the diplomatic bag and the cipher room. Sir Ralph had fastidiously averted his attention from their activities. Now, recalled from retirement, he found a naughty relish in what he had formerly shunned. These two had risen to their positions by very different routes; their paths had never crossed. Sir Ralph sported light herring-bone tweed, such as in peacetime he would not have worn at that season in London; brilliant black brogue shoes shone on his narrow feet. His long legs were crossed and he smoked a Turkish cigarette. The brigadier had bought his uniform ready-made. The buttons were dull. He wore a cloth belt. No ribbons decorated his plump breast. His false teeth held a pipe insecurely. An impersonal association, but a close one, united them. Their political sympathies were identical.

'It is a great thing getting control of Balkan Liberation shifted here from Cairo.'

'Yes, almost the whole Middle East set-up was hopelessly compromised with royalist refugees. We shall be able to use the few reliable men. The others will be found more suitable employment.'

'Iceland?'

'Iceland will be perfectly suitable.'

Lists were produced of the proposed liaison missions.

'De Souza got a very good report from the parachute school.'

'Yes. You don't think he'll be wasted in the field? He could be very useful to us here.'

'He can be very useful in the field. Gilpin failed. We can use him here until we open a headquarters in Italy.'

'Once our fellows get to Italy they'll be harder to keep under our own hand. They'll come under command of the army for a good many things. We've been accepted on the top level but we still have to establish confidence lower down. What we need is a good backing of conventional regimental soldiers in the subordinate posts. I see Captain Crouchback's name here, crossed off. I know him. I should have thought he was just what we need – middle-aged, Catholic, no political activities, a Halberdier, good record, excellent report from the parachute school.'

'Bad security risk, apparently.'

'Why?'

'They never give reasons. He is simply noted as unsuitable for employment in North Italy.'

'Entanglements with women?' suggested the brigadier.

'I should doubt it.'

There was a pause while Sir Ralph considered the fatuity of the security forces. Then he said: 'Only in North Italy?'

'That is what the report says.'

'In fact there would be no objection to his going to the Balkans?'

'Not according to this report.'

'I think he and de Souza might make a satisfactory team.'

For very many years Peregrine Crouchback's Christmases had been dismal occasions for himself and others. Bachelors, unless dedicated to some religious function or deluded by vice, are said to be unknown among the lower races and classes. Peregrine Crouchback was a bachelor by nature and the Feast of the Nativity was to him the least congenial in the calendar. As a child, as the mere recipient of gifts and the consumer of rich, rather tasteless foods, he had conformed and rejoiced. But he had matured, so far as his peculiar condition could be called maturity, young. In his early manhood, as his niece and nephews became the centre of celebration at Broome, he sought refuge abroad. After the First World War, Arthur Box-

Bender was added to the bereaved family; Ivo died but Box-Bender's children filled the nurseries at mid-winter. Finally Broome was emptied and Christmas ceased to be a family gathering. Uncle Peregrine did not repine. But between the wars, in a year whose quite recent date could have been established from the visitors' book but now seemed of immemorial antiquity, it had become habitual, almost traditional, for Uncle Peregrine to spend Christmas with some distant cousins of his mother, older than himself, named Scrope-Weld, who inhabited an agricultural island among the industrial areas of Staffordshire. The house was large, the hospitality, when he first went there, lavish, and one unloved, middle-aged bachelor less or more – 'Old Crouchers' even then to them, his seniors – did not depress the spirits of the 1920s. A forlorn relation was part of the furniture of Christmas in most English homes.

Mr and Mrs Scrope-Weld died, their son and his wife took their places; there were fewer servants, fewer guests, but always Uncle Peregrine at Christmas. In 1939 the greater part of the house was taken for a children's home; Scrope-Weld went abroad with his regiment; his wife remained with three children, four rooms, and a nanny. Still Peregrine Crouchback was invited and he accepted. 'It is just the sort of thing one must not give up,' said Mrs Scrope-Weld. 'One must not make the war an excuse for unkindness.'

So it was in 1940, 1941, and 1942. The children grew sharper.

'Mummy, do we have to have Uncle Perry here to spoil Christmas every year until he dies?'

'Yes, dear. He was a great friend and a sort of relation of your grandmother's. He'd be very hurt if he was not asked.'

'He seemed awfully hurt all the time he was here.'

'Christmas is often a sad time for old people. He's very fond of you all.'

'I bet he isn't fond of me.'

'Or me.'

'Or me.'

'Will he leave us any money?'

'Francis, that's an absolutely disgusting question. Of course he won't.'

'Well, I wish he'd hurry up and die anyway.'

And as Peregrine Crouchback left on the day after Boxing Day he reflected: 'Well, that's over for another year. They'd be awfully hurt if I didn't come.'

So it was in 1943. Loth to leave London he took the crowded train on Christmas Eve. Once he used to bring a Strasburg pie with him. Now the shops were empty. His only gift was a large, highly coloured Victorian album which he had extracted from 'salvage'.

That night, as always, they attended Mass. On Christmas Day they all made a formal visit to the library, now the common-room of the paid 'helpers', commended the sprigs of holly that they had disposed along the book-shelves and picture-frames and drank sherry with them before retiring to eat a middle-day dinner of turkey, an almost nefarious bird at that date, long cosseted with rationed food-stuffs. 'I feel so guilty eating it alone,' said Mrs Scrope-Weld, 'but it would go nowhere with the helpers and we couldn't possibly have reared another.' The children gorged. Peregrine and nanny nibbled. That evening there was a Christmas tree for the 'evacuees' in the staircase hall. On Boxing Day, as always, he went to Mass, walking alone through the chill morning, under the dripping avenue to the chapel on the edge of the park. Mrs Scrope-Weld had to milk and then do most of the work in cooking breakfast. One of the 'helpers' was there before him. They walked back together and she said: 'Perhaps this will be the last Christmas here.'

'Do you hope for that?'

'Well of course, everyone hopes for peace. But I don't know where I shall be or what I shall be doing when it comes. I've got sort of used to the war.'

Later he went for a long, damp walk with his hostess. She said: 'You're really the only link with Christmas as it used to be. It is sweet of you coming so faithfully. I know it isn't a bit comfortable. Do you think things will ever be normal again?'

'Oh, no,' said Peregrine Crouchback. 'Never again.'

Meanwhile Guy and Virginia were together in London. Virginia said: 'Thank God HOO doesn't make a thing about Christmas.'

'In the Halberdiers we had to go to the sergeants' mess and they tried to make us drunk. In some regiments, I believe, the officers wait on the men at dinner.'

'I've seen photographs of it. Peregrine's away?'

'He always goes to the same people. Did he give you a present?'

'No. I wondered whether he would. I don't think he knew what would be suitable. He seemed less loving after our fish dinner.'

'He told me you had Designs.'

'On him?'

'On me.'

'Yes,' said Virginia. 'I have. Peregrine had designs on me.'

'Seriously?'

'Not really. The thing about you Crouchbacks is that you're effete.'

'Do you know what that means? It means you've just given birth.'

'Well, it's the wrong word then. You're just like Peregrine correcting my pronunciation of homosexual.'

'Why on earth were you talking to him about homosexuals? You don't think he's one, do you?'

'No, but I think all you Crouchbacks are over-bred and under-sexed.'

'Not at all the same thing. Think of Toulouse-Lautrec.'

'Oh, damn, Guy. You're evading my Designs.'

It was all as light as the heaviest drawing-room comedy and each had a dread at heart.

'You're dying out as a family,' she continued. 'Even Angela's boy, they tell me, wants to be a monk. Why do you Crouchbacks do so little —ing?' – and again she used without offence that then unprintable word.

'I don't know about the others. With me I think, perhaps, it's because I associate it with love. And I don't love any more.'

'Not me?'

'Oh, no, Virginia, not you. You must have realized that.'

'It is not so easy to realize when lots of people have been so keen, not so long ago. What about you, Guy, that evening in Claridges?'

'That wasn't love,' said Guy. 'Believe it or not it was the Halberdiers.'

'Yes. I think I know what you mean.'

She was sitting beside his bed, facing him. Between them lay the wicker table-tray on which they had been playing piquet. Now she ran a hand, light, caressing, exploring, up under the bed-clothes. Guy turned away and the pain of the sudden, instinctive movement made him grimace.

'No,' said Virginia. 'Not keen.'

'I'm sorry.'

'It's not a nice thing for a girl to have a face made at her like that.'

'It was only my knee. I've said I'm sorry,' and indeed he was, that he should so humiliate one whom he had loved.

But Virginia was not easily humiliated. Behind her last, locust years lay deep reserves of success. Almost all women in England at that time believed that peace would restore normality. Mrs Scrope-Weld in Staffordshire meant by 'normality' having her husband at home and the house to themselves; also certain, to her, rudimentary comforts to which she had always been used; nothing sumptuous; a full larder and cellar; a lady's maid (but one who did her bedroom and darned and sewed for the whole family), a butler, a footman (but one who chopped and carried fire-logs), a reliable, mediocre cook training a kitchen-maid to succeed her in simple skills, self-effacing house-maids to dust and tidy; one man in the stable, two in the garden; things she would never know again. So to Virginia normality meant power and pleasure; pleasure chiefly and not only her own. Her power of attraction, her power of pleasing was to her still part of the natural order which had been capriciously interrupted. War, the massing and moving of millions of men, some of whom were sometimes endangered, most of whom were idle and lonely, the devastation, hunger, and waste, crumbling buildings, foundering ships, the torture and murder of prisoners; the condition in which Virginia's power of pleasing enabled her to cash cheques, wear new clothes, lave her face with its accustomed unguent, travel with speed and privacy and attention wherever she liked, when she liked, and choose her man and enjoy him at her leisure. The interruption had been prolonged beyond all reason. The balance would soon come right, meanwhile –

'What did Peregrine say about my Designs?'

'He didn't specify.'

'What do you think he meant? What do *you* think of *me*?'

'I think you are unhappy and uncomfortable and you've no one you're specially interested in at the moment and that for the first time in your life you are frightened of the future.'

'And none of that applies to you?'

'The difference between us is that I only think of the past.'

Virginia seized on the, to her, essential point. 'But there's no one *you're* specially interested in at the moment, is there?'

'No.'

'And you've absolutely loved having me round the place the last few weeks, haven't you? Admit. We get along like an old Darby and Joan, don't we?'

'Yes, I've enjoyed your visits.'

'And I'm still your wife. Nothing can alter that?'

'Nothing.'

'I don't exactly say you've a duty to me,' Virginia conceded with her high, fine candour.

'No, Virginia, you hardly could, could you?'

'You thought I had duties to you once – that evening in Claridge's. Remember?'

'I've explained that. It was being on leave from camp, wearing a new uniform, starting a new life. It was the war.'

'Well, isn't it the war that's brought me here today, bringing you, as I thought, a lovely Christmas present?'

'You didn't think anything of the kind.'

Virginia began to sing a song of their youth about 'a little broken doll'. Suddenly both of them laughed. Guy said: 'It's no good, Ginny. I am sorry you are hard up. As you know, I'm a little better off than I was. I am willing to help you until you find someone more convenient.'

'Guy, what a beastly, bitter way to talk. Not like you at all. You would never have spoken like that in the old days.'

'Not bitter – limited. That's all I've got for you.'

Then Virginia said: 'I need more. There's something I've got to tell you and please believe that I was going to tell you even if this conversation had gone quite differently. You must remember me well enough to know I was never one for dirty tricks, was I?'

Then she informed him, without any extenuation or plea for compassion, curtly almost, that she was with child by Trimmer.

*

Ian and Kerstie Kilbannock returned to London from Scotland on the night of Childermas. He went straight to his office, she home, where Mrs Bristow was smoking a cigarette and listening to the wireless.

'Everything all right?'

'Mrs Troy's gone.'

'Where?'

'She didn't say. Gone for good, I wouldn't be surprised. She packed up everything yesterday morning and gave me a pound. You'd have thought either it would be something more or just friendly thanks after all this time. I nearly told her tipping's gone out these days. What I mean is we all help one another as the wireless says. A fiver would have been more like if she wanted to show appreciation. I helped her down with the bags too. Well, she's lived a lot abroad, hasn't she? Oh, and she left you this.'

This was a letter:

Darling

I am sorry not to be here to say good-bye but I am sure you will be quite pleased to have me out of the house at last. What an angel you have been. I can never thank you or Ian enough. Let's meet very soon and I'll tell you all about everything. I've left a little token for Ian – a silly sort of present but you know how impossible it is to find anything nowadays.

All love
Virginia

'Did she leave anything else, Mrs Bristow?'

'Just two books. They're upstairs on the drawing-room table.'

Upstairs Kerstie found Pyne's *Horace*. Kerstie was no bibliophile but she had haunted the sale rooms and recognized objects of some value. Like Mrs Bristow's tip, she considered, it might have been something less or more. The elegant volumes were in fact Virginia's only disposable property, an inappropriate and belated Christmas present from Uncle Peregrine.

Kerstie returned to the kitchen.

'Mrs Troy left no address?'

'She's not gone far. I didn't catch what she said to the taxi driver but it wasn't a railway station.'

The mystery was soon solved, Ian telephoned. 'Good news,' he said. 'We've got rid of Virginia.'

'I know.'

'For good. She's been a sensible woman. I knew she had it in her. She's done just what I said she should – found a husband.'

'Anyone we know?'

'Yes, the obvious man. Guy.'

'Oh, no.'

'I assure you. She's in the office now. She's just handed in official notification that she is giving up war-work to be a housewife.'

'Ian, she can't do this to Guy.'

'They're going round to the registrar as soon as he can hobble.'

'He must be insane.'

'I've always thought he was. It's in the family, you know. There was that brother of his.'

There were depths of Scotch propriety in Kerstie, hard granite very near the surface. Life in London, life with Ian, had not entirely atrophied her susceptibility to moral outrage. It happened to her rarely but when shocked she suffered no superficial shiver but a deep seismic upheaval. For some minutes after Ian had rung off she sat still and grim and glaring. Then she made for Carlisle Place.

'Oh, good morning, my lady,' said Mrs Corner, very different in her address from Mrs Bristow, 'you've come to see Captain Guy, of course. You've heard his news?'

'Yes.'

'No surprise to me, I can assure you, my lady. I saw it coming. All's well that ends well. It's only natural really, isn't it, whatever the rights and wrongs were before, they are man and wife. She's moved in here in the room down the passage and she's giving up her work so she'll be free to take care of him.'

Throughout this speech Kerstie moved towards Guy's door. 'He will be pleased to see you,' Mrs Corner said opening it; 'he doesn't often get visitors in the morning.'

'Hallo, Kerstie,' said Guy. 'Nice of you to come. I expect you've heard of my change of life.'

She did not sit down. She waited until Mrs Corner had left them.

'Guy,' she said, 'I've only got a minute. I'm due at my office. I had to stop and see you. I've known you a long time if never very well. It just happens you're one of Ian's friends I really like. You may think it's no business of mine but I've got to tell you'; and then she delivered her message.

'But, dear Kerstie, do you suppose I didn't know?'

'Virginia told you?'

'Of course.'

'And you're marrying her in spite of –?'

'Because of.'

'You poor bloody fool,' said Kerstie, anger and pity and something near love in her voice, 'you're being *chivalrous* – about *Virginia*. Can't you understand men aren't chivalrous any more and I don't believe they ever were. Do you really see Virginia as a damsel in distress?'

'She's in distress.'

'She's tough.'

'Perhaps when they *are* hurt, the tough suffer more than the tender.'

'Oh, come off it, Guy. You're forty years old. Can't you see how ridiculous you will look playing the knight errant? Ian thinks you are insane, literally. Can you tell me any sane reason for doing this thing?'

Guy regarded Kerstie from his bed. The question she asked was not new to him. He had posed it and answered it some days ago. 'Knights errant,' he said, 'used to go out looking for noble deeds. I don't think I've ever in my life done a single, positively unselfish action. I certainly haven't gone out of my way to find opportunities. Here was something most unwelcome, put into my hands; something which I believe the Americans describe as "beyond the call of duty"; not the normal behaviour of an officer and a gentleman; something they'll laugh about in Bellamy's.

'Of course Virginia is tough. She would have survived somehow. I shan't be changing her by what I'm doing. I know all that. But you see there's another —' he was going to say 'soul'; then realized that this word would mean little to Kerstie for all her granite propriety – 'there's another life to consider. What sort of life do you think her child would have, born unwanted in 1944?'

'It's no business of yours.'

'It was made my business by being offered.'

'My dear Guy, the world is full of unwanted children. Half the population of Europe are homeless – refugees and prisoners. What is one child more or less in all that misery?'

'I can't do anything about all those others. This is just one case where I can help. And only I, really. I was Virginia's last resort. So I couldn't do anything else. Don't you *see*?'

'Of course I don't. Ian is quite right. You're insane.'

And Kerstie left more angry than she had come.

It was no good trying to explain. Guy thought. Had someone said: 'All differences are theological differences'? He turned once more to his father's letter: *Quantitative judgements don't apply. If only one soul was saved, that is full compensation for any amount of 'loss of face'.*

BOOK THREE

The Death Wish

I

The Dakota flew out over the sea, then swung inland. The listless passengers, British and American, all men, of all services and all of lowly rank, stirred and buckled themselves to the metal benches. The journey by way of Gibraltar and North Africa had been tedious and protracted by unexplained delays. It was now late afternoon and they had had nothing to eat since dawn. This was a different machine from the one in which Guy had embarked in England. None of those who had travelled with him that first sleepless night had continued to Bari. Crouching and peering through the little porthole, he caught a glimpse of orchards of almond; it was late February and the trees were already in full flower. Soon he was on the ground beside his kit-bag and valise, reporting to a transport officer.

His move-order instructed him to report forthwith to the Headquarters of the British Mission to the Anti-Fascist Forces of National Liberation (Adriatic).

He was expected. A jeep was waiting to take him to the sombre building in the new town where this organization was installed. Nothing reminded him of the Italy he knew and loved; the land of school holidays; the land where later he had sought refuge from his failure.

The sentry was less than welcoming.

'That's a Home Forces pass, sir. No use here.'

Guy still retained his HOO HQ pass and exhibited it.

'Don't know anything about that, sir.'

'I have orders to report to a Brigadier Cape.'

'He's not here today. You'll have to wait and see the security officer. Ron,' he said to a colleague, 'tell Captain Gilpin there's an officer reporting to the Brigadier.'

For some minutes Guy stood in the dark hall. This building was a pre-fascist structure designed in traditional style round a sunless *cortile*. A broad flight of shallow stone steps led up into the darkness, for the glass roof had been shattered and replaced by tarred paper. 'The light ought to come on any time now,' said the sentry. 'But you can't rely on it.'

Presently Gilpin appeared in the gloom.

'Yes?' he said. 'What can we do for you?'

'Don't you remember me at the parachute school with de Souza?'

'De Souza's in the field. What exactly is it you want?'

Guy showed him his move-order.

'First I've seen of this.'

'You don't imagine it's a forgery, do you?'

'A copy ought to have come to me. I don't *imagine* anything. It is simply that we have to take precautions.' In the twilight of the hall he turned the order over and studied its back. He read it again. Then he tried a new attack. 'You seem to have taken your time getting here.'

'Yes, there were delays. Are you in command here?'

'I'm not the senior officer if that's what you mean. There's a major upstairs – a Halberdier like yourself.' – He spoke the name of the Corps in a manner which seemed deliberately to dissociate himself from the traditions of the army; with a sneer almost. – 'I don't know what he does. He's posted as GSO 2 (Co-ordination). I suppose in a way you might say he was "in command" when the Brig. is away.'

'Perhaps I could see him?'

'Is that your gear?'

'Yes.'

'You'll have to leave it down here.'

'Do you suppose I wanted to carry it up?'

'Keep an eye on it, corporal,' said Gilpin, not, it seemed, from any solicitude for its preservation; rather for fear of what it might contain of a subversive, perhaps, explosive, nature. 'You did quite right to hold this officer for examination,' he added. 'You can send him up to GSO 2 (Co-ordination)' – and without another word to Guy he turned and left him.

The second sentry led Guy to a door on the mezzanine. Four and a half years' of the vicissitudes of war had accustomed Guy to a large variety of reception. It had also accustomed him to meet from time to time the officer whose name he had never learned, who now greeted him with unwonted warmth.

'Well,' he said, 'well, we do run across one another, don't we? I expect you're more surprised than I am. I saw your name on a bit of bumf. We've been expecting you for weeks.'

'Gilpin wasn't.'

'We try to keep as much bumf as we can from Gilpin. It isn't always easy.'

At that moment, as though symbolically, the bulb hanging from the ceiling glowed, flickered, and shone brilliantly.

'Still a major, I see,' said Guy.

'Yes, dammit. I was lieutenant-colonel for nearly a year. Then there was a reorganization at brigade. There didn't seem a job for me there any more. So I drifted into this outfit.'

The electric bulb, as though symbolically, flickered, glowed, and went out. 'They haven't really got the plant working yet,' said the major super-fluously. 'It comes and goes.' And their conversation was carried on in intermittent periods of vision and obscurity as though in a storm of summer lightning.

'D'you know what you're going to do here?'

'No.'

'I didn't when I was posted. I don't now. It's a nice enough outfit. You'll like Cape. He's not long out of hospital – got hit at Salerno. No more active soldiering for him. He'll explain the set-up when you see him tomorrow. He and Joe Cattermole had to go to a conference at Caserta. Joe's a queer fellow, some sort of professor in civil life; frightfully musical. But he works like the devil. Takes everything off *my* shoulders – and Cape's. Gilpin is a pest as you saw. Joe's the only man who can stand him. Joe likes everyone – even the Jugs. Awfully good-natured fellow, Joe; always ready to stand in and take extra duty.'

They spoke of the Halberdiers, of the achievements and frustrations of Ritchie-Hook, of the losses and reinforcements, recruiting, regrouping, reorganization, and cross-posting that was changing the face of the Corps. The light waxed, waned, flickered, expired as the familiar household names of Guy's innocence resounded between them. Then the anonymous major turned his attention to Guy's affairs and booked him a room at the officers' hotel. When the light next went out, the sun had set and they were left in total darkness. An orderly came in bearing a pressure-lamp.

'Time to pack it up,' said the major. 'I'll see you settled in. Then we can go out to dinner.'

'I'll just sign you in,' said the major at the entrance of the club. Guy looked over his shoulder but the signature was as illegible as ever; indeed Guy himself, entered in his writing, shared a vicarious anonymity. 'If you're going to be in Bari any time, you'd better join.'

'I see it's called the "Senior Officers' Club".'

'That doesn't mean anything. It's for fellows who are used to a decent mess. The hotel is full of Queen Alexandra's nurses in the evenings. Women are a difficulty here,' he continued as they made their way into the ante-room – this new, rather outlandish building had been made for a seminary of Uniate Abyssinians, who had been moved to Rome at the fall of the Italian Ethiopian Empire; the chief rooms were domed in acknowledgement of their native tukals and fanes. 'The locals are strictly out of bounds. No great temptation, either, from what I've seen. Thoroughly unsavoury, and, anyway, they only want Americans. They pay anything and don't mind what they're getting. There are a few secretaries and ciphereens but they're all booked. If you're lucky you get fixed up with a nurse. They get two evenings a week. Cape's got one – a bit long in the tooth but very friendly. It's easier for fellows who've been in hospital. Joe was in hospital when he came out of Jugland but he doesn't seem to have taken advantage. I have to rely on WAAFs mostly; they come through sometimes on the way to Foggia. They talk a lot of rot about Italy.'

'The WAAFs do?'

'No, no. I mean people who've never been here. *Romantic* – my God. That's where the club comes in. It *is* like a mess at home, isn't it? English rations, of course.'

'No restaurants open?'

'Strictly out of bounds. There's nothing for the wops to eat in this town except what they can scrounge off the RASC dump.'

'No wine?'

'There's a sort of local red vino, if you like it.'

'Fish, surely?'

'That's kept for the wops. Good thing, too, by the smell of it.'

The exhilaration which Guy had experienced at finding himself abroad after two years of war-time England flickered and died like the bulb at Headquarters.

'Shops?' Guy asked. 'I've always heard that there are some fine things to be found in Apulia.'

'Nothing, old boy, nothing.'

A civilian waiter brought them their pink gins. Guy asked him in Italian for olives. He answered in English almost scornfully: 'No olives for senior officers,' and brought American pea-nuts.

Under the blue-washed cupola where the dusky, bearded clerics had lately pursued their studies, Guy surveyed the heterogeneous uniforms and badges and saw his own recent past, his probable future. This was Southsands again; it was the transit camp, the Station Hotel in Glasgow; it was that lowest circle where he had once penetrated, the unemployed officers' pool.

'I say,' said Guy's host, 'cheer up. What's wrong? Homesick?'

'Homesick for Italy,' said Guy.

'That's a good one,' said the major, puzzled, but appreciative that a joke had been made.

They went into what had been the refectory. Had Guy been homesick for war-time London, he would have found solace here, for Lieutenant Padfield was dining with a party of three Britons. Since Christmas the Lieutenant had not been seen about London.

'Good evening, Loot. What are you up to?'

'I'll join you later, may I?'

'You know that Yank?' said the major.

'Yes.'

'What does he do?'

'That no one knows.'

'He's been hanging round Joe Cattermole lately. I don't know who's brought him here tonight. We try to be matey with the Yanks in office hours but we don't much encourage them off duty. They've got plenty of places of their own.'

'The Loot's a great mixer.'

'What d'you call him?'

'Loot. It's American for Lieutenant, you know.'

'Is it? I didn't. How absurd.'

Dinner, as Guy had been forewarned, included no succulent, redolent Italian dishes but he gratefully drank the 'vino', poor as it was; wine in any form had been scarcer and more costly than ever in the two months in London. The major drank nothing with his food. He told Guy in detail of his last WAAF and of the WAAF before her. The differences were negligible. Presently the Lieutenant came across to them bearing a cigar-case. 'I can't bear them myself,' he said. 'I think these are all right. Not from the PX. Our minister in Algiers gave me a box.'

'A woman's only a woman but a good cigar is a smoke,' said the major.

'Which reminds me,' said the Lieutenant, 'that I have never written to congratulate you and Virginia. I read about you in *The Times* when I was staying with the Stitches in Algiers. It's *very* good news.'

'Thank you.'

The Halberdier major having accepted, bitten, and lit the cigar he was offered, felt obliged to say: 'Bring up a pew. We haven't met, but I've seen you with Joe Cattermole.'

'Yes, he's the most useful fellow here in my job.'

'Would it be insecure to ask what that is?'

'Not at all. Opera. We're trying to get the opera going, you know.'

'I didn't.'

'It's the most certain way to the Italian heart. There's not much difficulty about orchestras. The singers seem all to have gone off with the Germans.' He spoke of the various opera houses of occupied Italy; some had been gutted by bombs, others had escaped with a little damage. Bari was unscathed. 'But I must rejoin my hosts,' he said, rising.

The major hesitated on the brink of so private a topic; then plunged: 'Did I gather from what that fellow said that you've just got married?'

'Yes.'

'Rotten luck being posted abroad at once. I say, I'm afraid I was talking out of turn a bit, giving you advice about the local market.'

'I don't think my wife would mind.'

'Wouldn't she? Mine would – and I've been married eleven years.' He paused, brooding over that long stretch of intermittent rapture, and added: 'At least, I think she would.' He paused again. 'It's a long time since I saw her. I dare say,' he concluded with the resigned, cosmic melancholy that Guy had always associated with him, 'that she wouldn't really care a bit.'

They returned to the ante-room. The major's spirits had sunk at the thought of the possibility of his wife's indifference to his adventures with the WAAFs. He called for whisky. Then he said: 'I say, do you believe that fellow's really going round getting up operas? What does he mean about "the way to the Italian heart"? We've just beaten the bastards, haven't we? What have they got to sing about? I don't believe even the Yanks would be so wet as to lay on entertainments for them. If you ask me, it's cover for something else. Once you leave regimental soldiering, you run up against a lot of rum things you didn't know went on. This town's full of them.'

In London at that moment there was being enacted a scene of traditional domesticity. Virginia was making her *layette*. It was a survival of the school-room, incongruous to much in her adult life, that she sewed neatly and happily. It was thus she had spent many evenings in Kenya working a quilt that was never finished. Uncle Peregrine was reading aloud from Trollope's *Can You Forgive Her?* Presently she said: I've finished my lessons, you know.'

'Lessons?'

'Instructions. Canon Weld says he's ready to receive me any time now.'

'I suppose he knows best,' said Uncle Peregrine dubiously.

'It's all so easy,' said Virginia. 'I can't think what those novelists make such a fuss over – about people "losing their faith". The whole thing is clear as daylight to me. I wonder why no one ever told me before. I mean it's all quite obvious really, isn't it, when you come to think of it?'

'It is to me,' said Uncle Peregrine.

'I want you to be my godfather, please. And that doesn't mean a present – at least not anything expensive.' She plied her needle assiduously showing her pretty hands. 'It's really you who have brought me into the Church, you know.'

'I? Good heavens, how?'

'Just by being such a dear,' said Virginia. 'You do like having me here, don't you?'

'Yes, of course, my dear.'

'I've been thinking,' said Virginia. 'I should like to have the baby here.'

'Here? In this flat?'

'Yes. Do you mind?'

'Won't it be rather inconvenient for you?'

'Not for me. I think it will be cosy.'

'*Cosy*,' said Peregrine aghast. '*Cosy*.'

'You can be godfather to the baby too. Only, if you don't mind, if he's a boy I shouldn't think I'll call him Peregrine. I think Guy would like him to be called Gervase, don't you?'

And Ludovic was writing. Since the middle of December he had without remission written 3,000 words a day; more than a hundred thousand words. His manner of composition was quite changed. Fowler and Roget lay unopened. He felt no need now to find the right word. All words were right. They poured from his pen in disordered confusion. He never paused; he never revised. He barely applied his mind to his task. He was possessed; the mere amanuensis of some power, not himself, making for – what? He did not question. He just wrote. His book grew as little Trimmer grew in Virginia's womb without her conscious collaboration.

It was the aim of every Barinese to obtain employment under the occupying forces. Whole families in all their ramifications had insinuated themselves into the service of the officers' hotel. Six senile patriarchs supported themselves on long mops from dawn to dusk gently polishing the linoleum floor of the vestibule. They all stopped work as Guy passed between them next morning and then advanced crablike to expunge his foot-prints.

He walked to the office he had visited the evening before. The morning sunlight transformed the building. There had once been a fountain in the *cortile*, Guy now observed; perhaps it would one day play again. A stone triton stood there gaping, last poor descendant of grand forebears, amid spiky vegetation. The sentry was engaged in conversation with a dispatch-rider and let Guy pass without question. He met Gilpin on the stairs.

'How did you get in?'

'I'm attached here, don't you remember?'

'But you haven't got a pass. How long will it take those men to learn that an officer's uniform means nothing? They had no business to let you through without a pass.'

'Where do I get one?'

'From me.'

'Well, perhaps it might save trouble if you gave me one.'

'Have you got three photographs of yourself?'

'Of course not.'

'Then I can't make out a pass.'

At this moment a voice from above said: 'What's going on, Gilpin?'

'An officer without a pass, sir.'

'Who?'

'Captain Crouchback.'

'Well, give him a pass and send him up.'

This was Brigadier Cape. The voice became a man on the landing; a lame, lean man, wearing the badges of a regiment of lancers. When Guy presented himself, he said: 'Keen fellow, Gilpin. Takes his duties very seriously. Sorry I wasn't here yesterday. I can't see you at the moment. I've got some Jugs coming in with a complaint. The best thing you can do is to get Cattermole to put you in the picture. Then we'll find where you fit in.'

Major Cattermole had the next room to Brigadier Cape. He was of the same age as Guy, tall, stooping, emaciated, totally unsoldierly, a Zurbarán ascetic with a joyous smile.

'Balliol 1921–1924,' he said.

'Yes. Were we up together?'

'You wouldn't remember me. I led a very quiet life. I remember seeing you about with the bloods.'

'I was never a blood.'

'You seemed one to me. You were a friend of Sligger's. He was always very nice to me but I was never in his set. I wasn't in any set. I wasted my time as an undergraduate, working. I had to.'

'I think you used to speak at the Union?'

'I tried. I wasn't any good. So you're going across to Jugoslavia?'

'Am I?'

'That seems to be why you're here. How I envy you. I came out in the new year and the doctors won't let me go back. I was there for the Sixth Offensive but I crocked up. They had to carry me for the last two weeks. I was only an encumbrance. The partisans never leave their wounded. They know what the enemy would do to them. We had men of seventy and girls of fifteen in our column. A few hours' halt and then "pokrit" – "forward". I don't know what my academic colleagues would have made of it. We ate all our donkeys in the first week. At the end we were eating roots and bark. But we got clean through and an aeroplane picked me up with the rest of the wounded. Didn't you have a pretty hard crossing from Crete?'

'Yes, how did you know?'

'It was all in the dossier they sent us. Well, I don't have to tell you what real exhaustion means. Did you get hallucinations?'

'Yes.'

'So did I. You've made a better recovery than I. They say I'll never be fit to go into the field again. I'm stuck in an office, briefing other men. Let's get to work.'

He unrolled a wall-map. 'The position is fluid,' he said, a curious official insincerity masking his easier, early manner. 'This is as up to date as we can make it.'

And for twenty minutes he delivered what was plainly a set exposition. Here were the 'liberated areas'; this was the route of one brigade, that of another; here was the headquarters of a division, there of a corps. A huge, intricately involved campaign of encirclements and counter-attacks took shape in Cattermole's precise, donnish phrases.

'I had no idea it was on this scale,' said Guy.

'No one has. No one will, as long as there's a royalist government in exile squatting in London. The partisans are pinning down three times as many troops as the whole Italian campaign. Besides von Weich's Army Group there are five or six divisions of Cetnics and Ustachi – perhaps those names are unfamiliar. They are the Serb and Croat Quislings. Bulgarians, too. There must be half a million enemy over there.'

'There seem to be plenty of partisans,' Guy observed, pointing to the multitude of high formations scored on the map.

'Yes,' said Major Cattermole, 'yes. Of course not all the regiments are quite up to strength. It's no good putting more men in the field than we can equip. And we're short of almost everything – artillery, transport, aeroplanes, tanks. We had to arm ourselves with what we could capture. Until quite lately those men in Cairo were sending arms to Mihajlovic to be used against our own people. We're doing a little better now. There's a trickle of supplies, but it isn't easy to arrange drops for forces on the move. And the Russians have at last sent in a mission – headed by a general. You can have no idea, until you've seen them, what that will mean to the partisans. It's something I have to explain to all our liaison officers. The Jugoslavs accept us as allies but they look on the Russians as leaders. It is part of their history – well, I expect you know as well as I do about Pan-Slavism. You'll find it still as strong as it was in the time of the Czars. Once, during the Sixth Offensive, we were being dive-bombed at a river crossing and one of my stretcher bearers – a boy from Zagreb University – said quite simply: "Every bomb that falls here is one less on Russia." We are foreigners to them. They accept what we send them. They have no reason to feel particularly grateful. It is they who are fighting and dying. Some of our less sophisticated men get confused and think it is a matter of politics. I'm sure you won't make that mistake but I deliver this little lecture to everyone. There are no politics in war-time; just love of country and love of race – and the partisans know we belong to a different country and a different race. That's how misunderstandings sometimes arise.'

At this moment Brigadier Cape put his head in at the door and said: 'Joe, can you come in for a minute?'

'Study the map,' said Major Cattermole to Guy. 'Learn it. I'll be back soon.'

Guy was well instructed in military map-reading. He did as he was told, wondering where in that complicated terrain his own future lay.

Next door Cape sat at his table staring resentfully at a gold hunter watch, handsomely engraved on the back with a crown and inscription. 'You know all about this, of course, Joe?'

'Yes, I told Major Cernic to report it to you.'

'Can you blame him?'

'But what am I supposed to do?'

'Report it to London.'

'It's the hell of a thing to have happened just when the Jugs were beginning to trust us.'

'They'll never trust us as long as they know there's an émigré government in London. Properly handled this might be the opportunity for repudiating them.'

'There's no doubt it's genuine, I suppose?'

'None whatever.'

'Not a political move?'

'Not on our part. It's exactly what it purports to be – a presentation watch inscribed in London to Mihajlovic as Minister of War. A Serb brought it out, who was ostensibly coming to the Partisans. Fortunately he got drunk at Algiers and showed it to a young American I know, who was passing through. He tipped me off, so the partisans arrested the agent as soon as he arrived.'

'He was going to have gone across? You know the odd thing about it is that it shows there must be a means of communication between Tito's chaps and Mihajlovic's.'

'Only through the enemy.'

'Damn,' said Cape, 'damn. I'd just as soon the fellow got his watch as have all this rumpus. What happened to the Serb?'

'He was dealt with.'

'This isn't soldiering as I was taught it,' said Cape.

Major Cattermole returned to Guy. 'Sorry to leave you. Just a routine matter. I'd pretty well finished my tutorial and the Brigadier is free to see you. He'll tell you where you are going and when.

'You are in for a unique experience, whatever it is. The partisans are a revelation – literally.'

When Major Cattermole spoke of the enemy he did so with the impersonal, professional hostility with which a surgeon might regard a malignant, operable growth; when he spoke of his comrades in arms it was something keener than loyalty, equally impersonal, a counterfeit almost of mystical love as portrayed by the sensual artists of the high baroque.

'Officers and men,' he proclaimed exultantly, 'share the same rations and quarters. And the women too. You may be surprised to find girls serving in the ranks beside their male comrades. Lying together, sometimes, for warmth, under the same blanket, but in absolute celibacy. Patriotic passion has entirely extruded sex. The girl partisans are something you will never have seen before. In fact, one of the medical officers told me that many of them had ceased to menstruate. Some were barely more than schoolchildren when they ran away to the mountains leaving their bourgeois families to collaborate with the enemy. I have seen spectacles of courage of which I should have been sceptical in the best authenticated classical text. Even when we have anaesthetics the girls often refuse to take them. I have seen them endure excruciating operations without flinching, sometimes breaking into song as the surgeon probed, in order to prove their manhood. Well, you will see for yourself. It is a transforming experience.'

Seven years previously J. Cattermole of All Souls had published *An Examination of Certain Redundances in Empirical Concepts*; a work popularly known as 'Cattermole's Redundances' and often described as 'seminal'. Since then he had been transformed.

Brigadier Cape's head appeared again at the door.

'Come on, Crouchback.' And Guy followed him next door. 'Glad to see you. You're the third Halberdier to join our outfit. I'd gladly take all I can get. I think you know Frank de Souza. He's on the other side at the moment. I know you've spent the evening with our G2. You haven't got a parachute badge up.'

'I didn't qualify, sir.'

'Oh, I thought you did. Something wrong somewhere. Anyway, we've got two or three places now where we can land. Do you speak good Serbo-Croat?'

'Not a word. When I had my interview I was only asked about my Italian.'

'Well, oddly enough that isn't a disadvantage. We've had one or two chaps who spoke the language. Some seem to have joined up with the partisans. The others have been sent back with complaints of "incorrect" behaviour. The Jugs prefer to provide their interpreters – then they know just what our chaps are saying and who to. Suspicious lot of bastards. I suppose they have good reason to be. You've heard Joe Cattermole's piece about them. He's an enthusiast. Now I'll give you the other side of the picture. But remember Joe Cattermole's a first-class chap. He doesn't tell anyone, but he did absolutely splendidly over there. The Jugs love him and they don't love many of us. And Joe loves the Jugs, which is something more unusual still. But you have to take what he says with a grain of salt. I expect he told you about the partisans pinning down half a million men. The situation, as I see it, is rather different. The Germans are interested in only two things. Their communications with Greece and the defence of their flank against an Allied landing in the Adriatic. Our information is that they will be pulling out of Greece this summer. Their road home has to be kept clear. There's nothing else they want in Jugoslavia. When the Italians packed up, the Balkans were a total loss to them. No question now of cutting round to the Suez Canal. But they are afraid of a large-scale Anglo-

American advance up to Vienna. The Americans very naturally prefer to land on the Côte d'Azur. But as long as there's any danger of an Adriatic landing the Germans have to keep a lot of men in Jugoslavia, and the Jugs, when they take time off from fighting one another, are quite a nuisance to them. The job of this mission is to keep the nuisance going with the few bits and pieces we are allowed.

'When the partisans talk about their "Offensives", you know, they are German offensives, not Jug. Whenever the Jugs get too much of a nuisance, the Germans make a sweep and clear them off, but they have never yet got the whole lot in the bag. And it looks more and more likely that they never will.

'Now remember, we are soldiers not politicians. Our job is simply to do all we can to hurt the enemy. Neither you nor I are going to make his home in Jugoslavia after the war. How they choose to govern themselves is entirely their business. Keep clear of politics. That's the first rule of this mission.

'I shall be seeing you again before you move. I can't tell you at the moment where you'll be going or when. You won't find Bari a bad place to hang about in. Report to GSO 2 every day. Enjoy yourself.'

Few foreigners visited Bari from the time of the Crusades until the fall of Mussolini. Few tourists, even the most assiduous, explored the Apulian coast. Bari contains much that should have attracted them; the old town full of Norman buildings, the bones of St Nicholas enshrined in silver; the new town spacious and commodious. But for centuries it lay neglected by all save native businessmen. Guy had never before set foot there.

Lately the place had achieved the unique, unsought distinction of being the only place in the Second World War to suffer from gas. In the few days of its occupation a ship full of 'mustard' blew up in the harbour, scattering its venom about the docks. Many of the inhabitants complained of sore throats, sore eyes, and blisters. They were told it was an unfamiliar, mild, epidemic disease of short duration. The people of Apulia are inured to such afflictions.

Now, early in 1944, the city had recovered the cosmopolitan, martial stir it enjoyed in the Middle Ages. Allied soldiers on short leave, some wearing, ironically enough, the woven badge of the crusader's sword, teemed in its streets; wounded filled its hospitals; the staffs of numberless services took over the new, battered office-buildings which had risen as monuments to the Corporative State. Small naval craft adorned the shabby harbour. Bari could not rival the importance of Naples, that prodigious, improvised factory of war. Its agile and ingenious criminal class consisted chiefly of small boys. Few cars flew the pennons of high authority. Few officers over the rank of brigadier inhabited the outlying villas. Foggia drew the *magistras* of the Air Force. Nothing very august flourished in Bari, but there were dingy buildings occupied by Balkan and Zionist emissaries; by a melancholic English officer who performed a part not then known as 'disc-jockey', providing the troops with the tunes it was thought they wished to hear; by a euphoric Scotch officer surrounded by books with which he hoped to inculcate a respect for English culture among those who could read that language; by the editors of little papers, more directly propagandist and printed in a variety of languages; by the agents of competing intelligence systems; by a group of Russians whose task was to relabel tins of American rations in bold Cyrillic characters, proclaiming them the produce of the USSR, before they were dropped from American aeroplanes over beleaguered gangs of Communists; by Italians, even, who were being coached in the arts of local democratic government. The Allies had lately much impeded their advance by the destruction of Monte Cassino, but the price of this sacrilege was being paid by the infantry of the front line. It did not trouble the peace-loving and unambitious officers who were glad to settle in Bari.

They constituted a little world of officers – some young and seedy, some old and spruce – sequestered from the responsibilities and vexations of command. Such men of other rank as were sometimes seen in the arcaded streets were drivers, orderlies, policemen, clerks, servants, and sentries.

In this limbo Guy fretted for more than a week while February blossomed into March. He had left Italy four and a half years ago. He had then taken leave of the crusader whom the people called 'il santo inglese'. He had laid his hand on the sword that had never struck the infidel. He wore the medal which had hung round the neck of his brother, Gervase, when the sniper had picked him off on his way up to the line in Flanders. In his heart he felt stirring the despair in which his brother, Ivo, had starved himself to death. Half an hour's scramble on the beach near Dakar; an ignominious rout in Crete. That had been his war.

Every day he reported to headquarters. 'No news yet,' they said. 'Communications have not been satisfactory for the last few days. The Air Force aren't playing until they know what's going on over there.'

'Enjoy yourself,' Brigadier Cape had said. That would not have been the order of Ritchie-Hook. There was no biffing in Bari.

Guy wandered as a tourist about the streets of the old town. He sat in the club and the hotel. He met old acquaintances and made new ones. Leisure, bonhomie, and futility had him in thrall.

After a brief absence Lieutenant Padfield reappeared in the company of a large and celebrated English composer whom UNRRA had mysteriously imported. On the Sunday they drove Guy out on the road south to visit the beehive dwellings where the descendants of Athenian colonists still lived their independent lives. Near by was a small, ancient town where an Italian family had set up an illicit restaurant. They did not deal in paper currency but accepted petrol, cigarettes, and medical supplies in exchange for dishes of fresh fish cooked with olive oil and white truffles and garlic.

The Lieutenant left his car in the piazza before the locked church. There were other service vehicles there, and when they reached the house on the water-front they found it full of English and Americans; among them Brigadier Cape and his homely hospital nurse.

'I haven't seen you,' said the Brigadier, 'and you haven't seen me,' but the nurse knew all about the musician, and after luncheon insisted on being introduced. They all walked together along the quay, Guy and the Brigadier a pace behind the other three. This place had been left untouched by the advancing and retreating armies. The inhabitants were taking their siestas. To seaward the calm Adriatic lapped against the old stones; in the harbour the boats lay motionless. Guy remarked, tritely enough, that the war seemed far away.

The Brigadier was in ruminative mood. He had eaten largely; other pleasures lay ahead. 'War,' he said. 'When I was at Sandhurst no one talked about war. We learned about it, of course – a school subject like Latin or geography; something to write exam papers about. No bearing on life. I went into the army because I liked horses, and I've spent four years in and out of a stinking, noisy tank. Now I've got a couple of gongs and a game leg and all I want is quiet. Not *peace*, mind. There's nothing wrong with war except the fighting. I don't mind betting that after five years of peace we shall all look back on Bari as the best days of our life.'

Suddenly the musician turned and said: 'Crouchback has the death wish.'

'Have you?' asked the Brigadier with a show of disapproval.

'Have I?' said Guy.

'I recognized it the moment we met,' said the musician. 'I should not mention it now except that Padfield was so liberal with the wine.'

'Death wish?' said the Brigadier. 'I don't like the sound of that. Time we were off, Betty.'

He took the nurse's arm and limped back towards the piazza. Guy saluted as Halberdiers did. The Lieutenant tipped his cap in a gesture that was part benediction, part a wave of farewell. The musician bowed to the nurse.

Then he turned towards the open sea and performed a little parody of himself conducting an orchestra, saying: 'The death wish. The death wish. On a day like this.'

Two days later, when Guy reported, the Brigadier asked: 'How's the death wish today? There's an aeroplane to take you into Croatia tonight. Joe will give you the details.'

Guy had made no preparations for this journey except to prepare himself. He walked to the old town where he found a dilapidated romanesque church where a priest was hearing confessions. Guy waited, took his turn at at length said: 'Father, I wish to die.'

'Yes. How many times?'

'Almost all the time.'

The obscure figure behind the grill leant nearer. 'What was it you wished to do?'

'To die.'

'Yes. You have attempted suicide?'

'No.'

'Of what, then, are you accusing yourself? To wish to die is quite usual today. It may even be a very good disposition. You do not accuse yourself of despair?'

'No, father; presumption. I am not fit to die.'

'There is no sin there. This is a mere scruple. Make an act of contrition for all the unrepented sins of your past life.'

After the Absolution he said: 'Are you a foreigner?'

'Yes.'

'Can you spare a few cigarettes?'

In Westminster Cathedral at almost the same time Virginia made her first confession. She told everything; fully, accurately, without extenuation or elaboration. The recital of half a lifetime's mischief took less than five minutes. 'Thank God for your good and humble confession,' the priest said. She was shriven. The same words were said to her as were said to Guy. The same grace was offered. Little Trimmer stirred as she knelt at the side-altar and pronounced the required penance; then she returned to her needlework.

That evening she said to Uncle Peregrine, as she had said before: 'Why do people make such a *fuss*? It's all so easy. But it is rather satisfactory to feel that I shall never again have anything serious to confess as long as I live.'

Uncle Peregrine made no comment. He did not credit himself with any peculiar gift of discernment of spirits. Most things which most people did or said puzzled him, if he gave them any thought. He preferred to leave such problems in higher hands.

2

Summer came swiftly and sweetly over the wooded hills and rich valleys of Northern Croatia. Bridges were down and the rails up on the little single-track railway-line that had once led from Begoy to Zagreb. The trunk road to the Balkans ran east. There the German lorries streamed night and day without interruption and the German garrisons squatted waiting the order to retire. Here, in an island of 'liberated territory' twenty miles by ten, the peasants worked their fields as they had always done, subject only to the requisitions of the partisans; the priests said Mass in their churches subject only to the partisan security police who lounged at the back and listened for political implications in their sermons. In one Mohammedan village the mosque had been burned by Ustachi in the first days of Croatian independence. In Begoy itself the same gang, Hungarian trained, had blown up the Orthodox church and desecrated the cemetery. But there had been little fighting. As the Italians withdrew the Ustachi followed and the partisans crept in from the hills and imposed their rule. More of their fellows joined them, slipping in small, ragged bodies through the German lines; there were shortages of food but no famine. There was a tithe levied but no looting. Partisans obeyed orders and it was vital to them to keep the goodwill of the peasants.

The bourgeois had all left Begoy with the retreating garrison. The shops in the little high street were empty or used as billets. The avenues of lime had been roughly felled for firewood. But there were still visible the hallmarks of the Habsburg Empire. There were thermal springs, and at the end of the preceding century the town had been laid out modestly as a spa. Hot water still ran in the bath house. Two old gardeners still kept some order in the ornamental grounds. The graded paths, each with a 'view-point', the ruins of a seat and of a kiosk, where once invalids had taken their prescribed exercise, still ran through boskage between the partisan bivouacs. The circle of villas in the outskirts of the town abandoned precipitately by their owners had been allotted by the partisans to various official purposes. In the largest of these the Russian mission lurked invisibly.

Two miles from the town lay the tract of flat grazing land which was used as an airfield. Four English airmen had charge of it. They occupied one side of the quadrangle of timbered buildings which comprised a neighbouring farmhouse. The military mission lived opposite, separated by a dung heap. Both bodies were tirelessly cared for by three Montenegrin war-widows; they were guarded by partisan sentries and attended by an 'interpreter' named Bakic, who had been a political exile in New York in the thirties and picked up some English there. Both missions had their wireless-sets with which to communicate with their several headquarters. A sergeant signaller and an orderly comprised Guy's staff.

The officer whom Guy succeeded had fallen into a melancholy and was recalled for medical attention; he had left by the aeroplane that brought Guy. They had had ten minutes' conversation in the light of the flare-path while a party of girls unloaded the stores.

'The comrades are a bloody-minded lot of bastards,' he had said. 'Don't keep any copies of signals in clear. Bakic reads everything. And don't say anything in front of him you don't want repeated.'

The Squadron Leader remarked that this officer had been 'an infernal nuisance lately. Suffering from persecution mania if you ask me. Wrong sort of chap to send to a place like this.'

Joe Cattermole had fully instructed Guy in his duties. They were not exacting. At this season aeroplanes were coming in to land at Begoy almost every week, bringing, besides supplies, cargoes of unidentified Slavs in uniform, who disappeared on landing and joined their comrades of the higher command. They took back seriously wounded partisans and allied airmen who had 'baled out' of their damaged bombers returning from Germany to Italy. There were also 'drops' of stores, some in parachutes – petrol and weapons; the less vulnerable loads, clothing and rations – falling free as bombs at various points in the territory. All this traffic was the business of the Squadron Leader. He fixed the times of the sorties. He guided the machines in. Guy's duty was to transmit reports on the military situation. For these he was entirely dependent on the partisan 'general staff'. This body, together with an old lawyer from Split who bore the title of 'Minister of the Interior', consisted of the General and the Commissar, veterans of the International Brigade in Spain, and a second-in-command who was a regular officer of the Royal Jugoslavian Army. They had their own fluent interpreter, a lecturer in English, he claimed, from Zagreb University. The bulletins dealt only in success; a village had been raided; a fascist supply wagon had been waylaid; mostly they enumerated the partisan bands who had found their way into the Begoy area and put themselves under the command of the 'Army of Croatia'. These were always lacking in essential equipment and Guy was asked to supply them. Thus the General and the Commissar steered a delicate course between the alternating and conflicting claims that the partisans were destitute and that they maintained in the field a large, efficient modern army. The reinforcements excused the demands.

The general staff were nocturnal by habit. All the morning they slept. In the afternoon they ate and smoked and idled; at sunset they came to life. There was a field telephone between them and the airfield. Once or twice a week it would ring and Bakic would announce: 'General wants us right away.' Then he and Guy would stumble along the rutted lane to a conference which took place sometimes by oil-lamp, sometimes under an electric bulb which flickered and expired as often as in the headquarters at Bari. An exorbitant list of requirements would be presented; sometimes medical stores, the furniture of a whole hospital with detailed lists of drugs and instruments which would take days to encipher and transmit; field artillery; light tanks; typewriters; they particularly wanted an aeroplane of their own. Guy would not attempt to dispute them. He would point out that the allied armies in Italy were themselves engaged in a war. He would promise to transmit their wishes. He would then edit them and ask for what seemed reasonable. The response would be unpredictable. Sometimes there would be a drop of ancient rifles captured in Abyssinia, sometimes boots for half a company, sometimes there was a jack-pot and the night sky rained machine guns, ammunition, petrol, dehydrated food, socks, and books of popular education. The partisans made a precise account of everything received, which Guy transmitted. Nothing was ever pilfered. The discrepancy between what was asked and what was given deprived Guy of any sense he might have felt of vicarious benefaction. The cordiality or strict formality of his reception depended on the size of the last drop. Once, after a jack-pot, he was offered a glass of Slivovic.

In mid-April a new element appeared.

Guy had finished breakfast and was attempting to memorize a Serbo-Croat vocabulary with which he had been provided, when Bakic announced:

'Dere's de Jews outside.'

'What Jews?'

'Dey been dere two hour, maybe more. I said to wait.'

'What do they want?'

'Dey're Jews. I reckon dey always want sometin'. Dey want see de British captain. I said to wait.'

'Well, ask them to come in.'

'Dey can't come in. Why, dere's more'n a hundred of dem.'

Guy went out and found the farmyard and the lane beyond thronged. There were some children in the crowd, but most seemed old, too old to be parents, for they were unnaturally aged by their condition. Everyone in Begoy, except the peasant women, was in rags, but the partisans kept regimental barbers and there was a kind of dignity about their tattered uniforms. The Jews were grotesque in their remnants of bourgeois civility. They showed little trace of racial kinship. There were Semites among them, but the majority were fair, snub-nosed, high cheek-boned, the descendants of Slav tribes judaized long after the Dispersal. Few of them, probably, now worshipped the God of Israel in the manner of their ancestors.

A low chatter broke out as Guy appeared. Then three leaders came forward, a youngish woman of better appearance than the rest and two crumpled old men. The woman asked him if he spoke Italian, and when he nodded introduced her companions – a grocer from Mostar, a lawyer from Zagreb – and herself, a woman of Fiume married to a Hungarian engineer.

Here Bakic roughly interrupted in Serbo-Croat and the three fell humbly and hopelessly silent. He said to Guy: 'I tell dese people dey better talk Slav. I will speak for dem.'

The woman said: 'I only speak German and Italian.'

Guy said: 'We will speak Italian. I can't ask you all in. You three had better come and leave the others outside.'

Bakic scowled. A chatter broke out in the crowd. Then the three with timid little bows crossed the threshold, carefully wiping their dilapidated boots before treading the rough board floor of the interior.

'I shan't want you, Bakic.'

The spy went out to bully the crowd, hustling them out of the farmyard into the lane.

There were only two chairs in Guy's living-room. He took one and invited the woman to use the other. The men huddled behind her and then began to prompt her. They spoke to one another in a mixture of German and Serbo-Croat; the lawyer knew a little Italian; enough to make him listen anxiously to all the woman said, and to interrupt. The grocer gazed steadily at the floor and seemed to take no interest in the proceedings. He was there because he commanded respect and trust among the waiting crowd. He had been in a big way of business with branch stores throughout all the villages of Bosnia.

With a sudden vehemence the woman, Mme Kanyi, shook off her advisers and began her story. The people outside, she explained, were the survivors of an Italian concentration camp on the island of Rab. Most were Jugo-Slav nationals, but some, like herself, were refugees from Central Europe. She and her husband were on their way to Australia in 1939; their papers were in order; he had a job waiting for him in Brisbane. Then they had been caught by the war.

When the King fled, the Ustachi began massacring Jews. The Italians rounded them up and took them to the Adriatic. When Italy surrendered, the partisans for a few weeks held the coast. They brought the Jews to the mainland, conscribed all who seemed capable of useful work, and imprisoned the rest. Her husband had been attached to the army headquarters as electrician. Then the Germans moved in; the partisans fled, taking the Jews with them. And here they were, a hundred and eight of them, half starving in Begoy.

Guy said: 'Well, I congratulate you.'

Mme Kanyi looked up quickly to see if he were mocking her, found that he was not, and continued to regard him now with sad, blank wonder.

'After all,' he continued, 'you're among friends.'

'Yes,' she said too doleful for irony, 'we heard that the British and Americans were friends of the partisans. Is it true, then?'

'Of course it's true. Why do you suppose I am here?'

'It is not true that the British and Americans are coming to take over the country?'

'First I've heard of it.'

'But it is well known that Churchill is a friend of the Jews.'

'I'm sorry, signora, but I simply do not see what the Jews have got to do with it.'

'But we are Jews. One hundred and eight of us.'

'Well, what do you expect me to do about that?'

'We want to go to Italy. We have relations there, some of us. There is an organization at Bari. My husband and I had our papers to go to Brisbane. Only get us to Italy and we shall be no more trouble. We cannot live as we are here. When winter comes we shall all die. We hear aeroplanes almost every night. Three aeroplanes could take us all. We have no luggage left.'

'Signora, those aeroplanes are carrying essential war equipment, they are taking out wounded and officials. I'm very sorry you are having a hard time, but so are plenty of other people in this country. It won't last long now. We've got the Germans on the run. I hope by Christmas to be in Zagreb.'

'We must say nothing against the partisans?'

'Not to me. Look here, let me give you a cup of cocoa. Then I have work to do.'

He went to the window and called to the orderly for cocoa and biscuits. While it was coming the lawyer said in English: 'We were better in Rab.' Then suddenly all three broke into a chatter of polyglot complaint, about their house, about their property which had been stolen, about their rations. If Churchill knew he would have them sent to Italy. Guy said: 'If it was not for the partisans you would now be in the hands of the Nazis,' but that word had no terror for them now. They shrugged hopelessly.

One of the widows brought in a tray of cups and a tin of biscuits. 'Help yourselves,' said Guy.

'How many, please, may we take?'

'Oh, two or three.'

With tense self-control each took three biscuits, watching the others to see they did not disgrace the meeting by greed. The grocer whispered to Mme Kanyi and she explained: 'He says will you excuse him if he keeps one for a friend?' The man had tears in his eyes as he snuffed his cocoa; once he had handled sacks of the stuff.

They rose to go. Mme Kanyi made a last attempt to attract his sympathy. 'Will you please come and see the place where they have put us?'

'I am sorry, signora, it simply is not my business. I am a military liaison officer, nothing more.'

They thanked him humbly and profusely for the cocoa and left the house. Guy saw them in the farmyard disputing. The men seemed to think Mme Kanyi had mishandled the affair. Then Bakic hustled them out. Guy saw the crowd close around them and then move off down the lane in a babel of explanation and reproach.

Full summer came in May. Guy took to walking every afternoon in the public gardens. These were quite unscathed. The partisans showed some solicitude for them, perhaps at the instigation of the 'Minister of the Interior', and had cut a new bed in the principal lawn in the shape of a five-pointed star. There were winding paths, specimen trees, statuary, a band-stand, a pond with carp and exotic ducks, the ornamental cages of what had once been a miniature zoo. The gardeners kept rabbits in one, fowls in another, a red squirrel in a third. Guy never saw a partisan there. The ragged, swaggering girls in battle-dress, with their bandages and medals and girdles of hand-grenades, who were everywhere in the streets, arm-in-arm, singing patriotic songs, kept clear of these gardens where not long ago rheumatics crept with their parasols and light, romantic novels. Perhaps they were out of bounds.

The only person Guy ever saw was Mme Kanyi whom he saluted and passed by.

'Keep clear of civilians' was one of the precepts of the mission.

Later that month Guy noticed an apprehensive air at headquarters. General and Commissar were almost ingratiating. He was told there was no military development. No demands were made. On a bonfire in the garden quantities of papers were being consumed. He was for the second time offered a glass of Slivovic. Guy had not to seek for an explanation of this new amiability. He had already received news from Bari that Tito's forces at Dvrar had been dispersed by German parachutists and that he and his staff, the British, American, and Russian missions had been rescued by aeroplane and taken to Italy. He wondered whether the General knew that he knew. A fortnight passed. Tito, he was informed, had set up his headquarters under allied protection on Vis. The General and the Commissar resumed their former manner. It was during this period of renewed coldness that he received a signal: *UNRRA research team requires particulars displaced persons. Report any your district.* This phrase, which was to be among the key-words of the decade, was as yet unfamiliar.

'What are "displaced persons"?' he asked the Squadron Leader.

'Aren't we all?'

He replied: *Displaced persons not understood*, and received: *Friendly nationals moved by enemy.* He replied: *One hundred and eight Jews.*

Next day: *Expedite details Jews names nationalities conditions.*

Bakic grudgingly admitted that he knew where they were quartered, in a school near the ruined Orthodox church. Bakic led him there. They found the house in half darkness, for the glass had all gone from the windows and been replaced with bits of wood and tin collected from other ruins. There was no furniture. The inmates for the most part lay huddled in little nests of straw and rags. As Guy and Bakic entered a dozen or more barely visible figures roused themselves, got to their feet and retreated towards the walls and darker corners, some raising their fists in salute, others hugging bundles of small possessions. Bakic called one of them forward and questioned him roughly in Serbo-Croat.

'He says de others gone for firewood. Dese one's sick. What you want me tell em?'

'Say that the Americans in Italy want to help them. I have come to make a report on what they need.'

The announcement brought them volubly to life. They crowded round, were joined by others from other parts of the house until Guy stood surrounded by thirty or more all asking for things, asking frantically for whatever came first to mind – a needle, a lamp, butter, soap, a pillow; for remote dreams – a passage to Tel Aviv, an aeroplane to New York, news of a sister last seen in Bucharest, a bed in a hospital.

'You see dey all want somepin different, and dis isn't a half of dem.'

For twenty minutes or so Guy remained, overpowered, half-suffocated. Then he said: 'Well, I think we've seen enough. I shan't get much further in this crowd. Before we can do anything we've got to get them organized. They must make out their own list. I wish we could find that Hungarian woman who talked Italian. She made some sense.'

Bakic inquired and reported: 'She don't live here. Her husband works on the electric light so dey got a house to demselves in de park.'

'Well, let's get out of here and try to find her.'

They left the house and emerged into the fresh air and sunshine and singing companies of young warriors. Guy breathed gratefully. Very high above them a huge force of minute shining bombers hummed across the sky in perfect formation on its daily route from Foggia to somewhere east of Vienna.

'There they go again,' he said. 'I wouldn't care to be underneath when they unload.'

It was one of his duties to impress the partisans with the might of their allies, with the great destruction and slaughter on distant fields which would one day, somehow, bring happiness here where they seemed forgotten. He delivered a little statistical lecture to Bakic about blockbusters and pattern-bombing.

They found the Kanyis' house. It was a former potting-shed, hidden by shrubs from the public park. A single room, an earth floor, a bed, a table, a dangling electric globe; compared with the schoolhouse, a place of delicious comfort and privacy. Guy did not see the interior that afternoon for Mme Kanyi was hanging washing on a line outside, and she led him away from the hut, saying that her husband was asleep. 'He was up all night and did not come home until nearly midday. There was a breakdown at the plant.'

'Yes,' said Guy, 'I had to go to bed in the dark at nine.'

'It is always breaking. It is quite worn out. He cannot get the proper fuel. And all the cables are rotten. The General does not understand and blames him for everything. Often he is out all night.'

Guy dismissed Bakic and talked about UNRRA. Mme Kanyi did not react in the same way as the wretches in the schoolhouse; she was younger and better fed and therefore more hopeless. 'What can they do for us?' she asked. 'How can they? Why should they? We are of no importance. You told us so yourself. You must see the Commissar,' she said. 'Otherwise he will think there is some plot going on. We can do nothing, accept nothing, without the Commissar's permission. You will only make more trouble for us.'

'But at least you can produce the list they want in Bari.'

'Yes, if the Commissar says so. Already my husband has been questioned about why I have talked to you. He was very much upset. The General was beginning to trust him. Now they think he is connected with the British, and last night the lights failed when there was an important conference. It is better that you do nothing except through the Commissar. I know these people. My husband works with them.'

'You have rather a privileged position with them.'

'Do you believe that for that reason I do not want to help my people?'

Some such thoughts had passed through Guy's mind. Now he paused, looked at Mme Kanyi and was ashamed. 'No,' he said.

'I suppose it would be natural to think so,' said Mme Kanyi gravely. 'It is not always true that suffering makes people unselfish. But sometimes it is.'

That evening Guy was summoned to general headquarters. A full committee, including even the Minister of the Interior, sat grimly to meet him. Their manner was of a court martial rather than a conference of allies. Bakic stood in the background and the young interpreter took over.

Guy would not have been surprised had they left him standing, but the second-in-command rose, brought his chair round the table for Guy, and himself stood beside the interpreter.

Kanyi's electric plant was again in difficulties. A single pressure-lamp lit the flat faces and round, cropped heads. All three military men were younger than Guy but their skin was weathered by exposure. All smoked captured Macedonian cigarettes and the air was heavy. The second-in-command offered Guy a cigarette which he refused.

The Minister of the Interior had a short white beard and hooked eyes that lacked shrewdness. He did not know why he was there. He did not know why he was in Begoy at all. He had enjoyed a sharp little practice in Split, had meddled before the war in anti-Serbian politics, had found himself in an Italian prison, had been let out when the partisans briefly 'liberated' the coast, had been swept up with them in the retreat. They gave him a room and rations and this odd title 'Minister of the Interior'. Why?

The interpreter spoke. 'The General wishes to know why you went to visit the Jews today?'

'I was acting on orders from my headquarters.'

'The General does not understand how the Jews are the concern of the Military Mission.'

Guy attempted an explanation of the aims and organization of UNRRA. He did not know a great deal about them and had no great respect for the members he had met, but he did his best. General and Commissar conferred: Then: 'The Commissar says if those measures will take place after the war, what are they doing now?'

Guy described the need for planning. UNRRA must know what quantities of seed-corn, bridge-building materials, rolling-stock and so on were needed to put ravaged countries on their feet.

'The Commissar does not understand how this concerns the Jews.'

Guy spoke of the millions of displaced persons all over Europe who must be returned to their homes.

'The Commissar says that is an internal matter.'

'So is bridge-building.'

'The Commissar says bridge-building is a good thing.'

'So is helping displaced persons.'

Commissar and General conferred. 'The General says any questions of internal affairs should be addressed to the Minister of the Interior.'

'Tell him that I am very sorry if I have acted incorrectly. I merely wished to save everyone trouble. I was sent a question by my superiors. I did my best to answer it in the simplest way. May I now request the Minister of the Interior to furnish me with a list of the Jews?'

'The General is glad that you understand that you have acted incorrectly.'

'Will the Minister of the Interior be so kind as to make the list for me?'

'The General does not understand why a list is needed.'

And so it began again. They talked for an hour. At length Guy lost patience and said: 'Very well. Am I to report that you refuse all cooperation with UNRRA?'

'We will cooperate in all necessary matters.'

'But with regard to the Jews?'

'It must be decided by the Central Government whether that is a necessary matter.'

At length they parted. On the way home Bakic said: 'Dey mighty sore with you, captain. What for you make trouble with dese Jews?'

'Orders,' said Guy, and before going to bed drafted a signal:

Jews condition now gravely distressed may become desperate. Local authorities uncooperative. Only hope higher level.

Next morning he received in clear:

P/302/B Personal for Crouchback. Message begins Virginia gave bath son today both well Crouchback message end. Kindly note personal messages of great importance only accepted for transmission Gilpin for brigadier.

'Query "bath",' Guy told his signaller.
Three days later he received

Personal for Crouchback. Our P/302/B for bath read birch. This not regarded adequate importance priority personal message. See previous signal Gilpin for brigadier.

'Query "birch".'
At length he received: *For birch read birth repeat birth. Congratulations Cape.*
'Send in clear Personal Message Crouchback Bourne Mansions Carlisle Place London Glad both well Crouchback. Message ends Personal to brigadier thank you for congratulations.'

Virginia's son was born on June 4th, the day on which all allied armies entered Rome.
'An omen,' said Uncle Peregrine.
He was talking to his nephew, Arthur Box-Bender, in Bellamy's where he had taken refuge while his flat was overrun by doctor, nurse, and his niece Angela.
The club was rather empty these days. Most of the younger members had moved to the south coast waiting for the day when they would cross the Channel. There was no air of heightened expectancy among the older members. They were scarcely aware of the impending invasion. Social convention, stronger than any regulations of 'security', forbade its discussion.
Box-Bender could not regard the birth of a nephew as happy. He had been disconcerted by Guy's marriage. He had counted the months of pregnancy. He regarded the whole thing as a middle-aged aberration for which Guy was paying an unnaturally high price to the eventual detriment of his own children's inheritance. 'Omen of what?' he asked rather crossly. 'Do you expect the boy to become Pope?'
'The idea had not occurred to me. Awfully few of us have become priests in the last generation or two. In any case I should hardly live to see his election. Now you suggest it, though, it is a pleasant speculation – an Englishman and a Crouchback in the chair of Peter – just about at the turn of the century, I suppose.
'Virginia has taken to religion in an extraordinary way during the last few weeks. Not exactly piety, you know; gossip. The clergy seem to like her awfully. They keep coming to call as they never did on me. She makes them laugh. They seem to prefer that to good works – though, of course, she hasn't

been in a state for them anyway. But she's a much jollier sort of convert than people like Eloise Plessington.'

'That I can well imagine.'

'Angela has been a great help. Of course you must know all about child-birth. It has all been rather a surprise to me. I had never given it much thought but I had supposed that women just went to bed and that they had a sort of stomach ache and groaned a bit and that then there was a baby. It isn't at all like that.'

'I always moved out when Angela had babies.'

'I was awfully interested. I moved out at the end but the beginning was quite a surprise – almost unnerving.'

'I am sure nothing ever unnerves you, Peregrine.'

'No. Perhaps "unnerving" was not the right word.'

In HOO HQ there was stagnation in the depleted offices. The more bizarre figures remained – the witch-doctor and the man who ate grass – but the planners and the combatants had melted away. In the perspective of 'Overlord', that one huge hazardous offensive operation on which, it seemed, the fate of the world depended, smaller adventures receded to infinitesimal importance.

'Brides in the Bath' Whale ordered not a holocaust, but a relegation to unsounded depths of obscurity in the most secret archives, of mountains of files, each propounding in detail some desperate enterprise, each bearing a somewhat whimsical title, all once hotly debated and amended, all now quite without significance.

Ian Kilbannock, without regret, realized that he had passed the zenith of his powers and must decline. He was already negotiating for employment as a special correspondent in Normandy. That was near home and the centre of interest, but competition was keen. Ian had his future professional career to consider. His brief experience as a racing correspondent seemed irrelevant to the Zeitgeist. The time had come, Ian believed, to establish himself as something more serious. There would be infinite scope, he foresaw, during the whole length of his life, for first-hand war 'revelations'.

The Adriatic was suggested and considered. Burma had been offered and evaded. It was plain from the reports he saw that it was no place for Ian. It might, on the other hand, be just the place for Trimmer.

'All Trimmer reports negative, sir,' Ian reported to General Whale.

'Yes. Where is he now?'

'San Francisco. He's been right across the country. He's flopped every-where. It isn't really his fault. He went too late. The Americans have heroes of their own now. Besides, you know, they haven't a fully developed con-sciousness of class. They can't see Trimmer as the proletarian portent. They see him as a typical British officer.'

'Haven't they seen the fellow's hair? I don't mean the way it's cut. The way it grows. *That's* proletarian enough for them, surely?'

'They don't understand that kind of thing. No, sir, he's been a flop in America and he'd be worse in Canada. As I see it we can only keep him moving west. I don't think he ought to come back to the U K at the moment. There are reasons. You might call them compassionate grounds.'

'There's a bigger problem in our hands – General Ritchie-Hook. He's had a bloody row with Monty and is out of work and keeps bothering the Chief. I don't quite see why we should be regarded as responsible for him. Ritchie-Hook and Trimmer – why should we be held responsible for them?'

'Do you think they could go as a pair and impress the loyal Indians?'

'No.'

'Nor do I. Not Ritchie-Hook, certainly. They'd soon stop being loyal if he had a go at them.'

'There's Australia.'

'For Trimmer that would be worse than America.'

'Oh, for God's sake settle it yourself. I'm sick of the man.'

General Whale, too, knew he had passed the zenith of his powers and from now on could only decline. There had been a delirious episode when he had helped drive numerous Canadians to their death at Dieppe. He had helped plan greater enterprises which had come to nothing. Now he was where he had started in his country's 'finest hour', with negligible powers of mischief. He occupied the same room, he was served by the same immediate staff as in the years of expansion. But his legions were lost to him.

There was stagnation at Ludovic's station, also. The staff-captain remained. The instructors had been recalled. No new clients appeared for the parachute course. But Ludovic was content.

He employed a typist in Scotland. He had chosen her because she seemed the most remote from enemy action of any of those who offered their services in *The Times Literary Supplement*. Throughout the winter he had sent her a weekly parcel of manuscript and received in return two typed copies in separate envelopes. She acknowledged the receipt of each parcel by postcard but there was a four-day interval during which Ludovic suffered deep qualms of anxiety. Much was pilfered from the railways in those days but not, as things happened, Ludovic's novel. Now at the beginning of June he had it all complete, two piles of laced and paper-bound sections. He ordered Fido to basket and settled down to read the last chapter, not to correct misprints, for he wrote clearly and the typist was competent, not to polish or revise, for the work seemed to him perfect (as in a sense it was), but for the sheer enjoyment of his own performance.

Admirers of his *pensées* (and they were many) would not have recognized the authorship of this book. It was a very gorgeous, almost gaudy, tale of romance and high drama set, as his experience with Sir Ralph Brompton well qualified him to set it, in the diplomatic society of the previous decade. The characters and their equipment were seen as Ludovic in his own ambiguous position had seen them, more brilliant than reality. The plot was Shakespearean in its elaborate improbability. The dialogue could never have issued from human lips, the scenes of passion were capable of bringing a blush to readers of either sex and every age. But it was not an old-fashioned book. Had he known it, half a dozen other English writers, averting themselves sickly from privations of war and apprehensions of the social consequences of the peace, were even then severally and secretly, unknown to one another, to Everard Spruce, to Coney, and to Frankie, composing or preparing to compose books which would turn from the drab alleys of the thirties into the odorous gardens of a recent past transformed and illuminated by disordered memory and imagination. Ludovic in the solitude of his post was in the movement.

Nor was it for all its glitter a cheerful book. Melancholy suffused its pages and deepened towards the close.

So far as any character could be said to have an origin in the world of reality, the heroine was the author. Lady Marmaduke Transept (that was the name which Ludovic had recklessly bestowed on her) was Lord Marmaduke's second wife. He was an ambassador. She was extravagantly beautiful, clever, doomed; passionless only towards Lord Marmaduke; ambitious for everything except his professional success. If the epithet could properly be used of anyone so splendidly caparisoned, Lady Marmaduke was a bitch. Ludovic had known from the start that she must die in the last chapter. He had made no plans. Often in the weeks of composition he had wondered, almost idly, what would be the end of her. He waited to see, as he might have sat in a seat at the theatre watching the antics of players over whom he had no control.

As Ludovic read the last pages he realized that the whole book had been the preparation for Lady Marmaduke's death – a protracted, ceremonious killing like that of a bull in the ring. Except that there was no violence. He had feared sometimes that his heroine might be immured in a cave or left to drift in an open boat. These were chimeras. Lady Marmaduke, in the manner of an earlier and happier age, fell into a decline. Her disease was painless and unspecified. Under Ludovic's heavy arm she languished, grew thinner, transparent, the rings slipped from her fingers among the rich covering of her chaise-longue as the light faded on the distant, delectable mountains. He had hesitated in his choice of title, toying with many recondite allusions from his recent reading. Now with decision he wrote in large letters at the head of the first page: THE DEATH WISH.

Fido in his basket discerned his master's emotion, broke orders to share it, leaped to Ludovic's stout thighs, and remained there unrebuked, gazing up with eyes of adoration that were paler and more prominent than Ludovic's own.

'What I long to know,' said Kerstie, 'is what went on between Guy and Virginia after she settled in Carlisle Place. After all there was a good month before her figure began to go.'

'It's not a thing I should care to ask her,' said Ian.

'I don't think I can now. We made it up all right after our tiff – it's no good *keeping things up* ever, is it? – but there's been a coldness.'

'Why are you so keen to know?'

'Aren't you?'

'There's been a coldness between me and Virginia for years.'

'Who was there this evening?'

'Quite a salon. Perdita had brought Everard Spruce. There was someone I didn't know called Lady Plessington and a priest. It was all quite gay except for the midwife who kept trying to show us the baby. Virginia can't bear the sight of it. In a novel or a film the baby ought to make Virginia a changed character. It hasn't. Have you noticed that she always calls it "it", never "he". She calls the midwife "Jenny". It was always "Sister Jenkins" in the days before the birth. They get on all right. Old Peregrine speaks of the child as "Gervase". They've had it christened already, as Catholics do for some reason. When he asks how Gervase is, Virginia doesn't seem to cotton on. "Oh, you mean the baby. Ask Jenny."'

When Virginia's baby was ten days old and the news was all of the Normandy landings, the dingy tranquillity which enveloped London was disturbed. Flying bombs appeared in the sky, unseemly little caricatures of aeroplanes, which droned smokily over the chimney-tops, suddenly fell silent, dropped out of sight and exploded dully. Day and night they came at frequent irregular intervals, striking at haphazard far and near. It was something quite other than the battle scene of the blitz with its drama of attack and defence; its earth-shaking concentrations of destruction and roaring furnaces; its respites when the sirens sounded the All Clear. No enemy was risking his own life up there. It was as impersonal as a plague, as though the city were infested with enormous, venomous insects. Spirits in Bellamy's, as elsewhere, had soared in the old days when Turtle's had gone up in flames and Air Marshal Beech had taken cover under the billiard table. Now there were glum faces. The machines could not be heard in the bar but the tall windows of the coffee-room (cross-laced with sticking plaster) fronted St James's Street. All heads were turned towards them and a silence would fall when a motor bicycle passed. Job stood fast at his post in the porter's lodge, but his sang-froid required more frequent stimulation. Members who had no particular duties in London began to disperse

Elderberry and Box-Bender decided it was time they attended to local business in their constituencies.

General Whale made an unprecedented move to the air-raid shelter. It had been constructed at great expense, wired, air-conditioned, and never once used. It had been a convention of HOO HQ that no attention was paid to raid warnings. Now General Whale had a bed made there and spent his nights as well as his days underground.

'If I may say so, sir,' Ian Kilbannock ventured, 'you're not looking at all well.'

'To tell you the truth I don't feel it, Ian. I haven't had a day's leave for two years.'

The man's nerve had gone, Ian decided. He could now safely desert him.

'Sir,' he said, 'with your approval I was thinking of applying for a posting abroad.'

'You, too, Ian? Where? How?'

'Sir Ralph Brompton thinks he could get me sent as war correspondent to the Adriatic.'

'What's it got to do with *him*?' asked General Whale in an access of feeble exasperation. 'How are military postings *his* business?'

'He does seem to have some pull there, sir.'

General Whale gazed at Ian despondingly, uncomprehendingly. Three years, two years, even six months ago there would have been a detonation of rage. Now he sighed deeply. He gazed round the rough concrete walls of his shelter, at the silent 'scrambler' telephone on his table. He felt (and had he known the passage might so have expressed it) like a beautiful and ineffectual angel beating in the void his luminous wings in vain.

'What am I doing here?' he asked. 'Why am I taking cover when all I want to do is die?'

'Angela,' Virginia said, 'you'd better go too. I can get on all right now by myself. I don't need Sister Jenny any more really. Couldn't you take that baby down with you? Old Nanny would look after it, surely?'

'She'd probably love to,' said Angela Box-Bender, doubtful but ready to hear reason. 'The trouble is we simply haven't any room for a single other adult.'

'Oh, I don't want to move at all. Peregrine will be quite happy with me and Mrs Corner once the nursery is cleared. Mrs Corner will be over the moon to see the last of it.' (There had been the normal, ineradicable hostility between nursing sister and domestic servant.)

'It's wonderfully unselfish of you, Virginia. If you really think it's the best thing for Gervase...?'

'I really think it's the best thing for – for Gervase.'

So it was arranged and Virginia comfortably recuperated as the bombs chugged overhead and she wondered, as each engine cut out: 'Is that the one that's coming here?'

3

In the world of high politics the English abandonment of their Serbian allies – those who had once been commended by the Prime Minister for having 'found their souls' – was determined and gradually contrived. The king in exile was persuaded to dismiss his advisers and appoint more pliable successors. A British ship brought this new minister to Vis to confer with Tito in his cave. The Russians instructed Tito to make a show of welcome. Full recognition for the partisans and more substantial help were the inducements offered by the British and Americans. Meetings 'at the highest level' were suggested for the near future. And as an undesigned by-product of this intrigue there resulted one infinitesimal positive good.

Guy had not dismissed the Jews from his mind. The reprimand rankled but more than this he felt compassion; something less than he had felt for Virginia and her child but a similar sense that here again, in a world of hate and waste, he was being offered the chance of doing a single small act to redeem the times. It was, therefore, with joy that he received the signal: *Central Government approves in principle evacuation Jews stop Dispatch two repeat two next plane discuss problem with Unrra.*

He went with it to the Minister of the Interior who was lying on his bed drinking weak tea.

Bakic explained, 'He's sick and don't know nothing. You better talk to de Commissar.'

The Commissar confirmed that he too had received similar instructions.

'I suggest we send the Kanyis,' said Guy.

'He say, why de Kanyis?'

'Because they make most sense.'

'Pardon me.'

'Because they seem the most responsible pair.'

'De Commissar says, responsible for what?'

'They are the best able to put their case sensibly.'

A long discussion followed between the Commissar and Bakic.

'He won't send de Kanyis.'

'Why not?'

'Kanyi got plenty of work with de dynamo.'

So another pair was chosen and sent to Bari, the grocer and the lawyer who had first called on him. Guy saw them off. They seemed stupefied and sat huddled among the bundles and blankets on the airfield during the long wait. Only when the aeroplane was actually there, illuminated by the long line of bonfires lit to guide it, did they both suddenly break into tears.

But this little kindling of human hope was the least impressive incident on the airfield that evening and it passed quite unnoticed in the solemnity with which the arriving passengers were received.

Guy had not been warned to expect anyone of importance. He realized that something unusual was afoot when in the darkness which preceded the firing of the flare-path, he was aware of a reception party assembling, among whom loomed the figures of the General and the Commissar. When the lights went up, Guy recognized with surprise those rarely glimpsed recluses, the Russian Mission. When the machine came to ground and the doors were open, six figures emerged all in British battle-dress who were at once surrounded by partisans, embraced, and led aside.

The Squadron Leader began supervising the disembarkation of stores. There was no great quantity of them and those mostly for the British Mission – rations, mail, and tin after tin of petrol.

'What am I supposed to do with these?' Guy asked the pilot.

'Wait and see. There's a jeep to come out.'

'For me?'

'Well, for your major.'

'Have I a major?'

'Haven't they told you? They signalled that one was coming. They never tell me anyone's name. He's over there with the gang.'

Strong willing partisans contrived a ramp and carefully lowered the car to earth. Guy stood beside his two Jews watching. Presently an English voice called: 'Guy Crouchback anywhere about?'

Guy knew the voice. 'Frank de Souza.'

'Am I unwelcome? I expect you'll get the warning order on tomorrow's transmission. It was a last-minute decision sending us.'

'Who else?'

'I'll explain later. I'm afraid in the whirligig of war I've now become your commanding officer, uncle. Be a good chap and see to the stores, will you? I've got a night's talking ahead with the general staff and the Praesidium.'

'The what?'

'I thought that might surprise you. I'll tell you all about it tomorrow. Begoy, for your information, is about to become a highly popular resort. We shall make history here, uncle. I must find a present I've got for the general in my valise. It may help cement anti-fascist solidarity.'

He stooped over the small heap of baggage, loosened some straps and stood up with a bottle in each hand. 'Tell someone to do it up, will you? and have it put wherever I'm going to sleep.'

He rejoined the group who were now tramping off the field.

'Right,' said the pilot. 'I'm ready to take on passengers.'

Two wounded partisans were hoisted in; then an American bomber crew who had baled out the week before and been led to the Squadron Leader's headquarters. They were far from being gratified by this speedy return to duty. There was a regulation that if they remained at large in enemy territory for some weeks longer, they could be repatriated to the United States. It was for this that they had made a hazardous parachute jump and destroyed an expensive, very slightly damaged aeroplane.

Last came the Jews. When Guy held out his hand to them, they kissed it.

As always on these night incursions Guy had his sergeant and orderly with him. They were plainly exhilarated by the spectacle of the jeep. He left it and the stores to them and walked back to his quarters. The night of high summer was brilliant with stars and luminous throughout its full firmament. When he reached the farm he told the widows of de Souza's coming. There was an empty room next to his which they immediately began to put in order. It was just midnight but they worked without complaint, eagerly, excited at the prospect of a new arrival.

Soon the jeep drove into the yard. The widows ran to admire it. The soldiers unloaded, putting the rations and tins of petroleum in the store room, de Souza's baggage in the room prepared for him. The Praesidium, whatever that might be, was of no interest to Guy; he was glad de Souza had come; very glad that his two Jews had gone.

'The mail, sir,' reported the orderly.

'Better leave that for Major de Souza in the morning. You know he's taking command here now?'

'Yes, we got the buzz from the air force. Two personal for you, sir.'

Guy took the flimsy air-mail forms that were then the sole means of communication. One, he noted, was from Virginia, the other from Angela.

Virginia's letter was undated but had clearly been written some six weeks ago.

Clever Peregrine tells me he managed to persuade them to accept a telegram for you announcing the Birth. I hope it arrived. You can't trust telegrams any more. Anyway it is born and I am feeling fine and everyone especially Angela is being heavenly. Sister Jennings – Jenny to me – says it is a fine baby. We have rather an embarrassing joke about Jenny and gin and my saying she is like Mrs Gamp – at least it embarrasses other people. I think it quite funny as jokes with nurses go. It's been baptized already. Eloise Plessington who believe it or not is now my great new friend was godmother. I've made a lot of new friends since you went away in fact I'm having a very social time. An intellectual who says he knows you called Everard something brought me a smoked salmon from Ruben's. And a lemon! Where does Ruben get them? Magic. I hope you are enjoying your foreign tour wherever you are and forgetting all the beastliness of London. Ian talks of visiting you. How? Longing for you to be back. V.

Angela's letter was written a month later: *I have dreadful news for you. Perhaps I should have tried to telegraph but Arthur said there was no point as there was nothing you could do. Well, be prepared. Now. Virginia has been killed. Peregrine too and Mrs Corner. One of the new doodle bombs landed on Carlisle Place at ten in the morning yesterday. Gervase is safe with me. They were all killed instantly. All Peregrine's 'collection' destroyed. It was Virginia's idea that I should have Gervase and keep him safe. We think we shall be able to get Virginia and Peregrine taken down to Broome and buried there but it is not easy. I had Mass said for them here this morning. There will be another in London soon for friends. I won't attempt to say what I feel about this except that now more than ever you are in my prayers. You have had a difficult life, Guy, and it seemed things were at last going to come right for you. Anyway you have Gervase. I wish papa had lived to know about him. I wish you had seen Virginia these last weeks. She was still her old sweet gay self of course but there was a difference. I was getting to understand why you loved her and to love her myself. In the old days I did not understand.*

As Arthur says there is really nothing for you to do here. I suppose you could get special leave home but I expect you will prefer to go on with whatever you are doing.

The news did not affect Guy greatly; less, indeed, than the arrival of Frank de Souza and the jeep and the 'Praesidium'; far less than the departure of his two Jewish protégés. The answer to the question that had agitated Kerstie Kilbannock (and others of his acquaintance) – what had been his relations with Virginia during their brief cohabitation in Uncle Peregrine's flat? – was simple enough. Guy had hobbled into the lift after their return as man and wife from the registrar's office and had gone back to bed. There Virginia had joined him and with gentle, almost tender, agility adapted her endearments to his crippled condition. She was, as always, lavish with what lay in her gift. Without passion or sentiment but in a friendly cosy way they had resumed the pleasures of marriage and in the weeks while his knee mended the deep old wound in Guy's heart and pride healed also, as perhaps Virginia had intuitively known that it might do. January had been a month of content; a time of completion, not of initiation. When Guy was passed fit for active service and his move-order was issued, he had felt as though he were leaving a hospital where he had been skilfully treated, a place of grateful memory to which he had no particular wish to return. He did not mention Virginia's death to Frank then or later.

Frank came to the farmhouse at dawn accompanied by two partisans and talking to them cheerfully in Serbo-Croat. Guy had waited up for him, but dozed. Now he greeted him and showed him his quarters. The widows appeared with offers of food, but Frank said: 'I've had no sleep for thirty-six hours. When I wake up I've a lot to tell you, uncle,' raised a clenched fist to the partisans and shut his door.

The sun was up, the farm was alive. The partisan sentries changed guard. Presently the men of the British Mission stood in the bright yard shaving. '

Bakic breakfasted apart on the steps of the kitchen. The bell in the church tower rang three times, paused and rang three times again. Guy went there on Sundays, never during the week. Sunday Mass was full of peasants. There was always a half-hour sermon that was unintelligible to Guy whose study of Serbo-Croat had made little progress. When the old priest climbed into the pulpit, Guy wandered outside and the partisan police pressed forward so as not to miss a word. When the liturgy was resumed Guy returned; they retired to the back shunning the mystery.

Now the sacring bell recalled Guy to the duty he owed his wife.

'Sergeant,' he said, 'what rations have we got to spare?'

'Plenty since last night.'

'I thought of taking a small present to someone in the village.'

'Shouldn't we wait and ask the major, sir? There's an order not to give anything to the natives.'

'I suppose you're right.'

He crossed the yard to the Air Force quarters. Things were freer and more easy there. Indeed the Squadron Leader did a modest and ill-concealed barter trade with the peasants and had assembled a little collection of Croatian arts and crafts to take home to his wife.

'Help yourself, old boy.'

Guy put a tin of bully beef and some bars of chocolate into his haversack and walked to the church.

The old priest was back in his presbytery, alone and brushing the bare stone floor with a besom. He knew Guy by sight though they had never attempted to converse. Men in uniform boded no good to the parish.

Guy saluted as he entered, laid his offering on the table. The priest looked at the present with surprise; then broke into thanks in Serbo-Croat. Guy said: 'Facilius loqui latine. Hoc est pro Missa. Uxor mea mortua est.'

The priest nodded. 'Nomen?'

Guy wrote Virginia's name in capitals in his pocket book and tore out the page. The priest put on his spectacles and studied the letter. 'Non es *partisan*?'

'Miles Anglicus sum.'

'Catholicus?'

'Catholicus.'

'Et uxor tua?'

'Catholica.'

It did not sound a likely story. The priest looked again at the food, at the name on the sheet of paper, at Guy's battle-dress which he knew only as the uniform of the partisans. Then: 'Cras. Hora septem.' He held up seven fingers.

'Gratias.'

'Gratias tibi. Dominus tecum.'

When Guy left the presbytery he turned into the adjoining church. It was a building with the air of antiquity which no one but a specialist could hope to date. No doubt there had been a church here from early times. No doubt parts of that structure survived. Meanwhile it had been renovated and repainted and adorned and despoiled, neglected and cosseted through the centuries. Once when Begoy was a watering place it had enjoyed seasons of moderately rich patronage. Now it had reverted to its former use. There was at that moment a peasant woman in the local antiquated costume, kneeling upright on the stones before the side altar, her arms extended, making no doubt her thanksgiving for communion. There were a few benches, no chairs. Guy genuflected and then stood to pray asking mercy for Virginia and for himself. Although brought up to it from the nursery, he had never been at ease with the habit of reciting the prayers of the Church for particular intentions. He committed Virginia's soul – 'repose' indeed, seemed the apt petition – to God in the colloquial monologue he always employed when praying; like an old woman, he sometimes ruefully thought, talking to her cat.

He remained standing with his eyes on the altar for five minutes. When he turned he saw Bakic standing behind him, watching intently. The holy water stoup was dry. Guy genuflected at the door and went out into the sunlight. Bakic was standing by.

'What do you want?'

'I thought maybe you want to talk to somebody.'

'I don't require an interpreter when I say my prayers,' Guy said. But later he wondered, did he?

The bodies of Virginia, Uncle Peregrine, and Mrs Corner were recovered from the débris of Bourne Mansions intact and recognizable, but the official impediments to removing them to Broome (Mrs Corner, too, came from that village) proved too many for Arthur Box-Bender. He had them buried by the river at Mortlake where there was a plot acquired by one of the family in the last century and never used. It lay in sight of Burton's stucco tent. The requiem was sung a week later in the Cathedral. Everard Spruce did not attend either service but he read the list of mourners aloud to Frankie and Coney.

He had met Virginia only in the last weeks of her life but he had long enjoyed a vicarious acquaintance with her from the newspapers. Like many men of the left he had been an assiduous student of 'society gossip' columns, a taste he excused by saying that it was his business to know the enemy's order of battle. Lately in the decline of social order he had met on friendly terms some of these figures of oppression and frivolity – old Ruby, for instance, at the Dorchester – and many years later, when he came to write his memoirs, he gave the impression that he had frequented their houses in their heyday. Already he was beginning to believe that Virginia was an old and valued friend.

'Who are all these people?' asked Coney. 'What's the point of them? All I know about Mrs Crouchback is that you gave her enough smoked salmon to keep us for a week.'

'Before we'd even had a nibble at it,' said Frankie.

'And a lemon,' said Coney.

The flying bombs had disturbed the good order of the *Survival* office. Two of the secretaries had gone to the country. Frankie and Coney remained but they were less docile than of old. The bombs came from the south-east and were plain in view in the wide open sky of the river. All seemed to be directed at the house in Cheyne Row. They distracted the girls from their duty in serving and revering Spruce. His manner towards them had become increasingly schoolmasterly, the more so as his own nerves were not entirely calm. He was like a schoolmaster who fears that a rag is brewing.

He spoke now with an effort of authority:

'Virginia Troy was the last of twenty years' succession of heroines,' he said. 'The ghosts of romance who walked between the two wars.'

He took a book from his shelves and read: '*She crossed the dirty street, placing her feet with a meticulous precision one after the other in the same straight line as though she were treading a knife edge between goodness only knew what invisible gulf. Floating she seemed to go, with a little spring in every step and the skirt of her summery dress – white it was, with a florid pattern printed in black all over it – blowing airily round her swaying march.* I bet neither of you know who wrote that. You'll say Michael Arlen.'

'I won't,' said Coney; 'I've never heard of him.'

'Never heard of Iris Storm "that shameless, shameful lady" dressed pour le sport? "I am a house of men," she said. I read it at school where it was forbidden. It still touches a nerve. What is adolescence without trash? I dare say you've not heard of Scott Fitzgerald either.'

'Omar Khayyam?' suggested Frankie.

'No. Anyway the passage I read, believe it or not, is Aldous Huxley 1922. Mrs Viveash. Hemingway coarsened the image with his Bret, but the type persisted – in books and in life. Virginia was the last of them – the exquisite, the doomed, and the damning, with expiring voices – a whole generation younger. We shall never see anyone like her again in literature or in life and I'm very glad to have known her.'

Coney and Frankie looked at each other with mutiny in their eyes.

'Perhaps you are going to say "the mould has been broken",' said Coney.

'If I wish to, I shall,' said Spruce petulantly. 'Only the essentially commonplace are afraid of clichés.'

Coney burst into tears at this rebuke. Frankie held her ground. 'Exquisite, doomed, damning, with an expiring voice,' she said. 'It sounds more like the heroine of Major Ludovic's dreadful *Death Wish*.'

Then another bomb droned overhead and they fell silent until it passed.

The same bomb passed near Eloise Plessington's little house where she was sitting with Angela Box-Bender. Directly overhead, it seemed, the engine cut out. The two women sat silent until they heard the explosion many streets away.

'It is a terrible thing to admit,' said Eloise, 'but, whenever that happens, I pray, "Please God don't let it fall on me."'

'Who doesn't?'

'But, Angela, that means, "Please God let it fall on someone else."'

'Not necessarily. It might land on Hampstead Heath.'

'One ought to pray, "Please God let it fall on me and no one else."'

'Don't be a goose, Eloise.'

These two women of the same age had known each other since girlhood. Charles Plessington had been one of the young men who seemed suitable for Angela to marry. He came of the same little band of landed recusant families as herself. She, however, had confounded the match-makers of the Wiseman Club by preferring the Protestant and plebeian Box-Bender. Eloise married Charles and became not only a Catholic but a very busy one. Her sons were adult and well married; her only family problem was her daughter, Domenica, now aged twenty-five, who had tried her vocation in a convent, failed, and now drove a tractor on the home farm, an occupation which had changed her appearance and manner. From having been shy and almost excessively feminine, she was now rather boisterous, trousered, and muddied and full of the rough jargon of the stock-yard.

'What were we talking about?'

'Virginia.'

'Of course. I'd got very fond of her this winter and spring but, you know, I can't regard her death as pure tragedy. There's a special providence in the fall of a bomb. God forgive me for thinking so, but I was never quite confident her new disposition would last. She was killed at the one time in her life when she could be sure of heaven – eventually.'

'One couldn't help liking her,' said Angela.

'Will Guy mind awfully?'

'Who can say? The whole thing was very puzzling. She'd begun the baby, you know, before they were re-married.'

'So I supposed.'

'I really know Guy very little. He's been abroad so much. I always imagined he had completely got over her.'

'They seemed happy enough together that last bit.'

'Virginia knew how to make people happy if she wanted to.'

'And what is to become of my godson?'

542

'What indeed? I suppose I shall have to look after him. Arthur won't like that at all.'

'I've sometimes thought of adopting a baby,' said Eloise, 'a refugee orphan or something like that. You know the empty nurseries seem a reproach when there are so many people homeless. It would be an interest for Domenica, too – take her mind off swill and slag.'

'Are you proposing to adopt Gervase?'

'Well, not *adopt* of course, not legally, not give him our name or anything like that, but just look after him until Guy gets back and can make a home for him. What do you think of the idea?'

'It's wonderfully kind. Arthur would be immensely relieved. I'd have to ask Guy, of course.'

'But there would be no objection to my taking him to visit me while we're waiting for an answer?'

'None that I can see. He's a perfectly nice baby, you know, but Arthur does so hate having him at home.'

'Here comes another of those beastly bombs.'

'Just pray, "Please God let it be a dud and not explode at all."'

It was not a dud. It did explode but far from Westminster in a street already destroyed by earlier bombs and now quite deserted.

'You've read *The Death Wish*?' Spruce asked.

'Bits. It's pure novelette.'

'*Novelette?* It's twice the length of *Ulysses*. Not many publishers have enough paper to print it nowadays. I read a lot of it last night. I can't sleep with those damned bombs. Ludovic's *Death Wish* has *got* something you know.'

'Something very bad.'

'Oh, yes, bad; egregiously bad. I shouldn't be surprised to see it a great success.'

'Hardly what we expected from the author of the aphorisms.'

'It is an interesting thing,' said Spruce, 'but very few of the great masters of trash aimed low to start with. Most of them wrote sonnet sequences in youth. Look at Hall Caine – the protégé of Rossetti – and the young Hugh Walpole emulating Henry James. Dorothy Sayers wrote religious verse. Practically no one ever sets out to write trash. Those that do don't get very far.'

'Another bomb.'

It was the same bomb as had disturbed Angela and Eloise. Spruce and Frankie did not pray. They moved away from the windows.

Frank de Souza kept partisan hours, sleeping all the morning, talking at night. On his first day he appeared at lunch-time.

'Better quarters than I'm used to,' he said. 'Until a few days ago I was living in a cave in Bosnia. But we shall have to do some quick work making them more comfortable. We've got a distinguished party coming to visit us. If I may, I'll leave the arrangements to you. I put the General and the Commissar in the picture last night. You'll find them very ready to help.'

'Perhaps you'd put me in the picture.'

'It's a very pretty picture – an oil painting. Everything is moving our way at last. First, the Praesidium – that's the new government – ministers of education, culture, transport – the whole bag of tricks. Officially, it is temporary, *de facto, ad hoc,* and so forth pending ratification by plebiscite. I don't suppose you saw much of them last night – they're a scratch lot collected from Vis and Montenegro and Bari. Two of them are duds we had to take on as part of the deal with the London Serbs. The real power, of course, will remain with the partisan military leaders. The Praesidium is strictly for foreign consumption. Now I'll tell you something highly confidential. Only the General and the Commissar know. It mustn't get to the ears of the Praesidium for a day or two. Tito's in Italy. He's a guest of honour at Allied headquarters in Caserta and from what I picked up from Joe Cattermole I gather it's on the cards he's going to meet Winston. If he does, he'll make rings round him.'

'Who'll make rings round whom?'

'Tito round Winston of course. The old boy is being briefed to meet a Garibaldi. He doesn't know Tito's a highly trained politician.'

'Well, isn't Winston Churchill?'

'He's an orator and a parliamentarian, uncle. Something quite different.

'All we have to do now is to square the Yanks. Some of them are still a bit shy of left-wing parties. Not the President, of course, but the military. But we've persuaded them at this stage of the war the only relevant question is: who is doing the fighting? Mihajlovic's boys were given a test – told to blow a bridge by a certain date. They did nothing. Too squeamish about reprisals. That's never worried our side. The more the Nazis make themselves hated, the better for us. Mihajlovic is definitely out. But the Yanks don't like taking our intelligence reports on trust. Want to see for themselves. So they're sending a general here to report back how hard the partisans are fighting.'

'As far as I know, they aren't.'

'They will when the Yanks come. Just you wait and see.'

Guy said, 'The thing that's been worrying me most is the refugee problem.'

'Oh yes, the Jews. I saw a file about them.'

'Two went out last night. I hope they get proper attention in Bari.'

'You can be sure they will. The Zionists have their own funds and their own contacts with UNRRA and Allied headquarters. It isn't really any business of ours.'

'You talk like a partisan.'

'I am a partisan, uncle. We have more important things to think about than these sectarian troubles. Don't forget, I'm a Jew myself; so are three of the brighter members of the Praesidium. Jews have been valuable anti-fascist propaganda in America. Now's the time to forget we're Jews and simply remember we are anti-fascist. You might just as well start agitating Auchinleck about Scottish nationalism.'

'I can't feel like that about Catholics.'

'Can't you, uncle? Try.'

When Guy went to church next morning at seven there were two partisans on watch. The priest in his black chasuble was inaudible at the altar. The partisans watched Guy. When he went up to communion they followed and stood at the side, their sten guns slung from their shoulders. When they were sure that nothing but the host passed between Guy and the priest, they returned to their places, watched Guy saying his prayers for Virginia, and followed him back to the mission headquarters.

At luncheon that day de Souza's first words were: 'Uncle, what's all this about you and the priest?'

'I went to Mass this morning.'

'Did you? That won't be any help. You've upset the Commissar seriously, you know. They made a formal complaint last night saying you had been guilty of "incorrect" behaviour. They say you were seen yesterday giving the priest rations.'

'That's quite true.'

'And passing a note.'

'I simply gave him the name of someone who's dead – what we call a "mass intention".'

'Yes, that's what the priest told them. They've had the priest up and examined him. The old boy's lucky not to be under arrest or worse. How could you be such an ass? He produced a bit of paper he said was your message. It had your name on it and nothing else.'

'Not mine. Someone in my family.'

'Well you can't expect the Commissar to distinguish, can you? He naturally thought the priest was trying to put something over on them. They searched the presbytery but couldn't find anything incriminating, except some chocolate. They confiscated that of course. But they're suspicious still. You must have realized what the situation is here. If it wasn't for our American guests, they might have made real trouble. I had to point out to them that the general was not only going to report back about the fighting. He would also be asked what Begoy was like now it's for the moment the capital of the country. If he found the church shut and cottoned on to the fact that the priest had just been removed, he might, I told them, just possibly get it into his noodle that this wasn't exactly the liberal democracy he's been let to expect. They saw the point in the end, but they took some persuading. They're serious fellows our comrades. Don't for goodness' sake try anything like that again. As I said yesterday, this is no time for sectarian loyalties.'

'You wouldn't call communism a sect?'

'No,' said de Souza. He began to say more and then stopped. All he did was to repeat 'No' with absolute assurance.

The battle prepared for the visiting general was to be an assault on a little block-house some twenty miles to the west, the nearest 'enemy' post to Begoy, on a secondary road to the coast. There were no Germans near. The garrison was a company of Croat nationalists, whose duty it was to send out patrols along the ill-defined frontiers of the 'liberated' territory and to find sentries for bridges in that area. They were not the ferocious *ustachi* but pacific *domobrans*, the local home-guard. It was in every way a convenient objective for the exercise; also well placed for spectators, in an open little valley with wooded slopes on either side.

The General pointed out that frontal assault in daylight was not normal partisan tactics. 'We shall need air support.'

De Souza composed a long signal on the subject. It was a measure of the new prestige of the partisans that the RAF agreed to devote two fighter-bombers to this insignificant target. Two brigades of the Army of National Liberation were entrusted with the attack. They numbered a hundred men each.

'I think,' said de Souza, 'we had better call them companies. Will the brigadiers mind being reduced to captain for a day or two?'

'In the Peoples' Forces of Anti-fascism we attach little importance to such things,' said the Commissar.

The General was more doubtful. 'They earned their rank in the field,' he said. 'It is only because of the great sacrifices we have made that the brigades have been so reduced in numbers. Also because the supply of arms from our allies has been so scanty.'

'Yes,' said de Souza, '*I* understand all that of course but what we have to consider is how it will affect our distinguished observers. They are going to send journalists too. It will be the first eye-witness report of Jugoslavia to appear in the press. It would not read well to say we employed two brigades against one company.'

'That must be considered,' said the Commissar.

'I suggest,' said de Souza, 'the brigadiers should keep their rank and their units be called "a striking force". I think that could be made impressive. "The survivors of the Sixth Offensive".'

De Souza had come with credentials which the General and Commissar recognized. They trusted him and treated his advice with a respect they would not have accorded to Guy or even Brigadier Cape; or for that matter to General Alexander or Mr Winston Churchill.

Guy was never admitted to these conferences which were held in Serbo-Croat without an interpreter. Nor was he informed of the negotiations with Bari. De Souza had all signals brought to him in cipher. The later hours of his mornings in bed were spent reading them and himself enciphering the answers. To Guy were relegated the domestic duties of preparing for the coming visit. As de Souza had predicted he found the partisans unusually amenable. They revealed secret stores of loot taken from the houses of the fugitive bourgeoisie, furniture of monstrous modern German design but solid construction. Sturdy girls bore the loads. The rooms of the farmhouse were transformed in a way which brought deep depression to Guy but exultation to the widows who polished and dusted with the zeal of sacristans. The former Minister of the Interior had been made master of the revels. He proposed a *Vin d'Honneur* and concert.

'He want to know,' explained Bakic, 'English American anti-fascist songs. He want words and music so the girls can learn them.'

'I don't know any,' said Guy.

'He want to know what songs you teach your soldiers?'

'We don't *teach* them any. Sometimes they sing about drink, "Roll out the barrel" and "Show me the way to go home".'

'He says not those songs. We are having such songs also under the fascists. All stopped now. He says Commissar orders American songs to honour American general.'

'American songs are all about love.'

'He says love is not anti-fascist.'

Later de Souza emerged from his bedroom with a sheaf of signals.

'I've a surprise for you, uncle. We are sending a high observing officer too. Apparently it's the rule at Caserta that our VIPs always travel in pairs, the Yank being just one star above his British companion. Just you wait and see who we're getting. I'll keep it as a treat for you, uncle.'

4

Ian Kilbannock's first day in Bari was similar to Guy's. He was briefed by Joe Cattermole and Brigadier Cape. Nothing was said about the impending battle, much about the achievements of the partisans, the failure of

Mihajlovic's *cetnics*, the inclusive, national character of the new government, and the personal qualities of Marshal Tito, who was at that moment in Capri awaiting the British Prime Minister.

Ian was the first journalist to be admitted to Jugoslavia. Sir Ralph Brompton had vouched for him to Cattermole, not as one fully committed to the cause, but as a man without prejudice. Cape had an unexpressed, indeed unrecognized, belief that a peer and a member of Bellamy's was likely to be trustworthy. Ian listened to all that was told him, asked a few intelligent questions, and made no comment other than: 'I see this as a job that will take time. Impossible to send spot news. If it suits you, I shall just look about, talk to people, and then return here and write a series of articles.'

He intended to establish himself now and for the future as a political commentator, of the kind who had enjoyed such prestige in the late thirties.

He was taken to dinner at the club by the Halberdier major. More direct than Guy, he said: 'I'm afraid I didn't get your name.'

'Marchpole. Grace-Groundling-Marchpole to be precise. I dare say you know my brother in London. He's a big bug.'

'No.'

'He's a secret big bug. I'm just a cog in the machine. How was London?' Ian described the flying bombs. 'My brother won't like that.'

While they were at dinner, Brigadier Cape came into the room politely, propelling a man in the uniform of a major-general, a lean, grey-faced, still old man, whose single eye was lustreless, whose maimed hand reached out to a chair-back to steady him as he limped and shuffled to his table.

'Good God,' said Ian, 'a ghost.'

He had sailed with this man to the Isle of Mugg in the yacht *Cleopatra* in December 1941; a man given to ferocious jokes and bloody ambitions, an exultant, unpredictable man whom Ian had taken pains to avoid.

'Ben Ritchie-Hook,' said Major Marchpole, 'one of the great characters of the Corps. He hadn't much use for me though. We parted company.'

'But what's happened to him?'

'He's on the shelf,' said Major Marchpole. 'All they can find for him to do is play second fiddle as an observer. He'll be in your party going across tomorrow night.'

Ostensibly the party which was assembled at the airfield next evening, was paying a call on the new Praesidium. It had grown since the simple project of sending an independent observer had first been raised and accepted.

General Spitz, the American, was still the principal. He had a round stern face under a capacious helmet. He was much harnessed with plastic straps and hung about with weapons and instruments and haversacks. He was attended by an ADC of less militant appearance, who had been chosen for his ability to speak Serbo-Croat, and by his personal photographer, a very young, very likely manikin whom he addressed as 'Mr Sneiffel'. Ritchie-Hook wore shorts, a bush-shirt, and a red-banded forage cap. His Halberdier servant guarded his meagre baggage, the same man, Dawkins, war-worn now like his master, who had served him at Southsands and Penkirk, in Central Africa and in the desert, wherever Ritchie-Hook's strides had taken him; strides which had grown shorter and slower, faltered and almost come to a halt. Lieutenant Padfield was there with his conductor who, it was thought, might help the partisans with their concert. The Free French had insinuated a representative. Other nondescript figures, American, British, and Jugoslav, made a full complement for the aeroplane. Gilpin was there with a watching brief for Cattermole, and an Air Force observer to report the promised cooperation of the fighter-bombers. He and the two generals specifically, and Gilpin vaguely, were alone in the know about the promised assault.

The Air Commodore in command turned out to see the party on board. The American General instructed Sneiffel to take snapshots of the pair of them. He called Ritchie-Hook to join them. 'Come along, General, just for the record.' Ritchie-Hook looked in a bewildered way at the little figure who squatted with his flash-light apparatus at the General's feet; then with a ghastly grin said: 'Not me. My ugly mug would break the camera.'

Lieutenant Padfield saluted General Spitz and said: 'Sir, I don't think you've met Sir Almeric Griffiths who is coming with us. He is a very prominent orchestral conductor as no doubt you know.'

'Bring him up. Bring him in,' said the General. 'Come Griffiths, stand with me.'

The bulb flashed.

Gilpin said: 'He ought to get security clearance before taking photographs on our airfield.'

Ian resolved to make himself agreeable to this photographer and get prints of all his films. They might serve to illustrate a book.

As the last glow of sunset faded they boarded the aeroplane in inverse order of seniority beginning with the Halberdier servant and ending after some lingering exchanges of politeness with General Spitz. A machine had been provided that was luxurious for these parts, fitted with seats as though for paying passengers in peace-time. Little lights glowed along the roof. The doors were shut. The lights went out. It was completely dark. What had once been windows were painted out. The roar of the engines imposed silence on the party. Ian, who had put himself next to Sneiffel, longed for a forbidden cigarette and tried to compose himself for sleep. It was far from his normal bedtime. He had worn the same shirt all day without a chance of changing. In the hot afternoon it had been damp with sweat. Now in the chill upper air it clung to him and set him shivering. It had not occurred to him to bring his greatcoat. It had been an unsatisfactory day. He had wandered about the streets of the old town with Lieutenant Padfield and Griffiths. They had lunched at the club and had been ordered to report at the airfield two hours before they were needed. He had not dined and saw no hope of doing so. He sat in black boredom and discomfort until, after an hour, sleep came.

The aeroplane flew high over the Adriatic and the lightless enemy-held coast of Dalmatia. All the passengers were sleeping when at last the little lights went up and the American General who had been travelling in the cockpit returned to his place in the tail saying: 'All right, fellows. We're there.' Everyone began groping for equipment. The photographer next to Ian tenderly nursed his camera. Ian heard the change of speed in the engines and felt the rapid descent, the list as they banked, then straightened for the run-in. Then unexpectedly the engines burst up in full throat; the machine suddenly rose precipitously, throwing the passengers hard back in their seats; then as suddenly dived, throwing them violently forward. The last thing Ian heard was a yelp of alarm from Sneiffel. Then a great door slammed in his mind.

He was standing in the open beside a fire. London, he thought; Turtle's Club going up in flames. But why was maize growing in St James's Street? Other figures were moving around him, unrecognizable against the fierce light. One seemed familiar. 'Loot,' he said, 'what are *you* doing here?' and then added: 'Job says the gutters are running with wine.'

Always polite Lieutenant Padfield said: 'Is that so?'

A more distinctly American, more authoritative voice was shouting: 'Is everyone out?'

Another familiar figure came close to him. A single eye glittered terribly in the flames. 'You there,' said Ritchie-Hook, 'were you driving that thing?'

As though coming round from gas in the dentist's chair Ian saw that 'that thing' was an aeroplane, shorn of its under-carriage, part buried in the great furrow it had ploughed for itself, burning furiously in the bows, with flames trickling back along the fuselage like the wines of Turtle's. Ian remembered he had left Bari in an aeroplane and that he had been bound for Jugoslavia.

Then he was aware of the gaunt figure confronting him and of a single eye which caught the blaze. 'Are you the pilot?' demanded Ritchie-Hook. 'Pure bad driving. Why can't you look where you're going?' The concussion which had dazed his companions had momentarily awakened Ritchie-Hook. 'You're under arrest,' he roared above the sound of the fire.

'Who's missing?' demanded the American General.

Ian then saw a man leave the group and trot to the pyre and deliberately climb back through the escape-hatch.

'What the devil does that idiot think he's doing?' cried Ritchie-Hook. 'Come back. You're under arrest.'

Ian's senses were clearer now. He still seemed to be in a dream but in a very vivid one. 'It's like the croquet match in *Alice in Wonderland*,' he heard himself say to Lieutenant Padfield.

'That's a very, very gallant act,' said the Lieutenant.

The figure emerged again in the aperture, jumped, and dragged out behind him not, as first appeared, an insensible fellow passenger but, it transpired, a bulky cylindrical object; he staggered clear with it and then proceeded to roll on the ground.

'Good God, it's Dawkins,' said Ritchie-Hook. 'What the devil are you doing?'

'Trousers on fire, sir,' said Dawkins. 'Permission to take them off, sir?' Without waiting for orders he did so, pulling them down, then with difficulty unfastening his anklets and kicking the smouldering garment clear of his burden. He stood thus in shirt, tunic, and boots gazing curiously at his bare legs. 'Fair roasted,' he said.

The American General asked: 'Were there any men left inside?'

'Yes, sir. I think there was, sir. They didn't look like moving. Too hot to stay and talk. Had to get the General's valise out.'

'Are you hurt.'

'Yes, sir. I think so, sir. But I don't seem to feel it.'

'Shock,' said the General. 'You will later.'

The flames had now taken hold of the tail. 'No one is to attempt any further rescue operations.' No one had shown any inclination to do so. 'Who's missing?' he said to his aide. 'Count and find out.'

'I don't see Almeric,' said Lieutenant Padfield.

'How did any of us get out?' Ian asked.

'The General, our General Spitz. He got both the hatches open before anyone else moved.'

'Something to be said for technological training.'

Gilpin was loudly complaining of burned fingers. No one heeded him. The little group was behaving in an orderly, mechanical manner. They spoke at random and did not listen. Each seemed alone, isolated by his recent shock. Someone said: 'I wonder where the hell we are.' No one answered. Ritchie-Hook said to Ian: 'You are not in any way responsible for that intolerable exhibition of incompetence?'

'I'm a press-officer, sir.'

'Oh, I thought you were the pilot. You need not consider yourself under arrest. But be careful in future. This is the second time this has happened to me. They tried it on before in Africa.'

The two generals stood side by side. 'Neat trick of yours that,' Ritchie-Hook conceded, 'getting the door open. I was slow off the mark. Didn't really know what was happening for a moment. Might have been in there still.'

The aide came to report to General Spitz: 'All the crew are missing.'

'Ha,' said Ritchie-Hook. 'The dog it was that died.'

'And six from the rest of the party. I'm afraid Sneiffel is one of them.'

'Too bad, too bad,' said General Spitz; 'he was a fine boy.'

'And the civilian musician.'

'Too bad.'

'And the French liaison officer.'

General Spitz was not listening to the casualty list. An epoch seemed to have passed since the disaster. General Spitz looked at his watch. 'Eight minutes,' he said. 'Someone ought to be here soon.'

The place where the aeroplane had fallen was pasture. The maize field lay astern of it, tall, ripe for reaping, glowing golden in the firelight. These stalks now parted and through them came running the first of the reception party from the airfield, partisans and the British Mission. There were greetings and anxious inquiries. Ian lost all interest in the scene. He found himself uncontrollably yawning and sat on the ground with his head on his knees while behind him the chatter of solicitude and translation faded to silence.

Another great space of time, two minutes by a watch, was broken by someone saying: 'Are you hurt?'

'I don't think so.'

'Can you walk?'

'I suppose so. I'd sooner stay here.'

'Come on, it's not far.'

Someone helped him to his feet. He noticed without surprise that it was Guy. Guy, he remembered, was an inhabitant of this strange land. There was something he ought to say to Guy. It came to him. 'Very sorry about Virginia,' he said.

'Thank you. Have you got any belongings?'

'Burned. Damn fool thing to have happened. I never trusted the Air Force ever since they accepted *me*. Must be something wrong with people who'd accept *me*.'

'Are you sure nothing hit you on the head in that crash?' said Guy.

'Not sure. I think I'm just sleepy.'

A partisan doctor went round the survivors. No one except Halberdier Dawkins and Gilpin had any visible injuries; the doctor made light of Gilpin's burnt fingers. Dawkins was suffering from surface burns which had rapidly swelled into enormous blisters covering his legs and thighs. He prodded them with detached curiosity. 'It's a rum go,' he said; 'spill a kettle on your toe and you're fair dancing. Boil you in oil like a heathen and you don't feel a thing.'

The doctor gave him morphia and two partisan girls bore him off on a stretcher.

The unsteady little procession followed the path the rescuers had trodden through the maize. The flames cast deep shadows before their feet. At the edge of the field grew a big chestnut. 'Do you see what I see?' said Ian. Something like a monkey was perched in the branches gibbering at them. It was Sneiffel with his camera.

'Lovely pictures,' he said. 'Sensational if they come out.'

When Ian woke next morning it was as though from a debauch; all the symptoms of alcoholic hangover, such as he had not experienced since adolescence, overwhelmed him. As in those days, he had no memory of going to bed. As in those days, he received an early call from the man who had put him there.

'How are you?' asked Guy.

'Awful.'

'There's a doctor going the rounds. Do you want to see him?'

'No.'

'Do you want any breakfast?'

'No.'

He was left alone. The room was shuttered. The only light came in narrow strips between the hinges. Outside poultry was cackling. Ian lay still. The door opened again; someone stamped into the room and opened shutters and windows revealing herself, in the brief moment before Ian shut his eyes and turned them from the light, as a female in man's uniform, wearing a red cross brassard and carrying a box of objects which clinked and rattled. She began stripping Ian of his blanket and pulling at his arm.

'What the devil are you doing?'

The woman flourished a syringe.

'Get out,' cried Ian.

She jabbed at him. He knocked the instrument from her hand. She called: 'Bakic. Bakic,' and was joined by a man to whom she talked excitedly in a foreign tongue. 'She's de nurse,' said Bakic. 'She's got an injection for you.'

'What on earth for?'

'She says tetanus. She says she always injects tetanus for everyone.'

'Tell her to get out.'

'She says are you frightened of a needle? She says partisans are never frightened.'

'Turn her out.'

So far as anything so feminine could be ascribed to this visitant, she exhibited pique. So far as it was possible to flounce in tight battle-dress, she flounced as she left her patient. Guy returned.

'I say I'm sorry about that. I've been keeping her out all the morning. She got through while I was with the General.'

'Did you put me to bed last night?'

'I helped. You seemed all right. In fact in fine form.'

'It's worn off,' said Ian.

'You'd just like to be left alone?'

'Yes.'

But it was not to be. He had closed his eyes and lapsed into a state approaching sleep when something not very heavy depressed his feet, as though a dog or a cat had landed there. He looked and saw Sneiffel.

'Well, well, well, so you're a newspaper man? My, but you've got a story. I've been down to the wreck. It's still too hot to get near it. They reckon there's five stiffs in there besides the crew. Lieutenant Padfield is het up about some British musician he's lost. What the Hell? There isn't going to be any concert now. So what? There'll be an elegant funeral when they get the bodies out. Everyone seems kinda het up today. Not me though. Maybe it's being light I don't shock so easy. The partisans were for putting off the battle but General Spitz works to a schedule. He's got to have the battle on the day it was planned and then get out his report and I've got to have the pictures to go with it. So the battle's tomorrow as per schedule. What say you come round with me and talk to some of these partisans? I've got the General's interpreter. He's not feeling too bright this morning but I reckon he can still hear and speak.'

So Ian gingerly set foot to the floor, dressed and began his work as a war correspondent.

No one could give a technical explanation of the night's mishap. Guy had stood at his usual post on the edge of the airfield. He had heard the Squadron Leader talking his peculiar jargon into his wireless set, had seen the girls run from tar-barrel to barrel lighting the path for the incoming aeroplane, had watched it come down as he had watched many others, had seen it overrun its objective, rocket suddenly up like a driven pheasant and fall as though shot half a mile away. He had heard de Souza say: 'That's the end of *them*,' had seen the flames kindle and spread and then had seen one after another a few dark, unrecognizable, apparently quite lethargic figures emerge from the hatches and stand near the wreck. He had joined in the rush to the scene. After that he had been busy with his duties as host in getting the survivors to their beds and finding in the store replacements for their lost equipment.

The partisans were inured to disaster. They had a certain relish for it. They did not neglect to mention that this was an entirely Anglo-American failure, but they did so with a rare cordiality. They had never been convinced that the allies were taking the war seriously. This unsolicited burnt-offering seemed in some way to appease them.

De Souza was very busy with his tear-off cipher-pads and it devolved on Guy to arrange the day of the newcomers. General Spitz's aide had been struck with a delayed stammer by his fall and complained of pains in his back. Gilpin now had both hands bandaged and useless. The two generals were the fittest of the party; General Spitz brisk and business-like, Ritchie-

Hook reanimated. Guy had not seen him in his decline. He was now as he had always been in Guy's experience.

Halberdier Dawkins said: 'It's been a fair treat for the General. He's his old self. Come in this morning and gave me rocket for disobeying orders getting his gear out.'

Dawkins was a stretcher case, and after arduous years in Ritchie-Hook's service not sorry to be honourably at ease. He submitted without complaint to his tetanus injections and basked in the hospitality of the Mission sergeant who brought him whisky and cigarettes and gossip.

The former Minister of the Interior reluctantly cancelled the *Vin d'Honneur* and the concert but there were sociable meetings between the general staff and their guests, the observers, at which the plans for the little battle were discussed. It was after one of these that Ritchie-Hook took Guy aside and said: 'I'd like you to arrange for me to have a quiet talk with the fellow whose name ends in "itch".'

'All their names end like that, sir.'

'I mean the decent young fellow. They call him a brigadier. The fellow who's going to lead the assault.'

Guy identified him as a ferocious young Montenegran who had a certain affinity to Ritchie-Hook in that he, too, lacked an eye and a large part of one hand.

Guy arranged a meeting and left the two warriors with the Commissar's interpreter. Ritchie-Hook returned in high good humour. 'Rattling good fellow that Itch,' he said. 'No flannel or ormolu about him. D'you suppose all his stories are true?'

'No, sir.'

'Nor do I. I pulled his leg a bit but I am not sure that interpreter quite twigged. Anyway, we had a perfectly foul drink together – *that* ended in Itch too – extraordinary language – and we parted friends. I've attached myself to him for tomorrow. Don't tell the others. Itch hasn't room for more than one tourist in his car. We're driving out tonight to make a recce and get the men in place for the attack.'

'You know, sir,' Guy said, 'there's a certain amount of humbug about this attack. It's being laid on for General Spitz.'

'Don't try and teach your grandmother to suck eggs,' said Ritchie-Hook. 'Of course I twigged all that from the word "go". Itch and I understand one another. It's a demonstration. Sort of thing we did in training. But we enjoyed that, didn't we?'

Guy thought of those long chilly exercises in 'biffing' at Southsands, Penkirk, and Hoy. 'Yes, sir,' he said, 'those were good days.'

'And between you and me I reckon it's the last chance I have of hearing a shot fired in anger. If there's any fun going, Itch will be in it.'

*

At eight next morning General Spitz and his aide, the British Mission, the partisan general staff, Ian and Sneiffel assembled beside the line of miscellaneous cars which the Jugoslavs had all the summer kept secreted, with so much else, in the forest. Guy made Ritchie-Hook's excuses to General Spitz who merely said: 'Well, there's plenty of us without him.'

The convoy set out through a terrain of rustic enchantment, as through a water-colour painting of the last century. Strings of brilliant peppers hung from the eaves of the cottages. The women at work in the fields sometimes waved a greeting, sometimes hid their faces. There was no visible difference between 'liberated' territory and that groaning under foreign oppression. Ian was unaware when they passed the vague frontier.

'It's like driving to a meet,' he said, 'when the horses have gone on ahead.'

In less than an hour they were in sight of the block-house. A place had been chosen 500 yards from it, well screened by foliage, where the observers could await events in comfort and safety. The partisans had moved out in the darkness and should have been in position surrounding their objective in the nearest cover.

'I'm going down to look for them,' said Sneiffel.

'I shall stay here,' said Ian. He was still feeling debauched by shock.

General Spitz studied the scene through very large binoculars. 'Block-house' had been a slightly deceptive term. What he saw was a very solid little fort built more than a century earlier, part of the defensive line of Christendom against the Turk. 'I appreciate now why they want air support,' said General Spitz. 'Can't see anyone moving. Anyway we've achieved surprise.'

'As a matter of fact,' said de Souza aside to Guy, 'things have not gone quite right. One of the brigades lost its way in the approach-march. They may turn up in time. Don't let on to our allies.'

'You'd think there would be more sign of life from a German post,' said General Spitz. 'Everyone seems asleep.'

'These are *domobrans*,' said the Commissar's interpreter. 'They are lazy people.'

'How's that again?'

'Fascist collaborators.'

'Oh. I got the idea in Bari we were going to fight Germans. I suppose it's all the same thing.'

The sun rose high but it was cool in the shade of the observation post. The air support was timed to begin at ten o'clock. That was to be the signal for the infantry to come into the open.

At half-past nine rifle-fire broke out below them. The partisan general looked vexed.

'What are they up to?' asked General Spitz.

A partisan runner was sent down to inquire. Before he returned the firing ceased. When he reported, the interpreter said to General Spitz, 'It is nothing, it was a mistake.'

'It's lost us surprise.'

De Souza, who had heard and understood the runner's report, said to Guy: 'That was the second brigade turning up. The first thought they were enemy and started pooping off. No one's been hit but, as our ally remarks, we have "lost surprise".'

There was no longer peace in the valley. For the next quarter of an hour occasional shots came, at random it seemed, some from the parapet of the block-house, some from the surrounding cover; then sharp at ten, just as on General Spitz's elaborate watch the minute hand touched its zenith, there came screaming out of the blue sky the two aeroplanes. They swooped down one behind the other. The first fired simultaneously two rockets which just missed their target and exploded in the woods beyond, where part of the attacking force was now grouped. The second shot straighter. Both his rockets landed square on the masonry, raising a cloud of flying rubble. Then the machines climbed and circled. Guy, remembering the dive-bombers in Crete relentlessly tracking and pounding the troops on the ground, waited for their return. Instead they dwindled from sight and hearing.

The airman who had been sent to observe them, stood near. 'Lovely job,' he said, 'right on time, right on target.'

'Is that all?' asked Guy.

'That's all. Now the soldiers can do some work.'

Silence had fallen in the valley. Everyone, friend and enemy alike, expected the return of the aeroplanes. The dust cleared revealing to those on the hillside equipped with binoculars two distinct patches of dilapidation in the massive walls of the block-house. Some of the partisans began discharging their weapons. None came into view. The Air Force observer began to explain to General Spitz the complexity of the task which he had seen successfully executed. The Commissar and the partisan General spoke earnestly and crossly in their own language. A runner from below came to report to them. 'It appears,' the interpreter explained to General Spitz, 'that the attack must be postponed. A German armoured column has been warned and is on its way here.'

'What do your men do about that?'

'Before a German armoured column they disperse. That is the secret of our great and many victories.'

'Well, uncle,' said de Souza to Guy, 'we had better begin thinking of luncheon for our visitors. They've seen all the sport we have to offer here.'

But he was wrong. Just as the observers were turning towards their cars, Ian said: 'Look.'

Two figures had emerged from the scrub near the block-house walls and were advancing across the open ground. Guy remembered the precept of his musketry instructor: 'At 200 yards all parts of the body are distinctly seen. At 300 the outline of the face is blurred. At 400 no face. At 600 the head is a dot and the body tapers.' He raised his binoculars and recognized the incongruous pair; the first was Ritchie-Hook. He was signalling fiercely, summoning to the advance the men behind him, who were already slinking away; he went forward at a slow and clumsy trot towards the place where the rocket-bombs had disturbed the stones. He did not look back to see if he was being followed. He did not know that he was followed, by one man, Sneiffel, who like a terrier, like the pet dwarf privileged to tumble about the heels of a prince of the Renaissance, was gambolling round him with his camera, crouching and skipping, so small and agile as to elude the snipers on the walls. A first bullet hit Ritchie-Hook when he was some 20 yards from the walls. He spun completely round, then fell forwards on his knees, rose again and limped slowly on. He was touching the walls, feeling for a handhold, when a volley from above caught him and flung him down dead. Sneiffel paused long enough to record his last posture, then bolted, and the defenders were so much surprised by the whole incident that they withheld their fire until he had plunged into the ranks of the retreating partisans.

The German patrol – not, as the partisan scouts had reported, an armoured column, but two scout cars summoned by telephone when the first shots were fired – arrived at the block-house to find the scars of the rocket and the body of Ritchie-Hook. They did not move from the road. A section of *domobrans* investigated the wood where the first aeroplane had misplaced its missiles. They found some smouldering timber and the bodies of four partisans. A puzzled German captain composed his report of the incident which circulated through appropriate files of the Intelligence Service attracting incredulous minutes as long as the Balkan branch continued to function. The single-handed attack on a fortified position by a British major-general, attended in one account by a small boy, in another by a midget, had no precedent in Clausewitz. There must be some deep underlying motive, German Intelligence agreed, which was obscure to them. Perhaps the body was not really Ritchie-Hook's – they had his full biography – but that of a sacrificial victim. Ritchie-Hook was being preserved for some secret enterprise. Warning orders were issued throughout the whole 'Fortress of Europe' to be vigilant for one-eyed men.

Lieutenant Padfield had not spent an agreeable morning in Begoy. His only company had been Gilpin and he had been troubled by a deputation of Jews who, hearing that an American was among them, had come to inquire about the arrangement UNRRA was making for their relief. The Lieutenant was no linguist. Bakic was surly. The conversation had been a strain on his spirits already subdued by the aeroplane crash. It was with great pleasure that, earlier than expected, the observers came driving into the town.

The death of Ritchie-Hook had changed the events of the day from fiasco to tragic drama. There was ample material for recriminations but in the face of this death even the Commissar was constrained to silence.

Sneiffel was jubilant. He had secured a scoop which would fill half a dozen pages of an illustrated weekly, the full photographic record of a unique event.

Ian was soberly confident. "You didn't miss much, Loot,' he said, 'but the object of the exercise has been attained. General Spitz is satisfied that the partisans mean business and are skilled in guerrilla tactics. He was rather sceptical at one moment but Ritchie-Hook changed all that. A decision of the heart rather than of the head perhaps.

'It's an odd thing. In all this war I've only twice had any part in an operation. Both have afforded classic stories of heroism. You wouldn't have thought, would you, that Trimmer and Ritchie-Hook had a great deal in common?'

Guy took it on himself to inform Halberdier Dawkins of his master's death.

The much blistered man displayed no extremity of bereavement. 'So that's how it was,' he said and added with awe at the benevolent operation of Providence: 'Hadn't been for going sick, like enough I'd be with him. He's led me into some sticky places I can tell you, sir, these last three years. He was fair asking to cop one. As you'll remember, sir, he always spoke very straight and more than once he's said to me right out: "Dawkins, I wish those bastards would shoot better. I don't want to go home." One thing for him; different for me that's got a wife and kids and was twenty years younger. Of course I'd go anywhere with the General. Had to really, and he was a fine man, no getting away from that. I don't know how I'll do about his gear. Ought to ship it back to the base. Maybe your orderly would lend a hand when they send to fetch us. It's a shame we couldn't bury him proper, but you can trust the jerries to do what's right, he always said. He wasn't a strictly religious man. Just so as he has his grave marked, he wouldn't want more.'

The partisans dug a deep common grave for the bodies in the aeroplane. They, too, were anxious to do what was right and offered the services of the village priest but since little was known about the beliefs of any of the dead, except Sir Almeric Griffiths who, Lieutenant Padfield said, was of Wesleyan origin and sceptical temper, a firing-party and a bugler performed the last office.

Later the Air Force made a daylight sortie with fighter cover to collect General Spitz and the remnants of his party. When Guy and de Souza returned from the airfield to their quarters they found the partisan girls already removing the bourgeois furniture.

'The captains and the kings depart,' said de Souza. 'What do we do now, uncle, to keep ourselves amused?'

There was not work for two liaison officers. There was barely enough for one. As the result of General Spitz's recommendations supplies came almost nightly in great profusion. The Squadron Leader arranged for them, the partisans collected them, Guy and de Souza were spectators. Throughout the last weeks of August and the first weeks of September the Commissar and the General were uncomplaining, even comradely. De Souza drove Guy in the jeep round the 'liberated' area visiting partisan camps.

'It seems to me,' said Guy, 'that they've got all they can use at the moment. If they're going to mount a summer offensive they'd better get on with it.'

'There's not going to be a summer offensive here in Croatia,' said de Souza. 'You might have noticed that we're moving troops out, as soon as they're equipped. They're going into Montenegro and Bosnia. They'll keep on the heels of the Germans and move into Serbia before the *cetnics* can take over. That's the important thing now. Begoy has served its purpose. They'll just leave enough men to deal with the local fascists. I have the feeling I shan't be staying long myself. Can you face the winter alone, uncle? Once the snow comes the landing strip will be out of service, you know.'

'I'd like to do something about the Jews.'

'Oh, yes. Your Jews. I'll make a signal.'

He got in reply: *Plans well advanced evacuation all Jews your area before snow.*

'I hope that's cheered you up, uncle.'

That was in the middle of the third week in September. In the middle of the fourth week de Souza came into their common-room with his file of signals and said: 'I shall be leaving you tonight, uncle. I've been recalled to Bari. Let me know if there's anything I can do for you there.'

'Remind them about the Jews.'

'You know, uncle, I'm beginning to doubt if you're fit to be left. You've an *idée fixe*. I hope you aren't going to become a psychiatrist's case like your predecessor here.'

It was not until dinner that de Souza said: 'I dare say you ought to know what's happening. Tito has left Vis and gone to join the Russians. He might have done it more politely. He never said a word to anyone. Just took off while everyone was asleep. Some of our chaps are rather annoyed about it, I gather. I bet Winston is. I told you he'd make rings round the old boy. Winston imagined he'd worked the same big magic with Tito he did with the British Labour leaders in 1940. There were to be British landings in Dalmatia and a nice coalition government set up in Belgrade. That's what

Winston thought. From now on any help Tito needs is coming from Russia and Bulgaria.'

'Bulgaria? The Jugoslavs hate their guts.'

'Not any more, uncle. You don't follow modern politics any more than poor Winston does. The Bulgarians have, as our Prime Minister might have put it, "found their souls".'

'I don't think you'll have a very busy winter. There won't be so much Anglo-American interest as there's been in the last few months. In fact they might close this Mission down before Christmas.'

'Any suggestion of how we're supposed to get out?'

'I'll leave you the jeep, uncle. You might get through to Split.'

It seemed to Guy then that he had never really liked Frank de Souza.

The officer in Bari who distributed educational matter had sent a huge bundle of illustrated American magazines, mostly of distant date. In the long hours of early October Guy read them, slowly, straight through, like a Protestant nanny with her Bible.

Days passed without his receiving any summons to general headquarters. Bakic did not like walking. Guy got some pleasure from tramping the autumnal countryside with the spy limping behind him. The church was locked up; the priest had left. Three members of the Praesidium were installed in the presbytery.

'What's become of him?' Guy asked Bakic.

'He gone some other place. Little village more quiet than here. He was old. Too big a house for one old man.'

On Guy's 41st birthday he received a present; a signal reading: *Receive special flight four Dakotas tomorrow night 29th dispatch all Jews*.

He went joyfully to the Commissar, who, as before, had received confirmation from his own source of authority, and coldly gave his assent to the proposal.

It seemed to Guy, in the fanciful mood that his lonely state engendered, that he was playing an ancient, historic role as he went with Bakic to inform the Jews of their approaching exodus. He was Moses leading a people out of captivity.

He was not well versed in Old Testament history. The bulrushes, the burning bush, the plagues of Egypt belonged in his mind to very early memories, barely distinguishable from Grimm and Hans Andersen, but the image of Moses stood plain before his eyes, preposterously striking water from rock near the Grand Hotel in Rome, majestically laying down the law in St Peter-in-Chains. That day Guy's cuckold's horns shone like the patriarch's, when he came down from the awful cloud on Sinai.

But there was no divine intervention to help the Jews of Begoy, no opening of the sea, no inundation of chariots. Guy was informed that no further assistance was required from him. A partisan security company was detailed to muster the refugees and examine their scant baggage. At dusk they were marched out of their ghetto along the road to the airfield. Guy saw them pass from the corner of the lane. It was the season of mists and Guy felt the chill of anticipated failure. Silent and shadowy the procession trailed past him. One or two had somehow borrowed peasants' hand carts. The oldest and feeblest rode in them. Most were on foot bowed under their shabby little bundles.

At ten o'clock when Guy and the Squadron Leader went out the ground-mist was so thick that they could hardly find the familiar way. The Jews were huddled on the embankment, mostly sleeping.

Guy said to the Squadron Leader: 'Is this going to lift?'

'It's been getting thicker for the last two hours.'

'Will they be able to land?'

'Not a chance. I'm just sending the cancellation order now.'

Guy could not bear to wait. He walked back alone but could not rest; hours later, he went out and waited in the mist at the junction of lane and road until the weary people hobbled past into the town.

Twice in the next three weeks the grim scene was repeated. On the second occasion the fires were lit, the aeroplanes were overhead and could be heard circling, recircling, and at length heading west again. That evening Guy prayed: 'Please God make it all right. You've done things like that before. Just send a wind. Please God send a wind.' But the sound of the engines dwindled and died away, and the hopeless Jews stirred themselves and set off again on the way they had come.

That week there was the first heavy fall of snow. There would be no more landing until the Spring.

Guy despaired, but powerful forces were at work in Bari. He soon received a signal: *Expect special drop shortly relief supplies for Jews stop Explain partisan HQ these supplies only repeat only for distribution Jews.*

He called on the General with this communication.

'What supplies?'

'I presume food and clothing and medicine.'

'For three months I have been asking for these things for my men. The Third Corps have no boots. In the hospital they are operating without anaesthetics. Last week we had to withdraw from two forward positions because there were no rations.'

'I know. I have signalled about it repeatedly.'

'Why is there food and clothes for the Jews and not for my men?'

'I cannot explain. All I have come to ask is whether you can guarantee distribution.'

'I will see.'

Guy signalled: *Respectfully submit most injudicious discriminate in favour of Jews stop Will endeavour secure proportionate share for them of general relief supplies,* and received in answer: *Three aircraft will drop Jewish supplies point C 1130 hrs 21st stop. These supplies from private source not military stop Distribute according previous signal.*

On the afternoon of the 21st the Squadron Leader came to see Guy.

'What's the idea?' he said. 'I've just been having the hell of a schemozzle with the Air Liaison comrade about tonight's drop. He wants the stuff put in bond or something till he gets orders from higher up. He's a reasonable sort of chap usually. I've never seen him on such a high horse. Wanted everything checked in the presence of the Minister of the Interior and put under joint guard. Never heard of such a lot of rot. I suppose someone at Bari has been playing politics as usual.'

That night the air was full of parachutes and of 'free-drops' whistling down like bombs. The anti-fascist youth retrieved them. They were loaded on carts, taken to a barn near the General's headquarters and formally impounded.

Belgrade fell to the Russians, Bulgarians, and partisans. A day of rejoicing was declared in Begoy by the Praesidium. The concert and the *Vin d'Honneur*, postponed in mourning, were held in triumph. On order from high authority a *Te Deum* was sung in the church, re-opened for that day and served by a new priest whom the partisans had collected during their expansion into Dalmatia. At nightfall the anti-fascist choir sang. The anti-fascist theatre group staged a kind of pageant of liberation. Wine and Slivovic were copiously drunk and Guy through the interpreter made a formal little acknowledgement of the toast to Winston Churchill. And next day, perhaps, as part of the celebrations – Guy could never discern by what process the partisans from time to time were moved to acts of generosity – the Jews received their supplies.

Bakic greeted him with: 'De Jews again,' and going into the yard he found it full of his former visitors, but now transformed into a kind of farcical army. All of them, men and women, wore military greatcoats, Balaclava helmets, and knitted woollen gloves. Orders had been received from Belgrade, and distribution of the stores had suddenly taken place and here were the recipients to thank him. The spokesmen were different on this occasion. The grocer and lawyer had gone ahead into the promised land. Madame Kanyi kept away for reasons of her own; an old man made a longish speech which Bakic rendered 'Dis guy say dey's all very happy.'

For the next few days a deplorable kind of ostentation seemed to possess the Jews. A curse seemed to have been lifted. They appeared everywhere, trailing the skirts of their greatcoats in the snow, stamping their huge new boots, gesticulating with their gloved hands. Their faces shone with soap, they were full of Spam and dehydrated fruits. They were a living psalm. And then, as suddenly, they disappeared.

'What has happened to them?'

'I guess dey been moved some other place,' said Bakic.

'Why?'

'People make trouble for them.'

'Who?'

'Partisan people dat hadn't got no coats and boots. Dey make trouble wid de Commissar so de Commissar move dem on last night.'

Guy had business that day with the Commissar. When it was ended Guy said: 'I see the Jews have moved.'

Without consulting his chief the intellectual young interpreter answered: 'Their house was required for the Ministry of Rural Economy. New quarters have been found for them a few miles away.'

The Commissar asked what was being said, grunted, and rose. Guy saluted and the interview was at an end. On the steps, the interpreter joined him.

'The question of the Jews, Captain Crouchback. It was necessary for them to go. Our people could not understand why they should have special treatment. We have partisan women who work all day and have no boots or overcoats. How are we to explain that these old people who are doing nothing for our cause, should have such things?'

'Perhaps by saying that they *are* old and *have* no cause. Their need is greater than a young enthusiast's.'

'Besides, Captain Crouchback, they were trying to make business. They were bartering the things they had been given. My parents are Jewish and I understand these people. They want always to make some trade.'

'Well, what's wrong with that?'

'War is not a time for trade.'

'Well, anyway, I hope they have decent quarters.'

'They have what is suitable.'

The gardens in winter seemed smaller than in full leaf. From fence to fence the snow-obliterated lawns and beds lay open; the paths were only traceable by boot-prints. Guy daily took a handful of broken biscuits to the squirrel and fed him through the bars. One day while he was thus engaged, watching the little creature go through the motions of concealment, cautiously return, grasp the food, jump away, and once more perform the mime of digging and covering, he saw Mme Kanyi approach down the path. She was carrying a load of brushwood, stooping under it, so that she did not see him until she was quite close.

Guy had just received a signal for recall. The force was being renamed and re-organized. He was to report as soon as feasible to Bari. Word had gone to Belgrade, he supposed, that he was no longer *persona grata*.

He greeted Mme Kanyi with warm pleasure. 'Let me carry that.'

'No, please. It is better not.'

'I insist.'

Mme Kanyi looked about her. No one was in sight. She let him take the load and carry it towards her hut.

'You have not gone with the others?'

'No, my husband is needed.'

'And you don't wear your greatcoat.'

'Not out of doors. I wear it at night in the hut. The coats and boots make everyone hate us, even those who had been kind before.'

'But partisan discipline is so firm. Surely there was no danger of violence?'

'No, that was not the trouble. It was the peasants. The partisans are frightened of the peasants. They will settle with them later, but at present they are dependent on them for food. Our people began to exchange things with the peasants. They would give needles and thread, razors, things no one can get, for turkeys and apples. No one wants money. The peasants preferred bartering with our people to taking the partisans' bank-notes. That was what made the trouble.'

'Where have the others gone?'

She spoke a name which meant nothing to Guy. 'You have not heard of that place? It is twenty miles away. It is not a place of good repute. It is where the Germans and Ustachi made a camp. They kept the Jews and gypsies and communists and royalists there, to work on the canal. Before they left they killed what were left of the prisoners – not many. Now the partisans have found new inhabitants for it.'

They had reached the hut and Guy entered to place his load in a corner near the little stove. It was the first and last time he crossed the threshold. He had a brief impression of orderly poverty and then was outside in the snow. 'Listen, Signora,' he said. 'Don't lose heart. I am being recalled to Bari. As soon as the road is clear I shall be leaving. When I get there I promise I'll raise Cain about this. You've plenty of friends there and I'll explain the whole situation to them. We'll get you all out, I promise.'

As they stood on the little patch before the door which Mme Kanyi had cleared of snow they saw through the leafless shrubs the lurking figure of Bakic.

'You see you have been followed here.'

'He can't make any trouble.'

'Not for you, perhaps. You are leaving. There was a time when I thought that all I needed for happiness was to leave. Our people feel that. They must move away from evil. Some hope to find homes in Palestine. Most look no further than Italy – just to cross the water, like crossing the Red Sea.

'Is there any place that is free from evil? It is too simple to say that only the Nazis wanted war. These communists wanted it too. It was the only way in which they could come to power. Many of my people wanted it, to be revenged on the Germans, to hasten the creation of the national state. It seems to me there was a will to war, a death wish, everywhere. Even good men thought their private honour would be satisfied by war. They could assert their manhood by killing and being killed. They would accept hardships in recompense for having been selfish and lazy. Danger justified privilege. I knew Italians – not very many perhaps – who felt this. Were there none in England?'

'God forgive me,' said Guy. 'I was one of them.'

5

Guy had come to the end of the crusade to which he had devoted himself on the tomb of Sir Roger. His life as a Halberdier was over. All the stamping of the barrack square and the biffing of imaginary strongholds were finding their consummation in one frustrated act of mercy. He left Begoy without valediction save for the formal application at general headquarters for leave to travel. He took his small staff with him. His last act was to send by the hand of his orderly the pile of illustrated magazines to Madame Kanyi. He gave the widows such remains of his stores as the Squadron Leader did not require. The widows wept. The Squadron Leader expressed the hope that he, too, would soon get an order of recall.

The road to the coast was free of enemy and passable by jeep. It led through the desolate Lika where every village was ravaged and roofless, down into the clement coast of the Adriatic. Forty-eight hours after leaving Begoy Guy and his men were under the walls of Diocletian at Split, where they found an English cruiser in harbour, whose company were forbidden to land. Partisans had the shore batteries trained on her. This, more than anything he had seen in Jugoslavia, impressed the sergeant. 'Who'd have thought the Navy would stand for that, sir? It's politics, that's what it is.'

There was a British liaison officer at Split who gave him an order that had come, to drive on to Dubrovnik where a small British force, mostly of field artillery, had been landed and then held impotent. He was posted there as liaison officer between this force and the partisans.

His task was to hear from the partisan commander allegations of 'incorrect behaviour' by the British troops and convey them to the puzzled brigadier in command who had come under the supposition that he was a welcome ally; also to hear demands for supplies – the contrast between the fully equipped invaders and the ragged partisans was remarked by the townspeople – and to receive clandestine visits from civilians of various nationalities who wished to enrol themselves as displaced persons. On his first day he made a signal: *Situation of displaced persons in Begoy area desperate*, and received in answer: *Appropriate authority informed*, but his further lists of exiles received no acknowledgement.

At length, in mid-February the British force withdrew, Guy with the advance-party. He was set ashore at Brindisi and drove up to Bari just a year after he had first gone there. The almond was again in flower. He reported to Major Marchpole. He dined at the club.

'Everything is packing up here,' said the Major. 'I shall stay on as long as I can. The Brigadier has gone already. Joe Cattermole is in charge. You'll be returning to UK as soon as you want.'

It was from Cattermole that he learned that the Jews of Begoy had escaped. A private charitable organization in America had provided a convoy of new Ford trucks, shipped them to Trieste, driven through the snow of Croatia, and, leaving the trucks as a tip for the partisans, brought the exiles to Italy. It was indeed as though the Red Sea had miraculously drawn asunder and left a dry passage between walls of water.

Guy got permission to visit them. They were back behind barbed wire in a stony valley near Lecce. With them were four or five hundred others collected from various prisons and hiding places, all old and all baffled, all in army greatcoats and Balaclava helmets.

'I can't see the point of their being here,' said the Commandant. 'We feed them and doctor them and house them. That's all we can do. No one wants them. The Zionists are only interested in the young. I suppose they'll just sit here till they die.'

'Are they happy?'

'They complain the hell of a lot but then they've a hell of a lot to complain about. It's a lousy place to be stuck in.'

'I'm particularly interested in a pair called Kanyi.'

The Commandant looked down his list. 'Not here,' he said.

'Good. That probably means they got off to Australia all right.'

'Not from here, old man. I've been here all along. No one has ever left.'

'Could you make sure? Anyone in the Begoy draft would know about them.'

The Commandant sent his interpreter to inquire while he took Guy into the shed he called his mess, and gave him a drink. Presently the man returned. 'All correct, sir. The Kanyis never left Begoy. They got into some kind of trouble there and were jugged.'

'May I go with the interpreter and ask about it?'

'By all means, old man. But aren't you making rather heavy weather of it? What do two more or less matter?'

Guy went into the compound with the interpreter. Some of the Jews recognized him and crowded round him with complaints and petitions. All he could learn about the Kanyis was that they had been taken off the truck by the partisan police just as it was about to start.

He took the question to Major Marchpole.

'We don't really want to bother the Jugs any more. They really co-operated very well about the whole business. Besides the war's over now in that part. There's no particular point in moving people out. We're busy at the moment moving people in.' This man was in fact at that moment busy dispatching royalist officers – though he did not know it – to certain execution.

Guy spent his last days in Bari revisiting the offices where by signal he had begun his work of liberation. But this time he received little sympathy. The Jewish office showed little interest in him when they understood that he had not come to sell them illicit arms. They showed no interest in the Kanyis when they learned they were bound for Australia and not for Zion. 'We must first set up the State,' they said. 'Then it will be a refuge for all. First things first.'

An old Air Force acquaintance from Alexandrian days had a flat in Posillipo and asked Guy to stay. For a journey such as his it was a matter of being fitted into an aeroplane at the last moment when someone more important failed.

On the day before he was due to leave for Naples, he was accosted by Gilpin who said: 'Before you leave I shall want your security pass back.'

'I'm afraid I've lost it.'

'That will be very awkward.'

'Not for me,' said Guy. 'I have a friend in Air Priorities.'

Gilpin scowled. 'I hear you've been making inquiries about a couple named Kanyi.'

'Yes, I'm interested in them.'

'I thought you might be. It didn't sound like Frank de Souza exactly.'

'What didn't?'

'The confidential report. The woman was the mistress of a British Liaison Officer.'

'Nonsense.'

'He was seen leaving her home when her husband was away on duty. They were a thoroughly shady couple. The husband was guilty of sabotaging the electric light plant. A whole heap of American counter-revolutionary propaganda was found in their room. The whole association was most compromising to the Mission. It's lucky Cape had handed over to Joe before we got the report. You might have found yourself on a charge. But Joe's not vindictive. He just moved you where you couldn't do any harm. Though I may say that some of the names you sent us as displaced persons at Dubrovnik are on the black list.'

'What happened to the Kanyis?'

'What do you suppose? They were tried by a Peoples' Court. You may be sure justice was done.'

Once before in his military career Guy had been tempted to strike a brother officer – Trimmer at Southsands. The temptation was stronger now, but before he had done more than clench his fist, before he had raised it, the sense of futility intervened. He turned and left the office.

Next day he settled in Posillipo.

'For a chap who's on his way home you don't seem very cheerful,' said his host and then changed the subject, for he had had many men through his hands who were returning to problems more acute than any they had faced on active service.

EPILOGUE

Festival of Britain

In 1951, to celebrate the opening of a happier decade, the government decreed a Festival. Monstrous constructions appeared on the south bank of the Thames, the foundation-stone was solemnly laid for a National Theatre, but there was little popular exuberance among the straitened people and dollar-bearing tourists curtailed their visits and sped to the countries of the Continent where, however precarious their condition, they ordered things better.

There were few private parties. Two of these were held in London on the same June evening.

Tommy Blackhouse had returned to England in May. He was retiring from the army with many decorations, a new, pretty wife, and the rank of major-general. In the last years he had advanced far beyond his Commando into posts of greater and greater eminence and responsibility, never seeming to seek promotion, never leaving rancour behind him among those he surpassed; but his first command lay closest to his heart. Meeting Bertie in Bellamy's he had suggested a reunion dinner. Bertie agreed that it would be agreeable. 'It would mean an awful lot of organizing though,' said this one-time adjutant. It was left for Tommy, as always, to do the work.

The officers who had assembled at Mugg were not so scattered as those of other war-time units. Most of them had been together in prison. Luxmore had made an escape. Ivor Claire had spent six months in Burma with the Chindits, had done well, collected a DSO and an honourably incapacitating wound. He was often in Bellamy's now. His brief period of disgrace was set aside and almost forgotten.

'You're going to invite everyone?' asked Bertie.

'Everyone I can find. What was the name of that old Halberdier? Jumbo someone? We'll ask the sea-weed eater. I don't somehow think he'll come. Guy Crouchback of course.'

'Trimmer?'

'Certainly.'

But Trimmer had disappeared. All Tommy's adroit inquiries failed to find any trace of him. Some said he had jumped ship in South Africa. Nothing was known certainly. Fifteen men eventually assembled including Guy.

The second, concurrent festivity was given in part by Arthur Box-Bender. He had lost his seat in Parliament in 1945. He rarely came to London in the succeeding years but that June evening he was induced to pay his half share in a small dance given in an hotel for his eighteen-year-old daughter and a friend of hers. For an hour or two he stood with Angela greeting the ill-conditioned young people who were his guests. Some of the men wore hired evening-dress; others impudently presented themselves in dinner-jackets and soft shirts. He and his fellow host had been at pains to find the cheapest fizzy wine in the market. Feeling thirsty, he sauntered down Piccadilly and turned into St James's. Bellamy's alone retained some traces of happier days.

Elderberry was alone in the middle hall reading Air Marshal Beech's reminiscences. He, also, had lost his seat. His successful opponent, Gilpin, was not popular in the House but he was making his mark and had lately become an under-secretary. Elderberry had no habitation outside London. He had no occupation there. Most of his days and evenings were passed alone in this same armchair in Bellamy's.

He looked disapprovingly at Box-Bender's starched front.

'You still go out?'

'I had to give a party tonight for my daughter.'

'Ah, something you had to pay for? That's different. It's being *asked* I like. I'm never asked anywhere now.'

'I don't think you would have liked this party.'

'No, no, of course not. But I used to get asked to dinners – embassies and that kind of thing. Well, so did you. There was a lot of rot talked but it did get one through the evening. Everything's very quiet here now.'

This judgement was immediately rebutted by the descent of the Commando dinner party who stumbled noisily down the staircase and into the billiard room.

Guy paused to greet his brother-in-law.

'I didn't ask you to our dance,' said Box-Bender. 'It is very small, for young people. I didn't suppose you'd want to come. Didn't know you ever came to London as a matter of fact.'

'I don't, Arthur. I'm just up to see lawyers. We've sold the Castello, you know.'

'I'm glad to hear it. Who on earth can afford to buy property in Italy now? Americans, I suppose.'

'Not at all. One of our own countrymen who can't afford to live in England – Ludovic.'

'Ludovic?'

'The author of *The Death Wish*. You must have heard of it.'

'I think Angela read it. She said it was tosh.'

'It sold nearly a million copies in America and they've just filmed it. He's a fellow I came across during the war.'

'One of your party in there?'

'No. We aren't quite Ludovic's sort of party.'

'Well, the Castello should be just the place for a literary man. Clever of you to find a buyer.'

'That was done for me by another fellow I met in the war. You may remember him. An American called Padfield. He used to belong here. He's become Ludovic's factotum now.'

'Padfield? No. Can't say I remember him. How's everything at Broome?'

'Very well, thank you.'

'Domenica all right, and the children?'

'Yes.'

'Farm paying?'

'At the moment.'

'Wish mine was. Well, give them all my regards.' A voice called, 'Guy, come and play slosh.'

'Coming, Bertie.'

When he had gone, Elderberry said: 'That's your brother-in-law, isn't it? He's putting on weight. Didn't I hear something rather sad about him during the war?'

'His wife was killed by a bomb.'

'Yes, that was it. I remember now. But he's married again?'

'Yes. First sensible thing he's ever done. Domenica Plessington, Eloise's girl. Eloise looked after the baby when Guy was abroad. Domenica got very fond of it. A marriage was the obvious thing. I think Eloise deserves some credit in arranging it. Now they've two boys of their own. When Domenica isn't having babies she manages the home farm at Broome. They've settled in the agent's house. They aren't at all badly off. Angela's uncle Peregrine left his little bit to the child. Wasn't such a little bit either.'

Elderberry remembered that Box-Bender had had trouble with his own son. What had it been? Divorce? Debt? No, something odder than that. He'd gone into a monastery. With unusual delicacy Elderberry did not raise the question. He merely said: 'So Guy's happily settled?'

'Yes,' said Box-Bender, not without a small, clear note of resentment, 'things have turned out very conveniently for Guy.'

MORE ABOUT PENGUINS,
PELICANS AND PUFFINS

For further information about books available from Penguins please write to Dept EP, Penguin Books Ltd, Harmondsworth, Middlesex UB7 0DA.

In the U.S.A.: For a complete list of books available from Penguins in the United States write to Dept DG, Penguin Books, 299 Murray Hill Parkway, East Rutherford, New Jersey 07073.

In Canada: For a complete list of books available from Penguins in Canada write to Penguin Books Canada Ltd, 2801 John Street, Markham, Ontario L3R 1B4.

In Australia: For a complete list of books available from Penguins in Australia write to the Marketing Department, Penguin Books Australia Ltd, P.O. Box 257, Ringwood, Victoria 3134.

In New Zealand: For a complete list of books available from Penguins in New Zealand write to the Marketing Department, Penguin Books (N.Z.) Ltd, P.O. Box 4019, Auckland 10.

In India: For a complete list of books available from Penguins in India write to Penguin Overseas Ltd, 706 Eros Apartments, 56 Nehru Place, New Delhi 110019.

Evelyn Waugh in Penguins

DECLINE AND FALL

VILE BODIES

BLACK MISCHIEF

A HANDFUL OF DUST

PUT OUT MORE FLAGS

SCOOP

THE LOVED ONE

THE ORDEAL OF GILBERT PINFOLD
AND OTHER STORIES

WHEN THE GOING WAS GOOD

WORK SUSPENDED WITH CHARLES RYDER'S
SCHOOLDAYS AND OTHER STORIES

and

THE DIARIES OF EVELYN WAUGH

Edited by Michael Davie

'An extraordinary, perhaps unique document, self-revealing, indeed often self-lacerating ... perceptive and stylish ... Bibulous and pious, gossip-gathering and gossip-provoking, pugnacious and scholarly, callous and touchy, it is the work of a haunted man' – Alan Brien in the *Sunday Times*.

THE LETTERS OF EVELYN WAUGH

Edited by Mark Amory

'A joy to read – riveting, subtle, outrageously funny, honest and touching – the effect is that of a work of great art, a self-portrait fit to hold its own beside anything by Rembrandt or Van Gogh' – *Literary Review*

'Some 650 pages of elegant gossip, ferocious malice, high seriousness, social observation and sheer lunacy (both real and inspired)' – *Sunday Telegraph*

and the autobiography of his early life

A LITTLE LEARNING